THE
HARVEST
OF
HATE

To my sons,
Angus and David

THE HARVEST OF HATE

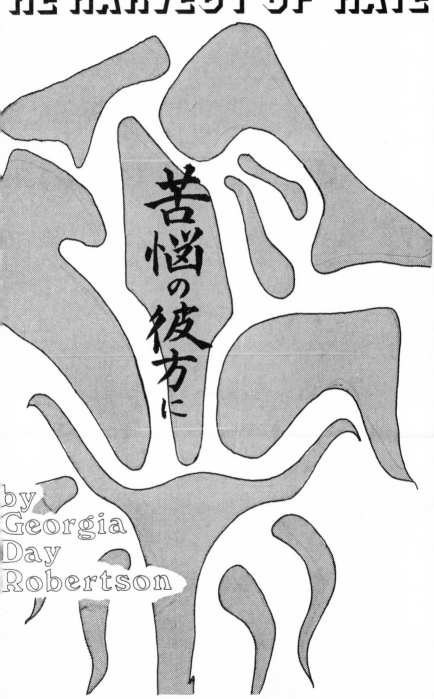

苦悩の彼方に

by
Georgia
Day
Robertson

FIRST EDITION

ISBN: 0-930046-08-0 KBF

FOREWORD 1

The hectic days of evacuation of the alien and citizen Japanese American population from the West Coast have been dimmed by the passing of almost forty years. As a person reads this novel, it brings back vividly what took place in many California communities. The story reflects the actual experiences that many Japanese American families had to live through during those uncertain years. The attitude of each person in the fictional family portrayed in *The Harvest of Hate* is expressed in such a manner as to faithfully capture their developing hope and despair.

Georgia Day Robertson has been thorough in her investigation of the various specific incidents that happened in the relocation centers, and her novel evidences a sensitive feeling as to why such events occurred. Perhaps this story will allow future Japanese Americans to better realize the trials and tribulations we all went through in order to establish our foundation here in the United States.

MOTO ASAKAWA
San Diego, California
July 29, 1980

FOREWORD 2

On several occasions, Georgia Day Robertson has told me that her reason for writing *The Harvest of Hate* was to acquaint the American public with America's concentration camps. After the closing of the War Relocation Center at Poston, Arizona, in late 1945, Mrs. Robertson returned to her native Midwest only to find that most of her relatives and former neighbors not only did not know about the evacuation and incarceration of tens of thousands of American citizens in barbed-wire-fenced, MP-guarded camps in dispersed, desolated areas in the United States, they refused to believe that such a thing had happened.

Mrs. Robertson wrote *The Harvest of Hate* over forty years ago while her Poston experience was fresh in her mind. It is a historical novel in that it portrays a fictional family of Issei (first-generation Japanese Americans) parents and Nisei (second-generation Japanese American citizens) offspring in a historically accurate setting.

Mrs. Robertson does not claim to be an Ernest Hemingway or a James Michener. But being neither Japanese nor an internee, she nevertheless manages to capture the feelings and emotions of those of us who actually experienced the evacuation and internment tragedies. The story, the characters, the detailed incidents all are far beyond merely plausibile--they happened to real people.

I first met Mrs. Robertson in 1944 in the second semester of my junior year at Poston II High School. She had been a math teacher in Poston III camp and supervisor of math teachers of all three Poston camps. Since Poston II had lost its advanced math teachers, Mrs. Robertson was sent to Camp II to fill in and also became the Vice Principal.

I remember her then as a stately, proud woman with silver-white hair, who made a tremendous impression on me when she guest-lectured in my advanced algebra class on logarithms with her homemade, ten-foot wooden slide rule. The following year I was in her trigonometry class, where she instilled my love for mathematics. After I graduated from Poston II High School in June of 1945, I was able to enroll at Iowa State College, her alma mater, without an accredited high school diploma, through her personal appeal to the Registrar. For this, I am forever grateful to her.

In the late 1940's, while I was away at college after military service, my family ran a farm and roadside vegetable stand in Garden Grove, California. Mrs. Robertson, by then having resumed her teaching career in Orange County, frequently stopped at my mother's stand to chat. We lost contact with each other until about seven years ago when she wrote to the California Institute of Technology Alumni Association to inquire about my whereabouts.

At long last, *The Harvest of Hate* is being published. This publication by the Japanese American Project of the Oral History Program at California State University, Fullerton, is sponsored by the Japanese American Council of the Historical and Cultural Foundation of Orange County. As one of the principal founders of both the Council and the Foundation, I am particularly pleased with this sponsorship.

As I write this Foreword a few days before Mrs. Robertson's 100th birthday, I can think of no greater birthday gift for her than the publication of her novel.

HIROSHI KAMEI
Anaheim, California
October 6, 1986

EDITOR'S INTRODUCTION

Except for cosmetic editing, the novel appears here consistent with its appearance as a submitted manuscript. The major editorial decisions reached in consultation between the author and myself were two-fold. First, we decided to include a chapter, Chapter VII, in the volume; second, we agreed that the present ending to the book was more satisfactory than an alternative one prepared by the author.

Many people have played significant roles in the preparation and production of this manuscript. Gaye Kouyoumjian typeset the manuscript and contributed some discerning editorial emendations. Eileen Pohl transcribed the interviews upon which the Afterword is based and penned a highly useful critique of the novel. Garnette Long assisted in the editing and preparation of the interview portion of the Afterword. Dr. Kinji Yada drew upon his experience as a wartime internee at the Manzanar War Relocation Center to give the novel an intelligent reading and he also prepared a helpful critical evaluation. Moto Asakawa and Hiroshu Kamei, both of whom were interned at the Poston center, took time from their busy schedules to write the eloquent and moving Forewords which precede this Introduction. Ruth Frey is responsible for designing the title page, as well as the dust jacket, for the book, while the Japanese calligraphy appearing on both of these was done by Yoshiko Koizumi (with the linguistic assistance of Masako Hanada and Yukiko Sato). Scott Howell gave generously of his computer knowledge to assist in the book's production, while Dr. David Pivar donated countless hours of his expertise in the area of desktop printing to ensure that the appearance of the book's printed pages would be commensurate with the quality of its contents. Shirley Stephenson, the Associate Director/Archivist of the CSUF Oral History Program nurtured the book's development from manuscript into published reality in a variety of ways, and the Oral History Program's director, Dr. Gary L. Shumway, gave freely of his boundless energy and his perfervid belief in the novel in the service of the book's manufacture. Debra Gold Hansen shouldered many of the burdens attendant upon an editor and did so with her customary humor, patience, and intelligence. Finally, I would like to thank the Special Collections of the CSUF Library, particularly Linda Herman, for bringing the manuscript to our attention, and the Patrons of the CSUF Library for helping to defray some of the book's publication costs.

ARTHUR A. HANSEN

I

Tom Sato drove the tractor into the shed and turned off the motor and lights. He had worked after dark tonight to finish the plowing rather than leave it over to the next week. Monday morning he would have to take time off to go to La Vista, the nearest town, to get the supplies his father had ordered at Wilson's Seed Store. Mr. Wilson had called that morning to say a shipment of fertilizer had come in. It was scarce this year, and only because Tom's father was such a good customer had the seed store man promised to fill his order out of the first shipment.

Tom climbed down from the high seat, his ears still ringing from the roar of the motor, and stretched his stiff arms and legs. No ranch life for him. The long hours of hard work this first year out of high school had convinced him he was not going to follow in his father's footsteps. He would go to college and learn an easier way to make a living.

He slapped the side of the dusty tractor with a grimy hand. "Noisy old thing, you're about ready for the junk heap. Dad says you've got to last another year, and then, who knows, you might get a trip to Japan as scrap iron." Not much sense helping Japan build up her military machine, but it wasn't his business. He let the thought drop.

If he could figure some way to get off the ranch ... When Tad got out of the army and got a good position, he might help pay for hired workers. Tom thought he could make his way through college by himself if he just had a chance.

Father Sato had laid out a killing program for himself and Tom for the coming year. High prices for produce and government prodding of farmers to grow more and more food had spurred him to the attempt to get everything possible out of his thirty acres. Although it was only early December, Father Sato had a work plan complete for the spring and summer ahead. The cucumbers, grown in cold frames, would be the first crop of the spring. At the same time the vines were growing and needing attention, there would be the tomato plants to bring in ready to fill the orders of the ranchers. Thousands and thousands of plants, for Tom saw the list of orders growing longer each week. His father wasn't turning anyone down. Then their own tomato field to be set and tended. Tom groaned at the thought of what lay ahead. Besides all of this new work, they were still harvesting the late summer planting of the bunch vegetables, carrots and the like, and hauling them to market.

Nothing but work, work, work.

Cars sped past on the highway in front of the ranch, some going west toward the city and the beaches, some east toward the mountains and the desert for the weekend. Lucky folks, Tom thought, with time to play and not too tired to enjoy it. He stood a minute watching the lights as they flashed for an instant on the row of his mother's blooming chrysanthemums which she had planted along the front edge of the yard.

Tom felt in his jeans pocket for a matchbook, struck a match, and held it close to his large wristwatch. Only ten o'clock. He had thought it later than that, for he had seen the lights go off in the greenhouse where his father was preparing the flats for the early tomato plants some time ago, and Father was not a man to quit work early. From daylight to long after dark, that was ranch life for you. Even in winter, for here in the sunny southland of California a rancher could work all the year-round.

No ranch life for him, Tom resolved for the unnumbered time as he started for the house. Malt, the fox terrier, which had been following him up and down the furrows since Yoshio had gone to bed, now limped along beside him. No siree, no ranch life for him. He was going to learn a profession like Tad had. He knew down in his heart that Tad wasn't coming back to help on the ranch while he went to college, but he had

2

played make-believe to keep his hopes alive. Yes, Tad had gone through the university, and now he could get a good position. Like Norio? A small, ugly voice came out of the subconscious. But Tom was too tired now to deal with the problems of discrimination which had indirectly killed his oldest brother, and his mind rejected the tragic memory as abruptly as an uneasy stomach ejects unwanted food.

Passing the garage, he stopped and felt the padlock to see if it were fastened. The new car was in there. Well, it was almost new, not yet a year old. The family had driven the Model A sedan for so long that this car would seem new for many years to come. Tomorrow was Sunday, the one day in the week that he could take the car out. He was glad his father was a Christian and not a Buddhist, for that meant they didn't work in the fields on Sunday. That was the one day in the week when the young folks could go pleasure riding. Other days it was drive the tractor, or the pickup, or the big truck; plowing, cultivating, trucking vegetables to market, delivering flats of plants. But come Sunday, dress up in your good clothes, take the new car out, load up with some friends, then sink down in the soft cushions behind the wheel and listen to the sweet hum of the motor as she purred along the broad Coast Highway at fifty, sixty, seventy--oh-oh, watch out for the black and white motorcycle of the state highway cop. Tom laughed softly to himself as he moved on toward the house.

At that moment a car came racing down the highway, curved into the drive on two wheels, and came to a sudden, skidding halt on the loose gravel beside Tom. Allen and Peg Sullivan bringing Mari home from the show.

"Say, you must have been getting almost thirty miles out of that old bus," Tom joked as he leaned a grimy elbow on the open coupe window.

"Thirty!" Allen exploded. "Why, I could give you a race. Want to get your car out and try it?"

Tom laughed at the idea and asked Allen how

about going riding tomorrow.

"Swell idea. About what time?"

"As soon as the folks get home from church and we have dinner. We want to have plenty of time."

"How about me?" Peg asked boldly. She was accustomed to the young Nisei's disregard for girls. "Am I included in the invitation?"

"Oh, sure," Tom answered quickly, with an embarrassed laugh. He was afraid he had been impolite. "Plenty of room."

"Then you be sure to come, too, Mari," Peg said. She turned to her brother. "Let's get rolling. I promised Mother we'd be home early." Mari thanked them for the show and went to the house.

"See you tomorrow," Allen called, as Tom stepped back from the car, and Allen shifted into reverse and shot out of the driveway sending a spray of gravel over Tom's shoes.

Tom went to the house and took off his shoes on the back porch. The cool boards felt good to his bare feet. He stood for a time, leaning against the porch post, looking up at the sky. It was overcast now, not a star in sight. Nothing but a high fog, he reassured himself. Couldn't think of having a Sunday spoiled by rain. The low ceiling of fog reflected the lights of the city ten miles to the west on the bay, a city which no longer slept but which worked the clock around in feverish haste to do its share in preparing for the defense of freedom, for was not America being called the arsenal of democracy? And besides, the fury of the Nazi hurricane which was snuffing out the lights of freedom in Europe with such rapidity had made the Atlantic look no larger than a pond. We must be ready to defend our own shores. The city, once quiet and aristocratic, a winter haven for eastern tourists of means, was now overcrowded and boisterous, a seething, milling concentration of defense workers, sailors, air force, soldiers, marines, and their wives and families, sweethearts, and the hangers-on who followed the men around.

Tom fancied he could hear the hum of machinery in the huge aircraft factory, so still was the night. Eight hour shifts and high wages. Those fellows had it easy, but it was not for him. Industry was allergic to the Japanese worker. That was the devil of it. Inside you could be the most patriotic, red-blooded American that ever saluted the flag, but outside you looked like a Japanese, and that's what you were to everyone--just another Jap. It didn't seem fair, but that was the way it was. All you could do was make the best of it.

He opened the kitchen door and closed it gently against Malt's persistent nose. He started for his room, then stopped in the middle of the kitchen as he became aware of a sweet, tempting odor, and realized he was hungry. He turned on the light and looked for the source of the tantalizing smell. Nothing in sight. He opened the refrigerator to see if its contents offered anything inviting. The chicken for Sunday dinner, some rice and raw fish, half a jar of daikons. He took out a bottle of milk and opened the dish cupboard for a glass, giving a low whistle of pleased surprise. A platter of cupcakes. Mari must have baked them between supper and the show.

"Plenty nice," he grinned as he lifted the platter down and admired the circular rows of pink and green dainties. He listened. All quiet in Mari's room. He took a pink one and downed it in a couple of bites, gulping the milk in between. How many could he eat without being noticed? For all his feeling of superiority as the brother, he feared his sister's temper, for she wasn't always the meek and lowly female her mother had tried to teach her to be. But hunger pressed him, made him temporarily brave, and he ate three more, washing them down with another glass of milk, and felt mildly satisfied. He rearranged the remaining cakes to fill the vacant places, replaced the platter, and went to his room. Shedding his grimy shirt and pants, he went to the shower. The water felt good, even though only lukewarm. Yoshio had probably used all the hot. The kid never thought of anyone but himself. The tepid water flowed over Tom's tired body like soft, caressing fingers, rinsing off the gritty sweat, soothing his sand-chafed skin. He finished off with a dash of cold, rubbing himself down until he felt all atingle. When he had donned the clean pajamas his mother had laid out for him, he went back to the bedroom which he shared with Yoshio, unwound the boy from the bedding which he had rolled about him like a cocoon, tucked the blankets in at the foot, and dropped into bed with a deep sigh of animal content. Yoshio hurtled over in his sleep, and Tom grabbed at the covers and anchored them under him. The December night was growing chilly.

It was almost forty years to the day since a young man of near Tom's age had arrived in San Francisco from Japan. Shigeru Sato was the name on his papers. Tom's father had come to this country like so many other young men, to seek a fortune and return to his native land. He had left behind him in the beautiful city of Hiroshima, on the Inland Sea, his father, a well-to-do merchant, his mother, and three older brothers. Being the youngest, he had little to look forward to in the way of aid in getting a start in life, so he had struck out early for himself. He worked in a market in San Francisco where he had secured a job soon after his arrival, but he did not like the cold climate and began to think of going further south. Slowly he worked his way down the coast: a cheap cafe in Salinas, gardening on a Santa Barbara estate, houseboy in a palatial residence on West Adams in Los Angeles. On this job he had days off which gave him an opportunity to mix with his own countrymen in the city, and when one of his new acquaintances told him he was going still farther south to work for a rancher, Shigeru decided to go along. He was city born and bred, but he was not afraid of work. He was always hoping with every move that he would find those wonderful wages that he had heard about before leav-

6

ing home.

When they arrived at the ranch, high on the mesa overlooking the sea, the warm sun above, and to the east the mountains dim in purple haze, Shigeru knew that whether there was a fortune to be had there or not, it was the place for him. He was pleased when he found the rancher had a job for him, too.

He worked so diligently that when the seasonal work was finished, Peter Vandenheuvel, a red-faced young Dutchman, offered him a year-round job on the ranch. Peter had shipped out from Holland on a cargo vessel when he was very young, to see the world, but when he arrived in the harbor of the southland he was sick of the sea and had seen enough of the world. He stayed ashore, worked for others until he could buy a ranch for himself, and was a good man to work for. Shigeru Sato stayed with him for nine long years, working hard, saving his money, and making of Peter a staunch friend. He had no thought of returning to Japan, but in his tenth year in the states rented some land for himself not far from Peter.

The five acres had a small house, little better than a shack, but it was a home, and he wrote at once to his brother to send him a suitable wife.

When he had brought his bride home on that hazy autumn day of 1914, the neat, straight rows of winter vegetables already made shimmering streaks across the golden loam. There was a war in Europe, and the farm prices were good. The future looked bright for the Satos.

Their first child was a boy whom they named Norio. It had pleased Father Sato greatly to have a son for his firstborn. The second and third were also sons, Tadashi and Tamotsu, who became Tad and Tom as soon as they started school. Their full names were too difficult for their schoolmates to handle. Then a daughter, Mari, and two babies who lived only long enough to die. They were girls, also, and then a boy, Yoshi.

A great sorrow had come to the family in the

7

death of Norio during his first year after graduation from the university. He had never been sturdy. When he had grown old enough to work, he had not been the help on the ranch that his father had anticipated. Sato was disappointed with his son's quick tiring and his lack of interest. Norio was always in a hurry to get through the work and get his head in a book. It was as if all his energy had gone into his mind. He grew up to be short of stature and extremely nearsighted, compelled to wear thick lenses constantly. His personal appearance was not at all prepossessing, and he was reserved and serious by nature, so he made few friends among the students. He was better known and liked by his teachers. At home he was the idol of the family. He mastered the Japanese language which meant so much to his mother who had never bothered to learn English. She said she could talk enough in one language; if she knew two, she might be talking all the time. She knew "how much" and "how many," and enough about money to care for the vegetable stand in front of the house, and could give simple directions to the children, but she could not carry on a conversation in English. So it was a great comfort to her that Norio could speak her native tongue. The other children looked upon their big brother as a sort of second father, for he assumed the responsibility of training them to be good Americans, a thing he realized early that his alien parents could not do. When he went away to school they missed him sorely and hoped that when he graduated he would secure a position near home. However, when he was graduated he could find no position anywhere. He had finished with honor. His professors gave him the highest of recommendations, for he was a brilliant student in his chosen field of chemical research, and there were many jobs opening up in that field. It was not enough. He had a Japanese name. That fact outweighed everything else.

Father Sato had made many sacrifices to send Norio through the university and was looking forward to the time when the boy would have the fine position such a brilliant student would be sure to secure.

Tad had met Norio at the train when he came home. No one had gone north to commencement as it was an expensive trip and Tad was graduating from high school the same night. Tad thought something was wrong when he saw his brother get off the train and come walking down the platform. Norio usually walked with the quick, springy steps of a short person, but now he moved along like a tired old man.

On the drive out to the ranch Tad waited to hear about Norio's plans, but when no information was forthcoming, he asked what he had in view.

"Nothing definite yet," his brother had answered in a tired voice, looking straight ahead through the cracked windshield. And then he had asked about the folks.

All that summer he waited for the letter that never came. He tried to help with the ranch work while he waited. Evenings he would go out to the packing shed with the others to pack crates or bunch vegetables ready for the next morning's trip to market. But soon he would be sitting, work forgotten, his hands dangling empty between his knees, his deep-set eyes staring into space. It was a heartbreaking sight for the others. They were so helpless to help the one they loved. Mother Sato would look at Papa-san and shake her head sadly. Sometimes he would say, "You and Norio go to the house and have some tea ready when we come in."

Norio began to talk of getting work in the city, anything he could get. But Tad, who was about to leave for his first year at the university, begged him to wait for something worthwhile.

"You don't need to worry about helping me. I'll get along all right. I've got a job where I can earn my room and board, and I've saved enough for registration and books. You just wait. You'll get what you want."

Tad left and Norio waited a little longer. Finally his pride would no longer allow him to live off his folks after all they had sacrificed for his education. He went into the city and found a job with a Japanese wholesale produce company trucking vegetables to the Los Angeles market.

Up at one o'clock those chilly fall mornings, driving through fog and later through rain, hunched over the wheel, wet, chilled to the bone, his weak eyes staring through the windshield. He began to cough. He lost weight. The crates of celery and lettuce became heavier and heavier. In January he had to give up. In February he died.

It was a crushing blow to the family and hardest of all on Tad. Father Sato had sent for him when they realized how bad Norio was, but Norio had slipped away before Tad reached home.

"They killed him!" Tad shouted at Tom, his voice strident with grief. They were standing in the room back of the garage which Norio and Tad had shared for so many of their boyhood years. Over the corner of the mirror on the old dresser hung the silk flag which Norio had won in an essay contest somewhere along the grades. The sight of it added to Tad's bitterness, and he jerked it down and threw it on the bed. "They broke his heart when they wouldn't give him a chance. He lived for just that one thing, and when he knew he couldn't do it . . . Honor student, and driving a produce truck!! God, Norio, why did you do it?" Tears ran down Tad's cheeks, and Tom went out and left him alone with his grief, for he could think of nothing to say. He felt as deeply as Tad the loss of their eldest brother, he sure did. Norio had never complained about injustice or discrimination, and who had suffered more than he from both?

At first Tad thought he would not return to the university. What was the use? You didn't need a degree to haul cabbage or spread manure. It was grief which drove him back a few days after the funeral. He couldn't stand it at home among the familiar things any longer. He would go back and get his things and find a job somewhere. On the campus, Dr. Billings, his mathematics teacher, talked him into staying on to finish the year, but he couldn't dissuade him from changing his course from engineering to business administration. He would never put himself in a situation where he would have to beg for a position. He would have a business of his own. Be his own boss. They would never grind him down like they had Norio.

Exactly who "they" were was pretty vague in Tad's mind. He had too many friends among the students and faculty already, as well as his many associations around home, to hold any grudge against white Americans en masse. He had never been wanting in popularity wherever he had been. He was naturally friendly and was attractive in his personal appearance. His shining black hair lay back from his forehead in a suggestion of a wave, and his eyes fascinated by their ability to flash like sunlight or veil themselves as inscrutably as a praying Buddha. His bronze skin gave him a beach complexion which others had to spend many an hour on the beach to attain.

No, the bogey "they" did not include any of his acquaintances. Neither did it mean those who governed his country. He was emotionally patriotic and interested in politics. Norio had seen to that. Every citizen has a responsibility to know what is going, Norio had taught his brothers. "They" was just someone else, spirit more than flesh and blood. Prejudice and discrimination, ignorance and injustice, all sired by selfishness and greed. These were the things which slammed the doors in the faces of minority groups in America, forced those people into narrow grooves, tried to keep them down economically, and feared and hated them when they prospered.

As Tad progressed through the university, his grief and bitterness seemed to become dissipated by the normal stream of his endless activites, and to all but the keenest observer, he appeared to be his old, happy, carefree self again. But not to Dr. Billings. He had Tad in for Sunday night supper as often as he could. And he realized that the resentment against things as they are had only settled into the subconscious and lay there like dregs at the bottom of a glass ready to rise at the first agitation and cloud the clear, sparkling wine of youth. He felt fearful for the young man's future, pondered over the problem of man's inhumanity to man, and hoped the way ahead for Tad would not be too rough.

The summer after Tad's graduation, Father Sato had made a trip to Japan. His mother was getting old and kept writing for him to make her a visit. Besides, he had a hankering to see his native land again. He took Tad with him. Mother Sato had refused to go, although she had never been back. She said they could not both be away from the ranch at the same time.

Tad had come home after commencement for a visit with his mother before he and his father left for Japan. Mother Sato had many messages to send to her folks.

"You should be going instead of me," Tad had said.

"No, no. Can't leave the children alone."

"You're one swell mother," Tad had said with affection. "I promise you I'll look up all your folks and tell them you're just as pretty as ever."

His mother hush-hushed him for such foolishness, and indeed Tad was a ready liar, for Mother Sato had long since lost her beauty. She was still on the plump side, but the fair skin of her youth was now tanned and leathery, burned by the sun, and toughened by the wind during the long years of working outside; her hands were the hands of a toiler.

Tad and his father had started off that day in July filled with great expectations, but came home in September disappointed and disillusioned. Father Sato found his brothers impoverished by government taxation to support the military. It pained him to see his mother deprived of the comforts of life in her old age, and he shared what little he could of his funds for the trip, promising to send something each month after he returned home. It pained him, too, to find his country completely under the domination of the military, and even his own brothers seemed afraid to talk freely with

12

him. Hiroshima, the beautiful city, was now surrounded by soldiers' barracks and defense activities, and the air was continually filled with voices shouting through loud speakers directing the residents in every phase of daily living. To Tad, the visit was nothing short of a nightmare. He might be thought a Japanese in America, but he certainly wasn't considered one here. Ignorant of the customs and speaking the language haltingly, he seemed uncultured to these people to whom custom was everything; and he felt that even his own cousins ridiculed him behind his back. He had looked forward to meeting university men and discussing the important issues of the day. But, although he met several who spoke good English, they froze like frightened rabbits if the subject of conversation turned toward political affairs.

He decided the people had no more freedom than in Hitler's Germany, and he was heartily glad when he was out of the country. He would have to make up some good stories to tell his mother, for his meeting with her folks had been no more satisfactory than any of the rest of the visit. Of course, they were glad to have news from her, they couldn't hide that in their eyes, but their words had been cautious and stilted. He would have to breathe warmth into them when he reported to his mother.

When they had been home a few days, Tad announced his intention of volunteering for military service. He said he didn't want to wait for the draft board to call him after he had started into business somewhere. His father, although surprised, remonstrated only mildly. He wanted his sons to be good Americans. But when Tom wanted to volunteer, also, telling his father what a competent worker the Mexican was who had helped out during the father's absence, Father Sato put his foot down. He needed Tom on the ranch.

Tom had watched Tad go with wistful eyes. How wonderful it would be to be in uniform and prove to everyone that you were a good, loyal American, ready to fight for your country!

13

Tad had joined the Army, as that was the only branch of the service open to Nisei. He would have liked the Air Force.

And Tom stayed on, plodding along with the work. He had been his father's right-hand man from the time he could handle a hoe. Not because he liked it, but because he was steady and willing. From the time he could tell a weed from a carrot, he had been the one to give up to Tad. But that was right; Tad was the elder. Tom would expect the same from Yoshio when he was old enough to work. That is, if he ever was.

If Father Sato had any thought of making a rancher out of his youngest, there were few signs to encourage him. Although the boy had been taught obedience to his parents, he found devious ways of avoiding anything bordering on work. He had a way with his mother and depended on her to intercede with his father.

Mari was the picture of her mother when she had crossed the Pacific twenty-seven years before to become the bride of Shigeru Sato. The same full, round face and laughing eyes, a heavy head of hair, and a small mouth which puckered when she concentrated on her lessons or her sewing. Here the likeness ended. Her hair hung loose around her shoulders instead of up in a high pompadour, and she wore short skirts and bobby socks to school instead of kimonos and tabis.

At home she was obedient and respectful to her parents, and she waited on her brothers, for she had been taught that the whole purpose in a woman's life is to be an obedient daughter, a subservient sister, a faithful wife, and a selfless mother. At school she was just another American girl of the middle class, perhaps a little more polite, an average student. Peg Sullivan was her best friend, and when possible they had the same classes. They were juniors now. Mari had early shown an interest in music, and in junior high she had played the violin in the orchestra. Her teacher had convinced Father Sato that Mari was talented enough to warrant his buying her a violin. Tad had found one at a bargain on the campus from a student who had soon tired of the pursuit of culture and had gone out for football. This junior year, her father had allowed her to go into the city once a month to take lessons. The maestro, in a rare moment of enthusiasm, had told her that her ability was above average. This had encouraged her enough to hope she might be chosen from her high school to play in the outdoor musical festivities in the city in the spring.

Such was the household of Shigeru Sato on this Saturday night in December. As they slept peacefully in their modest ranch home, in Washington, D.C., Saburu Kurusu waited for the morning to continue the peace talks with Cordell Hull, and Japanese carriers plowed their way through the Pacific toward Hawaii, their planes poised and ready for the attack which would startle the world, shake the United States to its very foundation, and scatter the Sato family to the four winds, one of them never to return.

II

Sunday morning Father and Mother Sato arose by habit an hour later than on weekdays but still a rising hour which would have seemed outrageously early for Sunday morning to city dwellers. After their favorite breakfast of fermented bean soup, raw fish, rice, and tea, Father Sato went to the fields to bring in the vegetables for market. This was the one chore which must be done on Sunday on the Sato ranch, for Mr. Kimoto must have fresh vegetables at his market in the city on Mondays.

Father Sato moved more leisurely than on weekdays. He stopped to look at the field Tom had finished the night before, and when his experienced eye had inspected it thoroughly, he smiled with approval. It was a neat, satisfying picture of even, parallel rows of golden furrows. The damp odor of recently worked earth was good in his nostrils. He could not have done better himself. Tom was a fine boy, a good rancher. He must think of some way to keep his son satisfied to stay on the ranch. Things looked very good to Father Sato, better than at any time since he had come to America. Another good year and he could buy more equipment, make the work easier, and share the profits with Tom. Give him five or six years of good prices like the present and he and Mother Sato could retire comfortably and turn the ranch over to Tom. He would be married by that time and would need a home.

Presently Mother Sato came out to the packing shed wearing an old sunbonnet to shade her eyes, for already the sun was bright and warm. She began to wash the vegetables which had been brought in, hosing and scrubbing them vigorously. When she had finished, they were ready to go into the most fastidious pot without further washing.

So the pair worked together as they had done for so many years, Sato bringing in the fine, crisp carrots, turnips, and beets, and Mother washing and bunching them ready for the market. When it was time to dress for Sunday school, they left the bunched vegetables under a fine spray to keep them fresh, and went into the house. They would pack them in crates that night and Tom would load them on the pickup truck, ready to haul to market in the early hours of the morning.

When the folks got back to the house, Mari and Yoshi were up, and Mari had fixed Yoshi's orange juice and a plate of bacon and eggs. Still dreaming of a lithe figure like that of the heroine in the picture the night before, she had limited herself to a glass of orange juice and a small slice of butterless toast. It had called for all the willpower she could muster, for she had bought some of her favorite coffee cake when she was in the city for her music lesson the day before. Why couldn't she be slender like Peg? Peg could eat cake, and candy, and ice cream, all she wanted, and she never gained a pound. Feeling very self-satisfied over her victory, Mari had done the morning housework in a hurry, the kitchen was left shining, and now she was in the living room going over her new violin lesson. She had the music propped up on the piano and had tried various baits to get Yoshi to turn it for her; but he, now in his Sunday suit, was sprawled in the middle of the floor looking at the comics.

Yoshi would accompany his folks to church. He was the only one of the children who went with the parents, for the service they attended was in Japanese, and one by one the other children had dropped out as they had grown up and reached a certain age of independence. They had rebelled against sitting through two hours of a service which they didn't understand, and the blunt reasons they gave for not going grated harshly on their parents' ears, attuned to gentle speech and gracious language. And now Yoshi was the only one left, and he went simply because he was still young enough to get a thrill out of going no matter where.

Mother Sato had sighed each time one of her flock had dropped out. She still marveled at the resis-

17

tance to her native tongue displayed by her offspring. Norio, of course, had been the soul-satisfying exception. Her heart would always bleed with grief for her firstborn. But the others--Tadashi, Tomatsu, and Mari . . . Their parents had sacrificed to spare the money to send them to Japanese language school when they were little, and with no visible results. They had played games, they had drawn pretty pictures, they had had a wonderful time with the other children--they had done everything but what they were there for. It was doubtful that any could write his own name. It was shameful. Then as they grew older and Father Sato needed them on the ranch, it had seemed sensible to discontinue the futile struggle. Mother Sato was as much at a loss to understand her American children as a mother hen with ducklings. She scolded and admonished and sometimes bribed and wheedled, but they were content to go on expressing themselves in a fair amount of good English and plenty of snappy American slang.

Mother Sato wondered at times at the unconcern of Father Sato. He seemed to take it for granted that the children would go to the young people's service at the Community Church in La Vista instead of going with them. She thought he was too easygoing with the children about some things, but she would not have thought of interfering. Mostly she was meek and quiet, and only on rare occasions did she get her spunk up. But when she did, the children had learned from experience that what she said went, and even Father Sato had learned to give in gracefully on such occasions. However, for the most part Father Sato ruled the family with a firm but gentle hand, never raising his voice. No one had ever heard him shout at his children. There was strength in his quiet nature, the strength and poise of a life whose roots went down, down into the centuries past, for Father Sato's life did not begin with his birth, nor was it bounded by that brief span which ends in death. Even in such commonplace acts as eating his food he communed with the ancient wise ones, poets and philosophers and warriors by whom the various dishes had been inspired. And an ability gained while still a youth in Hiroshima enabled him to enter at times into a world of unreality, where mysticism led him beyond the boundaries of the present into the realm of Centuries to Come. Although much of the symbolism and ritual he had learned so long ago and so far away was vague and dim in his memory, he was still acutely conscious of his connection with the past and future and hence unhurried and unruffled by the small incidents of this short present.

When Father Sato was ready for church, dressed in his dark suit and white shirt, his black tie neatly tied, he came out into the living room and sat down in his accustomed place, the worn leather chair by the front window, to read over the Sunday school lesson from his Japanese Bible while he waited until it was time to go. He commanded Yoshi to get up from the dirty floor, although there wasn't even a fleck of dust on it, and come sit on a stool beside him to keep himself clean.

Mari had turned from her lesson and was playing Christmas music now in preparation for the Christmas eve program at the Community Church. She appeared to be unaware of the presence of anyone in the room.

Mari had played in the grade school orchestra and had shown so much talent that her teacher had persuaded the Satos to let her go into the city to the maestro for lessons when she was older. She had made so much progress that he had told her only yesterday he was sure she would be chosen to represent her high school at the Spring Music Festival in the city in March. That would be a great honor, and she was dreaming of it now as she played. She pictured herself standing on the flower-banked platform before that great audience of music lovers, playing for them, receiving their applause. She would have to have a formal--red, a rich, velvety red. No, rose would be prettier under the lights and among the flowers, a dusty rose, like . . .

"Play 'Silent Night'," her father said.

Mari, impatient at the interruption of her

dreams, showed her impatience only by a shadow of a scowl passing across her face and began to play the number her father had asked for. She put aside the dreams and, giving her attention to the music, caused the violin to sing the lovely carol in tones of inexpressible sweetness. Father Sato let his Bible drop to his knees and, closing his eyes, gave himself to the enjoyment of the music. His daughter was talented. It was worth what they had put into her lessons to hear her play like that.

As Mari was finishing the carol, Mother Sato appeared in the hall door in her rayon print, to which there wasn't much fit because there wasn't much shape to Mother Sato. It was now time to go, and Mother Sato trotted out behind Father and Yoshi, giving directions to Mari as she went. Although she had lived in America and worn leather shoes for thirty years, she still walked with the quick, tripping gait of a wearer of clogs.

"Put chicken in at eleven. No make fire too hot."

"No, I won't. Don't worry. I can roast a chicken," Mari said absently and went on with her playing.

These two people who were her parents but with whom she had no intimate associations and little exchange of thoughts . . . they were people remote from her life, her plans and dreams. She lived in a different world.

Mari loved her father and mother, and in a crisis would have sacrificed anything for their sakes; the family ties were very strong when threatened from outside. But in the ordinary affairs of everyday living, they were strangers. There were times when she had been self-conscious and ashamed when her mother had come to a school program and could not talk with the teacher as the other mothers did. Mari, as well as her brothers, was separated from her parents by the barriers of language and conflicting cultures.

Father and Mother Sato were products of a civilization rooted in mystery and imagination, tradition and symbolism; Mari, one of a civilization of realism

20

and materialism, individual freedom and youthful, energetic pioneering. Her parents' civilization faced the past; Mari's, the future.

Father and Mother Sato started off to church, two humble little people reverently following in the footsteps of their Creator: six days had they labored, and on the seventh they rested and looked upon what they had done and saw that it was good.

Tom had wakened to the sounds of the music sometime earlier, and as he lay stretching and revelling in the luxury of lying in bed, he had heard his father getting into the car. He sat up in bed and looked out. It was a beauty of a morning, sun shining, fog cleared away, warm air sifting in the open window moderating the damp night chill of the room. Birds singing. It was like spring. If he could have ordered it, he wouldn't even have asked for anything as nice as this for a Sunday in December.

The car was backing out of the garage now. Tom listened intently to the sound of the motor. Dad doesn't give it time to warm up before he starts out, he criticized with his superior knowledge of the gasoline engine. Ah, but she is a beauty, though! A sleek, shining, lovely thing, like something alive, like a giant bird gliding along the drive and skimming silently down the highway, a dazzling streak of blue.

Tom lay back again lazily, hoping the folks wouldn't stay a long time after church talking to Pastor Tanaka like they did sometimes. It seemed as though they had no idea of time when they got to visiting with the preacher. The sermons he preached were long enough. Tom remembered the dreary hours he had spent sitting on the hard seats, swinging his legs fast to get the cramps out. He wondered that there was anything left to say once the service was over. He wanted to get dinner over early. The fine day was awasting; a late dinner meant a short afternoon for a drive.

After a catnap or two he got up and dressed leisurely and with care. He spent a long time before the mirror trying to make his hair lie back in waves like

21

Tad's, instead of standing on end. He put on more and more oil and with his fingers tried to push in the waves the way he had seen Mari do. But he got no cooperation whatever from his bristly, stubborn hair. As soon as he took his hands away it rose up and stood there in stiff, oily tufts, and Tom laughed at himself for trying. He got out his light tan sport shirt from a hanger in the closet and over it pulled the new blue turtleneck sweater he had bought for the Thanksgiving game at State College, the game Allen had starred in. Tad had been home from camp on leave then, the end of his basic. Sure looked swell in his uniform. Tom took a look at himself in the mirror--his sweater almost matched the car--gave his hair a last, futile stroke, and went out into the kitchen.

"Want me to fix your breakfast now?" Mari asked.

Tom sniffed of the chicken roasting in the oven and noted the kettles boiling on the stove.

"No. I'll wait till dinner. I'll find something." He went toward the cupboard.

"Well, don't eat any more of those cakes."

"What cakes?" Tom asked too quickly.

"What cakes!" Mari giggled. "You know well enough what cakes. You ate about half of them last night."

His sister's exaggeration betrayed Tom into confession.

"Why, I did not," he denied emphatically. "I only ate . . ." Tom laughed at himself and went on. "I ate three, and that's the honest to goodness truth."

"Well, don't eat any more. Please, Tom. Save them for tonight."

"Expecting company?"

"You could ask Allen and Peg to come home with us after the drive," Mari suggested. She looked for her brother's approval, but he made no comment. She should have left it for him to think of. Tom went out in the yard and picked a large orange from the navel tree at the back of the house. He sat down on a bench in the warm sun with Malt stretched out at his feet, and peeled and ate the orange while he watched down the highway for the folks returning from church.

As Tom and Mari were leaving that afternoon, Father Sato came out on the front porch, his wood carving and tools in his hands.

"Don't drive too fast," he called to Tom, more from habit than from any concern about Tom's speeding. He knew his son was a careful driver, and the pride he took in the new car insured the best care of it. Father Sato stood watching them go, his benign face aglow with content and satisfaction. Tom was a fine boy, a trusted son. And Mari was a good daughter, a hard worker indoors and out.

Tom glanced back as he was passing the house and, seeing his father still standing there, was moved to wave to him, an impulsive gesture, intimate and unusual, which left him self-conscious. But it surprised and pleased the little man who raised his hand promptly in response. Tom was long to remember that unique exchange of farewells.

When the car was out of sight, Father Sato went around to the back of the house and sat down on the porch steps with his carving. This was his favorite occupation on Sunday afternoons when he could be outdoors, sitting in the sun or shade as the temperature dictated; and over the years he had completed several pieces among which were real works of art. At the present time, he was working on a cat, carving it from a piece of wood taken from the end of an egg crate. He had learned by experience that this wood took the lacquer finish without soaking it up and left the clean cut of the chisel clearly visible which was one of the woodcarver's pleasures and satisfactions. This was not just a cat that Father Sato was carving but a very special cat. He had seen it in a frieze banding the wall of one of the famous Shogun temples at Nikko, the Sleeping Cat, done by the left-handed Jingoro, an exquisite bit of wood carving which he knew he was unworthy to attempt. But the design was simple, and he enjoyed trying with the colored postcard picture of the original as a guide. The figure was beginning to take shape now, and he stopped occasionally and, holding it up to the light, turned it about, viewing it with a critical eye.

Yoshi was doing bicycle tricks in the side yard between the house and the greenhouse and calling to his father to look at some new accomplishment every now and then.

"Look, Dad, I can ride around in a circle without ever touching the handle bars. Look out, Malt. Get out of the way. Now look what you've done." Yoshi picked himself up grinning. "Well, I could have done it if Malt hadn't got in front of me."

"Be careful you don't break your bicycle," Father Sato admonished.

Mother Sato dozed in her chair in the front room, lulled into a sense of security by Papa Sato's voice drifting in through the open doors as he talked with Yoshi. She had been very unhappy while Papa Sato was away in Japan during the summer and she hoped he would never go away and leave her again. She depended on him and was lost without him.

The home of Allen and Peg Sullivan stood on a knoll in the south part of the town of La Vista, with two large date palms standing like sentinels at either end of the long front veranda. The Sullivan family was in the yard, enjoying the warmth unusual for December, after the damp, chilly autumn. Mary, the oldest daughter who taught in a small coast town, was home for the weekend. Mrs. Sullivan and Little Bill, about Yoshi's age, were about to start for a drive over to La Jolla to see Little Bill's grandmother.

When Tom and Mari pulled up at the foot of the hill, Allen, Peg, and Jeanie, Allen's girl, came running down the path.

"Got room for me, too, in that snazzy car?" Jeanie asked boldly.

"Sure," Tom answered tolerantly." Plenty of

room for everyone."

Mari slipped into the back seat so that Allen could ride with Tom, and Peg and Jeanie climbed in with her.

"Where do you want to go?" Tom asked Allen.

The girls began to answer.

"Oh, let's drive down the Golden Strand and come back by the mainland," Jeanie suggested.

"No, that isn't far enough. We want to take a big, long ride," Peg put in. "Let's go up through Elsinore and then back over the mountains through San Juan and down the coast home."

"Yeah, that's a swell drive. Will you, Tom?" Jeanie flashed her most dazzling smile.

Mari had said nothing.

Tom looked at Allen, waiting for him to make his wishes known. What the girls wanted was inconsequential. It was for Allen and him to decide. With Allen it was just the opposite; pleasing the girls was the whole thing.

"Sure. Can't beat the circle drive for scenery if that's what you want," Allen agreed affably. "If we can get back in time. Jeanie and I have a date over at Sue's tonight."

"Get back in time? What do you mean?" Tom asked with a swagger in his voice. "Why, I could drive to LA and back before dark, easy."

The gang razzed Tom about having such a crush on his car and waved gaily to the family left on the hill as they started off. Tom was glad they were taking the inland highway instead of going up the coast, for his eyes were still tired from last night and the glare of the sun on the water would have been blinding at this time of day.

He sat back to enjoy himself. The car would almost drive itself, just a touch of his fingers on the wheel to keep it on the pavement. Good friends, a beauty of a day, no responsibility for the conversation. Allen and the girls had already started off on a steady chatter. Pleasant hours ahead with nothing to do but enjoy himself; yesterday's fatigue and tomorrow's toil forgotten. Carefree American youth out on Sunday parade.

Occasionally Allen pulled his attention away from Jeanie to tell Tom bits of campus gossip. He was in his first year at State, rode his motorcycle back and forth between home and the college, had already made a name for himself in varsity football. He was a big, husky blond, a good-looking fellow, his face a little too full to be handsome, lazy in appearance and motion, too young for the draft. His college years, filled with football and girls, stretched out attractively ahead.

"Want to bet on the Rose Bowl game?" he asked Tom. "I'll bet Oregon loses her shirt."

"Do you really think Duke can beat them? No, I'm not ready to place any bets yet. Want to wait and see if Duke's first-string men are all in the lineup. Two or three got some pretty bad injuries in that last game of the season back there."

"Yeah, I know."

Orange and avocado groves bordered the highway across the mesa and through the rolling hills. Once they got behind a truck loaded with crated cabbage, and Tom slowed and waited for a straight stretch of road to pass. Over the hills, they came out on the valley floor and drove through a town or two before beginning the steep ascent to the summit. At the top where the highway widened into a semicircle for sightseers' parking, Tom parked the car and they all clambered out and looked down over the low rock wall. Down in the valley far below the level floor looked like a vast checkerboard done in bright green and dull brown squares. Winter vegetables and alfalfa fields, leafless apricot orchards and plowed ground lying fallow till spring. Tom had brought his camera, a Christmas gift from his father, and he took pictures of the group, of Allen and Jeanie, and then one of Mari and Peg to finish out the roll. Restless to be on the move, they were soon off again. This time Peg, with a sisterly intuition, got into the front seat with Tom and let Allen ride with Jeanie.

This was all right with Tom, for he knew he must give his attention to the driving the rest of the way. The descending highway followed close on the edge of a deep canyon rich in beauty. Allen cuddled Jeanie close, Peg turned and talked with Mari, interspersing their conversation with exclamations as they caught glimpses of the scenery about them. Deep down in the bottom of the canyon a stream rushed along, plunging over large, white rocks, dashing itself into snowy foam. Across on the canyon wall opposite the highway, banks of bright green trees, washed clean by recent rains, glistened in the bits of sunlight which found their way into the canyon and fell upon the leaves.

Once out of the canyon, Tom relaxed a little as he drove along past the old San Juan Mission, its venerable walls concealed in a jungle of vines and trees, and on the few miles to the coast. Here the highway was one continuous stream of traffic. Everyone who had a car was out in it this bright, warm Sunday afternoon.

When they came to a string of roadside stands, Peg began to beg Tom to stop long enough to get some Cokes, as she was simply perishing with thirst. The sun was getting low, and Tom would have preferred to keep on going, for they were still nearly sixty miles from home. When all the others added their voices to Peg's, he pulled the car off to the side in front of a row of open-front shops selling everything from Cokes to cones to live bait.

While they were drinking their Cokes, Peg discovered some abalone.

"Since you and Jeanie have that date and can't go out to Satos' tonight," she began on Allen, "I think you ought to buy some abalone for us to cook at our house."

Allen remonstrated weakly and bought four. Tom, concerned for the car rug, found a gunny sack in the trunk, and Allen dropped the wet, slimy shells into it. Giving the top a twist, he threw it into the back seat.

"Now you and Tom can stop with us," Peg said to

Mari as they were getting into the car, "and we'll fry the abalone out in the barbecue, it's so warm."

"That'll be swell," Mari accepted readily. There was always a good time at Peg's house. "But you'll have to talk Tom into staying," she whispered.

"No better bait than an abalone to catch Tom with," Peg whispered back with a laugh. In the car she turned to Tom. "You and Mari are going to stop at our house to eat abalone tonight. We've still got some of that sauce you like so well with them, remember?"

"I sure do. Say, thanks, that'll be all right."

It was some time before he could find a gap in the traffic.

"Say, who's going to pound those things?" he asked suspiciously when he had gotten back on the highway again. He knew the menfolk sometimes helped with the women's work around the Sullivans'.

"I'll do it if you are too lazy," Peg joked, "although it's a hard job."

Tom grinned but made no offers. He knew well enough he would get roped in in the end.

"I'll pound if you'll cook," Mari said. "I never get them right. They're always tough when I do them."

"You leave them in too long," Tom told her.

"Mmm. Wish we didn't have that other engagement," Jeanie sighed.

"Maybe we could get Sue and Jimmie to come over," Allen suggested.

"No. I told you it was a party. It's Sue's birthday and it's a surprise on her. Her mother's giving it. I tell you we have to go."

The sun set blood red in the ocean before they reached the city. When Tom stopped at the first traffic light he noticed the people in the next car staring at him. Embarrassed, he looked straight ahead and tried not to see them. At the next red light it was the same. And the next. He flipped the rear view mirror and looked at himself to see what was the matter but could see nothing about himself to attract attention. Peg began to notice.

"Got your lights on?" she asked.

"Yes," Tom answered, uncomfortable.

There was something different about the streets, too. Usually filled with men in uniform around this time of day, sailors and marines swarming the streets on weekend passes, the sidewalks were practically deserted. Only here and there a lone uniform among the civilians, a serviceman with serious face, not hunting for fun and frolic.

Annoyed by the repeated stares, Tom turned off to the left on a side street, pretending to want to avoid the heavy downtown traffic, and took a shortcut through the city.

It was quite dark when they reached the Sullivan home.

Allen and Jeanie hurried out and started out the path, Allen swinging the sack of abalone in his free hand. Peg and Mari waited for Tom to make the car secure on the slope.

Mary Sullivan had been waiting for them on the veranda. When she saw the car lights she rose and came running down the hill, Little Bill skipping along beside her.

"Have you heard anything?" she asked as she came up to Allen and Jeanie. Even in the dark her face showed white. Something in her voice struck fear to their hearts.

"No. What's happened?" Jeanie was the first to speak.

Their words reached the car. Tom felt something like a piece of ice slipping along his spine. Something had happened. A dark premonition told him something had struck close to home. He was opening the door to get out, but he stayed his hand and listened.

"Pearl Harbor's been bombed." Mary spoke in a low, solemn voice. The four words exploded over the group like bursting shells.

"No!" Allen's loud voice shouted in violent protest. The thing was incredible. "When? The Japs?"

Tom slipped back in the seat and gripped the

wheel. The world stood still.

Allen and Jeanie turned, and they all ran down to the car together, Mary trying to talk but her throat so tense she could hardly speak the words.

"Early this morning they came over, waves of bombers. Oh, it's awful! So many of our boys have been killed, asleep in their barracks or drowned when they went down with their ships. There wasn't any warning! They didn't have a chance!"

"How awful!" Jeanie cried. She had a cousin on the *Arizona*.

"Why, the dirty doublecrossers!" Allen yelled. "They were still having peace talks in Washington." His voice was hot with fury. "We'll make them pay for this!"

"Yes, you bet we will!" Little Bill's shrill voice broke in. "The cops are picking up all the Japs and putting them in jail."

"Hush," Mary said, laying a restraining hand on the boy's shoulder. She was the first to realize the position Tom and Mari were in. She remembered the persecution of the German Americans in the last war, and the Nisei would have race prejudice to face besides. "Hush, Bill. You don't know what you're talking about."

"I do so. I saw them get old man Sera as soon as he brought his fishing boat in. You can just ask Mama. We were driving along the wharf, and I saw them pulling him off ..."

"Never mind now." Mary spoke more sharply. "The FBI were probably picking up someone they've had under suspicion."

"My God! This means war!" Allen exclaimed in a shocked voice, as if the significance of what had happened had just dawned on him. "Tom, do you know it? This means war between us and Japan." He had no more spoken the words than he realized what Mary had a moment before. He stopped, feeling hot and uncomfortable. But why should he? he asked himself. Tom was an American, the same as he.

"Yes, it sure looks like it," Tom said soberly,

keeping his voice even. "Come on, Sis, and get in. We'd better be getting home."

"But we are going to fry abalone," Peg cried. The words sounded silly, the whole afternoon, the light patter, their foolish laughing over nothings.

"No, we can't stay now. The folks, they'll be looking for us to come." Tom tried to sound natural, but it seemed to him that his voice was coming from way down in a deep, hollow cavern. His mind fought against recognizing that they were caught in a painful situation.

Everyone was trying to do the same. They had been such good friends for so long. It was embarrassing to suddenly feel strange in each other's presence.

Yet, in spite of their efforts to be at ease, an awkward silence fell over the group which no one seemed able to break. It was as if an earthquake had opened a crevasse--Tom and Mari on one side and the rest on the other, and the crevasse was slowly, inexorably widening as they stood there watching helplessly. Peg felt it and reached out and grabbed Mari, holding her tight as if to defy the irresistible force.

"Oh, isn't it just too awful!" she said incoherently. Then, laughing foolishly at her sudden display of emotion, she loosened her and said offhandedly, "Well, see you tomorrow."

"See you in English," Mari replied without emotion but with a toss of her head that threw her hair back from her face. It was a gesture of withdrawal familiar to Peg and something about Mari she had never been able to understand, that haughty air of withdrawal which shut everyone, even her best friends, out of certain phases of her life. "Don't forget the term themes are due tomorrow."

Mari got in beside Tom, and Peg grabbed a couple of abalone from the sack and thrust them into her hands.

"Well, take these if you can't stay. Papa Sato likes them so well. Tell him Peg sent them."

"Thanks," Mari said, taking the shells and dropping them on the rug at her feet, unnoticed by Tom.

Mary came to the car window. She had recovered her presence of mind, and her heart ached for the two in the car. Who knew what was ahead for them?

"Now don't worry, kids," she said in a voice warm with sympathy. "Everything will be all right, I know." She just wished she did know.

"Thanks, Miss Sullivan," Tom said with appreciation. "It's my folks I'm worrying about. We Nisei have nothing to worry about--we're Americans."

Mary winced before such a show of faith in humanity.

"Well, good night, children."

"Good night, Miss Sullivan. Be seeing you, Al."

"Yeah. So long." Allen was already turning toward the house, his hand holding tight to Jeanie's, his face set.

In the twinkling of an eye, things had changed for all of them.

Tom and Mari rode along in silence for a time. Then Mari's mind could no longer control her thoughts.

"Will there really be war?" she asked.

"Well, of course. You don't think we would let ourselves be attacked without fighting back, do you? Of course it means war."

"Tad will be in it," Mari mused, frightened. "Tad will be fighting Japan. Maybe his cousins that he met last summer."

"I'll be in it, too," Tom declared emphatically.

"You mean you're going to volunteer?" Mari asked in a weak voice.

"I sure am, as soon as Dad can find a man to help on the ranch. Nothing can stop me now."

All around them the night was so quiet and peaceful. They passed the familiar ranch homes, bright lights shining from the windows, families still united eating a Sunday night snack, people entertaining Sunday night guests, stars twinkling down the eastern sky, marking the mountain line where they ended.

At Harry Sakai's place the light was on in the barnyard, and Harry's wife was nailing up crates of cabbage, the two little children crying and tugging at her skirts. Harry was nowhere in sight. There was something strange about the picture.

"I never saw her working outside before," Mari said, puzzled. Harry's wife was a city girl and did not work in the fields as many of the other ranch women did.

"Harry's hurrying to get his cabbage to market," Tom explained condescendingly. To him, if a man were rushed with the work, naturally the women would help. But there was something strange about the scene at Sakai's. Tom stepped on the gas. The trip home from La Vista had never seemed so long.

"Tom." Mari broke the silence again as they turned the corner and could see their house all dark in the distance. "You know . . . what Little Bill said. Would they put a person in jail unless he had done something?"

"Don't be silly. This is America, not Germany. And don't say anything before Yoshi or the folks about what Little Bill or anybody else said."

"Yoshi has already heard everything on the radio. He always tunes in to get Jack Benny."

Tom didn't say anything. He was wondering why there weren't any lights on at the house. The folks must be out at the packing shed. He should have gotten home sooner to load the pickup. He began to have a protective attitude toward his parents. What would the war mean to them as alien Japanese? How would they feel to have America and Japan fighting, to have Tad and him fighting against Japan? Would the war make any difference to the Nisei?

Tom had scarcely turned into the driveway when Yoshi came dashing out from where he had been watching on the front porch and leaped onto the running board of the moving car.

"Hey, look out what you're doing! Do you want to get killed?" Tom shouted, grabbing the boy by the arm while he brought the care to a standstill.

"They took Dad away! They took Dad away!" Yoshi kept repeating. "The G-men were here. They took Dad away." His hands twitched nervously on the windowsill and his fingernails dug at the paint.

Tom felt something crushing on his chest. He couldn't breathe.

"When?" he managed to gasp. "What did they want with Dad?"

Yoshi felt better now that Tom was home, and he began to tell of the events of the afternoon with some relish over his own importance.

"They came in a big, black sedan. Harry Sakai was in it, too, and he looked awful scared and his nose was bleeding all over his clothes. Dad gave him his handkerchief when he got in."

Tom heard a strange sound beside him, like the sharp, frightened cry of a wounded thing, and then Mari was as still as death. As Tom listened to the words tumbling from his brother's mouth, he tried to piece in the gaps in the account. How had his father gone? Little Bill said they dragged Sera off the boat. Did they use force . . . he felt driven to ask, but instead hid cravenly behind the boy's omissions, afraid to know the truth.

"Where were they taking them?"

"I don't know."

"Didn't Dad tell you anything?"

"N-n-no."

"He must have," Tom insisted, trying to be patient with the kid. He knew if his father were leaving there would be a dozen things he would want to leave word about. "Think now. Wasn't there something he told you to tell me?"

"No. He didn't have any chance."

Tom was beginning to recover from the first shock. His father would tell his mother anything he wanted to leave word about--the ranch work, money, anything Tom would need to know about. Of course. He wouldn't trust it to the boy.

His mother. What a shock to her!

"Where is Mom?" he asked quickly.

Yoshi's voice changed.

"She's in the house," he said soberly. "She's crying."

"Come on, Mari, let's go in. She can tell us more about it."

"She don't know anything," Yoshi sobbed. "She didn't know Dad was gone till I told her."

"What do you mean?"

"The G-men wouldn't give him time. They took him ... They wouldn't let him go in the house ... He said goodbye to me. That's all. When I asked him where he was going, he didn't hear me, I guess."

"So they wouldn't let him see Mom." Tom could feel his anger rising. He got out and started for the house, followed by Mari and Yoshi, trying to make the things he had just heard from his brother seem like reality. His father was taken by the FBI. No. It didn't seem possible. He was standing there on the front porch when they had left, waving goodbye to them. How little did they know what a few short hours would bring! But why had they taken his father? He had never done anything against the country. Maybe there were other Japanese who worked for Japan here, but not his father. He was just a quiet, hard-working person who took little interest in anything outside his family and work. He had been willing for Tad to volunteer. Would he have wanted Tad to join the Army, fight against Japan, if he had been helping the other side? His father a spy, a saboteur, an agent of another country? It didn't make sense. It was too fantastic for him to believe that anyone could take it seriously. Then why did they want him? Where was he now? It seemed that he must find him when he went in the door, sitting there in the old leather chair reading his Japanese Bible and looking up as they came in with a smile of satisfaction on his aging face as much as to say, "Glad you are home again, children."

But when Tom opened the door, he was bereft of

all delusions. The house was dark; there was no sign of light anywhere. It was dark as pitch and there was an empty quality to the darkness, like a deserted house.

Then he heard a stifled sob, and with a quick motion of his hand he felt for the switch and turned on the light. He saw his mother sitting there crouched in the corner of a big chair, her face buried in her arms.

At the sight of her, even a greater anger swept over him. Anger at the Japanese for their attack, anger at the FBI for taking his father, anger at himself for being away enjoying himself when they came. If he had been there he could have talked to the men, he could have explained, told them his father was all right. Maybe they had come to the wrong place; there were other Sato families around the neighborhood. But if they wouldn't listen to him? Tom felt the first twinges of helplessness in dealing with the strong arm of the law.

Mother Sato sat up and tried to hide her tears when the children came in.

Mari took one look at her mother's dazed face, lost that haughty sense of self-sufficiency which had tided her over the scene at the Sullivans', and, bursting into tears, ran to her room. Yoshi's mouth was twitching with excitement as he looked from Tom to his mother, fear of the strange and unknown beginning to steal into his eyes. In that moment Tom realized that everything depended upon him, that it was for him to take some action to stabilize the family. If only Tad were home!

Tom labored to pull himself together, to free himself from the anger which was consuming him, muddling his mind. Time for that later on when he was in the fight. But now he must comfort his mother, quiet Yoshi's fears. This was America. Children should not have terror in their young faces; women should not have to huddle in the corners of their homes, bereft of husbands torn from them in violence.

Mother Sato's mind was in a state of confusion. She tried to tell Tom about the afternoon, now speaking rapidly in Japanese and then, reminded by his face strained by his effort to understand, changed over to slow, broken English.

She had run outside as soon as Yoshi had told her, but she was too late. The car had already backed out of the drive and was speeding down the highway toward the city. All she could do was stand on the porch and watch it go. Watch helplessly while the large, black sedan which was carrying Papa Sato away from her sped relentlessly on and soon disappeared around a curve. If she could only have seen him before ...

In a daze she had come into the house, not knowing where to turn for help or what to do. Then she had thought of the radio. Maybe she could find out something. There had been talk of war with Japan. Sometimes at night, when she and Papa Sato were alone in their room, he had told her about things he read in the Japanese language newspaper and talked about what might happen to them if war came. Papa Sato had always told her not to worry, that they would be treated justly.

From the radio came the dreaded news. The words which tumbled over themselves so fast as they came in loud, tense voices were familiar after two years of war news from Europe: bombs and planes, destruction and killing. But there were new words among them now, Japanese planes and Americans killed. Japan and America were at war. Papa Sato had been arrested. Tad would have to fight. Maybe Tom and Mari would be picked up somewhere along the highway and taken to jail.

It had all been too much. She had sunk down in the chair in a sort of dazed stupor. She did not remember how she had spent the remainder of the afternoon. The sound of Yoshi's voice calling to Tom had roused her to consciousness of her surroundings.

Tom drew the shades and locked the front door before he sat down to listen to the news still pouring from the radio. He found there was little he could say to comfort his mother or allay her fears.

"Now don't worry, Mom," he kept repeating. "Dad will be all right. Maybe he'll be home tomorrow when they find out they got the wrong man. There are other Sato families around here, you know."

"Yes. Some no good. No relation of ours. Why they take Papa away, no take me? He do nothing bad." Tom couldn't answer.

Mari came out when she heard the radio. She was not crying any longer. Yoshi said he was hungry, and she went to the kitchen and set out some supper, brewing a pot of tea for her mother. She took the plate of fancy cakes from the cupboard and set it on the table.

Tom looked ruefully at the little cakes as the family gathered around the table in silence. He remembered that, a long time ago--was it only that morning?-- Mari had said to save them for supper and he had asked lightly, "Expecting company?" What a gay, happy world that had been, the world they had been living in then! It had been Sunday morning and everything looked bright. Now it was Sunday night. His world had become dark and desolate, for it had turned its back to the light.

"Why did they have to do it?" he kept asking himself as he tried to choke down a sandwich with a glass of milk. He tried not to see the sober faces of his mother and Mari across the table or the empty chair at the end. War between the two countries might have had to come some time. But why did Japan have to start it this way? He flinched from the hate in Allen's voice. It would be that way all over the country. He could hear it in the voices on the radio. Wherever the name of Japan was spoken, it would be spoken with loathing and contempt?

The Sato family talked little as they sat around the table pretending to eat. The radio in the other room kept blaring out the terrible news. Twenty-nine hundred American boys killed. Planes destroyed before they could get off the ground. The *Arizona* sunk with all on board.

Mari pushed back from the table suddenly.

"I'm not going to school tomorrow," she announced. "I'm not going anymore at all. I'm going to quit." Tom and his mother, and even Yoshi, turned and looked at her, startled, as she stood leaning against the sink, her arms stretched out on either side, hands grasping the drain board, defiant of any opposition to her plans.

As the meaning of her words dawned on Yoshi, he began, parrot-like, to repeat her words. Going to school became dangerous and frightening.

"I'm not going either," he shrilled, sticking out a stubborn lip which trembled a little. "I'm going to quit, too."

Nothing could have aroused Mother Sato from her own grieving faster. Not go to school! Those were fighting words to Mother Sato. She had never wanted her children to miss even one day. And to quit! She looked from Mari to Yoshi and made a clucking sound of deep disapproval with her tongue against her teeth. The children must still go to school. She glanced toward the end of the table as if expecting to see Father Sato there, ready to take his rebellious offspring in hand. And then her eyes traveled around the table and rested on Tom.

At first Tom did not understand the message in them, for he had thought of his responsibility only in terms of trying to comfort and help his family, not of ruling them in his father's place. But now he could see as plain as day what was going through his mother's harassed mind. Papa Sato is away. Tadashi, the eldest son, is away. Tamotsu is the oldest son at home. He will take his father's place.

"Listen, Mom, have a heart," his youthful eyes pleaded at her. "I'm only two years older than Mari. She won't listen to what I say." A quick glance at the defiant girl standing at bay against the sink ready to counter the opposition of her mother which she knew would come, only served to convince Tom of the truth of his words. "You talk to her," his eyes said as they came back again to his mother's.

But his mother continued to regard him as the man of the family and waited for him to step forward and speak with the voice of authority. There was dependence and confidence in her tear-stained face. Tom could not fail her.

"Of course you'll go to school. Both of you," he said lamely, but gained confidence at the sound of his voice. "Where did you ever get the crazy idea you could quit?" He turned to Yoshi. "Now get to bed. Look how late it is."

Yoshi grinned up at Tom as if it were some kind of joke, but he met no answering smile on Tom's face. He got up slowly. "Okay," he said glumly, shuffling across the floor toward the door. "But if Mari don't go, I'm not either."

Mari had stood looking curiously at Tom. Always her brothers had ordered her around in the little things. "Hey, Sis, get me this," or "Give me that," and usually she had given up her playthings or, when older, other things, without too much resistance. But for Tom to order her to go to school after what had happened! What right had he? She was thrown off balance by his attack. She had expected the opposition to come from her mother, but now she turned to her as a possible ally. Mother Sato was saying nothing and looking at Tom. Now Mari recognized the right of the eldest male member of the family to command the others.

Tom, who could not know what was going on in his sister's mind, had risen from the table and was making his escape to the living room before his sister's storm of protest could break over his head.

"Tom," Mari called.

Tom stopped and stood in the doorway, surprised by the mild, wheedling tone of Mari's voice. That was just the way she spoke to Dad when she wanted to get her own way.

"Can't you see I simply cannot go to school after what has happened?" She tapped an impatient toe on the worn linoleum. "How could I ever look the other kids in the face?"

Tom hardened his heart. It was tough being the head of a family, making young people do things, before you were old enough to have forgotten how you would have felt under the same circumstances. Tom knew it would be punishment for him to face the rest of the school. The stares of the people in the other cars along the street that evening had sent him scurrying up a side street. But Mari must not be allowed to leave school in the middle of her junior year. And besides, the Nisei would be watched and judged by what they did now.

"You didn't have anything to do with the attack on Pearl Harbor," he argued, not giving any ground. "Do you want all the school to think you were afraid to come? That is what they will think of every Nisei who misses school tomorrow. If I were still in school I wouldn't let anything keep me out tomorrow." Tom was talking big now, getting the feel of authority.

"They ought to know how we'd feel," Mari countered, still in that plaintive, coaxing voice. "I know Peg would understand if I didn't go anymore. Anyway, what's the difference what any of them think? We won't have any place in anything anymore. Everybody will hate us."

Tom was afraid she was going to cry.

"You have the same right there as anyone, and you are going to go the same as you always have."

"But what if no one would speak to me? I simply couldn't stand it. What would I do?"

"You don't go to school to visit," Tom said sharply. This was worse than he had expected. "You want to graduate next year, don't you? If you drop out now, do you think it would be any easier to start in again later?"

This struck home. Mari had no answer. She hadn't looked that far. She certainly did intend to graduate and go to college, too. And she knew if she stayed out now, she never would go to La Vista again, for she would have lost face with the others.

41

She came over to the table and began gathering up the dishes. Mother Sato had been listening and sipping her tea, understanding little of what was passing between the brother and sister, but proud that Tom was standing firm.

"Well, maybe I'd better go," Mari conceded, the way one does who knows the deciding has not been hers at any time in the argument. "But getting on the bus in the morning, facing all the kids when I don't know how they're going to treat me . . . Why can't I ride in with you when you go for the seed?"

Tom relaxed, complacent in his victory.

"I'm not going in. I'm going to find out what's happened to Dad."

Mari muttered to herself as she turned on the tap and rinsed the plates and cups.

Tom remembered he had the vegetables to load for the morning trip to market and went out the back door, glad for an excuse to be alone for awhile.

On the porch his toe struck against something in the dark, and he stooped to pick it up. It was his father's woodcarving of the cat. Surprised to find it lying there, he felt around in the dark and found the chisel and gouge. To find them left carelessly on the porch told him better than any words of Yoshi's the pressure under which his father had left. No one was more particular than Father Sato about putting things away when he was through with them, and he insisted on all of the children doing the same. No farm machinery was ever left in the fields, nor garden tools standing out in the weather. The picture of what happened flashed across Tom's mind as clearly as if he had been watching it on a screen.

His father sitting here on the steps in the sun, absorbed in his carving, knowing nothing of what had happened out across the Pacific, indulging himself in this weekly retreat into leisure and beauty. Perhaps he would stop once in awhile to rest his fingers, and his mind would review the morning sermon, or recall something from Tad's last letter, or he would simply daydream trying to recapture the Japan of his love, the Japan which had been so completely taken from him by his last visit. These were the things his father talked about in leisure moments. Were they the subjects which formed the content of his mind when he was alone? Perhaps. Likely.

And then he had heard a car drive in. Tom's hand gripped tighter about the chisel handle. Looking up, Father had seen the black sedan and had laid down his carving and tools at once and gone to meet his guests. No Japanese would remain seated while a guest approached. And before his smile of greeting could die on his lips, he would have been faced by the law, arrested, and whisked away.

Tom leaned heavy-hearted against the porch post and looked off toward the city. Was his father there in the city jail? Or had he already been taken away? Would America have concentration camps like Germany? He rebuked himself for thinking such thoughts and went on out to the packing shed to load the pickup. Later, when he put the good car away, he felt something wet and slimy on the floor. He took out the abalone and threw them to the dog.

III

Tom was awakened at four-thirty the next morning by the loud clanging of the alarm beside his bed. Automatically he reached out and turned it off and jumped up at once as was his habit. But this morning he was groggy with sleep. A big day ahead, no time to waste, he mused, more asleep than awake, as he felt for the light switch in the dark and started for the closet for his work clothes. Get the vegetables in to market and then hurry home and get as many flats filled with dirt for the tomato plants as he could before time to go to town for the cucumber seed. Dad would want to be in there when Wilson opened the seed store.

Tom's half-open eyes fell on his good pants and sweater flung carelessly over the chair where he had left them the night before. His eyes flew open, and he stared at the mussy heap of clothing. He never left his things that way. Then the ugly events of the preceding evening came back to him. He couldn't even remember when he had come to bed. He had loaded the pickup and put the car away, and then he had gone into the greenhouse and sat down in the little room his father had partitioned off from the rest of the building and used for an office. Tipping back in the old swivel chair, briefly recalling the day his father had bought it at a used furniture place in the city--it had been sitting out on the sidewalk--Tom had tried to think. His mind had tried to encompass the meaning of the things which were happeneing to him and his family, but he could only feel.

He did not know how long he sat there or when he went in to bed. He had written to Tad, telling about their father. He only remembered the mental misery which engulfed him.

He was wide awake now. Everything was coming back to him. He knew he hadn't slept long. Yoshi had tossed and kicked all night and cried out in his sleep. Tom had heard his mother moving about in her room, and once he thought he heard sobbing. He wasn't sure whether it was coming from his mother's room or from Mari's or whether it was only his imagination, the memory of those hollow, grief-stricken sounds which had come to him as he had opened the door on his return home last night. Would he ever be able to forget them, or would they always be ringing in his ears?

Dad isn't here! He is gone! He has been taken away. I do not know where he is. I do not know what is happening to him. He is not here in the house this morning. We are here alone. He will not be here to guide the work of the day when I come back from the market. What will I do without him?

Tom dropped down on the side of the bed and buried his face in his hands. He felt lost and frightened. And then anxious. The responsibility which would fall to him if his father did not return soon seemed a greater burden than he could bear. He had never gone ahead with anything on his own; he had always worked under his father's directions. Father Sato had always handled the finances. Tom knew little about that side of ranching.

The habit of work soon drove him to his feet again. Mr. Imoto would be wanting the vegetables. As he went out through the dark hall and empty kitchen and on out into the dark outside, he felt that eeriness he always felt in being up alone in these last dark hours before the dawn when everyone else was asleep. There was always a mystery in the very aloneness. The others were there, yet not there--present in their physical being but themselves away in that mysterious absence called sleep.

He whistled to Malt as he went out to the shed and started the motor of the pickup.

Yes, Tom had always felt a sense of loneliness and mystery as he trucked the produce to market in these early morning hours, passing ranch houses familiar enough in the daylight or with the windows lighted in the evenings. But at this time of day they were unfamiliar groups of shadows, the distinctive landmarks around them shut from view.

But this morning he felt the weirdness of the predawn hour more intensely than ever, and his feeling of isolation from other people was keener. He was glad to have the companionship of the little dog who sat beside him on the seat, his pointed ears erect, his nose out the window sniffing eagerly at the damp morning air.

America's first night of war was ending. Men had been killed. Americans had given their lives, made the supreme sacrifice for their country without a chance to fight in her defense. Homes had been sleepless. Already the tears of grief were flowing. The whole country was aroused.

War! War between my father's country and my own, Tom thought. And then tried not to think. The world would still go on. People would still need food, and he would go on growing it and hauling it to market, carrying on the best he could until his father was home again. Surely it couldn't be long, for he was confident that his father was innocent.

Yet, in spite of his attempts to minimize or put aside the thoughts which were unpleasant to him, Tom knew that it was a different world he was living in. The evidence was too strong for him to ignore it. His mother's wan face and red eyes as she sat at the supper table last night were mute evidence of how their lives had changed. Tom knew it was more than grief which had stricken her to the depths. Even though he could not converse freely with his parents, he knew much of their culture and their philosophy. It was a great humiliation which had come upon the Sato family. The head of the family in jail! The Satos had been law-abiding people as far back in the past as it was possible to trace their individual family history; and beyond that their roots went back to the First Emperor himself, who had sprung forth from the union of the Sea God and the Sun Goddess and was the father of them all. In all the centuries since then the Japanese people had been taught to be law-abiding, meticulously following

46

rituals and rules which gradually developed through the ages into strict codes of behavior, reaching down to the least detail of personal living.

Now Father Sato had been arrested as an evil-doer, a lawbreaker, dragged from his home by government officers, held under suspicion, and regarded as a menace to the country in which he had lived most of his life. Tom felt the shame and humiliation, too, even though not so keenly as his mother. But mingled with these feelings there was another which was stronger, something warned him, something vague, yet sinister.

Was he safe? This was his first trip out into this new war world. Had he been wise to come? He began to feel nervous, and although he laughed at himself, and called himself foolish, and talked to Malt to drive away the feeling of isolation, forebodings kept returning. It was with a growing sense of insecurity that he drove along the deserted highway and into the outskirts of the city. He had often wondered what would happen if Japan and America ever got into a war against each other. He knew his family, like all other Japanese, would be affected, but he had never thought of it striking with such devastating swiftness. He had barely heard of the attack on Pearl Harbor when he learned that his father had been taken.

Where would it strike next? Would it be safe for them to go about their business as usual? Would it be all right for Mari to go to school today? Maybe he should drive around on the way home to see some of the other Nisei and find out what they were going to do.

He hadn't thought of any personal danger when he had started out from home, but here in the dark, deserted streets of the city he became more nervous. Anything could happen. This was a regular morning route for him; if anyone wanted to get him, there were plenty who had seen him pass in late spring and summer mornings when it was light. He slackened the speed of the pickup so as not to attract attention from a cop. Just then Malt gave a sharp bark at a cat on the sidewalk, and Tom started violently.

"Hey, pup, keep quiet. You seeing things? You and me both." He laughed and reached out and gave the dog a rub on the head. "Let me know before you let out another yelp like that."

The streets were almost as empty as the country highway had been. It was too early for change of shifts at the aircraft plants, and the servicemen on twenty-four-hour passes who were usually seen on the streets at this time were absent.

Still, out in a poor part of the residential section, a car swung around the corner ahead and stopped across the street. A man came across toward Tom carrying something in his hand. Tom felt prickly along his spine and his heart missed a beat before he saw that the man was carrying a couple of bottles of milk. Just another guy like myself out early delivering his produce, Tom thought, and was angry at himself for his fright.

"Now that ought to teach you," he told himself. "You are letting your imagination get away with you. Now pull yourself together and remember you're in the United States of America and not in Nazi Germany. You've got nothing to worry about."

But he had no sooner convinced himself of this than, as he got further down into the city, he began to wonder where the city jail was. He had never thought of the place before, but now that residence of unhappy men became a matter of the keenest interest to him. Would his father be there? Had he slept? Would he have a bed? Good food? Could he see him if he went there after he delivered the vegetables? Probably not so early in the morning. Did they have visiting hours at a jail like they did at the hospital? How strange to be wanting to know about visiting hours at a jail! Yes, he was living in a new world. He would come in later in the day and find out what he could.

As he came nearer the market Tom began to wonder about Mr. Imoto. How would his market be affected by the war? Would he still want vegetables? Or maybe Mr. Imoto had been picked up with the others.

The precariousness of their situation in a new era dawned upon Tom for the first time. What if no one would buy from the Japanese? That had happened up north somewhere when Japan attacked China. How much more likely a boycott now that Japan had attacked the United States. If Mr. Imoto had been picked up, what should he do with his load of produce?

An early streetcar clattered past with its sprinkling of passengers. Tom waited for it to pass and then turned the truck into the dark alley and drove down between the buildings, past rubbish boxes and garbage cans, turning in under the unloading shed of Mr. Imoto's wholesale and retail market. There he backed the truck up to the high platform. In the dim light of the few dusty bulbs hanging from the roof he could see Mr. Imoto standing waiting for him.

The proprietor of the market was a little warmer than usual in his greeting. Perhaps he had been wondering in turn about Tom, whether or not he would make the trip in. However, there was no sign of worry in his full-moon face. In fact, one glance at Mr. Imoto gave one the impression that he had never had a worry in his whole life. He was neither short nor tall, lean nor fat; his face was always merry as Santa Claus and a joke forever on his lips. But he was not easily taken in for all his good nature. Some ranchers mistook his easy, carefree disposition for that of a sucker and then hated him and called him names because they had not been able to put off on the "Jap" their wilted vegetables and specked potatoes which they couldn't sell anywhere else. They said he cared for nothing but money.

Tom didn't know much about that. He trucked his father's produce in and picked up the checks twice a month. Maybe Imoto wasn't generous, but he was square. He was an older Nisei, in his late thirties, and a power among the Japanese in the city.

"Hello, Tom," Mr. Imoto greeted in an easy drawl. "Hope you've got a good load for me this morning. We were sold out long before night Saturday."

"About the same as usual," Tom said with a

49

feeling of relief as he began to throw off the crates. "But I can bring more after this if you want me to. We've been selling what you didn't take wherever we could locally. Cuts your profit hauling stuff around that way."

"Well, bring me everything you have from now on."

Tom felt his spirits rising. It didn't sound much as if Mr. Imoto were expecting trouble. He finished unloading, found his empties, and threw them on the truck. He had hoped for an opportunity to talk to Mr. Imoto about yesterday. He couldn't have told him about his father, but maybe he could have found out what they did with the men the FBI picked up. But other trucks were beginning to come in now with their loads, and some empties from the smaller markets were coming to buy their supplies for the day. There was no chance to say anything.

Tom climbed into the cab and started the motor. Now Mr. Imoto came to the cab window.

"Say, Tom." He leaned closer to be heard above the motor without shouting. "Keep your chin up, boy." With a hearty laugh that flaunted trouble in the face, he turned away to the other trucks.

"Well, what do you know," Tom said to himself as he drove away. "Imoto's okay." This was the first time there had ever been anything but business between them. He began to feel a bond drawing him closer to Mr. Imoto, yes, and closer to all the Japanese. Tom's closest friends were his classmates at school, and since he had been the only Nisei in the class, he had not formed any intimate associations among them. Now he felt it would be a good idea for him to get better acquainted with the other Nisei around La Vista, and the Issei, too.

Passing the Sakai house on the way home he saw young Mrs. Sakai out already in the dim dawn trying to load some heavy crates onto the big truck, doubtless the crates they had seen her nailing up the night before. It was plain they were too heavy for her.

50

Tom turned his head away, embarrassed at watching the woman struggling futilely with the heavy loads, and drove past. It was no affair of his. The Satos and the Sakais had no dealings with each other. Norio and Harry had graduated in the same class at high school, but they had had nothing in common. That is, nothing except their Japanese ancestry. Their ancestry! The same feeling which had drawn Tom closer to Mr. Imoto was now pulling the Sakais into the orbit of his interest and concern. Father Sato and Harry Sakai had both been arrested. The security of both families was threatened.

Tom swung the truck around, with a twist of the steering wheel which sent Malt skidding off the worn leather seat, and went back. He turned the pickup into the Sakais' driveway and, getting out, approached the woman.

"Can I help you?" he asked.

When Mrs. Sakai turned toward him, he saw that she was crying.

"Oh, yes. Thank you," she said, trying hard to control her voice. "They are so terribly heavy for me."

She did not talk like the other ranch women, some of them, and Tom recalled hearing that she was a Los Angeles girl. Harry had married her when he was working up there. Tom had never met her before, and now he saw before him a poised, pretty young woman not much older than himself. Poised and pretty even with tears in her eyes and a break in her voice. He wondered how such a superior looking girl could ever have taken up with a fellow like Harry.

Tom lifted a crate to the truck, pretending not to see the tears.

"Harry got this much out of the field and crated," Mrs. Sakai said, seeming glad to have someone to talk to. "He was going to truck a load into Los Angeles today, but they came and got him last night." Her lips began to tremble and fresh tears rolled down her cheeks.

Tom busied himself with the loading, not

knowing what to say to the woman. Was there anything to say anyway in a case like this? He was wondering what she planned to do with the cabbage once it was loaded. Driving a loaded truck on the crowded highways and through city traffic was no easy job. Surely she wasn't thinking of trying to do it herself with a couple of little kids and a baby on her lap. He wouldn't have thought of asking her, but the woman herself seemed to sense that some explanation was due. When she could speak again she began to tell Tom her plans.

"I am going to pack a few things and take the babies and go home. I'll stay with my folks until Harry is home again. That is what he told me to do." So she got to talk to Harry before he left. Evidently they had no hopes of his early return as Tom had of his father's. "I'm going to drive the truck in," she went on. She seemed to be confident. Grudgingly Tom admired her courage. "My father is in the produce business, and he offered Harry a good price for his crop. He can scarcely get enough to meet the increased demand for fresh vegetables. Harry had planned to get it all harvested this week, but now . . ." In a graceful gesture, she brushed the hair back from her damo forehead with the tips of her long fingers. "Do you know of anyone I could get to do the work?"

"No, I don't," Tom answered reluctantly. Half a year's income would be lost to the young couple. "I'll inquire around if you want me to, but with labor the price it is and the cost of trucking to Los Angeles, it might not pay you to harvest the cabbage at all."

"No, maybe not," she said in a dull, hopeless tone.

The sound of babies crying came from the house, and Mrs. Sakai went in and left Tom to his work.

Presently she came out again with the two older children just as he was throwing on the last crate. Her expressions of appreciation for his assistance were so profuse that Tom was embarrassed and glad to get away. As he drove along home he mulled over the Sakais' plight. He knew Harry wasn't much good, but

52

he wondered if he wouldn't have been of more value to his country harvesting his fifteen acres of cabbage than he would be in jail.

His breakfast was ready for him when he reached home. His mother and Yoshi sat down with him, but Mari had not been able to wait when he did not come. She had eaten and was now standing by the front window watching for the bus.

Tom glanced in through the open door and saw her standing there so sober and quiet. No gay humming and keeping time with a tap-tapping of her toe as she usually did while she waited. Happy and gay, eager to get off to school and the good times there with Peg and the others. He began to have misgivings over his uncompromising attitude of the night before. His mother could not be expected to know what the Nisei might have to face. He should not have let her make the decision. She had never been a part of the community in which she lived; she couldn't be.

What if something did happen at school? Here he was, getting jittery again. He gulped his hot coffee and ate his eggs and toast with a relish, not in keeping with his uncomfortable state of mind. He had done a hard half-day's work before breakfast this morning. As he talked with his mother, explaining why he had been so late getting home, his mind was not on his words, but on his sister, standing there by the front window.

Unconsciously his mind was conditioned to trouble by the long line of unhappy experiences of his people in their struggle for a place for themselves in this country. Just as the white man was suspected and unwanted in the Orient, so the Oriental had met with distrust and prejudice in America. Sometimes it had been the Chinese who had been the victims of the professional anti-Oriental groups who fanned the flames of hate, fear, and prejudice, for reasons too insidious to be understood at a passing glance; sometimes it had been the Japanese who were thus victimized. This anti-Orientalism on the coast had always been a handy tool in the hands of politicians aspiring to city, state, or national offices; a promise to promote anti-Chinese or -Japanese legislation had proved to be a reliable mount to ride many a candidate to victory in closely fought contests. Rumor had it, even down to the present, that if one would travel the old highway through the Siskiyous of northern California and stop to scrape the moss from the faces of boulders turned toward the highway, one could still read such slogans as "The Chinese must go. Vote for O'Donnell."

Tom had heard these and other legends passed among his people over the years. Anti-Japanese riots in San Francisco, attempts to close the public schools to them, vigilante groups in the San Joaquin Valley shanghaiing laborers and shipping them out at night, alien land laws, and discriminatory immigration laws. And Japan had been a friendly nation then. But now there was a war on. Tom recalled the contempt in Allen's voice when he had heard of the sneak attack. Would the high school students feel as Allen had? Would this feeling react against Mari and the other Nisei students?

"Hot coffee, Tamotsu?"

Tom came to and realized his mother was standing over him with the coffeepot.

"Yes, thanks, Mom." He stirred in the sugar.

Things had changed since those early days, he reasoned within himself. And those incidents were directed against aliens. We are Americans, he said to himself. Everything will be all right.

Nevertheless, when he heard the familiar honk of the school bus, he pushed back from the table and, getting up, followed Mari to the front door.

"Good luck, Sis," he said, and Mari turned and gave him a look which said if anything happened he would be to blame.

The big, yellow bus pulled up at the gate as Mari ran out. Charley Mack, the driver, saw Tom standing in the door and waved. It was a gesture of friendliness, and Tom took it as a good omen.

The bus was always well filled by the time it came by the Satos, and Mari was the only Nisei to ride it. The students had had no opportunity to test their own reactions yet, when the door swung open and Mari stepped on.

Tom held his breath and watched.

"Hello, Mari." "Hi, Mari." He heard a chorus of voices shoouting, spontaneous, unrehearsed.

And some girl sitting near the rear called out, "Here's a seat by me, kid."

Tom's exhalation of relief was like the bursting of a balloon.

"Well, what do you know? I never heard so much fuss before when Sis got on the bus."

"Huh? What'd you say?" Yoshi asked, sidling up to Tom in the doorway.

"Nothing you'd know anything about. Watch the time now, and don't miss your bus." He went back to finish his coffee. High school kids were a swell bunch; if you were a good sport yourself, they'd never let you down.

Yoshi took the lunch box from his mother and started off down the road toward the corner where he caught the elementary school bus, swinging the box in one hand and playing with Malt with the other. After seeing Mari start out, he had made no further objections to going to school. Two other boys who lived down the road past the Sato ranch overtook him.

"Hi, Jerry. Hi, Bill," Yoshi said.

"Hi, Yo-Yo," the boys greeted offhand, and the three walked on together.

Tom and his mother talked over the situation together. It was decided that Tom would go on with Father Sato's plans, anticipating that Father Sato himself would soon be home again. The law would protect him from being held with no charges against him, Tom explained to his mother. That was in the Constitution. But Tom would not go to La Vista that morning. The cucumbers could wait one more day. Instead he would try to find out where his father was and see him if possible. He would want some of his clothes. Mother Sato had found his suit coat hanging on a nail on the back porch that morning, and she was gravely anxious for his health. He had been too warm, sitting there in the sun, and had taken off his coat. When he went, either he had forgotten to put it on or had not been given time. The nights were very chilly. He might have taken cold, and who would care for him if he got sick?

Mother Sato made up a bundle of things, some soap, and towels, and Papa Sato's toothbrush and razor, and some warm clothing. She tucked in a jar of Vicks in case he had taken cold. She trotted back and forth between bedroom and bathroom, relieved to be able to do something for Papa Sato, calling messages to Tom which he was to deliver when he found his father.

Tom took the bundle and the messages and was on his way out to the car when a motorcycle came streaking in the drive with the speed of a comet, and Allen pulled up just short of crashing the doors of the garage.

"Come on, Tom, jump on behind," he called. "We're all going into the city to join up, all the gang."

Tom walked over to where Allen was standing astride his machine. He was glad to see Allen, and he was more than pleased that Allen expected him to enlist with the others. If he only could. Here was his chance. No better, more undebatable opportunity to stand up and take his place as an American would ever come to him. But he knew he could not take advantage of it.

"You mean you're going to quit college?" he asked, playing for time. He dreaded having to tell Allen about his father, and yet he was afraid of seeing distrust in Allen's eyes if he refused to volunteer without giving a reason. If Allen suspected his loyalty, it would be the end of their friendship, Tom knew. His pride told him that.

"Sure thing I'm going to quit. We all are. We talked it over at Sue's last night. The whole gang was there, and we listened to the radio until way late." He named off the fellows, all seniors in Tom's class last year. "We're all going to try to get in the same outfit, and we want you with us. I told the fellows I'd come

56

out after you this morning. Come on, Tommy."

"Sorry, Al, but I can't go. I can't leave the ranch right now."

"Heck, we're in a war, boy. It comes first now. We've been attacked. We can't go on as if nothing had happened, going to school, raising vegetables. Come on, Tom, with the rest of us."

"How long do you think you could fight without food?" Tom teased, knowing how well Allen liked to eat and refusing to let his side of the conversation get serious. Wanting to tell Allen the truth, but unable to say the words.

"Oh, heck, there's plenty of old people to raise food. Let your dad get a man to help him. Want me to go with you to tell him you want to sign up? Your dad is swell. He'll want you to go just like he did Tad." Allen stood the machine up and looked about the place. "Where is he?"

"Dad isn't home," Tom said.

Allen gave Tom a quick look. Something in his friend's face told him that Father Sato's absence from home was not because of a routine trip to La Vista.

"They didn't . . ." he began, and then stopped, hunting for the right words.

Tom nodded.

"He was gone when we got home last night," he said in an aggrieved voice, as though there were some injustice in that fact.

"Well, I'll be damned! Father Sato picked up! The FBI must be getting pretty damn nearsighted. One good look at your dad would tell anyone he was okay."

There was an uncomfortable silence. Allen wasn't fluent when it came to expressing sympathy, but his heart went out to Tom, and the whole Sato family, for that matter.

"Say, I'm sure sorry. Sorry as all get out. Anything I can do to help? I can work on the ranch till I'm inducted."

Then Allen noticed for the first time that Tom had on his good clothes. "Going somewhere?"

57

"Yes. I'm going to try to find Dad and take these things to him. Why don't you ride into the city with me?"

A crisis in their friendship had been passed safely.

In the city they went to the recruiting office first and Allen explained to the boys about Tom's father and persuaded them to wait while he helped Tom find him. While Tom was waiting for Allen to come out, a couple of Nisei from La Vista came by and stopped to talk. One of them had been trying to see his father.

"They're all down at the jail," he told Tom, "but they won't let anyone in to see them."

"Well, I've got some things for Dad. I'll go around anyway."

The fellows gave him the location, and when Allen came out, he and Tom drove around to the jail. On the way Tom told Allen what the fellow had told him.

"I don't know whether I can get this stuff to him or not."

"Let me take it in," Allen said. "I bet I'll get to see him, or somebody's going to get his head bashed in."

Tom was loathe to give up seeing his father himself, but if Allen would have a better chance than he, he did not want his own desires to stand in the way of getting the bundle to his father. He finally consented to stay outside and let Allen go in first. He gave him as many of his mother's messages as he could expect Allen to remember, and with mixed emotions watched the big fellow march up the steps to the building. It was incredible that his father was in there and even more impossible to believe that he was in there and Tom would not be permitted to go to see him. There were a few other Japanese standing around, looking confused and beaten. They, too, must have members of their families in there.

Allen came out in a short time, red-faced and angry. He did not have the bundle.

"Did you see him?" Tom asked eagerly as Allen climbed in beside him and slammed the door.

"Yes, I saw him, all right, or I'd still be in there. But they weren't going to let me at first, and they sure don't mind being insulting. Your dad is all right. He was glad to get the coat and sweater. They didn't have any bedding last night, and he says it was kind of chilly. He says not to worry, to go on with what you planned on the ranch, and take good care of your mother."

Tom blinked back the tears. Before he could get his voice to ask anymore, Allen went on.

"Say, you remember that Sakamoto kid that graduated a year ahead of us? He was in there trying to see the old man. He was taking a nap when the officers came after him, and they wouldn't give him time to dress or even get his teeth. They dragged him off in an old bathrobe, and when his son brings his clothes and teeth down to him, they won't let him in. I'd be ashamed to call myself a man if I ever did such a cheap, mean, crawling thing as that. They finally let me take the stuff to him after they had opened it up and didn't find any heavy artillery in it. The poor old man is frightened out of his wits and sick into the bargain. One thing I know for sure, when I go to fight, it won't be for these jailkeepers, to make it safe for them to go on with their Gestapo methods."

Tom had never seen Allen so worked up over anything. In fact, he had never seen Allen get excited over much of anything before except a football game or a broken date. The new world in which they were living had changed Allen, too. He was no longer the happy-go-lucky friend of Tom's high school days, laughing at Tom's serious attitude toward his studies, always looking for the easy way himself. Allen was a man now, taking the responsibility of citizenship upon his broad shoulders, aroused and angered by injustice and man's inhumanity to man.

The two were nearer together now than they had ever been before. Tom went to the recruiting station while Allen signed up with the other fellows, and then they drove back out to the ranch. It had taken them so long that it was almost noon when they reached it.

Mother Sato came trotting out and was glad to have news from Papa. They let her think that Tom had seen him, and they did not tell her he had slept without covering all night. When she had drunk in every bit of information they had to tell and Allen had gone off on his motorcycle, she remembered to tell Tom the phone had been ringing ever since he had left. It was Mr. Wilson about the seed. Tom went to the phone and called the seed store.

"Does your father still want the things he ordered?" Mr. Wilson bellowed into the phone when he found out who was calling. Mr. Wilson, too, had changed.

"Why, yes, of course," Tom said quickly, thinking it strange the seed man would ask such a question. The seed had come in only Saturday.

"Well, you didn't come after it this morning, and fertilizer's hard to get now. There's plenty of good customers would be glad to get it if your old man don't want it." The insinuation in his voice left Tom more bewildered than ever. Mr. Wilson had always considered Father Sato one of his best and most regular customers, for he had been with him ever since the opening of the seed store twelve years before. Tom had often heard Mr. Wilson say this to his father, most often during Depression days when new customers were sought after and old ones were nervously wooed and pampered.

"Yes, sure we want it," Tom repeated. "I'll be in right after dinner." The receiver at the other end went up with a bang.

Tom puzzled over Mr. Wilson's strange actions as he ate his dinner and wondered if he really did want the stuff. His father had said to go on with the plans, but Allen hadn't been able to find out a thing about how long the men might be held before they would have a chance to clear themselves through a hearing, or trial, or whatever they would have. If his father were to be away very long, he didn't see how he could carry on alone, doing the work of two.

But there was the question of money. If they had to hire a lawyer to defend Father Sato, it might take more money than they had in the bank. Tom knew attorneys' fees were high, and it might take extra money to persuade one to defend an alien. If he didn't put out the cucumbers, the only income of any moment they would have before late summer would be that from the sale of tomato plants, and that might not be enough. The winter cucumbers were a quick cash crop, and there would be big money in them this year, for everyone had money and was spending it freely.

He put the problem to his mother.

"I can help till Papa comes," she said immediately. "See, no little ones anymore to keep me in house. I can weed. Set out plants."

Tom laughed.

"No little ones anymore. Time you had a rest."

His mother looked so tiny and tired.

"No, no. Too much rest no good. I can help. Yochan can work, too."

"Yes, that's right," Tom agreed heartily, glad that his mother was willing to see Yoshi put into harness at last. "It's time he was learning to work."

Tom could remember when he was the kid's age, getting up with his father mornings, his eyes glued shut with sleep, working in the fields until school time and at it again in the evening, sometimes until late at night. He had never played around with a dog all evening. He had never had a bicycle to ride around all day Saturday. Yoshi could be a real helper once he was broken in. And Mari liked to work outside better than in the house. They would get along someway without allowing his mother to do too much. And then there was always Jose Gonzalez during the rush season. He was a good worker for short stretches.

Tom drove into La Vista that afternoon. The

weather was not bright and balmy as it had been the day before. The sun glimmered feebly through a lightly overcast sky. It was a sullen war sun, Tom thought as he drove along. War, and we weren't ready for it.

The tension born of sudden attack was evident in the town. Men stood in little clusters on street corners and in front of the bank and post office, talking war. Newsboys were carrying the latest editions of the city papers. Tall, black headlines that could be read from a passing car screamed of the morning's declaration of war by Congress and of the attacks on Guam, Wake, Manila.

Tom parked the pickup in front of the seed store and went in.

"Hello, Mr. Wilson," he said cordially.

Mr. Wilson, a tall, angular man with sharp nose and short, thin mustache, was thumbing through some papers on his cluttered desk and grunted a response to Tom's greeting rather than actually speaking any words.

"This the stuff?" Tom asked, indicating the group of sacks standing together near the door.

"Yes, that's them. Here's your bill."

Tom had already shouldered one of the sacks of seed. Mr. Wilson's words took him by surprise. He intended putting it on the account as his father always did and making the payments according to the arrangement his father had with Mr. Wilson. He set the sack down and turned to the seed man. Mr. Wilson was holding out the bill and looking at him as though he were a stranger with whom he was dealing for the first time.

Disconcerted but trying not to show it, Tom took the bill and noted the amount. That would make a big hole in their bank account if he had to pay it all at once. Maybe he ought to wait. If he could get word to his father some way, ask him what to do ...

But no, Mr. Wilson wouldn't hold the seed. Tom took out his father's checkbook and reached for a pen on the desk. Good thing Father Sato had made a joint account of it when he went to Japan last summer. They'd be in a pretty fix now if Tom couldn't check on the account.

"Can't take a check," Mr. Wilson said crisply. "It will have to be cash."

This threw Tom into complete confusion for a minute.

"But Mr. Wilson, our check is as good as the cash. You can call the bank and find out. I don't have any cash . . . that much cash on me."

The man gave a short, unpleasant laugh when he mentioned calling the bank, and there was a malicious gleam in his eye. What was the matter? Maybe his check wasn't good.

"I want the cash," Mr. Wilson said shortly, and then turned away to take care of another customer.

Tom hurried out and down the street toward the bank. He found no change of attitude toward him among the people he met on street. Strangers paid him no attention and acquaintances said, "Hello, Tom," quietly. Their voices were serious; no one smiled. But no one was smiling at anyone.

In the bank he wrote a check and presented it at the window.

"I'm sorry, but you cannot draw on your account. All Japanese accounts are frozen as of this morning." The cashier's voice was cold.

"What?" Tom asked stupidly. Although he had had some forewarning from Mr. Wilson's actions, and although he had heard every word the cashier said, he could not comprehend the meaning.

"All Japanese accounts are frozen," the man repeated.

"I can't draw anything then? How long will it be . . . frozen?"

"I have no information in regard to that." Cold, steel gray eyes looked into Tom's worried ones without a change of expression.

There was a line waiting behind him, but Tom stood his ground at the window. Necessity had made him temporarily bold. The man at his shoulder tapped his foot impatiently on the marble floor.

"I'll draw from my savings account, then," Tom said stubbornly, reaching for his wallet.

"Savings accounts are frozen also," the robot said.

"But that isn't Japanese money," Tom argued, getting red. "That's my own personal account."

The man behind him laughed unpleasantly.

"You have proof of your citizenship?" the cashier asked.

"Birth certificate?"

"Certainly."

"Well, not here with me. I . . ."

"It will be necessary for you to present legal proof of your citizenship before you can draw on your account." With that the cashier reached around Tom and took the papers of the man next in line.

Tom picked up his check quickly and moved away from the window. He could not raise his eyes from the floor as he walked rapidly toward the door. He began to feel like a marked person. He alone of all the people lined up at the window could not draw on his account. He could not get the seed to plant his crop. He could not go to see his father although he was only ten miles away in the city. His face was burning hot from the humiliating encounter with the cashier. He wanted to get out in the open, back to the ranch.

"Howdy, Tom." A big, friendly voice boomed loud enough to be heard all over the bank, above the clatter of the typewriters and steady hum of business. "How are you?"

Tom looked up to see the red-whiskered face of old Peter Vandenheuvel beaming down upon him.

"Why, hello, Mr. Vandenheuvel. I wasn't expecting to see you out. How are you?"

"Not so good, Tom, not so good." The old man liked the Sato boys because they were always courteous to an old man and had time to listen to his complaints. "Some days I get around pretty well. And then again this rheumatiz gets to acting up and keeps me flat on my back for a week at a time. Guess I'm getting old."

He laughed as if he had made a good joke. "How are all your folks, Tom?   Your father got his cucumbers in yet?"

"No, not yet. But we have the ground ready." Tom was anxious to get away. Everyone was staring at them. "Well, I'm pretty busy these days. Guess I'd better be getting along."

"Yes, always a lot of work on a ranch. I'm glad to be rid of mine."

On his way back to the pickup Tom met Eddie Yamamoto. Eddie was in a dither. He pulled Tom to one side and began to talk in excited undertones.

"We're about to get kicked out of our home, Tom. Our rent's due today and our landlord says pay cash or get out. No notice nor anything, and he raised the rent ten bucks a month besides. He came over early this morning while we were at breakfast, and I heard him say to Dad, 'Pay cash or get out before night.' Well, Dad banked everything from the store Saturday and . . . Say, our funds are frozen, did you know that?"

"Yes," Tom said drily. "But what are you going to do if you have to move?"

"Gosh, I dunno. Mother had bought a lot of Christmas gifts for her friends, and she's out around the neighborhood now, trying to sell them to get the money. If she gets enough, okay. If not . . . guess we'll be on the street.

"You and Bill come over and sleep at our place," Tom invited quickly, feeling the bond pulling again. "There's Tad's room empty."

"Gee, thanks.   Sure hope we don't have to, though. Say, did you know the FBI picked up a lot of men yesterday, and they're still picking them up today. They got Harry Sakai for one, and guess who . . . Old man Sakamoto. He was in his pajamas in bed and they wouldn't even give him time to get his false teeth. Say, what do you suppose they wanted with that sick old man?"

"I wouldn't know. Well, come on over if you need a bed," Tom said, and hurried away.

He climbed into the pickup and sat there trying to figure out how he could get that seed before the store closed. That old buzzard knew all the time I couldn't get any money at the bank, he thought. That's the reason he wouldn't take a check. But why couldn't he have told me so I wouldn't go over to the bank and make a fool of myself? I'll never ask any favors of him again, and I hope Dad never buys another dollar's worth of stuff from him. He began to figure up just how much cash he could get together from all possible sources. Maybe he could get enough to go into the city and buy what he needed there. But the outlook wasn't encouraging.

His figuring was disturbed by a voice at the cab window. It was old Peter again.

"I just heard over at the bank about your funds being frozen, Tom. And I learned about your father, too. You should have told me. Mighty sorry to hear about it. Mighty fine man, Mr. Sato, yes sir, a mighty fine, God-fearing man." He mused along, as if talking to himself. "I hope he will soon be safe home again. Yes, I do that." Then he asked abruptly, "Do you need some cash, Tom?" He leaned over with difficulty and peered into the cab.

"We got caught a little short, but we'll get along all right." Tom would not have thought of letting the old man help him.

"Now, if you need any, Tom, I can let you have it. And glad to do it. So don't hesitate to say so if you need any."

"Thanks a lot, Mr. Vandenheuvel, but we'll get along all right. Wouldn't want to borrow money the way things are, but mighty swell of you to offer a loan."

Old Peter was not to be put off. Perhaps in those ten years when young Shigeru Sato had worked as a laborer on his ranch he had learned something about Japanese pride and reticence. And another memory, too, was stirring in his big heart. Bread cast upon the waters nearly two decades ago was about to return to the Satos.

Old Peter Vandenheuvel opened the door of the pickup and eased his huge, rheumatic frame laboriously into the seat beside Tom. There he sat for a minute, breathing heavily from the effort.

Tom sat back, impatient at the interruption. Well, there wasn't anything he could do, anyway. Doors were closed everywhere. He turned. Might as well listen to the old man awhile. Maybe he could forget things for a time.

"Tom, I saw you in the bank, and it's my guess you went there to get money. I hear all the stores are demanding cash from the Japanese on account of their funds being frozen. And you couldn't draw any, and you probably need some to finance your crops and are too proud to say so. Pride is a good thing, Tom, and I wouldn't want to see anyone without it. But when you let it stand in the way of your own and your family's best interests, then it's not good. Now I'm going to tell you something, and when I get through maybe you won't feel the way you do about taking money from me.

"The truth is, I owe your father quite a sum of money, and I'll tell you how it all came about. When you three older boys were little shavers--you weren't even walking yet ... Your folks were still living over there by me then. Your father did something for me that saved me hundreds of dollars. I had helped him out a few times when he first got married. He didn't have much to start with when he first leased that five acres. Well, I loaned him a team and plow to get his land plowed, and a few little things like that. Well, this year I'm speaking of, I was having my first full crop of strawberries off the ten acres I had put in on my place. Then, just about the time they were coming on, I fell from a ladder when I was up fixing the roof and broke my leg, my left leg here, and I broke it just a little ways above the knee. Well, there I was, flat on my back, and the whole income for the season out there in the field ready to be harvested. I thought I knew where I could get pickers, but when my wife started phoning around she couldn't find anyone who would come. Labor was scarce then just as it is now, and she couldn't find anyone. She kept on trying, and I wasn't too worried, for the days were cool and cloudy right then and the berries wouldn't ripen fast, and she would be sure to find someone. And then all of a sudden, overnight, the weather turned hot and the sun shone down like blazes, and I knew those berries weren't going to wait for anyone. They'd be a total loss if we didn't get someone in the field that very day. Well, your father came over that morning, Tom, the morning the weather turned hot. He knew I'd been hurt, and when he didn't see anyone out in the field picking strawberries he had gotten worried about the crop.

"To make a long story short, he took things in his own hands, got a crew in the field before noon of that day. I'll be doggoned if I've ever asked him to this day where he got them, but, my, how they worked! For three weeks they picked, and packed, and marketed the berries. My wife checked the crates and she swore they came in faster than she could count them. I don't know when your father ever slept himself, for he was working his own place at the same time. And I could hear the men talking out in the packing shed most of the night, it seemed like. Well, at the end of three weeks they had picked nearly five thousand dollars' worth of berries, and when I went to pay your father, he wouldn't take a cent more than enough to pay off the crew. He said I had helped him and he was just paying me back. All these years I've felt indebted to him, Tom, but I've never had a chance to square things up. You folks are kind of on the spot now, and maybe this is my chance. I'm going to feel right bad if you rob me of it. How much do you need?" He was already pulling out his wallet.

Tom couldn't speak for a minute. Somehow the story had made him feel that he could accept a loan from this man his father had once served so unselfishly, but it seemed too good to be real, and he was afraid to speak.

"I sure wouldn't want to hurt your feelings, Mr.

Vandenheuvel," he said at last. He took out the bill Mr. Wilson had given him and handed it over. "Here are the things I wanted to get today, but Mr. Wilson demanded cash. Could you let me have that much?"

Mr. Vandenheuvel took out his spectacles and adjusted them on his broad nose.

"Are you sure this will be enough?" he asked.

"Oh, yes, plenty."

"Well, it's too late to get in the bank today yet, but come on in and I'll write Wilson a check. I think he'll take one from me. You see, I own the building his store's in." The old man gave Tom a sly wink. "The man ought to be ashamed of himself. That's what war does to people, Tom. War's a terrible thing. Sets people against each other when there isn't any reason. Makes hate where there wasn't any before. A terrible thing. Yes, that's what it is. I'm mighty sorry to see it come to us."

"I don't know how soon I can pay this back," Tom said as they went into the store.

"Now don't you worry a minute over that. I'll fix it up with your father sometime. You've got enough on your young shoulders with your father away and Tad gone. Here, Wilson, is a check in full for the things Mr. Sato ordered."

"Why, thanks, Mr. Vandenheuvel. Well, glad you could get the money, Tom." Mr. Wilson began on a lengthy, red-faced explanation of how a man has to look out for himself when he's in business.

Old Peter interrupted unceremoniously. "Where's your men that do the loading around here? I don't recall as I ever had to load my own stuff."

"Guess they're working in the back room somewhere. Hey, Charley, come and put Sato's order on his truck."

When Tom reached home Yoshi was just coming from school, racing Malt down the road from the bus stop. Tom drove the pickup under the shed to unload later, and as he got out he saw Yoshi come out of the house with a piece of cake in his hand and start across the road toward the open mesa with the dog to chase rabbits.

"Hey, come back here," Tom called.

Reluctantly the boy turned back, resenting the interruption but regarding it as only temporary.

"What do you want?" he asked impatiently as he came up to Tom.

"I want you to help pick up turnips."

"Aw, gee whiz."

"Come on."

Tom took Yoshi to the field and put him to work.

When Mari came home she put on her levis and joined them.

"Oh, it was just awful when the president was speaking. Everything was as still as death in the room. It was in the history class. Henry Endo and Spike Fujita both cried," Mari told Tom. "And my throat ached till I could hardly stand it. But I wasn't going to let anyone see me cry. Everything was so solemn. And Peg looked so serious. I never saw her like that before, so . . . well, so kind of grown-up and sober. You know how she's always joking. Allen enlisted in the navy today, did you know?"

"Yeah. I went in with him."

"Everyone was so nice to me, and to all the other Nisei, too. Wouldn't it have been positively gruesome if I hadn't gone? Did you hear everyone when I got on the bus? After Congress declared war, Miss Winters gave us a long talk. She didn't try to have any lesson after that. She was just swell. She said we must be a united America without any conflicts or enmities among ourselves, and every American must be ready to do his duty no matter what personal sacrifice it calls for."

Tom told her about going to the jail, but Mari was in such a state of patriotic fervor at the moment that she stood ready to sacrifice the whole family if need be to win the war. However she did show a flutter

70

of concern for her father's safety.

"Do you think they will treat him all right?"

"There's international law to protect prisoners of war."

"That didn't stop Germany."

"But this is America," Tom said staunchly, but it had a sort of hollow sound to him after what he had been through.

"Well, you wouldn't think some of the traffic cops know it, the way they talk to you when they give you a ticket. If the FBI is anything like that I'd sure hate to be in Dad's shoes. When can we see him?"

"I don't know."

The three worked together until the shadows grew too deep to see any longer. Yoshi griped, and Malt walked dejectedly up and down the furrows, a puzzled look in his eyes.

Mother Sato had supper ready when they came in. It was a lonesome meal. Yoshi was the least affected by his father's absence. Revived by the food from the longest period of effort he had ever experienced, he rattled off the events of the day at school, switching from poor Japanese to English as he turned from his mother to Tom and Mari. On the playground at noon he had caught two forward passes for touchdowns.

"Heap big football star," Tom teased.

"Aw, I'd have been a big shot anyway even if I hadn't caught the passes," he bragged, throwing out his chest, "'cause I talked to the G-men yesterday. All the kids wanted to hear about it, and Miss Berry came over to see what was the matter. All the kids crowded just thick around me, and she thought there was a fight."

Yoshi's spirits continued to run high, unaffected by the silence of the others, until he saw that Tom was preparing to leave the table. Then he began to wilt visibly.

"Gee, I'm sure tired. Guess I'll go to bed right away."

"Oh, no you don't. Not for awhile yet. All

71

those turnips we brought in have to be washed and bunched yet tonight."

"Heck, I'm too tired to do anymore. Gee whiz, I've worked hours and hours already."

"Come on," Tom said.

"Aw, I'm tired." Yoshi looked toward his mother. Mother Sato had risen, and she laid a hand that trembled on the boy's shoulder. It was hard for her not to give in to her baby.

"Go with Tom," she said. "Mari and I will come soon to help, and it will not take long."

The boy realized then that his mother was no longer going to stand between him and the hard facts of life. He shook off her hand as a man who does not want sympathy, though his eyes were wells of self-pity. Somehow he managed to struggle to his feet.

"Okay. If I've got to, I've got to."

The boys walked out to the packing shed together. Tom thought of Eddie and Bill Yamamoto. Since they hadn't come over, their mother must have sold enough of the gifts to keep a roof over their heads for another month. Or maybe they had been lucky in finding a friend as he had done.

When Mother Sato and Mari had done up the supper work, they came out. Together they all sat around the workbench, bunching the cold, crisp vegetables for the market, Mother Sato's deft fingers doing a dozen to Yoshi's one.

Thus the family rallied around Tom as he endeavored to take his father's place, and the pattern was set for the winter evening on the Sato ranch.

IV

With the declaration in Washington that a state of war existed between the United States of America and the Empire of Japan, life changed for the people on the West Coast.

While the Satos and thousands of others in California who were linked with the enemy nation by ties of blood were facing the problems peculiar to their situation, the whole population was trying to adjust itself to a new world, a new way of living.

Reaction to the surprise attack upon the country was universal. No one was left unmoved, but emotions were varied. Some few unstable people were terror stricken; some loaded their cars with food and struck out for the desert, hoping to escape the destruction from the air which they were sure would come to the whole Pacific Coast. Some of these left heavy wagers behind with their taunting neighbors that San Diego, Los Angeles, and San Francisco would be in ruins within a month. But these few departures from the state were as grains of sand compared to the avalanche of arrivals which began to pour in from the East, brought to California by the labor demands of a rapidly expanding defense industry and an enormous program of war construction.

The newcomers filled every available house and apartment. New ones were built. People swarmed into them as soon as they were completed. And still they came. Villages grew to towns, towns to awkward, overgrown cities. And cities overflowed their boundaries, burst at the seams, overtaxed transportation facilities, public services, and food supplies.

Federal housing projects appeared to shelter government employees; thousands of trailers trundled together to form villages on wheels.

There was a general feeling of being too crowded.

Besides the workers who came--and they were only

a drop in the bucket--there were the servicemen, thousands of them, millions of them everywhere, crowding the buses, crowding the movies, milling about railway stations and hotel lobbies.

In some small communities, still sleepy from Depression days, detachments of troops appeared, set up their headquarters in empty buildings or in tents, and installed strange-looking equipment which they manned day and night. They created problems by their presence. While mothers, harassed by a thousand new anxieties, worried and disapproved, young girls fluttered around the uniforms like butterflies over a clover patch.

Air bases, and army camps, and naval flying fields sprang up like mushrooms overnight, and natty air corps cadets swaggered on the streets of the towns. Hasty marriages before the boys were shipped out became as common as movie dates before the war. Older men and women, still hungry from the lean years, rolled out at five in the morning, ate a hasty breakfast, and started off for the factory, their identification buttons pinned safely to their work jackets, leaving the children to get up later and fend for themselves until school time.

Everyone bought bonds through company payroll deductions, and many sold them as soon as they could and bought thick steaks, and new watches, and swanky clothes, and other things they had long done without.

Civilian defense was organized locally, and everyone had his job or responsibility. Emergency stations were designated in churches or club rooms, and cots and first aid equipment installed for victims of possible air raids. Buckets of sand and long-handled shovels became standard equipment for all patriotic homes, for what good citizen, even if careless of his own welfare, would allow a magnesium bomb to burn its merry way through his roof and cause a fire which would endanger his neighbor's house? People ceased to be units and became units in a community. Meetings were held where civilians were taught how to cope with poison gas and incendiary bombs, and air wardens and blackouts came into being. The curt, uncompromising voice of command outside the window growling, "Put out your lights," was a new experience to the American family, and some resented the intrusion on their privacy.

Observation posts were set up by the army and manned by civilian volunteers twenty-four hours a day. To these lonely stations men and women went faithfully day after day, week after week, without compensation, and did their two- or four-hour hitch, scanning the sky for planes. Women who couldn't tell a Mosquito from a B-17 stuck to their posts with the consciences of Puritans, fearful lest an enemy plane carrying death and destruction elude their vigilance; and when a plane passed within their ranges of vision, they promptly reported to the center the time, direction, and number of motors, the last being largely a matter of guesswork.

Women who did not take defense jobs gave liberally of their time to Red Cross and Nurses' Aid, grew victory gardens, and helped with scrap iron and wastepaper drives.

Selective Service was extended from one year to the duration and six months, and the age was lowered to twenty years. Boys rushed to join up with the navy and air corps to avoid the dreaded infantry. Territorial restrictions on disposition of troops was stricken from the books in Washington. Now the boys could be sent to any part of the world, and loaded transports were slipping out of the harbors under cover of night. Today the boys were here; tomorrow they were gone. The United States was in it up to her neck, and California was right on the front line.

And then, into what seemed to be an already saturated situation, a new and disturbing element was thrust.

It was well along in January--the war was almost two frantic months old--and the eyes of California were turned anxiously toward the sea and sky for the approach of the enemy, an enemy which had become more hated and feared with each new atrocity story printed in the press or broadcast on the air, an enemy which was barbarous, savage, without mercy. It struck terror to the heart, knowing the weak defenses on the coast, to contemplate the possibility of a Japanese invasion, when, lo! attention was called to the fact that an invasion had already been accomplished. The spotlight was turned upon the Japanese now living in the state by a barrage of stories in the press about the behavior of the Japanese in Hawaii at the time of the attack there, how those tricky, treacherous, cunning creatures who were American citizens by birthright showed their disloyalty by aiding the enemy in preparing for and carrying out the sneak attack on Pearl Harbor. They were handmade stories and smacked of fabrication, had one time to analyze them. Field laborers, it was said, had cut swathes in their cane fields in the shape of arrows pointing to important military installations; milkmen, making their morning deliveries at the time of the attack, turned their trucks crosswise and blocked the streets to keep officers from reaching their stations speedily; truck drivers drove their heavy trucks across the airfield and destroyed more planes than the bombs had done from the air. Other tales were passed about from one small group to another, always coming from someone who had heard it from someone who had seen it happen, so there was no denying it politely, even though one did not care to accept it. Among others was the one most terrifying of all, of how Japanese men had shot down women and children as they came out of their homes on their way to Sunday school that morning! Small wonder that the people of southern California, where the tale was circulated, sat, jittery, in their homes throughout the frequent blackouts and wondered if that little brown rancher across the way were cleaning his gun and getting it ready.

Parallel to the stories from Hawaii there were those which pointed out to the public the strategic position in which the Japanese of California had situated themselves, near harbors, and aircraft factories, and vital power lines.

Reason could have explained, but war does not cultivate and harvest reason as its crop. People lived through their emotions, and there was no time to reason or to think at all. Fishermen live by the sea and that is where harbors are found, and the Japanese ranches so far predated the aircraft factories built beside them as to make that accusation ridiculous to a rational mind. And to those unfamiliar with the laws restricting the use of land under power lines could have known that because of these restrictions it is cheaper to lease and may be used for farming. All of these stories pointing the finger of suspicion at the Japanese population as a group could have been seen as invalid by any high-grade moron, if there had been time for thought; but there was no time.

Pick up your load of riders and drive thirty miles to your defense job, get to the observation post to relieve the last shift, read the first aid lesson before class tonight, make the blackout curtains, finish that Red Cross sweater, work those extra hours at the store or office because the other fellow has been drafted, shop around for a good used tire, bake a cake for the USO party, write that weekly letter to John in camp. There was no time to think.

And so it seemed that men and women were allowing themselves to be used in an insidious campaign to create hate. These were people who had lived next door to Japanese aliens and their Japanese-appearing American offspring and had never given them a thought beyond the fact that they supplied high-quality fresh vegetables and luscious strawberries at a reasonable price. Now they began to see in these neighbors an enemy for whom they had been peering out to sea. Practical, hardheaded businessmen who had been dealing with these industrious immigrants for decades now became jumpy and saw the instruments of sabotage under every Japanese bed. Women who had seen their Japanese neighbors driving to town week after week for years suddenly became aware that the road led past a defense factory and rushed to the telephone to call the

77

FBI when they saw the familiar car pass. The more hysterical became veritable witch hunters, with all the fanatical zeal of a Salem judge. Calls to the offices of authorities became so numerous that a public announcement became necessary requesting the aroused, suspicious citizenry to leave the detection of spies and saboteurs to those trained for that work.

The string of defeats in the Pacific lengthened, heartbreaking reports of the hopeless struggle on Bataan strained nerves tight, the constant fear of attack kept the people jittery. Then came the mysterious middle of the night raid over Los Angeles. The antiaircraft went into action in a big way, and people for miles around rose from their beds and went outside to view the dazzling display of flak. What the guns were firing at no one knew then, and to this day no one has found out. Even the Secretaries of War and Navy contradicted each other vehemently a few days following. But, whatever it was, it had brought the war nearer. And the tempo of what now definitely appeared to be a planned campaign to rid California of the Japanese was stepped up by the papers. Editors dipped their pens in gall to write their editorials. "A viper is nonetheless a viper wherever the egg is hatched. . . . An American-born Japanese is a menace . . . unless hamstrung."

Public officials lost their dignity and screamed over the radio. "Change the Constitution if necessary, but get the Japs out. Never mind about citizenship, a Jap is a Jap. Get them out."

West Coast politicians in Washington met and inscribed a letter to the president. The language was polite, the sentiment was not. A Jap is a Jap. Get them out of our states.

And people read on the run, and began to repeat what they had read. A Jap is a Jap. Get them out.

It became a chant of hate ringing down the valleys of the Siskiyous, gathering volume and venom as it swept on southward toward the Gulf of Mexico. Those who did not join in were silent. They raised no counter-chorus for justice and fair play. There were

78

few who were clear minded enough to see the significance of what was happening, and their determined voices were but a murmur amid the deafening roar. They talked in terms of human rights and pled for selective evacuation, but there was no one to listen.

Belatedly, the newspapers retracted the stories they had printed of sabotage in Hawaii, but the retractions were neither given in headlines nor displayed prominently, and the hurried reader never saw them. Anyway, the damage had been done. The chorus was swelling. Primitive emotions were on the loose.

What had begun as the whispering hopes of a few interested groups now became the clamor of a war mad and unstable public. What would be the outcome? The fate of 100,000 souls hung in the balance.

V

It was a balmy afternoon in late February. Advance signs of spring were in the air. The open mesa was blue with lupine dotted here and there with the gold of poppies and patches of fresh, shimmering green sprinkled the foothills where shrubs were opening their new leaves. Above, the sky was a bluish white, and the warm sunshine, shifting through the fleecy clouds which lay in waves across the heavens, was barely bright enough to make soft shadows on the ground. In the distance, beyond the foothills, the mountain lines stretched dim in a lazy purple haze. It was a day for spring fever if ever there was one, a day for picnicking and fishing.

But Tom had long since forgotten what these things were. Today he was in the field west of the house picking cucumbers, the first of the crop. He crouched on his heels over the vines, carefully laying back the leaves to find the new fruits which were large enough to market. The lug beside him was nearly filled with the fresh green cukes, and he thought he would have at least ten lugs altogether to take in to Mr. Imoto in the morning which, as far as he knew were going to be the first on the market. Tom felt justly proud of his accomplishment, for he had labored against heavy odds.

More than two months had passed since that black Sunday in December which had by now come to be referred to with brevity and hate as Pearl Harbor Day, and Father Sato was still imprisoned. There were lines of maturity and strength about Tom's mouth which had not been there the day his father went away. Two months of carrying the responsibilities of the ranch during rush season, along with the heavy work itself and the anxiety over his father, had brought Tom from a responsible, hard-working, but carefree boy to a responsible young man who worked almost without resting and refused to retrench on any of the plans Father

80

Sato and he had made together.

Tom had not seen his father since the day of his arrest. But Mother Sato had. Yes, a few days after Father Sato had been whisked away by the government men, Allen had been able to find out for them that he had been taken with a group of other Japanese nationals to a camp near Los Angeles and that they could visit him during certain hours of the day. The Sakamotos were driving up to see the old man and asked Mother Sato to go with them. Tom planned to go later when he had the seed in and take the whole family.

Mother Sato had gone off in a great flurry of excitement that she was to see Papa Sato again. When she came home that night she looked as if she had come from a long siege of illness in the hospital. All of the life had gone out of her face.
"Did you get to see Dad?" Tom asked when he saw her. "Is he all right?"

Haltingly, she told her story.

When she had gotten there after the long ride she had discovered that all their conversation must be in English, so the much anticipated visit had turned out to be a few stammered phrases: "How are you?", "Don't worry," "I have food, I am all right," repeated over and over in the presence of a guard. All of the many things Mother Sato had to say to Papa, all her concerns and confidences, all the questions she had longed to ask, went unsaid.

Besides her own keen disappointment over the visit, it had been terrible for her to actually see Papa Sato under guard. And he had a bad cold and was very hoarse. What would he do with no one to take care of him?

All of that evening as they worked together in the packing shed, the children tried not to notice their mother's silent weeping. Frequently she sighed. The sighs were the worst. Tom thought they sounded like life seeping out of a person in a slow leak. Uncomfortable and self-conscious, he had tried to cheer his mother up, said things, little foolish things, to lighten the

81

leaden weight of a grief which was weighing her down. But when he joked about his father getting a good rest in camp, she looked as shocked and stricken as if he had desecrated a shrine.

Tom promised her another visit when he could be there to help with the conversation, but before they could go again, they had word that Father Sato had been taken to Montana. They heard from him as often as he was allowed to write. No formal charges had been made against him. He had had no trial. It was hard to understand how he could be deprived of his liberty without due process of law.

Tad had not been able to come home from camp on a weekend pass because of the distance, and his letters indicated that he was in great mental distress over his father's imprisonment and over the effect it might have on his mother. He wrote little about the war or any speculations as to where his outfit would land when it was ready for action, but he wrote long letters to Tom begging him to take good care of his mother and let him know about everything which happened at home and everything his father wrote them. One could tell that it was a severe punishment to Tad not to be able to come home or to do anything for the family at this time.

Tom was too busy to give the letters more than a hasty reading as he sat at the dinner table or dozed over them in the evening as he tried to write a brief answer assuring Tad that everything was all right and not to worry.

Tom had been rushed from morning till late at night, and it was seven days a week now. Sunday was no longer that day of rest and play toward which one looked forward with pleasure as one labored through the other six. Now it was only one day in seven, all of which were alike. Work. Mari took time to drive her mother and Yoshi to church and helped Tom the rest of the day. The folks rode home with a family who lived several miles on up the highway in the foothills.

Since that bleak day in December, the Sato family at home had gone about making their adjustments to the new situation to the best of their ability. They had tried to accept Father Sato's internment, inexplicable as it was, with patience and calm, and to shake off the fear and insecurity his sudden arrest and subsequent events had caused.

Fortunately their bank account was frozen for only a few days and then arrangements were made through the Federal Reserve Bank to release one hundred dollars a family each month, so they had been spared the hardship which a lack of funds to carry on would have brought upon them.

For two months the whole family had dedicated themselves to slaving on the ranch. Even Yoshi had done his share, although, it must be admitted, not with much dedication or much slaving, either. Mother Sato, and Tom, and Mari had toiled from dawn to late hours at night, doggedly, stubbornly, spurred on by the conviction that they would need money to free Father Sato, harassed by the urgency to earn while they still could. Who knew when the opportunity might end?

Tom had had a brief scare. They had worked hour upon hour, transplanting the tiny tomato plants into flats away into the nights until it seemed their eyes would go blind from the strain. More hours of weeding. Irrigating. Flat after flat, hundreds of them. Was there no end? Watching for insect pests. And then at last the greenhouse had been full of the flats of fine, strong plants ready for the early growers. It had been a beautiful sight to Tom. Soon the ranchers would be calling up, wanting their orders delivered. He had enough to meet every order his father had taken. And then Mr. Maberry had called and cancelled his order. He had mumbled something into the phone about having changed his plans and not wanting the plants. The following day, on a quick trip to town to get a piece for the tractor, Tom had seen plants in the field Mr. Maberry had prepared for his early tomatoes. Tom had slowed down. Yes, they were tomato plants all right. The man had gotten them somewhere else.

The possibility of a boycott loomed on the horizon,

and Tom had stood in the door of the greenhouse that evening and looked over the row upon row of flats of husky green plants. What could he do with them if no one would buy from him? He had neither the space nor the time to put out any now. These plants would be a total loss. What if all Japanese-grown produce should be boycotted? It was a frightening thought. His cucumbers! What if he could not sell them? And he was planning big on the tomato plants he would sell to the cannery growers later. They could ruin him in no time if they boycotted his stuff.

Tom hadn't kept up much with the news. The Satos didn't take a daily paper, and he wouldn't have had time to read it if they had. The radio had been confiscated by the FBI, along with Tom's camera and flashlight, soon after Pearl Harbor. Since he had finished marketing the winter vegetables, Tom had been cut off from one of his chief sources of news, Mr. Imoto at the market, for he had formed the habit of getting in a little early to have a talk with the proprietor before other trucks came in. Once in awhile some Nisei dropped around to the ranch with a new rumor, but not often. Mr. Imoto had told Tom of the hardships Japanese people in other parts of the state were suffering. It was worst in the cities where shops and factories had been closed on account of the war; fishing had been stopped, canneries closed, importing firms could no longer import. Many men had been taken away to internment and their families left penniless in a hostile community. The Japanese American Citizens League was raising funds to help the needy, Mr. Imoto had told Tom. The government relief funds which were for the purpose of taking care of such persons somehow managed to get so entangled in red tape that, when a Japanese family applied, none was forthcoming. Tom gave as liberally as he could and said he would give more as he sold his crops. Mr. Imoto told Tom one morning that some people were talking about trying to get all the Japanese out of California, and they had both laughed at anything so ridiculous.

Mr. Imoto himself was doing a flourishing business. He couldn't find enough produce to meet the demands of his customers, for the city was becoming more and more crowded every day. Naval officers and Army officers and their families were moving in. Defense workers arrived in droves. Thousands of new mouths to feed.

"Hurry up with your cukes, Tom," he kept saying. "They'll go like hot cakes at almost any price we ask. Everyone has money, and they're spending it fast."

So while some suffered from the hostilities, others prospered. With the Satos the prospects were splendid for the best year they had ever had on the ranch, even with Father Sato away. That is, if everything went well.

But if Tom couldn't sell his plants!

Sometimes he listened nights to the little homemade radio in the greenhouse office, the radio Norio had made. The war news was always bad. The United States wasn't ready to fight. She was losing everything in the Pacific. Tom was impatient to get into uniform. As if that would help any! The family was all anxious over Tad, but Mother Sato most of all. To a Japanese mother her son does not merely go forth to fight for his country, he goes to die for it; and her constant prayer was that he might get home for a last visit before he went into action. More frequently now, Tom heard vicious voices on the air, blasting at the Japanese in California. Someone seemed anxious to arouse the feelings of the people against them. Maybe that would account for the cancelled order.

Tom had a few anxious days, then men began to call for their plants; and he learned that, with most people, profits come before prejudices. Father Sato's old customers knew they could get sturdier, more productive plants from him than from anyone else around. Soon the greenhouse was empty again and the Satos more secure financially.

Tom began to feel optimistic and was inclined to spare Mari the money she was begging for to buy a formal. She had been chosen by her school to represent it in the Spring Music Festival in the city, and Tom wanted his sister to be as well dressed as anyone on the program. But he would tease her a little longer. She was getting pretty independent since Dad had been gone, and she had been working side by side with him in the fields.

Mari and her mother had found time to make blackout curtains, and they drew them carefully each night before they turned on the lights. The nearest siren was in La Vista and it was hard to hear it when the wind was from the west. They couldn't risk any light showing in a blackout; they might be accused of signalling. They had to be very careful of all their actions as the Japanese were being watched for sabotage. Mari heard stories at school of what the Japanese in Hawaii had done, and those reports reflected on the Nisei on the mainland.

Tom had not been able to find anyone to harvest Harry Sakai's cabbage, and it had burst and lay rotting in the field.

"What do you think was in the city paper today?" Mari said one day when she came home from school.

"Spill it," Tom said shortly.

"It was an editorial about the Japanese ranchers trying to sabotage the war effort by letting their crops rot in the fields. And it cited a cabbage field not far from the city as evidence. Why can't they be fair?" There was despair of justice in her voice. The unfairness of such an interpretation when people had lost their whole season's income was hard to take.

"If Dad doesn't get home soon we'll have stuff spoiling on the vines, too, and then I suppose we'll be accused of the same thing," Tom remarked ruefully.

He was beginning to lose patience with the slow government procedures. He was anxious about his mother, and Tad's worried letters didn't help him to throw off his worries. She was working too hard, but he couldn't stop her. His father's letters from Missoula had been cheerful at first; they were not to worry about him. He had recovered from his cold and was quite well. He implored the family to keep close in spirit during this time of enforced separation. Perhaps Tad would soon be going overseas. No one knew how long he himself would be detained, but they must keep tightly knit together spiritually until the time came when they would be reunited again. His words tore at their hearts, and Mother Sato and Tom each had their secret rendezvous with discouragement but came forth to face the family with determination on their faces.

Then Father Sato's letters changed. They began to show a note of despondency. Hearing boards had been set up by the Department of Justice, he wrote. Everyone must have a hearing. There were many men there, and he would have to wait his turn. It might be months, but he cautioned Tom to get in all of the necessary papers and references just in case he came up soon.

It had not been hard for Tom to find men around La Vista who would vouch for Father Sato's character, and Tad and Tom had both written personal letters to the Alien Enemy Control Unit. Then there was nothing left to do for him but wait, and hope, and pray. Waiting was hard, for they all wanted Father Sato home again so much.

Tom was worried about the films the FBI had taken along with his camera. He had taken pictures of Allen at the beach and the harbor, and some destroyers were in the background. And the ones taken up on the mountain showed an airfield. The officers had questioned him about them after developing them and had hinted that they would be used as evidence in his father's case. Tom had explained all of this in his letter, but he didn't know whether he would be believed or not. He knew the officer hadn't believed him that day when he told him they were just out for a drive and took some pictures.

That was one of the hardest things to endure-- suspicion. And no way to prove one's innocence. To have someone pointing the finger of doubt and asking, "Are you loyal?" And never believing your answers.

But in spite of the hard things, while Tom had tried to wait patiently for the good news that his father was coming home, he carried on at the ranch with a sense of satisfaction that he knew in his own heart he was loyal, that he loved his country dearly, and was willing to serve in this unheralded way until the opportunity came to prove himself. Maybe when Dad was home again and the summer season's work was over, he could enlist.

Now Tom bent over the cucumber fields as the afternoon shadows lengthened and gloated over the profusion of yellow blossoms showing from beneath the healthy green foliage. He had even outdone his father in bringing a cucumber crop to maturity. But how he would ever get the crop picked when it reached its peak was a poser. He couldn't let his mother work so hard. Several times he had had to put his foot down and make her go to the house when she looked ready to drop, but it would be hard to keep her out of the field if the crop were wasting.

He had been into town to see Jose one evening. He had found the Mexican boy dressed in flashy clothes and jingling money in his pockets, and he had known before he spoke that Jose was unavailable. Tom had scarcely recognized him at first in his new outfit.

"I got a job at Union Aircraft now," Jose had told him, disdaining an offer of ranch work. He was a riveter, he said proudly. Made lots of money. Overtime Saturdays. He pulled a handful of bills from his pocket and displayed them.

"Easy job. Eight hours and you're through." Was he thinking of the long hours of stoop labor he had put in for Father Sato? "Some days I just stand around. Nothing to do. No tools. No material. No nothing. When the boss comes through my lead man says, 'Go hide in a plane, Jose. I don't want him to see you fellows loafing around.'" Jose laughed and showed a row of snowy white teeth.

Did he know of anyone Tom could get? No. Everyone was working in aircraft.

Tom said he would get some of those idle Nisei in

the city, if he thought he could teach a city guy to do ranch work.

He was over three quarters of the field now and must finish before dark. Mari would soon be home from school to help, but he didn't trust Yoshi in the field yet. He might do more damage than good. Yes, Mr. Winters was right. It was the best looking field in the country.

It was queer about Mr. Winters coming over the other day and talking the way he had, Tom thought, getting back to his work after straightening to rest his back for a minute. It was the first time he had ever seen the man on the place, and, from the way he had talked, Tom hoped it would be the last. But it worried him.

Mr. Winters had come early in the morning while Tom was sprinkling the seed beds, and he had walked around inspecting everything with something of an air of possession.

"Nice lot of plants you have over there," he said, indicating the tomato seedbeds. "Must have near a couple of hundred plants altogether." He didn't seem to be talking to Tom, rather ignoring him as too unimportant to be noticed.

"More than that," Tom spoke up proudly. It was a source of great satisfaction to him that he had been able to get enough beds seeded to meet all the orders his father had taken.

Mr. Winters didn't appear to know Tom had spoken.

"And that's a mighty nice looking field of cucumbers, too. Ten acres. That's a lot of cucumbers, and they'll be a good price, though why any fool would pay thirty-five or forty cents for one cucumber is more than I know." Then, as if suddenly recognizing Tom's presence, he asked slyly, "How do you keep the mildew off them vines in wet weather?"

"My dad has a formula. We mix our own dusting powder," Tom said, and closed up. He turned off the water and stood waiting for Mr. Winters to make his errand known. He was quite sure his unfriendly neighbor

89

had not paid him an early morning call merely to admire the crops nor even to learn about mildew control on cucumbers, which the man didn't raise on his place. No hard stoop labor for Mr. Winters.

"Be too bad to let all this stuff dry up with the country needing food so bad. Maybe I could manage to take it off your hands, Tom, say for . . . well, how about four hundred dollars?"

"I don't understand," Tom replied, puzzled. Was Mr. Winters making him an offer for the crop in the field? Surely he couldn't think he could buy a four- thousand-dollar field of cucumbers for four hundred dollars, to say nothing of all those tomato plants. And why would he think he could buy at any price?

What Tom could not know was that Mr. Winters had come over expecting to find a very frightened "Jap" who would be shaking in his shoes and glad to sell out at any price and get out of the state. Mr. Winters was a man who did not miss any of the radio commentators who had made a crusade of getting the Japanese out of California, and he was fired with a consuming zeal to do his part in service to the southland.

But all that Tom could see was that the man was eyeing him curiously. He became a little less offhand, as though he had recognized the necessity of taking Tom into consideration if he were to make a deal.

"Well, that's more than I could afford to pay. There'd be nothing in it for me, by the time I'd hired men to pick the cucumbers. And those little plants aren't worth anything now; they're barely out of the ground." His eyes roved covetously over the ranch. "But just to help you out, I'll give you five hundred for the thirty. What do you say?"

Tom was dumbfounded. He could scarcely believe his ears. Mr. Winters was not making an offer for the crop, he was wanting to buy the ranch! And for the paltry sum of five hundred dollars! One acre of good vegetable land was bringing twice that or more. The very brazenness of the man's offer filled Tom with alarm, and a feeling of insecurity and uneasiness came over him.

"Our place is not for sale," he answered, trying to sound businesslike. But his voice was hollow and unconvincing.

"You'd better use your head and take anything you can get out of it while you still have a chance. When you're gone the government's going to take over all the Japs' property, and you won't get a cent out of it, I tell you. Now, do you want five hundred for the ranch and machinery, or don't you?"

Mr. Winters pulled his wallet from an inside coat pocket and counted out the money, holding it in one hand as bait. With the other he thrust into Tom's hand a paper on which he had scribbled the terms of sale.

"Just sign there at the bottom," he said eagerly. "I'll take care of the rest."

"But we don't want to sell, Mr. Winters. We aren't going away," Tom said, trying to give the paper back to the man.

"You'll have nothing to say about that," Mr. Winters snapped, growing impatient to close the deal. "Did they ask old Sato if they could take him away?"

Tom winced at the sneering reference to his father, but he held his temper.

"Well, my father is an alien. But we Nisei are protected by the Constitution. The government would no more take our land away from us than it would take yours from you," Tom said staunchly. But when he had spoken, things came up in his mind to shake him. He looked at the tall, lanky man standing there before him, so secure in his feeling of superiority and wondered if the FBI would go into Mr. Winters's house without a warrant and search it and carry off Mr. Winters's radio and camera. He could not have spoken his words with such confidence now that he thought of the things that had happened to his family. But he reasoned within himself that it was all because his father was an alien. There was little time for any thoughts to reach a logical conclusion, for Tom's declaration of rights under the Constitution had struck a sore spot in Mr. Winters, and his face grew uglier than ever. Tom thought for an instant that the man was actually going to strike him. Instead he burst forth in words, and his voice was as ugly as his hate-distorted face.

"Your land, your land," he shouted. "This is not your land. You never got it legally, your father robbed me of it, and I mean to have it. There isn't a court in the state would uphold your claim to it, and I mean to see that it gets to the courts." With a curse, Mr. Winters grabbed the paper from Tom's hand and strode away, muttering to himself, and leaving Tom with a new anxiety to vex his days.

Would Mr. Winters take advantage of the antagonism aroused by the war to rob them of their land? What made him so sure the Japanese would be leaving? Or was he only bluffing in order to get Tom to sell?

Tom was mulling these questions over now as he laid each large, crisp cucumber in the lug carefully, so as not to bruise it. Would Mr. Winters go so far as to take it to court? Tom grew bitter as he thought of the countless hours his father and Tad and he had spent pulling stumps and making the land tillable. If Mr. Winters had wanted it so badly he could have bought it before Father Sato. He had been there years before they had moved over. No. Mr. Winters didn't want it then, for it had been worthless stump land. But now ... Tom straightened up and surveyed the ranch. Not a square foot of it now that couldn't be planted. And Winters wanted it for five hundred dollars. Well, he should never have it at any price. What if it did get into the courts? They would fight it to the very last court in the land. Yes, they would take it to the Supreme Court before they would give it up.

At the sound of pattering feet, Tom turned toward the road and saw Yoshi come running from the bus like a frightened rabbit. The other boys who had gotten off were ambling along far behind him, swinging their lunch boxes and picking up stones along the shoulder of the road, then tossing them nonchalantly at the telephone poles.

92

When he saw Tom in the field, Yoshi swerved from the house and came dashing across toward him, unheedingly tramping vines as he ran.

Tom opened his mouth to shout angrily, when he saw the boy was crying.

"What's the matter?" he asked, straining the anger from his voice as the kid approached.

Then he saw. And he turned away. Nausea engulfed him in a brief, hot wave. On Yoshi's sweater sleeve was plastered a large blotch of saliva.

Before Tom could speak, Yoshi began to pour forth his woes.

"Them kids spit on me," he blubbered between sobs. "I never did a thing to them, honest. I got off the bus and they was off first and was waiting for me, and they did this," indicating the ugly smear on his sleeve, "and they said I wasn't wanted at school anymore 'cause my folks were killing American boys on Bataan. And then . . ." There was a long pause while Yoshi stood there shaking in convulsive sobs. "And then Billy Winters kicked me and called me names."

With that Yoshi threw himself down in the damp furrow and lay there crying as if his heart would break.

Tom stood looking down at the kid helplessly. First Mr. Winters after their land. Now Billy pitching into Yoshi. Were they going to try to make it impossible for them to stay?

Well, anyway, one thing was certain. Yoshi could not be shielded any longer. The time had come for him to learn the bitter facts of color and how to adjust his life to them.

Tom knew there was nothing he could do for the boy to alter the situation at school. He could tell the bus driver. Or the teachers. But that wouldn't change the boys' attitude toward Yoshi. It might only make it worse. And what was harder for a kid to face than the antagonism and ridicule of his schoolmates? Tom tried not to see the trickle down Yoshi's sleeve, but he couldn't keep his eyes from the loathsome sight.

The other boys had come along now and were passing the field, looking in. They couldn't see Yoshi down in the furrow among the vines, but they eyed Tom curiously.

"Hello, boys," Tom called, as if nothing had happened.

"Hi, Tom," Jerry Hatfield called back, but Billy yelled, "Slant-eyed Japs," but not too loud. And they all laughed and began to run down the road, shouting "Japs!" as they went.

Tom's impulse was to start after them.

"Steady now," he said to himself. "Stay where you are. Don't say anything nor do anything. You know you've got to keep still and take it."

With a tight grip on himself, he turned away from the fleeing boys and back to the prone figure on the ground. For the moment the cucumber picking was forgotten.

When a boy is tormented because he is poor, he mused, he has a better day to look forward to. He knows that he can work hard and save his money and eventually have a business of his own. Maybe become rich. There were plenty of examples to give him that hope. Anyway, he could take his place in society with no stigma attached. And when a farm boy is persecuted and ridiculed when he goes to the city to school, he knows he can soon learn the city ways and buy some new clothes and can look forward to the time when he will be accepted by the others. Even the boys who come to America from foreign countries, Swedes, Germans, Italians, Irish, and are laughed at for their strange customs and broken English. They know they can learn to speak better and learn the American ways, become naturalized, and eventually become a part of American life, indistinguishable from other citizens.

But if you have color, even a little, you are a marked person. Marked for life. You can never look forward to the time when you will be as the others. Even citizenship can't erase the color line. You have to plan your life on the basis of color.

It didn't seem fair, but that's the way it was. Yoshi

must be taught how to make the best of it. Sometime in the future, perhaps, things would be different. But Yoshi was living in the now.

Tom looked down at the kid and wished Norio were there. He knew how to talk about things like this so that it didn't hurt and you understood. It had been so easy for Norio to talk, he had the right words, and his voice was gentle and warm when he had things to tell you which weren't pleasant. Tom's mind flashed back to the times when his oldest brother had taken Tad and him out to his room and talked with them about different questions that bothered them. Sometimes it was this problem of being different. Norio knew so well the history and culture of both countries, America and Japan, that he was able to make the boys conscious of the fine things in both and cause them to be proud of their Japanese background and their American citizenship at the same time. Through him they had learned to accept petty discrimination without bitterness. He could not remember ever hearing a word of complaint or criticism from Norio, even when he had failed to secure a position after graduation. Only disappointment and, finally, hopelessness. And it was not until Norio's death that resentment had flared in Tad.

Tom was forced to admit that they were in a bad situation now. They must be prepared to meet with courage and self-respect whatever was in store for them at the hands of hysterical people. These were two things which no one could take away from you.

He stooped and laid a hand on the boy's twitching shoulders.

"Don't cry anymore, Yochan," he said gently, unconsciously using his mother's name for the child. "Get up and go wash yourself. And listen, don't let Mom know anything about this, do you hear? Don't you tell her a word. It would make her awfully sick."

Yoshi got to his feet slowly. His face was streaked with dirt and tears, but the storm of weeping had spent itself.

"Okay, I won't tell," he said hoarsely.

95

"Now go wash up in the greenhouse and leave your sweater in there. Hurry up before Mom comes out and sees you this way." Tom had been casting anxious glances toward the house as he had been standing there, afraid that his mother might come out to see if he needed any help.

Yoshi still stood there looking up at Tom, evidently waiting for something.

"Well, what do you want?"

"What are you going to do to those mean kids?"

"You mean the boys you ride the bus with, Billy and the others?"

"Yes."

"Oh, I don't know," Tom parried. "What do you want me to do?"

"I want you to help me beat them up," was the prompt reply, as Yoshi looked confidently at his big, strong brother.

Nothing I'd enjoy more, Tom thought. But you can't do things like that. You just have to take it. The kid must understand that.

"Well, we'll see about that later," Tom said, putting him off. "You go and clean up now, and then come back out here. I want you to help me awhile."

Mari came then and met Yoshi as he ran toward the greenhouse. Tom told her to begin picking at the other end of the row and to hurry, for it would be dark before they had finished.

"What's the matter with Yoshi?" she demanded, showing no inclination to hurry.

Tom told her briefly.

Mari was hot with anger.

"What are you going to do?" she asked.

"You know there's nothing we can do," Tom answered impatiently. He wanted to get the work done. "Yoshi will have to learn to take things the same as the rest of us have."

"But not that," Mari protested. "I'm not going to let anyone do such things to a brother of mine. Why can't we go away somewhere? No one wants us around here

96

anymore."

"You don't know what you're talking about," Tom shouted angrily, near his wit's end. "I can take care of things without any suggestions from you. Now get to work."

Mari opened her mouth to answer back, but closed it again without saying anything. Don't antagonize Tom, she told herself; at least not till after she got the money for the formal. But Tom was getting awfully short-tempered lately. Everything was going wrong. She was beginning to feel uncomfortable at school even if she had been chosen to represent the school at the music festival. Half of the Nisei had quit; she was the only one left in her class. She hoped Tom would let Yoshi stay home after this. It was an insult to the whole family to have him spit on. She tripped briskly down to the other end of the field, an empty lug in each hand, singing snatches of a song from the Hit Parade. "Never let anyone know how you feel," was her motto. The lower her spirits dropped, the louder she sang. And Tom, working down the row toward her and trying to figure out what was the best way to handle this latest problem brought on by the show of open hostility on the part of Yoshi's schoolmates, was annoyed by his sister's lightheartedness.

So they told Yoshi they didn't want him at school anymore, that his people were killing American boys. That didn't originate with those sixth-grade boys. They had heard talk at home. Billy Winters was at the bottom of it all. His father had gone away angry the other morning. He might even have put the boy up to doing what he had. Striking at the family through the children. Well, Yoshi would have to learn to take it, Tom argued stubbornly with himself. The boy was coming out to the field now. His face was clean except for a fringe around his hair.

Tom had him pick cucumbers alongside him until it was too dark to see.

Late that same night Tom was still up and working on his accounts in the little office in the greenhouse.

Everyone else was in bed. Mari's violin was silent at last. She was practicing every minute she could spare from work, and the sound of music, now loud, now soft, had drifted out to the greenhouse as Tom had been doing his accounts. But now everything was still, the way it is around a truck ranch at night. No sound of animals lowing and chewing; no chickens flapping and clucking on the roosts; no hogs grunting nor calves bawling. Vegetables made no sound as they grew. There was peace and quiet about growing fields. Tom liked it, and tonight the quiet was more soothing and restful than usual.

It was a chilly night after the warmth of the day, a reminder that fickle spring was only flirting with February.

As Tom sat hunched over the cluttered desk adding a column of figures, he heard soft sounds outside the door. Then there was the slow squeak of the hinges as the door was opened cautiously.

Tom wheeled about in his chair, startled. Who could be coming here at this time of night?

There stood Yoshi in the half open doorway in his pajamas, his feet bare.

"Oh, it's you," Tom said with relief. Then he knew that he must have it out with the boy. He had thought after Yoshi slept on it he might feel differently about going back to school, and he had felt secure in the belief that Yoshi was safe in bed and fast asleep. If they could get over this obstacle successfully, Tom had speculated, then perhaps he could let the larger problem go until Tad came home. He could talk to Yoshi, and, being in uniform, whatever he said would carry weight with their small brother.

However, any illusions Tom might have had were blown away by Yoshi's first words.

"I'm not going to school anymore," the boy announced stubbornly, forcing the issue. His tears of the afternoon were quite gone now, and he was fortified with righteous wrath. "I'm not going to let those mean kids do things to me." His mouth was determined, but his eyes pleaded with Tom to see it his way.

Why not let him stay out? Tom thought. At least until things get better. That would be the easiest way out of an unfortunate situation. No. He can't quit. Things might be bad for them as long as the war lasted, and that might be for years. Yoshi would have to face it sometime. But let him stay home until Tad came, or till Dad was back again. Let them make the decision. Tom was tempted to tell Yoshi to run along to bed and not worry, he wouldn't need to go to school the next day. He was tired and worried, and it was already late. No time to settle things tonight. But something inside him kept telling him this was the time and that he had a duty to perform.

"Come on in and shut the door," he said.

Yoshi responded promptly to the invitation, and Tom reached for an old coat of his father's from a nail on the wall and threw it around the boy's shoulders. Turning an empty crate on end he placed it beside his chair, and Yoshi perched on it, his feet drawn up under the coat. Impulsively Tom slipped his arm around the boy and drew him close.

The two brothers sat thus for a long time while Tom tried to figure out the best way to begin. He wished fervently that he need not tell the boy anything. Wished that he could protect him, that it were in his power to spare him the blight which discrimination and prejudice brought upon those who had color, as he spared the growing plants in the field from the deadly blights which would suck the life from them except for the protective sprays. But prejudice and hate were too extensive in their operation to be controlled by an individual. They could be eradicated only by whole communities working together for that purpose, and now it looked as if people were trying to spread rather than control these scourges.

Tom sat quiet so long that Yoshi began to squirm restlessly, and he finally turned and looked up into Tom's face with questioning eyes.

"Ever hear of Abe Lincoln?" Tom asked, with a

twinkle in his eyes.

"Course I have. Everyone has heard of him," Yoshi answered with disgust in his voice.

"Well, Abe Lincoln was a great American, one of the greatest that ever lived, I guess." Tom's voice was earnest now. Again he wished for Norio's gift of speech. It was not easy for him to talk, and when he felt deeply it was more difficult than ever. "And they hated him. They hated him so much they killed him."

Yoshi was very quiet now.

"Has anyone tried to do that to you?"

The boy shook his tousled head vigorously, but said nothing.

"No, but someone hurts you a little bit and you come running home crying. And now you want to quit school and make your father and mother ashamed of you. You'd throw away your chance to get an education just because someone called you a name. What kind of an American are you anyway? Or maybe you aren't one at all. Maybe you are a Tojo."

"I am not," Yoshi denied hotly. Tojo had become a bad word since the war.

"All right, all right," Tom placated. "But if you are an American, then be a good one like Abe Lincoln was. He wasn't afraid of anything or anybody so long as he knew he was doing his best for his country."

Yoshi considered this for a moment.

"Do you mean I ought to let those guys push me around?" he asked with a puzzled look in his eyes.

"No, I don't mean that . . . exactly. I think a fellow should stand up for his rights. That is, when he can. But when it's something you can't help; like the boys picking on you because . . ." Tom stopped. The kid looked so little and helpless as he cuddled close against him for warmth and for protection from threatened dangers. Yoshi had never known anything but friendliness from his schoolmates before. Tom took a deep breath, like one preparing for a plunge. "Like the boys picking on you because Mom and Dad are Japanese. Things like that you can't help, and so you have to learn to take what comes with your chin up. You have to be brave and go to school every day and get your lessons no matter what happens.

There was a long silence as Tom waited for Yoshi's reaction before he went on.

Finally the boy looked up at his brother. All the babyish expression was gone from his face.

"Is that why they did that to me?" he asked in an awed voice. His eyes were veiled as Tad's were so many times when he was shutting others out of his inner world. "Because Dad and Mom ... ?"

"That's one reason," Tom interrupted, and then went on quickly. If a surgeon wants to do a good, clean job he can't be squeamish about using the scalpel. "That, and because you yourself look different from the rest of the boys." Then he went on to explain how their ancestry gave them certain physical characteristics which set them apart and caused them to be thought of by others as Japanese rather than Americans. They usually even thought of themselves that way, Tom told Yoshi, and that was bad. If they wanted to be good citizens, they must always think and speak of themselves as Americans.

"If I had an American name like the other boys, wouldn't that be better?" Yoshi asked, surprising Tom by his question. "They laugh at my name, and nobody says it right."

"A good idea," Tom said, glad to get on a lighter subject for a minute. "You pick one you like and we'll all call you by it."

Tom himself suggested several, but none of them suited Yoshi.

"How did you get yours, Tom?"

"Oh, the boys at school just shortened my Japanese name the folks gave me. Tamotsu ... You see, the first syllable sounds almost the same as Tom. I didn't choose it myself. But lots of the Nisei do choose their own."

"I could be Joe. That sounds something like Yo, doesn't it?"

"Yeah, that's a good one. Joe Sato. Sounds all

right."

When that was decided, Tom went on to tell the things he still must say in order to finish what he had started. Better not have begun at all than to leave off at this point, giving the impression to the boy that his background was undesirable and the cause of all his trouble.

Out of the memory of Norio's talks to Tad and him, Tom garnered treasures from their parents' native land and presented them to Yoshi. The beauty of scenery was something he had never tired hearing about, and now he picked up a blue pencil from the cluttered desk and began sketching the place where their father had been born. He could see it as plainly as if he had been there, for he had had it described to him so many times. The little house on the hill looking out over the Inland Sea, with the garden of flowers and the tall woods behind it. And in front the sight of the tiny white sails of the fishing boats against the deep blue water. He told of the wooded mountains where his mother went with her family to the cherry blossom festivals when she was a little girl, and of the beautiful avenue of cryptomeria trees which once shaded the Imperial Highway all the way from Tokyo to Nikko and was the gift of a humble peasant.

"How far was it?" a sleepy voice asked.

"From Tokyo to Nikko? Oh, forty or fifty miles, I guess. Maybe more."

"Did one man plant all those trees?"

"Yes. He was a poor man who lived a long time ago, back in the days when the shoguns ruled Japan, and as he worked in his little patch of ground along the Imperial Highway, he saw great loads of fine gifts which wealthy subjects had imported from lands beyond the seas to present to their ruler as an expression of their loyalty and affection. Great bronze lanterns and chiming brass bells, and whole pagodas, beautifully carved, and many other expensive gifts, all going to Nikko to be placed in the wonderful temples there. And the poor man grieved in his heart that he had nothing to give."

102

Tom was conscious that he was quoting from Norio, and his elder brother seemed very near. "Then, one hot summer day, the Shogun himself passed on his way from Tokyo to his summer palace at Nikko. The heat was oppressive. The blistering sun beat down upon the Shogun and his equipage unmercifully; and the poor peasant, although he was not worthy to raise his eyes to look upon his ruler, felt very sorry for him, riding in the hot sun.

"That evening as the man walked in the deep woods behind his garden and saw the thousands of tiny saplings growing there, an inspiration came to him. He would plant these little trees along the king's highway. It would be a humble gift compared to buying fine brasses from abroad, but when the trees were grown, they would provide shade for the imperial head. And so he planted the little trees on either side of the highway the whole distance and tended them, and they grew into beautiful, tall trees. Even today, if you should go to Japan, you could ride along some twenty miles of Cryptomeria Avenue in a ricksha and enjoy the lovely, cool shade, for that many of the trees are still standing." And then Tom finished the story as Norio had always done. "Which do you think proved his loyalty best, the rich men who bought gifts for the Shogun, or the poor man who gave years of his life to planting and tending the trees?"

And the answer was the same as his and Tad's had always been.

"The poor man who planted the trees, of course."

Slowly and tenderly, Tom wove about the boy a protective covering of pride and self-respect.

Yoshi's eyes were starry as Tom switched to the American scene and told stories of boys of other races and nationalities who, sometimes through many trials, had made good and become great Americans: Jacob Riis and Andrew Carnegie, Booker T. Washington and George Washington Carver, Damrosch and Steinmetz.

He broke off suddenly and pulled out his watch.

"Hey, look what time it is! You'd better be getting

to bed before you catch cold."

"Yeah," the boy agreed. "I'd better get some sleep or I won't be up in time for school." He slid off the box and started for the door. In his eyes burned the fire of courage of one going forth to slay dragons. His head was high. He looked ready for any exigency, for any opportunity to prove that he, too, was made of the stuff of great Americans. He turned at the door and looked back.

"Tom." It seemed that the boy's voice had changed. It sounded older, and there was a quality of seriousness in it that Tom had never heard before. "You don't need to worry about me. What you told me is all right with me. And I'm not afraid of those guys anymore."

The baby of the Sato family was growing up.

"That's the way to talk," Tom commended, not talking down to the kid anymore. "You just be careful what you do, and don't be trying to start any trouble."

"Good night, Tamotsu," he said gravely. It was probably the first time he had ever used Tom's Japanese name.

"Good night, Joe," Tom responded.

They both laughed.

When Yoshi was gone, Tom went back to his accounts. But he was too sleepy to do anything now. He switched on the radio to check the time. The midnight news was just coming on. He was not going to listen, but the announcer's first words caught his attention.

"A news item of special interest to West Coast listeners who have shown increasing concern over the presence of so many Japanese on the coast was the signing today by the president of an executive order authorizing the War Department to set up military areas and to exclude any and all persons of Japanese ancestry from these areas."

Tom turned off the radio, wondering what this new presidential action would mean to him and his folks. He set his watch, and as he reached for the string to pull off the light, his eye fell on the calendar. The nineteenth of February, 1942. Tomorrow he was taking

104

his first cukes to market.

As he walked across the yard toward the house he reminded himself to ask Mr. Imoto in the morning what he thought of this latest news.

VI

Yoshi went to school the next morning. He had gotten up late after the previous night's vigil, and he had had to run to catch the bus, so there had been no chance for the other boys to continue with their persecution that morning. However, Tom had stood watching until he saw the kid safely on the bus, not that he had any idea what he would do if anything did happen.

Soon after Yoshi had left Tom started to the city with his load of cucumbers. Mr. Imoto beamed when he saw them, for Tom had been right; they were the first to come in.

"They are the best I've ever seen for the first ones, Tom. Or for anytime, for that matter. So uniform in size and color, they'll make an attractive display in anybody's market; and they're so crisp I believe one would shatter in a thousand pieces if you dropped it." Whimsically he took one of the slim green vegetables from a lug and dropped it on the cement floor. Sure enough, it split wide open lengthwise in a clean, sharp line. Mr. Imoto's jaw dropped, and he looked as surprised as if he had not predicted such a result. "Well, I'll be damned. I didn't think it would do it." Then he threw back his head as far as his short neck would permit and laughed a hearty laugh at himself.

Tom was greatly pleased over the praise he got for his produce, for he felt that it really was top quality; and it did a fellow good to hear a little appreciation when he had been working alone day after day in his fields. Tom would always consider that he was working alone until Father Sato or Tad came. Women and girls didn't count when it came to companionship. He was also pleased over the fancy price he had received. Yes, it was worthwhile, he thought, as he put the check in his billfold, to spend the extra money for fertilizer and plenty of water to get your cukes to market ahead of the others.

He was about to leave when he remembered to ask the produce merchant about the news on the radio the night before.

"I don't think it will have any effect on us, Tom," Mr. Imoto said. "It gives the Army authority to move anyone out, but it isn't likely they will do any more than get all the aliens away from military installations and other strategic areas. They'll probably leave the others to the FBI to sort out. They're still picking up fellows around here now and then. Sure is pitiful to see these old men, each one wondering if he will be the next. They all have their little bundles ready, nightshirt, toothbrush, and some soap and a towel. Maybe a bottle of medicine. Their faces are showing the effect of the long hours of suspense and waiting. Guess it's a relief to a fellow when they finally come and get him. But I don't think there'll be any moving of whole families, and I don't think the Nisei have anything to worry about at all."

"I hear something on the radio once in awhile about everyone getting out," Tom said.

"Yeah. The same old crowd that have always fought us, and some new recruits that the radio has produced. There's a lot of pressure from those groups, but the Army's got their hands full. I've an idea they will leave it to the FBI to sift out the dangerous ones. At least that would be the sensible thing to do."

"Yes. That's the way I feel," Tom said, climbing into the cab of his pickup.

"What do you hear from your father, Tom?"

"Nothing new. He's still waiting for his hearing."

"Well, don't worry. He's sure to be home as soon as he has that. They could never prove anything against him."

"No, I'm sure of that."

Yes, Tom was sure of it as he drove away, but maybe the government could still hold him after he had been cleared. It must have a lot of powers during war that the Constitution didn't cover.

107

As time for the school bus rolled around that afternoon, Tom found himself stopping work to glance down toward the corner. First he thought of walking down to meet the kid but decided that would be the wrong thing to do.

When he finally saw the yellow car coming along the highway and slowing down for the corner stop he felt a tenseness gripping him. But as soon as the boys got off in good order and started down the road much the same as usual, he began to relax.

Yoshi and Jerry were walking together, with the others ahead apparently paying no attention to them. When they came by the field where Tom could hear their conversation, he saw that Yoshi and Jerry were engrossed in the important business of dividing a banana between them, evidently a leftover from one of their lunches.

"So long, Jerry," Yoshi said, and came running over to Tom. With his mouth full of banana, he told Tom that Mr. Silvers, the bus driver, had seen what the boys did the day before, and he had given them a good scolding when they got on that morning. He had told them that if it ever happened again on the bus or anywhere on the way to school, he would go straight to their folks and their principal.

From Tom's memories of riding the gradeschool bus with Mr. Silvers, he judged a lecture from him would have more effect on the boys than the threat to tell their parents. For the boys, and the girls, too, had a very wholesome respect for the driver, who was a big, loud-speaking man.

It was a great relief to Tom to have an ally in Mr. Silvers, for now he felt it would be possible to keep the boy in school. No matter how determined they were to take what came, nor how eager Yoshi might have become for martyrdom, if things had gotten worse, Tom knew he would not have let him go on.

So the next time he went into La Vista in the evening when he would find Mr. Silvers at home, Tom took him an attractive basket of vegetables he had arranged from the family garden, celery and cauliflower and head lettuce, and some Fuerte avocados which were at their best now.

When he stopped at the Silvers's home in the outskirts of the town, he was met with a cool reception.

"Good evening," the man said, not asking Tom in.

"I sure appreciate what you did, Mr. Silvers, making the boys let my brother alone," Tom said, trying to ignore the rebuff and holding the basket out to Mr. Silvers. "I brought you a few vegetables. They don't amount to much but I thought maybe you could use them."

Mr. Silvers made no motion to take the basket.

"It's my duty to see that the children who ride my bus behave themselves and don't pick on anyone, no matter who he is," he said gruffly, emphasizing the last words to leave no doubt in Tom's mind as to what his personal feelings were in the matter.

Tom could see that the man did not want to accept anything, not even a basket of vegetables, from a "Jap," but still could not bring himself to be rude enough to refuse the offering outright. And Tom, in turn, could not very well withdraw his gift and walk away with it.

It was an awkward moment for them both. Since Tom had not been invited in, they still stood at the door in a sort of stalemate, which was broken by Mrs. Silvers coming to the door and taking the basket from Tom.

"Thanks," she said, with a suggestion of a smile on her lips, while her eyes were watching her husband with a sidewise glance.

She took the basket to the kitchen and emptied it and returned it to Tom, and he went away wondering whether he had helped or harmed their position by his call.

The spring warmth held. The days were unseasonably hot, with now and then an easy shower that caused the cucumbers to grow like Jack's fabulous beanstalk.

Tom and his mother picked from dawn till dark,

and Mari worked before and after school. Even then it was impossible to keep up with the fast maturing crop. Mr. Imoto told Tom of many idle Nisei in the city, and Tom went to see a couple of brothers who had been fishermen with their father in the tuna fleet. Of course, there had been no fishing since Pearl Harbor, and the fellows were tired of lying around, so they readily agreed to come out to the ranch. Then there was the little matter of money, too. But even their empty pockets were not sufficient to keep these lusty men of the sea at the backbreaking labor for twelve hours a day. At the end of three days they asked for their pay and went back to the city. Tom didn't think it would be worthwhile to bring anyone else out.

Mari stayed out of school part of the time, and Tom hired a couple of high school boys to work evenings and weekends. They had done ranch work in summers and proved to be good workers. Yoshi was allowed to pick regularly now, for the need was so great and he showed such a keen desire to help see the family through this emergency.

Since the night Tom had talked to him, Yoshi had ceased to look upon the family exclusively as the source of supply for his needs, his comforts, and his pleasures, but rather as an important and unique group to which he owed something and to which he must do something to champion and protect. He had become conscious of his responsibility as a member of a group. He had not only become family conscious, but family proud as well. The Satos were different, they had a rich and beautiful background. He could speak two languages and he had two names, Yoshi and Joe, and that was something none of the other boys had.

As the Sato family labored to harvest their crop with feverish activity, Malt roamed about, a forlorn bit of dog, bereft of his playmate. Sometimes he would follow Yoshi along the row, sitting beside him in the furrow with a reproachful look on his face. Sometimes he would go off alone and lie in the shade of the shed and wait for the folks to come in. Then he would get up expectantly, ready for a romp, only to see his young master stretch out flat on the ground and lie ther motionless, paying him no attention. Sometimes the family even forgot to feed him, and then he was heartbroken indeed and lay all night as close as he could up against the kitchen door, the tears running down his cheeks.

Mari had the festival on her mind, and when she worked in the field she wore long sleeves and gloves. She couldn't get up to play before an audience with sunburned arms and hands stained by cucumber vines. The festival was only a few weeks off now, and she schemed as she worked as to the best way to persuade Tom and her mother that she must have a fine dress to wear, a formal that would be as beautiful as that of anyone else on the program.

After working in the fields all day for a week, she found that she was getting too tired to practice at night. Her arms were too tired, they were stiff, and her fingers were not supple the way they needed to be to handle the strings and the bow. Finally it came to a choice between helping on the ranch or playing at the festival. After a desperate struggle with herself, Mari decided to sacrifice the greatest thing which had ever come to her and do her part to save the crop.

She told her mother and Tom as they all sat at the supper table on Friday night, too tired to get up and go on with their work.

"There are plenty of others at school who will be glad of the chance to get on the program. I can get out of it just as easy as that," she told them, trying to make it sound like nothing at all.

"You'll do nothing of the kind," Tom said positively.

"No. No," repeated Mother Sato. "You play. We find someone."

It was a great honor to the Satos to have Mari chosen. Mother Sato told Tom he would have to make some arrangements so Mari could have time to practice, even though some of the crop wasted. They would all drive in to hear Mari. She had been given four tickets for them, for Papa Sato might be home by that time.

"Can I go to my lesson then tomorrow?" Mari asked, planning her approach carefully.

"Sure you can," Tom said promptly to please his mother. She looked so worn and thin.

"Then I could get something to wear while I'm in the city."

"You've got a dress," Tom said, grinning exasperatingly. "What do you want with another one?"

"But I haven't anything suitable, and you know it," Mari argued, diplomacy forgotten in her extremity. "Everyone else will wear a formal dress, and I can't wear that old blue thing I wear to church and everywhere, short skirt and sleeves."

"Why not? That's a pretty dress. If it was good enough to wear to my graduation, it's good enough to wear anywhere." Tom was enjoying himself.

"Oh, you . . ." Mari began in despair. Then she turned to her mother. "Look here, Mom, I can't play if I don't have a new dress, a formal, you know, long down to the floor and no sleeves." She illustrated with appropriate gestures, helped out with a sprinkling of Japanese, while Tom tipped back in his chair and laughed.

Mother Sato's eyes, looking out from under sand-chafed lids, were puzzled. Ranch life had not included formal occasions, and this was the first time her daughter had been a participant in one.

Mari ran to her room and brought out the picture she had cut from a magazine. It was a kodachrome of a lady in evening dress, and Mari had been practicing the pose night after night in her room. She showed the picture to her mother.

"See, like this. Long, fluffy . . . everyone will be wearing one at the festival."

Mother Sato looked and smiled. She shared the universal interest of women in pretty clothes. This style wasn't what she had worn when she was Mari's age, but this was America.

"I could buy the material and make it myself," Mari wheedled. "It wouldn't cost much."

Mother Sato turned to Tom. He was still in a teasing mood, thinking the decision was still his and planning to hold out a little longer. Mari was getting too smart for a girl. She was even bossy at times. Let her beg a little longer, maybe it would put her in her place.

"Tamotsu, give Mari some money," Mother Sato said, and Tom recognized the voice of command.

"All right, Mom," he said respectfully.

"We want her look nice up there. Everyone be looking at her, say, 'Ooh, Miss Sato, how pretty she look.'"

Tom laughed and got up to go to his room for his billfold.

Mari gave him a triumphant glance as she began to gather up the dishes.

This was too much for Tom, and he had to have one last crack at his insubordinate sister.

"Don't waste the money buying material. Buy something already made, and then you'll have a dress that's fit to wear."

But Mari, with her mother on her side, no longer had to cater to Tom. She didn't bother to reply, but made a face at him and let it go at that. She had had two years of sewing at school, and she thought she was pretty good.

"This ought to be enough to get your dress and all the go-with-its you said you had to have," Tom said as he came back and handed her some bills. "Now come on out and get to work if you're going to have the day off tomorrow."

Mari needed no persuasion to take the day off. In the large department store in the city next morning she was fortunate in securing as a saleslady a pretty, grayhaired, motherly woman. When she learned the occasion for which Mari was buying and saw that the girl was none too sure of herself, she made it her special mission to pilot Mari around the store from one department to another, seeing that she was properly fitted with everything she needed.

The formal Mari decided on was taffeta, the color

113

of spring daffodils, a conservative basque type with shirring at the waist and shoulders. A pair of silver slippers made her look a full inch taller, and a sparkling bracelet and earrings to match, completed her outfit. She scarcely recognized herself when she looked in the mirror, that lithe, glamorous young woman with skirts sweeping the floor . . . Could that really be she, Mari Sato of the cucumber patch?

The saleswoman told her she looked beautiful and that no one on the program would surpass her in appearance. Mari loved the compliments and experienced a sudden revulsion against the ranch and her old, sweaty work clothes. She wished she need never go back but could always be dressed in fine raiment and live in richly furnished apartments.

Of course, her purchase had cost a little more than the amount Tom had given her. What woman ever found that her shopping cost a little less than expected? And she was unwilling to give up one thing she had selected, so she used the money for her violin lesson to pay the balance. The maestro would wait, and her mother would make Tom give her enough to pay for two lessons next time.

Mari left the store, hugging her precious boxes to her and walking on air. She had a light lunch at a dairy lunch place that was white and clean, and then went to her lesson.

The maestro was displeased with her. She knew he would be, for she had had no time to practice. But he would not take any excuses, and anyway Mari was not going to tell him she had been doing the work of a ranch hand ever since she had been in before. Instead she tossed her head saucily as he scolded and tried to do her very best when he was ready to begin the new lesson. Nothing could have dampened her spirits now that she had the coveted evening gown.

Her head still in the clouds, she boarded the bus for home. The unfriendly and curious stares from people on the bus and the withdrawal of the woman she sat down by as if Mari were a combination of smallpox and plague were all lost on Mari. Other times she would have been hurt and self-conscious. But today she was unaware that she had traveling companions, so busy was she planning how she would wear her hair, how she would look as she stepped onto the stage from the wings and walked out before a large, breathless audience.

When the bus approached La Vista she considered stopping off to show Peg her new finery, but Peg lived so far from the station, and, anyway, Mari was beginning to feel compunctions over leaving her mother to slave in the heat all day while she played the lady in the city. There was still an hour of daylight left when she reached home, and she hurried into her levis and shirt and went out to the field. Cinderella was back in the ashes.

For days the Sato family worked without respite, and even then some of the fruit was left to yellow on the vines. Whenever Mother Sato would find such a one she would pucker her lips and exclaim over it ruefully, "Ooh, too bad, too bad."

Tom was a machine. He started before daylight, and when dark drove him from the cucumber field, he ate a bite of supper and got out the tractor to work the ground for the tomato plants, or cultivate those he had out already. He was using the big truck to haul the cukes to market now, for the harvest had outgrown the capacity of the pickup. Mr. Imoto was selling the surplus on the Los Angeles market for him.

Mr. Imoto still seemed to have no worries, and as he was Tom's barometer, the disturbing rumors Tom heard from the other Nisei he discarded as rumors and nothing more. Anyway, a mind in a work-driven body does not wrestle long with difficult problems. He picked cucumbers, bossed his heterogeneous crew, tried to protect his mother from the heaviest work, marketed his crop, banked the money, and ate and slept when there was time left.

Yoshi came from school in a great state of excitement one afternoon. He ran across the patch to where the folks were working, shouting as he ran.

"They've put white papers on the posts!" he cried. They're all over everywhere. There's one right down here by the corner. Come on, Tom, and read what it says."

"What are they about, Joe?" Tom asked without looking up.

"They're about us, but they're too high. I can't see the fine print. The big letters on the top say 'To all persons of Japanese ancestry.' That means us, doesn't it?" Yoshi asked proudly. "Come on, Tom." He pulled at his brother's sleeve.

But Tom needed no urging now. He got to his feet at once and started down the road to the place where a fresh white paper was tacked to a telephone pole.

From Yoshi's description Tom had thought it might be the work of some Japanese-haters like Mr. Winters, trying to scare them all out of the country. But at first glance he recognized it as an official document. After those heavy black letters at the top had struck him in the face, his eyes fell to the bottom of the page of fine print. It was signed by the commanding general of the Western Defense Command.

Slowly, deliberately, Tom read each word of the fine print. Using the authority given it by the executive order of February 19, the Army had defined two military zones and designated them in the document as Military Area #1 by the first of May. Tom hastened to read the boundaries of this area. Certain sections of Washington and Oregon . . . He hurried on to California. There it was, the western half of California!

"That's us!" he exclaimed. "That takes us in."

"What does?" Yoshi asked.

Tom went on reading without hearing him.

The paper referred to German and Italian aliens, but it said *all* persons of Japanese ancestry. Such bold-faced discrimination from responsible officials was incredible. Citizenship, then, was to be disregarded. He couldn't believe it. It was there before his eyes, but he couldn't believe it. The general had overstepped his authority. The country would never stand for it. The president would remove him from his command.

"What is it?" Yoshi asked again, frightened by Tom's stern face.

"Just some Army regulations," Tom said absently. "You wouldn't understand."

They stood there so long that Mari quit work and came down to see what they were looking at.

"What does it say?" she asked when she saw the white paper on the pole.

"Read it," Tom said shortly.

Mari read it hastily and turned to Tom with fear in her eyes.

"What are we going to do? Where can we go?" It was more a cry of consternation than a question.

"The Nisei won't have to go," Tom said with assurance. "We can appeal to the president. He will give us our rights under the Constitution." Now that he had put his thoughts into words, he was sure he was right.

As they went back to work, Yoshi walked along beside Tom, conscious that this was something to do with their being a marked people. He took hold of Tom's sleeves to get his attention.

"Remember Abe Lincoln," he said shyly, looking up into Tom's sober face, a tentative smile on his lips.

"Yes. You bet we will," Tom answered, cheered by the kid's show of spirit.

While Tom and Mari, and the Nisei boys who were helping them, worked in the field that afternoon, puzzling over the flimsiness of their citizenship, in a bus station in a small town in northern California which served as an outlet and intake for the large Army camp nearby sat a soldier waiting for a southbound bus.

He had sat there for hours, motionless as a corpse, except for the intervals when the buses arrived. Then he would rise and go out to attempt to get aboard; but buses were crowded nowadays, and many made only routine stops at the stations. Unsuccessful, he would return to his seat and resume his frozen position, his eyes looking unseeing toward the littered floor.

He seemed unconscious of the crowds, mostly servicemen in uniforms like his own, which milled about him, tripping over his outstretched feet, brushing heavily against him as they dropped into adjoining seats. Like faraway voices he heard their conversations, planning their weekends in 'Frisco or griping over something not to their liking back in camp, the camp which they and he had just left, they for a few weeks, he for always. For the soldier was a Nisei, a volunteer, and in his pocket he carried a blue discharge from the Army because of his Japanese blood. He was Tad Sato.

Tad reached home Sunday around noon.

Tom had tried to keep his mother from going to the field with the rest of them that morning.

"Wouldn't you like to go to church this morning, Mom? Mari could drive you in, and you could ride out with the Tanimotos."

"No, no." Mother Sato's voice was decisive. "We can't rest yet." Then a glimmer of mischief flickered across her drawn face. "When all cucumbers picked, I go church twice on Sunday."

There was no way of handling this stubborn little woman. Tom had to give in and let her go to the field.

When they came in for lunch Mother Sato collapsed on the kitchen floor. Tom picked her up--there was no weight to her at all--and carried her into the living room to the couch. Mari ran for cold water and bathed her face and presently consciousness returned. She had given the children a bad scare, and they hovered around her as she lay there inert and jaded like a spent bird which, for lack of sanctuary, has been forced to stay too long in the air and drops at last, exhausted, to the ground.

Tom was for calling the doctor at once, but his mother would not hear of such a thing.

"Not sick," she insisted, pooh-poohing the idea. "Just tired. Today I rest. Tomorrow okay."

Mari opened a can of soup and, heating it, tried to

persuade her mother to eat. Tom added his efforts to hers. They were both stabbed wide awake now to what the last few months of anxiety and toil had done to their mother. How she had wasted away! Lying there on the couch, her shrunken body scarcely made a bulge in the blanket Mari had thrown over her.

"Yes, Mom, you've got to eat something or you won't have any strength," Tom urged, awkwardly. He didn't know what to do around sick people.

"Please try a little of soup while it's still hot," Mari coaxed.

To please the children, Mother Sato took a spoonful and made a wry face.

"Canned soup no good," she said childishly.

"Go fix her some rice and tea," Tom ordered Mari, with sudden inspiration.

But Mother Sato shook her head. She wanted nothing now except rest for her body and relief of mind from the dreadful anxiety over her man which pressed down upon her with the weight of a crushing stone.

Mother Sato had never fully recovered from the shock of Papa Sato's arrest. From that moment when Yoshi had rushed into the house telling her his father was gone, she had never ceased to worry about him. How was he faring today? What treatment was he receiving from his guards? Did he tell her all in his letters? Would they allow him to tell the truth? Seeing him at the mercy of his jailers that one time she had visited him had been anguish to her mind. As the weeks, and then months, went by, she began to imagine things. His letters were censored; he could not tell how bad things were. He was beaten and starved. Tom said he would be all right, there was international law to protect him, but she did not understand.

Then there was Tadashi. When he had volunteered there had been peace. She had been proud of her favorite son when he came home that Thanksgiving Day, so tall and straight and handsome. But now there was war; she might never see her boy again.

Left alone with her thoughts, for Tom and Mari

were always busy with their own affairs and never talked to their mother much at any time, she had been forced to create a world of her own in which the real and fancied dangers of her absent loved ones were magnified to such proportions that she could neither eat nor sleep. She had become the victim of brooding and imagination.

Her lifelong habit of hovering over the rest of the family at the table, waiting on them, had kept the children from noticing that their mother scarcely touched the food herself. And the hot tears which flowed unchecked down her hot cheeks as she lay alone in the dark nights were hidden from all human eyes.

At last her strength had given out. Her worn body would no longer obey her will.

So there she lay on the couch now, with Mari and Tom and Yoshi standing around helplessly, their faces shrouded in that gloom which closes down over a family when the mother is ill.

Already the responsibilities which had fallen on their young shoulders had seemed too heavy to carry-- the continued and unexplained detention of their father, the mounting antagonism against them in the community, the recent threat of eviction from their home--all these had been enough of a burden to bear. But now, Mother Sato down on her back . . .

Tom turned toward the couch and saw that his mother had dozed off.

"We'd better get back to work," he said to Mari. "There's nothing we can do for Mom. You stay and watch her, Joe. And if she wants anything, come tell me."

They were about to go when they heard a step on the front porch. Before they could even wonder who it might be, the door opened and in walked Tad.

"Tad!" Mari cried. Her face brightened at the sight of him, and she stood staring at him, unable to believe he was really there.

"Hello, Tom. Hi, Sis. How's everything?"

"Well, what do you know? Wasn't expecting to see

you walking in," Tom said. "How'd you get here? How long are you going to stay?"

Tom felt the old, familiar slap of greeting on his back, but as he looked into his brother's face he saw something different there. Something was wrong with Tad.

Yoshi had a hand in Tad's pocket.

"What did you bring me, Tad? Got any gum?"

Tad ignored Tom's question, gave Yoshi a playful cuff on the ear, and looked toward the kitchen.

"Where's Mom?"

Tom stood aside from the couch, and Tad saw his mother lying there.

"What's the matter?" he asked quickly, forgetting his own grievances.

Mother Sato had been aroused by the hubbub of Tad's arrival and, opening her eyes, she saw Tad standing over her.

"Tadashi!" It was a peal of ecstasy. Tears of joy ran down her cheeks.

"Hello, Mom. Surprised?" Tad said, grinning. But Tom noticed the break in his voice.

Tad sat down on the edge of the couch.

"How are you, Mom?" he asked gently. "Kind of lazy, aren't you, lying around like this in the middle of the day?"

Mother Sato looked up at him in a rapt sort of way, as if she were seeing a vision.

Mari felt her eyes blur. She hadn't known how her mother must have worried about Tad. She herself had been proud of his name on the honor roll at school and a star on the service flag for him. Besides, it gave her some reflected glory to have a brother in the service.

Tad was stricken by the change in his mother. Nothing in the letters from home had prepared him for it. The sight of her sunken cheeks, accentuated by the high cheekbones, and her thin hand lying on the blanket with no more flesh on it than on a bird's claw cut his heart to the quick and drove from his mind his own troubles which he had nursed all the way down on the bus with the idea of throwing them into the lap of the family when he reached home.

Now he made an effort to hide the depression and resentment which consumed him and tried to do something for his mother. How could she have changed so much in the short time since he had seen her? Less than six months, and she had turned into a haggard old woman.

"How are you, Mom?" he asked again, for his mother had not answered.

"I'm not so good," she said plaintively, now that she had a sympathetic listener.

"What's the matter? You've been working in the field," Tad accused, noting her dusty shoes by the couch. He turned and looked at Tom.

"I work some," Mother Sato admitted humbly.

"I couldn't keep her out," Tom said defensively.

"What's the big rush that you can't take time off on Sunday?" Tad asked. He had expected to find the family just home from church and ready to sit down to a good Sunday dinner. And he had pictured himself that afternoon, with all the folks around to listen, telling of what had happened to him and receiving comfort and sympathy from those to whom he was important and worthy.

He had tried to make his question to Tom sound offhand, but, in spite of himself, there was a note of irritability in his voice.

Tom noticed it and gave Tad a quick glance. Yes. There was something wrong. He began to feel uneasy. Could Tad be AWOL from camp? Was his outfit shipping out right away, and he was afraid to tell his mother? Had there been some incident on the trip home? Tad was hotheaded. He might not take the insults the way you had to learn to take them and keep still.

He explained to Tad what they were doing now and how he had not been able to get field labor on account of the defense plants.

"Regular old rancher, aren't you, boy? Sacrifice the

122

whole family for a lug of vegetables." Tad laughed, but not with good humor.

He turned back to his mother, dismissing Tom. And Tom and Mari went out.

"Do you suppose this is Tad's leave before he goes over?" Mari asked as she began to prepare some lunch for Tad and Tom ate a hurried snack so he could get back to work.

"I don't know any more than you do."

"He looks . . . Well, different some way."

So Mari had noticed it, too. Tom made no comment, but hurried through his lunch and went out.

In the living room Tad and his mother were visiting.

"You haven't eaten anything," he said, noticing the tray of untouched food, after awhile.

"I can't eat very good. I am all tight in here." Mother Sato made a vague gesture with her bony hand which could have indicated any locality between her chin and her waist. "I get all choked up and can't swallow."

"I know all about that," Tad laughed. "I got all choked up trying to eat the chow they serve up in the Army. I'm plenty hungry for some good home-cooked food. I'll get a nice, tender steak in town tomorrow, and we will make up a dish of sukiyaki. Bet that won't choke you up."

Mother Sato laughed with Tad and was better already for his coming. When Mari called Tad to lunch his mother was going to get up and come to the table, but Tad stopped her.

"Now you stay right where you are, Mom, and I'll bring my plate in here. Fix a plate for Mom, too, Mari."

But when Tad pulled up a chair and sat down beside the couch to eat with his mother, he found his appetite quite gone, and it was Mother Sato who emptied her plate.

Tad had thought he wanted to be alone with his mother, and now that Mari and Yoshi had gone back to the field and he knew they would be there till dark, he

123

found that it was not going to be as easy as he had thought to tell why he had come home. It was only three days ago he had been called into the CO's office and handed his discharge. There had been three other Nisei in his outfit kicked out at the same time. Blue discharges so they could never receive the benefits granted to veterans. His captain had hated it and told him so. And most of the fellows in his company had been swell. But there were a few who were glad to see him get it in the neck.

While his mother was finishing her tea Tad got up and wandered restlessly about the room, looking at the familiar things. He sat down in his father's chair a minute but too many memories began to roll over him, so he got up and went to the front window where he stood looking out across the mesa, talking to his mother about everything except himself.

To him, his discharge and the injustice of it were far worse than going to war, and he thought his mother would feel the same as he did. If he had known better, he could have spared her another moment of anxiety.

He asked about his father, and his face was ugly when he heard there had been no hearing yet. He was putting together the many pieces from the same pattern. His dad held without a hearing; his own discharge from the Army for no reason but his ancestry; the eviction notices to all persons of Japanese ancestry. The Constitution didn't mean a thing. That congressman knew what he was talking about when he said the Bill of Rights meant white people. Sure, newspapers like the Chicago *Tribune* would scream their headlines about the sacred Constitution when Roosevelt tried to do some renovating in Washington, but that document wasn't sacred enough or strong enough to stop the pressure boys.

"Mari is going to play at the Spring Music Festival later this month," his mother was saying. "She was chosen as the best musician in her school," she said proudly, speaking in her native tongue.

She can't do that, Tad thought. People are getting

too hostile, she might be booed by the audience. Didn't the folks know what was going on in the world? Tom with his nose in the ground and his childlike faith in his country. Tad didn't suppose Tom had even noticed the eviction notices. He still believed in fairies. Well, he'd soon let Mari know she wasn't going to get up and make a target of herself for all the hate and ridicule and contempt that was being stirred up in the state against the Japanese.

His mother was talking rapidly in Japanese. There was excitement and urgency in her voice, but Tad could not catch what she was saying. He did not answer, and she went on. Her voice became solemn and then low and heavy with sorrow. He caught a few words and knew now she was talking about the war. The war and him. How soon he would be sent away.

This was the time. Tell her now. Get it over with. It won't be any easier for her later. But, see, there's pride as well as sorrow in her eyes. See how she's watching me. She thinks I'm going to war, to fight for my country. She's proud of me, even though she believes I never will come back. Even though she thinks I may be fighting against her dear native land. But she's proud of me. Tell her I've been kicked out because an officer suspicioned me, was afraid I'd knife my country in the back, despised me for my Japanese blood. No. Not now.

But there was no use to have her brooding over the possible immediacy of his departure.

"Our outfit still needs a lot of training before it's ready to go overseas," he told her. It was true. "Too soon to begin worrying about that."

His words seemed to ease Mother Sato's mind. She smiled and sipped her second cup of tea with relish.

Tad went out to his old room adjoining the garage and found it in order as usual, with his civilian clothes laundered or cleaned and pressed, ready to put on. He shed his uniform quickly, throwing it carelessly over the foot of the bed, and put on a work shirt and a pair of blue jeans.

As he stood before the mirror running the comb through his short hair, his eye fell on Norio's flag, draped across the corner of the mirror. Quick, hot tears scalded his eyelids. We both know now what it is to be despised and rejected, he thought. He threw the comb down and turned away from the mirror with a curse, struggling to harden himself against this wave of emotion. The fear of allowing himself to be hurt was raising its ugly head again.

He must root out of his heart his love for the flag and crush that live thing that gripped his heart at the sight of it. All that the flag had stood for was gone anyway. Why should he have any emotion over it?

"Liberty and justice for all," he said bitterly.

He grabbed an old hat from a nail in the closet and went out. He didn't want to be alone.

When Yoshi saw him coming to the field he came running toward him.

"Where's your uniform?" he asked, disappointed to see his soldier brother in old clothes.

"I can't pick cukes in my uniform, boy. What's the matter with you?" Then, turning to Tom, "Where do I start, boss?"

"My name's Joe now." Yoshi went on talking. "Did you see what it said on the white papers, Tad?"

"Sure. They're all up and down the state. Just like the WANTED posters in the post office, aren't they? Only there aren't any photos on these." There was something foreign in Tad's voice. Yoshi didn't know what to make of it. He began to feel strange toward his brother.

"Yeah. No," he said uncertainly. It sounded like Tad was joking, but he didn't think there was anything funny about what the white papers said. Tom hadn't laughed when he had read them that day. But then Tad would know all about what Tom had told him about how they all had to be brave and take hard things. Maybe Tad was so big and strong he just laughed at hardships. Anyway, he was a soldier.

"Can I pick down here with you and Tad?" Yoshi asked Tom.

"Go back and finish your row first," Tom said. He thought if they were alone, maybe Tad would tell what was wrong.

But Tad went to work with those characteristically quick and effective motions which had always enabled him to do the work of two when he willed to do so, and he was soon far ahead of Tom on his side of the row.

It was not until that night when the two boys went out to Tad's room after supper--following an old custom--that Tom learned what had happened.

When they went in Tom saw that the uniform had slipped to the floor and lay there in a wrinkled heap. He picked the coat up and, shaking the wrinkles from it, got a hanger from the closet. The feel of the rough wool was good against his hand. Someday he would be wearing one of these.

"Never mind about that," Tad said casually, giving the clothes a studied, careless glance. "I won't be wearing it anymore."

Tom stood petrified, coat in one hand, hanger in the other, staring at his brother.

"Yeah, that's right. I got kicked out of the Army. I'll be in civvies from now on."

The words were spoken so casually that Tom had to go back and pick them up one by one and put them together again before he could be sure that he had heard correctly.

"How come?" he asked, and it was all he could do to get those two words out. His voice was low and hoarse with tension. He put the coat on the hanger, smoothing out the shoulders. The uniform of the United States Army. Tad was out. "Something happen?" as Tad did not answer his first question.

Tad was ready to talk now, and he poured out the whole story, finding relief with every word.

"All the Nisei in our outfit were discharged. And did you know that all the Nisei are reclassified in the Selective Service as 4C? Enemy aliens--that's what we are to the government now. How do you like that? And to think I volunteered because I wanted to fight for

127

freedom. What a laugh!"

Tom shrank from the bitterness in Tad's voice.

"Our fellows had some of the best records in the outfit. There wasn't a thing on the books against any of us, not even one AWOL. The CO just didn't trust us, and that's the whole, lousy truth. God, I'd like to get clear out of the country."

"Do you wish you'd stayed in Japan last summer?"

"Hell, no! There's nothing for us over there, either." Tad's voice was hard, and the corner of his mouth was twisted down in an ugly curl.

"If they'd only give a fellow a chance to prove his loyalty . . ." Tom began.

"Loyalty! To hell with loyalty! I'm through worrying about whether some dirty, selfish politician or some dumb cluck of an Army officer thinks I'm loyal or disloyal. What do I care what they think? I know my own heart. What more can a fellow do than offer his life?" Tad shouted. "But that wasn't enough," he added bleakly.

Tom felt sorry for him, but what could he do?

"Mom says they're still holding Dad without a trial," Tad said, changing the subject suddenly. "Just like Hitler's Europe."

"No, it's not," Tom defended. "He says he is being treated okay, and the Spanish consul, who is looking after them for the Japanese government, said so the other day. And he gets plenty to eat and can write home." Tom hesitated. "We don't write him anything we think will worry him," he said.

"I get it," Tad said drily.

In spite of the reason which had brought Tad home, Tom found it good to have him to talk to and to share the responsibility.

They began to talk of the white papers. Tom thought there would be a change in the orders. He didn't believe they would have to move. The ranchers wouldn't be moved until after the harvest anyway. Food was too important to the war.

Tad felt differently.

"But look how much of the food around here is raised by the Japanese. With the exception of oranges, avocados, and some tomatoes, they raise everything that's grown. Practically all the vegetables and all the strawberries. Why, there isn't a commercial strawberry grower in this part of the state that isn't Japanese. Do you think that with the food shortage, the government is going to move thousands of experienced ranchers off their places right in the spring of the year? Let the stuff they've put out spoil in the fields? It doesn't make sense."

"Well, I saw some fields where the government had done that very thing," Tad answered. "There's one right down the road between here and the city. I saw it as I came out. Acres of rotten cabbage."

"Yes, I know," Tom said wearily. "Harry Sakai's. You remember him?"

"Sure. He was that little guy in Norio's class. Tricky as a circus flea. So the FBI got him. I'll bet they had plenty on Harry. He's the kind that gets us all in bad. What became of his family?"

Tom told him the story as far as he knew it.

"I guess they found out Harry belonged to some Japanese secret societies in Los Angeles. They didn't have to have much to pick a man up or they wouldn't have taken Dad. They took Mr. Hanada, too."

"Bill's father?"

"Yes."

"Oh, sure. I remember now. I had a letter from him around Christmastime, and he said he had to leave the university and go home to take over his father's business. He sold the florist shop for a song. Everyone knew he had to sell."

The two boys talked on about the change the war with Japan had brought into their lives. Tad tried to get Tom to realize the situation as it looked to him. He had felt the rising tide of hate lapping at his feet. He had been refused service at the bus stops on the way home. Even his uniform had not protected him from insults. And he had seen the signs in store windows,

"No Japs wanted." It was not hard for him to believe that anything might happen to them.

But Tom was thoroughly indoctrinated with the principles of American democracy from his years in school, and he had not been disillusioned by experience as Tad and others had been. He discounted Tad's opinions as colored by the unfortunate thing that had happened to him. Finally Tad gave up.

"Any gas in the car?" he asked.

"Yes. Tank's full, " Tom said, wondering why Tad wanted to know at this time of night.

"Think I'll run into the city and see Bill," Tad announced, beginning to hunt around in the closet for a good suit.

"It's pretty late," Tom said, yawning.

"Oh, Bill never goes to bed before early morning."

Mari went back to school the next day, and Tad took the places of her and his mother in the field. He could do more than both of them without putting himself out. He had persuaded his mother to stay in bed that morning, but when they came in at noon she was up, shuffling about the kitchen trying to fix something special for Tad.

"If Papa Sato only come now," she said with a sigh as they sat down at the table.

"He'll be coming one of these days," Tad assured her.

Tad was restless. Even though he worked hard all day he wasn't satisfied to sit at home in the evenings with the others. By nighttime, Tom was ready to fall into bed and get some rest, but after supper Tad would shave, dress, and drive away, never telling anyone where he was going. Tom would hear him coming in when it seemed to him almost time to get up, and when he went out in the morning he would open the garage door and look ruefully at the shining blue car all streaked with dust and fog. He would get a cloth and carefully wipe the salty mist from the chrome and polish it till it shone like new again.

Tad usually went into the city and spent the evening with some of the other Nisei. From them he heard all the latest rumors. Everyone was going to be ordered from the coast. They were all to be evacuated from the state. Their property was going to be confiscated by the government. They were all, Issei and Nisei alike, going to be interned for the duration. The rumors flew thick and fast.

News of the Terminal Island evacuation was beginning to drift down the coast, and if it were a forerunner of what the rest might expect, it boded no good to anyone. The Department of Justice had given the Terminal Islanders thirty days to get off the island. Then suddenly the orders were changed. They must be out within forty-eight hours. There had been panic and consternation. Many of the men had been picked up by the FBI earlier, and the women were left to fend for themselves and their families. Many had nowhere to go, and no way to move their goods nor dispose of them there. Sharpsters appeared and bought boats and houses and furniture at prices ruinous to the owners. Trucks donated by the good people of Los Angeles made round trips between the city and the island all day and far into the night, moving out the people and a few necessary belongings amid laments and tears which made the drivers of the trucks wonder what all this fighting for democracy was about anyway.

When the evacuation had been accomplished, when the homeless women and children, long since deprived of their breadwinners, had been bundled into crowded emergency quarters, their lifetime savings invested in homes and stores and furniture suddenly shrunken to a few miserable dollars from the sharpsters' pockets, the whole affair had been ably reported by a Los Angeles columnist next morning in a single, humorous quip:

"Well, we got one island back from the Japs yesterday, Terminal Island."

It was grim humor to the evacuees.

Tad called around at Bill Hanada's house often, and the subject of Tad's discharge nearly always found a place in the conversation during the evening.

"You're better off than the fellows they kept in, the ones they pulled out of their outfits here on the coast and sent to camps back East. You know what's happened to them? They've been disarmed and given service jobs. Tony Matsui was demoted from corporal, and he's starting in all over again as a buck private with a job in the mess hall. And Sho Sonada is bartender in the officers' quarters. He hates it. They aren't trusted any more than you fellows, and you're lucky to be out altogether, if you're asking me."

Bill was short, heavyset, and as swarthy as an East Indian. In temperament he was self-assured and placid. In general demeanor he gave the impression that anything which happened to him he would be able to turn to his own advantage. The emotional stresses which pulled Tad apart were unknown to Bill.

"Sure I had to sell the florist shop cheap. But when I found out that the ones who wanted it and could afford to pay a reasonable price for it were going to take advantage of me, I let a guy who couldn't afford to pay anything much have it. He was sure tickled, for he had no idea he could get it so cheap." Bill grinned comfortably.

Bill had his ideas about their being classified 4C also, and Tad would have his say and then sit back and smoke while Bill aired his views.

"I don't like being classified an enemy alien by my government any better than the rest of you Nisei, but if my country doesn't want me to fight, that suits me just fine. I don't want to fight, either. I can see eye to eye with the Army there. What I want to do is get back to school and get my degree as soon as possible."

Bill's even temper helped to quiet Tad, and though Bill was the younger of the two, Tad came to depend upon Bill's judgment as they sorted over the rumors that each day produced.

Tad came home from the market one morning after trucking the cucumbers in and told Tom that Mr. Imoto and some other men were driving back to Colorado to look up locations back there somewhere, and he had told Mr. Imoto to be on the lookout for something for them.

Tom was angry and frightened. He and Tad fought over it, and Tad said he would go and take the family, and Tom could stay on the ranch and let somebody like Mr. Winters take a shot at him some night, if that was what he wanted.

The group of men went back in Mr. Imoto's big car and were gone about two weeks. When they returned they had a sorry story to tell. Mr. Imoto's smile was gone, and his eyes had fear in them.

Yes, they had found some good business opportunities around Denver, but it wasn't safe to try to move their families and belongings across New Mexico and Arizona. Crossing these states on their return they had often been afraid of physical violence. Anti-Japanese sentiment was running high. There were ominous signs in shop windows. "This restaurant poisons Japs and rats." On the barbershop in one town, "We shave Japs. Not responsible for accidents," and automobiles bore stickers saying, "Open season on Japs." It was all very disconcerting to these western pioneers facing east. Some gas stations refused service, and they came near being stranded more than once in the desert with an empty gas tank. One day they had travelled all day before they found a cafe which would serve them, and then, just as they were ready to eat, a crowd of rough looking men came in and surrounded their table. Each man was packing a pistol, and Mr. Imoto and his party were forced at gunpoint to get up from the table, leaving the food untasted, and get out.

Mr. Imoto swore he wouldn't make that trip across the desert again without protection, regardless of government orders. He advised Tad to stay where he was and wait.

The newspapers and radio were screaming for evacuation of these dangerous people. Public officials were adding fuel to the fire with their damaging statements. The uneasiness of the Japanese aliens and their

American offspring increased to the point where it was felt necessary to call a meeting and decide as a group what to do in case such orders should come.

VII

When the night of the mass meeting came, Tom said he wasn't going. He said it would just be a lot of arguing and excitement, and he thought the cooler everyone kept right now and the less they talked, the better. Anyway, he was too tired, and it didn't make any difference to anyone whether he was there or not.

But Tad wouldn't give up. He was determined that his idealistic younger brother should hear what was really going on around them, get his head out of the clouds where he imagined he could still see equal rights for all citizens under the Constitution. The boy had to get some sense in his head. They were right up against the possibility of being forced off their land, and Tom was still working twelve to sixteen hours a day tending the thousands and thousands of tomato plants he thought he was going to sell to the cannery growers later. No chance he'd be there to do it, but you couldn't tell him anything. He was as stubborn as Dad. It irked Tad, and also made him a little envious, when Tom took so much pride in doubling his production of plants this year in response to the government plea for more food, and when he talked about keeping faith with your country in time of crisis, that right now when she was losing her battles in the Pacific was no time to gripe and criticize and doubt. Tad remembered when he had felt the same way. He recalled with bitterness his high resolve when he had been on the way home from Japan the summer before, how he, too, had believed and was ready to die for freedom and democracy. What a fool he had been to volunteer. Now Tom was being just such a fool.

He kept at him until Tom finally gave in and had a quick shower and change.

It had taken some time to persuade him, and they were late getting started into the city. The large hall was filled when they arrived. It was not a secret meeting, permission had been secured from the authorities in advance, but no special police had been sent to that area. The regular officer on that corner watched the crowd gather but had no occasion to interfere as the orderly group assembled.

Tad and Tom found seats about half way down toward the front, and Tom surveyed the crowd as he walked down the aisle and estimated that there were four or five hundred present. They were young men for the most part, which meant that it was predominantly a Nisei crowd. They were orderly, but not quiet. There was a strong undercurrent of conversation in strained voices and some attempts at jocularity as now and then one of the younger fellows would shout out some wisecrack apropos of their situation, choosing to hide their real feelings behind a mask of bravado and laughter.

A tremor of strangeness and excitement took possession of Tom as he sat down and felt himself for the first time in his life in a large gathering which was exclusively Japanese. As he looked about the hall he spotted older men here and there throughout the crowd, men somber and with lines of worry in their faces. These would be the Issei, men who for many weeks, some of them, had had their little bundle of necessities ready in case the FBI came for them. They would be here tonight to have their say about the rights of aliens and to tell the younger men, the citizens, what they owed to their elders.

Mr. Imoto was to be the chairman of the meeting, and he was already on the platform when the Sato boys arrived. Tom looked twice before he recognized him as he sat there with his head down, shuffling through some notes. It was not the merry-faced market proprietor Tom was accustomed to greeting in the early dawn in the unloading shed, but a serious, businesslike man in a well-fitting dark suit, white shirt, and tie.

Even before the meeting opened the tension mounted. Basic emotions had been stirred to their depths by rumors of mass evacuation and detention. It would take skill and judgment and courage to handle the situation successfully and bring forth from the discussion anything constructive to justify their having come together.

Mr. Imoto called the meeting to order and stood waiting patiently for quiet, although it was some time before all of the talking stopped. Then he began to speak.

"We all know the purpose of this meeting," he said slowly, sadly. "Rumors have become more frequent and persistent that all persons of Japanese ancestry are to be removed from the West Coast and interned somewhere in the interior for the duration. Now so far these are only rumors and there has been nothing definite from the authorities themselves yet on the subject; but we have all seen and read the orders for us to be out of Military Zone Number One by May 1. Of course, under this order we can decide where we shall . . ."

"Oh, yeah? Where can we go?" someone yelled.

Mr. Imoto smiled slightly and went on.

"But the increasing pressure put upon the military by certain groups--I need not name them--leads some of us to believe that the present voluntary evacuation will not satisfy them and that they will fight for complete evacuation of all Japanese from the coast, and the military will not be able to withstand them. Besides, voluntary evacuation is not being successful. Too many states are closing their doors upon us. And as the gentleman said a moment ago, too few of us know of anywhere to go.

"Our senators in Washington are bowing to the hysterical demands of their people from the West Coast, and no one can tell what is ahead of us or how soon the blow will fall. As shocking and as unnecessary as this mass eyacuation and detention may sound to us, we should make ourselves ready. We should decide tonight on what course we shall follow if the order comes. It is better to act in unison and not to risk any untoward event which might reflect discredit upon us all. I think we should talk the matter over calmly and try to come

137

to a decision based upon good judgment rather than upon our feelings in this matter. Now let us hear what your opinions are."

Mr. Imoto had barely thrown the meeting open and turned to recognize the man with whom he had arranged to speak first and set the tone for the discussion when Tad Sato was on his feet, demanding to be heard. His face was flushed and his voice strident with unrestrained emotion. Tom fidgeted in his seat and felt as if he were sitting on the rim of an active volcano.

Reluctantly, Mr. Imoto gave Tad the floor.

Disdaining any introductory remarks, Tad plunged right to the heart of the subject.

"If we are ordered out," he shouted, "it will be absolutely unjust and unconstitutional, and I think we should oppose such an order in every possible way."

"How?" someone challenged. "Name a few ways."

Tad accepted the challenge.

"Well, there are at least seventy thousand American citizens involved in this proposed crime against humanity. Say ten thousand are disloyal or of dual citizenship."

"That's away too high," came a chorus of voices.

"Say five thousand, then."

"Still too high."

"Well, I want to be on the safe side. That leaves sixty-five thousand loyal Americans whose rights the government proposes to ignore and whose freedom it plans to disregard, if it interns us without any case against us. Sixty-five thousand--that is an army in itself. If we would stand for our rights under the Constitution of the United States and refuse evacuation, we could command the attention of the whole nation."

"All the attention we'd get would be a mass funeral."

"Didn't you hear what DeWitt's office said about using bayonets on us if we refused?"

"No, really, listen to me, fellows." Tad was definitely appealing to the younger Nisei. "If we all stuck together and were united in our attitude, as Mr.

138

Imoto suggested at the beginning, the authorities would have to give us some consideration. We could make such a national issue of it that we could not only secure justice for ourselves but for the aliens as well, and get what a lot of good people in this state are pleading for, selective evacuation after a proper hearing, the real American way of doing things.

"Do you think the American people are so engrossed in war that they have not time to think of anything else? They have time to listen to the radio commentators and to read the newspapers that are trying to force us out. They'll listen to us, they'll have to listen to the voices of sixty-five thousand citizens.

"Now about the president's order which gives the military authority to move people about as it pleases, is it itself constitutional? Does the president have the right to issue such an order, even in wartime? What about the Bill of Rights? The right of the state to move any and all persons of specific ancestry from certain areas of the country, or from the country itself, for if it can do one it can do both, is not democracy; it is rank totalitarianism. Such powers make the state supreme and put the interest of the state above the interest of the people. The individual has no rights. In Nazi Germany the theory in regard to the Jews is that no matter how good some Jews may be, the presence of any Jew in the country is a menace to the German state and to the greatest good of the German people. Therefore, all Jews may be removed, interned, or slaughtered.

"Aren't the white people of California taking that same stand? The presence of any person of Japanese descent in California is a menace to the state and must be removed. 'Get them out,' they are demanding. How does this differ from the Nazi attitude toward the Jews in Germany?

"Because this whole theory is un-American and violates the principles of democracy as set forth in the Constitution, we are obligated as loyal citizens to fight it, not only for our own sakes in this one instance where we are the victims, but for the sake of all who enjoy the freedom and opportunity for individual initiative, for which America stands." Tad for the moment was back to the day when he set foot again on the dear homeland after his visit to a totalitarian country, a day when the freedom and opportunity to be found in his country had never seemed so priceless before. "We are as much obligated to fight the foes of democracy in our own country as we are to fight them in another. We should be willing to take some risk in the fight to preserve our rights under the Constitution, and if we haven't got the guts to do that, then I say we deserve anything we get."

Tad sat down, trembling like a man with ague. His inflammatory words had stirred many in the audience, and there was loud shouting and applause. Mr. Imoto felt the meeting had gotten off on the wrong foot. He turned to recognize the man who was supposed to have spoken first, but another young fellow was on his feet and speaking without addressing the chair. The chairman decided it would be better to hear him out than to try to stop him. There was no damming up the emotions of the hotheads.

"I think Tad Sato is right, up to a point; but I don't think we can do much about preserving democracy when there is a war on. Everyone loses a certain number of rights during a war. So I say that if the army or navy consider that we are a menace or a threat to the country by our presence here on the coast, or that we are hindering or embarrassing the war effort, let's do whatever we're told without any back talk. But if this whole evacuation business has been cooked up by a gang of politicians and associated farmers · and would-be produce merchants, all of whom stand to profit handsomely by our removal, then let's fight it to the last ditch."

"Yeah, he's right."

"That's what I say."

"Let's get organized."

Cries of approval came from all over the room.

It looked as if the resisters were going to get control of the meeting. Mr. Imoto ran his hand back over his hair in a nervous gesture. But now Mr. Take Shigaki was on his feet at last, ready to make his speech.

He was a few feet from the front, and Tom leaned forward to see around the man in front of him. Mr. Shigaki was a professional-looking man, in his thirties, Tom guessed. He asked Tad about him.

"Lawyer," Tad answered. "Official of the JACL here in the south."

Mr. Shigaki was very conciliatory in his opening remarks. "What we have been hearing all sounds good," he said calmly. "What these men have suggested is doubtless what we all feel like doing. No one but a coward likes to take things lying down. After what I have seen in some of the homes where the breadwinner was picked up last December and the mother and little children have been left to fend for themselves, in many cases the unnecessary suffering and privation, the grief and anxiety, I feel like fighting, too. And the things I've heard about the evacuation of Terminal Island rouses my fighting blood, also.

"But let's stop and look at this thing with our eyes wide open for a minute. What possible good could come from resisting Army orders in time of war, no matter what the orders were? Suppose we are ordered out. Just what would happen if we refused to go? One thing is almost certain--we would be taken by force. So in the end we would have to go anyway. We would have gained nothing. And what would we have lost?

"If there were violence, some might lose their lives. And do you think for one minute that those who fell would go down in history as heroes fighting for the preservation of democratic principles? No. Not so long as we have a Hearst press in this country. To the American people these tragic dead would be represented as spies and saboteurs, and their resistance would be pointed to with fiendish glee as the final proof of their disloyalty. They would be worse than throwing their lives away.

"Is there a person here tonight who can honestly deny in his own heart that what I say is true?"

Mr. Shigaki stopped as if expecting an answer. He had been talking slowly, and his composure was having a quieting effect upon his audience.

"Let us try to see that no matter what the inconvenience to ourselves, we have an opportunity to make a real contribution to victory by carrying out in a peaceful manner all orders issued by the Western Defense Command. The government is plagued with many difficult problems now. A continuous string of defeats in the Pacific. The people demanding relief for the men on Bataan, and there is no way to get relief to them. Our unpreparedness, the conversion of industry to defense work is a race against time, the gearing of the public mind to the sacrifices and hardships of war, and along with all these vital and pressing problems, the presence of a large number of Japanese on the West Coast where the fear of a Japanese invasion is very real to the people--whether that fear is justified or had been created for propaganda purposes is beside the point. The fear is there.

"So if we are a vexing problem to our government, not through any fault of our own, then can we not show our loyalty best by putting the good of the country above our personal feelings and welfare and cooperating in whatever decisions are made to solve the problem?"

There were murmurs of agreement and assent from all over the hall, and, mingled with them, scattered loud protests. No matter how anyone might feel about evacuation, common sense told most of them that Mr. Shigaki had presented the only reasonable course open to them.

But Tad was not ready to give up yet.

He was up shouting for recognition before Mr. Shigaki was fairly seated.

"Cooperation with the authorities is no proof of loyalty in a case like this. It is more a confession of guilt. Men in all ages since the beginning of recorded history, when they have known in their own hearts that they were innocent, have always risen in defense of

142

their rights."

One didn't, Tom thought, wishing Tad would sit down, and he died on a cross.

"It is our right to protest injustice. Why should we submit meekly to being ordered out of our homes because some selfish, greedy persons and groups of persons have connived and planned and brought about a situation in which our removal from the state is demanded by the people?

"Who are the loyal Americans, anyway, we who have no guilt but our looks, or those who would risk the sabotage of the forty million dollar truck crop grown by the Japanese in order to get into office or grab a nice, juicy produce business for themselves at a small fraction of its real value? Let's not be played for a bunch of suckers. If we're not going to resist, at least let's not stoop to lick the boots of our oppressors."

"Tad's right. Cooperation in dirty business is no proof of loyalty. We all know, or we ought to, that this whole situation has been brought about by those who have taken advantage of the war with Japan to try to accomplish something they have been wanting for a long time--getting the Japanese out of California. All of this harping about national safety and the flag-waving patriotism is just a front. And when they do get us out, if we are saps enough to go like dumb, driven cattle, you'll find out then whether or not it was national safety they were concerned about. You mark my words, they won't let up on us once we're gone but will have some schemes for keeping us out. And it will be some nice, patriotic, democratic scheme, too, something that all the people, or most of them, will swallow just like they've done this idea of evacuation. You just watch and see. See if the newspapers let up on us. See if the hatred they've aroused against us is allowed to die out."

"We aren't gone yet," someone shouted as the fellow sat down.

There were laughs, and from the young hotheads, a wild burst of approval.

In the midst of the confusion, Bill Harada got up.

He looked as unperturbed as if he had risen to make a routine recitation in the mathematics class at the university. Bill had a big, strong voice, and he did not need to shout to be heard. The posture of his stocky body suggested complete relaxation, although he did not slouch.

"If we are ordered out," he began calmly, and the words which had sounded so inflammatory in the mouth of Tad now indicated nothing more than a possible contingency which should be given due consideration, "there will be only one thing for us to do and that will be to go. The only choice we will have is *how* we will go. I understand that that is the purpose of this meeting tonight, to come to some decision as a group on that point.

"We can go now on our own if everyone knows where to go and has the money to get there. With our bank accounts frozen, most of us couldn't get very far." He was interrupted by laughs. "Or we can wait and let the Army decide for us and take care of the transportation and living arrangements, or we can, as some have suggested here, resist and be taken by force, that is whoever is left after the resistance is broken.

"For my part, I intend to make the best of whatever happens. I believe that all citizens are subject to orders from the government in time of war. If it can take a fellow and put him in uniform and send him off to any part of the world to kill or be killed, then I believe it has the right to tell you and me where we shall go and what we shall do. I recognize that authority, and I stand ready to carry out any orders which are given me. But I do agree with Tad Sato on one thing. I see no reason why we should cater to the officials who are putting us out, trying to gain favor with them, as I have seen some Nisei doing with the Civilian Control men down here. I am making no bid for their friendship.

"Let us go, if we must, in a dignified and orderly manner, which will make it easier for all of us and which will bring credit to our people; but let the authorities who are doing this unjust thing to helpless women and little children, and to the aged and sick, let them be the ones to feel uncomfortable in our presence and do the catering, if any is to be done.

"We are the ones who are being inconvenienced, bereft of our possessions and disowned by our government. Have you ever seen a fellow hugging his draft board because they were putting him in the Army?

"This is war, and I am ready to do anything my country demands of me; but by what she asks of me she will be judged. I will know just where I stand as an American citizen, if I am interned for the duration, and my responsibility in the future will be determined by my status now.

"Well, I don't know that my opinion is worth anything to the rest of you, but that's just about where I stand on this question." And Bill sat down as calmly as he had gotten up.

"I am sure we are all glad to hear from Bill Harada," Mr. Imoto said. "He is one of the influential young Nisei of our community, and his levelheadedness will be a great help to us in whatever crisis we have to face."

Tad muttered something under his breath. He acted as if he were going to demand the floor again, and Tom wished heartily that he had stood firm on his intention not to come to the meeting. Then Tad suddenly sank back in his seat uneasily.

An older man had risen slowly and with great dignity and was ceremoniously addressing the chair. It was Dr. Kimura. A stir of expectancy swept over the audience, and many a Nisei shifted uncomfortably in his seat. Dr. Kimura was a man of around fifty, graying at the temples, an alien ardently pro-Japanese, and one of the few leaders among the Issei who had not been picked up by the FBI. He had had his medical training in Japan and Germany, but during his twelve years in the United States had learned to speak English fluently and with biting sarcasm.

He was held in great respect and some fear by the

Japanese of the city, especially the Nisei, who were often the victims of his contempt because of their pride in their American citizenship and their faith in America.

This was a bitter moment for the Nisei, to bare their backs to the lashes of stinging ridicule which the ready tongue of Dr. Kimura was sure to lay on them without mercy. Hadn't he always told them that no one considered them as Americans except themselves? Now their discharge from the Army after Pearl Harbor, their reclassification as enemy aliens by Selective Service, and finally, possible internment, all these had furnished the doctor with an abundance of ammunition.

"There are many things which confuse me in this awkward situation in which we find ourselves," he began in a taunting voice. "I see many thousands of honest, law-abiding, respectable, and worthy people ordered to move from their homes. It appears that they and their contribution to the community are no longer wanted; perhaps they have never been wanted. So they are being ordered to move. The orders have been posted conspicuously in public places so that everyone may know that these people have been singled out for this discriminatory action on the basis of ancestry alone.

"This is all very confusing to me, for I have been hearing so much about the superiority of the 'American way' over that of other countries, particularly since the beginning of the war. It seems that this superiority is regarded as so great that Americans must fight the whole world in order to preserve it.

"Then I look again at this group of people who have been ordered to move out of their homes, and I see that many of them, in fact a large majority of them, are American citizens," the doctor's voice here made the Nisei wince, "and presumably have the protection of a constitution against the very thing which the government now proposes to do to them. It is all very paradoxical, shall we say.

"Some young American patriots of Japanese descent have quoted to me from the Declaration of Independence that 'all men are created equal' and that they are endowed with certain inalienable rights, among which are the right to life, liberty, and the pursuit of happiness. And in the Constitution, which I have had the pleasure of reading myself, it says that 'all persons born in the United States are citizens of the United States, and no state shall enforce any law which will abridge the privilege of citizens or deprive any person of life, liberty, or property without due process of law.'

"Now the purpose of the national government, in specifically withholding from the states the power to deprive persons of these rights, would seem to my humble mind to be to insure these rights to the individual. However, the national government itself now proposes to break its own constitution. I am sure you will see how it could be possible that I might be puzzled by this strange contradiction of purposes.

"Again it is proposed to confine citizens for what is called military necessity, intimating that citizens of one color are dangerous en masse, which in turn presupposes that citizens of another color are loyal en masse. This proposed evacuation and internment will inevitably cause loss of property; many have already suffered severe financial losses through enforced evacuation. Some will not be able to stand the rigors of evacuation and life in an internment camp. They must die. Thus persons will be deprived of life, liberty, and property, without due process of law.

"To add to my great confusion of mind, I must witness the further disconcerting spectacle of some of these citizens organized into a citizens' league, showing a willingness, yes, a pathetic eagerness to cooperate with the government in its plan to deprive them of their rights, to do all in their power to aid the government in its intention to break the Constitution.

"In this way they seem to be wholly lacking in filial piety, for they desire to accept without protest the unjustified and cruel treatment meted out to their aged parents. For what is more cruel to the aged than to be deprived of the comfort and privacy of home in their old age?

"I feel obliged to inquire of these citizens as Elijah inquired of the prophets of Baal.

"Where are your gods of freedom and justice and liberty for all, about which you have boasted as blatantly in the face of older and wiser counsel?

"Cry aloud, for they may be sleeping, or on a journey. Dance about your altar of Americanism, cut yourselves with knives and lances--but, alas, I fear there will be no voice to answer, no one to speak up in your behalf, nor any to regard your predicament, and not one of you shall escape when this evacuation comes."

Few knew the scriptural source of his quotation, but no one missed the burning ridicule in his voice.

Now Dr. Kimura dropped his imagery and spoke in plain, condemning words.

"By your eagerness to cooperate, you have hastened the day and made evacuation possible. If your organization had taken a definite stand for your rights as citizens and the rights of your parents as peaceable aliens, things might never have reached this stage. As it is, you have upon your consciences a crime against your own people which no one envies you."

Kimura's right to speak freely his opinions, declared Mr. Imoto, was a privilege not granted to people in many countries of the world at that time. He called attention to the right of assembly which they were taking advantage of at that very moment, although many in the audience were aliens and citizens of a country with which the United States was at war.

With skilled hands he poured oil on the smarting wounds Dr. Kimura had left.

Then he spoke out boldly for quiet and orderly cooperation with the authorities in whatever decisions were made concerning their disposition.

Others followed his lead, speaking along the same line. Keep our heads. We gain more by willing obedience in the long run.

There were defeatists in the crowd. Sure, do whatever you are told. What difference does it make? The Nisei have never had a chance anyway.

And there were the hecklers who interrupted the speakers and threatened at times to break up the meeting.

Only Mr. Imoto's patience and calm, and his willingness to let every fellow have his say, brought order out of chaos each time.

It was an airing of grievances, a blowing off of pent-up emotions.

"What did I fight for in the last war?"

"How about the good Americans who bought new refrigerators from the Terminal Island evacuees for five dollars each?"

"And the one who bought my uncle's ten thousand dollar ranch up in the valley for five hundred dollars?"

Tom had been dozing through the last few speeches, but this remark brought Mr. Winters to mind. Why would anyone sell for so little? Wasn't it because they were too ready to believe the rumors which floated about? They had no faith in the fairness of the government. They should blame themselves, not someone else. Was there anyone here who wouldn't take a bargain if they could get it?

"Makes me boiling mad," an angry voice shouted.

"Why don't they move out the Germans and Italians, too?"

At last it seemed that everyone was about talked out, and Mr. Imoto was considering a vote, when a young man back in the far corner of the hall got up. His voice was so soft that at first it could scarcely be heard across the room, but as some began to catch the drift of his remarks, the hall gradually became as still as an empty room.

"I think we're getting excited about something which isn't ever going to happen. We haven't been moved out yet. Yes, I know you say orders are posted to move to some other area, but before the date on those posters comes, you'll see an extension of the time on and on through the summer until the season's crops are harvested; and by that time the situation may be changed. Time is on our side. The more this proposed

149

evacuation is publicized throughout the country, the less likely it is to take place. Especially the wrongness of evacuation on a racial basis will have become evident to everyone after more consideration has been given it, and there will be no evacuation."

"How about Terminal Island?"

"Terminal Island was a strategic military area, and it is suprising that it wasn't evacuated sooner. You could hardly expect the government to leave enemy aliens so near to military installations."

"How about citizens?"

"Let me say what I have to say. There is something we seem to have lost sight of in our excitement." The speaker's face shone as from some inner light. "All of us Nisei here tonight have been through the public schools. We have been drilled in the principles of democracy, and we should have more faith in the government and in the American people. We should know that our national government will not be stampeded to unjust action by race prejudice or by pressure groups. It will not violate the rights of its citizens, no matter what their ancestry. Local irresponsible or corrupt governments might do us violence, but not the national government.

"But if we lack that faith, and you don't need to pay any attention to my words, here are some statements from public officials to back up what I have said. The head of Civilian Control said in a speech in Los Angeles the other day, 'The American people won't stand for pushing people around. The American people wouldn't let their government do it, even if it were so inclined, and it isn't.' And this same official has promised that there will be no mass evacuation.

"Even the general of the Western Defense Command, and he is the one with the power to give the order, said recently that there was no plan for evacuation."

"Yeah, and he said last week there would be. Aliens and citizens alike," a cynical voice interrupted.

"The officials contradict themselves every time they

open their mouths," a heckler shouted.

The crowd laughed the quiet young man down. Things had gone too far now to believe in a miracle.

Tad fidgeted in his seat. Was it any use to try to rally his forces? This young idealist sounded like some of Tom's mooning. He hoped Tom didn't say anything.

This thought had scarcely passed through his head when Mr. Imoto began to talk.

"We haven't heard from many of the younger group of Nisei. I think they should have their say in this matter. In some ways, these boys will be more adversely affected by an evacuation than anyone else." He looked about, and his eyes fell on Tom. "Tom Sato, we'd like to hear from you. What do you think we ought to do in case the order comes?"

Tom felt very uncomfortable. He hadn't had the remotest idea of saying anything when he came and, after listening to the arguments, had been more certain than ever that he would not have anything to say which would be of interest to the crowd. Only when the young fellow in the rear had spoken did Tom feel that there was a kindred spirit in the audience.

Mr. Imoto and the crowd were waiting. Tom stood up.

"Don't make a fool of yourself," Tad said under his breath.

Tom stood there a minute, his hands on the back of the seat in front of him, his eyes on the floor.

"I guess I agree with that fellow there in the back who just spoke. It seems like we are trying to face a situation which just doesn't exist. It's hard to tell what you would do or how you would feel until you are actually up against a real situation. I just can't believe our government would force us out of our homes, men who are working on ranches raising food the Army needs so badly, they couldn't be spared, and women and little children and babies and harmless, crippled old men, why would anyone want to force them out? They couldn't do any harm to anyone. It just doesn't make sense. There are two sides, one working against us and

151

one working for us, that's the reason there is so much contradiction among the officials; and I believe the right side will win out, or I don't know what democracy is. A lot of us are doing work important to the war effort, and I think the thing for us to do is go right on working and not waste time worrying about what is going to happen to us. What kind of a soldier would a man be if he were all the time worrying about what was going to happen to him?"

"You have some good ideas for all of us, Tom," Mr. Imoto said, not satisfied with Tom's speech, "but you still haven't said what we should do if evacuation *should* come. Things can happen fast in wartime, and the local military authorities could order and accomplish it before the country as a whole knew anything about it."

"DeWitt says he can do it in sixty days," a helpful voice shouted.

"When I was back in Denver," Mr. Imoto went on, "the people I talked with there knew very little or nothing about our situation here. They read the headlines in the paper and that's about all they have time for. We don't get in the headlines in Colorado like we do in California. Even here in the city few people know what is going on. I talked with a man today who didn't know about the posters and the military areas set up. The Army under pressure could put this thing over before the people who would be the mostly likely to oppose it effectively knew what was going on. So, Tom, where will you stand in case of such an order?"

Tom fingered the back of the seat, his eyes down. Then he straightened himself and looked directly at Mr. Imoto.

"Well, I'll try to imagine it, but I still can't see it. It's like you were asking me what I would do if I went out to the field to work some morning, and when I got there the field wasn't there. Nothing but a big hole in the ground. It wouldn't make any difference what I did that day if my land were gone. And that's the way it would be for us Nisei if our citizenship were violated.

There would be nothing left for us but a big, empty space. We wouldn't have any country. It wouldn't make any difference what we did."

Tom sat down amid a deep silence. No one applauded, but there was a certain acclaim in the silence. His simple words were spoken with such sincerity that their meaning struck home to all. The loss, the utter loss. They had been so proud of their citizenship. Perhaps they had bragged a little too much to the Issei sometimes, those who couldn't become naturalized. But if it didn't mean anything . . .

"The boy's right," a sober voice spoke. "We will be like men without a country. Not by choice, but by the order of the Army under authority given it by the president."

Tom's faith in his country had stirred the wellsprings of emotion of the Issei as well as the Nisei. But the older men, more experienced in the competitive field, disillusioned by discrimination over the years, were less idealistic and more practical. They knew the evil of race hatred and what it made men do. They could see now all around them the flames of public hysteria being fanned into an uncontrollable conflagration. They could readily visualize evacuation. Among them were those who feared physical violence and would welcome some assurance of protection. They could not close their eyes to the fact that they could not continue to live on as they had lived before the war unless the government took some action to halt the vicious campaign being waged against them in their home state.

These older men were by training and disposition peaceful and respectful toward organized government. To resist official orders was unthinkable to them. Besides, resistance would harm rather than help their cause.

There were some, so scathingly referred to by Dr. Kimura, who had already accepted what they considered as inevitable and were eager to ingratiate themselves with the authorities by their ready acceptance and cooperation. In this way, some felt they might fare better in the detention camps, might get favors for themselves and families, and possibly be chosen for places of leadership and control over others in whatever communities would be set up for them for the segregated life which loomed so ominously on the horizon.

And, sadly, there were some, a few, who were ready to go so far as to seek favor with the FBI and hence immunity from investigation for themselves by handing over supposedly confidential information about other Japanese.

All of these groups threw their whole weight into the meeting now to bring the question to a decision. It was getting late. But the resisters were diehards.

Tad still fought for resistance. And he had a goodly following.

"What about the threat to use bayonets on us?" the crowd heckled him as he talked.

"Yeah. What about that? Where would we get -our-guns?"

Tad's lips tightened and his face became grim. He saw that he could no longer talk against the increasing opposition. With a final shout of defiance, he quoted from Patrick Henry. It was oratorical, but it was sincere.

"I know not what course others may take, but as for me, give me liberty or give me death."

Perhaps the uncertainty of the future was the one cohesive element which had held the meeting together. Regardless of the differing opinions, there was a general feeling of insecurity. If they should be interned, no one knew what their situation would be. Concentration camps. The very word struck terror to their hearts. The horror of such camps in Germany had become common reading. Resistance there had meant torture and death. Didn't the threat of the American Army colonel to use guns and bayonets on them smack of the same thing? When one was helpless to defend oneself and family what choice did one have?

Mr. Imoto began to sum up the arguments.

154

"I know that it is a profound shock to all Nisei to know that our citizenship does not stand between us and the treatment which is given to enemy aliens. We have seen it in the draft reclassification. We have seen it in the posted orders to leave Zone One. We may see it in mass evacuation.

"We need to prepare ourselves.

"Granted we know that mass evacuation is unnecessary from the standpoint of military necessity, for we know that only a small percentage of the Japanese are dangerous to the safety of this country, and most of them have been picked up already by the FBI, along with a number of innocent men. We know that evacuation is unnecessary for our own protection, as has been suggested by the authorities; for with a bare fraction of the cost and trouble of evacuation, this organized campaign against us could be stopped, and we would be safe where we are.

"Granted, too, that we are being victimized by war hysteria and prejudice fanned by political and economic interests for their own benefit;

"Granted that we are the innocent victims of public scorn and ridicule, and there's nothing we can do about it;

"Granted this evacuation will crush our old men, wipe out thirty or forty years of hard work. Many can never expect to be economically independent again. The Nisei will be hard hit economically and harder still in other ways, for we will be, as has already been stated, men without a country;

"Granted that if we are deprived of our liberty and confined in concentration camps without charges being brought against us and without benefit of trial, it is going to rob many of our young people of their ideals of democracy which they have been taught in the schools;

"Granted all of this--I ask you--what could we possibly gain from making any resistance to Army orders in time of war? Refusal to obey orders certainly will not change them. Refusal will only make us appear

155

more dangerous than we are now considered."

The vote was taken.

There was a large majority in favor of cooperation. Tom did not vote one way or another.

The resisters gave up. It was a democracy; the majority ruled. There would be no demonstration, no matter what came.

"Let us go on about our work," Mr. Imoto said, wiping the perspiration from his round face. "And keep calm and await orders. The meeting is adjourned."

There were two policemen on the corner as the men filed out and went their several ways.

A great gulf separated the two Satos as they rode home side by side, without talking.

VIII

Mari's excitement heightened with the passing of each day which brought the concert nearer. But when it was only two days away she began to experience a feeling of nervousness which mingled with the thrills of anticipation and robbed them of some of their pleasantness. Little tremors of premature stage fright rippled over her at the thought of walking out to the center of the stage before that large and critical audience. She had had one rehearsal in the concert hall already, and it had seemed a block from the wings to the place where she was to take her position. But all had gone well at the rehearsal. The maestro had been there to hear her, and, while he wasn't entirely satisfied, he had been pleased and said she would do her best at the performance. There would be only one more rehearsal and that was the night before the festival.

What if she should forget? Or make a mistake? She could never lift her head again nor face the others at school. Mr. Benton, the principal, and many of the teachers would be there; and Peg, and Mary Standish, who played the violin, too, and would be listening with a critical ear for the least little error. Her mouth went dry and her breath tight at the very thought of failing in any way.

Then a more terrible thought began to haunt her. What if the audience did not accept her? Suppose there would be nothing but a stony silence when she had finished her first number. How could she ever go on with the second? Oh, surely nothing that cruel could happen to her!

She had laughed at Tad's fears when he had told her she must cancel her engagement.

"The kind of people who go to the Spring Music Festival aren't like that," she had argued confidently. "They go because they love music, and who plays it isn't important to them. Music is like science. There are no

157

boundary lines between nations or colors." She had been very sure of herself then.

She had even defied Tad only a few days ago when he had come from the mass meeting in the city and said that he absolutely would not allow a sister of his to get up before a hostile audience. They had fought terribly about it, and it had taken the joint efforts of Mother Sato and Tom to end the quarrel, so bitter had it become. Tom and his mother had both taken Mari's part. Mr. Benton would not let her appear if he thought it wasn't all right, Tom argued.

"Mom just doesn't see what is going on, and you're too blind to see," Tad had flung at Tom as a parting shot and left the house. He might have said that Tom didn't know, either, for Tom had scarcely been off the ranch except for the quick trips to La Vista on business since Father Sato had been taken away. He did not see the stares Tad faced each evening when he went into the city. What he saw in the faces sometimes made him afraid for his own safety. Nor did Tom talk with idle groups of Nisei in the city as Tad did and listen to them harrying their minds with the latest insults from the papers or the newest crop of rumors.

Now with the festival only two nights away, Mari, in spite of intervals of doubts and fright, was dreaming and planning as she pressed out her billowy satin gown with careful, loving hands. Tomorrow night was dress rehearsal. Oh, she was going to love it! She was going to work hard at her music and be a real artist, spend her life on stage, wear beautiful clothes, have lots of money. She was so happy she began to sing as she pressed, light, joyous phrases, skipping from one air to another. The rest of the house was quiet, and Mother Sato, mending a pair of Yoshi's pants, smiled over her daughter's happiness. Tad had talked his mother out of going to the concert, but she was proud that her daughter was going to play.

Yoshi had gone to bed from the supper table. Now that he was working every evening he was barely able to keep awake through the late evening meal. Tom was dozing in his father's big leather chair; the farm magazine he intended to read slipped to the floor by his feet. Tad had dressed as usual and gone to the city. No one expected to see him again that night. Since the mass meeting he had been more restless, more frustrated than ever, but more quiet.

Mari took her dress to her room and hung it in the closet, and after standing back to admire its golden beauty for a moment, closed the closet door, got her violin, and went out by the living room fire to play awhile. A stiff breeze blowing off the sea had blown the fog in, and the evening was chilly. She never practiced in the living room if Tad were there, for he teased her so, making fun of her music and complaining about the noise. But Tom never minded, and her mother liked it.

Mari had scarcely begun to play when the whole family was suddenly alerted by the sound of a car careening into the driveway, brakes screeching. Tom sat bolt upright, wide awake. Mother Sato dropped her mending to her knees and looked up questioningly. Mari stood with bow in midair as she had been about to draw it across the strings.

Now someone was hurrying into the house, banging doors behind him like a windstorm suddenly blown up. Tad!

Yes, there he stood in the doorway to the kitchen, facing the family, his face as black as a thundercloud, his eyes darting forked lightning.

"They've put a curfew on us," he announced in a strained voice. His breath was coming hard, and he had difficulty getting the words past a constriction in his throat. Tiny beads of perspiration stood out on his forehead and glistened in the lamplight. He sat down heavily on the nearest chair, while the family waited for him to go on. What he had said made no sense to anyone. A curfew? What for? On whom? And who had done it? These questions were running through their minds. And Tad was looking like a crazy man, he was so mad.

159

"None of us can be out away from home after eight o'clock at night. Eight o'clock! God! What do they want to do to us, anyway? And we can't go more than five miles from home in the daytime even."

"Where did you hear all that?" Tom asked suspiciously.

"It's true, all right," Tad shouted angrily, catching the doubt in Tom's voice. He had brought home other news that had proved to be unfounded, but he resented Tom's attitude. "It's Army orders. It was published in the morning paper. The Haradas saw it and they heard it on the radio tonight. If we weren't all working so damned hard growing tomatoes we'll never have a chance to pick, we might know something that's going on, too. It's just lucky I dropped around by Haradas on the way in and found out before I got into the city. The highway cops are watching for us. I came home around by that narrow dirt road all the way to the corner down here."

Mother Sato had watched her son closely while he talked to Tom and she could not get the drift of his excited words. She knew that something was wrong, and a vague sense of fear and insecurity, which had been her constant companion since the day she went to the door and saw Papa Sato being taken away, deepened within her. Some new threat to their security had evidently arisen.

"What happen? You have accident? You hurt?"

In the unknown white people's world which revolved about her, Mother Sato had come to feel that there was plotting and danger.

"No, Mom," Tad said, but as he sat there hunched in his chair looking like a hunted animal which has temporarily made its escape but can still hear the baying of the hounds, his appearance was anything but reassuring. Mother Sato shook her head woefully.

There was nothing vague or indefinite in the reactions of Tom and Mari once their minds had taken in the strange news. If Tad saw it as an injustice, another slap at the Nisei and their citizenship, another link in

160

the lengthening chain of indignities which he had suffered at the hands of the authorities, Tom saw a threat to his successful continuance of ranch work. How would this new restriction on travel affect him? Five mile limit. That would allow him to go to La Vista, but what about marketing the rest of the cucumber crop? He had over two dozen lugs loaded on the pickup right now, ready for the trip to the city in the morning. Ten miles. If Tad had things straight he couldn't take them, and they would lose their crispness if they had to sit around a day or so. Maybe he ought to go see someone to find out what arrangements they had made for getting their stuff to market.

He got to his feet before he realized he couldn't go. Army orders said he couldn't leave home after eight o'clock. It gave him a queer feeling.

"Some of those Army officers are getting too big for their pants," he said.

To Mari the curfew had only one meaning: she couldn't go to the festival. She did not analyze the rights of citizens under the Constitution nor the injustices of racial discrimination. She wanted to go to the festival. The greatest moment of her life was only two nights away, and this thing, this obstacle, had risen up in her path to keep her from the realization of her greatest dreams.

"The festival!" she cried out in consternation. "How can I go to the festival?"

"You can't," Tad said bluntly. But there was no triumph in his voice.

Mari laid her violin and bow on the piano bench and stood looking helplessly from one to another. Mother Sato, Tad, Tom . . . each in turn lowered their eyes to avoid the look in Mari's. Each one was helpless to do anything, and they knew it.

"Why don't you call old Benton and see what he says?" Tom finally suggested, more to have something to say than for any other reason. The principal was a nice, friendly fellow, but not very effectual when it came to going to bat for someone.

161

But Mari snapped at the suggestion. Why, of course. Mr. Benton was the very person to see that she got to the city to take her part on the program. There was plenty of school spirit at La Vista High even though it was a small school. They would never let a spring festival come off in the city without a representative of their school appearing. She hurried to the telephone in the narrow hall between the living room and the kitchen.

"Hello, Mr. Benton," she said as soon as she heard the familiar voice at the other end of the wire. "This is Mari Sato. I've just heard . . ."

"Oh, hello, Mari. I guess you've heard the bad news by this time. Sounds bad, doesn't it?"

"Oh, yes. It's terrible! How can I get in to rehearsal tomorrow night?" Mari couldn't bring herself to ask about the fatal night just yet.

"Well, now, let's see. I was just thinking about that when you called. I talked to Mr. Ritchie after school. He's the Civilian Control officer here in La Vista, you know. He has charge of all the regulations concerning you folks."

Mari didn't know about Mr. Ritchie but she said yes politely, and Mr. Benton went on.

"He seems to think the Army is going to be pretty strict about enforcing the curfew, but we will see. I can let you know at school tomorrow."

"Thank you, Mr. Benton," Mari said weakly. He hadn't given her much to build her hopes on. "If I can't go, what . . . it would be too bad for our school not to have any place on the program."

"Well, I told Mary Standish to be ready for rehearsal tomorrow night, just in case," Mr. Benton said. "She was still here at school when I heard this evening so I spoke to her right away."

"Oh, yes, of course, there is Mary, and she plays better than I do." Mari's voice was trembling with disappointment and her eyes filled with hot tears. "But do you think she can . . . such short notice." She thought of the weeks she had been practicing.

An uneasy little laugh reached her ears. That was

162

the way the principal laughed when he was apologetic about something, when he had forgotten to do something he had promised the students or when he was about to make an announcement he knew would be unpopular.

"Well, to tell you the truth, Mari, I was afraid something like this might happen, something might come up to prevent you from being there, your family might move out of the community or something like that. So I have had Mary practicing on your numbers all along."

"Oh, I see. Well, everything will be all right then," Mari said, controlling her voice with effort.   "Well, thanks, Mr. Benton. Goodbye."

"Don't think I won't do all I can to get permission for you to be out that night, Mari, for I really want to see you have that opportunity. And it will be good for everyone else to see you there and hear you play, too. That is one of the things which make it hard for us to get a square deal for you folks now. You haven't made enough public appearances in programs and things. You aren't an integral part of community life. Well, I'll see Ritchie again tomorrow morning. This curfew order is new, and they may not want to start making exceptions the first thing. This war, you know, and Army orders are Army orders, no matter what we may think of them, so don't feel too badly if we can't get a permit for you. Goodbye."

"Goodbye," Mari said weakly.   She hung up and went into the kitchen for a drink.   So he had had Mary Standish practicing all the time.   Mari felt humiliated. She had sat in the same class with Mary all this time, not knowing that Mary was getting ready to play in her place, maybe hoping that she would go away or that something would happen. Mary was probably laughing at her when she talked about the concert and told the girls what she was going to wear. Mary wouldn't have to worry about what she would wear; she probably had two or three formals.   She was the doctor's daughter, and not only did she go into the city with her father and mother to concerts and balls, but they also drove often into Los Angeles to the theater or the opera.

It isn't fair, Mari thought. Mary has everything she wants, and all I want is just to play this one evening, and she takes that away from me.

Mari's thoughts still had not reached the point of analyzing the situation and rebelling against the discrimination involved. She still had not said to herself, "It is because I am Japanese that I may not be able to go."

She wasn't satisfied with her talk with Mr. Benton. She wanted to talk to someone else, someone who would more realize what this meant to her. Neither Tad nor Tom would know, and she couldn't talk to her mother. Mari longed in that moment as never before to be able to sit down beside her mother and have a good heart-to-heart talk, the way Peg did with Mrs. Sullivan. They talked over everything together, and Mrs. Sullivan always understood the problems of young people and was sympathetic and ready to help.

Suddenly Mari thought of the maestro and what he would think if he knew. He more than anyone else would know how she felt. She thought of calling him, but it was getting late and she had never called him outside of his regular hours at the studio. Would he think she was bold and maybe be angry with her? The maestro was very temperamental.

She decided to risk everything.

The music teacher's reaction was all Mari could have asked for. He had not heard of the curfew order, and when she told him he went into a rage and shouted and sputtered into the phone until she could not understand one word he said. When he had given vent to his emotions he became rational again and very serious. Emphatically he would do something about this curfew business. He would see about it the first thing in the morning, and Mari was to go ahead with her plans. He would call Mr. Benton when he had made the necessary arrangements.

Reassured, Mari started for her room when she heard someone coming up on the back porch. She turned back to see Peg and Allen come trooping into the kitchen without bothering to knock.

"Surprise," Peg said, grinning. "Everyone else in bed?"

"No, they're all in the room. Come on in."

Instinctively Mari knew what had brought them out at this time of night. They had heard and this was their way of saying that they were friends, and if the Satos couldn't go to see them or anyone else at night, then *they* would do the going.

"Hi, Tom. How are you, Tad?" Allen looked huge in his tight-fitting navy blues. Training had taken off some excess weight, but he was developing into a large and powerful seaman.

"Gee, we almost didn't stop. Couldn't see the sign of a light anywhere."

"Yes. Allen was going to turn around and go back home, but I made him come in."

"It's the blackout curtains. We pull them down every night, for we can't hear the siren very plain out here."

"I'll sure never forget the first blackout after Pearl Harbor," Allen said, taking a seat between Tom and Tad while Peg and Mari sat down on the davenport. "I was in the city that night. It was the worst mess I ever saw in my life. You should have seen it, Tad. Hundreds of people on the street that had come out of the shows wanting to get home, and mobs of fellows trying to get back to camp, and the streets as dark as pitch, and a row of dark streetcars two blocks long standing there. Taxis creeping along without lights, darn near running over people out in the streets trying to board the cars, and policemen shouting instructions and the taxis honking. Gosh, if there had been any enemy planes overheard they could have heard if they couldn't see."

Tad had cheered up some, and the three fellows began to hash over some of the old times before the war. That was safe ground where they could talk freely. Peg and Mari tackled the subject close at hand. Peg was just sure Mari would get to go, and Mari said, well, it didn't make so much difference since Mary Standish was all ready to substitute for her and Mary played better than she did. Peg contradicted her--Mari would have been much disappointed if she hadn't--and declared that she wouldn't go near the city herself if Mari wasn't going to play. Mari wouldn't hear of that and made Peg promise that she would attend the concert so that she could tell Mari all about it, and, more important still, bring her a program, for she was sure her name would be on it. It was too late now to print new programs. Mari felt all the time that the maestro would make good on his promise to get her there, but she enjoyed Peg's concern.

By noon the next day there was still no word from the maestro. Mr. Benton had not been able to soften Mr. Ritchie, but Mari still had one last hope in the maestro. He must be accomplishing something, it was taking him so long. He would take it all the way to Washington to get what he was after if he thought it would do any good. The maestro was like that. He wouldn't have been such a successful teacher if he hadn't been.

Mari was in history when a student came to the classroom and said she was wanted in the office. Her heart beating fast, she hurried down the stairs. The maestro had telephoned Mr. Benton, she thought. Would it be good news?

She went running into the principal's office, and there sat the maestro himself. He rose and came toward her. His face was sorrowful. She knew before he spoke. He had not known of the resentment against her people. He spent most of his time in the studio and did not know as much as he should of what was going on around him. Yes, it had been impossible to get permission for her to come into the city after dark. The officials had been disagreeable.

"It is a great disappointment to you, my child," he said in gentle tones which brought a lump to Mari's throat. "And it is to me, also. Things are bad now for you and your people. You will have to suffer persecution. I know what that is. But suffering will make a greater musician of you. You are young. You have time for concerts and many public appearances ahead, and you have real talent. Do not let anything cause you to give up your music." The music master hesitated and his eyes softened. "And do not let persecution rob you of your faith in your fellow man. There are more good people in the word than bad."

"Oh, thank you so much for your kindness," Mari said impulsively. She was deeply moved by the maestro's making the trip all the way out from the city to tell her personally of his failure. "I shall always remember what you have said."

The night of the Spring Festival was a dismal one in the Sato home. The weather was perfect, balmy and springlike, the roses were in bloom. There was a moon. Those in charge of the festival were regretting that they had not planned to have it in the Bowl as they had first considered. It was an ideal night for an open-air concert.

But there was nothing but gloom at the ranch. This was the night toward which everything had pointed for Mari for weeks past, and the family, varied though their emotions were, had shared in the anticipation. They had all been proud, even Tad, that such honor and recognition had come to one of them. Now, that honor and recognition had backfired. Mari Sato. That name would be on the programs for all to see, but Mari Sato would not be there. She would be conspicuously absent, and everyone in that great audience of music lovers would know why. Detained at home by Army orders because for some reason she was considered dangerous and not to be trusted by her country in time of war. This public humiliation the Sato family found hard to bear.

At the supper table they carefully avoided the subject. Yoshi came the closest to it when he rested his chin in a cupped palm and, trying to look important and mature, said, "I don't see why we have to stay home at nights. I don't see any sense in it myself."

"Listen to the wise man," Tom laughed.

"It's because people are afraid of us," Tad said sarcastically.

"'Fraid of who?" Yoshi asked, watching Tad to see if he were teasing. "Me?"

"Yeah, you, and Mom, here, and Sakai's little baby and old Grandpa Nishimoto. Afraid you might all go down to the harbor some night and blow up the fleet."

"Tad, you ought to be ashamed," Mari said, "talking to the kid that way. Don't you ever repeat that at school, Yoshi, nor anything else you hear said at home." She turned back to Tad. "You know how people can twist things around."

"Sure I know," Tad growled as he got up from the table. "Tad Sato is planning to blow up the fleet. His little brother said so at school."

Tad went out to his room to find something to read. If he were going to have to stay home nights from now on, he would have to find some way to spend his time. Tad had always been a great reader until recently, when his restlessness and confused state of mind made concentration on anything next to impossible.

He took a book at random from the rows on Norio's bookshelves, opened it, and began to read.

The book was *The Federalist*, and Tad had turned to one of the essays written by Madison.

"But what is government itself but the greatest of all reflections on human nature? If men were angels no government would be necessary. If angels were to govern men, neither external nor internal controls on government would be necessary. In framing a government which is to be administered by men over men, the great difficulty lies in this: you must first enable the government to control the governed; and in the next place oblige it to control itself. A dependence on the people is, no doubt, the primary control on the government; but experience has taught mankind the necessity of auxiliary precautions."

He stopped and read Norio's marginal notes on the paragraph, reread it, and went on.

Tom found work to do outside as soon as he had

168

finished supper. He had gotten permission to truck his vegetables into the city, and he carefully checked the tires on the pickup. He patched the tube, put a boot in the one which had blown out the other day, and hoped it would do as a spare to get home on in case one of the other worn tires gave out on the road. It was queer with his priority on tires as a rancher, but there were never any available when he went to buy one.

Because supper had been earlier than usual that night and it was too early to go to bed, Yoshi went out and had a light workout with Malt.

"I don't have much time for play," he explained to the overjoyed dog. "See, I've got to work all the time. But when school's out we'll go hunting like we used to and get a lot of rabbits." They tumbled over and over on the grass, Yoshi scuffing at Malt, and Malt rushing back at him to grab at his collar, sleeve, or pants leg and shake vigorously. Yoshi was the one in the family who was not trying to forget that this night humiliation and dishonor had fallen upon the house of Sato, for he had entirely forgotten about the concert.

Mother Sato and Mari did the supper dishes together, Mari drying them for her mother. Mother Sato was making a gallant attempt to be cheerful as she kept to her broken English, knowing that it irritated Mari to be spoken to in Japanese.

"Some strawberries ripe," she noted.

"Yes. I saw them today," Mari said listlessly.

"I pick tomorrow. Maybe have enough make short-cake. You ask Peg and Allen come over. Allen like shortcake most of anything."

"They were just over here. Just because we can't go anyplace we can't expect them to be running over here all the time."

"Ooh-ooh, they come all right. Eat strawberries. You ask Peg at school tomorrow," Mother Sato wheedled.

"I'm not going to school," Mari announced.

Mother Sato was still for a minute, thinking over what Mari had said and the reasons behind it. She washed at the same plate for quite awhile. Then she made sort of a grunt of acquiescence and put the plate in the draining rack. Mari rinsed and dried it, hung up the towel and went to her room.

It had been a hard day at school. Everyone knew, of course, that she was out of the festival on account of the curfew. Mary Standish had been awfully decent about it. She had expressed such genuine regret over Mari's disappointment that Mari could not doubt her sincerity and was ashamed for thinking as she had about Mary.

"I'm scared stiff, and I'd a hundred times rather see you up there tonight than to be there myself."

"It's a shame," the other girls said. They made no attempt to hide from Mary their sympathy with Mari. And Peg was all upset and ready to start to purge the earth of discrimination and injustice.

Mary had told Mari all about the dress rehearsal. The fellow from Corona Heights High had forgotten right in the middle of his flute solo, and he was so embarrassed. Everything else had gone off all right, and everyone had sent word to Mari that they were all for her and maybe next year she'd be there.

"And who do you think was there listening to us? Your music teacher, Mari. I could feel his eyes boring right through me while I was playing, and I knew he was comparing us. So after I was through I went out on the floor and asked him how I had done, and he said I was 'technically' near perfection. Now what did he mean by that, do you know?"

"He usually means what he says. He must have thought you did well, for he isn't often so complimentary," Mari had answered. She felt she did know just what the maestro had meant, and he wasn't being complimentary at all, merely polite. To the maestro, perfect technique was nothing at all by itself. A smoothly running gasoline engine has perfect technique, he would say to Mari, but it isn't music we hear coming from under the hoods of our cars. You must put something of yourself into your playing.

Yet in spite of all the kindness of the other students, Mari had suffered through the day. They pitied her, felt sorry for her. She felt set apart from the others, conspicuous as she had never felt in school before. By the end of the day she knew that she would never go back. Graduation or no graduation, she would never go back to La Vista High.

She turned on the light and looked at her lovely gown. She decided to dress. She had never had on all her finery together since that day in the store, and not the jewelry even then. She would dress just as if she were really going.

After her shower she combed up her hair the way she had decided to wear it, out of the way. She couldn't play with it hanging around her shoulders. When she had her hair and makeup done to her satisfaction, she slipped into her clothes and clasped the bracelet about her wrist. Fastening the earrings in place, she stood before the mirror, turning this way and that, lost in admiration of this strange young woman. The upsweep of her hair and the long skirts and sparkling jewels gave her an air of sophistication, she imagined. She wanted to be seen. She went out to show her mother, but she was nowhere about the house. Then Mari saw her trudging around out in the back, shutting up the chicken coops. Tom was fixing his tires, his hands and face grimy with greasy dust, and Yoshi was rolling around on the ground with the dog. She didn't know where Tad was.

Back in her room, Mari turned off the lights, her lips quivering with self-pity. Standing by the window, she looked out into the deepening twilight. The full bitterness of her disappointment swept over her. People would be coming to the festival now. She could see the cars driving up before the entrance to the hall, people going in, following the ushers down the long aisles, finding their seats, and sitting back comfortably for an evening of enjoyment.

It would not be long now before the program would begin. The excitement backstage would be at its height. She would have been fifth, following the chorus from

171

City High. Mary would be there; she was going to wear black. Would there be an announcement of the change in program? Mari felt her cheeks burn. Why should she have to suffer and be humiliated just because she was Japanese? She had done nothing wrong. People didn't choose which race they would be born into. It wasn't fair to be persecuted for what you couldn't help.

She snatched up her violin and began to play. The maestro had told her about the heartache and tragedy the composer had written into the music, but she had never understood. Now she thought she knew what he meant. The composition became her own, her escape from the pent-up emotions which she had tried to hide from others all day. Disappointment, insecurity, disillusionment went into the tones she brought forth from the violin.

It was not the bitterness and anger of Tad nor the frustrated longings of Tom to prove himself loyal, but a wail of helplessness. Helplessness to cope with this thing which was crushing the right to normal living out of herself as well as the other Nisei. Things she had never seen in the piece before now came to have meaning, became tense with pathos and suffering.

Tad heard . . . laid down his book . . . and listened. The music probed deeply into the bitterness and resentment which burned like acid in his heart. This cry of helplessness from his sister made him wild to fight for their rights, to fight their way out of this trap which was closing so steadily around them. He dropped his hands helplessly to his knees. There was nothing he could do. Their country had gone mad against them. One couldn't fight a thing like that. They must be passive, submit to whatever came. That was the hardest part, to submit. It was well-nigh unbearable. The old fears began to haunt him.

The maestro's words came to Mari as she played.

"Suffering will make a musician out of you."

She knew she had put something into her music which had never been there before. She had had to suffer to do it. Angrily she threw her violin on the chair.

She hated it. She hated music. She would never play again, if one had to suffer to be a musician. How horrible that something so lovely should only come up out of tragedy and hurt. She hated music. She never wanted to see her violin again. Bursting into tears, she threw herself down on the bed and lay there, shaking with convulsive sobs.

When the music stopped suddenly, two emotions struggled for supremacy in Tad, fear to face the future for what it might do to him and hatred for all those who had brought these troubles upon him and his people. Then a cord snapped and all hell was let loose. Hate burned upon fear and killed it with the venom of its hot breath. It was the hatred the wild and savage beast had for its captors. Accustomed to the freedom of the forest, now doomed to live within the narrow confines of a cage ...

Mother Sato went and listened at Mari's door before she went to bed. With a mother's quick ear she heard the stifled sobs and went in. Tenderly she helped the girl out of her finery and into her pajamas and tucked her into bed as she had done when Mari was a little girl. All the while she was murmuring comforting little phrases in her native tongue, her voice soft and soothing. She patted the hot, moist cheek and brushed the hair back from Mari's face as she sat on the edge of the bed, now crooning, now quiet. At last the sobbing ended and Mother Sato tiptoed out, closing the door softly behind her, and went to her lonely room.

IX

Events moved in rapid succession after the coming of the curfew, and every new development pointed to evacuation of some sort. The press was frantically calling upon the Army to save the country by getting the Japanese off the coast before there was a repetition of Pearl Harbor there. And the public was responding to the hysterical voices of the press and politicians by raising its voice of hate to a still more frenzied demand to be protected from the enemy in its midst.

Rumors flew thick and fast. There would be mass evacuation. There would not be mass evacuation. The aliens were to be evacuated. Camps were being built to confine them in. Everyone was to be taken to these camps immediately. It would take months to prepare the places for internment. Everything was confusion. No one knew what to do. Businessmen who were still doing business found that supplies were going to be hard to secure and bought up large quantities while they were still available, in case they were permitted to remain and carry on their business. Ranchers did not know how to plan. There were the orders to be out of Area Number One by the first of May, but few made any plans to go. Many of the states in the Rocky Mountain area, where land was available with irrigation water, had begun anti-Japanese campaigns of their own and threatened dire consequences to anyone settling within their sovereign borders. Colorado was an exception, and there had been some voluntary evacuations to that state; but the trip was hazardous because of the unfriendly states between. Men who had crops ready to harvest were working day and night to garner and sell all they could before they had to leave for somewhere. No one knew what their financial condition would be once the ranch was out from under them.

Tad and Tom worked to get the last cucumber out of the field, and Tom nursed his tomato plants along, giving them extra water to please Tad, who was sure they would all have to leave soon. A few weeks more and the cannery growers would be ready to plant.

Tom was still sure the citizens would not be evacuated; this May 1 deadline for moving out was still a month away. Anything could happen in that time. Father Sato kept writing to stay on the ranch until he got there. His hearing was coming up, and he was sure he would be free to come when that was over.

The conflicting statements from the authorities, the rumors, and the constant changing of orders which threw everyone into confusion and kept those who had the serious decisions to make for themselves and their families, were the very things which gave Tom hope.

They don't know what they are going to do. There are influences working for our rights as well as those working against us, and fair play will win out, he reasoned within himself as he went about his work, wasting little energy on worry. If Mom has to go, maybe they will fix it so she and Dad can be together somewhere when he is released, and that will be all right.

Mom is grieving over Dad, and she doesn't look very well. It would be good for her to get away from the ranch for awhile and have a good rest. Tad and Mari and I could carry on, and Mom and Dad could take Yoshi with them. Surely the authorities wouldn't separate a kid from his parents.

Yes, Tom was sure that order to move by May 1 would be changed, the date set ahead or something. He could not conceive of the government forcibly moving a large number of defenseless people on the basis of race alone. "All persons of Japanese ancestry," that's what the poster said. No. It would never be carried out. The order would be changed.

It was changed, and very soon, but not in the way that Tom had anticipated.

Three weeks after the curfew order and the Spring Festival came the new order reversing the one on the posters which were displayed so conspicuously and which were now becoming weathered and less white on the telephone poles. Whereas the original order had commanded that all be out of that particular area by the first of May, this new order said they were not to move either out of the area or from one place to another in the area. It "froze" all persons of Japanese ancestry just where they were. Voluntary evacuation had failed. Now the Army was going to tie them down where they were until it could make arrangements to handle the evacuation itself.

It was a strange quirk of fate that Tom should be the first to hear of the evacuation order when it came and to have to take the news to the family. That capricious old lady must have been in a particularly malicious mood that day to lead her to choose one of the least deserving upon whom to play her cruel tricks.

There had been another blowout on the pickup, and Tom had quit work and driven into La Vista that morning in early April to get a tire, any kind of tire, for now he was down to three. He took the good car and, since he was making a quick trip in and back, no one went along.

As he passed the empty store building in which Mr. Ritchie and his staff had set up the Civilian Control Offices, he noticed a crowd of Japanese gathered out in front, and across the front of the building in large blue letters which could be read for blocks was stretched a sign which read, "DATE OF DEPARTURE." He found a place to park the car and went back.

The crowd was divided up into little clusters, each standing before a certain column of names written on a large bulletin board which also reached across the entire front of the building. The faces of the people were solemn; the talking was in low tones, as one is wont to talk at a funeral.

Tom saw the list of names and, noting they were arranged alphabetically, went down the list till he came to "S." He would find his mother's name there, since she was the only alien in the family now Dad was away.

Saito . . . Sakemoto . . . Sanematsu. Tom's eyes ran

down the column rapidly.

Sato. There it was. Tom's heart missed a beat.

"Sato, Shigeko," he read. That was his mother. She would have to go. Now that evacuation had come it did not seem so simple sending her away as he had been thinking.

More Sato names. Yes, there were several Sato families. He read on.

"Sato, Tadashi." Why, that was Tad! A citizen! Was it because of what Tad had done at the mass meeting, speaking for resistance, that they had taken him?

"Sato, Tamotsu." Tom himself. He read on rapidly.

"Sato, Mari." "Sato, Yoshi." All of them. No difference between citizen and alien.

Tom was stunned.

He stood there like a man in a trance, reading names over and over again mechanically. He was aroused by hearing someone speak his name.

"Good morning, Tom. How are you this morning? Have you made any arrangements for your ranch yet?" It was the older of the Yamamoto boys. "I've just been in talking to the man about ours."

"Hello, Toshi. No, I've . . . I didn't know about . . . about this until now. I was driving past." The ranch? Yes. Making arrangements for the ranch? Of course. If they were all going to leave, have to make some arrangements for the ranch. Someone to irrigate the tomatoes. And sell the plants. And cultivate. And . . . Would they be gone a long time?

"We're going to sell our place," Toshi said. "Dad's old and not able to work anymore. If they keep him up there in that camp very long, it isn't likely he'll live to come back here again. And Ben and I don't plan to do ranch work. Our mother feels pretty bad, but we have to take what comes."

"Yes. That's right," Tom answered absently, as Toshi went off toward his car.

Tom wished he had asked more questions. What had the man said? Were there buyers for their ranches, and would the buyers pay good prices? What if you

177

didn't want to sell? Would the government try to make you? Would they use any pressure to get you to dispose of your property?

He looked up again at the date. April 8. That was only six days off. Tires forgotten, he hurried to the car and drove directly home to tell the folks.

As Tom drove along the familiar road toward the ranch he mulled over the implications of the new order.

Evacuation had come. What he had believed could not happen in America had happened. All persons of Japanese ancestry, the order said, south of Encinitas and north of the Mexican border were to be out of the area by the eighth of April. Those who wished could drive their own cars. That was all. No arrangements for moving furniture or personal belongings. That would all have to be left behind.

When he reached home he put the car away and went out to tell Tad. It would be hard to tell him. They had fought over this question of evacuation so many times, and Tom had been so sure. Now Tad had been proven right.

He went across the field to where Tad was picking cucumbers, trying to form the words he would say; but when he came up to his brother he stood there silent, unable to speak.

Tad looked up and read the news in Tom's face.

"When do we go?" he asked.

"Next week. The eighth. All of us." All of us. That was the part that stuck in Tom's craw.

Tad opened his mouth to say something sharp . . . stopped himself. Tom looked so forlorn Tad suddenly felt sorry for him.

"Go ahead and say it," Tom said. "I've got it coming. I guess I've been . . . well, kind of blind." He raised his eyes and looked about the ranch. He had often thought how good it would be to get away from it, to go to college, never have any long hours of hard, dirty work again. But now he looked upon the green acres with affection. He had put so much of himself into their care that now they were a part of him. Already he felt bereft at the thought of leaving them. It chilled his blood with fear to think that the tomato plants might die of thirst when he was gone.

"We'll have to decide quick what to do with the ranch," he said to Tad. "There's a man in the office in town who will take care of that for us. And one member of each family is to go in for instructions, too. You'd better lay off work and go in. We aren't going to have much time."

"I'm not going in," Tad declared firmly. "I'll have nothing to do with those damned officials. I've seen them around the city trying to act so friendly like they were planning a pleasure trip. I'll cram their damn breezy tongues down their throats if any of them start talking to me."

"The ranch is in your name. You'd have to sign the papers if we wanted to lease."

"Okay. I'll go along and put my John Henry to them. But you can do the talking. Do the folks know?" he asked, looking toward the house.

"No. I came to tell you first."

Tad could almost hear the words which went through Tom's mind but which he did not speak: "Because it was the hardest to, I wanted to get it over with."

"We'd better go in and tell Mom and see what she wants to do about the place." Tad picked up the lug of cucumbers and carried it to the end of the row where he set it down beside the others. Then together the boys walked toward the house. Momentarily they were drawn together again by this common tragedy which had claimed them both. Tad, with eyes wide open, and Tom, blind as a newborn kitten, had been struck by the same blow. Tad was prepared as much as one could be, so it was less of a shock to him. But Tom was staggering under the impact. Impulsively Tad threw his arm around his brother's shoulder. He still had that tender heart which couldn't bear to see hurt in another's eyes.

"Don't take it too hard, boy," he said. "A fellow has to wake up to the unpleasant realities of life some time.

And believe me, brother, it isn't easy. I know, for I felt like you do once. I used to think you could trust people and that this was the greatest country on earth, all that stuff." Tad raved on, and Tom scarcely heard. He was thinking of all the things to be done in six days. He knew it was nice not to be quarreling with Tad, but he didn't want his sympathy.

They found Mother Sato and Mari in the kitchen preparing the noonday meal. Mari had baked a cake and was putting the finishing touches on the thick white frosting at the dining table, which was already set. Their mother was busy at the sink. She looked up with a smile when they came in. She had seen them coming arm in arm across the yard, and it pleased her. Her two fine sons coming together so close and friendly. Maybe they had good news. Maybe Papa Sato was coming home. But one close glance at their faces told her it was not good news they were bearing.

Tom told them.

The only indication that Mari had heard was a jerk of the muscle of her hand as from an electric shock as she smoothed the knife blade across the still pliable frosting. Mother Sato set the dish of strawberries she had been preparing on the edge of the table and threw both hands in the air.

Go? Without Papa Sato? There were all of his things, his papers and letters, his farm machinery, the accumulation of two score years to be packed and shipped. They could not do it without him. How would they know what he wanted done with this and that?

A thousand memories ran through her mind. She looked about her. Her home for nearly twenty years. No, more than her home--her life. With the exception of occasional trips to town and the weekly attendance at Sunday service, all of the time of those years had been spent on the ranch. Mari and Yoshi had been born in this house and the two little girls who had died. Here Norio had spent his last years, and there were all the familiar things around her which had kept him close in her memory. His room, his books and pictures, the little rocking chair they had bought together, she and Papa Sato, for their firstborn. She could see her little boy sitting in it beside the fire evenings reading the books he had brought from the school library. Each of the other children had sat on it, and it was almost worn out, but still she called it Norio's chair. "I'll have to glue the rocker of Norio's chair," or "You want to sit in Norio's chair, Baby?" to the little ones who came to visit.

Suddenly she pulled herself out of her memories and was the one to get the others started on the big and bewildering job which was ahead of them.

"We must begin to pack," she said. "Many, many, oh so many things to take. Quick, Tad, Tom, get many big boxes. We pack right after we eat. Not much time."

"Wait a minute, Mom," Tom cautioned. "We can't take much in the car."

His mother's wrinkled face was blank. They were going to move and take only what they could haul on the car? Impossible! Why, they would have several truckloads.

Tad turned away from his mother's bewildered face and went out and stood on the porch, cursing under his breath.

"That's right," Tom continued. "Only what we can take in the car. We'll have to leave the rest. Store it somewhere or something." He didn't know any more than she did how or where.

At the table they talked over what they should do about the ranch and decided to try to find a suitable tenant. Since the time was so short they might do as well to leave it to the government man, but Tom wanted some assurance that Mr. Winters didn't get it. He didn't know whether they would have any choice or not if they put the leasing into other hands. However, there didn't seem to be any choice anyway. With all the things to be done there would be no time for any of them to go around trying to find a tenant, and no one had anyone in mind who might want the ranch.

"Are we going to Manzanar?" Mari asked. She had heard Tom say once that they were all going to be evacuated to Manzanar.

"I don't know where we're going," Tom answered. "I didn't stop this morning to ask any questions. We'll find out this afternoon, maybe. Tad and I have to go to town. I'll get some packing boxes in town, Mom, and we'll start packing up tonight."

"Yes. All right. You help tonight. I begin now."

It was a difficult afternoon for Tom, and one he would long remember with distaste. He and Tad went down the line of little tables in the big barn-like storeroom with an official in charge of some phase of the evacuation behind each. Tom registered for each member of the family and received identification tags for their luggage and for each of them. He was told that each one must wear his tag the day of evacuation, which made him wince and avoid looking at Tad. There were numbers on the tags. There were many others there registering, getting their tags and going down the line arranging to lease or sell their homes, to store their possessions, and to dispose of their crops or business.

Tad maintained a glum and insolent silence as Tom discussed the leasing of the ranch with the Farm Security Administration man. The official was cordial, although businesslike, and to the point. He assured them he would have a tenant soon, there were several people inquiring for ranches of that acreage. Tom did not feel that he could say anything about Mr. Winters, but he did say that he wanted to lease with the understanding that the place would be vacated when they were able to return. The man made a note of that, not appearing to think there was anything unusual about such a request. Tad made the necessary signatures, and before they left the table they were urged to carry on with the ranch work right up to the day of leaving, and warned that any neglect or destruction of crops would be considered sabotage. It was hard for Tad to keep silent now.

"I'm going outside a minute," he said to Tom, and

his face was red with anger. "I'll go look around for some boxes while you finish up here."

Tom nodded. It was a relief to him to have Tad gone. It took someone with more self-control than Tad to go through this ordeal without blowing off, and before Tom was through he was more glad than ever that Tad was not along.

He found that the departure had been set up a day. They were to go the seventh of April. And they could not drive their cars and go anytime before but must all go together on the train. Everyone was to be at the Santa Fe station in the city at five-thirty on the evening of the seventh.

Tom was still smarting under the warning not to destroy his crops as he went on to the table where he would see about storing the goods. And the car, now, too. When the very thought of his tomato plants being neglected or dying for want of water made him positively ill, to have a stranger warning him made him angrier than anything which ever happened to him. It was not a quick-tempered variety which made him want to rush out where he could let off steam without getting into trouble, but a slow burning, deep, permanent type. Like the burning of peat land it would go on, unquenched and unquenchable. In the years to come he would be just as angry at this gross lack of understanding as he was now. How little these people who had been sent to handle them knew about them!

The Federal Reserve Bank had been delegated by the government as the agency to handle the storage of personal property and passenger cars. The man in charge advised Tom to sell everything. However, when he saw that Tom was not to be persuaded, he agreed to store the things and handed out a form to be filled in. Tom read the conditions carefully and reread them as the man tapped impatiently on the little table, for Tom could not believe his eyes. The goods would be stored at the owner's risk, and the bank would not be liable in any way. Neither was any insurance available. On inquiring, he found that cars would not necessarily be stored inside but might stand on vacant lots. He knew too well what the damp salt air would do to the paint job on a car even in a few weeks. What if they were gone a year, two years, maybe more?

Thanking the bank's representative politely, he declined to accept the services. In all of the conversation the man gave the impression that he viewed the departure of the Japanese as a permanent thing and saw no reason why they wanted to keep and store their possessions.

Before Tom left the building he had taken care of everything, even to getting the dates for the family to take their various inoculation shots at the health department set up in the Japanese church.

He found Tad at Nishimoto's Cafe, drinking a cup of coffee. The place was all torn up, and Eddie was helping his father pack away the things they planned to store. The building was leased.

"Well, so long, Eddie," Tad said, getting up when he saw Tom in the door. "Be seeing you in Manzanar."

"Yeah. That's where they told us to have our mail forwarded. Guess that's our destination. I'm glad we're going to get to stay in California. I was afraid they might send us out on the desert somewhere."

There was new consternation at home when Tom told his mother they were going on the train and could take only what they could carry. When he first said "train," she was pleased, thinking that meant they could ship their things, but when he got it through her head that only hand baggage could go, she was disheartened. She had sorted out the minimum of things they must take and had planned to have Tom make a rack for the top of the car so that all could be loaded on.

She had been torn by the many decisions she had had to make, deciding what could be destroyed, what could be left behind, and what they simply must take-- clothing, bedding, and keepsakes too precious to allow out of their possession. Now she must go through with it all over again. Only what they could carry! Why, that would be no more than the most necessary clothing.

When Yoshi came home from school he found the house in confusion, chairs and davenport piled high with books and pictures, boxes of letters, winter clothing, curtains from the windows. When he heard they were going, he ran to his room and began to haul out and sort over his own possessions, piling on the bed the ones he would take, his books and games, and his favorite sweater among them. He was wild with excitement and ran from room to room, afraid of missing something of the many activities going on. Later in the evening a new thought came to him which made the train trip ahead less attractive.

That night while Tom was working in his room after supper, gathering a few of his own things before starting on the family packing, he heard pounding on the window. The sounds seemed to be coming from the garage. He found Yoshi nailing slats across the top of an old apple box.

"What are you doing?" Tom asked. "You can't pack anything in that."

"I'm making a crate for Malt. You have to have a crate when you take a dog on the train. Jerry told me so. That's the way he brought his dog out from Missouri."

Tom could think of nothing to say. He had forgotten all about Malt and what they would do with him. But there was one thing sure, they couldn't take him.

"You can't take Malt," he said brusquely, his own affection for the little dog making his voice harsh.

"I can so," Yoshi retorted stubbornly.

"No. Now listen to me." Tom stooped down beside the boy. "We can only take what we can carry. That's Army orders." He thought that would make an impression on Yoshi.

But to the boy his dog was the most important thing in the world to him, now that there was a threat of separation. The Army was something vague and faraway, something which thrilled you in a general way when you saw soldiers marching on the screen at the movies or a big brother home on leave in his fine uniform, but powerless to influence you if your dog's welfare was at stake.

"I can carry Malt," he said quickly.

"But you've got your clothes and all those other things you've got laid out on your bed."

"Aw, I don't care about them. I don't need any clothes but what I wear. I want to take Malt." His lips began to quiver. The dog had been sitting there with ears erect, as if he were aware that the conversation was vital to him. Now he moved over and laid his nose on Yoshi's knee.

Yoshi grabbed him up and hugged him close.

"Don't you worry, Malt. We're not going to go off and leave you behind. No, sir. We wouldn't do that. Leave you here all alone with nobody to feed you."

He was talking to Tom through the dog, hoping to work on his feelings; but fear was in Yoshi's eyes. It had not occurred to him as the remotest possibility that the family would go away and leave the dog behind.

"Of course we won't leave him here alone," Tom said irritably. "We can get someone to keep him for you. Even if you took him you don't know whether you would have anything to feed him or not where we are going. It isn't likely the government will feed everyone's dogs. And you couldn't carry Malt and enough food to feed him for a long time, too."

This was something Yoshi had not thought of. He considered it for a time, stroking the dog's slick hair along his back as Malt sat soberly on Yoshi's knee. A vague sense of insecurity began to creep over the boy. He was going to a strange place. He had never been away from home even overnight. Suppose the Army wouldn't give him food for his dog. He wiped his sleeve across his eyes, and Malt gave a quick lick at his face.

"Maybe Jerry would keep him for me," Yoshi said in a tremulous voice. "His dog got run over."

"Yes. I bet he would. You watch for him when he goes by to school in the morning and ask him."

Yoshi considered the significance of Tom's words.

"You mean I don't have to go to school?" There was an unmistakable note of relief in his voice.

"No, kid, Joe. You've been a good American, going all this time when it hasn't been easy. But you don't have to go anymore. We'll drive down and get your books or whatever you have sometime tomorrow. We're going to need you at home to help us get ready to leave."

Tom tossed the apple box on the pile of crates and put the hammer and nails away in their place in the shed and, leaving the boy and dog to themselves, he went into the house. He hated leaving Malt behind almost as much as Yoshi did. If dogs didn't have so much confidence in you it wouldn't be so hard to desert them, he thought. If Jerry wouldn't take Malt they might have to take him to the pound. No, someone might get him who wouldn't treat him right. It would be better just to have him put to sleep. But Yoshi would have to be kept in ignorance of this.

These last days at home were a nightmare. Every minute meant a decision to make, and it was exceedingly difficult to make important decisions under such pressure for time. What to do with all the things they could not take? No place had been found yet for storing the goods and car, and Tad was spending a great deal of his time running around trying to find a suitable storage where they could be reasonably sure of the safety of their things.

When he had a little time from this and packing the stuff in his room--mostly Norio's things--he went through his father's papers, sorting out some of the most important to take with them and tying the others in neat bundles, some to go to the safety deposit box at the bank and some to store with the other things. Some, mostly letters written in Japanese, he laid out to be destroyed.

Mother Sato was suspicious that after they had left all Japanese goods would be searched by the officials and anything from Japan which might be found would be used as evidence against their men in internment.

Even if that did not happen, there were things too precious to be desecrated by unfriendly hands, so she destroyed many things which were intimate and prized. With tears flowing quietly down her bronzed cheeks, she took the bundles written in Norio's fine Japanese script, one bundle for each year at the university, untied the strings and, reading bits from the pages, dropped them one by one into the fire which was kept going from morning till night, burning the things they could bring themselves to part with. Photographs of her folks in Japan followed the letters into the fire, after she had taken a last, loving look at each face through her tears.

It was while the Satos were in this travail of making decisions that two men came out to the ranch one morning. It was the morning of the fifth, so there were only two days left, and still no arrangements had been made for the things they must leave. Tom and Tad were doing some cleanup work in the greenhouse when they saw the car drive in, and they hurried to the house. The men were already inside, their hats on and cigars in their mouths, trying to bargain with Mother Sato for the furniture.

They nodded to the boys when they came in and told them they were buyers. They knew the folks were leaving soon and might want someone to take the furniture off their hands. They made a show of being friendly.

"Twenty-five for the refrigerator and fifteen for the furniture in each room," the heavyset one clipped off glibly without ever looking at the things. It was plain to be seen that this group of sharpers who were buying up Japanese goods had agreed on the prices they would pay so there would be no bidding against each other. They knew the people had no choice; they had to go. And many would not be able to find storage in the short time left to them.

"Seventy-five for the car," the other said.

The family looked about the room from one to another in astonishment and dismay. The refrigerator was only a year old, and the car was like new. Most of the furniture was old and had been bought when prices were much lower than now, but it was in good condition and couldn't be replaced for many times what they were being offered.

The men stood puffing on their cigars and watching the Satos curiously.

"Well, if you don't want to sell now, we won't press you. But if you change your minds, phone us before you go and we will give you the same prices we have offered you now. We won't take advantage of you." The heavy man with the sagging chin took a card from his pocket and handed it to Tom, who took it mechanically.

"You'll find my phone number on there."

The men made a move to leave without actually going.

The folks did not know what to do. They had found no place to store their things, and they knew if they sold they couldn't hope to get a better price. The buyers were all together in this.

Tad's eyes flashed fury, and the corner of his mouth twitched from the stinging whips of white heat that lashed at his insides. Had he been less indignant he would have cursed the greedy sharpers and ordered them out of the house. Had he been more so, he would have thrown them out bodily or made the attempt. As it was, he could neither speak nor act.

Tom didn't want to sell the things, confident that they would yet find a place to put them, and he was always thinking that . . . well, they weren't gone yet. Something might happen. And even if they did go, they might not be gone very long.

Mari wasn't interested one way or another. It didn't make any difference to her. She was mainly concerned with how she was going to get everything she had to take with her into two small suitcases.

The boys turned to their mother. She was the one to decide. The things represented a lifetime of saving for her and Dad. Certainly neither of them would give their consent for these unscrupulous racketeers to take the stuff unless she was willing.

Tad turned his back on the buyers and tried to explain to his mother that he had still found no place to store the furniture and that if they left things in the house vandals might break in and destroy or steal them; that some folks who had moved voluntarily and sent trucks later to get their things had found their houses stripped. But if she wanted to keep her things, he would still keep trying to find a place to put them.

Mother Sato looked about calmly at their possessions. She was undisturbed by the contempt on the faces of the men as they watched her and unhurried by their growing impatience.

"No. We not sell," she announced at last. "Too cheap. Papa Sato would not like it." She was firm. With polite curtsies of dismissal she bowed the men toward the door. And the men, who had come to take advantage of some scared and cringing "Japs," were disconcerted by the unruffled dignity of Mother Sato and allowed themselves to be bowed out the door.

When the men were gone Tad locked the front door and swore that if another white man set foot on the place he would kick him off. They all felt somewhat shaken by the experience.

As it happened, the next person who came to the ranch was warmly welcomed, for he was a friend coming on quite a different errand. The boys had returned to their work at the greenhouse after the buyers had gone and had been there only a short time when another car drove in and out of it climbed old Peter Vandenheuvel. He shaded his eyes with his hand and looked about the place. Seeing the boys, he came hobbling over to where they were. He was sorry to hear they were leaving and wanted to know if there was anything he could do to help.

The boys were still too proud to ask favors and did not know of anything Peter could do for them anyway, so Tom thanked him and asked him if he wouldn't come to the house where they could sit down and talk awhile.

"No. No, thank you, Tom. I'll have to be getting on

190

back. I just thought I'd come over and see if everything was all right. What are you going to do with all your things, boys?" Old Peter wasn't satisfied that there was nothing he could do. Blasted proud, this Sato family. Got it from the old man. "Got a good place to store everything? Or are you going to sell? If you're going to sell you'd better wait and let me do it for you after you're gone. You always have to take a big loss when you sell in a hurry."

Tad went ahead stacking empty flats in the corner while Tom did the talking.

Tom told the old man about the buyers and how his mother had decided not to sell, but that they still hadn't made arrangements for storage. However, he was sure they would find a suitable place.

"Well, bring them right over to my place. I've got that big double garage--cement floor, nice and dry all the year round, you can put your things right in there. I'll see that the mice don't get into them."

"But your car! You use your garage, don't you?" Tom felt the offer was too good to be true. They couldn't crowd the old man even if he were so willing.

"Oh, I sold my car yesterday, Tom. The fellow's coming after it today. That's the reason I have to get back home. Can't get tires anymore and, well, I'm getting too old to drive a car anyway, and too crippled up. Might kill somebody."

Ugly old Peter's rough, red face looked to Tom like an angel's, and the fringe of straw colored hair around his bald head like a halo. He could scarcely find words strong enough to express his gratitude. Even Tad was softened by the genuine friendship of the man and quit his work and walked with him to the car along with Tom.

"Just bring them over anytime," Peter called from the window as he started off.

This left only the farm machinery and the car and trucks now. Tom finally decided to leave the machinery and trucks in the hands of the Farm Security Administration, hoping for the best. They were storing them in an empty warehouse in La Vista, and the outlook didn't seem too bad, unless the warehouse filled up and the rest were put on the vacant lot outside. No passenger cars were taken there, and their last day at home came with no arrangements for the car. Tom had it washed and polished until it looked like new. He had found time to do it somehow in the middle of everything else.

He and Tad had been picking cucumbers every minute they could spare from preparations to leave. They didn't get as good a price now as earlier but every cent counted, for the day they left the ranch their means of making a livelihood would be gone. There would be no income except the small amount they would get from the rent, and the place wasn't leased yet.

Mr. Winters passed in his car several times these last days, driving slowly, looking in. To Tom he was like a buzzard circling overhead, waiting, waiting, waiting.

The only time he felt like destroying his seedbeds was when he saw Mr. Winters pass, but down in his heart he knew he would rather have even Mr. Winters have the tomato plants than to have them dry up and die.

Mrs. Sullivan called that last evening at home to offer a place for the car in their garage in case the Satos hadn't made other arrangements. Allen had just sold his motorcycle and Mary had decided to take the family car up to school for awhile, for she could get tires and gas on her priority. And that solved the last of the problems. Tomorrow the last things to be done and then go to the train. Peg was going to drive them into the station.

There was one more errand Tom must do yet tonight. Jerry had consented to keep Malt while they were gone.

"We'd better take the dog over tonight," Tom said to Yoshi at the supper table. "We'll have too much to do tomorrow."

"Okay," Yoshi replied briefly and slipped from the table with a half-eaten chicken drumstick concealed in his hand.

When Tom went out after finishing supper to get out the car, he heard the boy taking a farewell of his dog.

"Now, Malt, I'm going away and I can't take you with me. See? Don't you get to thinking I don't want you just because I went off and left you. I couldn't help it. Are you listening to me, Malt? I can't help it. I have to go. Jerry will be good to you and give you plenty to eat, but don't forget, you belong to me. You wouldn't forget me, would you, Malt?"

All the time Yoshi was talking, his voice shrill with grief, the dog was sitting licking the last taste of chicken bone from his jowls and listening attentively, as if trying hard to understand what he was being told.

When Tom started the motor and whistled for the dog, Malt and Yoshi both came running from behind the garage. Malt jumped into the seat beside Tom, but Yoshi drew back.

"I don't want to go," he said.

"All right," Tom replied, closing the door. He had never seen Yoshi so cut up over anything.

When he had driven away, Yoshi watched the car down the highway and then ran and beat his fists against the side of the garage, his face contorted with grief he could not contain.

Tom took the dog to Jerry and told him he had better tie him up a few days until he got to feeling at home over there. Jerry held Malt in his arms, and Tom reached out the window and gave him a pat on the head.

"So long, old fellow. Be good." Then he drove away in a hurry, not looking to see how Malt was taking this being left behind. His eyes were smarting and he wondered how the windshield could be so blurred when he had washed it that very day.

X

The Satos ate their lunch, the last meal in their own home for many, many months to come, in picnic style on the back porch. Table and chairs had been stored that morning along with the other furniture in old Peter's garage. Mrs. Sullivan had insisted they all come in there for lunch, but the family was too busy and worn out to want to stop and dress for lunch. So when Mari drove the car over to the Sullivans's to leave in their garage and Peg took her home, Mrs. Sullivan slipped a kettle of rich vegetable soup into the car with some bowls and spoons. Allen had promised to jack up the wheels and take out the battery and said he had a large tarpaulin he could cover over the car to protect the finish from dust and salty fog. So this took one job off of Tom this final day.

No one was hungry. Mother Sato ate a little soup and drank her tea. The others ate unconsciously from instinct of self-preservation. The future was blank, empty, insecure. No one knew where or when they would eat again.

Yoshi tossed the crust of his sandwich away and quick tears sprang to his eyes when no eager jaws snapped it up.

As soon as he had finished Tom went out to the field to turn off the irrigation water. He had had it running for two days, giving everything on the ranch a last good soaking, hoping it would last until a tenant could be found. He had phoned before lunch, and no one had leased the ranch yet. The official told him there were several buyers looking for ranches at the right price and asked again if he would be willing to sell if they could not lease. Tom would like to have known if Mr. Winters were one of the buyers; however, he didn't consider asking, for the place was not for sale, so what difference did it make who wanted it?

As he looked over his field of sturdy young tomato

plants and the seedbeds where thousands upon thousands, almost ready for the growers, had made a solid mass of shimmering deep green, he could not bear to take the life-giving water from them. Maybe a little more would make the difference between life and death to them. He decided to let the water run a little longer. Peg wasn't coming till four-thirty, and most of the work was done. He would just sit down and wait a few minutes and then turn it off.

It was a lovely spring afternoon. The sun was more than warm, it was getting real summer heat into it. The open mesa was abloom with wild mustard, and the soft, balmy air was scented pleasantly with the faint odor of orange blossoms from nearby groves. It was a day made for pleasure and happiness and love. Sorrow and hate ill-fitted it.

This was the first real moment of leisure Tom had had since the news broke. There had been no time for brooding nor for introspection over the thing which was happening to him. And there had been little time or freedom of mind for thinking. Besides, Tom had not wanted to think. He had unconsciously avoided it for days. Now his time at home had almost run out. In a short time he would be leaving, under compulsion, driven out because of his ancestry. He had been repudiated by his government, branded as an enemy alien. All of this was contrary to what he had been taught about democracy. This had brought about a bitter conflict which he was bound to have to face some time and resolve within himself. It was inconceivable that he could go on indefinitely in a mental and emotional vacuum.

In the past he had been able to face his problems objectively and come to reasonable judgments. Would he be able to do so in this present situation? Or would he, like Tad, surrender to bitterness and resentment and lose his faith in American ideals? It was well that Tom could fight his battle here in his fields with his growing plants. This was his world.

He was still unable to comprehend how his government could deprive citizens of their rights under the Constitution on such shaky grounds. Military necessity and their own protection. That was what the Army said. Hadn't the very general who gave the evacuation order said publicly that there had been no acts of sabotage on the coast? And hadn't the newspapers denied the reports of sabotage in Hawaii, although belatedly? This same general had also stated that various rumors of attack upon the Japanese people along the coast, when traced to their sources, had proved false for the most part. But even if these attacks had taken place, was the government too weak to protect her citizens and their parents from violence? Was it just to confine the innocent rather than the guilty? Where would such a policy lead to, confining people to protect them from the criminal element of the nation?

This fact of evacuation had come to Tom as a profound shock. He had been so sure. To him citizenship had indisputably been a guarantee of equal rights and privileges in the eyes of the government. Individuals were sometimes prejudiced and unfair and sometimes even fanatical to the point of perpetrating acts of physical violence against helpless minorities. And isolated cases of officials in power misusing it against minority groups. But not the government. The national government could not be prejudiced. It could not stoop to such a petty act of discrimination against any group of its citizens. And yet it had.

He felt an urgency to restore it in his own mind to its former high position of dignity and infallibility. There must be some mistake. Even yet new orders would come. The evacuation would be cancelled. Dates had been changed, transportation had been changed. This indicated things were still in a fluid state. Everything was in confusion among the authorities. But the real American spirit would emerge from the confusion and triumph before this hideous thing was allowed to happen. That liberty loving spirit which had made America great, the spirit of Washington and Jackson and Lincoln was not dead.   Of Patrick Henry and Franklin and Wilson.   The people would yet speak out for the rights of their fellow citizens.   Even yet, though the hour of ignominy had almost struck, he would hear the bells of liberty ringing out clear and strong above the din of vitriolic hate and unjust accusation.   And those ugly little voices would be hushed from very shame.

Tom sat there on the bank at the edge of the field, looking off in the distance toward the mountains, and listened.   Listened in his mind to the great utterances on behalf of freedom throughout the history of the United States--the stirring words Norio and he had read together, passages from his books at school.   He raised his tired eyes to the mountain peaks to the east and listened as if expecting to hear the voice of a new defender of liberty.

The afternoon was quiet.   There was no sound but the droning of training planes far overhead.

He began to take stock of himself, trying to find in his own life some shortcomings which had brought this thing upon him and made him deserving of it.   He felt a sudden eagerness welling up within him to be able to put the blame on himself, to exonerate his country.   Had he failed as a young American?   Had the Nisei as a group failed?   Had they fulfilled their obligations and responsibilities as good citizens?   Had they been aggressive members of their communities, standing up for the fundamental rights of others in times of persecution and discrimination?   What contribution had he made to the life of his community?   He was forced to admit that he had never thought of it before.   He had taken advantage of all the opportunities which the freedom of his country had offered: education, making money, going where he pleased, speaking his opinions freely among his associates.   But what had he and the other Nisei given in return?   Had they championed the rights of other minorities?   What about the Dust Bowl immigrants to the state?   They had been preyed upon by some of the same pressure groups which were now ousting the

Japanese from the state. Had the Nisei been forward in speaking out for them, or had they laughed and called them Okies along with others? The answers were not to his advantage. He could see now how the Nisei themselves must shoulder some of the blame for evacuation.

They had not even championed their own rights. They had been acquiescent in the face of evacuation. Tom began to see Tad's side of the question. He had been right. They should never have allowed this to happen without first making a protest which could be heard across the country from border to border. He had been a fool, an ostrich with its head in the sand. If he had foreseen, if he could have believed this possible, he would have joined with those who wanted to resist. He recalled his poor, childish speech at the mass meeting. How the others must have laughed to themselves!

Didn't the American colonies protest against the oppression of their government in England? Where would the country be today if they had not, if they had submitted meekly? Would it still be a colony of the British Empire? Was it a proof of weakness or loyalty when the Nisei organizations had shown a willingness to cooperate with the authorities?

Well, it was too late to ask and answer those questions now. Evacuation was no longer a possible tragedy to be debated over. It would soon be a fact. No voice of a savior of democracy had spoken out with a voice firm enough to make itself heard, and one thing he had said the night of the mass meeting he did not disavow now: if their citizenship were violated, there would be nothing left. This he was experiencing as a truth. Emptiness engulfed him, swept into the spaces where faith and love and loyalty had been. Yes. Evacuation was a fact. He would have to go.

Someone else would till his fields, harvest his crops, reap the financial gains from his labor, while he idled in an internment camp. Without the income from the ranch the family would soon be penniless. All his hopes, plans, and dreams for the future were gone. College, a career, marriage, all out of the picture.

Unsteadily he gazed upon the blank film of his future.

A queer feeling came over him at the thought that tomorrow he would be living in a strange place. He had heard much of the concentration camps of Germany and Russia, and he recalled those things he had heard now. He had never dreamed that he would be in one of those camps in his own country.

Insecurity gripped him, and he began to be afraid. He groped around in the empty dark for some way to accept this strange thing which was being done to him without losing his balance. He must find some reasonable way to make the best of it. It was too overwhelming to accept in blindness.

He shifted his position to ease a cramped leg. He must think straight, without emotion, think about it as if it were happening to someone else. He must build a new foundation under him. He had put all his trust in his citizenship. He had thought it a Rock of Gibraltar. Believed in it, depended upon it, would have given his life to defend it. And then came the waves of war hysteria and race hatred and beat upon it, and it had washed away like shifting sand. And he was left floundering in a choppy sea of dismay and confusion.

He must find a new footing, one which could not be washed out from under him. It must be built upon something over which he himself had control. It must be built upon faith in himself, in his own resources. He took inventory. What had he left? Evicted from home and all the freedom of normal life, made a ward of the government, regarded as a criminal by his fellow citizens, disloyal and ready to stab his country in the back, and, most unbearable of all, denied any opportunity to prove himself otherwise. The inventory did not find much to build on. He was still an American. Some public officials had advocated robbing him of his citizenship along with other Nisei, but they had not succeeded in bringing that about. Yes, he was still a citizen, though that had lost its meaning. Was this internment to be his contribution to the war effort, his sacrifice in the interest of national security? An inglorious part, indeed, for any true American. But it was something. And Tom was in that state of mind where he would grasp at anything to keep his head above water. He was a citizen. He knew he was loyal. Then he would carry on as a good, loyal citizen should. He would take his orders from the Army as any good soldier did and carry them out faithfully. He would make his citizenship mean something again. He would show that he was made of the same stuff as the early pioneers who had endured hardship and privation as they pushed their way westward and made their contribution to the building of America. He tried to persuade himself that going willingly to a concentration camp took as much courage as hewing homes from the virgin forests and preserving life against the attacks of savages. He could not entirely convince himself, but he had found a starting point. Viewed in this light he was ready to accept evacuation as a service to his country. He could face ignominy, suspicion, and repudiation in the same spirit. In this hour of introspection he had discovered that affection can be a one-sided affair. He loved his country, but she despised him. However, that would not keep him from continuing to love her and serve her no matter what she did to him. He would keep his loyalty unblemished by disloyal thought or word or deed. Tom had won the victory.

He came to with a start and jumped to his feet just as he heard a voice from the house calling, "Tom. Tom. Where are you? It's time you're getting dressed." It was Mari calling from the back porch.

The sun was halfway down the western sky. Tom turned off the water quickly and hurried to the house.

When he came out into the living room after finishing his packing and getting dressed for the trip, he found the others ready. To see them all there in their good clothes on a midweek day looking so solemn reminded him of the day of Norio's funeral. He could see his father sitting there where the big leather chair had always been by the door, grief-stricken and silent.

200

What would he think if he could see his family now? What would Norio think?

Tom added his two bags to the pile of luggage in the center of the bare floor, and Mari handed him the identification tags. He attached one to each bag, and the third he fastened to the lapel of his coat and sheepishly stuck it inside his pocket. Mari had pinned her tag to her jacket and slipped it inside where it didn't show. She had her chin tilted at an impudent angle, and one could tell that no evacuation official nor anyone else would see any tears or kowtowing from her.

Tad, the only one who had not dressed for the occasion, came in from the porch, his tag slung around his neck and dangling across the front of an old, worn sweatshirt. He was trying to cover up his distress by joking about everything and everybody. His loud voice and raucous laughter were mirthless and harder for the others to bear than his gripes and bitterness had been. He began to try to tease his mother into a smile.

But Mother Sato was weeping silently, with Yoshi tugging at her sleeve and begging, "Don't cry, Mommy. Please don't cry."

Soon they heard the honk of Peg's car. Mari grabbed up the baggage that she was to carry and marched out to the car with her head high, never looking back. Mother Sato and Yoshi followed, carrying smaller bundles. Yoshi was crying, too, now. Tad gathered up all he could carry and went staggering out, clowning the motions of a drunken man as he sang loudly, "California, Here I Go."

Tom locked the door.

Tears came with this final act of separation. They were not so much from grief over leaving home, although this was the only home he remembered, but more the quick tears of panic of a child who finds itself deserted.

Although he had been able to rationalize and to make his decision to go as a good soldier, he felt none of the ecstasy of a martyr to buoy him up. As he took the key from the door and put it in his pocket and walked out to the car, his mind moved in the midst of an illimitable emptiness which stretched out in every direction beyond the boundaries of his comprehension and which defied him as the limits of the universe defy the scope of human thought.

In the midst of this vast emptiness he moved and hugged to him, with the passion of a miser grasping his gold, his two priceless possessions, faith and hope. Faith in himself and hope that some day he could restore his faith in others and win their faith in him. Faith that he could carry out, through thick and thin, the program of willing service he had set for himself; and hope that the opportunity might come for him to vindicate himself, for him to again take his place as a free individual in a normal society and as an accepted American.

Tad and Mari had climbed into the front seat with Peg, so Tom squeezed into the rear seat with his mother and Yoshi and the mound of baggage. Seeing the mailbox, he asked if anyone had thought to look for mail, and since no one had he got out again and went over. The farm paper and a letter from Father Sato addressed to Tom. Father Sato took turns addressing his letters to different members of the family. As Peg started the car Tom let himself look back for one last look at the ranch and saw Malt running down the road as fast as his legs could carry him, his ears lying back against his head. A piece of rope was dangling from his collar. When he saw the car start he tried to quicken his speed, his short legs working like triphammers in his supreme effort to catch up. But as Peg shifted into high the little dog was soon left behind. Tom saw that no one else had noticed the dog and he did not say anything, for there was not time to go back. They must be at the station on time. He was no longer Tom Sato, rancher, managing his own affairs, giving orders. He had now become Tom Sato, evacuee. Others would give the orders from now on.

On the ride into the city Tad kept the girls laughing with his jokes. Tom opened the letter from his father and read it. It was very brief and it did not take long. His father had had his hearing and been found guilty of the charges against him, it said.

"What did he say?"

"Has he had his hearing?"

"When is he coming?"

They were all asking for news. This was no time to tell them the truth. Tom was to wish later he had broken it to them then, bad as it was, but he stuffed the letter back into his pocket.

"Oh, he just wrote to let us know he was all right. Didn't say much."

"Has he heard about us leaving?"

"He didn't say anything about it."

Soon they were in the city, and from the top of the hill going in the view of the bay was always a beautiful one, although now the large number of gray ships of the Navy which rode at anchor in the harbor added a foreboding note to the bright blue of the sea. When they reached the downtown section, Peg guided the car skillfully through the heavy traffic. Tom looked at his mother and saw her shrinking back in the corner of her seat, her eyes lowered, and he reached over and rolled up the window as if that could in some way shut out the curious, ugly stares which followed them down Broadway.

These people hate us, Tom thought. They are strangers, have never seen us before. But they hate us. You can see it in their eyes. They would be glad to see us killed. Why? Why? Why? The words kept drumming on his mind as they passed slowly through the evening traffic down Broadway to the Santa Fe station.

XI

Many generations of liberty-loving Americans have wept over the tragic tale, immortalized by Longfellow, of the deportation of a hapless population from the land of Acadia. This incident in the British colonization of the New World still stirs the heart. Condemned as cruel and needless, that uprooting of industrious and peace loving French farmers; sympathized with as innocent victims those 6,000 souls as they look back from their boats and watch the flames of their burning homes and fields . . .

This deportation occurred some twenty-one years before a great human document declared to the world that man is possessed of certain inalienable rights, among which is liberty. The sin for which the Acadians were punished was their refusal to take an unconditional oath of allegiance to the British sovereign.

Still, nothing more cruel or intolerable was done to them than to resettle them in the English colonies from Massachusetts to Georgia, with some going as far south as Louisiana. They were not herded into crowded quarters in internment camps. They were not put under guard.

Now, nearly two centuries later, what was this strange action on a railway station platform in that democracy of the New World which had become so great a defender of liberty and justice, so jealous of these two priceless possessions of man that she had crossed the seas twice in two world wars to champion them?

What had brought about this gathering of confused and bewildered people, milling about their baggage, anxiously guarding the few things they had been permitted to take with them on their banishment from home? Banishment not to some other favored garden spot but eventually to a dead and barren desert. Would another Longfellow arise to immortalize their tragedy? Would he have to write of their southland ranches as the other had said of the Acadian lands:

"Waste are the pleasant farms
And gone forever the farmers"?

Would he write of separation and heartbreak, of warped and twisted lives, as the fruits of evacuation ripened to harvest?

In the light of history how would this extraordinary deportation be judged? Would future historians, reviewing this period of World War II from the vantage point of hindsight, record the greatest defeats to America as those wreaked upon her at Pearl Harbor and Bataan? Or would they be forced to conclude, from the events that followed, that American democracy had been dealt her deepest injury when a general of the United States Army had permitted his race prejudice against some of his fellow Americans to lead him to refer to American citizenship as a scrap of paper while no one arose in his presence to challenge him in shocked indignation?

Whatever the causes leading up to this final abortive action, whatever the judgments of history at some future date, here they were on the station platform, part of a group of over 100,000 people of Japanese ancestry who would be moved from the states bordering on the Pacific. Deportees, unwanted in California, ordered out by the Army on the authority given it by the president. The same Army whose uniform some of these boys had worn so proudly only·a short while before, and that some had worn in honor and glory in World War I. There had been no refusal to sign oaths of allegiance here. Many had sent letters to their president affirming their loyalty. Their organizations had written.

But here they were, nevertheless, outcasts awaiting shipment to an unknown destination. "A Jap is a Jap" had won out over the sentiment so dear to the hearts of so many generations of Americans that "All men are created equal."

Peg pulled the car up to the loading zone since there was no place near the station where she could park, and the Sato family climbed out.

Peg would have clung to Mari in a tearful farewell, for it was their first long separation and her heart was full. But Mari slipped out of the car seat after Tad in a quick gesture of withdrawal. Although she was not conscious of the forces impelling her to become suddenly aloof from her closest friend, instinctively she felt that there was a gulf between them now too wide for intimacies. She had become conscious of the barrier of race between them for the first time in all the years they had been in school together. Peg was an individual free to come and go as she pleased. She could go on to school tomorrow, and the next day, and the next, while she, Mari, would be shut up in a camp somewhere, and regarded as a dangerous person because of her looks. Her pride forbade her to show any affection for Peg or any grief over leaving her.

"Now be sure to write," Peg begged, bewildered by this new Mari who was busy with the baggage and avoiding her eyes.

"Yes. I will," Mari said lightly, as if it were of no consequence either way, and with her hands full she said, "Goodbye" airily and turned away.

Mother Sato bowed many times and thanked Peg for her kindness, and Peg, wounded by Mari's coldness and touched by the pathos of the polite smiles on Mother Sato's drawn face, let the tears run unheeded down her own cheeks as she cried and tried to laugh and be cheerful at the same time.

Tom had managed so he would be the last to leave, for he wanted to tell Peg about Malt.

"I'll drive out past the house," Peg said readily. "He's probably there . . ." She stopped. There waiting for the folks to come home. "He knows me so well I won't have any trouble getting him to go back to Jerry's with me."

"I hate to bother you," Tom began, but Peg stopped him.

"Don't be silly," she said almost harshly, irritated by such diffidence at a time like this. Her young eyes swept the crowd on the platform with a compassionate glance. Mari and the other Satos were already merging with the group. Mari had never looked back, and her head was high. "I'd die if I couldn't do something for you folks."

"Well . . . thanks a lot. Guess I'd better be getting this stuff on the train. It may start pretty soon. Goodbye, Peg." There was a huskiness in Tom's voice in spite of the casualness of his words.

"Adios. Good luck," Peg said. It sounded silly, but what was there to say? Words hadn't yet been formed for such occasions.

As Tom turned away he was conscious of the breaking of the last link which bound him to his old life. Unless Allen should come before they pulled out, from now on everything would be new and strange. He hurried to catch up with the rest of the family.

There was a mountainous heap of baggage on the platform beside the train, and men were busily loading it into the baggage car. More people were arriving all the time, some brought to the station by friends, some on the streetcars, struggling with their bags and bundles of bedding.

There were young and old, rich and poor, weak and strong. The 1,500 persons brought there by Army orders were from all stations of life. There were the humble peasant farmers and wives in dark suits and white shirts and chain-store dresses. There were the well-to-do and sophisticated city dwellers with all the style and savoir faire of the elite. There was a small group of college girls in bright sweaters and sleek slacks, one with her identification tag and her Phi Beta Kappa key mingling with ironic intimacy on her sweater front. There were high school boys, scowling and angry over the stupidity of the Army, and young men from the university cut deep by the knife thrusts of suspicion at them. There were babies in baskets, and a bride and groom who had married at the last minute to keep from being separated in different camps.

There were the old. And the crippled. And the blind. There was an old man dying of cancer. And one

207

on crutches barely able to stand. Some crippled with rheumatism and others worn out from age and hard work. Pathetic figures.

There were little tots, toddling on their first uncertain steps, already tired and fretful, reflecting in their unhappy faces the strain under which their parents had labored the past few days. Anxious lines around the eyes of tired fathers and mothers as they tried to comfort their children and wondered what was in store for them. Would there be good food? Would there be *any* food? Milk? Would there be medical care? What would happen to their little ones now that the parents were no longer able to look to their welfare?

There were quiet, acquiscent little women, Issei women. What flight of the imagination would be required to regard them as dangerous!

The military dragnet had been no respecter of persons. It had been drawn through the designated area with merciless efficiency, into the sanctuary of the old and infirm as well as the able, and had dragged them forth from the comfort and warmth of their firesides and the beds to which they were accustomed. Here they stood, many with difficulty, desolate and shivering in the chill evening air from the sea, waiting to entrain for internment . . . and for some, death. Pullman accommodations had been provided for the sick and aged, and they were being put on board as rapidly as possible. The swarming people who filled the platform to overflowing were unusually orderly for such a large number under difficult circumstances, and there was something incongruous in the presence of military police stationed at intervals the entire length of the platform. Towering over this throng of subdued little people, they looked as much out of place as stage settings left inadvertently from a previous act. The young people eyed these guards with unbelief and resentment.

There was a veteran of World War I limping about on an artificial foot; he had left his own in France a quarter century before. He was wearing a worn and faded overseas cap at a jaunty angle and was stumping about talking to everyone, trying to boost morale.

"Hey! Where are you going, Charley?" someone yelled.

"Military secret," the vet retorted with a resounding laugh which brought some smiles where scowls had been.

There was Mr. Imoto, dressed in new tweeds and flashy tan oxfords, looking very much as if he were starting on a world tour. His expensive, new cowhide luggage stood out among the worn suitcases and lumpy bundles like "a Nisei at a meeting of the Native Sons," Tad quipped when he saw it. Tad had found Bill Harada who, in a neat gray suit and navy tie with tiny white dots, was leaning comfortably against the station, smoking a cigarette. Although the two were worlds apart in their opinions and reactions to what was happening to them, they liked each other, and the university was a common bond between them. They were to see much of each other in the months ahead.

Yoshi tugged at Tom's sleeve and pointed to a couple near them who had brought a small dog, a Pekingese, in a large clothes basket. The basket was half full of cans of dog food, with the dog perched unhappily on top. Apparently this was all the couple had brought, for it was a load for two. Yoshi looked up accusingly at Tom, and Tom felt more guilty than the incident itself would have occasioned, for he did not know what had become of Malt, although he knew Peg would do all she could to find him.

Tom kept watching the street for Allen as they waited their turn to go aboard. Seats were assigned, and each family had to wait their turn.

Passing sailors from the Navy Landing at the foot of Broadway threw cursory glances at the strange gathering, and Tom overheard one tell another, "They're shipping the Japs out."

"What the hell for?" asked the other, apparently from the East.

At last the Satos's names were called, and they moved over to the steps of the coach to which they were

209

assigned. At that moment not only Allen but the whole gang came racing across the fast emptying platform, laughing at the remonstrances of the MPs as they pushed up to the steps. Navy blue and the air corps olive mingled with motley array of civilian attire.

There was time only for hasty sketches of conversation.

"Gee, sure hate to see you go, Tom."

"You ought to be going with us instead of . . ." Broken off in embarrassment.

"What are we fighting for, anyway? That's what I'd like . . ."

"Be sure to write."

"Hey, Al. Drop a bomb with my name on it." Tom was being hurried up the steps now. "Hope you get a bunch of Zeros."

"Yeah, I sure will, Tom."

"So long. Be seeing you when it's over."

"So long, Mari. Goodbye, Mama Sato. Take care of yourself."

Mother Sato turned as she was about to enter the car and smiled wanly. Allen was a nice boy. He never forgot to speak to her.

"Where's Tad?" someone asked.

"He's inside, I guess."

"Well, tell him goodbye for us."

The fellows left as abruptly as they had come.

Tom followed the family down the aisle to their seats. Honor for Allen and the rest of the gang . . . disgrace for him. But he would carry on now, and some day his chance would come. Someday he, too, would be in uniform.

Tad, who had been standing talking to Bill, came now and, shoving Yoshi over, dropped into the seat beside Yoshi and his mother. He laid his head against the back of the seat and closed his eyes. All the expression drained out of his face, and he looked as ghastly as a corpse.

"It's harder on Tad than any of us," Tom thought. "Maybe if I hadn't been so stubborn we could have

210

moved on our own, like he wanted to. Then he wouldn't have had to go through this." He felt guilty as he looked at his brother's haggard face.

Everyone was on now. The platform was cleared of Japanese. Only the friends who had come to see them off were still standing, waving and smiling, and then drifting away. The folks inside with their faces against the windows smiled back, trying to put up a good front for their friends, and little children waved tiny American flags they had brought. The military police had taken their positions at either end of the coach. The forced journey seemed about to begin.

There was an air of expectancy among the older children, for most of them had never had a train ride before. Yoshi, occupied with inspecting every part of the car his eye could reach, leaned across his mother to work the window shade up and down, spelled out the words in red letters on the glass box which enclosed a shiny new axe, and, when he saw someone else getting a drink, swaggered down the aisle to the drinking fountain.

Tired people who had spent the last week in feverish preparations for leaving and the weeks before that in anxiety and suspense over what might happen sat back with something of relief that the suspense was over. The thing so long dreaded had come at last. Now they knew the worst.

Manzanar. The name meant little to them. A place up north, on the east side of the High Sierra. Some had been told to have their mail forwarded there. Some had had no information. The sources of information had been undependable and contradictory. They could only wait and see.

Seven o'clock came and the train still stood in the station. Folks began to get restless. Had something happened? Did some new danger threaten, or was the delay because of new and better plans? Eight o'clock.

Tad still sat there like a graven image, just as he had done in the bus station up north that day he was discharged from the Army. He spoke to no one, and no

211

one dared to say anything to him.

Children who had been hungry for hours were crying now.

"Why are we sitting here, Mama? Why don't we go home?" a shrill voice piped out frankly. Who could have given an answer which would have satisfied the fairmindedness of a child?

"Home, Mommy. Want to go home," a tiny one wailed.

Soon after eight o'clock lunch boxes were distributed, Each contained a sandwich, cookies, and an apple. And, yes, praise God, a bottle of milk for each person. Expectancy soon turned to disappointment. The sandwiches were stale, and some were moldy and could not be eaten. Parents went without to give to the children.

Sometime during the evening the train pulled out of the station and up the track a mile or so to the yards. There it stopped again and, as the hours wore on, it appeared they were going to spend the night there. No explanation was given for the delay, and no one was allowed to get off the train. Waiting became as hard as work.

Tad got up suddenly, as if something within him had reached the limit of endurance, and joined a group of young people in the back of the coach, where some music was starting up.

Yoshi curled up in the space left and, laying his head in his mother's lap, dropped off to sleep. Mother Sato sat like one in a trance. This thing which was happening to her and her family had left her in such a state of confusion that she herself knew not whether she was actually going through it or dreaming. She laid a loving hand on the boy's shoulder in a protective gesture as if to shield him from whatever hardships or privations were ahead for him. Little did she see now the pitfalls ahead for Yoshi and hundreds like him who were going into internment, pitfalls which were to give her far more concern than a bit of physical discomfort for her youngest.

212

Tom and Mari dozed and shifted often in an attempt to find more comfortable positions.

"Haven't we started yet?" Mari asked, rousing up. "Oh, I'm so tired I could lie right down in the aisle and sleep. Want anything, Mom?" As if there were anything she could get for her mother.

Tad was strumming the uke and loud voices boomed through the coach. "Deep in the heart of Texas." Clap, clap. "I don't want to set the world on fire. I just want to start a flame in your heart."

An elderly man, trying to sleep, raised his head and looked around at the young people indulgently and lay back again. It was as if he said, It is hardest for them. His life had been lived. It didn't make much difference what happened to him now. And besides, he had his country, Japan, to go to if he were treated badly here. There would always be a place for him there. His country would always welcome him. But these young people . . . They had nothing left. They didn't belong anywhere now.

As the night deepened the music changed to softer harmonies.

"There'll be bluebirds over
   the white cliffs of Dover."

At last one of the college girls took the uke from Tad and, sitting on the arm of the seat, began to play and sing softly.

"On a hill far away
   Stood an old rugged cross;
   An emblem of suffering and shame."

Her low voice could be heard to the farthest end of the crowded coach. Those who listened were reminded there was another one who had suffered shame and disgrace. He would understand and give comfort and strength to bear whatever came.

"So I'll cling to the old rugged cross
   Till my burden at last I lay down."

The cross seemed lightened. Someone to help with the weight of it. The singing stopped. Hearts had been soothed. Dewy-eyed, the girl handed the uke back to

213

Tad, and he came and sat in the seat assigned to him behind Tom and Mari and went to sleep.

When the train finally got on its way Tom looked at his watch. It was half-past one. The shades were all pulled, and no one could look out during the trip.

Daylight found everyone tired and cross, although expectant. Where were they? Would they be at the end of their journey soon? There was complaining.

"It isn't as bad as being crowded on the boxcars for days on end like the Germans did," Tom defended.

"Do you have to compare the United States with the Nazis to make her look good?" a sarcastic voice asked. "That should make us proud. Is America to be commended because she interns innocent victims with less torture than the Nazis?" The voice of the older Nisei was ugly, and it could not be ignored. He had made a point. Tom was silenced.

It was around ten that morning that they reached their destination. At first no one knew where they were, although they knew they were still in the southland from the orange groves and the palm trees. Then someone discovered the grandstand.

Santa Anita! The racetrack.

There was a flurry of excitement. Getting off the train after the long ride, stretching their tired limbs, looking about to catch some inkling of what they were in for.

Tom saw the barbed wire fence and took his eyes away quickly, walking through the gate looking straight ahead. Even then he couldn't keep from seeing the watchtowers all around the enclosure and the guards sitting up in them behind machine guns. He hadn't thought it would be like this.

When the Satos had had their physicals and were assigned to their quarters, a guide went with them to show them the way. He was a Nisei from San Pedro who had been there some days and seemed as anxious as a real estate salesman to sell the place to the newcomers.

"Of course, there are a lot of things to be done yet

before we can really get organized and going good," he breezed on, not noticing the silence of his audience. "We've got some baseball teams already, though. Need some good pitchers. Either of you fellows play?"

"No. We play checkers," Tad said glumly, before Tom could speak up.

The guide took the hint and remained silent for a few steps.

"When do we eat?" Tad asked.

"Well, that's about the worst part of the camp right now," the guide began apologetically. "But it will be all right as soon as they get the other mess halls completed. You may have to wait in line awhile."

"How's the food once you get it?" Tad continued.

"Why, it's not so good now, but . . ."

"Yeah, I know. It will be better soon." Then Tad turned to Tom and said out of the corner of his mouth, "One of those damned bootlickers."

The Sato quarters were a long way from the gate, and they passed one long row of buildings after another before the guide finally stopped before a door.

"Well, here you are," he said cheerfully, pushing the creaking door open and standing aside to let them pass. Then he disappeared.

Mother Sato stepped inside, followed by her family. They set down their baggage and looked appraisingly about them. They were in a low-ceilinged room about ten by twenty feet, partially divided into two sections by a low partition. The rough walls were covered with a thin coat of whitewash, and the floors were freshly painted asphalt.

Mari sniffed the air curiously. Tom saw her and he, too, began to be conscious of a peculiarly unpleasant odor.

Tad laughed harshly.

"Sea Biscuit lived here. Maybe even Man o' War. We ought to be proud." His voice was bitter.

Yes. They knew they were in the stable where horses had been kept. The low partition divided the stall from the feed room. The whitewash and paint had

215

not been able to cover up the stench of ripened manure.

Yoshi looked beaten.

"We're not going to live in a barn, are we?" he asked plaintively.

"Sure, kid. Anything's good enough for us. Maybe they'll feed us oats for lunch."

Yoshi grinned sheepishly, not knowing whether his big brother was joking or not. He turned to his mother.

Tears were streaming down Mother Sato's cheeks. They were to live in a stable. Her family had never had fine houses to live in, but they had always been clean and respectable. She and Papa Sato had worked and sacrificed that their children might have advantages. Now they were to live in a stable. What would Papa Sato think when he came? Even in their darkest hours, when crops had failed and money was scarce, when they were getting their start in America, they had never come to that. They had seen to it that their children had an education. There was Tad with a degree from the university, and Tom with his high school diploma, and Mari and Yoshi both good students, all of them good children. Living in a stable. Mother Sato would have laid down her life if by so doing she could have spared her children this indignity.

With the coming of darkness that first night spirits sank. The time had been occupied since arriving in standing in line for meals, standing in line at the washrooms, and in getting their mattress covers fitted with straw for their cots. Now the Sato family were together in their quarters again. Tad had sworn after the unappetizing lunch of rice and tea--eaten in sodden clothes after standing in line two hours in a heavy drizzle--that he would not go back to the mess hall that evening if he starved to death.

However, after the others had been gone some time, he realized he was hungry and there would be no raiding the refrigerator later in the evening like he did at home, and he went over. Being late he had to take what was left--cold potatoes and a slice of moldy bread. Suspicious little teeth marks on the crust gave away the secret that mice had tried it first. He had washed down the potato with some tea and had just returned to the quarters looking sullen and dropped down on his cot.

Tom and Mari were expressing their opinions of their surroundings. Tom was restless with nothing to do--no night work with the tractor, no produce to truck to market in the morning, no irrigation water to turn off before he went to bed. He was homesick.

The letter from his father burned in his pocket, and he was sorry he had not told the folks when he first got it. It would have been better then, there at home, even if they were just leaving, than to tell them here in this dreadful room, this horse stall. Tom was discovering that there is no good time to tell bad news.

Tad had brought an old newspaper he had picked up at the mess hall, and he began to read aloud from the pages. "Multimillion dollar race track at Santa Anita, the world's most beautiful and luxurious racing plant, yesterday opened its gates as an assembly center for Japanese evacuees.

"As nearly as possible, the evacuees will live lives as normal as can be arranged under the circumstances.

"They will have the freedom of the grounds."

"Hell," he exploded, throwing down the paper.

They called it an assembly center, but to Tad and Tom and Mari and all the others the place had barbed wire around it and armed guards in the watchtowers, and you daren't walk outside the gate under penalty of death. You visited your friends--if you had any--through the fence, so if it weren't an internment camp, then it was just another place by the same name. It was easier for Mari to submit to the insult of it; she had been taught submission. But to Tad and Tom, trained as Japanese boys to think of themselves as "gods fallen from heaven," this confinement without charges or a hearing was unspeakable. Tad felt it was more than he could bear.

While they lounged there griping, Mother Sato was unpacking the things she had brought to make their quarters more cheery. She had rested that afternoon while the others were filling the mattresses, and she was feeling brighter.

The boys had set up her cot and Mari's behind the low partition where they would have some little privacy, and from time to time she would come out bringing something to brighten up the room. A paper shade with flowers painted on it which she put over the single light bulb hanging from the ceiling, a large calendar from Wilson's Feed Store, the one which had hung in the kitchen by the hall door and had a brightly colored picture of woods and stream and an Indian in a canoe. It still had the month of March on it, and when she had hung it to one of the large spikes which stuck out all around the wall, Tom looked up and saw where he had marked the day he had set out his tomato plants. The cloisonne vase Papa Sato had brought her from Japan on his last trip was brought out, balanced on the narrow window sill a minute and put away till a suitable and safe place could be found for displaying it.

Now Mother Sato came and stood in the half-door with something in her hand. She shook it out and held it up proudly. It was Norio's little silk flag.

The children looked at it in rebuked surprise. Not one of them had thought of bringing one. When Tom saw so many people with them on the train, he had thought about it and wondered why he hadn't brought one. He had asked Mari if she had. He said it would be nice to have a flag for the Fourth of July and times like that, but Mari had not thought of it, either. It had been their mother, the alien of the family, who had thought of it. Mother Sato would like to have been an American, would have been proud to take out citizenship papers and be an American citizen with her children. But she was barred by the laws of the country from doing so. Nevertheless, she was jealous for her children's rights and privileges.

"Too many Japanese here," she said with deep concern, speaking mostly to Yoshi. "You might forget you in America. Now you can look at flag every day-- remember." She looked about the stable for a place to

218

display it. A knothole in the rough studding yawned vacantly, and Mother Sato thrust the flagstaff into it. There the doughty little flag which had such an important mission to fulfill unfurled itself and spread its colors out as far as it could reach over the whitewashed boards as if by covering some of the rough, ugly wall it could lessen by that much the shame which had come upon its family.

Mother Sato gave a reproving look at Tad as she turned to go back to her unpacking, but she did not say anything. Where she had found the flag after Tad had packed the things in his room and thrown the things he did not want to keep into a trash box to be burned would remain a secret between them.

Tad felt he never wanted to look upon the Stars and Stripes again. It brought back too many unhappy memories. Things he wanted to forget, to put out of his life forever. Things at camp when he was in uniform getting ready to go out and fight to save democracy in the world, good things when he belonged, when he was just another G.I.; things back in high school when he used to snap to attention and salute the flag saying, "with liberty and justice for all" and thinking it meant something; things at the university, going down with a bunch of students to picket the docks and keep scrap iron and oil from being shipped to Japan. They all carried little flags then and wanted to keep their country out of war, wanted to stop arming her potential enemy. Yes, there were a lot of things Tad wanted to forget that were all tied up with the red, white, and blue. Now it maddened him to see it turn up here; this was no place to prod the emotions when they were already spent. The air in the room became stifling to him. He got up from his cot and went to the door.

"Say, I'm glad you brought that, Mom," Tom said, not knowing what was the matter with Tad.

"Mom thinks of everything," Mari added. "You just see if everytime you want anything she doesn't go bring it out. I don't suppose you brought a thing for yourself in your suitcases, now, did you?"

219

"Oh, yes. I brought two dresses. Everything I need." The mother was pleased with Tom's and Mari's assurances, for she was afraid Tad was angry with her.

"You going somewhere, Tadashi?" she asked as she saw him go outside.

"Yeah. I'm going to walk around outside and get some air before I go to bed." His words were commonplace enough, but there was something ominous in his voice. She wanted to run and call him back.

When Tad was outside in the dark he stood for a minute drawing great, deep breaths of air to clean the vile stench of the stable from his lungs. But even outside the odor persisted. His head was a ball of fire, and the cold, greasy potatoes he had eaten for supper were churning about like stones in his stomach, growing harder every minute. As he stood there miserably, the revolving searchlights played across the grounds and the pointed barbs on the new wire fence glistened like sparks of fire as the light caught them in its piercing white rays.

Tad heard a stifled sound from the stable next door, and he held his breath and listened, tense. A woman's muffled sobs. No privacy for sorrow here. He must not listen.

A light breeze sprung up from the east, and the sweetness of orange blossoms mingled with the fetid odor of the stables in a sickening blend.

A quick attack of nausea seized Tad and he ran toward the latrines beyond the racetrack, but he could not reach them in time. He stepped aside from the path and stooped over to vomit. Again and again he bent almost double, still retching violently long after his stomach had been emptied. At last the convulsions stopped, and he lay down on the dew-laden grass, weak from the effort.

Despair overtook him. It was a frightful thought that one could become ill and die here in this unorganized camp where thousands of people had been thrown together even before adequate plans had been set in motion for taking care of the well. He became morbid, hopeless, irrational. He went back in his mind and began to mull over all the circumstances of Norio's death. He recalled the day he had come home for the funeral, how he had insisted on going into the room alone, how he had stood and looked down upon what had so recently been his scholarly, warm-hearted brother, and the sight of the dead face had terrified him. It couldn't be that Norio would never speak to him again. It was an awful thing to have life go out of a person.

"Oh, God, don't let me die in a place like this."

It seemed to Tad now that Norio had had little to bear in comparison with what had happened to the rest of them. It was hard for one so brilliant and ambitious not to be able to secure a position, but to be knifed through the very vitals which a man lives by: character, pride, honor, self-respect, freedom. If disappointment had broken Norio's heart and robbed him of his desire to live, what would this internment do to him?

Had he been right about Norio? Was it possible for the impact of the emotional upon the physical to be fatal? Could acid bitterness of soul poison pure red blood? Could eating in leaden misery cause the digestive processes to stop while one died of slow starvation? Could the deadly weight of mental anguish lie so heavily upon the chest that the heart could no longer beat nor the lungs draw in air?

He was suffocating. Panic gripped him. He raised himself on his elbow and looked about him, wild-eyed. Here and there around the grounds he would see figures moving in the dark, moving aimlessly, others like himself, all caught in a trap. The glare of the searchlight fell full upon him, and he cursed it for hunting him out in his distress and robbing him of the privacy kindly night had given him.

He thought of escape. What chance? The sentries behind their machine guns and the high fence had enclosed him so securely that he could feel the prick of each jagged barb in his flesh. He soon discarded the

221

thought. Only a dead man could get out of there.

No, there was no physical escape. But there were other possibilities. He felt too weak and sick to reason now. He was too confused and helpless to do anything for himself. If only his father had come home before they left, if he could have been with them during this ordeal, how much easier it would have been. Maybe he will come soon. Maybe he is already on the way. Tad buried his damp, cold face in his sleeve and sobbed like a small boy for his father. Imprisoned as a dangerous enemy alien. His father's words the morning they left Japan came to him. They were standing by the rail taking a last look at Fujiyama as the steamer headed out to sea. Tad knew his father had been disappointed over his visit, everything had been so changed; but the sadness in his eyes now Tad mistook for regret over leaving.

"You can come back often, Dad, now that we kids are all grown up. It will be more like it used to be when the war with China is over."

There had been a mistiness in his father's eyes as he shook his head.

"No, son. I will never come back to Japan. I do not want to come again. I find I am an American now. I cannot be a citizen, but I have lived there so long that I am an American at heart."

Tad got to his feet and began to weave about like a blind man. Several passed him as he tried to find his way back to his quarters. One man started to speak, but diffidence stopped him from intruding on another's troubles. All were heartsore and weary in the camp tonight.

If Tad could have talked with someone that night, someone whose feet were firmly on the ground, whose belief in the ultimate triumph of right and justice was unshakeable, how different the months ahead would have been for him and his family! But he was surrounded by other displaced persons like himself in an artificially created community where fear and insecurity in greater or lesser degree were the common

222

experience of all. Even while he was stumbling along, caring little where he went or what happened, a high school boy in quarters not far from the Satos, unable to accept the disgrace of his father's arrest and the internment of his mother and little brothers and sisters in a horse stable, was sitting on the edge of his cot in the dark, deliberately tearing his army blanket into strips and knotting them into a noose.

There were some in the camp who could have helped, older men who had gone through the fire of racial hatred and discrimination in years past and had come out philosophers. They could have guided those boys who were taking evacuation so hard. They could have told them that it is what is inside the man which makes or unmakes his life, not what is done to him from without. Later these men would make their influence felt in the days of internment in the permanent camps, but it would be too late then to help some. They would already have chosen to walk down the wrong side of the road.

Tad approached the Sato quarters. He had found his escape as he had done since his discharge from the Army, in bitterness and resentment toward all authority and a determination to resist with all his strength until he was a free man again.

He struck a match to find the right number, and in the dungeon like darkness inside he struck another to locate his cot. By the flickering light he saw the letter from his father lying on the floor where it had fallen from the pocket of Tom's coat. He picked it up and read the brief message at a glance. The match burned to his finger tips, and he dropped it to the bare floor where it flickered out unheeded.

Found guilty!

Tad dropped down on the rustling straw mattress with his clothes on, drew his knees tight up against his stomach to ease the gnawing emptiness, and prayed for sleep.

XII

The long caravan of busses made its way across the desert through the dead of the night. The passengers had been told before they started that they were to travel at night to avoid the heat of the day; and, as they sweltered in the stifling heat of the crowded busses, they wondered what it must be like on the desert in the daytime.

The Satos were on the move again. They had been held in the assembly center along with thousands of other evacuees for several months while permanent camps were being constructed. Now they were being taken to one of these camps on the Arizona desert.

Life at Santa Anita had become more comfortable as the camp became better organized. There had been plenty of recreation and plenty of time for it. Tom and Mari and Yoshi had entered into the games and club and school activities and, if they would have admitted it, had had a good time. Yoshi had kept in touch with Jerry, so he always had the latest word on Malt's new life; and Peg and Allen had driven up once to see Mari and Tom. They kidded about having to visit through the fence and pretended it was a great joke; but there were deeper currents underneath, running parallel to the laughter. Allen and Peg were shocked and hurt to see their friends behind barbed wire, and Tom and Mari were so humiliated by the situation that they could not enjoy seeing and visiting with them and were relieved when Allen said they would have to start back because he was due at his ship in two hours. He had already had one trip to the South Pacific and had seen action.

Mother Sato had had leisure for the first time in her life, and, in spite of her concern over Papa Sato's failure to clear himself--he had been moved to a camp in New Mexico after his unsuccessful hearing--she had made many friends and had gained in weight. Surrounded by so many other Japanese-speaking people, she had found plenty of company, and there had been classes and recreation for the older people, too. Flower arrangement, and painting, and sewing were a few of them.

Only Tad had remained aloof from the activities of the camp. He had joined himself to a group of like-minded fellows all bent on sabotaging any efforts on the part of the camp administrators to make the place as livable and constructive as possible, under the circumstances. Since the assembly center was under military discipline, they had to work undercover, using intimidation of those who cooperated as their main weapon. They were a disturbing element and kept themselves in a state of hot rebellion, as well as causing constant anxiety to their families.

As the permanent camps throughout the Rocky Mountain area were completed, groups of evacuees had been moved out along through the spring and early summer. Many had gone on ahead to settle in the Arizona one as each unit was ready. Now it was August, and the third and last unit there was ready to receive its unwilling residents.

The caravan had stopped at Desert Center, well-named, for it was the only stopping place in the one hundred and fifty mile stretch across the open desert from the Arizona border to Indio in the Coachella Valley of California. It had been two in the morning, and it was hotter than the hottest summer day they had known, even on the ranch. The whole, great, empty out-of-doors was like one mammoth, overheated room. There was no way to get away from it. It surrounded them, it was everywhere, there was no escaping it. No matter how much you suffered from it, there was no relief. There was something alarming to the people from the cool coastal areas about this weird, unnatural heat in the middle of the night, knowing that they were sentenced to live with it as best they could for no one knew how long.

It seemed that they had left civilization when they had pulled out of Indio. No more lights of towns were to be seen along the highway. No touch of man's hand in citrus groves and date gardens. No more roadside stands tempting thirsty people to buy the sweet Coachella grapefruit juice or a tall date malt. It had all been open desert in its virgin state, desolate and forbidding, as it spread out before them, drenched in the floodlights of a full moon.

Back from the highway, scarcely visible even in broad daylight, stretched miles and miles of army tents, their olive drab blending with the desert sand. Men in training for desert warfare--air forces, medical units, armored divisions. Quantities of equipment arranged in orderly rows--tanks, jeeps, big guns.

Once the caravan was delayed behind a slow Army convoy, and all along the way for miles signs warned of danger from night maneuvers. Occasionally a jeep went tearing past on the dirt road paralleling the pavement, throwing a cloud of sand through the bus windows into perspiring faces.

Dawn had come at last after an endless night of discomfort, and the sun had risen out of the sand in the cloudless eastern sky, a huge ball of heat and blinding glare, lighting up the burnt earth and making the sandy wastes look even more bleak and desolate than they had under the more kindly light of the moon.

As the sun climbed higher it beat down upon the tops of the busses with a broiling intensity, converting the interiors into veritable ovens which threatened to cook the very flesh of the passengers.

The sight of green trees along the Colorado Rover told them that the end of their journey was near. Soon they were crossing the long river bridge. California was left behind; they were now in Arizona. The little town of Parker was just ahead.

Parker, gateway to the camp at Poston, sat on the open desert, halfway between Phoenix and Indio. Sat there beside the Colorado in the empty desert like a creature who had lost his way and had squatted in the barren sands near water, the accumulation of his living scattered in heaps of rubbish about him. In its isolation, it had become suspicious and crafty and inclined to show its ugly teeth to strangers.

When the government moved in to construct the camp for Japanese evacuees on the Indian reservation some twenty miles below the town, the place worked itself into a frenzy of suspicion and hate. Some businessmen hurried to paint large signs on their doors warning, "Japs keep out," and the barber's was the largest of all. Did he not have three sons in the service? His patriotism knew no bounds. "Keep out Japs, you rats," his sign read.

So those in charge of transportation of the evacuees hurried their charges from train to bus at the dirty little station or drove the overland bus travelers along the edge of the town and whisked them away from the place. Once they were safe in the camp below, they were not allowed to go to Parker.

So all summer long the busses crowded with their unwilling passengers had been lumbering through the town and off to the south along miles of narrow roads covered deep with fine dust. Winding between cotton fields, along rows of tamarisks with lacy foliage drooping under the weight of powdery coating, past unpainted Indian shacks half-hidden by high banks of irrigation ditches, until finally they rolled out into a wilderness of mesquite and creosote bushes. Here the camp had been built.

Into this shell of a town of black tar paper barracks, named Poston for a government engineer of earlier days who had looked out over this bleak expanse of wasteland and dreamed of a beautiful valley full of the green of growing things, the first evacuee residents had been moved in May; and since then, block after block had been filled until a city which was second in size in the state of Arizona had come to Parker's very door.

But her hermit days living on crusts had made her blind to the opportunity for better things which had been thrown in her very lap. She had owed her continued existence economically to a few ranchers along the Colorado, the Indian agency nearby, a scattering of

Indians from the reservation, and the small government colony at Parker Dam. Two or three small churches struggled to keep her soul alive.

Blinded by ignorance and prejudice, the businessmen of the town did not foresee the thousands of dollars which would go out of camp to mail order houses each month because the residents of the camp were not allowed to shop at Parker. They did not foresee the cooperative stores which would spring up in the new community through necessity to meet the demand of human needs and desires, and which would do a million-dollar business the first year.

No, blind little Parker, you did not foresee, did you? Neither did you foresee the still greater wealth which lay at your feet. Even the angels in Heaven would have coveted your opportunity. A beaten people, thousands upon thousands of them, passing through your portals. Being brought into internment, weary and hopeless and baked by the heat. How much a cup of cold water would have meant then. Later there would be those who would pass through your town again, going out timidly to freedom in a strange world beyond the Rockies. How much a friendly word of cheer would have meant to them, instead of the send-off of sticks and stones you gave to some.

But you missed your chance. So you will flourish for a time, like an obnoxious weed, on the troops in the desert and their wives and familes who have come to live in your midst. Greedily your saloons and stores will supply them with liquor and groceries. You will sell more than you have ever done before, but it will be only a drop in the bucket to what you might have had. In your niggardly greed you will sell bottled whiskey across the counter to the Negro troops from Boise, even, although you cannot bring yourselves to let them sit down at the tables, for you hate them almost as much as you hate the Japanese.

But when the troops are gone and your stores are empty of customers again, what then? Will you, standing idle, waiting for a sale, think of the gold mines to the south which you might have worked to your advantage and, since a good deed never dies, your everlasting glory?

It will be too late then. You will have no choice but to go back to your subsistence living again. And the mighty Colorado, wise in eternal values, who has seen civilizations come and go throughout the centuries, will continue to flow serenely by your borders, keeping her skirts unsullied from the rubbish which litters your soul and street, by the heavy border of trees along her banks. And she will have a story to tell of how she opened her heart to these lonely people and succored them and murmured soothing words as they sat on her shores and fished and thought of home and happier days, while they rolled the acid pill of bitterness on their tongues.

The Sato bus was at the head of the caravan, and the driver turned off the highway at the western outskirts of the little town and took the gravel road south. One by one the other busses swung around the corner, following.

The young people began to watch eagerly for anything of interest in the surroundings which might give promise, for they knew they were getting near to the camp now.

"Look! There's some sycamore trees," Mari pointed out. And the dusty tamarisks bordering the highway looked pretty after the long hours of nothing but barren emptiness. Maybe it wasn't going to be so bad on the desert after all. They had had nightmares thinking about it. There were mountains all around the horizon to break the monotony of sand dune and distant skyline. Needle-like peaks to the north and red sandstone bluffs to the east eroded into facades suitable for magnificent temples to the gods. And across the Colorado, rising from its banks, was a lofty range with here and there a rocky peak standing out above the others.

The gravel road soon ended, and the busses were tire-deep in dust. Choking clouds of it, powder fine, rolled up from the wheels and poured in the windows. It settled in the rivulets of perspiration running down

229

hot faces. When one tried to wipe it away, it smeared into grotesque masks until soon the travelers were a ludicrous sight. Elderly men, who up to this time had maintained their poise and dignity in the most trying circumstances, were now no longer venerable. People could scarcely recognize their own families. They looked at each other in silence. They were a comical sight. But no one laughed.

There was no laughter in them. They were hot and tired and disgusted and scared. They were well aware of the fact that they had not suffered only intense hardship or physical torture as people all over the world had suffered in bombed and occupied countries; but it was because this was so unnecessary. This was the thought that tantalized them and aggravated every discomfort or inconvenience into a major irritation. They knew, most of them that there was no reason why they should not be back in their own homes now instead of here on this scorching desert. They should be home carrying on their work, profiting while business and prices were good, so that they would have something for the lean years. But, no, they must be idle. And endure every indignity and inconvenience. For what? For no good reason.

The heat was growing worse every minute with the ascent of the sun toward the zenith; and the rapidly increasing temperature raised new apprehensions in the already harried minds.

The sun was like a huge furnace heating the whole outdoors to oven temperature. There was no shade, no escape from its fiery rays. How could one live in such a place? How could they keep their children well in it? What would happen if anyone fell ill? Would there be doctors? Medicine? Both were scarce during war. Would the government bother to send scarce items to them? Or would they be forgotten once they were all out of California? Other fears pestered their minds. They felt so insecure because they were helpless to do anything for themselves. Would there be plenty of water, an unfailing source? Would there be sufficient

food? There was already talk of a food shortage in the
country.   They looked out the windows through the
clouds of dust at the dry, brown earth, and contrasted it
with the lush productivity of their home communities,
the abundance of fruit and vegetables, milk and eggs
always available.   Only the dusty mesquite and dry,
dead bushes. Not an edible thing in sight. It would be
possible to starve here. Everything they would eat in
the days to come must be shipped in.   Would the
government forget them under the pressure of war?

These and other vital questions clamored loud for
answers from some where as their overstrained minds
turned them over and over, while the busses plowed
slowly through the dust to Poston.

In spite of the heat and the forebodings, Mother
Sato napped fitfully; and Yoshi, worn out by the long
night of wakefulness, slept soundly with his head on his
mother's shoulder.   The mother opened her eyes now
and then, but took no interest in the passing landscape,
being in no hurry to see what she knew could not be
good.

When she judged from the rising state of expectancy among the other passengers that they were almost
there, she reached in her bag and brought out some
cleansing tissues with which she began to wipe the dust
and sweat from her face and Yoshi's.   She only
succeeded in smearing it and making their appearance
worse than before. The boy grimaced in his sleep and
turned his face away. Mother Sato looked around at the
others.

Tad had shed his shirt, and his T-shirt, damp with
perspiration, had collected dust until it was the color of
the desert. He was slouched down in his seat, looking
out the open window through half-closed lids. This insolent drooping of the eyelids until only a narrow slit of
an opening was left had become a habit with him. It
gave him a devil-may-care appearance and, together
with the scornful curl of lip, completed the impression
of insolence and contempt. Mother Sato looked now at
her eldest son and shook her head sadly. He had be-

come a stranger to her. And they used to be so close. He never talked with her anymore, so she could not know how he felt, what was going on inside him. If only Papa Sato had come--all those long days at Santa Anita with lots of time to talk together--she was sure he could have won Tad's confidence.

She turned to Tom and Mari. They were both watching out the window for the first sight of their new home.

Tom caught side of some long, low sheds, black and ugly through the dust.

"Heh, look! I hope that isn't it," he said, laughing at the possibility. The beautiful surroundings of Santa Anita had unconsciously built up false expectations for this new place.

"There it is!" someone shouted.

Everyone craned their necks to see.

It was a depressing sight, the long rows of tar paper barracks with not a sprig of green in sight.

"What a hell of a place to live," Tad muttered without moving his lips.

"We'll have to plant some trees and flowers. Maybe they're all right inside," Tom suggested.

The bus pulled up before a group of frame buildings painted gray. Everyone got up and crowded the aisles, eager to be off where they could stretch tired limbs and find a drink of water.

But no. Not yet. A man had come abard, one of a volunteer group of Nisei who had come to the camp early, before the influx of population, to help the administration prepare for the people. These men stood squarely with the administration policies and were out to sell the place to each group of newcomers.

This man now began to make a speech. Everyone sat back again, disgusted.

"Fine time to pick to make us a speech," Tad grumbled, trying not to hear anything said. "They've got us here. There'll be plenty of time to lecture us."

Tom gave the man his attention in spite of Tad's mutterings. He wanted to get all the information he

232

could. After all, this was where they were going to be; he wanted to know how to make the best use of whatever was available to make life profitable, and maybe agreeable.

The Nisei talked first in English and then briefly in Japanese. He outlined the plans of living, urged everyone to sign up for work of some kind and to cooperate with those who were trying to make the place an ideal community which would have the best interest of all at heart. The fellow adopted a sort of Chamber-of-Commerce tone in describing the possibilities of the place, but his enthusiasm was largely wasted on the weary listeners.

Tom caught a little of the spirit. He was ready to get to work at something again. Santa Anita had been a long vacation. Work would be good.

The speaker ended by saying the administration-- puffing out his chest a little as he identified himself with that all-powerful body which was to run the camp--knew they were all tired from the long, hot ride and would make the routine of checking in as speedy as possible. If there were less than five in a family, they must be prepared to have others living in the same room with them. Secretly, each Sato was glad that there were five.

The passengers began filing out, parents clutching tightly to their children.

In this first contact with the administration, they found it as good as its word. After a hurried physical once over, fingerprinting, and an opportunity to sign up for the Work Corps, the Satos were off again, this time to the third and newest unit of the camp a few miles on further south. On their way down the narrow dirt road they passed the second unit, which looked more forlorn, if possible, than the main camp had done. A few miles on beyond, they came to the section of the camp to which they had been assigned.

It was truly the "end of the trail." There the road stopped. On beyond there was no human habitation to be seen, no sign of life. The block to which the Satos had been assigned was at the farther end of the camp, and the bus stopped before the mess hall for that block, where the family climbed out along with several others. The thermometer outside the wide door of the mess hall barracks registered one hundred and twenty degrees.

To the new arrivals who exclaimed over such a high temperature, one of the "old-timers," who had been there three months and who was standing watching the procession of the arrivals, a bit of excitement in his empty day, said superiorly, "Oh, that's nothing. It was fifteen degrees hotter last week."

Two shining new garbage pails filled with ice water were sitting just inside the door, waiting for the new people.

"Drink all you want," the reception committee invited, as they dipped up the water, filling paper cups. "You may never get another cold drink around here."

Of course, everyone was dry, no drinks since Desert Center; but some drank with caution, sipping the icy water slowly. Others, especially the young people, drank in great gulps, cupful after cupful, and then found themselves doubled up with cramps in a short time.

After they had had their drink and had sorted out their baggage from the heap the baggage truck had dumped before the mess hall, the Sato family started out to find their "apartment," as the family rooms had been designated by someone with an unjustified degree of optimism. They were to be in Barracks Number Eight, and they found it to be a corner barracks, with their apartment "A" on the west end, with the double rough wooden doors opening out onto a small platform two steps above the ground level.

Tom threw open the doors, and they all looked in. The room was twenty-by-twenty-four feet. There was no ceiling, nor interior walls, only bare, rough boards above, below, and around them. There were knotholes in the walls, through which one could see readily into the next apartment where people were also moving in. There were two regulation army barracks windows in

234

the north and two in the south. The room was bare of furniture, except for five army cots. Every place which would hold it was covered deep with the fine dust.

"Nothing here that water can hurt," Tom said cheerfully. He was sort of forcing a "Boy Scout on a camping trip" attitude. "I'll see if I can find a hose and wash the place out. Make it cooler, too."

He went back to the mess hall. Everyone was after the same things, hoses and brooms and buckets to clean up their rooms. Some were belligerent and demanding. Tom discovered the right approach got what you wanted from the block manager's office. He returned to 8A and hosed out the room from roof to splintered floor, the water running through the wide cracks in the floor to the ground beneath. Tad sat on the stoop outside the door, leaning on his elbows, groaning with pain from drinking too much ice water. Yoshi was off already. He had found some boys he had known at Santa Anita.

"Mmmm, smells nice and clean," Mari remarked as she came in refreshed from her shower. She sniffed the clean smell, thinking of the stable they had just left yesterday which had never entirely lost its odor of horses no matter how many disinfectants and deodorants and colognes they had squandered on it.

"Yeah. Nice place," Tad retorted. "We're coming up in the world. Maybe the next time we move, we'll have a chair." Bitterness was eating Tad up, and he was never heard to say a pleasant word to anyone. He felt better now and got up and helped move the bags inside. He got a towel and some clean clothes out of his and started for the showers.

"Heh, Sis," he called back. "Where are the showers? Any hot water?"

"See those two short buildings down there in the middle of the block? The first one is the men's and the next is the women's. And then that long one at the other end is the laundry. Yes, the water's scalding hot, and it comes out fast."

It was convenient not to have to walk so far to the latrines as they had at the assembly center, but the

235

complete lack of privacy in bathing or taking care of the other needs was not pleasant.

Tom set up his mother's cot first, so that she could lie down and rest awhile before time for the evening mess. The water had cooled the air in the room a little, but the sun was getting around to where it came in the open door.

"We'll have to grow some vines to shade the door," Mari said.

"I could build a trellis over the porch if I can get some lumber," Tom planned vaguely. Everything was so strange. He didn't know yet whether he could go to town. Some of the fellows who had gone to Granada had written him they went into town shopping whenever they wanted to; but he had rumors that it was different at Poston, that the nearest town wasn't friendly to the evacuees. Well, he would soon learn the ropes and know where he could get the things he would need to fix up the bare room into a home. Tom had a surprise in store when he was to find out where people in camp got their lumber.

He and Mari took a couple of the army blankets and curtained off a corner for Mother Sato's and Mari's cots to give them a little place to themselves, and Tom found a few nails in one of his pockets and pounded them in the wall above the knotholes. They hung clothes on the nails to shut off the view of the next apartment. This would do until they could find a better way. When he had done all he could with what he had to make the place comfortable, he went for his shower.

Around five-thirty the mess hall gongs began to clang. They were makeshift affairs; any old piece of metal which would make a loud noise when hammered on would do. There were triangles, and straight iron bars, and broken pieces of old wagon tires; and one block boasted a real bell, which someone had secured from back home, maybe a discarded church bell, which pealed out the call to chow in genuine style three times a day. The gong in the Sato block was a short piece of railroad rail suspended from an arm of wood nailed to a post. When beat upon with an iron rod by an evacuee who could put his resentment against evacuation into the beating, it could make a din which was capable of rousing an opium addict out of his deepest dreams. The Satos soon learned to distinguish its melodious tones from those of the other gongs in nearby blocks; but today this sudden clatter coming from all directions at the same time, with new ones breaking in at short intervals, sounded like the beginning of a riot.

Tom ran to the door and saw everyone heading for the mess hall at a sprightly pace.

"Come on," he said, lighting out, not waiting for anyone. "It's time to eat."

It was nice not having to wait in line. The family had followed Tom promptly, for everyone had a good appetite, and they all went in and sat together on one side of a long, picnic-type table with board seats nailed to the table at each end.

They saw and nodded to many of their Santa Anita acquaintances who had preceded them to the camp and some friends who had come all the way from La Vista with them; but there were many strangers in the large room, and the family which faced them across the table they had never seen before. There were the father and mother and two sons, one about Tad's age or slightly younger, and the other a handsome lad in his early teens. His coal black hair and long black lashes with his unusually fair complexion gave him a striking appearance, even without the charm of manner and the high degree of intelligence which one noticed later. There was something very appealing, too, about his modest self-assurance.

It was easy to see that the boy was eager to talk to these new people, but he held back, knowing it was for his parents or his older brother to begin.

The evening meal of cold wieners and boiled potatoes, with bread and jam for dessert, left ample time for conversation. Tad gulped his food and left the table, not having uttered a word to anyone. The father and mother engaged Mother Sato in conversation, and

Haruo spoke to the young people, addressing himself particularly to Tom. Haruo was the older brother and the younger one was named Mas.

"Just come today?"

"Yes. Came through in the night from Santa Anita," Tom answered.

"It must seem pretty hot to you here after Santa Anita. We don't mind it so much, for we have it plenty hot at home up in the San Joaquin Valley."

"I've never been inland. I didn't know it could be like this anywhere," Tom said with a grin as he mopped the rivulets of sweat from his face.

Mas broke into the casual remarks about the weather. His mind never dwelt on small talk.

"Say, if you're just new, you'd better tell them about some of the things down here, the scorpions and things like that."

"How about telling them yourself," Haruo said, with a look at Mas which showed a deep affection for his younger brother. "You know a scorpion when you see one, and that's more than I can say. Mas has been reading up on all the flora and fauna of the desert since we came down; he'll be a specialist if we stay here long."

"Well, I guess you'd better tell us anything we ought to know," Tom said. "We're all pretty green about living on the desert. What kind of an animal is a scorpion, anyway?"

"A scorpion is an invertebrate of the order of arachnida; that's the scorpions, spiders, and mites, among others. You find them in tropical regions, and they are all sizes, from two inches long up to eight. Each of the front legs has a pair of pincers, and the tip of the tail has a poisonous sting in it."

Yoshi and Mari were taking in all Mas was telling. It wasn't helping any to lift the spirits which the unsavory meal had lowered to rock bottom. Life on the desert looked anything but attractive.

"Gee whiz, I don't see how they can bite anything, with their pincers on one end and their stinger on the other," Yoshi said, scoffing at the idea.

238

"Maybe they're acrobatic," Tom remarked, and they all laughed. The laughter left no feeling of strangeness between the young folks.

"Do they ever really sting anyone?" Tom asked.

"Oh, yes. They surely do. There are about twenty species in Arizona, and two of these are known to be deadly poison. Both of them are found around here. So you must learn to recognize them if you want to live. I found one in my bed when I turned the blanket back one night."

"Oh, boy!" Yoshi shouted. "Did you kill it?"

Mother Sato turned and spoke reprovingly. Children didn't shout at the table.

"I certainly did, but not until I had had all of the family see it so they would recognize one again. You saw it, Haruo."

"Yes. I remember. But it looked just like the centipedes back in California to me, all legs."

"There is no similarity," Mas said in a positive manner. "This one was about two inches long and was yellow, sort of honey color. That's the most deadly one there is."

Mari looked about at the open, screenless windows and had visions of swarms of the deadly things flying in the rooms at night on their murderous missions and stealthily stinging the whole family in defenseless sleep.

"Can they fly?" she asked Mas, horrified.

Even Father and Mother Endo laughed at this.

"Has Mas been scaring you newcomers with his scorpion stories?" Mr. Endo asked kindly. "Fortunately, they do not have wings. Why the Creator gave them a poisonous sting I do not know, but he was good enough not to give them wings to make it easier for them to use their sting."

"Why, no one could live here if scorpions could fly," Mas declared.

"That would be all right with me," Haruo said.

Mas looked up at his brother, a shadow crossing his face. He knew it hurt Haruo to leave college and come to the camp, and he could not bear to see him hurt. But

Haruo was smiling, so Mas went on enlightening the Sato family.

"If you ever get stung, send for a doctor right away, and while you are waiting for him to come, keep the stung spot immersed in cold water."

"Where would you get a doctor here?" Mari asked.

"Yes, and where would you get any cold water?" Tom put in. "I turned on the tap to get a drink this afternoon and thought it was tea running out of the faucet."

"It gets colder if you run it long enough. The sting is something like a bee sting, only it doesn't swell; it gets numb, and you begin to have pain in other parts of your body. And then you have convulsions, and that's the end."

Mas went on describing the scorpion and finally agreed to bring the one he had killed and mounted over their apartment so they would be left in no doubt if any of them met up with such a monster some night.

"Which barracks are you in?"

Tom had to think.

"Eight A," Mari said.

"Have you got any rattles? You know, off of rattlesnakes?" Yoshi asked.

"No. But I can show you some. The cook killed a big snake under the mess hall here yesterday. It had seven rattles, and he's got it stretched up outside. Do you want to go and see it?"

Mas took Yoshi out the side door, and Tom and Haruo went out together. Mari and her mother went back to their apartment.

"Want to look around a little?" Haruo asked.

"Yes. Sure." Tom felt the heat of the evening sun burning his neck. "But it's kind of hot now."

"You'll soon get used to it. There's a ball game going on over by the firehouse. We'll go over there. That's a good way to forget the heat. They're playing the semifinals."

Haruo was right. As they watched a good game with plenty of excitement on the sidelines, the fans yelling for one side or the other because the players came from their hometown--there wasn't so much block spirit now as there was to be later on--it was easy to forget the heat, even to forget for a few minutes that you were in a concentration camp.

After the game, Haruo escorted Tom around the camp, describing the layout.

"You see, the camp is laid out in blocks, like any town, eight barracks on each side, and in between, where the alley would be at home, are the latrines and the laundry. You have to know your way around pretty well, especially at night, or you find yourself in the wrong place. The women are always having to shoo some nearsighted old man out of their showers. The mess hall is two barracks put together side by side, and back of the mess hall on the opposite side of the block is the recreation hall. In between is the oil tank where the oil for the cook stove is stored. Every block is the same."

They stepped to the door of the recreation hall and looked in.

"Just like all the others, except there are no partitions. And nothing else, either. But we'll get the room fixed up somehow, when the weather gets cooler. They say they are going to use the rec halls for schoolrooms in the other units, but we've got a whole block set aside for school.

"The fellows and girls have a deuce of a time about dates here. No place to get together and no place to go except church Sundays. A fellow doesn't want to go to a girl's apartment and sit around all evening with her mother and father and all the little kids. And the whole bunch crowded into one corner by five or six beds. Once you've tried it, you'll know what I mean. And the parents of the right kind don't want their girls running around the camp at night; and I don't blame them from some of the things I've seen. The girls can use the library for an excuse to get out in the evening and then meet their dates and go strolling around, but it's not much fun. When we've got the rec hall furnished, we can have dances and parties and have a place to come for a social evening."

It sounded to Tom like life as usual. Dates and dances and girl trouble.

"There's a canteen over in the next block to ours," Haruo said as they were on their way home. "Want to walk around that way? Maybe they've got ice cream tonight. A nice guy running it. Say, he's from down your way, maybe you know him. His name's Imoto."

Imoto. Could it be the same Mr. Imoto of the market?

"Well, I could surely eat something more after that supper," Tom said, turning with Haruo toward the canteen.

"We usually can," was Haruo's short reply.

The canteen seemed to be the center of interest. People coming from all directions. People going nibbling on candy bars to satisfy the hunger which the inadequate supply of food at the table had failed to do.

Tom didn't recognize the canteen manager as his old friend at first glance. Most of the man's weight had melted off in the heat, and his present dishabille was not characteristic of the city market owner as Tom remembered him.

Mr. Imoto himself was the first to speak.

"Hello, Tom. Sure glad to see you."

"Well, what do you know! Imagine finding you down here."

"Why, I've been here since last June, over two months now. Tom's an old standby of mine," Mr. Imoto said to Haruo. "He and his dad raise the best vegetables in San Diego County. Just come in today? I saw a string of busses headed this way when I was up in Unit One this afternoon. Well, this is quite a place, Tom, quite a place. Guess we'd all like to be getting that cool breeze from the ocean tonight, wouldn't we?" He wiped the beads of sweat from his face. It wasn't round like the full moon anymore, but it was still merry.

Now Tom could begin to see the Imoto of the market.

"I'm doing a million dollar business here, Tom. And I make sixteen dollars a month."

Tom didn't know what to say. It embarrassed him to see a prosperous businessman reduced to this level. But the little black eyes which looked into Tom's were twinkling, and Tom could see that Mr. Imoto was making the best of it until he could do something else.

"Did you sign up for work, Tom?"

"Yes. I asked for agriculture, but I don't know what I will get. They told me they are going to clear and plant thousands of acres, and I thought that would be about the most important thing a fellow could do for his country now, besides fighting."

"Tom, you're all right. I see so many fellows in here who are bitter and warped. I don't hardly see how they will ever get straightened out again. It sure does me good to hear someone talk like you do."

"Well, I'm still an American, and I want to act like it."

Other customers were coming in. Mr. Imoto leaned across the counter and spoke to Tom in a low voice.

"I wouldn't say things like that out in the open, if I were you. I can't explain why now, but you'll find out for yourself soon enough." Then, raising his voice, he said, "I could have used you in the canteen, Tom. Well, come in again."

There was no ice cream and no cold drinks, so the boys each got a candy bar and went out.

The sun was dropping below the California ranges across the river. Welcome departure to the sweltering campers. Once a day a gasp of relief went over the camp as that glaring ball of torture sunk out of sight and the softer lines of twilight crept over the place, hiding the ugliness. Not that it got much cooler after the sun had set, but the dark was kinder to the eyes.

"Well, I guess that's about it," Haruo said after pointing out the school block, now empty and dark, but which the people had been promised would house a school when the weather was cooler, and the rec hall in Block 329 which was used as a church. "Mail comes to

243

the block manager's office and you get it there. Tanimoto is manager in our block, a good guy, lots of pep. He gets all he can for us."

"Seems accommodating. I got the hose from him."

"I forgot to tell you we have been promised a movie once a week, but I don't know when they will start or what they will be like."

When they reached the home block, Haruo asked Tom to come into his apartment awhile. Mr. and Mrs. Endo both spoke excellent English, and there was a comradeship between them and their children which the Sato family had never known. The Endos had a cooler, and the room felt chilly to the boys coming in out of the hot night. Tom asked about the cooler and thought he would try to get one, but Mr. Endo said the summer would be over in another month and it would take longer than that to get one and have it installed, the way things moved in Poston. Haruo and his father had made chairs and a table out of scrap lumber and had put up shelves for their books. Mrs. Endo had made pretty ruffled curtains to hide the ugly barracks windows, and soft pads for the chair seats and backs. And Mas's share in making their room more homelike was a bouquet of zinnias which he had grown in a box outside. The place was quite livable, though crowded with four in a room.

When Tom left, Haruo made an excuse to walk home with him.

"Want to see where you live," he said. He and Tom had clicked from the beginning, and he seemed loath to let Tom go.

They sat down on the steps and talked some more.

The long desert twilight had deepened into soft dark night. Hot, starlit night. Everyone was outside, except the few who had coolers.

They talked of evacuation and what they thought about the government's action; and Tom found that Haruo thought the same as he did about the fundamentals. This pleased him and drew him closer to his new friend. Haruo was older than Tom and had had a year and a half of college.

"I don't mind it so much for myself, this being shut up down here," he told Tom. "It isn't going to influence me one way or another. But Mas. I hate it for him. Now look, he's starting his sophomore year this fall. If they do have a high school here, what kind of a school can it be? Bare rooms. No laboratories, no library, no gymnasium. No anything that makes a school good. And what kind of teachers will come to a place like this to live? The administration is planning to house them over in the school block in the same bare rooms we all have. Maybe there wouldn't be anyone willing to teach Japanese with the war on. Someone who couldn't get a job anywhere else, maybe. But what kind of school could they run? It isn't likely any teachers from California will come."

"I don't know about that," Tom said quickly. "I don't believe most of the teachers swallowed that newspaper propaganda. The ones in La Vista, that's our home school, were swell to the Nisei as long as they stayed in school."

"Well, we'll have some kind of classes whether any outside teachers come or not. A lot of the college students are getting ready to teach. A busload of fellows and girls go up to the Indian school to a training school that's been set up especially to get them ready. Maybe you know Bill Harada. He comes from your part of the state. He's going to teach math."

Tom nodded. He was watching the sky. There was a constant display of sheet lightning along the horizon to the south and east. The soft flashes of light playing across them and the overheated night air enveloping them gave a sense of unreality to Tom. He felt he was dreaming of being shut in a hot, dark oven, and the bright points of light above him were sparks of fire in the firebox of the immense stove. If he could only wake up and get the door open so he could get out again where it was cool and fresh!

Mother Sato and Mari and Yoshi came in from where they had been sitting with some neighbors on their homemade benches, said good night, and went inside to bed.

"There are other reasons why I hate to have Mas here," Haruo went on. He seemed to be trying to tell Tom something, in a roundabout way. Things he felt he should know at the beginning of his enforced sojourn here. "The way we live in camp, with everyone dumped in here together, no privacy or real home life, the young fellows don't act the way they did back home. They are all pretty darn sore about being here and living this way when most of them have been accustomed to much higher standards at home. Good home, good car to run around in, and the best school buildings in the country. They've let down. They do a lot of things they never did before. Some even take things that don't belong to them. You can't blame the kids too much. Nothing to do to keep them out of mischief. And they think anything they can get from the government belongs to them, lumber for basketball backstops, tools and materials to make things out of. So far I don't see any change in Mas. Mother and Dad expect the same of him that they did at home, and he seems to take it for granted. But some of these kids, their parents can't even correct them without getting insolence and profanity thrown back at them. If they do that with their parents, I don't know what they'll do to the teachers when school begins."

"I don't think we'll have any trouble with Yoshi. He's just a kid yet, and he's always been easy to handle. Of course, it isn't the kind of place I'd choose for him or any of us, but I think he'll be all right."

Tom was really thinking about Tad. What was this place going to do to him? Santa Anita had been so offensive to him that the family had been afraid at first that he was not going to survive evacuation. He hadn't eaten for days and grew so thin and depressed that Mother Sato, after crying and pleading with him to no avail, asserted her authority and ordered him to go to the clinic. She also found ways to send outside for fresh fruit and other tempting foods to whet his appetite after the medicine the doctor gave him had eased his indigestion. But Santa Anita had been heaven compared to this barren place. What would the isolation and discomforts of the desert do to Tad?

"Our students have always had a reputation for high standards of scholarship and for good behavior," Haruo said. "But with everything so different, makeshift school, no school or community traditions or stability, no spur to study to try to outdo the other students because maybe you are looked down on because of your race. There will be just one big gang of mad kids, all the same color. I'm glad I didn't sign up to try to teach them." Haruo shook his head.

Tad came slowly along the dusty road, looking in.

"Is that you, Tom?"

"Yeah. This is the place," Tom answered, chuckling.

"Good thing you were out here, or I never would have found it. I forgot our number. How is anyone to sleep in this beastly heat?"

Haruo got up to leave.

"Wring out a bath towel and put it over you. It works swell. Good night."

XIII

Mari had been with her mother more constantly in the fifteen days since they had come to the desert camp than at any other period of her life since infancy. At Santa Anita there had been so many activities in which she had joined with the other girls--sports and clubs and lectures and community sings, among others; and besides, the unsavory atmosphere of the stables, and, in contrast, the beauty of the grounds and the cool mornings and evenings, kept the evacuees outside their quarters much of the time, so Mari saw little of her mother except at meals or bedtime.

But here it was different. It was too hot to walk or sit outside during the daytime. Only the necessary errands were done, like walking across camp to the post office for stamps or a money order. Mari and Mother Sato sat around their barracks quarters all day, day after day, stirring about only enough to do the things which might bring some relief. They hung wet towels over the windows, hosed the floor several times a day, and sprinkled the ground around the door outside. Their long hours of leisure were consumed in this one-sided battle with the heat.

The whole camp was apathetic. Many of those who worked did so half-heartedly and gave the impression that they were incompetent and irresponsible. Those who did not work lay around their barracks or grouped themselves in one barrack or another and aired their grievances over the injustice of sending them to a place like this. At Santa Anita they had felt themselves still a part of the world outside. Friends had come to visit them; even strangers who were sympathetic had come and brought gifts of food and words of good cheer. Transcontinental trains rushed by on their way east, or approaching the end of their long trail west. Streetcars rumbled past day and night, and heavy traffic moved on the wide boulevard. Green trees and bright flowers met their eyes at every turn, and orange groves and vegetable gardens nearby were assuring.

Here there was nothing except complete isolation. There was no fence around the camp, only a guard station at the north end and one seven miles below at the south border. Anyone could walk out of camp in between day or night and strike off across desert to--death--not freedom. For how long would a person last on those vast, sun-beaten stretches of uninhabited sand without shelter or water?

Thrown in with strangers and forced to live the communal life with them without personal or family privacy, people became suspicious of one another. Instead of being drawn together into a cohesive unit through the common bond of their unhappiness so that they might build together a community life as comfortable and agreeable as possible under the circumstances, their reaction to their situation and to each other was more like that of a series of negative poles, actively repelling one another. Their similarity of experience threw them apart rather than drawing them together. There was almost no tendency in these first stages of camp life to organize socially or to work for constructive civic development. There developed a competition, where things were scarce, for each family to get their share or more of what was available. Stealth and cunning came into play in getting special rations, an extra carton of milk to take to one's quarters, oranges and apples when they were on hand at the mess hall, a loaf of bread and some butter. They could not all have these extras--those who got them became objects of dislike and envy and suspicion. People built little mental walls around themselves behind which they hid until such time as they could find out whom they could trust.

So Mari and her mother were much alone. Tad had found many of his Santa Anita gang and one or two of his university friends, and Yoshi divided his time between trips to the canteen and play with some of the other boys of the block who had made an excavation under one of the barracks which they kept damp and which provided a cool place to lie and read and talk about home on the long, hot afternoons. Tom was working with a bulldozer, clearing off the mesquite.

Mother Sato was losing her battle with the heat. On this fifteenth day of their life in the camp, she suffered a heat stroke.

Now the boys had come home in the evening for mess, and Mari was watching a chance to tell them without her mother hearing. Mari had been worried for days. She could see her mother failing a little each day. Then the women had come carrying her home from the laundry while Mari was bundling up the clothes, ready to go over.

They had put her on the cot and put hot towels on her head while they took turns fanning her in an effort to help her get her breath. Mari had been dreadfully frightened. One woman told her an aged grandmother in another block had died of the heat the week before, and another family had lost their newborn babe at the hospital in Unit One because there was not enough moisture in the air to sustain the new life. This had not helped to quiet Mari's fears for her mother.

It was not until after supper that she had her opportunity to speak to Tad and Tom. Mother Sato had insisted on getting up before the boys had come home and went to the mess hall as usual. She did not want them to know and worry. What could they do? Now she had gone to the latrine to brush her teeth and bathe her hot face.

"We've got to do something about Mom," Mari said hurriedly as soon as she was out of hearing. Mari wanted to say what she had to say before Tad got away for the evening.

Tad slouched back on his cot, then raised up again and gave a quick, angry brush to the mattress which, with its covering of fine dust, felt as gritty as sandpaper against his bare arm. There was always dust everywhere. The eyes, scalp, lips, never free from the irritation. It sifted in at the tiniest cracks; there was no shutting it out.

Tom was reading. That was his escape each evening. It was an old book by Ralph Conner, donated to the local library, which some unselfish evacuee had been good enough to start, by a friend in California. Her name was in the front of the book. It was a story of the north woods, and Tom was far away from Poston. His eyes were inflamed from the cloud of dust in which he worked each day, and the light from a single bulb hanging from the ceiling was not good for reading, but he was not conscious of either.

Mari now addressed herself to Tad as the most likely to hear, as he was not occupied with anything more exacting than a study of the boards in the roof.

"I tell you we've got to do something about Mom. She's sick."

Tad laughed unpleasantly.

"I haven't heard her complain," he said in a voice that ridiculed Mari's fears.

"It's the heat. She can't stand it."

"Phooey! You're the one that can't stand anything. Can't do anything but gripe about everything." The words came with poor grace from Tad, for no one in the family had been a poorer sport or met the hardships which had come with less courage, but Mari did not argue with him. He only wanted to start a quarrel, and she had more important things to accomplish. The boys must be made to see the seriousness of the situation.

Tad didn't try to provoke his sister further. He was feeling pretty pleased with himself. He hadn't signed up for work at first, declaring he wasn't going to work for fourteen dollars a month for the government or anyone else. This camp wasn't his idea. Let the government employ workers at a decent wage to maintain it instead of having the nerve to appeal to the conscience of the people to get them to do the necessary jobs, cooking and washing dishes, trucking supplies down from the warehouse in Parker, emptying garbage, plowing up the dust into fields. All the dirty work out in the heat, while the big boys ate in their air-conditioned offices and bossed the show and drew down

251

fat government salaries. No. He was too smart to let himself be used that way. Tom was a fool to do it. Working like a slave at slave wages in dust so thick he had to wear a mask and coming home at night as grimy as a miner. There was a little unwilling admiration for Tom in Tad's heart, but he would not have admitted it.

However, when Tad found out that he could teach classes in the school which was to be opened later, he changed his mind about going on the government payroll. He announced one morning that he was going to attend the Training School, and he had been going every day. He was very secretive about his change of heart; but from the malevolent gleam in his eye when he talked about teaching, one could see that he had not chosen that occupation purely from altruistic motives.

"I know you never hear Mom complain, but that's because she doesn't want to make things harder for us. And she doesn't say anything about the food, either, for the same reason, and goes to the mess hall every meal so we won't notice, but she scarcely eats a thing."

"No one eats in hot weather," Tad said scornfully. "Especially when they aren't doing anything. That's what's the matter with you and Mom, you haven't got anything to do. Now if you had to get up and start out early every morning like I do, and study and listen to lectures all day, you'd forget all about the heat. Anyhow, the chow they dish up here--who does eat more of it than they have to?"

Mari was angry now.

"So we don't have anything to do? Who do you think provides you with a clean shirt to wear to school every day, and cleans clothes for Yoshi, and who do you think washes Tom's black, dirty overalls?"

Tom looked up from his book at the sound of his name.

"Heh! What's all the row about? How do you think a fellow can read?" he said with pretended indignation.

"Mom had a heat stroke in the laundry today," Mari said flatly.

"Well, why didn't you say so in the first place?" Tad

252

demanded. Anxiety replaced the taunting tones.

Tom laid down his book. Fear and insecurity began to drum on their minds with blunt, jarring fingers as always happened when an emergency arose. They had to stay where they were whether they lived or died, and no one seemed to care much about them one way or another.

Tad's anxiety made him bitter.

"Well, what do you want us to do? Send her to Mission Beach for a week?"

"No, Tad. I know you can't do that. But can't you think of something? I know Dad would if he were here."

The boys were silent. What could even their father have done? He would be as helpless as any of them in this situation.

"I could make a cooler if I had a fan," Tom said.

"But just try to get a fan. I had a fellow looking all over Los Angeles for one for me to bring down, and he couldn't find any. I'll bet everyone in Poston has tried to buy a fan this summer."

"I'll write to Peg. She'll get one for us," Mari said confidently. "Peg will get one if anyone can."

She got out her box of stationery and found it was gritty with dust. Could the dust sift into her violin case? she wondered. She would wrap it in many folds of newspaper and tie it securely. Of course, it didn't make much difference what happened to it; she never intended to play it again, and certainly not here. It was silly to have brought it all this way.

Tom snatched a piece of her paper and began to figure the materials he would need.

"Make a list," Tad said, "and I'll see you get the pipe and lumber and stuff."

"Got a drag with someone on the warehouse crew?" Tom kidded.

"Don't worry your head about that. Anything we get around here is coming to us."

Tom didn't ask any questions. If they had to have a cooler for their mother's sake, let Tad get the material

253

any way he could. Steal it? His mother's life or his conscience? His conscience didn't seem very important.

Yoshi came in, his body and swimming trunks dripping wet. In spite of the thermometer reading of 110 at eight in the evening, he was as cool as a cucumber. The small boys had solved the heat problem in this land of excessively rapid evaporation. He flopped down comfortably on his cot, indifferent to the puddle which collected in a hollow in the mattress.

"Get your muddy feet off that cot," Tad shouted.

"Sez who?" Yoshi yelled back impudently.

"Shh! Everyone can hear you," Mari said, looking up from her writing.

"Yes. Pipe down, kid. You're getting too big for your britches. You're in for a good trimming down."

"Oh yeah? Who's big enough around here to do it?" Yoshi challenged, grinning impishly at Tad. He wriggled the fast drying mud from between his toes.

Tad made a threatening pass at him but did nothing more. He was no help in handling Yoshi in his father's absence but was always ready to pick a fuss with him.

Mother Sato returned. She had stopped outside to visit with Mrs. Hayashi awhile. She made Yoshi get up and go out to wash his feet, while she brushed off the cot carefully, then sat down with a deep sigh.

Mrs. Hayashi had a husband in internment in the same camp with Papa Sato, and the two women had been sharing the news in their letters. International law in regard to prisoners of war protected their husbands in some way. The women didn't understand about it, but they did understand that the men had much better living conditions than their families in Poston.

Yoshi came back with clean feet, kicked off his slippers, and went to bed. Turning his face away from the light, he was soon asleep. Tom looked over at the back of his tousled head and wondered about the things Haruo had said. Was Yoshi changing? He had never heard him talk so saucily to Tad before. Maybe they should keep a closer watch on him.

Tad was watching his mother cautiously over the

top of a book on social studies he had brought from the Training School.

"Feeling all right, Mom?" he asked. "How about the heat?"

"Keep out of sun--all right. But that sun--ooooo, bad. I think the devil made the desert sun. Makes my head go this way." She made a gesture of circular motion. "You keep out of sun, too. Wear hat like Tom."

"How about in the laundry today? That wasn't in the sun."

Mother Sato gave Mari a quick look of reproof.

"Oh, that laundry--full of hot water--steam. Everybody wash. Next time I wash at night."

"Next time let Mari do it, and you take it easy," Tad said. "This is no place to get sick."

"That's right," Tom echoed. "We don't want anyone sick around here. If it takes as long to get a doctor as it does to do everything else, a person could get well while he was waiting." Tom decided not to say anything about the cooler until he was sure he could get the materials. He gave Tad the list and hoped for the best. That was the only thing he could think of to help the situation. Mari had promised to make her mother keep quiet during the day, and they talked awhile about their father, trying to cheer her and ease her mind. Maybe he would get another hearing. They had heard that some of the other men who had been convicted the first time had been released on a second hearing.

Mother Sato seemed brighter, and they turned out the light and went to bed.

There had been one more thing preying on Mother Sato's mind, and Tom remembered hearing her express her fears when, the next day, he learned that residents could order rice through the administration. He ordered a 100 pound bag which would be a bulwark against the starvation she feared for her family if the food shortages outside became worse and the government forgot them.

Within a week a package and letter arrived from

Peg. She had shopped all over the city for the fan, she wrote, and then found one in Charley's secondhand shop in La Vista, of all places. It was a good one, too. Someone had brought it with them from the east, Charley had told her, and traded it for a gas heater when they had found the evenings so chilly. Allen had completed his special training and had shipped out again the day Peg wrote, so they were all feeling kind of low. Be sure to write and let her know if the fan was all right.

Tad went off that night after dark and came back with lumber and nails and a length of pipe sufficient for the short distance to the connection at the corner.

Tom worked evenings, and when the cooler was on the platform outside the south window, one of the maintenance men he knew came over and helped hook it up. The Satos now joined that small and envied group of aristocrats--those who had coolers.

Tom flipped the switch, and as the cool air began to circulate through the room, Mother Sato nodded her head with satisfaction.

Tom was enthusiastic over the program of the Agriculture Department. Great things were planned, so he had been told. Some of the older men, the more experienced Issei ranchers, listened with skepticism to the plans on paper and the promises of the head of the department, and many felt they could do better if left to themselves to till the soil. But Tom and some of the other young fellows drank it all in, for it was something big to fill in the vacant space left by evacuation from home and repudiation by the government. Tom felt he might have even a greater opportunity for service here than on the thirty acres at home. The sky was the limit here. Thousands and thousands of acres of fertile desert land. All it needed was water and that was on the way in canals from Parker Dam. Four million tons of vegetables for the local camp annually--that was the goal to aim at first. Then later when more land could be cleared, vegetables for the other camps where the

256

weather or soil was not suitable for producing for local needs. But this was not all. They would grow for the Army, too. All this seemed like a tremendous undertaking; but it was only the beginning. The evacuees were to be allowed to grow a large surplus which they could sell on the open market and receive the profits. Here was an opportunity which Tom had never even dreamed would come his way. It gave him a chance to earn for the family and for himself. It put meaning into his future again. The war wouldn't last always. They would be out again some day. To go into the free world again financially solvent--perhaps college was not a futile dream after all.

Each day brought more cleared ground and the irrigation canals a few feet closer. Everything would be ready for a huge planting of winter and spring vegetables.

Some projects had already been undertaken and had ended in failure. Mistakes had been made. Seventy thousand guayule plants had died. Tomato fields had burned up in the summer sun. Willie Soto, who worked with Tom, pointed out these things as indicating their own labor would come to naught; but Tom had sized Wille up as antiadministration the first day they had worked together, so was not influenced by Willie's suspicions.

The head of Indian Affairs had been in Poston before the Satos came, and he had advised the residents in a paternal manner to make the best of things and be prepared to remain there from five to ten years. That gave the place the kind of permanency needed to inspire people to develop the land; but the older men were not gullible. They were willing to work, would be glad of the opportunity to earn during the years they must stay there, but they didn't care to work for the Indians for nothing, they said. They wanted things in writing. They were not satisfied with the ready promises given them by men who had no power to keep them, men who might be removed from their positions at any time themselves. They wanted concrete agreements in writing from the government. These they did not get, and the enthusiasm of many waned.

But Tom went on about his work every day, always on time, and usually the last one to quit in the evening. Then back to his block, a shower, mess, and a candy bar or cold drink at the canteen. Maybe a chat with Mr. Imoto if he weren't too busy. Often a walk and talk with Haruo. Then an hour of escape from camp in a good story in the comfort of their cooled apartment. This was his life. He was fairly content for the present.

Mari had been invited to join a club. The Cactus Club. It wasn't very exciting or flourishing. Just an excuse for a bunch of girls to get together and try to have some fun. Later they would do more--have dances and picnics to the river and hikes to the mountains when it was cooler. Were they allowed to go to the river and mountains? Mari had asked. Sure, if anyone could walk so far. It was a long hike through the dust to the river. Three or four miles at least. Maybe some of the fellows who drove maintenance trucks would take them if they promised them a good feed. It was strictly against the rules to use government trucks and gas for pleasure trips, but the fellows did it anyway and got by with it. Mari didn't know whether she liked the girls or not, but she said she would join the club.

Tad and Bill Harada had some hot arguments evenings after their return from the Training School. They were still as far apart as they had been the night of the mass meeting back home. How much water had run under the bridge since then! Bill still said, take everything which comes along and turn it to your advantage. Tad said, tear down the rotten and unjust and build something new and worthwhile in their place.

"But you can never get rid of all the injustice and greed and hate," Bill argued. "There will always be those things in the world, so find a way to turn them to your good. Now look at us down here. I've got time to do things here I've never had time enough to do before. I can read and study hours on end. The government supports me and makes this leisure possible. That's fine.

I can spend my money for books I've always wanted instead of for rent and food. I'd be silly not to take advantage of it.

"More than that. By teaching this year I have a chance to influence others. I'm dead sure I would never have been a teacher if I'd stayed at home. I'll try to shape these kids into real, independent Americans who will not defer to others, who will think for themselves and demand their rights, who will believe in no superior race, not even their own, but who will know superiority is an individual thing and comes as a result of what a man is and does."

"Good oratory, Bill. But I'll spend my last drop of energy working under cover against the administration for the way we are treated. I will oppose every Nisei who cooperates with it and takes advantage of the positions they get in that way and use to lord it over the rest of us. I'll show them up to the pupils in my classes. I'll teach them that resistance and antagonism are the only weapons the administration will recognize and that we must use them to gain respect and consideration. These Ad. fellows aren't any too sure of their jobs themselves. They don't know anything about running a place like this. They've never had any experience. They want to succeed. And I'll show them they can't do it unless they treat us right. There are plenty of us who think the same way."

"And if the organization of the camp fails, who will be the worst sufferers?" Bill asked. "If I have to be here I'd a darn sight rather have the place run smoothly. You're forgetting that all the government men here aren't bad. Just because some of them have the swell head and some hate us so they can hardly bear the sight of us walking upright, that's no reason to condemn the whole crowd. Now take our unit administrator. There isn't a better, more open-minded man anywhere than he is. If he can't get the things we need, we know it isn't his fault, it's the higher-ups somewhere along the line from here to Washington. If he could have his way he'd have a cooler in every apartment and food equal to his

259

own on every mess hall table. That's just the way he is. And his wife is tops, too. Ever been up to their barracks?"

"No, and I never want to be."

"They live in a tiny room about a quarter the size of ours. It's finished inside and that makes it look nicer, but it sure is small. And how about the prof who has come here to organize and direct the schools? Is he the kind of a fellow you want to antagonize and fight?"

Bill always came out ahead. Tad was confused. "They" were still something indefinite to him, someone he couldn't bring out in the open for a fair contest.

The Satos awoke one morning to the howling of the wind. Tom got up and looked out. He rubbed his eyes and looked again. He couldn't see the barracks only a few feet away. The air was filled with a swirling mass of dust.

It was the first dust storm for the Sato family.

No one went to work that day.

Mother Sato had to cling to Mari and Tom to keep from being blown away when she went to breakfast that morning.

The wind whisked about like a wild beast on a rampage, carrying with it fine sand which cut and blinded. It blew doors shut with deafening bangs, and before one could make them secure, whipped in from another direction and snatched them from one's hand to crash them out against the side of the building again. It seemed that everything loose must surely be dashed to splinters. Windows rattled like chattering teeth. Eddies of wind caught up stones and gravel and loose trash from the ground and whirled them high into the air as they traveled forward across the camp at the speed of a tornado. Unfortunate people caught in these eddies could only stop and clutch at their clothing with one hand to keep it from being whisked off while they threw their free arms over their faces for protection against the flying debris.

Dust sifted through cracks and settled thick over

the rooms. It got into throats and nostrils, and people coughed and sneezed.

"There won't be any movie tonight," Mari said gloomily that afternoon as she stood at the window looking at the storm. "It's a dust blizzard. People could get lost in it just like they do in a snow."

It was true. People were shut in just as completely as if it had been a true blizzard.

"If those damned engineers hadn't been so smart and scraped all that growth off the ground, we wouldn't have all this loose dirt to blow around," Tad complained.

All through the afternoon the wind kept up. Tom worked on some stools he was making of mesquite so they would have something besides the cots to sit on; and they could take them to the movies, too, for there would be no seats provided.

About four o'clock the wind left as suddenly as it had come, leaving behind it dust-filled apartments and red-eyed, nerve-wracked people. Everyone went to work to clean themselves out. Brooms and hoses and even shovels were used before the rooms were clean again.

At the mess hall that evening it was announced that the picture would be shown as planned. After the windy day a movie would be a welcome diversion.

XIV

They were sitting out on the firebreak after the movie, a half dozen fellows from the surrounding blocks who had started a tentative acquaintance in mess halls or washrooms or at work but were still in the process of feeling each other out. This strange atmosphere of suspicion which pervaded the camp had kept even Tom and Haruo from fully accepting and trusting each other, as congenial as they had found each other's companionship.

Haruo and Mas were in the group, and Tom and Willie and a younger boy named Harry. That was all any of them knew about him. And then there was a stranger that no one knew at all.

Mas was hardly one of the group. He lay on the ground, his arms under his head, looking up at the stars. At times something in the rapid-fire conversation going on about him caught his attention, but for the most part he was lost in his thoughts. When he had first come to the camp in the late spring he had run across a copy of the *Desert Magazine* at the block manager's office. In it he had read an article about the many kinds of precious and semiprecious stones to be found on the desert. On the occasional hikes to the mountains with his father he had found a beautiful moss agate into which nature had woven a design of mountains and trees. He had heard that there was a lapidary in camp, and he planned to have him cut and polish the stone into a suitable size and shape for a pin for his mother for Christmas.

Willie was sitting on the ground, his hands clasped around his knees. He was a small, hollow-chested, scornful fellow with a continual scowl on his thin face. He had been snatched out of his first year of college by evacuation and was sore as a boil about it. He had been sitting on one of the trucks during the movie, and so had Henry, the younger boy, who would have been too lazy to carry out a stool even if someone had made one for him. The stranger sat on a low stool made out of mesquite, similar to the ones Tom and Haruo had made. He hadn't opened his mouth, but he was giving careful attention to what the others were saying. The expression of contempt on his face was not completely hidden by the starlit night.

Tom looked at him suspiciously from time to time and wondered why he had stayed after the movie was over.

The air was still shimmering with heat. Yet in spite of the hot evening and the cruel lashing of the wind the camp had taken that day, between two and three thousand people had turned out to see the picture. From all directions they had come, beginning long before it was dark enough for an open air show, converging on the firebreak where it had been announced the picture would be shown, carrying their homemade seats of all designs of construction, ranging from three-legged stools to rustic armchairs with cushions, according to the ambition and originality of the designer.

Movie night was to become a weekly event in the isolated lives of these people--an event which was the red-letter day on their calendar--for there was nothing else in the way of amusement at that time. The sumo matches attracted only a small crowd of Issei, and the stage plays which were being started were all in Japanese and did not draw on the young people for their audience.

Each one, as he arrived at the firebreak, chose his own location. There was no plan for seating arrangements, but by the time it was dark enough for the picture to be flashed on the screen suspended from the oil storage tank back of a mess hall, the large crowd had somehow miraculously seated itself in an orderly fashion in the vacant block between the buildings which was known as the firebreak.

Around the back of the crowd some young fellows had driven government trucks in defiance of administration orders and had parked them in a semicircle skirting the audience. The trucks were filled to capacity, fenders, hood, and body entirely covered with young men and boys. It was a car, and any kind of car was a touch of home. Tad was sprawled on the hood of one of them with some of his gang.

Mother Sato and Mrs. Hayashi had sat together, Yoshi was with his friends, and Mari sat with some of the girls she knew. Thus the ties of the Sato family were weakening, as were those of the other families.

The picture had been a great disappointment, an old, worn-out film of the early thirties which had wound its dim, flickering way across the screen, barely visible at times. Frequent guffaws from the crowd on the trucks had drowned out the music and words.

At the end the trucks had gone roaring off, throwing a cloud of dust in the faces of the pedestrians and missing some of them by a hair's breadth. The older people shook their heads and wondered what was to become of their young people if they had to stay here long.

Now the little group clustered together on the empty, littered firebreak were expressing their opinions of the picture.

"Some film. And a Navy picture at that," Willie griped. The Navy had never been open for enlistment to the Nisei. "What a laugh. Suppose the Ad. think we will get all hepped up over seeing the flag and want to be nice, good little Americans and do whatever they tell us to."

"That must have been the original talkie," Henry drawled in a good imitation of Henry Aldrich.

"Not quite that old," Haruo said. "But I saw it when I was in grade school."

"And I thought we were promised a good picture every week," Henry groaned.

"Promises. Phooey!" Willie snorted. "Promises, promises, that's all we get down here. We were promised lumber to make partitions and furniture, and the only way to get a piece of lumber around here is to go out some dark night and find it before somebody else does. And cash advances to be made to us if we worked, and

264

instead of that we have to wait months after our wages are due and then fight to get the twelve dollars per coming to us. Don't put any stock in their promises. Just some more big talk like all the other hot air the administration's been blowing off. They seem to have the idea they can sell this hellhole to us. A screwy idea. They must think we are pretty damn dumb."

To Willie nothing in the camp was right. Everything was unfair. The better a thing looked the more suspicious he was of it. The more the administration did to make the place comfortable and the people satisfied, the more sure he was that they were being worked for something.

"The Colorado River Valley, most fertile land, a second valley of the Nile," he quoted oratorically, imitating a pep talk from one of the Agriculture Department personnel. "Make the desert bloom with our wonderful gift for farming. The devil take them. If we did make it bloom we'd soon have to give it up. Someone else would want it as soon as they saw it was valuable. Look at Imperial Valley--Japanese labor developed that sun-baked pile of sand into the rich vegetable and melon country it is today. And who has it now? The same way up in the San Joaquin. That river delta was nothing but a swamp. Now it's the best potato land in the state. And who has it? And a dozen other places I could name." Willie's voice was rising. "Our dads made the desert of sunny California bloom all right; and where are the old boys now? Some of them in prison camps, and others burning up in this damned place." He was shouting now. Mas turned from the stars to regard him curiously. "And now the Ad. had the nerve to ask them to start all over again at their age and make another Salt River Valley out of this dust bowl. And slave labor at that." Willie ended with a curse.

The atmosphere was charged.

"They get twelve dollars a month," Tom said in a light voice, trying to loosen up the tension.

"Twelve dollars and board and room," Haruo added

in the same tone. "Don't forget the swanky apartments."

"And clothing allowance," Henry put in. "Three bucks a month. That ought to keep a fellow in socks."

Everyone laughed at Henry. They usually did wherever he went. That is, all but the stranger. He made a kind of breathy sound between his teeth which sounded like an enraged gander.

"Well, we may make a good thing out of this deal while we're here, anyway," Tom said, "no matter who gets it afterwards. It's a good land. You can tell that from the size of the vegetables people have grown around their barracks this summer. If we can't go back to California, maybe we can buy some of it. My dad isn't old. He can ranch it for years yet."

"You can't buy a foot of this land," Willie growled. "It belongs to the Indians and goes back to them, with all the development our labor has put into it, when we leave. If we were really smart we wouldn't do a lick of work while we're here."

"For my part, I'd rather work," Tom said quickly. "Lying around here with nothing to do--that is the worst thing I could think of."

"Here, too," Haruo echoed. "Time goes faster when you're busy. Just as well work and make the best of it. We're here, and there is nothing we can do about that. We won't gain anything by bucking the administration all the time. You'll only get yourself in bad, Willie."

The stranger, who had been listening and nodding his approval of Willie's attitude, now spoke for the first time.

"That is the reason we are here," he said. His precise enunciation gave him away at once as a Kibei. "If your so-called Japanese American organizations had not been so weak and foolish as to cooperate with the authorities while we were still in California, they could have prevented evacuation."

His taunting accusation left the others silent with surprise.

"In Japan the Americans treat the Japanese with dignity and respect. Here you permit them to discriminate against you and you cater to them, trying to gain favors or be noticed by them. Here there are many who try to ingratiate themselves with the authorities instead of demanding consideration and fair treatment for all. In Japan you are looked down upon because you want to be Americans and allow yourselves to be treated as inferiors. Over here the Americans do the same.

"I attended the Imperial University," he offered by way of information. He told them his name was Hideo Yano and that he had been in Japan since he was five years old. "The students at the university do not have the money to spend that you do in America, but we are regarded with respect and we enjoy a social equality you have never known in America. When we graduate we have an opportunity to go to the top in our chosen profession. I have one more year at the university, and then I will have a fine position with the government. In Japan the government honors her scholars. What does it do in America? Puts them in concentration camps." When one of the boys started to protest, the Kibei went on determinedly. "When the University of California presented her awards at Commencement last June, where was her honor student with the highest scholarship rating? Was he there to receive the recognition of the faculty and the plaudits of the students for his great achievement? No. He was incarcerated in a concentration camp. What were the charges against him? He had Japanese blood."

None of the fellows had known of this incident, and they were silenced for a minute.

"But the Japanese government puts people in camps who have done nothing wrong. I know of one, an American missionary . . ."

"You have been misinformed," Hideo said firmly.

Then he went on eulogizing Japan.

"When she gets her industries organized in the newly acquired islands, Java, and Borneo, and others rich in natural resources, she will need many trained men, engineers, chemists, accountants, and businessmen

267

to run her factories and her rubber and sugar plantations. Great opportunities await the graduates of her universities. What do you have to look forward to when you graduate? Raising cabbage or chickens, or driving a truck, or mowing the lawn or growing flowers for some cinema star. You think you are Americans, but no one considers you so except yourselves. Evacuation should have proved that to you. And you never will be."

The other fellows had listened to Hideo's long tirade with mixed emotions. Tom thought of Norio and winced. There was too much truth in what the Kibei said to dismiss him lightly. He could cause a lot of trouble in camp with his talk. He wondered if Tad knew him.

Willie was inclined to be approving.

"I think you've got something there. We never have had a square deal."

This bothered Haruo, to see Willie falling for this pro-Japanese line. He addressed himself to Hideo.

"If you like Japan so much why aren't you over there fighting on her side?" he asked. He thought perhaps the fellow was one of those dual citizenship cases, born in the United States and registered by his parents at a Japanese consulate, thus making him a citizen of Japan, too.

"If I were in Japan I would not be in the army. I would be at the university. Students are exempt from military duty because of their importance to the nation in other capacities. But unfortunately I came to this country to visit my father, who was an importer in San Francisco, and the war which the United States forced on Japan began, and I could not get back. Now I am here in Poston. And my father is in a prison camp." His voice was ugly with hate. It was not the resentment and bitterness of the boys who really loved America but had been repudiated by her, but poisonous hate, hot and malicious.

Haruo turned and looked at Mas.

"Look at the size of those stars," Mas said softly when he saw he had his brother's attention. He stretched, and his body was as relaxed as a cat's. His face was free from any strain or disquiet.

Haruo had thought he would send him in to bed, for the conversation wasn't developing into anything he wanted him to hear, but he decided he was safe where he was. Maybe he had some insulation within himself which would make it possible for him to live through this thing, in the midst of all this disintegration and lowering of standards, and not be touched.

"You said you were born in this country?" Tom asked.

"Yes. In San Francisco. My mother died when I was born because the doctor did not come when he was called."

"You are an American, then, yourself. Weren't you afraid to come to the states on account of the draft? Or were you willing to fight in the United States Army if you were?"

Hideo looked around furtively before answering. He had lived too long in a country where one could be executed for talking, if overheard by the secret police.

Henry noted the glance and was sharp enough to understand it.

"Don't worry, Tojo," he said impudently, "there's no Gestapo around here."

Tom and Haruo laughed, but Willie continued to regard Hideo with considerable esteem.

"I don't owe this country anything," Hideo burst out indignantly. "Why should I fight for it?"

"Here, either," Willie echoed. "I wouldn't know what I was fighting for."

An electric shock went through the other boys. Those were dangerous sentiments.

"There's a lot of important things we are fighting for," Tom began staunchly. "The four freedoms . . ."

Hideo interrupted, his voice stinging with ridicule.

"You talk of freedom here?" With a sweeping gesture of his long arm he took in the rows of black barracks shrouded in soft darkness, barracks which housed confused, unhappy people, little children deprived of the comforts of home, the aged who saw nothing ahead but that dread of all proud people, dependency. Even as he gestured the lights of a jeep with change of guards came glaring down the highway, passed, and headed on toward the south guard station. They all saw, and it was as if the heavy boot of oppression had crushed down upon them.

"Oh, well, this thing isn't going to last always," Tom said, getting up and stretching and pretending he hadn't seen the guards. "We're just temporary war casualties. We haven't got too much to gripe about. You can't deny this is a good, safe place to ride the fighting out." He hated himself for talking like a coward, but someone had to say something. You couldn't sit there in silence with the MP's jeep running through your brain like a car on a race track and a voice yelling through a megaphone at you until it seemed everyone in the group could hear it, "You're under guard. You're under guard. Don't forget for a minute, you're under guard. You're dangerous. You're disloyal."

Anything to say, no matter how stupid, was better than listening to that.

Willie took up the conversation.

"Do you think Japan's going to win this war?" he asked Hideo.

"Of course," Hideo answered promptly. "She has won already, but her enemies will not admit it. Take a map and look at her present position in the Pacific. She has everything now except Australia and Hawaii, and she can take them whenever she is ready."

"She didn't get Midway," Tom retorted.

"How about the Battle of the Coral Sea?" Haruo asked. The boys didn't have many American victories to counter with, but they were determined to make the most of what they had.

Hideo was unabashed. He took off his glasses and wiped the perspiration from his face.

"That is the news you read in the American papers." He was condescending now.

Tom saw that the talk was going on, so he shed his

shirt and spread it on the ground to lie on. The mesquite stool was getting hard after several hours.

"You do not know what actually happened at Midway Island," Hideo went on arrogantly. "You should know you cannot depend upon the news you read in the American papers. Are the things you read about yourselves in the California papers true?"

"No, but . . ." Haruo began.

"Hell, no," Willie broke in.

"You see," Hideo triumphed. "And you don't see the truth about the war, either. I know what the papers say about the battle at Midway is not true because I have seen the power of the Japanese Navy and Air Force. That news was printed to encourage the people who have had nothing but defeats and make them willing to carry on a war that is already lost."

"If Japan has such a powerful military machine, why has it taken her so long to lick China?" Haruo asked. "China doesn't have any at all, in the modern sense."

"The Chinese are fools," the Kibei retorted, making that queer, breathy sound again. He was angry now. Haruo had touched a sensitive spot. "The Chinese are fools," Hideo repeated. "They do not know what is good for them. Japan wants to establish a coprosperity sphere for all of Asia, but China still prefers to fight for the continuance of white supremacy in the East. As soon as she sees the truth she will know that Japan is her friend."

"If the Japanese military would treat the people better in the occupied areas, wouldn't that help the Chinese to recognize their friendly intentions?" Haruo asked, holding the advantage, so he thought. "Torturing and killing civilians doesn't make friends."

Hideo laughed unpleasantly.

"It is hard to talk to you," he said, "because you have been kept in ignorance of the truth. You have a distorted view of the real situation.

"The Japanese have made friends wherever they have gone. The little children crowd around them when

271

they go into a town until they have to stop marching to keep from trampling them. The soldiers give the children candy . . ."

"Poisoned?" Henry asked.

"I have seen many pictures taken in China and sent back to Japan so that we might all know what our army of occupation was doing." Hideo ignored Henry's flippancy.

Haruo had listened to all he intended to. He was going to shut this braggart up or get rid of him.

"I think you are the one who has been kept in ignorance," he said. Maybe the Kibei was sincere and really believed what he said, but it was time he was learning better. "I have heard people talk who were in Nanking at the time that city fell to the Japanese, and the things they tell me are horrible, almost beyond believing. And I know they are telling the truth. They are fine, honest men and women who would have no reason for making up frightful atrocity stories. This was long before we got into the war with Japan that I heard them. They said they couldn't tell the worst, but what they did tell . . . well, the things those Japanese soldiers did, you wouldn't think human beings could be so low."

Hideo's cocksureness was puncture proof.

"You don't need to look so far for cruel and inhuman treatment. You can see it with your own eyes all around you here and know it is true. Old people dying of heat because they've been put where there is no escape from it. Isn't that murder? Sick people dying for lack of medicine or the special diet essential to their condition. Thousands suffering mental torture every hour of the day. How do you think these things sound to the Japanese government when it hears how its nationals are being tortured by the enemy over here?"

"I'm not trying to whitewash anything the Army has done to us here," Haruo said. "But I do say it is nothing compared to the brutality and ruthlessness in Nanking."

Hideo got up stiffly and picked up his stool. Without any formal leave-taking he left the group and

272

made his way across the firebreak to Block Three.

Willie had gone through the motions of getting up to accompany him, but had received no invitation and so sank down again.

When Hideo had gone the conversation turned to the outside. ·

"I wonder how things are going back on the ranch tonight," Tom mused. They didn't get much news from their tenant. "I'd sure like to be back there."

"Did you live on a ranch? So did we. What did you grow?" Henry had roused up at the first word about back home. He had napped off and on during Hideo's discourse.

· Tom told him about the cucumber crop and the tomatoes he had planned to raise.

"We'd be right in the middle of the tomato harvest now. I don't know whatever happened to the plants. The tenant never tells me anything."

"Sure tough having to leave things that way," Haruo sympathized. "Didn't it give you a funny feeling right in the pit of your stomach when you knew you really had to go?"

"You're telling me!"

"It was something you can't forget, even if you live to be a hundred."

"Where did you come from, Willie?"

"Up near Salinas. Know anything about that part of the state? Too bad. That's the garden spot of California, richest soil. To own a good ranch up there is to guarantee you'll be a millionaire some day. Never saw such vegetables. If I'd tell you how big, you wouldn't believe me. Lettuce so crisp if you drop a head it shatters like glass."

"Listen to the boy. Were you a member of the Chamber of Commerce up there?"

A couple of fellows had come up and stood listening to Willie. One of them broke into the conversation.

"Them sharks sure fleeced my dad out of everything." The others turned at the sound of his voice, aware for the first time of their presence. "The old man

273

was picked up Pearl Harbor day when he came in with his fishing boat. Those thieves got the store, house, boat, everything, for four hundred dollars. And our new Buick for forty-five. They gave a neighbor of ours just five bucks for a brand new refrigerator."

"What the devil did you sell out so cheap for?"

"Hell, what else could we do? We had only forty-eight hours to get out. Those guys called up and said they were the FBI and told us if we didn't sell our stuff to the buyers who came around, the government would take it after we left. Four hundred was better than nothing."

"That sounds like the Terminal Island evacuation."

"You're right, brother. That's where we're from. First they told us we had thirty days to get out, and we began looking around for a buyer for the house and a place to store our furniture and the boat. Then all of a sudden the time was cut to forty-eight hours. There wasn't time to do nothing. Somebody sent trucks down from Los Angeles, some church people, I guess, to haul us out. It took all day and night to get everyone out. It was awful working at night. We couldn't have any lights, they wouldn't let us hold flashlights even. We had to get some white person to hold them for us. Guess they were afraid we might signal Tokyo or something with them. It cost so much to live in LA that all we got now is what my brother here and me make--twenty-four bucks a month between us."

"The government ought to have to pay you back for all you lost on that deal," Willie demanded.

"If they will help the old man get another boat when he gets out, we'll get along all right. He's the best fisherman on the Pacific Coast."

The boys walked off as unceremoniously as they had come. One of them hadn't uttered a word. Just a couple of guys from Terminal Island, whistling as they walked away into the desert night.

Willie went on with his story.

"When the Army told us to move away from the coast, we went inland. Sold all our stuff and went over into the valley to live with an uncle of mine."

"Sell your ranch, too?"

"We didn't own the ranch. Dad leased twenty acres and we had it all in strawberries. They were getting ripe when we left. We sublet it on a share-the-crop basis, but we never got much out of it, and neither did the man who leased it. He didn't know anything about growing strawberries, and he wouldn't listen to anything Dad tried to tell him.

"We rented thirty acres over by my uncle's and put it in tomatoes. We thought we were safe because the officials had advised us to move to the valley when we left the coast. And then we got ordered out of there, too, just when the plants were about half grown. It's not having a damn thing to say about what you are going to do that is the worst.

"I stayed in college till the folks got their date of departure. There was a bunch of fellows in my room the night the wire came from my dad. I didn't know how to tell the guys, and I knew I would have to catch the midnight train home to get there in time." Willie stopped talking. He was reliving those moments. He was much softer now than when he had been castigating the administration earlier.

"How did you?"

"How'd I what?"

"How did you tell the fellows?"

"Oh, I didn't tell them. I waited until they were all gone out, and then I grabbed my things and stuffed them into my suitcase and called a taxi and went to the station."

"Didn't say goodbye to anyone?"

"Hell, no. And I never want to see any of those fellows again. I'll go to another college to finish, if I ever do finish. Maybe I'll go east when I get out of here."

"Heck, I don't feel that way at all about the fellows at State. I'd go back there anytime. They sure were swell."

"The men were all right where I was, too, all during that campaign against us. But I just don't want to see

275

them again, that's all."

"The first I knew about evacuation," Haruo said, "was when I saw the order stuck up in the post office. Even had one in the college station. 'All persons of Japanese ancestry' in big black letters you could read all over the place. Someone came up behind me while I was reading and stood looking over my shoulder. I didn't turn around to see who it was, but I felt my neck and ears getting hot and I wanted to shrink up real small and crawl out under the door where no one would see me. Then someone put a hand on my shoulder and said in a friendly voice, 'Looks like you picked the wrong ancestors, Endo.'

"I whirled around, and there was Eddie Carlson, a senior and a swell guy. He's in the Air Force now. He went around with me the day I checked out and told everyone I was under Army orders to go.

"I never actually realized what was happening to me, though, until I was on the bus and pulling out of town. When we drove past the campus and I saw the other students strolling around . . . well, I guess you never really know what freedom means until you lose it. I had the most empty, all-gone feeling. Don't think I'll ever forget it."

"I'm sure I'll never forget it, either," Henry said. "I had a girl back at Fresno High. Gee, she sure was pretty. A little bit of a thing with a lot of hair hanging around her shoulders in pretty waves and big, soft eyes that made your heart turn over when they looked up at you with that come hither expression."

"Oh, boy," Willie exclaimed, forgetting to scowl. "Heh, what's her block number?"

"Yeah. Give, fellow. What's her block number?"

"That's just the trouble," Henry groaned. "She isn't here. Her folks got sent to Manzanar and mine to Poston. Now what chance have I got?"

"Sure tough luck. But maybe she'll wait for you. You're something of a sheik, you know, Hank."

"I may be an old man by the time I get out of here. Anyhow, one girl's as good as another just so she's got plenty of oomph. I've already picked out a couple of cute ones here, but how am I going to get acquainted? I'm bashful."

"Going to school this fall?" Haruo asked. "That's a good place to meet them."

"Yeah. I've got to finish that one semester I missed while we were moving around. I would have graduated at Salinas if we hadn't had to leave. Now imagine having Poston on my diploma to show my kids and having them asking, 'What were you doing down there, Daddy?'"

No one could keep from laughing at Henry, he was so forlorn. He even laughed at himself.

It was cooling off a little now. A waning moon was rising over the mesa, and the coyotes began yapping nearby in the mesquite. Most of the lights had gone out in the barracks windows. Haruo wakened Mas, who went running on ahead of the others. Henry lit a cigarette as he started off alone toward his block.

"There was a lot of truth to what that Kibei said," Wille commented as he walked along with Haruo and Tom.

"Yes," Tom admitted. "Some."

"It would be nice to be the same as everyone else at college." Willie's voice was dreamy. "Live in a frat house, take your date to the dances and dance with all the girls."

"We have the same opportunity that anyone has in classroom, and that is what counts," Haruo said quickly. "And only a small percentage of the students participate in social affairs anyway. There's hundreds of fellows who go to State who never attend a dance or party the whole four years. An occasional movie date with some girl who doesn't belong to any social set."

"But that's different. They could if they wanted to."

"That's just where you're wrong. A lot of them couldn't. There are more reasons than one for social unacceptability. I've heard of students starting to college and then dropping out after the pledges are announced because they didn't make a frat or sorority."

"I even heard of a girl who committed suicide," Tom recalled.

"Social life and campus politics are both run by small groups of students, and the big majority have no part in either. And I believe it's the same in Japan, too. There are leaders who run things, and the others go to classes, join athletic teams, and plug. And I'll bet Hideo is not one of the leaders, either. He doesn't sound like any big shot to me."

Willie was somewhat deflated. He couldn't contradict Haruo, but he still liked the picture Hideo had painted of student life in Japan. He had always believed that he would be a great social lion if he only had the chance.

"Just the same, that boy knows what he's talking about, and I want to see more of him." He was almost defiant in his attitude toward the others.

"I'd advise you to keep away from him and others like him around the camp," Haruo warned. "Those guys are dangerous."

"That's my affair," Willie retorted stiffly.

They parted on a sour note.

Tom turned off toward his barracks. He felt apprehensive of the future in camp. He had become aware of the existence of conflicts within the group of Japanese itself, conflicts which were later to tear it in twain. He could see that it was not a case of evacuees on one side and the administration and all it stood for on the other, as Tad said, but that there were elements within the evacuee group working against the others with ends in view more inimical to their best interests than anything the government had done to them. He was beginning to understand what Mr. Imoto had meant when he warned him not to advertise his loyalty.

278

XV

Early in October a new and powerful influence came into the life of the camp. Schools opened.

The heat of the summer had been slowly relinquishing its dominion over the desert and giving way to the cooler nights of autumn. Although the day temperature was still around the hundred mark, that seemed relatively cool to those who had endured the summer.

On the surface, an atmosphere of listlessness and indifference lay over the camp. A casual observer might have concluded that the people had accepted their lot and that their emotional reactions to evacuation had been burned out by the summer heat, but such a conclusion would have been wrong. Beneath this layer of apparent lethargy the fires of resentment burned deeper with each added day of privation and discomfort and were constantly refueled by the mounting list of grievances against the administration.

Tom had not seen Hideo again after their meeting on the firebreak, but he and Willie worked together every day, clearing the mesquite, and from some of Willie's mysterious remarks, Tom got the impression that there was a group of pro-Japanese vigilantes being organized to work under cover and control the camp to their own liking through intimidation of the residents.

Willie, apparently under Hideo's influence, was convinced that Japan would win the war and seemed to feel that he was going to profit from it in some way if he got in with the right crowd here in Poston.

At first Tom had laughed at Willie when he made offhand remarks about how he might be making big money on a rubber plantation or that he was making plans to go out to college after Christmas to get ready for a big engineering job in the Pacific. Tom kidded him over thinking Japan could whip the United States and asked him how such a dumb fellow got into college in the first place. But when he saw that Willie was serious and became very angry under his joking, Tom learned to keep quiet. But it worried him. There was something going on undercover that he couldn't get his fingers on, but he knew it was there and that it wasn't good.

About this same time, Tom was losing his enthusiasm over the agricultural program. The plans had hit a snag. The irrigation project was months behind schedule, he learned. There would be no water for fall planting. There was evidence of poor management everywhere; the men who were doing the work did not agree. One would tell Tom to do one thing, and another would come along and stop him and put him at something else. The dust kept his throat and lungs irritated and his eyes sore. When he went to get his pay at the end of the first month, he found that his name was not on the list and he would receive nothing. Twelve dollars wasn't much, but he had planned to get some things he needed; and it irked him that the payroll office had been so careless when he had been willing to put out a good day's work every day in the heat to help put the program over.

Things went on in the same haphazard pattern in other departments. Blundering and inefficiency--that was what it looked like from the evacuees' side. That the delays in getting needed machinery and other equipment and supplies and the fizzling out of plans due to the tangle of government red tape, the fact that the administration was working under two bosses, the Indian Service and the War Relocation Authority, and the lack of experience on the part of all the administrators in running a camp of this nature, bothered and exasperated some of the administration officials even more than it did the evacuees, Tom and others, of course, could not know. They saw only the frustration and delays and gradually lost interest.

With the coming of autumn there were some half-hearted attempts at organizing social groups such as the club Mari had joined, and some group organizations from their former lives had been transplanted. The sumo exhibitions and the Shibai, or Japanese theatre, were drawing larger crowds, as the young people began to take more interest in things Japanese since their American contacts were cut off. But these few efforts toward satisfying the gregarious urge were only isolated cases in this large community of seething, milling individuals who were largely still strangers to each other, living in a strange setting, and all definitely at sea.

Now toward the end of September there were unmistakable signs of activity in the school block. Yoshi came home with the first news to the Satos. There was a man over there, a big, tall man with sandy hair walking around looking at the barracks. Next, several Issei were employed as school janitors and set to work cleaning out the dust-laden buildings. Finally the grapevine, the only vehicle of communication, passed the word around that the man was to be the new principal of the school they had been promised. The promises had been taken with mental reservations. There were many other promises yet to be kept. Even the knowledge that a director had been among them all summer preparing for the opening of schools and that some of the Nisei had been going to Training School had not been conclusive evidence for the more skeptical, and they represented the majority by this time. They had been told there would be no mass evacuation from California, too. They had been credulous enough to believe that one. But not anymore.

Anyway, the parents said, what would a school amount to, taught by the young Nisei who were inexperienced and just out of school themselves? And they couldn't believe that any experienced teachers, who could get a good position anywhere now with the teacher shortage, would voluntarily come to Poston and live under the conditions there. So the attitude had been a wait-and-see, hope-for-the-best attitude.

Now that the activities around the school block became convincing, interest began to pick up. Men, employed as gardeners, began to beautify the school grounds. Girls with commercial training were employed as secretaries in the office the principal had set up in the corner barracks. Soon advance notices of school

281

registration were posted in the mess halls.

Then the teachers from outside began to arrive and take up their residence in the barracks assigned to them in the school block. Some came by train and rode the old covered Army truck down from Parker. Some drove their own cars in and parked them beside their barracks and came and went as they pleased.

Grateful as parents were to see these teachers, their outbursts of merriment as they settled themselves in their rooms rang out across the adjoining blocks with a harsh note as it fell upon the ears of those who had come to Poston in such sorrow and heaviness. It had been no adventurous lark to them. Or did the sound of genuine laughter echoing through the camp loosen the grim lips into a smile? Who knows?

Parents stole interested glances at the teachers as they walked past the block. They were too polite to stare openly. What kind of people had come to teach their children in this crucial situation? Were they capable? Would they be understanding and kind?

Now that a school was assured, a new problem began to plague the minds of parents. The attitude of their children, notably those of high school age, toward the prospective school was contemptuous. What good would such a wacky school be? They didn't want to have anything to do with it. No teachers were going to come in there and boss them around. They adopted a defiant attitude, daring any white teacher to try to tell them what to do. Those who were not defiant but genuinely concerned over their education had little hope that they would receive any credit at real schools outside for any work they did here.

When it was announced at the mess halls that each pupil was to bring his own seat as there were no chairs for the classrooms, there was a howl of derision. School was a joke. Some of the high school boys declared they would not go. Parents who had insisted on having the education of their children provided for now began to fear that the children themselves were going to sabotage the efforts. They had become rude to their parents.

Suppose they offended their teachers or demoralized the school and the teachers became discouraged and left?

So the school opened under inauspicious circumstances on a bright, crisp October morning. Teachers crowded into the office to get last minute instructions and to ask the question which was in everyone's mind, "Have the books come yet?" How could they carry on without library or textbooks?

Bill Harada looked professional in a fresh shirt and tie, but Tad had chosen to show his contempt for his position by careless grooming. He had put on an old Army shirt from which he had ripped the insignia, but the stitching still showed, and a pair of worn khaki pants. As he stood near the door talking with a group of Nisei, he bristled with antagonism each time one of the outside teachers passed and spoke. He got his room assignment and went there and sat down to wait for his first class.

Mari got ready for school much as she would have done at home, wearing a plaid skirt and a pretty green sweater of light weight. She had shampooed her hair the night before and left it overnight in pincurls, her permanent was about gone. She combed it out carefully and let it fall in rings about her neck. Picking up the stool Tom had made for her, she started off.

She was soon joined by other girls who were also headed for the school block. The boys, rather sheepishly carrying their stools, strode by ignoring them, nevertheless doing a great deal of shouting and horseplay to attract attention.

At school nothing which had been ordered had arrived. There were no books nor pencils, no seats or desks. No blackboards or maps. In some barracks there were only low partitions between the rooms so that each class heard not only their own teacher but all the other teachers the length of the barracks.

It was education on the Mark Hopkins basis, teacher and farm boy sitting on a log, except that in classes where the Caucasian teachers, as they were called, were presiding, there were many farm boys and girls and many city boys and girls on one end of the log, and be-tween them and the teacher was a great gulf fixed--a barrier of race.

In the students' heated, irrational minds, the teacher stood for the race which had persecuted them, discriminated against them, and finally driven them and their parents from their homes into isolation and internment on the desert. To them the teacher was the embodiment of all the forces which had robbed them of their freedom and their right to go to a good school. They knew they were at an advantage here, for the teacher belonged to a minority group in Poston. It made some a bit heady. They would show him, or her, how it felt. Back home they had been spread out over the state with only two or three Nisei, maybe, in a school with Caucasian pupils and a Caucasian teacher; but here the teacher stood alone. To many a frustrated youth it seemed a chance to get even for all that had happened to him. In nearly every class there was a group hell-bent on breaking it up, and the more domineering they found their teacher, the more insubordinate they would be.

It was the impact of teachers with a program upon a solid wall of resentment and anger, and deep under-neath the sting of wounded pride. It was the teacher's personality and resourcefulness against the mass resentment which had been building up from the day the white posters appeared on the telephone poles back in California. The situation was full of dynamite. Who would win? How long would school last before the lid would blow off?

In the classes which had Nisei teachers the situation was different. Students and teachers were in sympathy with each other, understood each other, were bound together with ties of a common experience, and there was no barrier between. Those Nisei teachers, who were able to look at what had been done to them objectively, gave splendid leadership for their students in helping them to adjust themselves, in leading them out of the fog into a normal state of mind which made it possible for them to pursue their studies with profit, even under camp conditions. Others, like Tad, were not able to do this. They had not been able to get their own feet on firm ground, so they could not help their students, but rather floundered with them in the condemnation of the government, the Army, and the administration. In those classrooms there was a continual airing of grievances and a wallowing in a morbid sea of self-pity.

It was an unfortunate circumstance which divided the faculty into two economic groups. The Caucasian teachers were on the Civil Service payroll and received substantial salaries from the government. They had comfortable furniture in their barracks rooms and ate at the personnel mess where the food was known to be much superior to that served in the block mess halls. The Nisei teachers received the prevailing camp wage for professional people, eighteen dollars a month. Doctors and dentists and lawyers received the same. They lived in unfurnished barracks rooms with their families, sometimes seven or eight in a room, and ate in the communal mess halls. It will be forever to the credit of the Nisei teachers and a tribute to their tolerance that they overlooked these inequalities as well as they did and kept the friction to a minimum.

Tad, ridiculing some queer-looking specimen among the Caucasian teachers--and there were some museum pieces--said to Bill, "And to think that old discard gets over two hundred a month for doing the same work the government pays me eighteen dollars to do."

"You knew what you would get when you signed up to teach," Bill reminded him coldly.

"Sure. I knew it."

"It doesn't make any difference to me what I'm paid. I want to help these kids go on with their education--that's why I'm teaching."

"What the hell do you think I'm teaching for, the money?" Tad asked angrily.

"I'm not sure what you're teaching for," Bill said shortly, "but I hope it isn't what I think it is."

Tad laughed harshly.

285

This was as near as they ever came to quarreling, although they stood on opposite sides of nearly every question.

Sometime before school opened, a group of parents, concerned over the unpromising situation, had met and laid plans for a parent-teachers' organization. Then they plodded through the dust and the heat, going from block to block trying to sell their idea to others. Considering the deadly lethargy with which any constructive ideas were met, their success was surprising. School held a respected and important place in the minds of the people. Some had labored all summer in the heat to make adobe bricks for a school building which was to be built some day, and many of the crew were old folks who would have no children in school. Yes, the camp residents had a high regard for education.

It was felt that the organization could be a go-between for parents and teachers, could interpret the concerns and problems of the parents to the teachers and the program and goals of the teacher to the parents. Also, it might be able to acquaint the teachers with the background and personality of the Nisei student under camp conditions. Many of the teachers had come from the Midwest and the East, and some had never seen a Japanese face before coming to camp.

A reception was planned for Friday night of the first week of school honoring all of the faculty and welcoming the new members who had just recently come in from the outside. It was the first community-wide social event to be given in the camp, and the civic-minded few who were back of it were determined that it should be a success.

Mrs. Sugiyama came over to school a day or two after it opened to ask Mari Sato to play a couple of violin numbers on the program. Mrs. Sugiyama, who had been chosen to head the new organization, was a slender young matron, stylish looking even in the cotton print she was wearing, and a woman of poise and refinement. She had a couple of small boys in school, and it was she who had first suggested that the parents form an organization. Her seriousness and her confidence had been responsible for encouraging many parents to try to do something to make the school a success.

Mari came hurrying to the school office, wondering why she had been called out in the middle of a class. The students had learned already that the principal had some funny ideas and one could expect most anything from him. She was surprised to find a strange woman waiting to see her and more surprised still when she found out what the woman wanted.

"Oh, no, I couldn't," Mari refused at once, not giving the request the slightest consideration. "I don't play well enough. There are lots of other people here who must play much better than I can." Mari was not being humble. She was stubbornly set against playing. She had been robbed of the one opportunity which had meant more than anything that had ever happened to her. Certainly she would not play here. No, indeed. She was even incensed that she had been reminded of the happier days back home. Yes, each month she spent away from California enhanced the happiness of those days, until now Mari, in common with many others in the camp, remembered only the nice things back home, the good times they had had, the cool weather, the comforts, the easy chair by the radio, riding in the new car. All the hard work, the snubs, the unpleasantness was forgotten. They remembered only the roses of prewar days; they had forgotten the thorns. California had become a Garden of Eden from which they had been banished without having sinned. And so they tortured themselves, recalling the golden days as the Jews did by the rivers of Babylon when they remembered Zion, and fumed against the forces which had cast them out and doomed them to live in this barren land.

Yes, the very mention of her violin aroused anger in Mari.

"Now, don't be so modest. Of course you can play well enough," Mrs. Sugiyama urged gently, understanding the independent toss of Mari's head. "And we do want you so badly. Don't you think you could play for us just this one time?"

"No. No, really I couldn't. I--why, I haven't played for--for just ages." She could say "not since the night of the Spring Festival." And then asking her to appear in a barracks mess hall. Well, she wouldn't, and no one could make her.

"We think the reception is quite important. We parents want to meet the teachers and make them feel we appreciate their coming here to teach our children. And we want to honor the Nisei teachers and show them we have confidence in them, too. We must make a success of this very first affair, and a good program always helps to put things over. But we can't have a program unless the ones who are able to give good performances are willing to take part." Mrs. Sugiyama's voice was smooth and kind but earnest and persuasive at the same time.

Mari showed no signs of weakening.

"I'm sure you can find someone else."

"Well, I don't want to keep you from your class any longer," Mrs. Sugiyama said, rising.

Mari stood up and reached to open the door for her.

Then Mrs. Sugiyama seemed to come to a decision. She reached out and laid a restraining hand on Mari's arm.

"I know all about the Spring Festival, Mari."

"You do!" the girl exclaimed in surprise. She had been wondering who had told her that she could play. "Then you live in the city?"

"Yes. I have never lived anywhere else until now. I have been on the Festival Committee myself in former years. I couldn't even attend this time." She smiled wryly. There was no trace of resentment in her voice. "So you see now why I know you would do so much for our program. Anyone who is invited to play at the festival has got to be good. Besides, I have heard the maestro speak of you. He has great faith in your future."

288

Mari remembered how he had told her not to let anything interfere with her music; but he did not know anything about life in a concentration camp. Or did he?

"If you are letting that disappointment," Mrs. Sugiyama was going on in a quiet voice which could give no offense, "keep you from sharing your gift with others, then I think you are making a mistake. There is a very fine violin teacher from Los Angeles here in camp. I am sure she would take you if you want to go on with your lessons while you are here. And if you would have played for us Friday night, how much pleasure it would have given us. We have so little to enjoy here." Mrs. Sugiyama turned to go.

Now it was Mari who hesitated, with her hand on the knob.

Seeing someone who knew about the festival and the maestro and everything was like a breath of home.

"Well, I don't know about my violin down here, all this dust and the air so dry. The strings might all snap if I tried to tune it."

The woman smiled to herself. She was glad she had helped to break down whatever was blocking Mari, more glad of that than of having her on the program, much as she wanted that, too.

"Find out this evening, will you, and let me know tomorrow. You can send word by Sammie; he is in the third grade room."

Mari promised, and Mrs. Sugiyama left, satisfied.

Mari, seeing that her class had been dismissed, went on home walking with a lighter step than usual. She found her violin case among the luggage under the cot, brought it to the door, and took out the instrument. With her handkerchief she wiped off the fine particles of dust which had sifted into the case and stroked it gently, like some live thing. Then she tightened the strings and drew the bow across them softly, so that no one in the next apartment could hear.

"You going to play?" Mother Sato asked, excited at seeing her daughter taking an interest in her music again.

"I'm just going to see if it's all right," Mari said, noncommitally.

When Haruo stopped by on his way from work to see Tom, Mari was fretting over not being able to tune her violin. She told him about the reception, and he knew just the person to play her accompaniment. She was a senior, too, Yuri Takeda, and lived in Block 311.

"Why don't you go over and see her tonight? I'll show you where she lives."

So Haruo walked over with Mari after supper.

The sun had set, and the long twilight had begun. The air was still warm enough to enjoy sauntering, and Haruo took the longest way. He had thought of Mari only as Tom's sister before, but as he looked at her now with the afterglow of the sunset on her hair and felt the softness of her body as she brushed against him when she stepped on a rough place in the road, he began to think of her as a person in her own right, and a very attractive one.

And as is often the case when an inexperienced young man becomes interested in a girl, he began to talk about himself.

"I went up to Camp One to the Student Relocation Office today," he told Mari, "and I can get into Barton University next semester if I want to go."

"Oh, that's wonderful--to get out of here. When do you leave?"

"I don't know yet whether I'm going or not."

Mari turned and gave him a puzzled look. She knew how much he wanted to go on with his education.

"It's on account of Mas. I think maybe I ought to stay here this year anyway and help him over the worst. By then the place ought to be better organized, and he will be adjusted to camp life. Or maybe by that time I could take him out with me."

"Mas is all right. I don't think you need worry about him. He's about the least affected by the evacuation of any kid I know."

"Yes, but school is going to be rugged with the heat put on the students who want to study and get something out of it. Mas stayed after class the first day to ask the teacher something, and a gang of fellows waited for him and razzed him all the way home. And he said they weren't fooling, either. It's hard for a boy to stand up against the ridicule of the other fellows. If Mas is going to keep up his high school standard of scholarship, I think he is going to need all the moral support I can give him."

"Maybe so." Mari was thinking of some of the boys in her classes who seemed determined to block everything the teacher tried to do and laughed at the idea of doing any studying. "But to give up a chance to go outside." Her voice indicated that she thought Haruo was wonderful for making such a sacrifice.

They passed the main canteen, and, seeing the door still open, Haruo suggested they go in and have a cold drink. Their errand began to take on the nature of a date.

At the Takeda barracks Yuri agreed readily to accompany Mari and suggested they go over to the church then, since Mari had brought her violin, and to begin practice right away. The time was short.

She invited them inside while she explained to her folks, and it was like stepping out of Poston into a city apartment. Yuri's father was an artist of some renown, had exhibited in some of the better galleries of the East, and was well known in art centers on the West Coast. They had been evacuated from San Francisco, where they still owned their beautiful home overlooking the sea. Being an artist, Mr. Takeda had not endured the sight of the rough board walls and splintery floors of the barracks for long. The walls and ceiling were now done in wall board of some type and tinted a delicate green, with a fresco around the molding. The floor was covered with a thick, light colored linoleum, which in turn was almost hidden under soft, heavy Oriental rugs. Since Yuri was the only child, they did not have all the space taken up with beds as was the case in the larger families, but had them curtained off at one end, leaving a nice though small living room richly furnished with a selection of their own furniture shipped down from San Francisco. Mari sank down unbelievingly in one of the large easy chairs and could scarcely keep from staring around at the other things, a carved coffee table with a bowl of brightly colored petunias, a wide mirror with gold frame on one wall reflecting a pair of tapestries on the other, a low bookcase full of books.

Mr. Takeda was pleased when he saw her enjoying the flowers. He was very proud of his petunias. He had grown them in a small plot outside the door, only four or five plants, he told her, because water was scarce until the irrigation ditch would come. Then he planned to build a miniature Japanese garden with a teahouse and arched bridge and a pool full of golden lilies.

Mr. Takeda was taking internment in stride, for he was finding many things to paint on the desert and was thoroughly enjoying himself here, while he and his family lived off the government. They were comfortable; they had food delicacies sent in from outside to supplement the mess hall menus, and they had more leisure for reading and music than they had had at home.

Mrs. Takeda told Haruo that she and Mr. Takeda would bring Mari home when she was ready, as they always went for a walk before retiring, and Haruo was to stop and tell Mrs. Sato so she would not be worried.

As neither of the girls suggested that Haruo go with them to the church, he left reluctantly, thinking maybe he hadn't made as good use of the time on the way over as he might have done.

"What a funny place to have church," Mari exclaimed when she and Yuri went into the barracks and saw the rows of crude, backless benches on either side of an uneven aisle and the otherwise bare ugliness of the building in the dim light of a few bulbs hanging from the ceiling.

"The building doesn't count," Yuri said philosophically. "It's what goes on in it that matters."

292

"Yes, I suppose so." But Mari didn't think she would feel as if she were in church in a place like that.

When Mari had the instrument tuned, they played through a lively little piece first to get acquainted with each other.

"You play beautifully," Yuri said, looking up at Mari with real pleasure in her face.

"Do you really think so? I believe the violin sounds better than it did. I haven't played for six months."

"I've heard it is good for a violin to have a rest. What are you going to wear?"

"I hadn't thought about that."

Yuri suggested formal dress, but Mari didn't know.

"Do you think it would look right--in a place like this?"

"Surely. Why not? This is where we live, isn't it? Formal dress is always proper for an evening performance. Because we have to live on an Indian reservation is no excuse for going around in a blanket. It's just an alibi for the people who want to let down. All we ever see is people shuffling around in their old clothes, unless there's a funeral, and shoes covered with dust. Come on, what do you say? Mine is black. What color is yours? Yellow? A perfectly striking combination. We should get a write-up in the Poston *Chronicle* society column."

All Mari wanted was to be convinced. She had worn the new gown once at Santa Anita--a ball to celebrate something, she didn't remember what.

The night of the reception, Mari wore her old shoes and carried her silver slippers to the mess hall in the school block, where the reception was to be held. She held her long skirts up out of the dust which was ankle deep in the road, and Tad walked beside her, carrying her violin case. He teased her unmercifully all the way about being overdressed and making a show of herself, and she could see that everyone was staring at her as she passed the buildings, so by the time she reached the mess hall she was all distraught.

She changed into her slippers in a dark corner back

of the pantry, and found Yuri, who was poised and cool and looked as if she had just stepped from her cab.

Already quite a crowd had gathered, and as Mari looked around the poorly lit room and saw only the dark faces of the Issei and a few teachers congregated at one table, she thought of the great concert hall back in the city where she was to have made her debut, the beautiful tapestried walls, the brilliant lights, the stage banked with roses, and the rich, velvety curtains which lifted silently and left you standing there breathlessly before your waiting audience. What a thrill that would have been! But here. How could she play here? What inspiration? She saw her mother come in with Mrs. Hayashi and sit down at one of the bare board tables. What would her mother care about the music she was to play? What would any of them care? Only a few would appreciate it, a few like Mrs. Sugiyama. The others would rather hear a record of that horrible Japanese music like they had at the Shibai. She wished she had not told Mrs. Sugiyama she would play. She walked gingerly over the floor lest the long, loose splinters pierce the silver slippers and sat down beside Yuri on the plank seat where Yuri had spread a newspaper to protect their dresses.

They made a pretty picture, and Mother Sato watched them and smiled contentedly. The children were both in school and Mari was playing her violin again. If only Papa Sato could be here to see her tonight. But she would have something good to write him.

Mrs. Hayashi sat beside Mother Sato and looked at the teachers, trying to pick out one she felt she could talk to about Kenji. He had been giving her a great deal of anxiety ever since the day his father had been arrested shortly after Pearl Harbor. Kenji had adored his father, and when he was taken away the boy had become morose and quiet. He had quit school at once, although it was months before they left home, and stayed at home all the time, refusing to have anything to do with his friends. But since he had come to camp he had changed. She thought he had gotten into bad company. He had become aggressive and was belligerent toward all authority. Mrs. Hayashi could do nothing with him. He had refused to register for school on the day set for registration, but when the day came for school to open, he had gone. She thought if she could tell his teachers about him, maybe they could do something to get him interested and keep him going.

Tom and Yoshi had had no reason for attending the reception. Tom had gone to bed early, and Yoshi had slipped out and joined a gang of wanderers which finally turned up in the mess hall, where they took turns standing on an orange box to look in the window.

"Heh, that's my sis," Yoshi said, grabbing another boy off the box when he heard the violin. "Let me get up there, will you?" He was already up, balancing precariously on tiptoe, for the box wasn't high enough for his short figure.

When the program was over, many parents came and thanked Mari in their gentle voices and their halting English, their faces showing so much pleasure that she was glad she had played. She knew it wasn't because they had enjoyed the music so much, but they appreciated what she had done and the fact that she had dressed for them as she would have done for an audience back home. It gave them all a lift to see her and Yuri in their lovely gowns. It put beauty into the drabness of their day.

But if the older people got a lift out of them, the Nisei teachers, who were the only young people there, were practically boosted into the stratosphere. They crowded round while they drank their tea and ate the small cakes, full of plans for the winter season.

"I didn't know you girls could play."

"We'll have to start an orchestra to play for the dances. Can you play the good ol' rhythm, Yuri?"

"Gee. You look wonderful, Mari."

"You look so grown-up with your hair done that way."

Tad's eyes were all for Yuri, but she pretended she

didn't notice.

"How about shoving the tables back and having a dance when the old folks go home?" he said, looking at Yuri.

She flashed him an impersonal smile and said she was going home with her folks. Tad didn't know what to make of her. Girls were not usually immune to his charms.

There was no chance to dance anyway. Mrs. Sugiyama shooed everyone out when all of the cups and plates had been washed and put away by the volunteer committee.

"I'm sorry," she said, and it was no mere courtesy speech, "but I promised to leave everything the way I found it if they would let us use the mess hall for the reception. We'll have to get our recreation hall furnished so you will have somewhere to dance. That will be the next thing now. If you will back me up, I'll see if I can get some furniture from the administration."

"To the limit," Bill Harada said. "You ought to be able to. I saw at least three warehouses full of it up in Camp One."

Tad didn't say anything. He was still glum over Yuri's coolness. If he had her in his class, he'd flunk her. Besides, earlier in the evening he had had an argument with Miss Brown, one of the core teachers, over evacuation, and she had bested him in the argument. He was angry with himself because it made no difference to him what she thought. She had intimated that she thought human beings ought to do better than keep whining around like wounded animals when they had been hurt. He thought she was hitting at him.

School muddled along through the autumn, unsteady, faltering. There were no traditions to give it security, no loyal upperclassmen to give it equilibrium, no interschool contacts for competition, and still no books or equipment. Some teachers gave up and left. Some broke under the strain and left. One was taken out in a straitjacket, and one died.

The Sato block got much firsthand news about the teachers because one of the block women was employed to care for the teachers' barracks. Mrs. Imoto, no kin to the erstwhile market proprietor, had decided it would be nice to earn a few dollars to buy things for the grandchild which was coming soon and so had made a trip to the employment office.

The Imotos had had money when Mr. Imoto had the store, but the store had gone for a song when people knew he had to sell. Now they were determined to save what little they had in the bank to help them make a new start some day. Mrs. Imoto was on the payroll as a full-time employee, working eight hours a day, but she had found that she could get the twenty beds made and brush up the middle of the floor a little in a couple of hours, or three at the most, when she used the wet mop.

Yes, she could tell all about the teachers. They had upholstered chairs in their rooms and beds with springs and mattresses, no straw-filled ticking. She always took time to sit down awhile in one of the easy chairs. She would lay her head back and close her eyes and imagine she was back home in Oakland.

Some of the teachers were friendly, she told Mother Sato, and talked and laughed with her even though she didn't know much English. Some of them tried to learn Japanese words from her. She liked to clean the rooms of the nice ones, but the one that had the cats, Mrs. Imoto made a terrible face when she told about her. And there was one who put a big padlock on her door and wouldn't let her go in. She didn't care, it made one less room to clean, but it did pique her to be locked out. One or two tried to boss her around like she were a common servant and complained that she didn't keep their rooms clean. What did they expect for twelve dollars a month? Mrs. Imoto asked Mother Sato with disdain.

As time went on, the pupils also began to classify their teachers into the friendly, sympathetic group, and the group who looked upon them as inferiors, thought an internment camp was just where they belonged, and even used threats to work against their return to California after the war if they didn't behave in classes.

Miss Brown, with whom Tad had tangled at the reception, was placed by the pupils in the friendly class, although they knew she was no softy. She was Mari's core teacher, a woman in her early thirties, and a graduate of a California university. She was sympathetic and deplored evacuation as undemocratic and unworthy of the America they all loved, but she believed in accepting facts and not allowing this to ruin their lives.

"You should study just as much here as you did at home," she told her senior students, "or even harder, for it isn't going to be easy to do the work of the senior year under the handicaps you have. No quiet place to study and so few books for so many students."

"What good will it do us to graduate here?" they asked her. "You don't think any college will accept our credits, do you?"

She could only answer that she hoped the school would be good enough to become accredited.

She pleaded with them earnestly to keep their faith in democratic principles of government and preserve their loyalty as citizens as one of their most precious possessions.

The boys, and some of the girls, laughed at her for this, and argued with her, always coming back to evacuation as the final proof of the worthlessness of their citizenship.

Miss Brown would plant her feet firmly on the wide floorboards behind her desk and stand her ground. She had to make them see objectively, to get them out of themselves.

When they were discussing possible units of study, some wanted to study slavery in the South.

"That's what we are, slaves," they told her. "We ought to study about the Negroes and learn more about how they were treated."

"You're more in the position of the white people in the South after the war than you are of the slaves."

And she read from *Gone With the Wind* the description of the way the southerners were treated by the carpetbaggers.

It was a new idea to them. They began to see that minority groups weren't always racial. They studied the history of child labor in the United States, the exploitation of little children which was only stopped as laws were made against it. They learned of the position of the Irish at one time, and how they had won a place for themselves in America, and they were gently reminded that they were only the second generation of Japanese. They must be patient, for social progress was slow. Gradually as the months passed the students began to relax, lose some of their tenseness, and become rehabilitated to a more normal way of thinking. They, with seniors from other classes with constructive programs, began to plan the activities for their senior year.

Yoshi said little about school at home, and when any of the family asked him about it, he said it was okay. But his actions were taking such a turn for the worse that Tom decided to investigate. He talked to other families who had children in the same room and found that the seventh grade teacher was inexperienced and incapable of handling a roomful of children with no books and nothing else to keep them busy. The parents were all worried about it, but what could they do? Maybe when the books came . . .

In spite of its shortcomings and the unhappy circumstances which created it, the school was to become one of the most stabilizing influences in the community.

The school accomplished something which the administration during the whole period of internment was never quite able to gain completely, and that was the confidence of the people.

XVI

Tempers were getting short in the crowded quarters. The reserve born of suspicion and the veneer of politeness which block residents had shown toward each other was rapidly wearing off. People no longer tried to keep their voices down for fear of having their family differences overheard in the next rooms. They didn't care; and some family could be heard quarreling up and down the length of the barracks almost any hour of the day or night. Differences which had at first been carried on in lowered voices, as folks accustomed to privacy felt ashamed to have their family bickering aired in public, were now shouted in unrestrained tones.

Parents screamed at their children. Children, hitherto obedient and respectful, shouted back, insolent, defiant.

"I don't have to listen to you anymore," was heard often. "The government's taking care of me now." Unwittingly the administration had contributed to the breakdown of parental authority. It had permitted only citizens to vote in the newly formed local camp government, and only citizens could hold office in the Community Council. This relegated the Issei parents to the background without power or authority in the community. The children followed the administration's example and refused to recognize the parents' authority in the family, either.

Another factor which caused continual differences between parents and children was the concern of the parents to save some semblance of family life in the midst of this communal form of living. They worried over the constant absence of their children from their presence, the freedom with which they roamed about the camp, their independence of their parents. Who knew what they were doing? The easy familiarity between boys and girls of high school age shocked them, walking about the camp holding hands or with arms

300

about each other. There was always irritation caused by trying to keep the girls at home in the evenings. There was too much freedom. Mothers and fathers did not want their young girls gadding about the camp after dark.

There were bickerings between the young folks themselves, who were irritated by the inconveniences of living conditions and angry at being there.

Few families sat together in the mess hall any longer. There was a tendency to congregate in age groups at the different tables. Table manners sank to an all time low among the children as a natural consequence of the new life of general carelessness and defiance of all authority and rule. A new language sprang up among the young people which, along with a manner of speaking with the lips half open slurring the words, came to be known as Postonese.

The Sato family, which had come to be looked upon with considerable respect in the block, was beginning to show signs of fraying and disintegrating. They no longer ate together. Tad had never eaten with the others since that first night, but usually the others had been together once a day anyway. After school began, Mari started eating with some of her new acquaintances from her classes, and Yoshi did the same, in spite of his mother's remonstrances. Tom often went to breakfast before the others and was not ready for supper when they were. Mother Sato, left alone, found friends among her block neighbors who were likewise deserted by their children.

Tad had grown increasingly irritable with each succeeding week, and it was a blessing he spent so little time in the apartment. He was impatient with Tom because he kept on working in the fields even after they had failed to get the irrigation water in time to plant.

"We will have much more to plant in the spring, when we do have the water," Tom answered him.

"You don't know whether there will ever be any water for irrigation," Tad would come back.

He was angry because Tom and Mari were trying to

make an adjustment to their new way of living and to make the best of it. It annoyed him beyond words for either of them to show any enthusiasm for anything around the camp. He did all he could to turn his pupils against their Caucasian teachers, and he wanted Mari to hate hers. It made him furious to have her like Miss Brown, although he couldn't dislike her himself and often had long talks with her after school. He ridiculed Mari for studying so hard, working for good grades so she could go to college.

"You don't think you'll get credit at any college for what you do here, do you?" he would ask contemptuously, arousing uncertainty and a sense of futility in Mari's mind.

He found satisfaction in meeting his students each day and reviewing with them the wrongs and injustices the American people had meted out to them and to other racial minorities. He also enjoyed defying the principal.

Mr. Harrison was inclined to be domineering, and the experienced teachers accustomed to that attitude on the part of principals scarcely noticed it; but to the Nisei teachers the dictatorial nature of the school system was surprising as well as disagreeable, and many besides Tad resented it. Even Bill Harada rebelled against rules arbitrarily set up for him to follow and came into open conflict with the principal before the year was over.

Apart from his activities as a member of the school faculty, Tad had allowed himself to be drawn into a group of companions who were potentially dangerous. He had thought when he made his decision that first night in internment to resist authority that he would be a free agent to choose his own, independent course of action wherever he was sent to permanent camp; but he had found, on coming to Poston, that the road he had taken was traveled by many others, some of whom were determined upon going much further than he had planned.

Tad had not thought of perpetrating acts of physical violence against those who did not follow his policy of resistance and noncooperation; and by the time he learned that others did, it was too late for him to withdraw. He would be suspected and watched, and the next time the FBI came to camp to investigate someone, Tad would be accused of being an informer and would be due for a beating.

The way in which these cruel and mysterious beatings were carried out was enough to make one think twice before doing anything which might incriminate him with the undercover boys.

Torn by emotional conflict within and fear and suspense from forces without, Tad became moody and sullen. He ceased to show any concern for his mother's welfare. Although the weather was delightfully cool and bright now, she could not seem to gain back the weight she had lost in the heat, and her face was pinched and drawn. Her mind was constantly plagued with the same fears and insecurities as plagued the minds of other women with family responsibilities whose husbands were separated from them in internment. There came rumors of family camps being prepared where families could go to live with their men who were prisoners, but Mother Sato kept hoping that Papa would be cleared.

Tad neglected the little attentions he had always shown his mother and which she expected and enjoyed. His coming home had once been the bright spot of her life, but when he came in from school each evening with a frown on his face, he didn't seem to see her as he threw down his bunch of papers to grade and went out again. If she did not feel like going to a meal, Tad paid no attention, did not even know she hadn't gone; and it was Tom or Mari who brought her a tray.

This neglect from her eldest son, and favorite if she would have admitted it, made Mother Sato sad as she sat in her barracks alone after the children had left in the mornings and pondered over the change which had taken place in her family. The children heeded their father. He had always had a way with them, and he

303

would find one now to draw them together again before the rifts became too wide. There were so many problems with which she felt unable to cope. She had never known the truth about Tad's coming out of the Army, but she sensed that there was something about it which had been reponsible for this change in Tadashi. Once at Santa Anita when they were alone in the stable and Tad seemed to come nearer to her and need her help, she had tried to talk to him about it, to find out what it was, and he had spoken rudely to her for the first time in her memory. When she had chided him for disrespect toward his mother, he had become angry beyond all reason, had begun to use bad words she had never heard him use before, and hurried out, banging the door behind him. She had never dared question him about it again.

Mother Sato spent many long, anxious hours over what to do about Yoshi, her little boy, and he was growing so far away from her. After he was dressed and off to breakfast she would see little of him for the rest of the day. Only running in after school to beg for some money to go to the canteen. They had had so much trouble over his demands for money that Tom had finally put him on an allowance; but it hadn't done much good. He was out of money by the middle of the week and asking for more. When he couldn't get it out of Tom, he would wheedle it out of his mother, a nickel at a time.

Mother Sato was afraid not to give it to him. There were stories around camp about children, and grown-ups, too, who were seen stealing from other residents because they were without funds themselves. Driven to it by a pride which could find no way to hide poverty from the ever-present eyes of other residents.

So far Yoshi had never gotten into any trouble, but his mother was always afraid. He played football with the other small boys after school, and after dark a crowd congregated on the firebreak and lay on the ground and talked, mostly about what they did back home and the pets they had. Malt became a super-dog

304

as the tales of his prowess grew with each telling. The nights were getting frosty, and the boys would carry in some dead mesquite from the environs of the camp and build a fire to gather round. Sometimes older fellows, idle, bitter, and disgusted, too cowardly to defy authority openly, joined the boys and promoted fights between them, encouraging a general attitude of belligerence and insubordination. Mother Sato wanted him at home evenings, but she found she had to bow to the circumstances. Yoshi would not sit alone with her in the barracks evenings, or with her and Tom, when all the other boys were outside. She knew she could not expect him to.

Mari was always finding an excuse to go somewhere after supper, too. One night it was a club meeting, and then it was study. Several girls had to use the same book, she explained. There was nothing to do but let her go. Sometimes some boy would walk home with her, and they would sit out on the stoop in the dark and talk. Usually there would be another couple with them, but not always. It was very disconcerting to Mother Sato, who could never become accustomed to the American freedom of association of the sexes.

No, she could not cope with the influences which were working to mold the lives of her brood. She imagined she could see disintegrating processes working even in Tom. He showed less interest in his work and was short-tempered at times and withdrawn from others.

The physical environment of the camp was a symbol of the life the evacuees lived. It was a desert life, barren of the normal growing things of the spirit, such as kindness and honesty, ambition and courtesy. A desert life where only the tough, hard, ugly things could exist. Selfishness, trickery, suspicion, and bitterness.

The Japanese had always had a great love for their homes. They had spent money on them, if they had it, to make them comfortable and beautiful. Family privacy and integrity were held sacred. Here life was communal. There were cases of three families living in

305

one room. It was intolerable. The reaction of these to such desecration of their private lives influenced the attitude and thinking of others. All drifted toward carelessness. There was no such thing as family life, couldn't possibly have been. Crowded rooms made it impossible to keep children at home in many instances. A family of six or seven could not have stood the strain of stumbling over each other in the close confines of a single, crowded room day after day. Their wounds were still too tender.

There were those with far broader experience than Mother Sato who were concerned with what the camp was to do to their young people. As they looked about them at the empty, boundless desert, they could not help wondering why the Army had thought it necessary to confine them in such cramped quarters.

As the parents brooded and worried, the Nisei themselves were facing trials they had not foreseen. Those who were loyal found themselves more severely tested here than on the outside. Since the night after the movie, Tom had found himself more and more involved in a swirl of intrigue, intimidation, and underground activity.

When people had first come to Poston, the potential troublemakers had lain low for a time, not knowing what the policy of the administration might be toward the evacuees. Would it rule with a stern hand? Would there be anything similar to concentration camps in Europe? Would there be executions? When the administration was found to be friendly and considerate, in attitude if not always in practice, fear of punishment waned, cliques began to form quietly.

Tom had soon found friends besides Haruo, with like ideas and purposes.

As this first group of American-born Japanese had grown into manhood and womanhood on the West Coast and had graduated out of high schools and colleges into the economic world, discrimination against them had been a force which all had had to face. In the public mind there seemed to be no distinction between these educated, English-speaking young Americans and their Oriental parents.

While they had all faced the same problem of discrimination, they had not reacted alike. They could have been divided roughly into three groups.

First, there were those who believed they would never get anywhere in America and that their best chance was to go to Japan for their higher education and make their home there. Thus they could escape the constant barrier of race prejudice which blocked them in this country. Of those who followed their reasoning and went to Japan, some were disappointed and disillusioned, for they found that they were less equipped to live there than in their native land. Others, endowed with a capacity for adjustment or with more training in the Japanese language and culture, were happy and able to make good in the homeland of their parents. There was also a residue of this first group who, although they believed they would have a better chance in Japan, lacked the initiative or funds to go. They stayed in America, got their education here, but were unhappy, disgruntled, critical. These made fertile soil for the agitators to plant their seeds of dissension.

The second group might be called the defeatists. They felt there was no place for them either in America or Japan. They didn't expect to get a break anywhere, and there was no use to try to do anything. They were a helpless, downtrodden minority in their own eyes and felt sorry for themselves. They had never felt that American citizenship had any meaning for them, and evacuation had convinced them that they had been right. It didn't make any difference how much you did, you would never get anywhere, so why try?

The third group, and by far the largest, were those who believed they could win out and build successful careers for themselves in their own native land. They believed in themselves, and they believed in the inherent fairness of the majority of their fellow Americans. Because of these beliefs, they were perhaps the hardest hit emotionally by evacuation; but they were the first to recover and put their shoulders to the wheel to make their sojourn on the desert as comfortable and profitable as possible. When the policy of the government concerning the evacuees changed in the fall of this first year and they were permitted to seek employment in certain unrestricted states, the leaders of this third group were the first to leave the camp and get into the normal stream of life in the world outside.

However, as long as they stayed in camp, they stood for cooperation with the government officials, whom they looked upon as fellow Americans, in the difficult job of running the camp. They took the criticism of others and were often threatened if they took this action or that. These loyal Nisei had to watch their tongues, for it was not healthy to talk about loyalty or to defend the government, and anyone who was fool-hardy enough to defend evacuation on any grounds whatever was in danger of a night visit from the vigilantes.

In camp the defeatist group was passive and submissive in appearance. Inwardly they were brooding and bitter. Despondency led to attempts at suicide.

Hideo was an example of those educated in Japan.

That evacuation was a military necessity, it is doubtful if any Nisei would have agreed. The Nisei knew their own people; they knew how few were enemies of the United States. How few had sabotage in mind. They knew their parents for honest, hard-working people who had made great sacrifices for their education. They knew they dreamed of their youth in Japan and loved their native land, but dangerous, no.

When evacuation was made on a strictly racial basis, with those of German and Italian ancestry excluded, and came as the culmination of a short and vigorous campaign by newspapers and pressure groups in California, it would have been impossible to believe that military necessity was the criterion without doing violence to one's intelligence.

Tom Sato often tried to explain to himself why he had such an abiding faith in democracy after what had happened. Of course, he had had it preached to him all through school, but so had all the Nisei, and they didn't all feel as he did. He had been little influenced by the ideologies of his parents' country, for there had been little exchange of ideas between them and him. He had read good things about Japan, and he had read things he didn't like. Neither was personal. He liked his own country. He knew that in a democracy there was a greater degree of individual freedom than in many other forms of government, and that meant freedom to make mistakes, even on the part of the officials. If you believed this, you had to be willing to be a victim of these mistakes at some time; but you could remember that most of the time you could enjoy the fruits of freedom. To have your constitutional rights set aside temporarily was not sufficient cause for throwing everything overboard. Where politicians got into office through free elections there would always be selfish and unprincipled men who would exert pressure or use deception to get the votes, and highly organized and powerful financial groups would exert pressure to gain their own ends. In time of war, high public officials were too busy to give their personal attention to the welfare of small, unorganized, and politically unimportant minority groups. This was a weakness of democracy.

But, all in all, the United States was the best country in the world, and he was going to wear the uniform and fight for it before the war was over. Rumors were circulating--they had been traced to someone in the administration--that the Army was going to take the Nisei again. As soon as they did, he would volunteer. He didn't talk about it, for he had discovered that there were small but powerful groups organized in camp for eliminating just such fellows as he. They were powerful because they ruled by intimidation, and the people felt they had little personal protection from the police force, which was known as Internal Security. The evacuee police were not allowed to carry arms. They would have been ineffective against a vicious band armed with clubs and ball bats. And one could easily be beaten to death before the slow communication system in camp would get word to an armed government official, much less get him from his personnel quarters in the farthest unit of the camp to your aid in time.

There was no way to protect oneself. The tension at times, especially after a beating had taken place, was well nigh unbearable. Nisei who were suspected of reporting pro-Japanese agitators to the FBI were soundly beaten with the approval of many good people in the camp who felt they were getting what they deserved. Their minds could not bridge racial barriers and see one Japanese reporting on another, no matter what the reason, as good or justified; and such people were despised. There were those suspected of being informers of the FBI before evacuation, and it was thought that many of the arrests by the FBI were made as a result of some Nisei reporting on someone against whom he had a grudge.

"If I ever find out that anyone lied to the FBI about Dad and got him picked up, I'll kill the louse," Tad had threatened.

Whether or not there was any truth in these accusations, it made for uneasiness and suspense among the people.

On a dark night an apartment would be entered by masked men, and the victim would be beaten with clubs or ball bats to within an inch of his life. The frantic family could do nothing. Then the invaders would leave as mysteriously as they had come, and if by any chance any one of them had been recognized, they had no fear it would be reported. The victims' folks were too terror stricken for that.

Many of those who suffered beatings had to be hospitalized, and the lives of some had been despaired of; but up to this time, no one had died, although some had been cruelly bludgeoned beyond recognition. One was an old man who had been beaten by mistake.

It was terrifying. You could be next. You had to

310

be careful what you said.

Tom continued to work hard each day, even though there was not much heart in it. He found his escape in reading at night, keeping aloof as much as possible from the swirling eddies of destructive human emotions circling about him. But he could not close his eyes to the effect that the generally unwholesome environment was having on Yoshi.

At last things came to a head.

The Sato family, their nerves stretched taut by the strain under which they were living, were in the midst of a family quarrel. It grew louder and louder, and the families up and down the barracks shook their heads sadly to hear the fine Sato clan falling into the bad ways.

It had begun at noon, when Yoshi had asked Tom for money. It was Saturday, and there was to be ice cream at the canteen that afternoon. There had been defiance in his voice when he had asked, for he knew his allowance was not due till Monday. But there was none of the begging and wheedling he ordinarily used when his money was gone too soon. He was standing outside the mess hall door when Tom came out from lunch.

"I want a dime," he demanded.

"I don't have any," Tom said truthfully. He had just come from the fields, and he never carried money to work. "Anyway, you are supposed to make your allowance last all week. You spend more money at that canteen in a week than all the rest of us put together."

"Mom will give it to me after you go to work."

"I don't work this afternoon, so you're out of luck." Tom started to explain to the boy how little money they were making now and that he should be more careful with what they gave him.

"Aw, shut up your big mouth," Yoshi yelled at him and ran around the corner of the mess hall, throwing back a string of foul language at his brother.

Tom started to go after him to take him home, but several people were coming out of the mess and he didn't want to make a scene before them. Too many had heard the boy already.

He walked slowly toward his apartment, thinking of the night he and Yoshi had had the talk in the greenhouse. The comparison between that roguish, lovable little kid and this impudent, hard-boiled gamin who had slipped around the corner like a fugitive from the law brought home to him forcibly the extent to which the child's actions had changed. How much has he changed inside? How deep had it gone? He felt pretty sure that if he tried to talk to Yoshi now as he had that night, he would be laughed at.

No one saw Yoshi all afternoon. Tom went over to the next block to the basketball court in the late afternoon, and on the way home Mr. Imoto called to him as he passed the canteen.

"Can you stop a minute, Tom? I want to tell you something."

Tom went inside. Mr. Imoto was alone.

"I hate to tell you this, Tom," he began, leaning his elbows on the counter and looking down at the floor. "But I think you folks ought to know. Yoshi and another boy took some ice cream bars from the canteen this afternoon. I was going over some bills, and I looked up just in time to see them scooting out the side door with their hands full. I didn't go after them, for I don't think anyone else saw them. There were only a couple of fellows in then, and they were looking at the magazines."

Tom fumbled for words.

"Well, thanks for telling me. I'll pay for whatever he took. I guess it was my fault; I wouldn't let Yoshi have any money."

Tom took his coin purse from his sweater pocket.

"I don't know how many he took. I'll just charge it to the government. You can't blame two kids. They see other people taking what they want around camp and they don't distinguish at their age between a piece of lumber that doesn't belong to you and an ice-cream cone that doesn't. We're all to blame. I would have given

312

them something if I had known they didn't have the money. I try to be friends with all the boys. Well, I just thought I'd better tell you."

"Glad you did. I'll see it doesn't happen again." Empty words. How would he see? Give Yoshi all the money he wanted? What would they do when the money was gone? All checks and no deposits--their bank account couldn't last forever.

After mess Tom had gathered the family together.

"I want you to hear this, too," he told Tad as he got hold of him after mess before he could get off somewhere for the evening. It was the first time for weeks that they had all sat down together in their apartment. And now they were having a general family showdown, with the quarrel circling widely around Yoshi.

The boy sat on his own cot alone, his chin propped on a pair of grimy hands, sullen and impenitent. However, he was quiet, for this sudden show of family solidarity had impressed him. And he was a little frightened over having been caught.

Mother Sato was thoroughly aroused and soundly berated them all for their indifference and carelessness about their obligations as members of a family. Now shame had come upon them. She threatened Yoshi with dire punishment when his father came.

The children understood barely half of what she said, for she spoke rapidly in her excitement, using her native tongue, but they were painfully conscious that everyone else in the barracks could--that is, all the Issei.

"Don't talk so loud, Mom, please," Mari pleaded.

Tad was laughing one minute, regarding it as a pretty smart escapade, getting something right out from under Imoto's nose; and the next he was threatening to lick the hide off of Yoshi. The idea of a Sato stealing! He ought to be put out of the family and have to live somewhere else. He wasn't fit to belong to the Satos anymore. He was a disgrace to them all and ought to be turned over to the police. Then Tad decided to take his punishment into his own hands.

"I'll teach you never to do a thing like that again."

He went outside and cut a short length off the government hose where a neighbor was watering his castor beans.

When he grabbed the boy by the back of the neck and had jerked him off the cot, the rest of the family turned on Tad, and the quarrel became more heated.

He should be ashamed to think of whipping the boy. He was the last one in the family to do the punishing. What kind of an example had he set for Yoshi since he had come to camp? If anyone got a beating, he was the one that needed it. Only in anger would Tom and Mari have talked so to Tad, but in the excitement all repression was swept away. They had borne with him mostly in silence since long before evacuation. Now they told him what they thought about the way he had acted. Mother Sato joined in and aired all of her grievances.

Tad finally loosed Yoshi's collar to give his attention to defending himself. He became livid with anger, and the shouting grew louder and louder as each tried to make himself heard.

"If that's the way you all feel about me, I'm the one to get out of the family," he said finally in a hoarse, edgy voice. And with that he fled the room.

There was a frightened lull after he had gone. What had they done?

Recalling the origin of the quarrel, they turned to Yoshi again. He kicked at the piece of hose Tad had dropped to the floor and winked hard to squeeze back a tear which was about to slip out on his cheek. Tad had given him a scare, and he was more ready to listen to Mari when she told him what pupils in school thought about one who took what didn't belong to him.

Mother Sato was crying now, and Tom was just sitting on his cot looking at Yoshi. The boy was getting pretty tired of the whole business.

"Aw, skip it," he told Mari. "Nobody else knows. Mr. Imoto won't tell anyone."

"Maybe not this time, but if it ever happened again."

That was what they were all afraid of. Where was this going to end? How could they protect him from something much more serious?

"Well, you don't think I'd do that again, do you? What are you all getting so excited about? If I had Malt here, or my bicycle, or something to do, I wouldn't have to run around with those mean kids all the time," he complained, bidding for sympathy.

"Why can't I have Malt, Tom? The cook said he would give me enough meat scraps to feed a dozen dogs."

"We'll see," Tom said tentatively. He didn't know much about psychology, but it looked to him like rewarding misbehavior to promise Yoshi anything right now. "If you could have only one, which would you rather have, Malt or your bicycle?"

Yoshi's face brightened and he considered. He couldn't decide between the two. If he had his bicycle he would be the envy of all the other boys, but it would be nice to have Malt to play with and to sit by him in the evenings.

Still, it wasn't the kind of a place for Malt somehow, with all the other families around all the time; besides, he might get bitten by a rattlesnake, he was always running off across the open spaces.

"I'd rather have my bicycle," he decided.

"Well, we'll see," Tom began again. "If your report card is good next time."

There was a knock at the door, and Mrs. Hayashi bowed and asked deferentially if Mrs. Sato were going to English class. Mother Sato bowed and apologized profusely for not being ready and invited Mrs. Hayashi in to wait while she ran to the latrine to bathe her red eyes. Then the two women went clipping off together, for they were late. Mrs. Hayashi had waited discreetly until the uproar in the Sato apartment had subsided before she called for Mother Sato.

As they left, two senior girls came by, calling for Mari. Mari brushed her hair and put on some powder and perfume and told Tom she was going over to the teachers' barracks to get some help on her English. The other girls giggled, and the three started out. Tom thought it queer to be studying on Saturday night.

He was left alone with Yoshi, who made no move to leave. Instead he got up and came over to sit down beside Tom.

"I was going to pay for that ice cream," he said in a low voice, "when I got my allowance Monday."

Tom didn't say anything.

"I was, honest. Don't you believe me?"

Still Tom remained silent. He sat looking at the floor. Mustn't let the kid work him. If Yoshi got off too easy this time, it might be something worse next.

"You tell Mama, and all of them, will you, huh? Tell them I was going to pay for it. Tell them, will you, Tom?" Yoshi's voice became coaxing. "You ought to know I wouldn't steal anything. Remember?"

"Remember what?"

"You know. Honest Abe." The boy's face was wistful. He needed to be restored to the family confidence. He, too, suffered from feelings of insecurity in this place.

"Sure, I remember," Tom said, covering up the surprise he felt. Yoshi hasn't changed so much. Just on the surface. If we could get out of camp now, he'd be all right.

"Want to go for a walk? I have to see a man over in Block 311."

Tom chose the road around the outer edge of the camp so they would not meet so many people, and as they walked along leisurely hand in hand, they began to talk about the ranch. About little, silly things like the day the water tank ran over and flooded the backyard before they could get the power turned off, and what a fine time the ducks had swimming that day; and the time Malt had chased the three cats up a tree all at the same time and how funny they looked sitting there on a limb. Then the conversation came back to camp, and Tom asked Yoshi where he learned to talk as he had that noon.

316

"All the fellows do."

"No. Not all of them. I know better than that."

"Well, most of them. You can't be just a sissy. All the men talk like that."

"What men?"

"In the latrine."

Tom felt he would be willing to give ten years of his life if it would get Yoshi out of there and back on the ranch. And they had been in camp only three months. What would a year do? Two years? Five to ten years like the Commissioner of Indian Affairs had said?

Yoshi was still all right in intention, but how could an eleven-year-old be expected to stand up against such a disintegrating environment?

After Tom's errand was completed, the boys had another good talk as they returned home. Yoshi told Tom all about school and how they acted in his room. The teacher wasn't any good, he said. She couldn't keep order so she couldn't teach them anything, for they couldn't hear what she said. He hated school. He wanted to go back home to La Vista.

"Why do we have to stay here, Tom?"

What could Tom say? Could he make Yoshi believe that they were kept there because they were considered dangerous? Would he want to? Or could he make him believe that the people back in California were dangerous and they were there for protection? Those were the reasons he had been given. He would feel foolish repeating them to Yoshi.

"It's Army orders," he said. "And good soldiers take orders and don't ask questions."

When they reached home, Tom said, "We'll have our showers and get to bed. That will please Mom, to find you in bed when she comes home."

"Yeah. You tell her I was going to pay."

"You tell her yourself," Tom said.

A little later when his mother came in, Tom heard a whispered conversation over Yoshi's cot which appeared to end in satisfaction for both parties. Then Mother

Sato went to bed.

"Have you seen Tadashi?" she asked from behind the curtain.

"No, I haven't, Mom; but it's way too early for him yet." He tried to sound unconcerned, but he, too, was worried. He had never seen Tad so angry. And they had said more than they should. And where was Mari? Wasn't his mother concerned with her? She would be if she knew some of the things that were going on around camp. He lay listening. Finally he heard Mari's voice outside, and the low voice of--not one of the girls she had gone off with--but of some strange fellow. He strained to hear better, but he could not recognize the voice as anyone he knew. If only she would date with Haruo. But, no, she had to slip off pretending to be going to study and then pick up some strange man. She'd be getting in trouble like some of the other girls. He heard Mari say good night, then a long silence, and a little laugh. Steps going away, and Mari coming in the door humming happily to herself. She tiptoed through the dark room back to her cot, and he could hear her still humming after she got in bed.

Tom couldn't go to sleep. He kept mulling over the events of the evening and listening for Tad. He tried not to listen, for Tad might not come home at all tonight. Sometimes he stayed over at the bachelors' barracks. The place had a bad reputation.

It was after midnight when Tad came. Tom was still awake. Tad had been drinking heavily, and he came stumbling in the door and turned on the light. He had brought another man with him who was also drunk, and they were talking loud as Tad staggered about the room, gathering up his things.

His folks didn't want him anymore, and he was going to move out, he told the other fellow confidentially in a voice which could be heard a block away. They didn't treat him right. He didn't have to take it, because he had plenty of friends. They had a bed all waiting for him over at the bachelors' barracks. He was stuffing his clothes in his suitcase. Yoshi pulled the blanket over his head and peered out, frightened, from underneath.

Mother Sato got up and slipped on her robe and came out to see what the commotion was all about. When she saw Tad's condition she tried to hush him up. He swore at her. Angrily she jerked the shirts from his hand, and Tad, too unsteady on his feet to keep his balance, fell back against the wall and struck his head against the sharp corner of the window frame. A trickle of blood ran down in front of his ear.

Tom was up now, trying to get the other fellow out of the place. When he had him outside, he closed and bolted the doors and watched through the crack until he saw him move off toward the firebreak. He turned at the moment that Tad had grabbed up the piece of hose and raised his arm to strike his mother.

"Tad!" he shouted, attracting his attention long enough for him to get between them and take the blow. It wasn't hard, but it was a terrible thing to see Tad strike at his mother. It seemed to sober Tad a little, and Tom persuaded him to go to the shower, where Tom turned cold water on him while Mother Sato made coffee with trembling hands and Mari cried into her pillow and wished she had died before she ever came to Poston.

When Tad had had a couple of cups of strong coffee, they bandaged his head and got him to bed.

Mother Sato stood looking down at her two boys. Yoshi, who pretended to be asleep, the first in the family to take something which didn't belong to him. Her baby. She shook her head sadly. "Bad boy. I shall have to write Papa Sato," she murmured to herself. "It will hurt him, but he will have to know."

Then she turned to Tad, who was already breathing heavily in drunken sleep. Tadashi. Her eldest now that Norio was gone. The first one to drink the bad *sake*. Her face grew old, her heart weary. She laid an extra blanket over the foot of each cot. It would be cold before morning.

After the light was out again and all was quiet, Tom still lay awake. He felt he could never relax enough to sleep again. He listened now to Tad's heavy breathing, now to a stifled sob from Mari, the happy little tune gone from her heart, and, hardest of all to bear, those long, drawn out sighs from his mother's cot. If only his father could come. He was the only one who could help now. Tom buried his face in the rough mattress and fought for courage to face the endless days ahead.

XVII

Tom was awakened by the clang of breakfast gongs. He opened his eyes and looked about. Yoshi's cot was empty. Tad was still asleep. From force of habit, Tom leaped out, pulled on his clothes, and gave his face a hasty dash of cold water at the communal wash trough on his way to mess.

He had no appetite for food. Why hadn't he turned over and gone back to sleep, stayed unconscious for as much of the long, monotonous, drab day as possible? Tom wanted to avoid thinking. He wanted escape from a consciousness of the continually deepening depression of their situation. Working days with their physical activity brought weariness at evening, and the body's enjoyment of rest eased the pressure on the mind. But the long weekends with nothing to do, nowhere to go for a change of scene, no way to escape from the tensions which hung over the camp like stagnant, poisonous air, were interminable.

It was then that thoughts you couldn't avoid crept in, haunted your mind. You wanted to be loyal to your country. You wanted to believe she was right. So you kept rationalizing, trying to believe you were serving by being here, trying to feel that you were proving your loyalty by being a good internee. The mask began to wear thin, and you were afraid sometimes that there would be holes you could see through, and then you wouldn't be able to deceive yourself any longer. Your faith and your hope would be gone, and there would be nothing left.

Tom felt uncomfortable over the thought of facing Tad after last night. He was ashamed for Tad and ashamed that he had seen him in such a condition, heard his silly babbling. He wished he didn't have to see Tad today. Nor Mari, either. Nor Yoshi. He didn't want to see any of the family. He felt a sudden craving for privacy. A need to be an individual again, planning his work, running his own life, with an opportunity for solitude when he was surfeited with people. He thought of the ranch with a yearning which brought a sting to his eyelids. He dreaded to enter the mess hall, to face other residents of the block. Were they whispering among themselves this morning about the Sato family row? Were there nodding heads with knowing smiles over Mari? Everyone in the block would know by this time that she had been out late the night before.

Tom took the first table inside the door and sat down on the end of the bench as inconspicuously as possible. The Endo family, all together as usual, had beckoned him to their table, but he had pretended not to see. There was only one man left at Tom's table, and the bare boards were strewn with dirty dishes and drops of syrup from the pitcher. Some cold griddle cakes were left on the plate. He scooped one up and downed it with a cup of hot coffee which a woman had brought him, and got up. Haruo came by his table, and they went out together. Haruo threw an arm around Tom's shoulder as they walked along, a familiar gesture, but this morning with his nerves all on edge it meant to Tom that Haruo was trying to show his sympathy. He resented it; he didn't want pity from anyone.

"How about going to church with me this morning?" Haruo invited. "There's a new preacher going to preach, a young fellow who has been in prison camp for nearly a year. Well, he was picked up right after Pearl Harbor, and he just got out last week. They didn't have a thing on him."

Go to church? Why not? It would help to pass some of the day. The preacher might be from the same camp Father Sato was in, and he could get some firsthand news.

"Sure, I'll go--once. What time is it?"

"Good. The service starts about half past ten. I'll stop around for you."

Tom didn't want Haruo to see Tad.

"Don't bother. I'll come over when I get dressed."

322

Tom had a shower, shaved, and got his good suit down from the nail on the wall. It was the first time he had worn it since the day he left home. Although Mother Sato had thrown a shirt over the shoulders, the coat was gray with fine, powdery dust.

Tad was still in a dead slumber, his mouth sagging, a leg hanging over the edge of the cot in a clumsy fashion. Tom tried to avoid seeing him as he reached across the cot to hand his coat to his mother, who took it and gave it a thorough brushing. She was pleased that Tom was going to church.

"You not going to church?" Tom asked, noting that his mother had not dressed. Even during the heat she had never missed a Sunday, often going in the evening, too. As she had said when they were so busy picking cucumbers back home, when the work was over she would go twice on Sundays.

"No. Not this morning," she said. Her voice was toneless.

There was quite a group gathered outside the church barracks when Tom and Haruo arrived. As they joined the crowd and talked with those they knew, Tom eyed the ugly building and felt it wouldn't seem much like going to church in a place like that.

The Japanese service for the Issei was going on, and he could hear the chant of the preacher's voice rising and falling with the peaks and troughs of his subject. The Issei preacher was an elderly man whom Mother Sato described as having "too many words" when she would come in from the service. So there was a long wait outside for the service to end. Many more young people arrived to swell the crowd. Everyone was dressed for the occasion, not so much as they might to go to church back home, Tom thought, feeling a little stiff in his suit and tie, but more than for any other occasion where young folks gathered. Too, it seemed to be a most cheerful crowd, everyone talking and laughing, trying to keep their voices down, but even then they must have made stiff competition for the preacher

323

droning away inside the building.

The morning was bright and cool. The mountains around the horizon stood out sharp and clear against the deep blue sky. Birds come south for the winter were singing in the mesquite. The dry, clear air carried a pungent fragrance and the caressing coolness of a tender hand. Bright sunshine, which two months ago could have struck one down, now sparkled with good cheer and invited the waiting crowd out of the chilly wind from the north and around to the south side of the barracks into its warmth.

It seemed that Haruo knew nearly everyone, and he kept presenting Tom to fellows and girls he had never seen before, mostly from the northern part of the state. There were some of the girls he had heard Mari talk about, pupils in her classes at school. One was Yuri Takeda. He had heard Tad speak of her, too. But Mari had never asked Yuri to come to her barracks, because she was ashamed of the emptiness of it after having seen how the Takedas lived, so Tom had never met her before. Tad had said she was a city girl who put on airs and thought she was too good to associate with common people.

Tom liked Yuri at once. He did not think her haughty. She was friendly and unaffected and did not giggle the way so many girls did when a fellow tried to talk to them. She made Tom feel comfortable talking with her, which means a great deal to a boy who is shy around girls. She was also pretty, which was no handicap to this immediate liking he had formed for her.

The piano began to play and the music drifted out through the little paned windows as the audience sang the closing hymn. And then the Issei came filing out, dressed in their Sunday clothes. For a minute Tom imagined he was waiting for Father and Mother Sato to come out, and then they would all drive home to the ranch together to a good Sunday dinner.

When the Issei had emptied the hall, the young people went in. It was just another barracks like the ones they lived in every day. Hymn books lay on the backless benches, rough seats made of scrap lumber and mesquite by the members of the congregation. The regulation barracks windows were curtained with burlap. An old piano, donated by a church in California and trucked down by the Army, sat near the side wall at the front of the room. On it stood a bowl filled with large, yellow chrysanthemums. To the uninitiated they would have passed for real flowers, even at close range. Paper flowers were the answer to the craving for color in this land of brown earth and black barracks.

The pastor, a young man not much older than Tom and Haruo, took his place on the low platform at the front and opened the service, resting his Bible and notes on a rough pulpit which had been made by a devoted member of the congregation, an Issei who had found comfort in putting his idle hands to work. Heavy dark green draperies hung across the back of the platform, hiding the ugly, unfurnished wall behind.

By this time the building was filled, a few hundred young souls had come in a spirit of worship. It was the most wholesome atmosphere Tom had experienced in Poston. He began to feel something loosening inside him as they rose to sing the first hymn, a slackening of the tension which had stretched his nerves tight. With Haruo's deep, strong voice on one side and Mas's soft soprano on the other, Tom joined in the singing without fear of being heard.

Now the hymn was over, and the pastor was reading the scripture. The first sentence caught Tom's attention.

"If God be for us, who can be against us?"

He had heard it many times in Sunday school and Young People's back in the days when no one knew what it meant. Now he was listening as a man under condemnation from his fellow men.

"He who did not spare his own son," the pastor read on in an earnest voice, "but gave him up for us all, will he not also give us all things through him?

"Who can bring any accusation against those whom God has chosen? God pronounces them upright. Who can condemn them?

"Who can separate us from the love of Christ?

"Can trouble, or misfortune, or persecution," the voice was slowly laying the words upon the ears of the audience, "or huunger or destitution, or danger of the sword?

"No. For in all these things we are more than conquerors through him who loved us."

Tom felt a release from bondage, the beginning of a freedom of spirit which he had not known since that bleak December day almost a year ago, the day the war began, the day he came home and found his father gone.

After the scripture reading a girl sang. Tom did not notice her at first, for his eyes were still on the pastor. He had been in a prison camp. Even though he did not know Father Sato, he could tell them what the camp was like, how they were treated, whether Father Sato only wrote the good things.

When he drew his mind back to the service, he saw that it was Yuri singing. One of the Caucasian teachers was playing her accompaniment.

> This is my Father's world
> And to my listening ears
> All Nature sings and round me rings
> The music of the spheres.

She was beautiful, he said to himself, more beautiful than any girl he had ever seen before. And her voice was glorious, rich and sweet like the singing of angels in Heaven. It was more; she sang as if the words were her own and she was speaking them to her audience. It was no mere rendition of a hymn.

> This is my Father's world
> And let us ne'er forget
> That though the wrong seems oft so strong
> God is the ruler yet.

The sermon began with evacuation, as most sermons

in camp did in those early days. Some never got beyond it. They had had trouble, the young man said, there was no denying that. It was not something to be denied, anyway, skirted around, or shut up inside to brood over, or turned away from by some escape mechanism. It was something to be faced.

They had known persecution. They had had misfortune come upon them through no fault of their own. Some were tasting the bitterness of poverty for the first time. But there was nothing to fear from these things. They were powerless in themselves to hurt. The thing which was to be feared above everything else was what you were allowing these things to do to you.

Have you become discouraged and depressed? Have you given up? Have you allowed your troubles to make you resentful? Are you getting careless, lowering your standards of behavior? Are you harboring thoughts of revenge?

Young people squirmed uncomfortably under the blast of questions.

Are you hugging your misfortune to you so closely that you are shutting off the sight of God?

Troubles can be used as fire is used to purify gold, as the storm and rain are used to wash the air clean of dust. What use are you making of the tempest of emotion which blows about you? Are you blowing with the wind, this direction, that direction? Are you defeated?

It seemed to Tom the sermon had been prepared especially for him on that particular morning. He began to see how his family might weather this gale of evacuation after all, if they got the right anchors down.

The pastor went on, leading his listeners' thoughts on, up and up, to the mountain top of vision from which they could see victory. "We are more than conquerors through him who loved us."

When the service was over there was no lingering around the church, for everyone must get back to his block before the gong rang for Sunday mess, which was the same time as on weekdays.

"Come on," Haruo said when Tom wanted to wait to

see the pastor. "He's going to live in camp, you can see him anytime."

A section of the crowd trooped down the middle of the road toward Tom's block.

When the three boys dropped out, Yuri called to Tom.

"Be sure to come over to the singspiration tonight."

Turning to Haruo, she said, "You see that he comes."

The crowd went on, the girls laughing, the fellows kidding. Tom's face was red.

"How do you like Yuri?" Haruo asked tactlessly. He had been wanting to bring Tom and Yuri together.

"Oh, she's all right, I guess." He wouldn't let Haruo see how he felt about her, for fear of being laughed at. Haruo would know that Tom wasn't in Yuri's class. Haruo was disappointed and decided that Tom just wasn't a woman's man.

Tom cut across the block to his apartment with a light step. He found Tad nursing a pounding headache, lounging on his cot in a sloppy sweatshirt.

"Where the hell have you been?" he asked when he saw Tom in his good suit.

"To church."

The ridicule Tom expected did not come. Tad was feeling too sorry for himself to waste any energy on others.

"I feel gosh awful," he groaned.

"Want an aspirin?"

"Yeah. Have you got some?" Surprised. Did Tom ever take aspirin?

"No, but I can get some from Willie. He always has a supply."

"Well, don't tell him who it's for."

Tom laughed and ran out to catch Willie before he went to mess.

Tad took some aspirin and, pleased with Tom's attention, decided to go to mess with him.

"I can bring your dinner over," Tom offered.

"No. I think I'll go over. Come on, Mom. There's

the gong."

Tad put his mother between Tom and himself and took her arm, but it was more to steady himself than to help his mother as they stepped down the two steps off the stoop.

"See. You've got a couple of dates. I'll have to tell Papa on you." Tad was making a gallant effort to be gay. He didn't remember much about last night. When he had left the apartment he knew that he was going to do something to forget for awhile, or even for good; and after he had had a couple of drinks over at Suki's apartment, he began to feel awfully good. After that he didn't remember much. But he was ashamed, for he knew he had disgraced himself and had brought shame upon the family.

They attracted attention as they went into mess together. The contrast in appearance in the two sons was sharp and impossible to ignore. Tad, bleary-eyed and slouchy, came shuffling in in an old pair of slippers; Tom still wore his Sunday suit, and walked with the assurance of a man who had a source of strength upon which he can draw in any emergency.

Those who had known the Satos back home shook their heads. What had happened to Tad? He used to be such a fine fellow, so friendly and so popular. It was the evacuation. Too many others were getting like him. But Tom hadn't changed, as far as they could see. Of course he had grown older with his responsibilities. He was a fine boy. He must be a great comfort to his mother.

XVIII

The sky was red and gold with the brilliance of a desert sunset. The school block was quiet, the buildings empty. Only the two barracks occupied by the teachers showed signs of activity. Another day's struggle in the classroom was over, and the disorderly groups of displaced children had gone home to their barracks. Now it was near time for the evening mess.

Julia Brown and two other teachers came out of her door and cut across the block on their way to the personnel dining hall some three quarters of a mile away in the group of light gray frame buildings which housed the administrative offices and the residents of the administrative staff. As they turned their faces toward the glowing sky, they saw a long figure silhouetted against it, a tall, lean figure, standing at the foot of the flagpole in front of the school office, lowering the flag. Taking down the flag was the work of the janitors, but they often forgot it in their hurry to finish their cleaning after school and get away; and the sight of Tad Sato performing their neglected duty was a familiar one to the teachers.

"Isn't it strange the way he never fails to see it if that flag is left out?" Julia said to her companion, a girl who had come all the way from New York state to teach in the camp.

"Yes. It is. When he is so antagonistic toward the government, and so bitter."

Tad folded the flag neatly across his arm and went into the school office. If he had seen the girls, he did not give any indication of it; and they did not call to him as they would have done at any other time. They sensed this was a ceremony not to be interrupted. Although they often commented about it among themselves, no one ever said anything to Tad.

Tad was liked by all of the teachers who had come in from the outside, and the more one liked him, the greater the frustration one felt over not being able to do anything to help him resolve his conflicts and emerge from the welter of emotions which imprisoned him.

"If he could ever get over evacuation," Julia said, lamenting her own helplessness before the wall he had built around him. "It is like a disease, slow working, that eats away at a person until there is nothing left. And he's so brilliant and has the best manners of any of the Nisei. Aren't his manners just perfect? It's funny. To me he is the most Americanized of any of them, and still he has taken evacuation the hardest."

"Maybe that is the reason he has. He's proud and independent. I don't think he'll ever get over it. His attitude has become chronic with him now. I think he'll always be disgruntled and unhappy."

"Yes, and he isn't the only one, from what I see in my classes."

No one could contradict this, dismal prophecy that it was. They walked on in silence for a time, watching the colors change in the western sky while in their minds they contrasted the beauty of Nature with the ugliness of human relations gone mad. They followed the road now between the blocks with the dark faced people all around them. Men sitting idle on the stoops outside their doors or on rustic benches under dusty shelters which had been built to keep off the hot sun during the summer. Men and women everywhere, sitting, sitting, sitting. Looking, looking. At nothing. Young people, high-school age, college age, ambling about aimlessly, with a sloppy, nothing-to-do, nowhere-to-go air about them. Baffled faces, sullen faces, hard faces that made one wince to look at them.

No merry "Hello, Miss Brown," or "Hello, Miss Stevens and Miss Currie," but a rude turning away as the teachers passed, with some an intentional insult, with others, fear of being persecuted by their fellow schoolmates if they were friendly; and still others in confusion and embarrassment because they knew not what to do. Children running, playing, lost in the clouds of dust their feet kicked up.

Miss Stevens broke the silence.

"I have always thought it was sad to see an old person sitting idle with time hanging so heavy on his hands. Here it's all ages. I have never seen anything so depressing."

"What a devilishly destructive thing hate is," was Julia Brown's reply.

"What do you mean? That hate causes war, and war, this?"

"What I mean is much more direct than that. You aren't from California, are you, Marge?"

"You haven't heard me bragging about New York yet? You are fortunate. But what do you mean about hate and this?"

Julia hesitated. She loved her home state as much as anyone, but not the evil in it.

"Well, some day I hope the whole story of the plot behind evacuation will be brought out in the open; and then the world will know that what we see here is not a breakdown of democracy, not a product of military necessity in time of national emergency, but truly a harvest of hate.

"Hate was sown like wild oats in California after Pearl Harbor. I don't know anything about what went on behind the scenes, but from what I heard and read myself, I know that enough hate against the residents of Japanese ancestry must have been engendered to have driven them out of the state, war or no war. And this is the harvest. What a one!"

Julia went on pointing out the many hardships and sufferings which she felt had unnecessarily been brought upon an innocent people.

"Don't you think you are exaggerating?" Miss Currie, an older teacher broke in. "After all, these people aren't being tortured or starved. I think the government is being very considerate of them."

"No, they are not being tortured physically as the people in concentration camps in Europe. However, there are forms of torture just as cruel, and some are harder to bear."

They were interrupted by a fourth teacher, who came puffing up behind them. Miss Walton was one of the oldest women who had come to Poston to teach, but she could outwalk any of the others. Now she was in a state of mental agitation.

"Have you girls heard about Takio Kimura's father?" she asked, panting for breath. "They found him hanging from a mesquite tree this evening."

"Oh, no!" Julia Brown cried in distress. "Oh, poor Takio. And all those little brothers and sisters, too. What will they do?"

"Yes. Seven children altogether," Miss Walton went on. "Miss Simmons, the missionary from Japan, just came from there, and Mrs. Kimura told her he went off after breakfast this morning, and when he didn't come back she became worried. She said he had been acting queer the last few days and was very despondent. When he hadn't come back by late afternoon, she went to the block manager, and a searching party was sent out. He was just out of sight in the mesquite and had been dead for hours, the doctor said."

"How could he do it, with all those children depending on him?"

"Maybe that is why he did it--he couldn't see any way that he could ever support them again."

"Takio told me once that they had had a nice little ranch all clear and the man who bought it when they left had tricked his dad and only had to pay a fraction of what he had promised."

"Mrs. Kimura has always sent for oranges and canned milk and soup whenever I went to Parker," Miss Walton said. "Last Saturday when I stopped to see what she wanted, she told me they didn't need anything. I wonder if their money was gone. I wish now I had brought something anyway. These people are so proud it is hard to know what to do for them."

"I feel so sorry for Takio. It is a big responsibility to fall on the shoulders of a sixteen-year-old."

They had reached the mess hall. In the sky the last bright color had faded into somber gray. The dusk was cheerless, the desert empty and sad. The desolate howl of a lone coyote pierced the still air.

The teachers hurried into the brightly lit room, to the companionship of friends and the cheer of good food.

"Harvest of hate." The New Yorker shivered as she hurried to close the door against the dark loneliness behind her.

XIX

The lowering skies of the desert winter came in mid-November. The nights were frosty and the sunless mornings chill. No stoves had arrived for heating the barracks. The sharp wind whisked in through the cracks around the windows and up through the wide spaces between the floorboards, and Army blankets felt stiff and scratchy and impossible to tuck in against the draft sifting down one's neck. Straw mattresses were cold.

The unheated barracks were cheerless places, as families shivered into their clothes those dull, gray mornings. It was Army life, not suited to women, nor old men, nor little children. The sun which had beat down so mercilessly upon the helpless community only a few weeks before, burning and glaring like a giant demon determined to singe the whole puny population off the face of the desert, now did not appear at all. Or if it did, it shone with a sickeningly pale light through a thinly overcast sky and "gave at noon a sadder light than waning moon." There was no warmth in it at all.

Gray November ended and December came with its shorter days and longer, cold, dark evenings, and still no stoves. Ice formed on pails of water left out overnight. Those who had brought winter clothes with them found that what had been adequate to keep them warm in the milder climate of the coast did not suffice for the lower temperature here.

Poston life came to take on a picturesque appearance as necessity drove the people outside the barracks to sit around great bonfires of mesquite, which were built up each morning and evening. Fortunately there was an abundant supply of wood lying in tangled heaps under the growing trees surrounding the camp. And it was fortunate, too, that the Army had not yet fulfilled one of the regulations for all evacuee centers, building a barbed-wire fence around it.

After the ordeal of getting up in the cold and eating breakfast in the unheated mess halls, fingers stiff and teeth chattering, the residents poured forth from their rooms and gathered around the fires. In the firebreaks, in the clear space immediately surrounding the barracks, even between rows of buildings regardless of fire hazard, the cheering campfires sent their crackling flames heavenward, first dozens of fires, then hundreds of them. Little fires where two or three boys held their own council. Big fires with shelters of burlap staked up around them for protection from the biting wind. Some groups made excavations and built their fires below the surface of the ground, and sat down in there in cozy comfort away from the reach of the chilly north breezes.

And so the community life came to center around the fires, and people were drawn together there as they had not been in the communal mess halls where there was hurry and noise and barely elbow room at the tables.

Men, weary from uncomfortable, sleepless nights and lack of daytime comforts, angry at the government for placing them here and giving so little care to their welfare, sat around the fires, untrained in leisure, and their idle hands made mischief of their minds. They sat stooped over the crude benches, backs cramped and aching, and brought out all their grievances since the beginning of evacuation and mulled them over. Not one had been forgotten, no matter how insignificant. Their losses, their present economic plight when they should have been earning while prices were good, the pauperizing of their children who would have to support them when internment was over, the broken promises of the administration about pay for their work, the cotton picking fiasco. All were gone over. They had made good money picking cotton for the growers in the fields between Poston and Parker, and the growers were glad to have them save the crop and bragged on their picking, but the administration had suddenly withdrawn permission for them to go to the fields. Army orders, it said. No one knew.

They complained of the food, and they shared their anxiety over the danger of falling ill, living under such conditions. Disturbing rumors about the hospital in Unit One had circulated about the camp. The care was inadequate, there was no medicine, the doctors were careless; while the appointed personnel had sat around in air conditioned offices during the summer heat, newborn babies had died in the hospital for lack of moisture in the air. No coolers had been provided for the babies' ward. Dead bodies were carried out at night so that no one would know how many were dying. So the rumors had passed from block to block until the hospital had become a place of terror rather than one to give them a sense of security against fear of illness. There was no freedom of communication between the units, and when rumors spread there was no way of checking on the truth of them. The fear of falling ill became greater with the coming of cold weather.

The food was insufficient still, and there was no special diet for those who were ill with chronic diseases. The diabetics ate at the same table with the others, and there was no insulin available. No provision, except milk, was made for young children. All of these things were to be corrected in time, but no one knew. It was thought that the steward was not spending the government allotment for food to provide their tables; and some of the blocks had poor cooks, who spoiled what food was provided. Cooks, who played favorites in handing out food, became the most powerful people in the blocks.

Constant changes of policy on the part of the administration was another grievance which was aired around the fires. The stupendous plans for building up the community and developing the land which the administration had sold to the residents with such high-powered sales talk in the early months, were being abandoned, or revised and rigorously pruned. Now the talk was of relocation--get the people out of camp. No, not back home to California but to some new location

337

east of the Rockies. Who wanted to go there? queried the Issei of each other. Besides, there were many strings to the opportunity to get away from camp. There must be hearings to determine loyalty, and investigations by the FBI to make sure there was nothing in one's past which could be brought up as an obstacle between you and freedom. Then, if you passed the hearings and investigations--how the words jarred on super-sensitive minds--there was still employment somewhere out in that great unknown beyond the Rockies.

The uncertainty as to the treatment they would receive in the outside world was a deterrent to the Issei in taking advantage of the opportunity to go out, and it was ignored. Strangely enough, the Los Angeles newspapers, which had so soundly castigated them before they left California and were still whooping it up against them, were the only papers sold at the canteens. They were the only daily source of news from the outside world, and their constant attacks on Issei and Nisei alike were not reassuring. It was as the young man had prophesied at the mass meeting--they had not let up once the Japanese were evacuated from the state. A train wreck near Parker was blamed on the evacuees. They were accused of caching quantities of food taken from government warehouses in camp for the Japanese airborne troops when they arrived. They were accused of trying to poison the Los Angeles water supply at Parker Dam, although the camp was some twenty miles down the river from the dam, and the Colorado River, in common with all others, flowed downstream. No, relocation was not attractive. Besides, how could a man with a family expect to support them at war prices by starting out now?

The rift between the Issei and the Nisei, who were taking a place of leadership in the camp, was widening. The elders blamed the Nisei for the lack of consideration the government was showing them. Weren't the Nisei the only ones eligible to hold office on the council? Why didn't they demand better food? What had they received in return for their willingness to

338

cooperate in evacuation?

Construction began on a camouflage net factory in the camp. A war industry. Rumor flew through the block that the residents would be expected to work in it at camp pay. The protest which arose was like thunder, threatening, rumbling. Some of the administrative personnel accused the people of trying to sabotage the war effort. The people accused the administration of exploitation of labor. Work necessary to the welfare of the camp, yes, they would do that for fourteen dollars a month, but not defense work for which workers on the outside were paid that much a day in some cases.

And so they talked around the campfires, aired grievances in the morning before work, and work began late on these cold mornings. Some did not go to work at all. The Nisei sat with their elders and listened. Their Japanese contacts were stronger now than they had ever been.

Along with the grievances there was another element which greatly influenced the attitude of the Issei and formed a part of their conversation. It was the firm belief at that time that Japan would win the war. Each new Japanese victory in the Pacific strengthened that belief. Newspaper reports of American gains were discounted as propaganda to bolster the morale of the American people, for they were read alongside unfounded accusations against the readers themselves. What grounds for credulity?

The elders began to speak of returning to Japan when the war was over. They had always planned to go back someday. Most of them had come to America in their youth, as Father Sato had done, with the intention of returning home when they had made their fortunes. Father Sato's experience had been common to many. They had not realized their dreams. They had found only hard work. They had stayed on year after year, getting into business for themselves, leasing a piece of land or buying through their children, but still looking forward to the day when they would return to their beloved homeland.

They had made homes here which had the aspect of being permanent, and had reared children who turned out to be strange offspring with an indifference toward things Japanese, which was puzzling to their parents.

Finally their plans to return home had dispersed into the vagueness of dreams. Their place had been taken by the nearer things which had come to bind them to America with the bonds of permanence. They had made friends and business connections in their communities which they valued highly. They had attained economic security at various levels. And, most binding of all, the future of their children was in America, their native land. Their roots had gone too deep; they were no longer able to make the break.

With evacuation, all of these roots had been pulled with one mighty heave. Many of their friends had deserted them in the hysteria of war, their business connections were gone, their homes sold or left in the care of unknown tenants, and their children no longer Americans in good standing. There were no roots holding them. Evacuation had done what they had not been able to do for themselves. Uprooted, they now talked fondly of returning home to Japan.

Always around the fires they talked of Japan, the Japan they remembered, and the young people listened with increasing interest. They, too, were uprooted. Few of the elders realized the change which had taken place in the Land of the Rising Sun in the thirty or forty years of their absence. To them she was still the Japan of the turn of the century, the country of their boyhood, beautiful, peaceful, beloved. When there had been war, it had not come to their own soil, and they remembered only the glorious victories, and the security, and the etiquette and custom they loved so well, the beautiful wooded hills, and the dainty gardens looking out to sea.

As the young people listened some of them began to look upon it as a good land. Perhaps--perhaps their happiness lay in that direction. Their own country had repudiated them. Was it futile ever to expect equal rights with others under the Constitution? The confused minds of the young Nisei were fertile soil for planting the seeds of loyalty to another country. This talking around the fires was softening them up for the more intense campaign the "pressure boys" were to conduct a few months later.

Tom would stand around the fires, first with his face to the fire and then his back, trying to warm all sides. He brought wood and replenished the fire when it grew low. Rubbing his hands together to loosen the stiffness of his fingers, he listened to the talk of the older men. The future was uncertain, and things in the past which he had accepted unemotionally stood out boldly now as he heard of the good life in Japan. The government there was zealous for the rights of her nationals; this country would have to pay some time for the way she had treated the Japanese on the West Coast, they said. It felt good to know that some politically powerful body cared. He recalled Hideo's attractive picture of student life in Japan. Tad hadn't liked it there, but what Tad had said a year ago had been forgotten in the swift moving events.

As Tom left the fires and went to work in the field those cold, gray mornings, grading the land to irrigate, his mind was plagued with the many questions the talks around the fire had raised. Would Father Sato want to go back? Or Mother Sato? Neither had ever mentioned it. What was he preparing this land for? The dazzling plans for reclamation of this rich bottom land had been discarded. His work had come to have no more meaning to him than the moving of dirt from one place to another. Who know but that when the land was ready they might abandon their plan to plant it? Maybe he ought to get outside and work at something worthwhile. Willie was going after Christmas to college somewhere in the east, and he was more disagreeable than ever. The hearing was an insult to any decent American, he complained bitterly. Tom looked forward to the day he would leave.

Tom went doggedly about his work, trying to summon back the old feeling of satisfaction that he was doing something for his country. As he drove the tractor through the dust-clouded days, often choked with dust in spite of his mask until he could scarcely breathe, he went back in his mind to his years in school, the pride he took in the flag salute each morning, the thrill which came from listening to Mr. Grant teaching the Constitution, reading from the great statements regarding human liberty. When he found he had forgotten things, he went to the library evenings and huddled over a book, his neck hunched down into his sweater collar as far as possible to shut off the cold wind blowing through the cracks in the walls.

With what sweat and toil, what sacrifice and tears, this country had been born and nurtured! His own problems became diminutive and finally lost in the vast expense of two centuries of the doings of a new people in a new country, of the making of a new government based on the premise that all men were created free and equal.

It was still a new country, he thought, as time measured the progress of civilization. He must not be impatient. He must help it through its present crisis. He must be a good citizen. He knew now that he would never want to live anywhere else.

Haruo was a great help to Tom in his struggle toward these conclusions. They spent many an evening together, usually in the Endo apartment, with Father Endo listening to the radio turned low and Mother Endo knitting a warm sweater for Mas, while the boy worked on his lessons. When the cold came the family scene moved to their own campfire in front of their barracks on the firebreak; and often other Nisei, trying to preserve their loyalty, found refuge around the Endo fire. For here there was no condemnation of the government, no eulogizing of the emperor, no plans for returning to Japan.

Haruo had decided to go outside after the first of the year, not to college but to work so that he might help the family to get out sooner. His one obsession was to get Mas away from this poisonous environment. The place had become a psychological nightmare of intrigue and pressure and intimidation. The mental life was like a stagnant pond. No outlets. No intake of fresh ideas.

The wartime life which gripped the people on the outside, drawing them out of themselves into a feverish rash of activities for their country, did not penetrate the isolation of the camp. War was remote. There were not enough contacts with the outside to bring it near. Young people stewed in their own juice. They lounged about in enforced idleness and licked their festering wounds. There were many Nisei like Tom and Haruo who were fighting the same battles and winning their victories. Some were losing in the fight.

One morning while Tom was working he saw truck-loads of posts being hauled down the road toward camp. When he went to mess at noon there were fence posts already set along side of the block next to the mess hall. All morning the old men who did not work had sat over the smoldering embers of the morning fires and looked on stolidly. Mothers, hovering over their babies in the barracks, trying to protect them from cold and disease, stopped to look out the small windows in mute rebellion. They were to be fenced in. The young folks coming from offices and school shrugged their shoulders when they saw, and tried to pretend they didn't care; but underneath a new resentment flared and was reflected in the behavior at school that afternoon and in the flippancy of office girls at their typewriters.

Besides the resentment over being put behind barbed wire after they had been here for months without an incident, there was the practical problem of how to secure wood for the fires.

The Army had put a large crew on the construction job, and the fence was soon completed.

When the supply of firewood inside the fence was gone, like the miracle of the walls of Jericho, the wires of the fence dropped to the ground at convenient intervals and let the wood gatherers pass out into the

343

mesquite. The Army had built the fence. Orders had been carried out. It was satisfied. The wires lay undisturbed on the ground the remainder of the winter.

Boys and girls went from the fires to their classrooms emotionally upset and unstable and sat there in physical discomfort. The boys were insolent and overbearing, unable to accept the authority of the makeshift school. Pupils sat all morning in the unheated rooms, fingers soon too stiff to hold the pencils. After an hour they would be chilled to the bone. Girls in cotton prints and light sweaters shivered miserably. Some days it was so cold that the classes moved outside around the campfires to carry on their work. Trucks were used to bring great loads of wood for the little children.

A few books had come, and there were now chairs to sit on, and camp-made tables for desks, but there was still little enough to command respect or pride in their school. The pupils were in a frame of mind to listen readily to Tad and others who preached the same philosophy of resentment and hate, and to scorn the wise counsel of those among the faculty who took the longer view. Tar paper was torn from the barracks, doors broken off their hinges, the new tables which their fathers had made, defaced, and some of the sturdy chairs the government had purchased for the school rooms, broken. There was a general campaign of destruction of government property. The school was helpless to change the attitude, for the principal and teachers who raised their voices against this destruction were representatives of the government and came under the same classification as the officials responsible for the internment. Such words as right and wrong, duty and responsibility, fell on deaf ears.

It was natural that everyone in school would have a cold. Overheated from the bonfires, chilling in the cold rooms, their colds were not slight ones but heavy, frightening. Tight, hoarse coughing. All of the Satos were afflicted. So were the Endos. There was no protection against them and nothing to do for them.

Haruo noticed one morning as he and Mas were

344

dressing that his brother was breathing with great difficulty. The exertion of pulling on his shoes had left him gasping, and he was shaking like a quaking aspen leaf.

"You'd better go to the clinic this morning," Haruo said, "and get something for that cold."

"Yes, I think I should," Mas wheezed. "I don't believe I could sit in class this morning, I am so cold."

When Haruo came home from work at noon he saw a crowd standing around outside his door. They made way for him silently as he came up the path and went in.

Inside, his mother sat with her face buried in her hands, weeping. A screen had been placed around Mas's cot. His father laid a trembling hand on Haruo's shoulder.

"Mas has just passed away," he said in a quavering voice.

Quick pneumonia, they called it. Yes, they had called a doctor, but Mas had choked to death before he came.

Haruo went around the screen and stood a moment, the tears streaming down his cheeks. He could not believe it.

The Endos were not at mess that day, nor the next. Friends carried their meals to them.

Tom went to see Haruo.

"If we had been home this wouldn't have happened," Haruo said, and his voice was so cold that it chilled the marrow in Tom's bones. He could find no words to say to one so grief stricken, and if he had he doubted that Haruo would have heard him, for he sat like a man in a trance, staring straight ahead.

The whole block mourned the passing of the boy. The school mourned. No pupil had so endeared himself to the teachers in the few short months of school as Mas had. His interest in his work and his poise in the midst of the confusion and writhing of the other boys had been an inspiration and encouragement. His sudden death had struck terror in the hearts of parents. It

345

deepened their resentment over being there, for they felt helpless to protect their loved ones from a similar fate. There was mute despair.

Tom sat watching his mother and Mari making red paper carnations for the funeral. Couldn't the government have found some better way to solve the problem of its enemy aliens and their families? he asked himself. Now and then Mother Sato would lay down her work and rub her hands to limber up the stiff joints.

The church barracks was a mass of roses and chrysanthemums and carnations. Mas lay in the casket in his black suit and a snowy white shirt, tranquil, sleeping, handsome. His classmates filed by in awed silence and went out with wet eyes. The young pastor looked on with compassion.

The day after the funeral, a truck came around the block unloading the stoves. The days of the campfires were over.

XX

It was late afternoon of the day of the Christmas Bazaar. As winter had approached with its melancholy atmosphere of dull, chilly days, and thoughts of spending Christmas in such a place as Poston began to trouble the minds of the leaders of the camp, there was talk about what could be done to make the holiday season more cheerful, especially for the children. There were some parents who would be able to look after their own; but there were many who had suffered too heavy losses at evacuation, and some who had little laid by when the blow fell. Their children would have no Christmas at all.

It was unthinkable that, in this communal life where the boundary lines between families had grown so dim, one child should burst forth on Christmas morning shouting with joy over his armful of shiny toys while another, who sat on the same stoop with him day after day, should be left to look on, forgotten and empty-handed. No. Such a thing as that should not be allowed to happen, said those who were foresighted and public-spirited enough to see beyond the boundaries of their own personal grievances on this first Christmas in internment. It would be dismal enough spending the holidays here, but no child should be left without a gift.

The city council, presented with the problem of raising the money to buy for hundreds of children, had conceived the idea of a bazaar. Everyone who could would make something to sell; and those who had money would buy. Thus two birds could be killed with one stone. People could do their Christmas shopping in camp, and money would be raised for the kiddies. Plans had been laid, and busy hands had been at work for several weeks. Over in the barracks where Industry held forth--Industry was the misnomer for the department which had become the art center of the camp-- many idle hands with artistic bent had found work to do, woodcarving, water colors, inlay creations, and other things of beauty. Hand-decorated Christmas cards had been turned out by the hundreds, each with a touch of the desert on it; it was hard to keep them back until the day, for customers bought as fast as they could be made. Exquisite woodcarvings had slowly come into being. Old men had gone off to the mountains and come home at evening time, backs bent with the load of ironwood they carried, ironwood in grotesque shapes which lent themselves well to the artist's imagination. Thin slabs of mesquite, with the white ring of wood around the outside, had been decorated with bright sprays of holly and a brave "Merry Christmas" and were on sale for a quarter, ready to go into any barracks and do their share in fostering the holiday spirit and announcing to all that Christmas could come to Poston as well as to San Diego, or Reedley, or to the old ranch back home.

Scores of things had been made in other departments. Sweaters, and mittens, and blouses, and huge bunches of paper flowers, poinsettias and chrysanthemums, roses and carnations. There were also clusters of desert holly gathered from the desert mesas, white leaved and frosty, and sprigs of desert mistletoe, with its white, rosy-cheeked berries, plucked from where it grew on the mesquite.

The bazaar was the first constructive venture on a community-wide basis, unless one counted the parent-teachers organization, and a new spirit of alertness and interest had been generated. Booths had been built in the recreation hall in Block 344; and in the mess hall of that same block, hot dogs, of all things, were to be served. Real hot dogs with all the fixin's, just like back home. Yes, and hamburgers, too. And chili. It had taken a great deal of diplomacy and persuasion to get the makings; meat was not available in camp for such a use. Mr. Imoto had been appointed chairman of supplies, and he never gave up until he had secured the consent of the authorities to purchase on the outside, and the plans were assured of success. Just the announcement had been an uplift to the young people.

Tom Sato had been chosen as one of the chefs. Haruo had been the other one decided on, but that was before Mas died. Now he had withdrawn. He could not bring himself to enter into the hilarity which the bazaar had set off in the camp. At the very time that laughter was coming to Poston, fate had dealt him a blow which made him feel he could never laugh lightheartedly again.

Mother Sato, as she sat alone in the barracks that afternoon of the bazaar, smiled wanly as she thought of how her children were as excited over these indigestible foods they called by such weird names as hot dogs and burgers as she had been in her youth over the annual all-day excursion to the mountains in cherry blossom time. Yoshi shrieking through the room hunting for a lost nickel and finally spying it on the ground beneath the floor, where it had fallen through a crack. Mari all alive again with excitement, preening herself before the small mirror hanging on a nail, pulling on her best sweater. She was going to preside at the booth where the water colors were displayed. She and Yuri. Afterward, they were going to fill up on hamburgers or chili, or maybe both, and go over to the church to practice carols.

"The water colors are perfectly beautiful. I wish you could see them. Don't you think you could . . ."

Mother Sato had shaken her head. She was too hoarse and her throat too sore to talk.

Beautiful desert scenes. The artists had discovered beauty on the desert to which those whose eyes were filled with self-pity had been blind.

"How could I have missed all this?" Mari had said to Yuri as they arranged the pictures the night before.

"I might have, too, if it hadn't been for my father. I have seen the lovely things about the desert through his eyes. He can see a picture in even the barracks against a sunset sky."

Mother Sato was not only alone in her barracks that afternoon, but she was almost the only person left in the

349

block. Everyone had turned out to see the bazaar. She had been miserable with a cold all week, and today she felt worse. There had been a flu epidemic in the camp, and she had stayed home from the mess hall and her English and flower arrangement classes, hoping that by avoiding people she could escape the dread disease; but she believed she was coming down with it in spite of all her precautions. Up to the time the administration had issued orders against the use of electrical equipment in the barracks, she had been cooking some of the rice Tom had bought and making a cup of tea over the hot plate. After the order, which had been made necessary by a succession of blown fuses, Tom or Mari had brought her food from the mess.

She pulled her stool closer to the stove as the late afternoon grew cooler and kept to her knitting by an effort of will. She was trying to finish a sweater for Yoshi, a heavy one, not one of those stretchy store things, but something substantial and warm to protect him from the cold as he sat in the drafty school room. He would still need it even though there were stoves, for the wind would still blow through the cracks. She was going to give it to him for Christmas. Her eyes watered, and her knitting was interrupted constantly by the necessity of wiping her eyes and her dripping nose. Her head became tighter and tighter, until it seemed a bursting pressure would be reached soon.

Tom and Mari would be away until late. Tadashi, no one ever knew where he was. She sighed, and the deep breath caught in her throat and brought on a spell of coughing. And Yoshi, nothing could drag him from the block where the crowds would be gathered, not until the last light was out. This was a great day for the children of Poston. Not one of the Satos would come home for supper. Mother Sato began to consider the possibility of using her hot plate anyway, in spite of the order. The immediate need for the comfort of a cup of tea was great, but a deep-rooted spirit of submission to authority was strong. While a rather feeble struggle went on between the two opposing forces, Mother Sato heard the sound of pans and dishes from the mess hall and knew that Cook Kato was in the kitchen, preparing the evening meal. She would go over there and get hot water for her tea. She stood up, and her head spun. She took a few unsteady steps toward the door and threw out a hand to the wall to keep from falling. The mess hall was too far away. She could not make it there and back. She tottered back to her chair and sank down, exhausted. She picked up the knitting and sat there holding it in her lap. She was thoroughly lonely and miserable. She wished fervently for Papa Sato.

In his letter she had received the day before, he had admonished her not to worry. He had plenty of good, nourishing food, he had written, and a fine wood heater in his room with plenty of fuel to keep the fire roaring. She felt angry with him because he was comfortable and repented at once and bowed her head reverently while she thanked the good God that he was well and had not been mistreated, and with deep humility she besought the All-powerful One to bring him back safely to his family soon.

The shadows deepened. The mess gongs began to clang. Mother Sato turned on the light. Maybe Mrs. Hayashi would stop in to see how she was. She heard the voices of people returning from the bazaar and hurrying to mess. She glanced at the little teakettle full of water sitting on the hot plate, and an expression came over her face which Papa Sato and the children would have recognized as Mother Sato preparing to assert herself. With high disregard for the administration order, she reached out and plugged in the cord. There was no disheartening sputter. The coils began to glow. Soon the teakettle was singing blithely. She crept about the room, bringing the cup and the tea and some leftover soup.

Food brought little enjoyment, the tea was tasteless on her coated tongue, and she did not finish the third cup.

Her eyes were too blurred to see the stitches in the dim light from the ceiling bulb, and she finally gave up and went to lie on her cot, shoving the unfinished sweater into the suitcase underneath.

She began to chill, and reached out and pulled the blankets from Mari's cot over on top of hers. When she got warm, she would put them back. There she lay chilling until the Army cot shook on its wobbly legs like an old man with shaking palsy. After a time the chill left and a great heat swept over her, her lips burned with thirst, and rational thoughts were burned from her head and replaced by fragmentary, vague, will-o'-the-wisp fantasies. Poston vanished. She was at home. Papa Sato was there, and they were all preparing for a trip to Japan. Home to Japan.

Over in Block 344 the evening session of the bazaar was in full swing. It was the most gala occasion in the brief history of Poston. A continuous line of people had been filing through the building since the doors had opened at one o'clock, and the evening crowd promised to be just as large. Truckloads had come pouring in from the other units to swell the crowd and to go back with their arms full, leaving the Christmas gift treasury richer for their attendance. Money was flowing freely from the pockets that had it. The administration people were buying heavily of the rare art pieces; the teachers were patronizing the booths generously. The success of the venture was already assured.

In the mess hall, Tom and Willie, who had been drafted in Haruo's place, decked out in white aprons and caps, were presiding over the big kitchen stove, an oil-burning relic of World War I camps, turning out hot dogs and hamburgers with assembly line speed, yet not nearly fast enough to supply the demand of the horde of eager youths who crowded round the counter and lined up to the door of the long mess hall and out into the road. The dimly lit mess tables were dotted with groups or couples who preferred to eat sitting and to make their delicacy last as long as possible. All were trying to squeeze out of the occasion something of the carefree happiness of the dear old days back home.

Only a year ago, some were thinking--could it have been only *one* year ago?-- they were pulling the family car up to their favorite hamburger joint and sitting there talking and laughing with their friends while they munched to their hearts' content. There was much good-natured banter flying back and forth among the tables. Yes, laughter had come to Poston.

Mari and Yuri were released from duty at their booth at seven, and they hurried over to the mess hall, fearful that the supply might run out before they could get there.

"Two hamburgers, please," Yuri ordered from Tom in mock solemnity.

"Onions?" he asked politely, as befitted a waiter. His face, already burning from the stove, was not too hot to feel the inner warmth which crept over it at the sight of Yuri. He could never feel indifferent nor just ordinary with her as he did with other people; yet he never felt uncomfortable in her presence as he did with most girls.

"Sure, we want everything," Mari put in.

"Careful, girls," Willie cautioned. "Eating onions won't get you any dates." Willie had laid aside his grouch, and his usually scowling face was boyish and pleasant with its rare smile.

"Phooey! Who cares about dates?" Mari retorted saucily.

"I'll have to tell Haruo that," Willie teased. "Maybe we can get him to spend one evening playing bridge with the rest of us fellows."

"Coming over to practice when you are through here?" Yuri asked Tom, catching his eye when he turned from the stove with a neatly browned hamburger on a turner.

"Yes. Sure. We won't be here much longer. We're about cleaned out of everything."

There was a groan of disappointment all along the waiting line as far as his voice had carried.

"You come, too, Willie. A little music will do you good," Yuri said.

"Oh, yeah? Let me tell you, you are talking to a musician. I had my own band back home." Willie hadn't given out that much information about himself since he had come to Poston.

"Why, Willie. Why didn't you tell us . . ." Yuri was interrupted by a shout from Yoshi, who had come up, breathless.

"Tom. Hey, Tom. Come on home quick. It's Mom." The boy had elbowed his way through the crowd up to the counter. His face was frightened. Seeing Mari there, he grabbed her hand and began pulling her toward the door.

Tom dropped the mustard paddle and handed Yuri the hamburger.

"Let someone else have it. I'm going with you," she said quickly.

The four hurried through the dark across the blocks to the Sato barracks, plying Yoshi with questions as they went.

"I went home to get a dime, and Mom didn't know me. She wanted me to find Tad to go on the boat," Yoshi explained, feeling his importance. Now he had Tom and Mari, his fright had worn off.

"She must be what our neighbor back home calls 'flighty,'" Yuri said. "Every time she gets a little temperature, she doesn't know anyone and says the most outrageous things." She was trying to minimize the seriousness of the situation.

As they passed Dr. Nakata's barracks, Tom ran in and asked the doctor to come over, and he said he would follow as soon as he could get his bag.

They went in the open door just as Yoshi had left it when he had darted out, and Mari crossed the room and pulled back the blanket curtain. It was the first time Yuri had ever been in the Sato barracks, but Mari thought nothing now of the comparison between the old Army cots and ugly blankets and the fine furniture over at Yuri's.

Mother Sato looked up at them with bright, burning eyes, with no sign of recognition in them. She began to talk rapidly in Japanese about the thing which was first in her mind.

"Do any of you know Tadashi Sato?" she asked, looking from one to the other anxiously. "The boat is going soon, and I cannot find him. We cannot go without him."

Tom and Mari stood dumb with anxiety.

Yuri dropped down on the edge of the cot and patted the thin, hot hand.

"Yes, I know Tadashi," she said in Mother Sato's native tongue. "And I will find him for you. Now don't you worry, he will be here in time for the boat. Here are Mari and Tom. And Yoshi. See, they are all here."

Mother Sato looked at the trio vacantly and shook her head.

"No. They have all gone aboard with Papa Sato. I am waiting for Tadashi."

Dr. Nakata came in and, after taking Mother Sato's temperature, said to Tom, "We must get your mother to the hospital right away. She has a severe case of influenza, I think. I will go and phone for the ambulance to come at once."

The hospital! Ambulance! Frightening words in this insecure and uncertain atmosphere. Although they dreaded to have their mother taken away, neither Tom nor Mari thought of objecting to the doctor's orders.

"Yes. She'll be better off there," Yuri said, seeing their worried faces. She helped Mari slip a coat on her mother, and Mari tied a scarf around her head to protect her from the cold wind which was whipping around the corner of the barracks.

After they had watched the ambulance drive away, Yuri said, "I must go over to the church now. They will be waiting for me to play. Are you coming, Mari?"

"No. I couldn't sing now," Mari answered, and her voice broke a little. "I'll stay with Yoshi. You go, Tom."

Yuri turned to Tom. "Coming?"

"I'll walk over with you," Tom said absently. "I'll be right back," he said to Mari.

The three Sato children sitting there alone that

evening found that even an ugly barracks room could be more desolate when Mother was gone. Yoshi had lost interest in the bazaar and did not want to go back, although Tom offered to give him a dime. He lay on his cot and listened to Tom and Mari talking about their mother and how suddenly she had been taken ill. They knew she had a terrible cold.

They were surprised by Tad coming in early. He had run home to get Tom's heavy football sweater, for the night was sharp, and some of his crowd had a secret session planned down by the river. Tad was surprised, too, to find Tom and Mari at home, for he had seen crowds still going through the bazaar; but a ready barb was always on the end of his tongue.

"Well, was the bazaar a success?" he asked sarcastically. He hadn't gone near. It was run by a bunch of bootlickers of the administration.

As neither answered, Tad looked about the room.

"Where's Mom?"

"She's sick," Tom said.

"Sick?" Tad's voice changed. "What's the matter?" He walked over and pulled back the curtain and said in a soft voice, "Mom?" Then he saw that the cot was empty.

"Where is she?" he demanded.

"The doctor took her to the hospital a couple of hours ago." Tom braced himself.

In the excitement of getting their mother off to the hospital with the least possible delay, Tom had not thought of trying to find Tad and consult with him first.

The storm of Tad's wrath broke over their heads. Mari bowed to it, offering no resistance. Yoshi turned face down on the cot and cried for his mother. Tom was left alone to face the fury of his older brother.

"You fool. Why did you let them take her? Why didn't you ask me? Hospital. That is no hospital; it's nothing but a dirty morgue. Full of dead people the doctors didn't know how to cure. If those doctors were any good the Army would have them. It wouldn't leave

356

a good doctor down here to take care of us. They want us to die, every last one of us. You don't know anything about what goes on at that hospital, do you? You don't know any more about what goes on around here than you did back home. If you'd listened to me and moved out when we could, we would never have been in this God damned place." Tad stopped for breath.

"The doctor said she'd have to have something done for her right away. Her temperature was away high. He thinks she has the flu. What could we do for her here?"

"I can take care of her. Better than they will up there. I'm going after her and bring her back."

Tom gasped.

"Tad! You wouldn't dare! She's awfully sick."

Tad laughed as he started for the door. Tom followed him. Would they let Tad bring her away from the hospital? Would they keep a patient against the wishes of the family? Tad was the older; he would have the authority to speak for the family.

"It might kill her, Tad. Don't do it. You wouldn't want to be responsible."

"You should talk. Who's responsible now?"

"I'm going with you, then," Tom said stubbornly, when he saw Tad was determined to go.

Tad refused to have him and rushed out like a madman.

Tom went back and sat down and buried his face in his hands, praying that the doctor would not allow Tad to take his mother from the hospital.

Tad nursed his wrath as he walked across the dark camp in search of a government car. It was seven miles to the hospital. His anger drove out any anxiety over his mother. He was furious that she was in the hospital, that was all now. He experienced a feeling of exaltation that he was getting even with the administration in some way by defying the regulation about official cars. He had a new grievance against the administration. It was to blame for his mother being ill. No stoves for so long. This was no place for a woman. Summer heat.

Poor food. Cold, drafty barracks. Hell! How had anyone stood it?

Camp life wasn't bad when you were in uniform and had a cause to work and fight for. The sense of well-being after a physical workout, the uplift of physical accomplishment beyond anything you had been able to endure before. Muscles hard as nails. Ah, yes, Army life was good for strong young men. But for women of Mom's age? And little kids? And sick old men? Had the government no shame? No heart? Bah! What did the big shots care for anyone who didn't have a white face? And to think that once he had been proud to be an American.

He found official car number twenty-seven standing in front of Toru's barracks. He drew a deep sigh of satisfaction. He had been afraid that Toru might have it out somewhere himself. Tad reached in the window and felt along the dash. Yes, the key was in the ignition where Toru had left it. Good ol' careless boy, Toru. The barracks was dark, and Tad was glad he could get away without answering any questions.

The night was biting cold, and the icy wind whipped in the broken car window and cut through Tad's thin sweater as he stepped on the gas and sped out of camp onto the crooked, dusty road. A heavy cloud of the powdery silt hung in the air behind him and finally settled on the dead mesquite leaves which still clung stubbornly to the squatty trees.

The lights of an approaching car caused no slackening of his speed. Grudgingly he pulled over a little and went careening on, forcing the other car from the road in a blinding spray of dust. He laughed exultantly when he saw the shiny side of a sedan and, above the roar, heard a hearty curse on the "Japs" as he dashed past. The private car of one of the staff. Sure of that. No evacuee was allowed to have his car. They were all stored back in California somewhere, rotting their tires, rusting out in some leaky warehouse, or sold to some patriotic white American for a song.

A coyote loped across the road some distance ahead

and slunk off into the dark, an ugly, mean-appearing animal, mad at the world. The wide expanse of desert and sky stretched out before Tad, but it gave him no sense of freedom. Instead it pressed upon him, the emptiness, the isolation. What more ideal prison than a camp in the middle of the desert! Miles of open, water-less sand to be traversed to reach a hiding place. Fool-hardy would be the man who tried to escape from here.

But being alone, he could be himself. No need to pretend. No need to cover up what was going on inside one's mind. The tightness of his mouth, which drew his lips into an ugly sneer when he was in the presence of others, loosened, and his eyes, which were wont to look out through half-closed lids in an insolent expression of contempt, now lifted to the sky for quick glances at the nearness of the cold, blue stars. There was loneliness in his dark eyes, and suffering. Thwarted hopes and lost ideals. Defeat and despair, twin demons, fought for the right to paint the expression of his face.

He passed the lights of Unit Two. On his right the personnel quarters, frame buildings painted light, and on the other side and back some distance, the evacuee barracks. Segregation? Oh, no.

As he approached Unit One, he began to form some definite plans for his mother. He would send outside and get the medicine she needed. Dr. Nakata would tell him what to get, and he would write to, no, he would wire, Johnny Katayama in Denver. Johnny had been smart; he had moved away before evacuation. Now he was a free man, selling eggs from his own poultry ranch. Sure, the people bought from him. When people wanted fresh eggs or anything else, they didn't care where they got them from. Yes, Johnny was free. Free. What was it like? How long had it been? Nearly a year now ... Oh, don't drag all of that stuff out and look at it again.

Tad parked the car in a dark space between two buildings and walked over to the front entrance of the hospital. It was a large building made of several bar-racks joined under one roof.

Habitually he put on his mask as soon as he entered the door and came into the presence of someone again. He slouched across the lobby to where he saw a Nisei girl sitting at a desk and stood looking down at her with an insolent stare. He hated these Nisei who worked for the administration as much as he hated the administration itself.

"Is there something I can do for you?" the receptionist asked politely.

"Yeah. There sure is. I want to get my mother out of here, and you can tell me where to find her."

"Did you receive word that she was to be released tonight?"

"They just brought her in without my knowing about it. I want to take her home."

"You will have to talk to Superintendent Stevens. Here she comes now." The girl was evidently relieved to see Miss Stevens.

Tad turned and saw her coming along the narrow corridor toward him, a tall, slender Caucasian woman in stiffly starched uniform. Her gait was brisk and her manner efficient.

"Miss Stevens, someone wishes to speak to you."

The woman stopped suddenly as she was about to pass, whirled about, and looked at Tad.

"Yes. What is it?" she asked brusquely.

Tad wavered an instant under her scrutiny, but he was not going to allow himself to be routed by one of the bigwigs of the administration.

"I have come for my mother. You have her here somewhere. Sato is the name. Mrs. Shigeru Sato."

The superintendent surveyed him coldly.

"She was brought in this evening. She is very ill."

"The doctor brought her without my consent," Tad explained. "I do not wish to leave her here."

Miss Stevens tried to read the meaning back of his words by studying his face. What she saw was what she saw on so many young faces, even among the young Nisei who worked on the hospital staff--antagonism and distrust and a desperate attempt to hide one's own feeling of inferiority.

"Oh, I see," she said crisply but not unkindly. "Come with me, please."

Tad had expected something else. Refusal. And superciliousness and highhandedness. He had thought he would have to put up a fight for his right to take his mother home. In spite of himself, he found the superintendent inspired confidence. She certainly seemed to be a competent person. He followed her down a long corridor and was forced to abandon his nonchalant, shuffling strides in order to keep up. He took quick glances into wards as they passed open doors. There he saw regulation hospital beds with springs and mattresses, and there were many nurses, some in white and some in stripes, hurrying about, caring for the patients. It was still visiting hour, and many visitors were sitting beside beds chatting with their sick ones, not appearing to be alarmed to have them confined there.

Miss Stevens turned off into a short hall leading to another ward. As she did so, a nurse stepped out of a room off the hall. The superintendent spoke to her.

"Mrs. Sato? She is in here," the nurse answered, indicating the room she had just left. "Dr. Jeffers wanted her in a private room tonight, she is so ill." The nurse looked at Tad. "He doesn't want her to have any company."

"This is her son," the superintendent said, smiling. "He wants to . . ." The young Nisei nurse eyed Tad with interest. He began to feel uncomfortable and hoped the superintendent would not say what he had come for. "He wants to see her."

They went in, and the nurse continued on her way down the corridor.

Tad looked at his mother lying on a comfortable bed, and he saw the narrow army cot and the straw mattress she slept on at the barracks. He went to her and leaned over the bed.

"Hello, Mom."

She stared up vacantly.

"It's Tadashi. Don't you know me, Mom?" There

was coaxing in his voice.

"Her temperature is very high. That makes her dreamy. Why don't you leave her here tonight while we do everything that can be done to bring it down? You can stay here with her if you wish. I'll have Nurse Imoto put up a cot for you."

Tad felt foolish. He had come to fight and found no opponent.

Before he could answer, the doctor came in. He gave Tad a cold look.

"This is Mrs. Sato's son," Miss Stevens said quickly. "This is Dr. Jeffers, Mr. Sato. Dr. Jeffers has just come to Poston."

"Oh, yes. Good evening," Dr. Jeffers greeted.

"How is she, Doctor?" Tad asked, ignoring the introduction. It frightened him to have his mother fail to recognize him. He was feeling less and less like taking the responsibility upon himself of removing her from the hospital. He recalled Tom's anxious words. "It might kill her." He could believe it, now he had seen her for himself.

"Your mother is very ill. Her temperature was high and still rising when she was brought in." The doctor leaned over and read the chart. "But I believe we have it checked now. I have put a special nurse on her case tonight, and we are doing everything possible for her. It is influenza."

The superintendent looked at Tad. She seemed to be telling him to ask the doctor, if he still wanted to take his mother out; but if he didn't, it was just between her and him. She wouldn't say anything about it.

Tad looked again at the frail little woman on the bed. Tom had been right. He wouldn't dare. He said nothing. The nurse came in with a fresh ice pack.

"Where is your father?" the doctor asked Tad.

"He is not here," Tad said unwillingly. Then fear gripped him.

"I see," the doctor said quietly. There was no need for an explanation. Although he had just come to camp, as the superintendent had said, he had spent several

362

months in another evacuee center. The problem of the broken families was the same in all.

"Should we send . . ." Tad began, but could not finish.

"Oh, no. This is just a case of flu, and it hasn't been so severe this winter. So long as she doesn't get pneumonia afterward."

That decided Tad completely. Mas had died of pneumonia. And one of the men in the bachelors' quarters, too.

"I told the young man he might stay here tonight if he wishes," Miss Stevens told the doctor.

"I don't think I'd better," Tad said hurriedly. "My sister and brothers will want to know how Mother is. I'll have to get back."

"If there is any change for the worse in the night, I will have the nurse call the clinic in your unit," the doctor said.

"Thank you, Doctor Jeffers," Tad said, turning to leave.

The clinic. That was too slow. They might not even bring the message to him until morning. He knew some of the Nisei who were on duty over there. But the clinic had the only telephone he knew of in his unit except in the offices, and they were all closed at night.

The superintendent overtook him as he walked back down the corridor toward the entrance. Tad was hungry for a talk with an outsider. However, he could not let the barriers of resentment down.

"Now, don't worry about your mother," Miss Stevens said as she passed. "Nurse Imoto is a graduate nurse and one of the most competent. Good night."

Tad went out satisfied that his mother was in good hands, but worried about her nevertheless. She didn't know me, he thought. She looked so strange. She didn't know me. He hurried around the corner and looked into the dark shadows where he had parked. Yes, the car was still there. He got in and started off at a slower speed than he had driven up.

Suppose his mother should get worse during the

night. The clinic might not let him know. There must be some surer way. Mr. Bronson must have a telephone in his apartment, but could he go to the unit administrator and ask a favor of him? Hadn't he told Bill once he had never been to Mr. Bronson's quarters and never wanted to go? The thought of his mother lying there on the hospital bed, so frail, so strangely away from them all in her illness, convinced him this was no time to hold grudges. He stepped on the gas. If he hurried he might reach the camp before the Bronsons retired. He had no idea of the time, but it must be getting late.

To his great relief, there was still a light in the personnel quarters as he drove through the gate. He parked the car on the side of the office buildings opposite the quarters, entered the quarters, and walked down the narrow hall until he came to a door with Mr. Bronson's name on it. He realized he was chilled to the bone. He knocked on the door.

The door was opened promptly by Mr. Bronson himself. If he felt any surprise at seeing Tad, he carefully concealed it.

"Good evening. Come in."

Tad stepped inside the tiny room.

"Celia, this is Tad Sato. This is Mrs. Bronson, Tad. He teaches down at the high school, Celia." Tad avoided Mrs. Bronson's eyes. There were so many other things her husband could have said to identify him. She probably knew them all. The administration had its blacklist, the fellows who had the guts to stand up against them. It saw to it they never got any privileges around camp. He'd been a fool to come in here.

"Hello, Tad. Here, take this chair. It's the most comfortable," Mrs. Bronson said warmly. She was very gracious to all of Mr. Bronson's Japanese guests.

Tad felt ill at ease. He had come to ask a favor because he was up against it and had to. He didn't want to fraternize with them.

"Well, thanks, I can't stay. My mother is ill, and ..." He hesitated. Now that he was in the presence of Mr.

364

Bronson, who represented the hated administration to Tad, he found it hard to go on. It was bitter as gall to him to have to ask a favor. But a night of anxiety over his mother, maybe having her grow worse and asking for him and no way to know, that was worse. She could die, and that outfit up there wouldn't tell him until the block manager's office opened in the morning, so they could call nice and easy. He couldn't stand it not to be able to get word during the night.

"Oh, I'm sorry to hear that," Mr. Bronson had said kindly, but Tad had scarcely heard him. Now the man's next words reached him, made it easier for him to make his request.

"Is there anything I can do for you?"

"Yes," said Tad, swallowing his pride. "She's in the hospital. If she should get worse in the night, well, you know, everything's closed up in the blocks at night. No way to get a message through."

"That's easily taken care of," Mr. Bronson said. "I'll call the hospital and ask them to call me if they have a message for you."

"Wouldn't it be quicker in an emergency to have them call the Internal Security Office?" Mrs. Bronson suggested. "There would be someone there already up and dressed."

Tad cursed himself for not thinking of that himself. It would have saved him from this humiliation.

"It might be quicker, but not so sure," the man said. "The officers might be out on a job. I'd better have the hospital call here, and then I can call Security or the fire department, whichever I can get."

The fellow's got brains, Tad thought. And both Mr. Bronson and his wife appeared so concerned, as if it were one of their own folks, that Tad felt himself relax a little.

"Thanks a lot," he said, and gave the woman a smile.

"How about a cup of coffee?" she said.

"No, thanks. I'd better be getting along." He was thinking of the official car standing outside. He must get it back before Toru discovered it was gone and alerted the police.

"Then good night. And don't worry. If a message comes, my husband will see that you get it at once."

Tad thanked them and said good night. Then he hurried out and started the car with as little noise as possible. The barracks were all dark on Toru's block, so he felt safe. He parked the car and went across the camp.

Tom and Mari looked up as he came in, and their faces showed the strain they had been under as they waited. When they saw he was alone, that he hadn't dragged his sick mother home with him, they began to ask questions. Was she better?

"You didn't expect her to get well while I was there, did you?" Tad said gruffly. Then he softened. He knew Tom and Mari were suffering the same as he was. Their common anxiety drew them close.

There was no thought of going to bed. They sat and talked, Tad jumping up now and then to walk the floor.

"She didn't know me," he kept saying.

"The fever does that," Mari told him. "It doesn't mean anything."

Finally, Tad's pacing got on Tom's nerves.

"Why don't you sit down? You're not doing anyone any good, and you make me fidgety."

They heard a car. Tad rushed to the door. It was an Internal Security car making the rounds.

"They drive around all night just for the fun of it," Tad said, closing the door. "Why don't they stay in the office so someone could get them if they were really needed?" He dropped down on his cot and put his head in his hands.

Tom looked at him and took pity.

"Why don't you go over to the Fire Hall and call the hospital?" he said.

"That's what I'll do." Tad jumped up, glad for action. "I'll get Mom's nurse. She'll tell me the truth."

When he came back, Tom and Mari knew from his face he had good news.

"Her temperature is down, she's responding to the medicine, and Nurse says the doctor told her the crisis has passed," Tad said, all in one breath. "I told her to stay with Mom anyway, and she promised she would." Tad stretched out on his cot without undressing and fell asleep. He was like a man spent.

Tom took a deep breath and got up and set the alarm clock.

Mari went behind her blanket curtain and made ready for bed.

XXI

Tom had intended talking things over with his mother ever since the night the Army had made its announcement. Of course, he would volunteer. From the minute he had heard the news there had never been any question in his mind about that. At first he had taken for granted that his mother would feel the same way he did about it. Oh, of course, she wouldn't like to see him go, but she would know it was his duty and the right thing to do.

But much had happened since that night. A great deal of opposition had arisen against the Nisei going into the Army, perhaps to fight against Japan. There was criticism of an all-Nisei unit. That was discrimination, as was the acceptance of volunteers, instead of drafting the boys the same as they did the other citizens.

The pressure groups, always on the borderline of violence, seized on this opposition as a golden opportunity to foment more trouble and unrest. There were threats against any Nisei who would be so spineless as to volunteer. Tom had received his share, nothing definite, veiled, vague hints, innuendoes, references to the mysterious attacks on undesirables the previous autumn. You couldn't pin anything down, or trace anything to its source. Rumors passed from mouth to mouth, the origin soon lost sight of.

During the days preceding the arrival of the recruiting team, Tad began to have a real concern for Tom's safety. Although Tom had never confided in him, he had talked to others at first, and to talk in Poston was to publish. Tad tried to warn his brother one night just before the Army mobile unit arrived, hoping, for his safety's sake, to scare him into changing his mind. But he met with little success.

"I'm not kidding, Tom," he said finally, with a shrug. "You could get hurt."

"'Fraid cats don't volunteer for military duty in

time of war," Tom scoffed. "Give your advice to those who scare easy."

"Well, don't say I didn't warn you, wise guy," Tad growled with impatience. He didn't say any more, but promised himself he would do all he could to protect Tom from violence if the kid persisted in his crazy decision to join up.

Secretly, Tad was envious of Tom's eagerness, of his constant and unshaken faith in his country, of his burning desire to serve. Tad could remember when he, himself, had felt that same way. It was a glorious sensation, something he was certain he could never recapture. He never permitted himself to really think about the past few years, his experience with the Army and all that, but still he cherished and nurtured all the hate and disillusionment engendered by the injustice, and loudly denounced and ridiculed all the nobler and finer sentiments which had once so deeply affected him.

But a human cannot completely control his emotions, and in spite of himself, and in the face of vehement denials to himself, Tad felt an envy for Tom, who still had all his ideals intact. Also, he sensed that, regardless of Tom's weasely acquiescence to the camp authorities, Tom was a stronger character than he, more like Norio, and it humiliated him, because he was the elder brother.

Tom, of course, was unaware of any of these inner feelings toward him. Tad's own course of action since he had arrived home with his discharge from the Army had been abominable and aggravating beyond bearing, except on a few occasions, like during the critical illness of Mother Sato, and there was no outward sign that he had anything but contempt and criticism for Tom.

Now the Army mobile unit had been in camp for a week, and the recruiting was being done by blocks. So far not many Nisei had volunteered; in fact, the number was surprisingly low, and the recruiting officers were being badly heckled during the pep talks they were giving. Embarrassing questions were being asked, and things weren't going according to schedule.

369

To add to the confusion, the administration decided to put on a camp-wide registration at the same time in an effort to separate the pro-Japanese from the others. The evacuees had approached the opening day of registration in a state of ferment which was not calmed any by the ill-fated questions of loyalty, to which a "yes" would leave the Issei without a country, and a "no" which would immediately classify them as undesirable aliens in a country at war. The absurdity of requiring Issei to answer this question was soon recognized by the authorities and a more suitable one substituted, but not until damage had been done.

Feeling ran high against the government among some of the more resentful Issei. They were angered at being asked to renounce Japan when American citizenship was denied them. The government had no right to ask them to do it. All of the old animosities over discriminatory naturalization laws flared anew. Rumors flew thick and fast. What was the registration for, anyway? What was to be the fate of those who answered "no" to the loyalty questions? What new mental cruelty was being prepared for them?

The Japanese were still strong in the war despite two cheering American victories in the Coral Sea and at Midway. These victories were discounted by many in camp as American propaganda. The pro-Japanese were still arrogant, hoped to return to Japan, and some even boasted of important positions they would hold in the new Japanese Empire embracing all the islands of the Pacific.

The camp pot of emotion boiled and seethed, and the rabble-rousers tended the fire with glee and venom, snatching upon every misstep of the administration for fresh fuel. Every personal grievance of the people, every denunciatory headline in the outside newspapers-- the governor of California had just announced at a meeting in the East that a Jap was a Jap and they should be kept in custody, so he was quoted in a Los Angeles daily--even complaints of pupils in school and of patients in the hospital; everything was carefully garnered and laid on the fire of mounting emotions.

In this welter of confusion, intimidation, fanaticism, and, sometimes, righteous indignation, some of the young men beacame hopelessly lost. Besides, they had their own personal problems to solve. Their resentment against evacuation, their duty to their country. Should they volunteer? Should they not? It was hard to think straight.

Through it all Tom had been able to keep his head, and his decision to volunteer remained firm. Although he knew now it was not so simple as he had thought at first, it never occurred to him to change his mind. Constantly while he was at work scooping out the big irrigation ditch which was to bring the water to Camp III by spring planting time, his face was turned to the future. How great to get out of camp! What satisfaction and peace of soul to be wearing the uniform of his country, to be recognized as a loyal citizen. He could scarcely wait. His block was last on the list, and it seemed as if the day would never come.

But now he was not nearly so sure about his mother's attitude. She had been willing for Tad to join the Army after he came from Japan, and she had always stood with Father Sato in encouraging the children to be good Americans. How much had evacuation changed her? And how much of the talk against the boys volunteering had reached her ears? What would he do if she opposed him? He had never once defied his parents in his whole life. To do such a thing was almost as unthinkable as to give up his plan to volunteer. He knew if he could explain to his mother how he felt, what it would mean to him, what it would do for the whole family to have a soldier in the army, he knew she would understand. But you couldn't explain things of the heart in a smattering of two languages. He knew that some of the Nisei, when they had difficulties with their parents over problems vitally affecting their futures, sought the aid of an interpreter; but Tom shrank from baring his soul to a third party. He tried to think of someone he would even consider for such a delicate task. Mr. Imoto? No, he could never be confidential with Mr. Imoto about family affairs. It had been bad enough to share Yoshi's disgrace, but there had been no help for that. Haruo's father? A possibility, if things reached an emergency stage.

Tom had written to his father as soon as he knew the Army was opened to Nisei volunteers, but he had had no answer yet. He thought he would wait until he heard before he said anything to his mother. He was confident of his father's approval.

And so Tom dillydallied until the very day before their block registration. He had said nothing to Mother Sato of his plans, and she had not questioned him. But she had commented on other things during the days of recruiting which brought little encouragement to Tom.

Mrs. Imoto's son in Block 308 had volunteered.

"Too bad. Too bad," Mother Sato said. "Mrs. Imoto very sad." And again she laughed about the old Issei women signing their willingness to fight for the U.S.A.

"Mrs. Hayasi and me make good soldiers," she quipped, but there was little humor in her voice. In fact, it was as nearly bitter as Tom had ever heard from her.

On the way in from the irrigation ditch that February afternoon, he knew he could no longer delay the talk with his mother. He would tell her as soon as he got to the barracks. Perhaps a letter had come from Dad, and then things would be easy.

The air was a still, sullen cold. The sun had been unable to break through the haze all day but cast a diffused glow of murky light completely without warmth. As he drove into the car pool and climbed down from the seat on stiff legs, he shivered in the late afternoon chill.

"Going to be cold tonight, Mr. Mano," he said to the watchman at the pool gate.

"Yes. Plenty cold. Maybe wind, too."

"Hope not."

Tom cut across the blocks, walking rapidly past the canteen and on down the line of black barracks to his apartment.

Mari had just come from school, and Yoshi stood huddling over the stove, warming his red, chapped hands and sniffling with a cold. Mother Sato sat on the end of her cot nearest the small window, mending a pair of almost unmendable socks for Tad. She looked up as Tom came in, and a shadow of anxiety moved across her tired eyes.

How bad she looks, Tom thought. She's never really recovered from the flu.

"Hello, Mom. Any mail today?"

"Nothing for you," Mari answered.

Tom's face darkened with disappointment. "Did any of you hear from Dad?"

"There weren't any letters for anyone," Mari complained. "I don't see why Peg doesn't write."

Tom suppressed a gripe at Mari for always thinking of herself and took another long look at his mother. He was going to have to break the news to her tonight, somehow. Again he noted the thin face and the slow movement of her hands as the needle moved back and forth. He felt relieved that Mari and Yoshi were there. It gave him an excuse to put things off a little longer. He got a towel and started for the showers. Yoshi dashed out the door ahead of him.

"Got to get some more practice before dark," he yelled back as his mother called to him.

When Tom came back, his mother was alone. He hung up his towel, stuffed his soiled clothes in the laundry bag, and took a clean shirt from the row Mari had just ironed and hung on the wire stretched across the corner of the room. As he pulled on his shirt and began to button it, he turned resolutely toward his mother.

"Mom," he began. Mother Sato looked up from her darning. "You know we all have to register tomorrow, don't you?"

"Yes, I know," his mother said in a thin voice. Then she forced a laugh and continued. "I say I fight for your country."

"Aw, Mom, you know the Issei don't have to answer that one. That was just a mistake."

"Mrs. Motoyama in Camp I did."

"But that was just at first, because they . . ." Oh, let it go. He couldn't explain it to her, these blunders by a well-meaning administration. "Well, now the Nisei can volunteer, you know. We can go in the service just like anyone. Like Allen, and . . . and Jim and the other fellows back home."

"Yes, volunteer, not draft like others."

Tom was taken back. How did his mother know about the fierce arguments over draft versus volunteer going on around the camp?

"Allen wasn't drafted," he parried. "Nor Jim. They both signed up the very next day after Pearl Harbor." As soon as the words were out he knew he had said the wrong thing.

"Day after they took Papa-san," his mother reminded, accusingly.

There was no doubt in Tom's mind now where his mother stood. He was going to have to persuade her.

"Can't you see, Mom, it's a lot better to volunteer. It gives us Nisei a chance to prove ourselves. Draft, you have to go. Volunteer, you go because you want to. Shows you're a good citizen. Then everyone knows you're okay."

Mother Sato merely grunted and went on sewing. Tom waited. The room was quiet except for the sound of voices floating in from outside, as the residents of the block returned from their day's work and made ready for the evening meal. The rough, bony hands shook a little as they guided the needle out and in between the strands of yarn. It became evident to Tom that as far as his mother was concerned, the matter was discussed and settled.

"Well, I just wanted to tell you that . . . that . . . well, I've decided . . . that is, I think it's the thing for me to do. Volunteer." At least he had it out. The signs of struggle were in the tiny beads of sweat on his forehead.

Mother Sato laid the sock on the top of the sewing basket, stuck her needle in the ball of yarn, and laid the ball on top of the sock. Then she folded her hands in her lap and looked up at her son.

"You ask Papa Sato about this?" she demanded.

"Sure, I wrote him. But he hasn't answered yet. You know he would want me to go."

"You wait, you hear."

"No, I can't. We have to sign up tomorrow. This is the last block, and then the recruiting team will be leaving the camp. I can't wait. I'll miss my chance."

"One man no win a war."

"I know that," Tom said, getting angry. "It's not because I think I'm so important. It's just that . . ." Here he was stymied. How could he explain so she would understand?"

"Tamotsu, you wait. Draft, you go."

Before Tom could protest further, Mari came rushing in, her face rosy with the cold. When she found out what they were discussing, she immediately took Tom's part.

"About time someone in the family did something we could be proud of. The way Tad acts, he's giving all of us a bad name. And Yoshi, too," she complained. She began fixing her blown hair before the cracked mirror. "I know I'd go if I were a fellow. I'd go anywhere to get out of this horrible place."

Her mother hushed her and began a rapid stream of words aimed at Tom. She had risen from the cot and stood over him where he had sat down to put on his shoes. He could understand only a word here and there, she talked so rapidly, but he knew she was using everything possible to keep him from going away. Her illness, their poverty since the tenants had left the ranch, her loneliness without Papa Sato, her anxiety over Yoshio. Only Tom's presence could help her bear all these burdens.

"I'm sorry, Mom, but I have to go," Tom interrupted.

Mari broke in before her mother could start again.

"I'll be through school in June. I can work. I can

375

go outside and get a job and send money home. What can Tom do for you that the rest of us can't? You ought to give Tad a good talking to. Make him take some responsibility."

Her mother ignored her, pushed her words aside. But the little woman was getting tired now. The conflict had upset her, sapped her energy. She moved the sewing basket from the cot to the floor and gave it a push under the cot with her foot. Then, as if she no longer had the strength to oppose her stubborn children, she lay down and began to weep softly.

Tom gave his sister a hopeless glance. Then he turned away from them both and looked out the window to the somber evening. He could never win her consent. He would have to go without it. The blare of the trumpets was in his ears, his eyes blinded by the splendor of battle. The little, shrunken woman on the cot was, at that moment, only an obstacle in his path.

The door flew back on its hinges, and Tad strode in and closed it with a bang. He was in an evil mood. He looked about the room, trying to find something to growl about. Mari was innocently polishing her nails. His mother was lying down as she usually was when he came in. Tom was still at the window. He did not turn when Tad entered.

Tad threw his sweater down and reached across the cot for his towel. Then he heard the low sobs.

"What's the matter with Mom?" he asked the others accusingly.

Neither Tom nor Mari had a ready answer.

Mother Sato sat up and wiped her eyes.

"Tadashi," she said, and there was a stern note in her voice. It caused them all to turn to her. "You tell Tamotsu he cannot go to war. You elder brother. He will obey."

A shock of surprise shook the room, each one feeling it in his own way. Mari's hand slipped, and the brush smeared the nail polish across her finger as she looked anxiously from one brother to the other. She could sense the drama of the situation. Tom felt a burning anger welling up in his throat. He could scarcely breathe. To think that his mother would enlist Tad's aid against him! What if Tad were older? Hadn't he sold his birthright over and over again since evacuation? Tom thought of his own efforts to carry the load after his father was taken, how he had tried to spare his mother all he could. And Tad . . . Tom couldn't believe his ears. Had his mother really said the words?

Tad himself was utterly unprepared to carry out his mother's request. Having been the black sheep of the family for so long, he was unable to rise to the position of authority to which his mother had raised him. And it humiliated him that he hadn't the courage to speak the command to Tom. He sought refuge in righteous anger.

"So that's it. You've been telling your mother you're going to volunteer, I suppose. Now see what you've done with your damned, cheap, flag-waving patriotism? Do you want to kill her? You're nothing but a coward, striking a sick, helpless, woman."

Tom angered him still further by refusing to answer his taunts.

"Tom's got a right to go if he wants to," Mari said. "It's his country."

"His country," Tad sneered. "Then why doesn't he tell *his* country that he and his family would like to go back home where they belong? *His* country. Who wants a country that has kicked every one of us in the face? Nobody with any guts, with any family pride. It's a disgrace to the Sato blood in his veins to want to offer himself. I've already warned you, Tom. Now I . . ."

"Don't pay any attention to him, Tom," Mari shouted.

"Mari, you keep out of this!" Tad screamed at her.

"Yes, Mari, keep out. This is between Tad and me," Tom said bitterly. Then he turned on Tad, flames and anger shooting from his eyes.

"What right do you have to tell me what to do?"

"You heard what our mother said," Tad answered,

hiding behind his mother's skirts. "I'm the head of the family. I'm taking Dad's place."

"Since when?" Tom's voice was as withering as a desert wind.

Tad looked away, unable to face Tom. He was fighting himself, trying to gain the stature to force Tom to stay. Not able to do so, he resorted to threats.

"If you defy your own family, there are those here who will see you don't get by with it. There are people here who are determined that you damned fool hotheads don't dishonor the Japanese blood in you."

"Who's going to know I have defied anyone? Who's going to report me?"

"There are ways of finding out."

"Informers?" It was plain this wasn't meant for a question, but an insult.

Again Tad's eyes shifted, and Tom laughed. It was an ugly laugh.

Already stung by the insult, Tad was angered beyond control by the laugh. He lunged at Tom, his fist clenched. Mother Sato cried out and rushed between them. The blow went over her head. It missed Tom, for he had seen it coming in time to dodge. He grabbed his sweater and ran for the door. In the doorway, he turned and shouted at Tad.

"And while you're informing, tell your heavyweight friends I'll do my duty to my country as I see it and for them to keep their dirty hands off me. I've got friends, too, and we can darn well take care of ourselves."

It was an empty boast, and a silly one. No one could protect himself against the cowardly attacks of the pressure gangs if they decided to move in on one; but Tom was beyond reason. He slammed the door and was gone.

The room became very still. No one had ever seen Tom, the good-natured, easygoing one of the family, blow up before. It gave them all a feeling of uneasiness. He had stood for stability, a rock to lean against in uncertain times, and now the rock had erupted and left them without support. For the first time they real-

378

ized and appreciated what Tom had meant to them during the hard days since Pearl Harbor.

Tom's outburst had been like a dash of cold water in Tad's hot face. It lowered his temperature and made him conscious of immediate concerns. Had anyone heard Tom shout defiance of the muscle men? These lousy barracks had ears. If anyone had heard, it might mean trouble for all of them. He had never intended to inform on Tom. What did Tom take him for, anyway? He had only wanted to scare him. He had failed his mother, too. He could see the look of reproof on her drawn face. And he had made a spectacle of himself attacking Tom. What if the blow had fallen on his mother? Tad's eyes filled with misery, and he drew a veil down over them to hide it from the others.

Mother Sato realized her mistake in setting Tad against Tom, and worry over her third son tied her aching head into tight knots. She hadn't been fair to him, but she couldn't let him leave her. On that she was adamant.

Tom walked rapidly around the block, trying to calm himself. The sudden convulsion of temper had frightened him. It was like being insane, not knowing what you were doing. After awhile he went into the washroom and crowded in at the tin trough to dash cold water over his face. He felt weak and sick after the anger had drained away.

As he came out, he saw Mr. Endo standing there. They walked along together toward the Endo apartment. Should he ask Mr. Endo to talk to his mother for him?

"I had a letter from Haruo today," the man said.

"Suppose he's started into classes by this time," Tom said.

"Oh, yes. He entered as soon as he got back East. Now he's wondering if he ought to quit and join the Nisei battalion."

"Sure. He'd want to volunteer. How do you folks feel about it?" He'd find out where Mr. Endo stood before he enlisted his services of intercession.

"We want him to decide for himself," Mr. Endo

began. "However, I have a letter ready to mail, advising him to do nothing in a hurry. There are many angles to this thing, and he will see them for himself when he thinks it over."

"I don't think I know what you mean, Mr. Endo. It looks like a great opportunity for the Nisei to me."

"The majority don't seem to agree with you. I hear not many are joining up. I think it is just as well they don't. The Army should draft them the same as it does the rest of the young men. This is still discrimination."

Tom was impatient. This was a typical Issei point of view, but he would have expected something more liberal from Haruo's father. He knew he could get no help from him.

They reached the Endo apartment, and Tom hurried on before Mr. Endo could ask him in. The man was right about one thing, Tom thought. This was a question everyone must decide for himself. No one could make your decisions for you, not even your own parents. Tom dodged out and in among the people milling around the block like ants, men home from work, children from school and games, women scurrying back and forth between laundry and barracks bringing in clothes before the mess hall gong.

Yoshi shouted from the basketball court as Tom passed. "Heh, Tom, look! Watch me drop one in. Heh, can't you hear anything? Lookee!"

"Yeah. Good work, kid. Keep it up," Tom called back absently. His mind was hunting for a quiet place to think. He wasn't ready to go back to the barracks and face his family yet. He had to be alone. There was only one place where that was possible, out in the mesquite, away from the crowded camp. He left the block and struck out into the desert, among the small, bare trees.

Tad saw him go, stood at the window and watched him until he disappeared in the tangle of squatty trees, then glanced apprehensively around at the adjoining grounds. Had anyone else noticed Tom's departure? This was a strange time to be leaving the camp.

As soon as Tom was out of sight of the confusion of the camp, he sat down on a fallen tree spared from the winter fires and tried to organize his mind.

The thing he wanted to do more than anything in the world was now within his grasp. When he had first heard the news, he was afraid to believe for fear it was just another rumor. Then, when it became official, he was in a dither lest the Army cancel the order, as they had done so many times before evacuation. It was too good to be true. Not until the mobile unit arrived did he feel sure. He had walked around past the administration area where the unit was parked when he came from work each day just to look at it and reassure himself. It was out of his way, but it was worth it. Not to take advantage of the opportunity he had waited for so long was incredible.

Of course, he had obligations to his parents, and he had always tried to fulfill them. But he was a man now and had obligations himself, too, and to his country. Which was stronger? Which came first?

Didn't other parents, millions of them, have to give their sons, who were as much to them as he was to his? Thus he reasoned, and a voice answered back, "not out of concentration camps." But there were parents in the camps who were giving their sons. Hadn't Mr. Endo said it was for Haruo to decide? And Haruo was all they had, now that Mas was gone, Tom argued doggedly with the voice. No, they have each other, came the retort; Mr. Endo is not away in a prison camp, and Mrs. Endo is a strong, healthy woman, not weak and spent with illness and anxiety.

Tom drowned out the voice by fanning his resentment toward his mother for appealing to Tad. Let Tad take care of her. She had always been partial to him.

The setting sun shone forth below the clouds before it sank behind the mountains and set the world aflame with color, breathtakingly beautiful. Gradually the light faded, and a somber gray twilight settled over the desert.

The supper gongs began to clang.

From habit, Tom rose to go. But, no, he wasn't ready yet. He hadn't decided a thing. But what was there to decide? He was going to volunteer, wasn't he? Or was he? For the first time, he became conscious of the fact that there was a question about it, that the matter was in doubt. He might have to give up his dreams.

Now he could not sit down and think quietly. He began to walk rapidly away from the camp. He wandered about aimlessly in the mesquite, fighting to bolster his wavering decision. This thing means too much for me to give it up for anyone, even my own mother. His thoughts wandered far afield. He thought of Allen, somewhere out in the Pacific. Both in uniform, they would be back on a basis of equality again. Be funny if they'd meet someplace overseas. They could compare their experiences and fight over the Army and Navy. He thought of Yuri. If he were doing something worthwhile, he'd have more of a right to try to win her. A tractor driver grimy with desert dust couldn't be very romantic to a girl like Yuri.

Gradually he came to see that there was some selfishness in his plans. Tad was wrong about cheap patriotism. It wasn't cheap to want to defend your country in time of war. It wasn't cheap to want the respect and confidence of your fellow citizens. These were legitimate and honorable goals. But were his more personal ambitions as worthy?

Dark came on.

Still Tom walked, without sense of direction, hopelessly bogged down in a welter of contradictory thoughts. He went over the scene in the apartment, trying to understand why his mother appealed to Tad. It wasn't like her to do such a thing. Even though Tad was her favorite after Norio, she had never set one son against the other. She had always been fair in dealing with her children. Then how could she have done this, and after the way Tad had acted, too? Finally he realized that only under tremendous stress would she have done so. If it meant that much to her, maybe he ought to give the whole thing up. Give it up? What was he thinking about? Heck, he wasn't getting anywhere. He might as well go back to camp and sleep on it. Things might look better in the morning.

He reversed his direction and made his way slowly through the dense dark. A coyote gave its lonely howl not far away, and he felt around on the ground and found a stout stick for a club. Then he heard other sounds, tramping feet breaking dry twigs, voices. His heart skipped a beat. Was he being followed? He stopped stock still and listened. The voices came nearer. Tom thought of making a run for the camp. Then the sounds receded and were lost in the distance. Must have been a crowd returning from a hike to the river. He drew a deep breath of relief and started on.

Tom walked for some time, and still no lights in sight. A light breeze sprang up and quickly developed into a wind that picked up puffs of dust and blew them into his eyes. It was a cold wind, coming off the snow covered mountains to the north. He quickened his pace. He was anxious to get home, for it was plain a full-fledged dust storm was in the making. He walked on and on. Nothing but darkness ahead. He knew he hadn't been that far from camp. He had lost his way.

The wind increased. The air became filled with the powdery silt. There were no landmarks from which he might have been able to fix his position. On a moonlit night, or even on a clear night with the bright stars shining overhead, the familiar outlines of the mountains to the west, south, and east would have guided him. But this miserable dust shut him in. He might wander around all night and get further and further from camp. He decided to hole in and wait for daylight.

He tried to scoop out a shelter from the wind, but underneath the surface the ground was hard, so he gathered brushwood and built a windbreak and stretched out close against it.

The wind penetrated his thin sweater, and soon chills were running along his spine. He would have to keep moving.

He knew the wind must be coming from the north. No wind blowing up the arroyos from Mexico could pack such a frigid wallop. He would keep moving east.

The hours wore on, and Tom was no nearer to finding his way out of the pathless desert. The immediate task of reaching camp drove all other thoughts from his mind.

When he returned to his problem again in the bitter cold hours after midnight, his mind was cleared of the muddle. There in the solitude, engulfed in blinding dust and chilled to the bone by the whipping wind, the way his duty lay opened up before him like a well-defined road. It became crystal clear that he could not leave his mother under the present circumstances. How could he ever have considered doing so?

To answer that was to recognize that he, too, had been a victim of personal disintegration since coming to Poston. He had a son's duty to his parents which he could not delegate to any other member of the family. He would have to give up his cherished dreams for the present.

The decision brought him no joy, only a dull sense of relief that the struggle was over. And a stubborn resentment. He felt that fate had dealt him an illegal blow. All he wanted now was to get home and out of this blinding dust.

Where the devil was he, anyway? Maybe he had gone too far south and missed the camp. In that case, he would be east of it. Should he turn and retrace his steps? He didn't know. He had no idea where he was.

Suddenly the dust became so thick he had to hold his arm over his face to breathe, and his feet sank deep in soft sand. He had come to an open space like a windbreak up the mountain side. Could this be the old road to Blythe? If so, he could follow it back to camp. The road from Parker to Blythe had long since been abandoned, and the sand was too deep for passenger cars to negotiate it, but sometimes a truck managed to get through. He felt sure he was right about the road and turned into the cold wind. The driving sand blasted against his face like millions of tiny needlepoints.

Suddenly the world of dust around him lit up with a yellow blur. Startled, he stopped, and above the roar of the wind he heard the rumble of a laboring motor. Turning quickly, he saw the headlights bearing down upon him. He leaped off the road to let the car pass. Who would be traveling this abandoned road at this eerie hour of the night? Instead of plowing past, the car, which he could now see was an Army jeep, slowed and stopped a few feet beyond him.

Wary now, Tom drew farther back into the mesquite and crouched behind a pile of brush.

"What are you stopping here for?" a thick voice growled.

"Didn't you see that Jap?"

"Naw. I didn't see anything. Come on, let's get going. We're late already." Other voices mumbled their agreement.

"But I saw him, I tell you. Right there in the road in front of the car. We'd better take a look and see. Might be one of them trying to get away."

A bunch of fellows piled out of the jeep, and by the car lights Tom could see they were in uniform. Military police from the camp guard station doubtless. His first impulse was to step out and tell them of his plight, but when he saw them staggering about, the worse off for a night in a Blythe bar, fear gripped him, and he withdrew still further back into the brush.

"He went off on this side," the one who had spoken first said. He must be the driver, for he was the most coherent of the five. They all began beating about in a ludicrous fashion, as if they were trying to flush a rabbit, bumping into each other in the dark, falling, fighting, and cursing each other as the sand choked their throats.

Tom watched and listened with mixed emotions.

Finally their interest in the hunt waned, and they drifted back toward the car. Tom rose and went toward them. The temptation to hitch a ride back to camp was

385

strong. Would they believe him when he told them he was lost, or would they turn him in at the police station? What rumors would the pressure group, who hated him for his loyalty, start about him trying to escape the night before registration? If he were going to volunteer, it would scotch any rumors, but now . . . He decided it wasn't safe to risk it.

He stood motionless while the men climbed clumsily into the jeep and drove off. The taillights disappeared in the dust.

"And to think I wanted to wear the uniform so I'd be considered the equal of other Americans." He snorted with disgust and spit onto the sand.

He slogged wearily through the sand, following the jeep. He was sure of his directions now. As he struggled along, the wind died down and the dust began to settle. At last the lights of the camp came into view. Then the dim outline of the black barracks. He left the road to avoid the little cubbyhole of a guard station at the south end of the camp and skirted around toward the west and his block.

Wandering all night on the desert, his wounds had healed. His temper was spent. He was tired and hungry. The long hours had built a buffer zone between the past and its dreams, and the future with its black realities. His fight with Tad and his determination to defy his mother belonged to the past. The future was too vague and uncertain to inspire any plans.

As he came into his block, he was surprised to see a light in his apartment. When he saw a man standing in front of his barracks, he stopped suddenly and took a tighter grip on the club he still carried.

"Is that you, Tom?" It was Tad's voice, low, worried.

"Yeah."

"Are you all right?"

"Yeah. I'm okay."

"I was afraid something might have happened to you." No need to explain what. "Where have you been?"

"I went for a walk and got lost," Tom admitted,

feeling silly. He dropped down exhausted on the step.

"Heh, don't sit here in the cold. Come on inside."

Tad had kept a fire going, and the room was warm, so warm that Yoshi had kicked off his blankets, and they lay in a heap on the floor, covered with a thick layer of dust sifted in through the cracks. Mother Sato, hearing voices, had come out from her curtained cot. She picked up the blankets and shook them gently and laid them across the foot of Yoshi's bed. A cloud of dust filled the room. Yoshi sneezed and threw himself over on his back, sending more dust into the air.

"Anything to eat?" Tom asked his mother, who was regarding him out of hollow eyes.

"I make some tea."

"Heck with tea," Tad said. "This boy's been walking all night. He needs some real food. Wait a minute. I'll get you something."

Tad went out and returned in a few minutes with a loaf of bread, a carton of milk, butter, generous slices of roast beef, and a big hunk of chocolate cake.

"Well, what do you know?" Tom grinned with pleasure through his grimy face. "How did you ever . . ."

"Ask no questions, boy. Fall to."

Mother Sato, after satisfying herself that Tom was all right, no longer the rebellious son but ready to bow to her wishes, went back to bed and left the boys to themselves.

Tom needed no urging to eat. He was glad for once that Tad had a drag with the cook. He must have more than a drag. He must have a key to the mess hall, as Tom had suspected once or twice before.

When he had finished, they sat on talking. Tad showed no triumph over Tom's decision.

"I'm glad," he said. "I don't believe you will ever regret it. It would have dealt Mom a low blow if you had gone."

"Yes. I know it now. We've got to think of her first while Dad's away."

The brothers were very close. It was a precious

387

moment, but one which could not be prolonged, for so delicate is the fabric of human emotions that to grasp and hold it is only to tear it in twain. While their fellowship was still warm, Tom got up stiffly, found a towel and soap, and went to the showers.

XXII

It seemed to Tom that he had barely closed his eyes when the breakfast gong began clanging. With difficulty he opened his dust-irritated eyes and looked around. Mother Sato, Mari, and Yoshi had gone to breakfast. Tad was still sound asleep.

"Good old Tad," Tom thought with a nice feeling of warmth inside. "I guess I gave him a scare." He lay there stretching and yawning, reliving the rediscovery of his brother a few hours earlier.

"I should never have accused him of squealing on me," Tom thought with regret. And that thought got him around to what day it was. The great day. The day of enlistment. By night he'd be in the Army. So long had he had this goal in mind that for the moment his decision of the night before was wiped out. Tom threw back the blankets and leaped out of his cot. Then it struck him like an avalanche that set him reeling. Not a big day for him. Just another day to eat and work and listen to gripes, with a little time off from work to run over to the block to register.

He began to realize how tired he was from his battle with the wind the night before. He sat down on the cot and inspected the blisters on his heels which were aching like bee stings. And his toes were red and sore. He didn't think he could run the tractor. He couldn't even stand to put on shoes.

He picked up one of the old tennis shoes he had worn yesterday. All shot to pieces plowing through the sand last night. The other one was just as bad. He tossed them into the apple box which served as wastebasket. A choking puff of dust rose as they landed. The floor was covered with a layer of dust, everything in the room gray with it.

When Tom was dressed, he looked down at Tad still sleeping, was going to yank off the blankets, hesitated, and decided against waking him. Before last night he wouldn't even have thought of rousing Tad. But things were different this morning. They were brothers again.

As he walked over to the mess hall, Tom was looking forward with pleasure to some real companionship, like they had had on the ranch. He felt because he had sacrificed his most cherished desires for his mother's sake, Tad would feel that he, too, had obligations. Brighter days were ahead. And they day would come when he could do what he wanted to do. He even found himself whistling as he limped along in his bedroom slippers.

He must see Hitoshi and Mitsuro. They had planned together that they would all enlist when it came their block's turn to register. He hated to have let the fellows down when they had all solemnly sworn they would stick together and not let the pressure boys scare them out. Would they suspect he had got cold feet? And a lot of other fellows knew he intended to volunteer. And they all knew where Tad stood. Well, they'd have to think whatever they wanted to. A man had to live his own life and make his own decisions and be free to change his mind if he needed to. And he didn't have to fall over himself to explain to everybody, either.

But what about Yuri? She knew how he'd been all hepped up about going into the Army. And now he had the chance. She'd wonder about it. And it wasn't so easy to say, let her think what she wanted to. Her opinion of him was important. He wouldn't want her to think he was a slacker. Of course, if she knew the facts, she'd know a fellow couldn't defy his sick mother. But who was going to tell her? He knew he wasn't.

The mess hall was almost empty. Only a few stragglers and not much food left. Some cold toast and a sticky jar of jam almost empty. He didn't care. He wasn't hungry after the big feed Tad had spread for him. He didn't know why he had bothered to come over. Must have been pure habit.

Tom got a cup of hot coffee, and over it mused uncomfortably about Yuri. He'd talked too much, wanting to impress her. He should have kept his mouth shut. He'd had visions of coming back to camp in his uniform for a last visit before he went overseas and sort of sweeping Yuri off her feet. Be nice away off in some strange country, thinking of her as his girl and getting letters from her. And he'd answer and say things he'd never been able to say face to face. But that dream was all over now. He was still just plain, unglamorous Tom Sato, ag worker with dust in his hair. Fat chance to make an impression on a city girl like Yuri.

Well, he'd better get out and hunt up Hitoshi and Mitsuro. They must have had their breakfast early. No sign of them coming now.

Tad finally got up from his cot, driven out of it by his mother, who was in a hurry to get at the after-storm cleanup. Before he went to school, he was in a devilish mood. As if ashamed of his softness with Tom the night before, which to him was a display of inexcusable weakness, he set out with a vengeance to regain his stature as a martyr, at least in his own eyes. He snapped at his mother and sister. He gave Yoshi a cuff on the ear when the boy, dodging Mari's broom, stepped on Tad's foot. The blow sent Yoshi staggering against the wall, eyes stinging with hot tears. He heaped curses of revenge on his brother, but he was careful to whisper them so his mother wouldn't hear.

Tad laughed and went on searching for his clothes. He refused to tell what he was looking for and was tearing the apartment apart. He shuffled his feet through the deep pile of dust Mari had swept up, sending it scattering.

"Oh, Tad, look what you've done! If you'd only tell me what you're looking for, maybe I would know where it is." Mari was still cross with Tad because of the way he had talked to Tom the evening before, and the two had been fussing ever since Mari came from breakfast.

"Well, if you'd only leave my things alone, I could find them myself," Tad fired back. Then his eyes fell on some typewritten sheets on the table.

"What have we here?" Tad said, picking up the

papers. "Been typing a love letter to Haruo so he can be sure to read it?"

"That's my English theme," Mari squealed. "You leave it alone." She dropped the dustpan and rushed across the room to grab the paper, but Tad held it out of reach.

"Not a letter at all. Well, I'll have to see what you're writing themes about. 'What Democracy Means to Me,'" Tad read in a taunting voice, holding the paper high over his head. "Democracy means freedom and equality," he went on. "In a monarchy there are titled people and common people, and in a dictatorship no one has any rights but what the dictator gives them; but in a democracy the people elect their own, that is, they govern themselves. Everyone has a vote so all the citizens have an equal say in choosing the officials. I like a democracy best, because I know when I am old enough, I can vote for the president of my country . . ." Tad broke off, furious.

"What putrid rubbish. When you're old enough to vote, you'll still be rotting in a concentration camp." Tad wadded the papers into a ball and threw them into the waste box. "How do these damned Caucasian teachers have the nerve to teach about democracy in a place like this?"

"Oh, Tad, you've ruined my paper," Mari cried with tears in her eyes. She pushed Tad aside and retrieved the crumpled papers, trying to smooth them out. "I have to hand this in first period. There's no time to do it over. I'll just tell Miss Brown and the whole class what happened to it."

"Do that. I wish you would. And tell Miss Brown I said if the teachers haven't any more judgment than to teach such rot, the Nisei ought to have more guts than to fall for it. Haven't you got any pride? Haven't any of you? Do I have to have pride for the whole family? I suppose you can hardly wait to get up there to register today, so you can answer 'yes' to all those questions."

"Of course, I'll answer 'yes' to the loyalty questions. Won't you?"

Tad didn't answer, and Mari stared at him with startled eyes.

"Tad, you wouldn't dare!" she exclaimed.

Tad turned away from her gaze and went on ransacking the place.

Mari laid the theme on the table and took up the broom. There was a frightened look in her dark eyes. Would Tad refuse to declare his loyalty?

Right then Tom opened the door, stepped over a pile of dust, and stood grinning at Tad, who was throwing articles out of a suitcase.

"Looking for something?" he asked with a tease in his voice.

Tad looked up, scowling. Tom should have been warned.

"Save your corny remarks for your own weasely crowd."

Tom studied his brother's face for a moment. Tad must be joking.

But the face was as hard as the words.

Tad had exhausted the places to look, and he turned to Tom.

"Seen anything of my old sweat shirt?" he asked.

"The last time I saw it, you were in it," Tom ribbed, determined to keep cheerful.

"Turn off the comedy, will you?" Tad shouted.

"I know where your shirt is," Mari said, in a gloating voice. "It was nothing but an old rag full of holes, and I tore it in two. Half of it I used for a mop, and half for a dust cloth. See, Mom's using it now."

If Tad hadn't been speechless with anger, Mari would never have been able to finish her words of triumph. The disreputable old sweat shirt had become a symbol to Tad, like sackcloth to the martyrs of old. He had worn it when he left home, instead of a good suit as Tom had done. He always wore it in his darker moods, as the most potent protest against discrimination and evacuation. It showed contempt for his persecutors. And he wanted it above everything else today to wear when he went to register.

And now there was half of that prized symbol, dangling from his mother's hand as she dusted off the table.

"Let me have that," Tad shouted, snatching the rag from his mother. "Get the other piece and sew them together," he demanded.

Mother Sato, unaware of the conflict among the children, pulled at one end of the shirt.

"No good. Full of holes. You put on good shirt."

Limply Tad loosened his hold on the disputed piece of cloth.

"Well, of all the . . ." His fury choked him. He looked at Mari, and Mari, glancing at the rumpled theme paper, tossed her head and laughed.

"You can wear my sweat shirt if you want to," Tom said. "It's clean, and I won't be needing it today." Come back, Tad, come back, was ringing through Tom's mind as he spoke.

"Who said I wanted a *clean* shirt?" Tad shouted. "The lousier the better."

Tom gave his brother a puzzled look. He couldn't know that Tad was a man imprisoned. By himself. Only during those long night hours of deepest anxiety which ended in unspeakable relief when Tom returned safely, only in those hours when Tad was not thinking of himself, was he completely free.

What Tom saw convinced him that he could get nowhere with Tad now. He turned and left the apartment, confused and disheartened. He went to the block manager's office and phoned the Ag. Office about his blistered feet and was excused from work for the day. From there he went to Hitoshi's apartment to wait until it was time to go to register.

By evening Block 324 had completed their registration. And those Nisei who were going to volunteer had done so. Each registrant had taken his silent stand. For each one, another piece had been added to this crazy quilt of evacuation. The decisions had been made, the die cast. That evening, the Army mobile unit left the camp.

Next day the authorities began to tabulate the results. The total number of volunteers was disappointingly low. The number of citizens answering "no" to the loyalty questions was alarmingly high. Those charged with the duty of checking the papers looked at the thick pile of what they had begun to call the "No-No" answers and shook their heads. Surely there couldn't be that many Nisei ready to throw away their prized citizenship. Some had made notations beside their negative answers. "I would have been willing to fight before evacuation," some wrote. Thus, this was a hasty action taken in revenge, and with realization of the full consequence of their action. These must have counsel and protection of their citizenship.

Facilities were set up for interviews with all the "No-Nos." It took a long time. Many were glad of the chance to change their answers. Some had not known what it meant to forswear allegiance to the emperor of Japan. Afraid it might mean loyalty to Japan, they had considered the negative the safer answer. When the interviews were all over, only a small hard core of "No-Nos" were left. These still refused to pledge their loyalty to their country. Tad was one of them.

His family was shocked. So were Tad's real friends, who knew Tad was as loyal an American as they themselves were. Mother Sato and Tom wrote separately to Father Sato. Ordinarily they did not worry him with family cares, but each one had come to the conclusion, without confiding in the other, that this was an emergency with which only the head of the family could cope.

Father Sato wrote to Tad. Then there followed an exchange of letters between them, Tad always explaining and defending his action and imploring his father to understand. Father Sato, begging, all but demanding, that he reconsider. Tad stood his ground.

He was equally deaf to the arguments and attempts at persuasion of his friends in camp. Miss Brown and Bill plotted to get Tad over to Miss Brown's room in the teachers' barracks one evening where they could talk to him together.

Miss Brown had been to Parker the evening before, and she opened a box of chocolates she had bought at the drugstore. The three sat eating candy and exchanging camp gossip for awhile, Tad and Bill, as usual, bathing in the luxury of the soft upholstered chairs.

Presently the teacher brought out a bottle of wine, laughing as she set it on the table between the two Nisei.

"I hope you appreciate this, after what I went through to get it past the guards," she said. "Mrs. Madden went with me to Parker."

At mention of the librarian, the fellows both laughed. It wasn't a laugh of ridicule. The woman was delightfully unique, so much so she was amusing to others.

"Well, when we started home," Miss Brown continued, "she saw my bottle and said she'd better put it in her handbag until we got past the guard station. You know that carpetbag of hers she carries everywhere?"

"One of the never-to-be-forgotten landmarks of Poston," Tad said. He was in a good humor and all unaware he was the victim of a plot.

"Well, she put the bottle in it, down in the bottom under all that trash she carries around. I told her she'd better get her identification card out so she wouldn't have to open the bag at the guard station, and I supposed she did."

Miss Brown poured the wine into small, flowered cheese glasses and passed them over to Bill and Tad.

"But she didn't. We got to thinking about the war, and before I knew it there was a flashlight motioning us to stop. I pulled the car up beside the MP and showed him my card and waited for Mrs. Madden to produce hers. There she was, pawing around in that bag. I knew no one could ever find a little card in that mess in the dark. I thought she'd have to take everything out. Goodbye, wine, I said to myself. Then the MP flashed his light into the bag to help, and what he saw must have given him the creeps, for he said, 'Well, never mind this time, Mrs. Madden. But be sure you have your card ready after this.' And he waved us on."

After a hearty laugh, Bill raised his glass.

"Here's to one human MP," he said.

"Yeah. Yeah," Tad said grudgingly.

After they had a couple of glasses, Miss Brown thought Tad was softened up enough to be reasonable. She gave Bill a questioning glance, and she took the slight lifting of his eyebrows as a sign to go ahead. They had been discussing some of the problems of the evacuee students as they drank. For no matter where a conversation started, it was bound to end up with something to do with evacuation. So it came naturally for Miss Brown to go a step further than the students and speak of Tad's own personal difficulties.

"Tad, you're not going to stick to your guns and let them ship you off to Tule Lake, are you?" By this time, rumor had it that Tule Lake Relocation Center in nothern California was to be used for the disloyal until they could be repatriated to Japan.

"I don't know as I understand what you mean," Tad parried. He was still relaxed.

"I mean, aren't you going to change those negative answers? We all know you're just as loyal as Bill, or me, or any other good American. Why punish yourself and your family?"

Bill squirmed a little over having his loyalty compared to Tad's. Bill prided himself on having taken evacuation in stride.

"Loyalty?" Tad asked. The wine had warmed him, and his voice was soft. "What is loyalty? Someone cheats you out of your rights, kicks you when you're defenseless, curses you as a dirty Jap, and you lick his hands. Is that what you mean by loyalty? That's the devotion of dogs, not human beings. I don't want any of that kind for myself."

"Are you classifying me and all the other Nisei who declared our willingness to fight for our country as no better than dogs?" Bill asked. He stared across the table at Tad, and his voice had an undercurrent of anger.

397

Miss Brown began to wonder if she hadn't made a mistake in having Bill present when she talked to Tad.

"I'm only speaking for myself, Bill," Tad said quickly. "I follow my convictions and let others follow theirs. And I'm ready to take the consequences."

He doesn't realize how far-reaching those consequences are going to be. His life will be ruined, his family heartbroken. These thoughts ran through the teacher's mind as she tried to figure some approach which would break through the barriers Tad had built around him. She knew she was getting emotional but she didn't try to restrain herself. She couldn't bear to see a fine young life thrown away.

Finally she burst out with a sob in her voice.

"Change your answers, Tad, before it's too late. And get out of camp. You're just simply festering in here."

Her concern was so apparent that Tad was touched.

"I'm sorry, Miss Brown. I'd like to please you. You've been good to the students and a friend to the Nisei teachers, and I'd like to do something to show my appreciation. But I can't do what you say. It would be the easiest way, but the most craven."

"I'm sorry you see it that way, Tad. But I'll never give up hoping until the books are closed on you and your chance is gone."

"That won't be long now," Bill said. "We'd better go, Tad. It's getting late."

Bill got up and pulled on his sweater. Tad followed, and, after goodnights, the fellows left.

Bill was no help, Miss Brown thought. I'll have to find a chance to talk to Tad alone soon. But she never did. Tad avoided her.

Registration had brought another headache to the administration besides trying to salvage the citizenship of disgruntled Nisei. Many of the Issei, being aliens and feeling mistreated by evacuation, as well as having many grievances over regulations in camp, had pledged loyalty to their emperor and expressed a desire to return to Japan as soon as possible. With this declaration, families began to split wide open. A new and powerful wedge was being driven between the alien parents, whose hearts had turned longingly toward their native land, and their American-born offspring, who loved their own country and desired to remain in America as fervently as their parents wished to leave. It was a tragic situation, and many were the heartbreaking sessions which took place within those barracks walls as spring came on that year.

Emotions ran high.

As Tad remained adamant in his decision, Mother Sato wrote again to Father Sato concerning the problem. What did Father Sato think about the whole family going with Tad to Tule Lake and eventually to Japan? She was very much upset and confused. She had never had to make far-reaching decisions for the family. Should she go to the office and sign up for repatriation for them all? Would Father Sato hold Tom and Mari to any decisions which were made? She couldn't bear to see the family broken up. If they could not keep Tad with them, then shouldn't they all go with him? Would not Papa Sato write as soon as he could? for her mind was troubled and she could not sleep.

Father Sato's reply was prompt. He was not in favor of repatriation. He did not want to return to Japan to live, and he was certain Mari and Tom did not want to go, and he would never try to force them to do so. Wait until he came. He was sure he could reason with Tad and persuade him to change his negative answers. No, he didn't know how soon he would be free to come, but he had faith it would be in time. She was to make no decisions.

Mother Sato was comforted and relieved. She tried to share her husband's faith, but it was hard. She was too close to the situation.

The volunteers left for training camp in the East, where they would join the Nisei from other centers and the volunteers from Hawaii to form the 442nd, which was destined for fame. Tom, indeed, might have won the medals and decorations which would have confirmed him as a patriot in the eyes of all if he could have been one of those fellows, half-eager, half-reluctant, who clambered on to the Army bus at the departure station one evening.

Tom was there to see them off. A large crowd of relatives, friends, and students, and many other well-wishers had gathered to say good-bye. No one had heard a word of complaint from Tom since the day of registration, but what is he thinking now as he stands at the outer rim of the crowd in the gathering dust, watching?

The evening sky is clear, and the lingering afterglow of sunset penetrates the darkness of the covered truck and lights the faces of the row of fellows sitting there waiting to be off. The goodbyes have been said, and the serious faces look down upon mothers silently weeping, and grave-faced fathers, and among them the brothers and sisters and friends, trying to smile and cheer and give the boys a real send-off. Mingled with the pangs of separation from their families is the suppressed excitement of getting out of camp and suddenly changing their status from prisoners to soldiers. What a topsy-turvy world. Soldiers going off to war and leaving their parents in a concentration camp!

As Tom watches, he mentally places himself in the truck with the others, and feels some of the thrill of going. He experiences a sudden feeling of remorse that he had ever given up. His mother had no right . . . He might in truth be going with the rest, instead of remaining in a camp which had become a breeding ground for psychological pressures too heavy to bear. He should have stood his ground, and brought honor and glory to the Sato name. He thinks of Tad, and spits on the sand at his feet.

There comes a brief moment of silence as the bus is about to start. In the evening stillness the sound of stifled sobs comes to Tom's ear. Mothers weeping over their sons, some they would never see again. He imagines his own mother standing there, weeping for him. In her weakness perhaps leaning on Mari for support.

And he knows he could not have gone. There would have been no joy or triumph in his heart. Only self-condemnation. He had made the right decision, and he is glad he did. Nothing else would have been right. But his time would come.

"So long, fellows," he calls to Hitoshi and Mitsuro. "Good luck." And with that, he turns and walks away.

The motor roars, drowning out the sobs; the wheels begin to turn; the boys were off.

The crowd quickly disperses, not looking at one another, fanning out in small groups toward the several blocks. Are they aware they have just witnessed one of the strangest events in the history of democracy?

Tom had little time to brood. The next day a letter came from his father, begging him to hurry with some new references for his trial. No one knew when it might come up, and he was getting anxious, for he feared he didn't have all that he needed to clear himself.

Tom had already written with confidence to some of the businessmen in La Vista whose names his father had suggested. Two had not replied; the others had excuses. They did not feel they were well enough acquainted with Mr. Sato to give a character reference, or they did not think it wise to sponsor an alien in time of war. Tom did not want to tell his father that his old acquaintances had refused to vouch for his good character and to ask for other names. So he wrote to other men on his own initiative.

Tad was no help. He said he'd been away from La Vista too long to remember anyone, and anyway he didn't think any of the Japanese had any friends back there. Mother Sato was eager to help and kept suggesting people with whom Papa Sato had done business, but in most cases she didn't even know the names. That big dark man from whom he had bought his first tractor. He had been friendly. Or the tomato grower who lived fifty miles up the valley. He said he came so far because Mr. Sato was an honest man, and he liked to do business with him. Sometimes Tom could remember the names, but he had no idea of the addresses.

As the weeks passed and Tom had no references to send, Papa Sato's letters became more and more anxious, almost peevish at times, which wasn't like him, and showed what a terrible strain he was under. He seemed to feel the family was letting him down. Why didn't they send references? His trial might come at any time. Some men had had theirs and had returned to their folks in the camps.

Now it was the end of April. I can't fool around with this trial and error method any longer, Tom thought. Surely there must be someone who will say a good word for Dad. If he could go back a few days and see one person after another until he found someone who would give him what he wanted . . .

He went to the administration office and explained the situation and asked permission to go home under guard. His request was refused. However, the administration promised to do what it could to get the needed papers.

Tom knew how slowly things moved through government channels. He couldn't depend on that. All day in the field, watching the irrigation water fill the furrows between the new green vegetables, he mulled over the problem; and when he went home to the barracks that night, he thought he had a solution. He must ask a favor of their own personal friends back in La Vista.

He confided in Mari because he needed her help. He knew Peg's mother had considerable influence in the community. Would Mari write to Peg to ask her mother to see some of the prominent businessmen? Tom himself wrote to Mr. Vandenheuvel.

Now he had done all he could. Nothing now but wait for results.

He had not long to wait. In less than a week, a thick, long envelope came from Peg to Mari.

"Well, what do you know? Well, what do you know about that?" Tom kept repeating as he looked through a mist dimming his eyes at the wealth of material Mari handed him when he came home from work that evening.

"One from Mr. Johnson at the Farmers' Bank. Dad never even banked there. And one from Mr. Welch, written on his Farm Machinery Company stationery. I wrote him and he never even answered. I'll bet Mrs. Sullivan really worked him over. Dad's spent thousands of dollars in his store."

"The Welches and Sullivans go to the same church," Mari said.

"I'll get these off to Dad tomorrow," Tom said, "to cheer him up. And not wait to hear from Mr. Van. I can send his later."

When it came, it had a big surprise. There was not only a long letter from the old man eulogizing Father Sato--not that that would have any weight with a trial board even though it brought tears to Tom's eyes--but there was an enclosure. A brief but valuable note from the chief of police in La Vista, saying he had known Mr. Sato for years, and Mr. Sato couldn't possibly be guilty of the charges against him. It sent Tom sailing on clouds. That letter alone ought to clear his father.

Not until after the letters were sent off and Tom's mind relieved of that worry did Mari share Peg's letter with him.

"'I wish we could be together for graduation,'" Mari read to Tom as she sat on the stoop while Tom planted cantaloupe seeds beside the barracks, "'but since we can't, wouldn't it be fun for us to wear identical dresses? I think so, so Mother is making two. You know we can wear each other's clothes just dandy, unless you've got fat lazing around down there in that resort. Ah, me! No dishes to wash. Can't you make room for me? Mother says she hopes the letters are okay.'"

"How are you going to pay for a fancy dress?" Tom asked.

"There's a P.s. to the letter," Mari answered. "She says 'Don't be stuffy about the dress, nothing expensive, simple dimity, powdery blue, pretty. It will be my grad gift to you, so don't expect anything else.'"

Mari folded the letter and waited for Tom's approval.

Tom took his hoe and shaped the edges of the melon bed neatly.

"What are you going to give Peg?" he asked. "You'll have to send something nice. You can't send a cheap little gift when she's giving you a dress. Money's pretty scarce right now."

"I've already got her a present. Yuri's father gave me a picture for her."

"You didn't ask him for it?"

"Of course not. It was Yuri's idea."

Tom leaned on his toe, looking down at the ground.

"Well, I guess it's all right. I'd like to send Peg something myself. She sure got us out of a fix."

XXIII

During the late winter and spring, the other members of the Sato family had been so deeply involved in their own problems and those of the absent member that Yoshi had been left pretty much to follow his own inclinations. The few restrictions which had been placed on him were gradually and unconsciously relaxed, and he was quick to take advantage of his freedom. No one seemed to notice whether he was around or not, and he began to stray farther and farther from his own block. He had grown tired of practicing basketball, for he never got to play in the games. The other kids said he was too short and too slow. Then, when spring came he was expected to be the flunky for the bigger fellows, running after balls, carrying the bats out to the field. He thought he was too big for that kid stuff. He was restless to be doing something exciting on his own.

One evening after school he walked home with Fumiki, a boy who lived in one of the blocks on the far side of the camp. Fumiki appeared to be as much on the loose as Yoshi. At the time of evacuation his father had been ill with some disease which required a special diet. Fumiki didn't know what it was. But when he was brought to camp where he couldn't get the food he needed, he had died after a few months. Fumiki said he had an older sister and four younger brothers. His mother was having a hard time. He told Yoshi all of this without any show of emotion, his voice without expression, fatalistic, helpless.

This evening the two boys ambled along between the barracks, swinging their idle hands and talking about the things they used to do back home, riding their bicycles after school, going to the movie on Saturday, and to the beach in summer.

It was the hour of the day when the Poston streets were full of people. Office workers going home, men coming from the fields and the shops. As the boys

405

passed the Main Canteen they saw a procession filing in.

"Must have ice cream today," Yoshi commented off-handedly, feeling in his pockets for the change he knew wasn't there.

"Yeah, that or something else special," Fumiki agreed with feigned indifference. He, too, was broke.

They went on.

After awhile they began to get tired of just meandering around talking and were trying to think of something else to do to kill time, when they met up with Harry. Harry was in the ninth grade and didn't bother to notice the smaller boys, except when he decided to beat one up just for kicks. But now he fell in with Yoshi and Fumiki, which sent a tingling along their spines. They were not afraid of Harry out here in the open with everyone around. Besides, he was real friendly with them now, and they swelled with pride.

They both knew that Harry stole things at school, pencils and fountain pens and things like that from the teachers' desks, but stealing from the government wasn't considered a crime in camp. Even some of the teachers had swiped lumber from the construction projects to make backstops for the basketball hoops, and some of the honest old Issei, who had never in their lives taken anything that didn't belong to them, went out at night and got lumber to make shelves and cupboards in their barracks to make them more liveable. So they didn't hold it against Harry.

Harry hated school and all of his teachers, the Caucasians most, because they were smarties and tried to make a fellow behave when they hadn't any right to. They could drive their cars and go anywhere they wanted to. But if a fellow tried to have a little fun they would jump down his neck. Harry rebelled against authority of any kind. And his father, long before he had died that first year in camp, had given up the struggle to control him in this abnormal situation. No privacy in which a father could admonish and discipline his son. What was a man to do? He had given up and left the boy to the community government and the school, and then he had died. Neither organization was doing much for Harry. And the boys in his class had begun to avoid him. Harry was lonely this evening.

"Where are you guys going?" he asked as they swung along.

"Nowhere special. Just walking around. Any harm in that?" Fumiki said. Yoshi kept still.

"Want a candy bar?" Harry took out of his baggy pocket a handful of ten-cent bars he had stolen from the canteen during rush hours. He tossed one to each of the boys.

They walked on aways, munching the candy.

"Say, let's go over where they're building the new school and see if the workmen left anything lying around," Harry suggested as he caught sight of a corner of the low adobe walls. The other boys fell in readily with the idea. It was something to do. There was still an hour left before supper to be got rid of some way.

And so began an association which was to lead to trouble for Yoshi and shame for the whole Sato family.

After a few minor thefts which provided the boys with money to buy ice cream and candy at the canteen, Yoshi and Fumiki began to grow bolder under Harry's tutelage. Harry was a smart operator, and they had never been caught. Harry decided they were ready for a really big deal now.

Yoshi knew it was wrong to steal. But down here in camp it was different. And Harry said the government had robbed every one of their dads by hauling them away from their ranches and businesses, so when he got money out of the desk drawer in the principal's office, when Old Fat Face had him there for discipline, he was just taking back a little of what his folks had been robbed of. Yoshi thought of his father, who had always made good money on the ranch and was now in a prison camp over there in New Mexico where he couldn't earn a cent, and Harry's reasoning sounded convincing.

So he was willing enough when Harry suggested they break into one of the rooms in the teachers' barracks the night of the PTA meeting.

"Those teachers must have a lot of money around. You know what they get paid?" Harry asked. The boys were sitting on the stoop of Harry's apartment, talking low.

"No, I don't know," Fumiki said, "but I bet it's a lot more than the Nisei teachers get. Nineteen dollars a month. Chicken feed."

"I'm here to tell you it's a lot more. Do you know some of those smartie white faces get over two hundred dollars a month?"

That sounded like riches to Yoshi. He guessed one of them wouldn't miss the little he and the other boys would take.

When night came on the day of the meeting, the boys went into one of the rooms easily, through the unlocked door. It was just as easy to find the handbag in the upper drawer of the dresser. Two tens, a five, and six ones. Harry counted it out while Yoshi and Fumiki held matches.

"We'll take the five and the ones," Harry said. "Someone might get suspicious if I tried to change a ten." Harry was smart. He divided the ones between the other boys and kept the five for himself, because he was the brains of the outfit, he said.

Yoshi felt prosperous. He hadn't had that much money since he had left home. But how was he going to enjoy it without his folks finding out he had it?

He sent one dollar back to Jerry to buy a new collar for Malt. The old one would be worn out by this time, and if Jerry had to spend money on the dog he might get to thinking Malt belonged to him. The rest of the money gave him a good deal of trouble. He spent it as rapidly as possible, and had to go over to the Main Canteen, for Mr. Imoto would wonder where he got so much money all of a sudden.

The theft was reported, and the police questioned several suspects, men who had been doing some petty thieving around the camp, but the boys were never suspected. That made them even bolder.

As the days grew hotter and longer, it seemed to get

harder and harder to kill all the time the boys had on their hands. One hot evening in late May, when the bright stars in the blue-black sky hung barely out of reach and there was no moon, the three boys went venturing over into the administration area, which was off limits to the evacuees.

They wandered about aimlessly, past the motor pool, which was protected by an eight-foot wire fence and a heavy, padlocked gate, out and in around the warehouse barracks, all padlocked, too, and the windows boarded up. Nothing very interesting. Then taking a cautious look over toward the housing units where the Caucasian personnel lived and, seeing no one outside, they moved over in that direction.

The burning heat of the evening had driven everyone indoors to the coolers. The grounds were deserted. But several staff cars were parked in front of the long, low buildings. The boys walked along the line of cars on the street side, Harry feeling in each one for a carelessly left key.

"Hey, here's one," he whispered, beside the open window of a Ford coupe. "Let's take a ride."

"Can you drive?" Yoshi asked, a little scared.

"Can I drive? Why, I used to drive the tractor all over the place back home," Harry lied. "What do you think I am, a baby or something?"

He opened the door and climbed in.

"If you guys don't want to go, okay by me." He started the motor. No need to worry about the noise. The coolers inside the building would drown it out.

Yoshi and Fumiki ran around the car like jack rabbits and jumped in beside Harry. It was the first time Yoshi had been in a car since he left home, and it was a big thrill. He held his hand out in the breeze as the car sped out the gate and up the highway toward Camp I. Harry couldn't drive so good, but he managed to keep on the road, and there wasn't much traffic at night.

When they got to Camp I, Harry turned and started back without entering the camp. No use to press his luck too far. When they got back, he parked the car

409

where he had found it, and the boys got back to the evacuee area safely without being seen.

It had all been so easy it gave Harry an idea. It would be the biggest job they had pulled off yet. They would steal a car and hide it down in the mesquite somewhere off the road, and they could have a spin every night. Sometime they might just drive right out of camp and go east somewhere.

He was so preoccupied with his plans that he was immune to the sarcasm of one of his sharp-tongued teachers, who called the students "Japs" and appeared to have a grudge against them because they were living off the government. As if they'd asked to.

When Yoshi went home that night of the ride in the Ford, he had an uneasy feeling. After lights were out and he lay in his cot beside Tom's, he said, "Why can't we have our own car down here, Tom?"

"No place to drive it," Tom mumbled, half asleep. "And no gas. We wouldn't be eligible for a ration card."

"Yeah, I guess not. But it would sure be nice just riding around camp these hot nights. Step on the gas and feel the wind blowing in your face. You can't get up any breeze just walking."

Something clicked in Tom's mind like a weak alarm clock jingling. He realized he hadn't seen much of the kid recently. Wondered what he'd been doing. What made him think about the car? Since the worst of the heat, the ag workers had been getting up at daylight so they wouldn't have to work in the middle of the day, and Tom was drugged with sleep.

"Let's get to sleep, Boy," he said. "I've got to be up at four." He turned over and was asleep.

Yoshi's chance to talk things over, maybe tell Tom about the ride, was gone. By morning Tom had forgotten all about Yoshi's sudden interest in a car. A week later, when he read in the Poston *Chronicle* about a car being stolen, there was no connection in his mind between the two.

After a few days and an extensive search, the police found the car three miles south of the camp on an abandoned road, hub deep in sand and everything combustible burned to a crisp. The police thought it was the work of young hoodlums. Older men would have known better than to try that old road.

Everyone in camp was talking about the incident and speculating as to who the thief might be. More than one parent was jittery, afraid to learn the truth.

Yoshi began staying close to home evenings and froze like a frightened rabbit every time he heard a knock on the door. Tom noticed and asked the boy if someone had threatened to beat him up.

"Tell me, and I'll take care of him," he said.

Yoshi shrugged him off.

Mother Sato was sure the boy was ill. He didn't want to go to the mess hall to meals. She tried to doctor him with her favorite remedies, but Yoshi would have none of them.

"I'm all right. Just let me be. Just let me alone, I'm okay."

Then one afternoon the news broke. Harry had been picked up for questioning about something else, had admitted the theft of the car as well as the other robberies, and had named Fumiki and Yoshi as his accomplices.

The two boys were taken to the police station and questioned, then turned over to their parents with orders that they should stay in their own blocks and not be outside their apartments after dark. Nothing further would be done, the officer told Tom, until it was known what action the owner of the car decided to take.

The Sato family were stunned. Everything else, Tad's defection and imminent departure, Father Sato's trial, Mari's graduation and her application for entrance to a college near Philadelphia, everything was driven completely from their minds by the bitter knowledge that the youngest of the family was known all over the camp as a thief.

XXIV

It was Sunday evening in the middle of June. And stifling hot. Tom had just had his third shower of the day and, in a fresh T-shirt and clean blue jeans, was stretched out on his cot which he had pulled out into the center of the room, directly in front of the cooler. The little homemade contraption was running at full capacity, but was totally inadequate to compete with the overheated world outside. The room was hot.

Mother Sato sat by the window in the last light of day, reading from her Bible, fanning and nodding intermittently. She had the limp appearance of a wilted plant. Mari, getting ready to go to the evening singspiration at the church, was the only wide-awake one in the room. Yoshi lay on the floor, languidly turning the worn pages of a comic book he had already read a dozen times.

Now and then Mother Sato looked down on the tousled head of her baby and sighed deeply.

Yoshi had been cruelly disillusioned about Harry, whom he had accepted as a pal and to whom he had given all the loyalty and devotion of a twelve year old to a middle teenager. And Harry had lied to him and Fumiki. He had said the car was an abandoned one. The owner had quit Poston and gone east on the train. Harry said a man at the garage said he could have it for ten dollars and he had paid for it. Now all they had to do was go get it. He wanted Yoshi and Fumiki to go with him. When they had wanted to go right away, he said, no, they'd have to wait till dark, it was too hot to go in the daytime.

When they did start after the car, the boys found it wasn't in their camp but in Camp II, and they had to walk the four miles. Harry wouldn't let them thumb a ride. Yoshi didn't know why then, but he did now.

When Yoshi saw the car, he thought it looked pretty good for ten dollars, but it was dark and he couldn't tell too much about it. It wasn't until after Harry, stuck in the sand, spun the wheels until he set the tires on fire, got scared to see the car burning and told them it was stolen. He made them promise never to say a word about it.

"You fellows are in this just as deep as I am. If you keep your mouths shut, no one will ever know who did it."

As they had stood and watched the burning car, Yoshi had thought there wasn't going to be much evidence left. But he was mad at Harry for lying to them.

Now he was madder than ever, and hurt, too. When Harry got caught, he named him and Fumiki just the same as if they had known all the time they were stealing a car. It was a blow. But even if Harry had been unfair to him, Yoshi didn't intend to squeal on Harry. So he had never explained, either to the police or his folks. When any of the family tried to get him to tell why he had done such a terrible thing, all he would say was, "Leave me alone. I haven't done anything. Can't you leave me be a minute?"

Tom thought Yoshi was innocent, but since he couldn't get anything out of him, there wasn't much he could do about proving it.

Yoshi was very hard to live with. The case was still pending. The car had belonged to a teacher and was estimated to have been worth around eight hundred dollars. The Satos expected to pay Yoshi's share. That would be a hardship. But they could never buy back Yoshi's good name.

"Well, tomorrow's the day for Dad's second hearing," Tom said, speaking what had been in his mind all day. A letter had come from Father Sato, and the exciting news had taken some of the heat off Yoshi. "He ought to be coming pretty soon now."

"Did he ever say how long the hearings last?" Mari asked, turning from the mirror with quick interest. She had to let the Relocation Office know soon whether or not she was going to accept that scholarship. Father

413

Sato had given a tentative consent, but Mother Sato insisted Mari wait till he came before she made any final arrangements.

"I was talking to a fellow in Block 2 this afternoon," Tom said. "His father came home last week. He said his hearing lasted only one day, and he left the prison camp the next."

"Why, he could be here by Wednesday, then," Mari cried.

"Jee-ez!" Yoshi muttered under his breath. He was the only one who wasn't looking forward to his father's return.

Mother Sato's nodding head came up with a start.

"You say he come Wednesday?"

"Yes, he could be here then," Tom said.

"Three days. Papa-san been gone long, long time. Long, long time," the woman chanted like a spiritual.

"So many things have happened," Tom said. "Makes it seem longer than it is. Only a year and a half. Seems a lot longer."

Mari was ready to start.

"Aren't you going over to the church tonight, Tom?"

"Do I look like it?" he asked, laughing and looking down at his work pants. "No, it's too hot to sing. Besides, I don't feel like singing hymns."

"We could take Yuri home after the service."

"It's still too hot."

Mari left.

Father Sato's return meant something different to each one of the family.

To Tom, besides the grateful relief at having his father free again and cleared of the false charges, it meant a chance for him to make plans for himself. The Nisei Division was still open to new recruits. He would enlist immediately.

To Tad, who had as much reason as Yoshi to dread facing his father, there was no reluctance whatever. He was eager to have someone to talk to who would understand, and he was sure his father would when they talked face to face, man to man. He always had. In his heart, Tad was desperately unhappy and needed sympathy more than criticism.

To Mari, it was the bright prospect of getting out of camp and going to college. She had no doubt her father would be pleased when he heard she had the scholarship and a nice job in a doctor's home, working for her room and board. He would want her to go.

But to Mother Sato, the return of her husband meant the most of all. No one would ever know how lost she had felt during his absence. The grief over his imprisonment and her worry over Tad and now Yoshi had been too much for her to bear alone. Only the hopes of Father Sato's early return had kept her going.

No one considered the possibility that he might not be cleared. They knew he was innocent. Their hopes were running high.

On Monday another letter came. The hearing had been postponed until July.

It meant another wait.

Mother Sato felt July would not be soon enough. It was rumored the government might begin shipping out the disloyal anytime now. It would take a long time to move them all, but there was no way of knowing who would be taken first. Summoning all her courage, she decided to go to the administration office herself and intercede for her Tadashi. He was a good boy. He had always been a good son until something happened to him when he was in the Army back in California. She didn't know what it was, but it had hurt him. He was proud and sensitive like most young men with Japanese blood in their veins. He had had too much to bear. But he was a good American. She knew he would never do anything to harm his country. She must make the authorities understand how it was with him. They must not take him away from his family.

It would be a long walk to the office, and she knew how sensitive she was to the rays of the burning sun, but she would go in the cool of the morning. She knew there was no such thing as "cool of the morning" on the desert this time of year. The sun came up with withering intensity the minute it cleared the cloudless horizon. But it would be worse later in the day.

When all but Yoshi were away one morning, she put on her Sunday best, got out her old parasol, and started out.

"Where you going, Mom?" Yoshi asked. He was sitting glumly on the stoop, his chin in his hands. She mumbled something he didn't hear, but he noted the good dress and the hat which she wore only to church and funerals. Since it wasn't Sunday, she must be going to a funeral. Kind of early in the day for one of those, he thought. Maybe people were dying so fast in this hot weather, he mused mournfully, that it took all day to bury them. He watched her until she disappeared around the corner of the laundry, then went back to feeling sorry for himself.

In the corridor of the long building Mother Sato inquired where to go. When she entered the indicated door she saw many people waiting in chairs along the wall. She was glad to drop down into a vacant one. Her face was burning and her head throbbing. Soon she began to feel chilly in the cold room.

When at last her turn came, she found herself across the desk from an interviewer who knew no Japanese. The young woman was brusque with efficiency.

"I Tadashi Sato's mother," Mother Sato began hesitantly.

Quick hands flipped through a file of cards and drew one out.

"Yes. What is it you want?"

"No want him sent away. He . . ."

"It says here he has answered 'no' to both of the loyalty questions and has repeatedly refused to change his answers."

Mother Sato winced at the crisp, accusing voice.

"Tadashi good American," she said stubbornly.

"I am afraid, Mrs. Sato, that we can scarcely call anyone a good American who refuses to defend his country in time of war and will not forswear loyalty to our enemy, the emperor of Japan."

416

Mother Sato understood few of the words, but the hard voice conveyed the meaning.

"But Tadashi . . . evacuation change him . . . hurt him in here." She laid a thin, trembling hand across her heart.

"Many American boys are being hurt," the woman snorted. "Many are being killed. But they are dying loyal."

The little woman was bewildered. If she could talk in her native tongue, she could make the interviewer understand. A thought came.

"Tadashi once go Japan to visit. No like Japan. Soon he come home, join Army. Volunteer."

"You say he volunteered? Well . . ." The interviewer spoke to a man at the next desk.

Mother Sato took hope as she waited.

"I'm sorry, Mrs. Sato," the girl said, turning back to her. This time the voice was a little softer. "But there isn't a thing anyone can do for your son unless he changes his answers. Is that clear?" She replaced the card in the file and called for the next in line.

Mother Sato rose and bowed politely.

"How soon they take him?"

"The departure date has not been announced."

Mother Sato bowed again, thanked the interviewer, and backed away.

As she walked down the long corridor, she bent her head low to hide the tears which blinded her eyes.

"Is there something I can do for you, Honorable One?" a voice beside her spoke in Japanese.

Mother Sato brushed the tears away and looked up into the friendly face of Miss Carlson, a graying woman past middle age who had been a missionary in Japan for long years.

Relieved to find someone who would understand her, Mother Sato burst into a torrent of words.

"Come into my office where it is cool and we can talk without interruption," the woman invited.

In the small office Mother Sato poured out her heart, beginning with the day Father Sato had been

417

taken away. The listener appeared to have plenty of time and did not hurry her. But when she was through, there was nothing that could be done to help Tad.

"Unless he changes his answers, no one can do anything. He must speak for himself. He is of age and responsible. I am so sorry, Mrs. Sato. I know how much it means to you to keep your family together, and I pray that your husband will soon be with you again. Perhaps if I talked to Tadashi . . ."

No, Mother Sato did not think it would do any good. She would tell him what Mrs. Carlson and the interviewer had said. She must go now. She had stayed longer than she had intended. It would be getting hot.

She stepped out of the cool building into the blazing inferno of a midday sun. She raised her parasol and started out on the half-mile walk across the treeless waste to her own barracks, moving with slow, shuffling steps. She was defeated, hopeless.

The dinner gongs began to clang.

Two nurses, starting out from the clinic for the staff mess hall, saw her fall. They picked her up and laid her in the back seat of the car, then hurried back to the clinic.

"She's light as a feather," Nurse Grover said as they carried her in.

As soon as Mother Sato was conscious so that they could find out who she was, they took her home and left orders with Mari to keep her quiet and not let her get out in the sun.

Mari skipped school that afternoon to be with her mother. Exams were over, and the classes were just marking time.

When Tad came home from the mess hall and learned what his mother had done for his sake, he was very uncomfortable. Since registration, he had been gradually getting his eyes opened about some of his cronies. He'd teamed up with them when he came to camp because they were bitter like he was. Of course, they had all given negative answers to the loyalty questions. But not for the same reason that he had. They had no respect for their country. They were eager to go to Japan. Now they only wanted to cause trouble. He wanted to break with them, but they were cruel and dangerous. He didn't know how to do it without the risk of being beaten up, perhaps even killed.

His mother's intercession in his behalf shamed him. He began to show her more consideration. She took it as a sign of weakening, and she began again to try to persuade him to change his mind before it was too late.

"I'll do anything else in the world for you, Mom. But I can't do that. But don't you worry. Everything will work out all right in the end." He didn't think so, but her sad face drew the words.

Mother Sato shook her head and longed more fervently than ever for the quick return of Father Sato.

As the time approached for the July hearing another letter came. The hearing had been postponed again. Now the family became plagued with doubts. Was the father to be released at all? They felt helpless. The letter had said there were many cases to be heard and the board had not gotten to his yet.

July sizzled through. The repatriates were packing to leave. The family adjoining the Satos were going. It was welcome news for the Satos, because they had been unfriendly, suspicious, and inquisitive from the beginning. The children, emboldened by the breakdown of parental discipline, poked holes in the paper Tom had pasted over the knotholes between the apartments and peeked through. Sometimes they had pushed rubbish through, burnt matches, cigarette butts, even scraps of food. After Tom had nailed boards over the holes they had found other ways to be unpleasant. It would be good riddance when they were gone.

The processing of the disloyal had been a painful procedure. The administration did not want to make any mistakes. The door was being left open to the last possible minute for anyone who wanted to change his mind. Now the tedious job was nearing completion. The date of departure was drawing near. Packing boxes were a common sight over the camp. They made it look as if half the population were leaving.

Tad made no gesture toward getting his things together, but the atmosphere around the Sato apartment was that of a family with a member doomed.

Mother Sato had allowed Mari to go ahead with her plans since the date of Father Sato's return was so uncertain, and Mari would be leaving in early September.

"Yuri's going to stay in camp," she told Tom one evening. "Aren't you glad?"

"What difference does it make to me? I won't be here. I'm going to enlist as soon as Dad comes."

"What if he won't let you?"

"He will. I think he'll want me to."

"Yuri's father thinks she's too young to go out alone. Anyway, he thinks in another year they can all return to San Francisco and she can enter the university. Yuri says if she can't do that, then they are all planning to move east somewhere to live."

"That'll be nice for them," Tom said absently. If Yuri leaves California, he was thinking, then I never will see her again.

"What do you suppose Yuri is going to do this fall?" Mari asked.

"How would I know?"

"She's going to work in the school office, attendance clerk. The new buildings will be done when school opens. The office where she will work is really swell, air conditioned, too. Isn't it nice she got the job?"

"If that's what she wants to do," Tom said.

"Oh, Tom, you make me so mad. I could tell you something you'd like to hear, but I'm not going to when you act like this."

"There's just one thing I want to hear," Tom said, looking out the small window, "and that's when Dad's coming. Heh, there's Harry Yamoto running across the block like the Devil was after him. Looks like he's coming here."

Tom jumped up and opened the door for the block manager, whose face was beaming like a full moon. He handed Tom a piece of paper.

420

"This telegram was just phoned down from Parker. I knew you'd want it right away." Then he politely withdrew.

Tom read the few words and called to his mother, who was dozing on her cot. His voice was choked with emotion. "Message from Dad."

He cleared his throat and read aloud.

"'Hearing over. Cleared on all counts. Will arrive Poston Friday night. Shigero.'"

"Friday! That's tomorrow," Mari cried. "Oh, goody, goody, he's coming at last."

"Well, what do you know? He's really coming," Tom said, his face breaking into a big grin. He looked at Yoshi, who was glumly looking down at the floor.

Mother Sato got up and her eyes swept the cluttered room.

"We must clean house," she said calmly.

"Listen to Mom," Mari laughed. It was easy to laugh now. "We've been waiting nearly two years to hear this good news, and all Mom says is, 'We must clean house.'"

"Papa-san very neat, likes everything clean in his house, his greenhouse, his tool shed, everywhere. What would he think of this?"

Now the children glanced around. It did look sort of messy. Housekeeping had been neglected during the heat. They tried to see the place through their father's eyes. Then they began to look at themselves through his eyes, too.

"I wonder what he'll think of the whole layout here," Tom said. "Ourselves included."

"Do you suppose he's changed much?" Mari asked of no one in particular.

"Not as much as we have, I'll bet," Tom wagered. "He's not going to like what we've let the camp do to us."

"What we let it do!" Mari exclaimed in anger. "You don't 'let it,' it just does things, and you don't know it until you look back to the way you were before you came."

"Yeah. Maybe you're right."

421

Tom looked at Yoshi, now leaning against the wall, looking idly out the window, hands buried in empty, baggy pockets, a picture of utter boredom. He was pretending to have no interest in the good news which had rejuvenated the rest of the family. He's changed more than any of us, Tom thought.

Then he looked at his mother and thought of her as his father would remember her--plump, strong, saucy, able to do a day's work in the field along with the men and then go into the house and cook up a meal for everybody. How frail she looked now. He began to feel a twinge of conscience that they had kept his father in ignorance of her condition. It was going to be a shock.

Tad came in. He looked around at smiling faces.

"What's going on? You all look like you'd just inherited a million bucks."

"Better than that," Tom said, handing Tad the message.

Tad read it at a glance.

"Well, it's about time. 'Cleared of all charges.' They were phoney in the first place. What's the government going to give him for the years of illegal imprisonment? I know. Nothing, absolutely nothing." After he had relieved himself of his venom, he could share in the pleasure of the others.

Then his eyes fell on Yoshi.

"What's the matter with you, Vinegar Face? Don't you know your Dad's coming back?"

"I ain't deaf," Yoshi growled.

"Wise guy. Well, I guess you know when he gets here you'll get what's coming to you. You've nothing to celebrate about."

After the car theft, Tad had wanted to whip Yoshi within an inch of his life, but Mother Sato had refused to let Tad touch the boy.

"Well, it will sure be great to have the old man home again," Tad said, throwing his hat in the corner and stretching out on his cot. "Tomorrow night. On that late train from Phoenix, I suppose. It's the only night train. You want to get yourself dolled up a little,

Mom. You look kind of puny."

"I'll give her a shampoo and put her hair up tonight. It looks nice when it's got a little curl in it," Mari said.

Mother Sato, busying herself straightening up the odds and ends on the shelf, turned and said, "Papa-san no like my hair curly . . . like movie star."

They all laughed together. Even Yoshi joined in.

XXV

This was a red letter day for the Satos. And friends in the block shared their joy with them.

It was a wilting hot August morning. The night was still hot when it gave way to the day's sun blazing over the peaks of the distant mountains with a blinding, fiery brilliance.

Mari and her mother were as busy in the little apartment as if they had a ten-room house to clean. Father Sato could not arrive before ten-thirty at the earliest; and it might be later, for the night train was often late, and then it took a long time for the MPs at the gate to the camp to go through all the luggage of incoming evacuees. But Mother Sato had been up since dawn, her meager strength multiplied by eager expectation. She had washed the curtains and dried them soon after, for it took little time for laundry to dry in the dry heat. Now they were ready to hang as soon as Mari had finished washing and polishing the windows.

Mother Sato sat making some draperies out of flowered material Tad had brought from the canteen. They would be used to partition off a small corner of the room for Papa Sato's cot and hers.

Tad got an extra cot from the block manager and a tick which he had filled with straw. They were out on the front stoop, ready to be brought in when the cleaning was done. Tad was staying home this morning to save his mother as much as he could, but she was not to be stopped in her rush to have everything in order when the head of the house returned. Every last grain of dust had to be removed, every cobweb swept down from the rafters, the rugs shaken mightily, and the floor scrubbed to whiteness.

When Mari hung the draperies, there was barely room left for her to stand beside her cot. But what difference did it make? She would be gone soon. And Tad would be, too, she thought with a pang. That was the only thing that kept this from being a perfect day. Maybe Tom would be going away, too, if the Army took him. His joining the Army had never seemed real to her.

Tom was working as usual. He could have had the day off. His foreman had offered him a holiday. Father Sato's return was recognized as the important event that it was. But Tom said there were enough hands to do the work at home, and the fields were shorthanded. The cantaloupes were ripening faster than the men could pick them. Secretly Tom preferred to work. It would make the time go faster.

In the middle of the morning Tad gave Yoshi a quarter and ordered him to go to the barbershop and get his mane cut. When he came back considerably improved in looks, Mari sent him out to water his mother's zinnias to get him out of the way.

Carelessly he turned a full stream from the hose on the flower bed and washed out a couple of plants. He hurried to reset them, but the hot sun wilted them in a few minutes, and he yanked them out of the ground and threw them under the barracks. As Tad had said, this was no celebration for Yoshi, and he was miserable over facing his father. He wished he was big enough to fight Harry. He'd sure like to bloody his nose, lying like he did to Fumiki and him.

At the mess hall at noon, neighbors bowed to the Satos and smiled. What was one family's joy or grief was the joy or grief of them all.

"Your dad coming?" one of the boys said to Yoshi.

"What's that to you?" Yoshi snapped.

"Nuthin'. I just wanted to know. What's eatin' ya?"

"Nuthin'. Sure he's comin'. It ain't no secret."

"You don't act very glad."

Yoshi stuck his hands in his pockets without replying. He swaggered over to his barracks and sat down outside, out of sight of the door so Mari wouldn't see him and put him to work.

Wasn't he glad his father was coming? Was he afraid of him? He never had been; he guessed he wasn't

425

now. He was thirteen and ready for eighth grade in the fall. He was big enough not to be afraid of anybody. If his dad got too smart with him, he'd tell him off.

Mari spotted him through the window and called to him. Yoshi got up and took his time getting into the house. His jaw was thrust out, ready for trouble.

Evening came at last. Sundown gave merciful relief to weary eyes.

After supper was over and the last little things done, the children sat around their cots talking and waiting, although it was still some hours to train time. Mother Sato had run over to see Mrs. Tanaka. Mr. Tanaka would not be released from prison camp. He had not been cleared, and Mrs. Tanaka and her children were going to join him later in a family camp in Texas which was being built for such cases.

Presently Mother Sato returned and sat down on a stool by the window. Her thin face was serene. She did not join in the conversation, nor did she seem to be listening.

"Hell, it's only nine o'clock," Tad said after a long time. He got up and stretched. "Think I'll run over and see some of the fellows."

Mother Sato watched him go, an anxious look in her eyes.

"Don't worry, Mom. He'll be back in time," Tom said, guessing her thoughts.

The minutes passed as though reluctant to give way to one another. The group sat watching the clock. Sometimes they talked, sometimes they sat in silence. The cooler droned. Now and then a cricket came through a crack in the floor and went shooting through the air. Yoshi batted at them with the evening copy of the Poston *Chronicle*, which he had rolled and unrolled until it was limp.

Miss Brown's arrival came as a welcome interruption. She had some paper sacks containing the items Mother Sato had ordered from Parker. Tea and lemons. Cookies and candy. Pajamas and shirts for Papa Sato.

"I hope these shirts are all right. There wasn't much

choice."

"Nice," Mother Sato said, feeling the cloth. "Thank you very much. I have trouble you."

"Oh, no. I was so glad I could do something for you. I'm so sorry I couldn't get any oranges, but there wasn't a one in Parker today. But I'll be going in tomorrow. There should be some then. Aren't you excited about your father coming, Yoshi?"

"Yeah. Sure."

When Miss Brown was gone the family couldn't seem to get down to the inactivity of waiting again. Mother Sato busied herself putting the groceries away, and then hung the shirts on hangers. She would press one before breakfast so Papa-san would have a clean one to wear to the mess hall. She laid the pair of pajamas on Father Sato's cot. Then she sat down facing the clock.

Mari thumbed through a school book. Yoshi lay down and went to sleep. Tom, up since four, found himself nodding and jumped up and began to walk around the room.

Ten. Ten-fifteen. Ten-thirty. He might come any time now. And Tad wasn't back.

A truck rumbled down the street. Tom rushed to the door. A police car rolled past.

Tad brushed past Tom and came in, and Tom closed the door.

Tad went and sat on the cot at Yoshi's feet.

"Time for the truck," he said. His face was showing signs of strain. A muscle in the corner of his mouth twitched, and he tried to control it. He went over and looked in the mirror and saw the droop of his eyelids which gave an insolent look. He must remember not to peer at his father through half-closed eyes. How long had it been since he'd looked a man squarely in the eye?

Eleven o'clock came and went.

"Train must have been late," Tom suggested.

Half-past eleven.

Under the surface passiveness, dire thoughts began to gather. Had Father Sato been detained at the prison camp? Had the authorities cooked up something else against him? Had there been an accident? Foul play? There were plenty of people gunning for "Japs" outside. All those fantastic imaginings which torment the minds of those waiting for belated loved ones.

Tad roused Yoshi.

"Get up, kid, and comb your hair. You're a sight."

"Sez who?" Yoshi sat up, yawned, and said he was going to undress and go to bed.

"You heard me," Tad said. "Comb your hair and slick yourself up a bit. Dad will be here any minute now."

"Who's going to make me?" Yoshi said, sticking out his tongue at Tad and beginning to unbutton his shirt.

Tad leaned over and gave him a cuff on the side of the head. Yoshi howled, jumped up, and doubled his fists. It looked for a minute as if Father Sato might arrive in the middle of a free-for-all. But Yoshi drew back sullenly before he reached Tad and went over to the mirror, where he gave his hair a few careless strokes with his comb. While he stood there, the rumble of wheels brought the rest of the family to their feet.

This time they were not disappointed. The Army truck pulled up in front of the barracks.

Tad and Tom rushed out to the street. Mother Sato and Mari followed them out the door, but stopped on the stoop.

"Hello, Dad. How are you?" the sons chorused as Tom took the battered suitcase his father handed down from the truck. It was the same one Tom and Allen had taken to him at the city jail that bleak Monday morning in December. Tad reached up and took his father's arm as the old man began to climb down.

"Kind of awkward getting out of these fancy taxis," he said with a laugh. "Can you see the step?"

"Yes, Tadashi, I can see it all right. How are you all?"

"Just fine. Everything's swell now you're here."

When Father Sato had both feet safely on the ground, the truck rumbled off, leaving the three men standing there in a little group, surveying each other in the dim light of the street lamp.

Yoshi stood leaning against the door, watching. Except that he was heavier, Father Sato looked just as he did the day he was taken away. He had on the same dark Sunday suit pants and white shirt, with his coat neatly folded over his arm.

At sight of the familiar figure, something snapped inside Yoshi like the breaking of a string drawn too tight. There stood his father, emblem of the security and family solidarity which had been the foundation of his childhood and which unconsciously he had missed so much. All of the bad which had attached itself to him like barnacles since he had come to camp suddenly sloughed off, and the boy ran out past his mother and Mari, shouting with a terrible sob in his voice.

"Oh, Papa, you're back. You're back."

He grasped his father's arm in both hands and hung on desperately.

Father Sato was deeply moved. The older brothers looked away, surprised and embarrassed by this show of emotion.

"Yochan, my little son. How good to see you again." The father's voice trembled. He seemed to be struggling for control. Then he held the boy off at arm's length and looked at him fondly. "But you are not little anymore. How you have grown!" He handed Yoshi his coat to carry, and Yoshi was glad to have something to do after his outburst. He brushed a tear from his eyes with his free hand and, looking at his father, began to grin.

"You've grown, too," he joked. "You're fat."

"So I am. So I am. My suit is very tight. I could just get into it this morning. I may have to give it to you. Yes, I've grown fat and lazy with nothing to do." The man sighed.

Now the four started for the stoop, Yoshi holding his father's arm as if he were afraid he might get away. Tad and Tom walked behind them.

"Hello, Dad," Mari said, and laughed foolishly.

Then remembered to bow.

"Shigeru! You are here." Mother Sato's voice was low, emotionless.

"Yes, I am with you all again."

They went inside. In the brighter light the man took one look at his wife and drew in a quick breath.

"You are ill," he said.

"No," was the quick answer. "No, I am well."

"Then you have been ill."

"A long time ago, yes. But now I am well again. You remember me when I was heavy. Now I am slim, and you are the one who is fat. But the heat will soon melt off the pounds."

"I had little to do and plenty of good food. Here I hope there will be work to do."

"You won't suffer from good food here," Tad said, unconsciously lapsing into the bitter accusations which had become a habit. "There they had to treat you right; international law compelled them. But here they can get away with anything. We have no protection, not even our citizenship."

His father regarded him thoughtfully.

"You are looking very well," Father Sato commented drily.

"Yes, sir, I am," Tad said respectfully. "I guess we always have enough."

Mother Sato and Mari began fixing food, and Tom set the old suitcase at the end of a cot, got some soap and a towel, and took his father out to the washhouse to clean up.

As soon as they were out of the door, Father Sato turned to Tom.

"What is wrong with your mother? She looks very bad."

"Well, she's never been good since the day you left. That hit her hard, you being dragged off that way. She worried a lot, and she worked too hard in the field trying to take your place. I couldn't stop her. And the heat and cold here are both hard on her. These barracks . . . it's like living outdoors. It's been hard on all the older folks."

"She said she'd been sick. I am sure the heat and the cold could not have done this to her."

Tom knew he could not hide anything from his father, now that he was here.

"She was pretty sick with the flu last winter. She was in the hospital awhile."

"Why didn't you write to me about her?"

Tom squirmed.

"Well, we didn't want to worry you, and there wasn't anything you could do away off down there."

"I could have prayed."

The quiet strength of his father made Tom feel like a grain of sand that had tried to protect a granite cliff from high seas.

"I can see now we should have written. I'm sorry, sir, that we didn't. Tad did try to send a wire when she was the worst, but it got lost in the office; and by the time we found out it hadn't got off, Mom was better. She'll be all right now you're here. To have you imprisoned has been the worst. And Tad. When that gets settled one way or another. Don't you think you can do something with Tad? I think he's pretty miserable over his decision."

"I intend to try."

Father soaped his hands and held them under the tap, washing off the grime of travel.

"There's not much time left," Tom warned. "Not more than a couple of days, maybe three. The administration usually gives a day of grace when they put out their ultimatums."

"I will talk to him when the time is right."

When they went back to the apartment tea was ready, and the family drank and ate and talked. Mother Sato ate with more relish for her food than she had shown since Papa-san went away.

Yoshi was wide awake now and sat on his cot beaming at his father. After Tom had eaten, his eyes began to droop, and finally he could hold out no longer and lay back and went to sleep.

Father Sato wanted to know about everything since he had left. He was like a Rip van Winkle, for he had had no outside news.

He asked Yoshi how he was doing in school. Would he be in the eighth grade when school started? How had he done in the seventh?

Shamefaced, the boy admitted he hadn't done so well and began to make excuses. First, they didn't have any books, and in the winter the classrooms were so cold you couldn't do anything but shiver. There was no library, and some of the teachers weren't much good. A lot of Nisei girls were teaching in the elementary school, and they couldn't do anything with the kids.

"Then I suppose all the pupils did poorly, with so many handicaps," Father Sato said, smiling. Yoshi got the point.

"It is late and past time you were in bed," the father said to his youngest.

Yoshi, without protest, undressed and lay down with his face to the wall, away from the light.

Now there were only Tad and Mari and their parents. They went on visiting and drinking tea. The cookies and candy were gone.

Father Sato asked Mari about her plans and was pleased with the arrangements for her to go to college. Perhaps he could help some later with her expenses, but she must work now to pay her way, and not accept gifts from others.

Finally the father turned to Tad, who braced himself as his father spoke.

"And you, Tadashi. Are your plans the same as when you wrote me?"

"Yes, sir, they are."

Father Sato shook his head sadly.

"You were always the stubborn one," he said.

He was silent for a moment, and Tad gathered his defenses ready for the struggle against his father's arguments.

"I think we should get some rest now," Father Sato said quietly. "Tomorrow we will talk it over together."

XXVI

When Father Sato was ready for breakfast the next morning, he joined Mother Sato, who was waiting on the stoop.

"Where are the children?" he asked. "Should we not wait for them to come?" He looked out toward the washhouse.

"Tom is in the field already, and Mari and Yoshi have gone to the mess hall. And as you can see for yourself, Tadashi is still sleeping."

"What kind of family is this?" the man said in a grieved but gentle voice. "Don't you eat together?"

Mother Sato lifted her shoulder in a Poston shrug.

"What can one do? None of the families eat together. The young ones eat with their friends. Do you want our children to be different?"

The last gong rang.

"Come on, Shigeru, or there will be nothing left."

Father Sato went, shaking his head. He must do something about this.

As he entered the mess hall he saw a group of boys seated at a table near the door. They were high-school age and talking and laughing like rowdies. As he and Mother Sato looked for two empty seats together, he saw Mari at a table filled with girls of her own age. He was half through eating before he saw Yoshi. He was leaving with two other boys, and the trio slouched through the door like ragamuffins.

Old acquaintances bowed and smiled as Father Sato looked around the room. He recognized several of his neighbors, but the people at his own table were strangers.

There were pancakes for breakfast, cold and soggy. And coffee. He would have liked tea. After breakfast he stopped outside the mess hall and talked with the group of men who were waiting there to greet him. They all noted how well he looked. Mother Sato went

433

on to the apartment. The mess hall doors closed.

Presently Tad came over.

"Good morning, Dad," he said.

"Good morning. You have missed your breakfast, Son. The doors are closed."

Tad started to laugh, then checked himself.

"Yes, sir, it looks like it. Well, I'll go around to the kitchen door. Maybe I can get a handout of a cup of coffee."

The men standing with Father Sato kept their faces blank, showing nothing of surprise or amusement over Tad's deceit.

When Tad came out after a better breakfast than any of the family had had, he saw his father sitting alone under the vine-covered arbor which the men of the block had built between the two rows of barracks. Not ready yet for the showdown with his father, he would have gone off in another direction; but his father called to him.

When Tad was seated on the rustic, mesquite wood bench, the other men, who had been sitting near, got up and walked away, leaving the two men alone.

Father and son sat in silence for a time, as if each was waiting for the other to speak. Then Father Sato broke the silence.

"Tell me about yourself since I saw you last," he said in a kindly manner.

Suddenly Tad was ready and eager to pour out his heart. At last he had a sympathetic listener. He could unload the heavy burden he had been carrying for so long. He began with going back to camp after Thanksgiving and how everything was going fine when the attack on Pearl Harbor came. After that it was hell. The CO was suspicious of all the Nisei and could hardly wait until the orders came to kick them out. He went to the apartment and brought out his discharge papers to show to his father.

"It is not good to scratch a sore and keep it bleeding," Father Sato said. "It is better to let it heal."

Tad recalled Miss Brown's words about festering,

but he said nothing.

"This is not a dishonorable discharge, is it?" his father asked, puzzled over the wording.

"No, but it might as well be. It deprives a fellow of all the privileges the government gives to GIs. It's called a blue discharge."

Then Tad began an account of the time he spent at home between his discharge and evacuation, becoming more bitter all the time. He took his father through those galling days at Santa Anita, then the life in the permanent camp at Poston, finishing with the registration and the hated loyalty questions.

Father Sato listened intently, not interrupting.

"Do you wish to go to Japan to live?" he asked quietly when Tad was through.

"Dad, you know I don't. You know how I felt about Japan after our visit there."

"You consider yourself a loyal American, then."

"Yes, sir, I do."

"Then why did you refuse to declare your loyalty?"

"Because they had no right to ask me unless they were going to ask every other citizen in the country the same questions. That's why."

"Could you not have left the questions unanswered? Was it necessary to give a false impression?"

"That would have been the same as saying no. They would have taken the blanks to mean that. You don't know how they are here. Always suspecting everything you do."

"Tadashi, I think you have used poor judgment. And you have given answers which were not true. There are better ways of defending one's rights and convictions. You have harmed yourself, and you have done an injustice to your family."

Tad slumped with disappointment. His father had failed him. He began to feel resentment against his own father rising in him, and it alarmed him. He was afraid to speak for fear it would show in his voice. He began to excuse his father. He hadn't been in camp long enough to know what it was like. If he could have come

435

sooner. How could his father be so forgiving for having been held a prisoner so long without reason? Not a word of complaint had escaped him since he came. No use now. He would have to defy his father as well as his mother and Mari and Tom. They were all against him.

"What will you do when you are sent to Japan?" Father Sato asked.

"I don't think I'll ever be sent. There are too many Nisei from all the camps in this with me. The government isn't going to rob all of us of our citizenship when there's been time to think it over."

"But you can't be sure. You should be considering the possibility of spending the rest of your life in Japan."

Tad winced at the thought. He'd as soon be dead.

"Have you considered what your action might do to your mother? She looks very frail."

"She'll be all right now you're here," Tad said. "She looks better already. Anyway, I'll be with you again when the war is over." Tad spoke with a confidence he did not feel.

"You will not change your mind, then?"

Tad bit his thin lips and looked out across the sun-baked firebreak. Beyond it men were putting the finishing on the adobe school buildings, painting the window frames, laying the forms for the walks between the long, low buildings. Over their tops to the north he could see where the spikes of Needle Mountain pierced the cloudless sky.

He tried to form the words he knew he had to say. His father sat waiting for his answer. He had to speak.

"No, sir. I can't. A fellow has to do what he thinks is right."

Father Sato sighed deeply.

"The men who crucified Christ thought they were doing what was right. A person can be mistaken." He seemed to be talking more to himself than to Tad. Then he turned and looked squarely into Tad's eyes.

"You are a hard-headed boy. I will pray that things

436

will come out all right for you."

There was nothing more to be said. The men rose just as the first dinner gong began to clang.

Mother Sato, who had seen them talking and guessed the topic of their conversation, came out to meet them. She saw nothing in their faces to encourage her. Together the three walked over to the mess hall.

After dinner, when Father Sato told his wife of the talk he had had with Tad, she began to feel him out about their going to Tule Lake with Tad. There would be only Yoshi to take, for Tom and Mari had their plans. Father Sato refused to listen. He said he had other plans.

That afternoon he went to the Relocation Office with Mr. Ohashi, who was making plans to leave for the Midwest in a few weeks. While there, Father Sato started proceedings for his own relocation. That evening he and Tom went over the bankbooks and accounts together. What they found was distressing.

It was the middle of the following morning that Tad came running home from the canteen. A shipment of T-shirts had come in and he wanted some money to get a couple. He hated to ask his father for money the second day he was there, but if he waited until Tom came from the fields, it would be too late. The fellows were buying them up like women at a bargain sale.

Father Sato was watering the grass beside the barracks.

"Hey, Dad," Tad panted, "could you let me have a couple of bucks? I want to get something at the canteen. I can pay you back when I get my clothing allowance."

His father turned off the water and sat down on the stoop in the shade. He took out his handkerchief and wiped away the sweat which was trickling down his face.

Tad chafed at the deliberate slowness of his father.

"I don't have any money, Tadashi."

"Well, just write a check, then. Guess Mr. Imoto will take your check all right," Tad said with a laugh.

"Make it for five and I'll get a shirt for Tom, too."

"I cannot write a check, either. There is no money in the bank to draw on."

Tad looked at his father in disbelief. Was this refusal punishment for his refusal to give in? No, his father had never lied to him. If he said there wasn't any money in the bank, then there wasn't. But how could it be? There always had been.

"Why . . . why . . ." Tad stopped. Then he said in a thin voice. "So it's all gone."

"With everything going out and nothing coming in, even a substantial account cannot last always."

"But the rent from the ranch?" The T-shirts were forgotten now in the face of this calamity.

"Hasn't Tom told you that the tenant moved and that he failed to make payments the last several months?"

"Yes, I guess he did. I'd forgotten. What are we going to do? You can't live in a place like this without a little money of your own to buy some comforts. No money in the bank." It was beyond Tad's comprehension.

"I am making plans to go outside to work," Father Sato said. "A farmer in Iowa wants a man, I learned at the Relocation Office yesterday."

Tad's face reddened to the roots of his hair. He pictured himself in voluntary idleness at Tule Lake while his father labored on a farm and maybe his mother worked in a farm wife's kitchen back in Iowa. And they would send money to him at Tule Lake to buy some of the comforts of life he was talking about. The thought was unbearable.

"No, Dad," he fairly shouted. "Never. Not as long as I have two good hands, I'll never let you go out and work for someone who might be a slave driver. I'll go myself and get a job. And you can stay here and take care of Mom."

"Would you sacrifice your convictions for us?"

"To hell with convictions."

"Tadashi!" the father exclaimed, and his voice

betrayed his emotion. "Your head is as hard as the stones bordering the garden, but your heart is as tender as the lilies that bloom in the pool. You are a good son and not lacking in filial piety."

Tad straightened his shoulders and stealthily brushed away a tear.

"That's because I have a good father and mother," he said, his voice light. And his heart felt lighter than it had for many a month. He had committed himself and there was no turning back now. And as much as he dreaded the ordeal he must endure before he would be able to get clearance from camp, he sincerely did not want to turn back.

They began to discuss details. Tad must get into action at once, for this was the last day to change the answers. Then there would be a hearing, and FBI clearance, and a dozen other obstacles. It would be difficult, but not impossible.

When Tom came in for the midday rest, he found the family in the midst of a celebration. Mari had produced a dollar from her travel fund and had bought cookies at the canteen, and Mother Sato had brewed tea. But Tad thought tea was too weak a libation to drink to his health and his success in finding a job outside, and he had remembered a friend who had a well-stocked cupboard hidden away from the eyes of the authorities. Cups of *sake* were going the rounds when Tom came in, with Yoshi content with a bottle of coke.

"What the heck's going on?" Tom asked, looking from one smiling face to the other.

"Tad isn't going to Tule!" Mari shouted, her tongue a little thick. "Isn't that great?"

"Well, it sure is. When did all this happen?" Tom looked at Tad, and Tad nodded toward his father. Tom was puzzled. Dad must have used a stick of dynamite to dislodge Tad from his bulwarks. But he'd have to wait to find out. Everyone was too happy now to explain, and he was too happy to want to know.

Tom's clothes were wringing wet with perspiration and his face was burning like fire. He doused it with water his mother poured into a small basin, dried his face and hands, and took the glass Mari had filled for him.

"Here's to Tad," he said, raising his glass. "And here's to Dad."

They drank and laughed together, and Father Sato smiled and was pleased with his family.

Yoshi finished his coke and cookies while the others talked, and when the dinner gong rang he said he wasn't hungry and wasn't going to the mess hall. Father Sato, however, had other plans. The family would all go together and sit together. This was a good time to start.

"I feel silly," Mari whispered to Tom as they all went into the mess. "Everyone's looking at us."

"Let 'em look," Tom said, unconcerned. "I'm hungry."

That afternoon Tad went to the office and changed the answers on his registration form. His action only aroused suspicion. What was he up to now? His hearing was set for the following day.

Tad was no more reconciled to evacuation than he had been before he changed from no to yes on the loyalty questions. He still felt it was an insult to the Nisei to ask them to declare their loyalty. He was just the same inside, but he must not let the board know he was. He'd have to butter them up. He hated the thought. He was going to have to bow down to the administration at last.

Something of his old self-assurance began to come back to him. He'd made himself liked in the university, and he'd got along well with the other fellows in the Army. Now he had to make himself liked by the examining board.

But when the day of the hearing came, Tad's resentment was burning so deep that he wondered whether or not he could go through with it without losing his temper and shooting off.

That morning he shaved and put on a pair of khaki pants and a light sport shirt Mari had laundered for him the night before. He combed his hair with unusual care. He was consci⌐us that he made a good appearance as he walked into the hearing room with his father. Tad had asked his father to go, for he felt his presence would be a brake on his own actions if things got too hot.

There were three people sitting on the hearing board this morning, an elderly man with grizzly short hair that appeared to bristle at the sight of a "Jap", a middle-aged woman, large and mannish in appearance, and a young fellow with a sheaf of papers on the desk before him. He was the one in charge, and as Tad looked his inquisitors over, he felt it was a streak of luck to have one who looked human.

"Good morning," the young man said in a cheery manner, but not too much so. "You are Tad Sato; so it says here on my paper. And is this your father?"

"Yes," Tad said, thawing a little.

The man got up from his chair, came around the desk, and offered his hand.

"How do you do, Mr. Sato? I am Pat O'Connell. This is Mrs. Easterbrook and that is Mr. Belter at the end." The woman murmured something by way of recognition of the introduction, but Belter never so much as raised his eyes from a spot on the floor to which he was giving his undivided attention.

"Sit down, men, and make yourselves comfortable," O'Connell said, indicating the row of chairs facing the desk. "This may take quite awhile."

From Belter's actions Tad had formed the opinion that the man didn't care much more for O'Connell than he did for "Japs," and that made him feel the young man was a friend of the Nisei. But when the session began the first question made him wonder if he was right about that.

"Your tardiness in changing your answers makes you like a brand snatched from the burning," O'Connell said briskly. "You are the first university man I have interviewed who was Tule Lake bound right up to the wire. What caused you to change your mind?"

Belter suddenly showed interest. He turned his head slightly, as though he were a little deaf and didn't want to miss Tad's answer. Then, before Tad could say anything, he took the questioning out of O'Connell's hands.

"There are other questions that come before that one," he said.

Sharp, deep-set eyes full of animosity bored into Tad's. Tad's eyes never wavered, but he made his hands relax to keep them from clenching into fists.

"Why did you refuse to swear allegiance to the United States in the first place?"

"I didn't feel anyone had the right to ask me to without asking every other citizen the same question."

"So you didn't think the government had a right, eh? Don't you know the government has the right to ask a citizen any question it wants to in time of war?"

"I suppose it has," Tad conceded.

Belter looked down at the paper before him on the desk.

"I see that you served in the Army for a time."

"Yes, sir, as a volunteer."

"Didn't you swear to your loyalty when you volunteered?" The man stressed the last word with a tinge of sarcasm.

"That question was asked of all of us, sir. It was not a racial affair."

The hearing wasn't going very well. Mr. Sato looked a little anxious. It was a relief to have the young man take over again.

"You couldn't be a little oversensitive, could you?" O'Connell asked in a friendly manner. The voice was like music after the gruff burr of Belter.

"We've stood for a lot," Tad answered.

Belter snorted.

The questioning went on and on. Mrs. Easterbrook delved deeply into Tad's past. He judged she was an ex-teacher, for she seemed more interested in his education than anything else.

After she was through, O'Connell began to ask Tad

about his Army record. Would he be willing to give the name of any officer he had trained under as a reference?

"Yes, gladly. Captain Standish would know most about me, I think."

"Couldn't be Miles, could it?" O'Connell joked, and Tad smiled faintly. He wasn't in a joking mood.

"I think it was Morris," he said. "But I'm not sure. Naturally we didn't call officers by their first names."

"I'll try to get a reference from him. Do you know where he is now?"

"No, I have no idea. He was with the 3rd Armored."

"Aren't they training out here on the desert now?" O'Connell asked, looking at Belter and Mrs. Easterbrook. "Seems to me I've met some men from the 3rd in Parker."

"Don't ask me. There's thousands of men training between here and Indio, but I have no idea what the units are."

"I think we are capable of reaching a decision without any help from the Army," Belter said.

"Are you satisfied we have all the information we need?" O'Connell asked the other board members. "If so, I think we can close the hearing."

Tad breathed a sigh of relief and started to get up.

"Not so fast, O'Connell," Belter said. "I'm not through yet with this fellow." He turned on Tad. "When did you change your answers to the loyalty questions from no to yes?"

"He has told us that already," O'Connell said impatiently.

"I want to hear him tell us again."

Tad took a tight grip on himself as he sat back in his chair. He must not antagonize this man more than he was already. He was older than O'Connell and might have more influence with the administration. Tad regretted the young man had not been able to bring the hearing to a conclusion, for he didn't know how much more he could take from Belter.

He turned and looked at his father. If he had

known what Belter had in mind, he would have known this gesture was a mistake, but he received strength from the calm, passive face beside him.

"I made the change yesterday, sir."

"The last possible day. And what happened two days before this?"

"I don't understand what you mean."

"Didn't your father return from a prison camp in New Mexico where he had been detained since Pearl Harbor?"

My God, is he going to drag my father into this? Tad thought bitterly. His eyes sought O'Connell's with mute appeal. But O'Connell avoided him. He was as helpless as Tad to shut off Belter. Tad had to answer.

"Yes, sir, from New Mexico and a number of other places where he had been held."

Belter's face broke into a grin of triumph, and he turned to talk to Mrs. Easterbrook and O'Connell.

"Now I have an idea those Issei sitting around those prison camps do a lot of plotting, and I just figure Mr. Sato decided his son could do more to help Japan if he were a free man on the outside than he could sitting around up there at Tule Lake. So he gets released, comes to Poston, and right away, almost the next day, the son rushes up and changes his answers in the registration papers."

Tad clung to the arms of his chair to keep from striking the man.

But Belter had gone too far. O'Connell's Irish dander was up. He had done his homework on the Sato family before the hearing, and he knew the accusation was preposterous. He banged his fist on the desk and said, "The hearing is closed." His eyes were blazing.

Belter made no attempt to go on, but from the expression of cunning on his face, one could guess that he wasn't through with the case. He would work behind the scenes. He and Mrs. Easterbrook walked out together.

"You will be notified as soon as a decision had been made," O'Connell said to Tad.

444

It was over. Tad and his father walked slowly back to their block in the stifling heat.

"That Belter will never let me get out if he can help it," Tad said.

"Be hopeful, Son. You did well. We will not be idle while we wait."

That afternoon, Father Sato was out rounding up his friends among the Issei, men who had cooperated with the administration, men who served on the local council and had influence with the authorities. They might be needed.

That same evening, O'Connell went into Parker, where he was sure he would find someone from the armed forces either at the drugstore fountain or dancing at the Corral. He learned that the 3rd Armored was on the desert somewhere around Desert Center, and after a long wait he got Captain Standish on the line.

"Yes, this is Standish. Who are you?"

"Well, you don't know me. I'm Pat O'Connell on the staff at Poston. You know, where we've got the Japanese interned. Do you remember a fellow named Tad Sato who was in your outfit before Pearl Harbor?"

"Tad Sato. Sure, I remember him. You got him over there at Poston? Like to see him. The army lost a good soldier when they let him get away."

"You think he's okay, then?"

"What do you mean? Of course he's okay. I don't get you."

"Well, is he loyal? Or would he work for the Japs?"

"Fatheads, fatheads everywhere. In the Army, and now you got them down in that camp. Can't you tell a real guy when you see one?"

O'Connell didn't know whether to be glad or sore.

"Tad wants to go outside and get a job, but we've got to be careful whom we release. Got the politicians breathing down our necks. And Tad has been in a lot of funny business since he came to camp. I just wanted to make sure he's okay, loyal and all that."

"Well, you can take it from me he's all right. I wish I had him in my outfit in place of some of the jerks I

445

have to put up with. And let me tell you, if the government had put me in a concentration camp, I'd have kicked the walls clean out of the barracks. Good for Tad. Whatever he did, I'm on his side."

O'Connell laughed.

"Well, thanks a lot, Captain."

"If you don't mind, call me Major."

"Oh, I'm sorry, Major. Well, so long."

"Just a minute. Would it help any if I came over there and put in a word for Tad Sato? I'd like to see him again, anyway."

"It would sure make my job a lot easier," O'Connell said.

They set a time when the major was free, and O'Connell got together in the project director's office some of the top men of the administration to hear the major. He didn't bother to tell Belter. Belter didn't have a much higher opinion of the Army than he did of the Japanese. An officer's reference wouldn't carry any weight with him. He knew Belter had been carrying tales to the FBI before whom Tad must appear, but he thought those fellows would get Belter's number pretty quick.

O'Connell also asked permission of the project head to ask Tad up to the office so he could have a visit with his former captain. That presented an opportunity for Tad to meet the head man, and he made a good impression.

Now O'Connell had done all he could. It was up to the big shots to make the decision.

Tad's session with the FBI was better than he had expected. The men were curt and thorough, but they were fair. Now all he had to do was wait.

While he waited, he wrote letters to Take in Chicago and to Bill Kudo, who was working in defense in Detroit, and asked them about job opportunities.

The waiting period was hard. He must get out and earn some money. His mother needed medicine and some good food to add to the dismal camp diet. They all needed a lot of things. And the thought of having

446

gone through that ordeal with Belter all for nought drove Tad crazy. If he wasn't cleared, he'd blame it all on Belter, and he thought he would kill him.

Mari was busy sewing, getting ready to go off to college. Tom had contacted the recruiting officer and would go to Phoenix with the next group who were taken for their physicals.

Each day, truckloads of packing boxes marked for Tule Lake were being hauled to the station in Parker for shipment. Soon the repatriates and their unwilling children would begin the exodus. Tad watched the trucks go with the feelings of a man pardoned at the door of the gas chamber.

The days passed. A week since the last hearing. Ten days. Tad became more and more anxious with each passing day. Then the block manager came with a phoned message. He was wanted at the hearing room. Tad went with his fingers crossed. Was he going to have to endure another questioning?

O'Connell met him at the door. He was grinning.

"Tad Sato, you've been cleared for relocation," he said. "Go and get yourself a good job."

"Thanks a lot. I know I owe you for this. I won't forget it."

"Well, it wasn't easy after the reputation you made for yourself since coming to Poston. But I'm glad you made it."

Tad felt like a free man as he hurried over to the employment section of the Relocation Office to find out what jobs were listed.

XXVII

Tom was taking down Tad's and Mari's cots and folding them up. He was thinking of how soon he, too, would be leaving, and his father would be returning his cot and mattress to the block manager.

Tad and Mari had left the night before, taking the ten o'clock train to Cadiz, where they would catch the main line train to Chicago. Since there had been few leaving from Camp III, the whole Sato family had been allowed to ride in the truck to Camp I to see them off from the departure station there. They had stood and watched with mixed feelings as the truck rolled out the gates of the center, past the guard station and on toward Parker. It was a bright, moonlit night, and the mountains to the north, east, and west were plainly visible.

"Well, two of the family are free," Yoshi said, grinning up at Tom.

"Not quite. They'll be under guard, or at least have an escort, till they get to Cadiz, because that's California. But when they get on the through train to Chicago, then they'll be on their own."

"Are they that suspicious of citizens?" Father Sato said sadly.

"It's just routine, Dad. We're excluded from California, so we can't enter the state except under guard."

It seemed lonely and empty in the apartment this morning. Father Sato had started working in the warehouse. Tom had given up his job with the Ag. Department, for he had thought it wasn't worthwhile to start on another month. Anyway, when one of his father's friends found this easy job in the warehouse for Father Sato, who was afraid after two years of idleness that he could not stand the heavy work in the fields, someone needed to be with Mother Sato. Yoshi would soon be in school. This morning he was out on the firebreak playing ball while Tom helped his mother.

"What shall I do with these old mattress covers?" Tom asked his mother. "I'll burn the straw, but these ticks ..."

"Very dirty," Mother Sato said, eyeing the dusty covers. "You empty straw, I wash."

Tom stopped on his way to the door. He began to realize how much they were going to miss Mari. Who was going to do the laundry?

"I'll ask the manager," Tom said. "Maybe they just burn the old ticks, too, along with the straw."

He found that they didn't, so after he had emptied the straw in the incinerator, he took the ticks over to the laundry and ran them through the machine. He hung them on the line, feeling pretty smart over his first laundry job. They looked clean, too.

When he turned around and saw a row of men outside the washroom watching him with grins on their faces, he didn't feel so smart over doing a woman's work. He hurried back to the barracks.

"Get to Chicago today?" his mother asked when he went in.

"Heck, no. It will take a couple of days, anyway."

"Then Mari go on alone. Not let her leave be better." Mother Sato was worried. The great outside unknown was filled with perils.

"Take is going to meet them in Chicago, and he and Tad will put her on her train. Haruo and Willie will be there when she gets off and take her where she's going to live. She'll be safe enough on the train. Now stop worrying and be glad Mari could go to college. She'll make you proud of her. She's smart, and she'll be a good student."

"Proud now. Mari good daughter."

"And Tad with a good job. Soon he'll be sending you lots of money." Tom was thinking how crazy it all was. One day Tad behind barbed wire like a dangerous enemy and the next working in a defense plant.

"And I'll send you some of my big Army pay," he went on, trying to get his mother's mind off her worries.

449

"You can buy yourself some fancy dresses."

"Where I wear new dress?" Mother Sato said, laughing.

It was good to hear her laugh like she used to do so much back home.

"Oh, to church, to night classes, make all the other women envy your fine clothes." Mother Sato was studying English at night school.

"Better places to spend money," Mother Sato said, as she swept the dust from where the cots had stood.

Tom looked at the clock. The hours were dragging. Would tomorrow never come? He could scarcely contain himself until he could be off to Phoenix for his physical.

His mother was thinking of this, too.

"Tomorrow you go. Birds all fly from nest, leave it empty."

"You'll still have Yoshi," Tom reminded. "He'll keep you and Dad busy. Say, Mom, did you ever tell Dad about the stolen car and all that?"

"No. He wait. Plenty of time."

"Yes, I guess so. Yoshi is different since his father came. He won't be getting into any more trouble. I don't think he ever had anything to do with stealing a car. I hope Dad can get the truth out of him."

"He will," Mother Sato said confidently.

Tom looked around the room for something to do, and, not seeing anything, said, "I guess I'll go over and collect my last month's pay. Sure hope it's there. Wasn't the last time I went. I might want to buy something in the city." With that, he swaggered out. Talking about being in the city made him heady.

As Tom passed the open door of the adjoining apartment, he said a cheery good morning to the man stuffing last things into a packing box. All he got was a surly look, but his daughter, a junior in high school, came toward the door with swollen red eyes.

"Hello, Tom," she said, and gave him a wan smile.

Gee, sure tough on her, Tom thought as he went on.

Tom left at five the next morning on the truck

which would take him to Parker to get on the train. His father got up and put on a robe and went out with him to wait for the truck.

"It would have been nice for you if you could have gone when the other boys went," Father Sato said to Tom. "But you did right to wait."

"It was hard, but I'm glad now I did." He could go with a clear conscience. His father was there to care for his mother, and he was going now with her blessing.

"You have always been good to your mother, Son. You will have no regrets."

Praise from his father was always sweet to Tom's ears, but it meant more than usual this morning. It made the day perfect. When the truck came, he sprang in with a light heart.

Four other fellows, all strangers to Tom, were picked up in Camp II, and in Camp I their escort, Mr. Bradford, a young man from Internal Security, joined them.

It was the first time Tom had been out of the camp since the day he arrived, and everything was a thrill. Even the dust-covered smoke trees were something different. And the shacks of the Indians weren't much to look at, but they were houses, not barracks. The cottonwood trees were a pleasant change from the everlasting mesquite. An Indian girl, milking a cow, waved as they passed, and the boys waved back shyly.

At Parker, the little railway station was dirty, ill-smelling, and very hot, even at this early hour. The train was hotter, and crowded. The drinking water tanks were emptied, and Tom was disappointed when he walked forward, his mouth savoring a refreshing drink of ice water.

But nothing could dampen his high spirits. He went back and sat down and watched out the window for the sight of a ranch. He saw nothing but vast stretches of desert with now and then a little town. Bouse, Salome. Then Wickenburg, which was a little larger. Giant saguaros everywhere.

By two that afternoon the boys were through with

their exams. They were pretty well acquainted by this time, and when Mr. Bradford, who had proved to be a most pleasant escort, asked them what they wanted to do in the time left before they must go to the station, the answer was unanimous. They wanted to go downtown and see the stores.

Tom bought a pocketknife for his father and a pair of hose for his mother, and he found he had enough money left to buy a basketball for Yoshi. He had kept a little for himself, and he and the other fellows gorged themselves on hot dogs and candy, ice cream and cokes, until Mr. Bradford, sometimes a little misty-eyed, wondered if they would live to get back to Poston.

When they reached Parker that night, they saw long lines of empty coaches on the siding. They had been brought in to take the people to Tule Lake, Bradford told the boys. Tom thought of Tad, a free man in Chicago doing a man's job for his country, and he shivered in the heat to think of what a narrow escape he had had.

Home in camp again, the hard period of waiting began for Tom. How soon before he would hear the results of his exams? He wasn't concerned about the physical. He was strong as an ox. But there had been some other tests. Now his dream was so near reality, it was difficult to wait.

School opened, and Tom somehow managed to be passing the building about the time Yuri was leaving the office in the evening. He would walk home with her, saying it was about as near for him to go that way on his way to his block.

On Friday he was late, not knowing that school closed earlier on Fridays. It made his heart beat faster to find Yuri still there, talking with some students on the sidewalk. He didn't know whether she had waited for him or not, but he could think she had.

When they reached Yuri's apartment that evening, Yuri's mother invited him in. She had made some cupcakes and frosted them with a pretty pink icing. They ate the cakes and drank iced tea, and while they were enjoying themselves, Mr. Takeda came in. He showed a satisfying interest in Tom's plans.

"A fellow who volunteers from a place like this is a real patriot," he said.

"Well, I guess a loyal American volunteers from anyplace where he finds himself," Tom replied.

Although both Yuri's parents made him feel at ease with their friendliness, he couldn't help comparing their luxuriously furnished apartment with his own, and realized the great gap between the Takeda and Sato families as far as money and culture were concerned. He didn't think he would be the kind of son-in-law Mr. Takeda would choose. He wondered if he should say anything to Yuri before he left.

The same week school opened, the exodus to Tule Lake began. Besides the folks next door, there were several other families in the Sato block who left. And in the adjoining block, so many went that the mess hall was closed, and the remaining occupants came to Block 324 for their meals.

Letters came from Tad and Mari, brief because both were busy. Each promised to write more later. Tad had gone to work the day after he arrived and lived in the same house with Take. He said they had a swell trip after they got rid of their escort at Cadiz. It was a woman, and she watched them like a hawk. He said the men could hardly get away from her to go to the men's room. Mari was thrilled with everything, the college, the doctor's family where she was working. Everybody was just wonderful. None of these black looks like they had had from Caucasians in California before evacuation. It was great to be out of camp.

Each day, Tom was at the block manager's office when the mail came. Nothing for him from the recruiting office. Not till the twelfth day after the trip to Phoenix. That day the letter came. He didn't open it until he had walked over to the edge of the camp, stepped over the strands of barbed wires which lay on the ground, and found a little shade under a mesquite tree. Even then he waited. What that envelope con-

453

tained meant so awful much to him. He sat there turning it over, reading the postmark, the date, the address. Mr. Tamotsu Sato, Block 324, Poston, Arizona. When he could get no further reponse from the exterior, he carefully tore off the end of the envelope and took the letter out.

Its contents had the effect of a hand grenade exploding in his face. He had failed to pass the physical. He had some spots on his lung. He had been rejected.

Tom sat there for a long time, not moving. Then he shoved the letter back into the envelope, got up, and walked directly across the camp to the warehouse to tell his father.

It was almost time for the noon mess, and Mr. Sato left his work and walked with Tom back toward the home block.

He had tender words of sympathy for his son in his deep disappointment, but his chief concern was for Tom's health. Tuberculosis was a dreaded word in the country from which he had come. There many had the disease. Many died of it. He had lost a sister in her youth. But she had been sickly and pale and grew thinner day by day. He looked at Tom. Tanned a deep bronze. Robust, vigorous, the picture of health. He could not believe that the boy was ill.

"We must have Dr. Nakata look at you," he said. "The Army doctors are very busy now. They may not have time to give as careful an examination as they should. Mistakes can be made."

Tom made no objection. He had been rejected by the Army. What another doctor said wouldn't change things any.

In his barracks, Doctor Nakata gave Tom as thorough an examination as was possible with the equipment he had. He didn't find anything to cause worry. Some old scars, he thought.

"But you must report to the Public Health Office, Tom," he said. "That is the regulation. All suspected cases must be reported, as well as the known ones."

After he had given Tom the location of the office,

he said, "I don't advise you to go back to work in Agriculture. There is too much dust. No use taking any risks in case this does develop into something definite. Take it easy awhile. There's no more favorable climate in the whole country for TB than where you are right now. Rest and eat, and don't worry. In a couple of months I'll take another look at you."

Tom and his father agreed they would say nothing to Mother Sato. No use to worry her. Let her think Tom had failed one of the other exams. Tom put the letter away in his suitcase and tried to act as if nothing had happened.

That evening, Yuri waited awhile after school, and when Tom didn't come, she went on home alone.

At Public Health, Tom was given the works: tests, X-rays, a questionnaire on family history. If the spots on his lungs were caused by tuberculosis, it was no longer active, was the decision. The advice was the same as Dr. Nakata's. Rest, eat, don't worry. Come back in a few months.

Mother Sato began to ask questions. What exam had Tom failed? She'd heard the talk around camp about why this one and that one had been rejected. Some weren't smart enough, some had poor eyesight, some were too small. What was wrong with her son?

Since the diagnoses of the doctors in camp had been so encouraging, Father Sato decided to tell her the truth.

She was glad Tom was not going away. She began to pamper him. Tom accepted her fussing over him as he accepted everything else, like a person in a trance.

When a week had passed and Tom had not shown up after school, Yuri waylaid Yoshi outside his classroom one afternoon. Surely Tom hadn't left camp without saying goodbye.

"Hello, Yoshi," she said, as the boy came hurtling out of the classroom onto the lanai. "Have you heard from Mari yet?"

"Ye-yes," Yoshi stammered, while the boys with him nudged him, giggled, and went on to their next class.

"The folks had a letter."

"How does she like it, being outside?" Yuri asked, giving the boy a winning smile.

"I dunno. All right, I guess. Who wouldn't?"

"You must be lonesome with Tad and Mari both gone, and Tom going soon, I suppose."

"Tom isn't going," Yoshi said. "Well, I've got to get along to my next class." He turned awkwardly and sped down the lanai.

Tom isn't going. What does that mean? Did he change his mind? Didn't he go to Phoenix after all? No, she knew he would never have willingly given up his plans to serve his country. Had his mother and father put pressure on him?

Yuri wished with all her heart that Mari were home so she could go over to the Sato apartment. But with her gone, there was no excuse. Maybe Tom would be waiting to see her when school was out that evening. He did not come, and Yuri went home to write to Mari and see what she could find out from her.

However, Yuri did not have to wait to hear from Mari. The word that Tom had been rejected soon was circulating around the camp. Finally it was recorded, with the reason, in the Poston *Chronicle*. His friends were sympathetic outwardly, but secretly congratulated him for not having to go. Not to Tom, of course. They kept their words in the hearts.

Tom lived alone in his world of disappointment. He couldn't share it with anyone. Since the day he had been forced to leave his growing crops on the ranch, nothing had hit him so hard. If he could go to some other recruiting office, he might be accepted. But that was impossible so long as he was shut up in camp. If he were on the outside. That's what he would do, get clearance for relocation, go out and get a job, and then try again.

He talked to his father. Tom must stay until they knew positively that his health was good.

"He who desires and offers to serve is as worthy as he who does," the father consoled.

It was poor comfort to Tom, but he accepted it, quit struggling, and began to take an interest in the camp activities, since he was no longer dead tired from long hours of work in the fields. It was a pleasanter place now the disgruntled who were always ready to sow the seeds of dissension were gone to Tule Lake. Several projects were planned to add to the comfort and pleasure of living. A swimming pool was started, to be ready for the next summer, and an open air auditorium with stationary seats was soon under construction. When it was completed, the residents would no longer have to carry their own seats to the movies, and there would be shade overhead for the events which took place in the daytime.

The baseball season was about over, but Tom went out for practice so he would be ready to join the team in the spring. He felt as good as he had when he was working ten hours a day. He couldn't see any reason why he should sit around idle all day.

Father Sato had quickly learned the Poston motto that the Lord helps those who help themselves, and he had appropriated the empty apartment next door for the use of his family. Tom helped him cut a door in the wall between the two apartments, and with lumber which was still to be had for the taking, they put up a partition in the annex making two bedrooms, one for Father and Mother Sato and one for Tom and Yoshi. To have a bedroom again was a luxury. Now that Tom wasn't working, he didn't have money to buy even a picture for the wall, but he had Yoshi bring home some drawing paper from school along with some crayons, and he made some sketches which he thought were pretty good.

When the Endos left early in October, Father Sato bought their davenport and chair, and a bed, table, and lamp. Mr. Endo would gladly have given them to him, for Haruo had rented a furnished apartment for them not far from the college, but Father Sato insisted on paying. It would be on the installment plan, as Tad sent money home. However, after much urging on the part of both Mr. and Mrs. Endo, he did accept as a gift their linoleum, a pretty marbled brown and white. The apartment was much more homey with the splintered floor boards covered and with something comfortable to sit on.

When the remodeling was finished, Tom thought he might as well work again. He needed that twelve dollars a month. Dr. Takata took another look at him and said there was no reason why he shouldn't be working, but warned him again not to go back to the dusty fields. So Tom went to the local employment office and found there was a job open in Industry.

In the beginning, the administration plans for Poston had been on a ten to fifteen year basis. Agriculture was to be developed on a large scale, with evacuee farmers selling the surplus crops for profit to themselves. So with Industry. Those who had made their living by making things with their hands, from cabinet makers to artists, would be given the opportunity to continue their work in the center.

But when the government policy changed Poston into a temporary stopping place on the way to permanent relocation of the evacuees in the unrestricted areas of the country, these grandiose plans were curtailed. Less land was irrigated, only the needs of the community being considered in planning the crops; Industry became only busy work for those of artistic tendencies while they waited. One of the barracks which had been given over to this department was named the Mojave Room, and in place of the double rough doors at the front there was a wide, custom-built one on which was the name in fine letters. This gave the place an air of distinction.

When Tom went to see Mr. Kawai, who was in charge of Industry, the man was reluctant to take on a fellow from Agriculture. What could he do with a man who had done nothing but ranch work?

"Did you have any art work in school?" he asked.

"I had a couple of years of shop," Tom replied.

"Think you could make picture frames?"

"I don't know why not." Tom was as unimpressed by the exclusive art center as Mr. Kawai was with him.

"Well, come over tomorrow and we'll see what you can do." The man was sure that a few days would be all Tom would want of it. He looked at the rough hands and was convinced that they were not for making the finer things.

And so Tom started on the first indoor job he had ever had. At first he didn't think he would like it, but the weather was cooler now, and with the windows and doors thrown open, the crisp autumn air circulated through the rooms gave him no feeling of being shut in.

He didn't have much to do at first. Mr. Kawai said nothing about picture frames. There was an ever-increasing demand from the Caucasian personnel in the three camps for the place cards, stationery, bookmarks, and the like, on which the girls working in Industry put colorful little sketches of desert scenes. Tom was put to work as a paper cutter. He took his job as a joke. It was not work. When he wasn't busy, he spent the time making sketches on scraps of paper, shoving them under something when anyone came near.

After he had been there about a week, Mr. Kawai came into the workroom with one of Mr. Takeda's watercolors which he had framed to hang in the Mojave Room. And he was in a hurry. The project head was bringing some outside guests down to see the Mojave Room sometime over the weekend. The place had gained quite a reputation in all the camps. The man he wanted to do the work was not there; workers had a habit of coming only when it suited them. He had to give the work to Tom.

He explained carefully what he wanted and told Tom to go into the salesroom and look at the pictures hanging there. From the frames he could get an idea of the fine work required. This must be something worthy of holding a painting from the hand of the great Takeda.

Mr. Kawai was a dapper little city man with a toothbrush mustache. His life had been lived among the exquisite imports in his art shop in San Francisco, and to him a rancher could be nothing but a clumsy clodhopper. He hurried out before Tom could start, for he could not bear the agony of watching Tom work.

Tom was impressed with the importance of making a frame for Mr. Takeda's picture. He hadn't seen Yuri since the trip to Phoenix. Maybe he would never see her.

When he had measured the picture and decided on the width of the frame, he was still not ready to begin the work. He propped the picture up before him and studied it. It was very simple. A group of trees silvery green; on the ground surrounding the group, the barren sand was dotted with tiny flowers which caught the blue of the sky in their cups and waved in the breeze like tiny flags. A mountain in the distance. That was all. But it was beautiful.

"What kind of trees are these?" he asked Florence Yamamoto, who was decorating place cards across the table from him.

"Smoke trees."

"Oh, sure. I saw some on the way to the station."

"Mr. Takeda is always painting smoke trees."

"I don't wonder. They're pretty. What color of mat should I use?"

"How about sand?"

"No, there's too much sand in the picture. I think a contrast would be better. How about this? It's darker." He placed the large sheet alongside the picture.

"Oh, yes. That's exactly right. You're an artist, Tom."

"Hardly." But he was pleased.

When Mr. Kawai came in after dinner, prepared for the worst, he was both surprised and pleased. Tom was bent over his work, and with all the girls chattering as usual, he did not hear Mr. Kawai come.

"Well, how is it coming?" the man asked, although he could see it was coming very well indeed.

"I don't think you can really tell about something like this until it is finished and the picture is in it,"

Tom said.

That pleased Mr. Kawai. Maybe he had misjudged the rancher. He looked at the hands and noticed the sureness of their touch. If he had seen Tom transplanting thousands of fragile seedlings from seedbeds to growing flats, he would have known that all work on a ranch was not accomplished by mere brawn.

"Take all the time you need," he said, giving Tom a pat on the back. Then he slipped away.

After the others had gone that evening, Tom stayed on to finish. When the frame was completed, the wood sanded and waxed to a velvet finish, he placed the picture in it and stood back to assess the result of his work. The picture and frame blended into one; each was a part of the other.

While he was standing there admiring his work, Mr. Takeda came in. He was surprised to find Tom still there. Most of the workers left on the dot, or even a little early.

The artist took his picture into the salesroom, with Tom following. There he hung it on the wall beside his others. Tom thought his was the best, and hoped Mr. Takeda would say it was. But he didn't. He looked at it a minute, then went back to the workroom to pick up some materials for his art class that night. Tom started out the front door, but found it was locked. He went back through the workroom.

Mr. Takeda was holding some scraps of paper in his hand, studying them intently.

"Do you know which one of the girls did these?" he asked.

Tom's face was hot. It was some of his sketches. He thought he'd thrown them all into the wastebasket.

"Oh, that's just some of my doodling when I didn't have anything else to do."

"Young man, you have talent, and you must not belittle it. You must do something with it." He held up one paper on which Tom had drawn two Issei picking melons in the early dawn. There was only a faint glow of the coming sunrise in the sky. "Of course, you need

461

study and hard work. But the spark is there."

Tom laughed.

"Never ridicule genius, even in yourself. Come to my class tonight, Tom."

Tom was afraid to refuse, for fear of offending Yuri's father, which showed he still had hope of resuming his friendship with her. So Tom became a regular member of the art class and took a lot of ribbing from his former fellow workers of the fields.

Tom and his teacher had many disagreements. Mr. Takeda wanted to make a landscape painter out of his star pupil. Tom wasn't interested. He wanted to paint pictures of people doing things, men working in the fields, boys at their games around the camp. It was one picture of Tom's that won his teacher over to his way of thinking. It was a watercolor of a lone man out in the mesquite in a dust storm. In the dying light of day, the dim figure, arm raised to protect his face from the swirling sand, peered uncertainly into a world from which all guiding marks had been obliterated, and gave the impression to the viewer that he was lost, hopelessly lost.

When Mr. Takeda saw it, he gave in.

"Follow your own inclinations, Tom," he said. "I will help you all I can."

It was at art class one night that Tom saw Yuri again. She and her mother had come over to walk home with her father. While they waited for him to gather up his materials, Tom and Yuri talked outside the school building. Nothing was said about why Tom had quit coming to see her after school. They just took up where they had left off a month before. After that evening they spent much time together.

It was very pleasant in the Sato household that autumn. Tom wondered how they had ever lived so long with Tad. In the evenings he would sit back on the soft davenport and watch his mother's contented face as she knit a sweater for Yoshi, and his father reading the newspaper or the Bible, and Yoshi diligently studying at the desk his father had made for him for the purpose of increasing his interest in his schoolwork.

Gradually, Tom began to realize that he was satisfied to be here. It bothered him at first. Then he said to himself, why not? This is a good place. Lots of friends and no worries. His father out of prison, Tad back to normal and sending home money, Mari getting her college education. Maybe she and Tad would help him through the university sometime. And a girl like Yuri to go around with. It was only when he looked into the future that he felt some stirring to get out of camp.

Although Tom followed the war news in the paper, it all seemed faraway and had nothing to do with him. In the Pacific, Lae had been captured, and now the fighting was around Guadalcanal. Allen's ship was out there. He might be in the battle. The day of quick victories for the Japanese was over, and those Issei who had straddled the fence for some time between asking for repatriation and staying in Poston, and who had decided to stay, began to feel more satisfied with their decision. Japan might not win the war after all. Life in a defeated country could be a miserable one.

Camp life moved on an even keel that autumn in Poston. There was little of the ferment of the first two years. The new school buildings had given prestige to the school in the eyes of the students who had hated the barrack classrooms. Many Nisei teachers left to relocate in the east, and new Caucasian teachers were brought in to take their places. Some were good. Some were not.

Tad sent a check every month, and Father Sato bought medicine and food delicacies for Mother Sato with some of it, and put the rest away as a nest egg for Tad. He prayed daily that Mother Sato would get through the coming winter without an attack of flu. She had gained a little weight, but her health was not improving as he had hoped it would.

The Christmas season came on. Early in December, Mr. Takeda had hung some of Tom's pictures in the Mojave Room for the Christmas trade, and someone bought the one of the man in the dust storm. Tom had named it *Alone*. He thought anyone was crazy to pay money for his work. At first, he wished he had not let this one go on exhibit. Then almost at once, he was glad it was gone. It would always have been a reminder of that night and his struggle. A struggle which had no meaning now and the remembrance of which left him reaching out vaguely for something beyond his grasp.

There was no dust storm this year as there had been their first Christmas. The Satos opened the large parcel which had come from Tad, and a small one from Mari, and presented each other with small gifts they had bought at the canteen. It was a quiet Christmas.

But the new year, 1944, soon ruffled the peaceful water of the center. Selective Service was extended to cover the Nisei, and all of the young men in camp who had reached the age of twenty had to register. Tom went with the others. Tad registered in Chicago, and back in Philadelphia, Haruo and Willie signed up. All over the country, the Nisei had lost their 4C status and were now subject to the draft the same as any other American.

Relocation was slowed. Young men, subject to military service, were reluctant to move their families out, perhaps to be left alone in a strange place if the men were called. Some families who had been so satisfied they had made the right decision when they chose not to ask for repatriation, now did request that they be transferred to Tule Lake. Some young men announced openly that they would refuse to go. Tension was building up again by the time the first draftees were due to start for Phoenix.

XXVIII

Tom found a letter from Tad waiting for him when he came home at noon one day in early April. His mother handed it to him and stood waiting to hear the latest news from her favorite son. Some sixth sense caused Tom to decide not to open the letter right then. Tad usually wrote to his mother and father. Since it was addressed to him this time, it just might contain something the folks were not to know. The clanging of the mess hall gong gave him an excuse.

"Kind of thin. I guess there's not much news in it," he said, feeling the envelope. "We'd better get over there to mess if we want anything to eat. There's Dad and Yoshi coming now." He tucked the letter into his shirt pocket. "With all those folks from 323 eating over there now, a fellow is lucky if he gets a slice of bread." He was exaggerating. Food was plentiful, and much better than at the beginning of their days in Poston.

Tom finished his meal before the others, and Father Sato excused him. He went back to the barracks and sat down in the shade of a flourishing little elm, one of a row planted along the street to bring restful shade to the desert dwellers. He tore open the envelope and took out one sheet of paper. It took only a minute to read the few words.

"Oh, my gosh!" he exclaimed. It was hard to believe. He read the note again.

"Dear Tom, Guess what. I've been drafted. That is, I've been called to report to the draft board. April 26th. That's two weeks yet. My boss is trying to get me off, says this is a war industry and I'm needed. But I'm not banking on it. I'll send a wire when it's definite. Your brother, Tad."

After his surprise, Tom's first thought was that Tad would be the one to wear the uniform, not him. This warned him that hope had not died in his heart. Immediately he threw up a barrier to protect himself

465

against further disappointment.

How would he tell his father and mother? He knew it had never occurred to them that once Tad had been kicked out of the Army, the military would be brazen enough to reach out and draft him. Although his mother had escaped a bout with the flu during the winter, she was not very well. Now she complained of a pain in her chest. Dr. Nakata had advised them to protect her from heat, heavy work, or shock. Her heart was tired, he said. This news would certainly be a shock.

Father Sato, coming from the mess hall, saw Tom with the letter in his hand and came and sat down beside him on the bench to rest a few minutes before he had to go back to work.

"Mama-san says you had a letter from Tadashi. What is the news?"

Tom handed him the letter. There was no easy way to break the news.

"S-oo-o." There was more than surprise in Father Sato's voice. The draft had been operating for a couple of months now in the camp, and there had been fellows, resentful and disgruntled like Tad, who had refused to go. The FBI had picked them up and taken them to Yuma to the jail. Would Tad refuse? How would his mother take it, either if he went overseas to fight or if he went to jail? Was the family facing another crisis?

Tom waited for further reaction from his father, having no idea what was going through his mind.

"Do you think Tadashi will answer the call?" the father asked, turning and looking intently into the face of his third son.

Now Tom knew what concerned his father most.

"Sure, he'll go. Didn't you read what he said? Tad's all right now. But they've sure got their gall to draft him."

On his way back to work, Tom met Larry Sakai from La Vista. When he told Larry about Tad, Larry let out a roar.

"Oh, no! That couldn't happen to anyone. Now

they're not only drafting their prisoners of war, they're drafting their discharges." He laughed and kidded about it all the way over to Industry.

That night, after Mother Sato had come from her English class, she and Father Sato sat talking as they tried out the fine new cooler Tad had sent.

"Tadashi spend all his money on us," the woman said. "I will write him to put more in the bank. Tamotsu hasn't told me what the letter said. Is Tadashi sick?"

Then Father Sato, with gentle words softly spoken, prepared his wife to face the possibility of giving her son to fight for his country.

She took the news with great calmness.

"He will make a brave soldier," she said proudly.

They all waited anxiously for further word from Tad.

If Tad were inducted into the Army, it would mean a change in Tom's life. He felt he must go outside and find work. And what about Yuri? Tom was mulling over these things as he walked home from work one evening. As he walked past the new auditorium where they were decorating for the first commencement exercises to be held there, he thought of last year, when Mari and Yuri had graduated. He could see her now as she sat straight and prim in her ruffled yellow dress on the backless plank bench. A stage had been built for the graduates, while parents and friends sat on their homemade stools on the sloping hillside. Was it then that he knew he wanted Yuri? Or was it a long time before that? He thought it was the first time he saw her. That morning at church when she had sung, "This is My Father's World."

How much the camp had changed. The barracks were almost hidden now by vines and trees. The castor beans had grown at the corner of his barracks higher than the roof and had spread out their large, divided leaves like hands to hide the ugliness of the worn tar paper now frayed by age or maliciously torn by hands venting their spleen against the government. There was more than one mark of Tad's resentment there, now hidden by the green leaves and by the sweet pea vines which had grown like weeds up the side of the building under the expert care of Father Sato. Their tips were feeling for the eaves, and from top to bottom they were a mass of fragrant flowers of many colors.

Tom had seen much of Yuri during the winter, and although he had spoken no words about his feeling for her, there was a bond between them. A bond they both fought against, for different reasons. Tom because he hadn't enough to offer a rich girl, Yuri because of pride. Tom had never spoken his heart; she was not going to let herself fall for him. She couldn't understand him since his rejection by the Army. It seemed to her he had lost all ambition. He had refused to talk about his rejection, and he didn't talk about having any plans to do anything. And so they struggled against their bonds, but could not break them and pull apart. Tom thought if he were away where he wouldn't be seeing Yuri all the time, he could forget her. Now if Tad went, it would give him a chance to get out. Not that he wished for Tad's induction for that reason. He could go out anyway. Dr. Nakata had given him a clean bill of health. He might even be drafted, although he had been classified 4C for real after his physical, not just because of his race.

On reaching the barracks, Tom found his father and mother sitting outside, waiting for the supper gong. After a shower and change, he joined them.

He noticed how quiet they had become in recent months. Back on the ranch they never sat in silence like they were doing now. His mother was always chattering in Japanese wherever she was, in the house, the fields, in the packing shed getting the vegetables bunched for market. Even in their room at night Tom could hear them in that quick, rhythmic foreign tongue. He hadn't thought of it before, but now they seldom talked in that lively manner. They just sat in seemingly quiet contentment with one another. Tom noticed, too, how old his father looked. He had aged ten years in the last two. He had looked well when he came from prison camp because he had taken on weight. But a close look showed the tiredness in his eyes, and his shoulders were stooped; and as he got up to move his chair out of the sun, his motions were slow, heavy. Tom knew his father would never be able to do the hard work on the ranch which he had done before evacuation.

This awareness of his father's aging and the fact to be faced that Tad might be out of the picture as an earner if he were disabled by the war brought Tom to the realization that he must be prepared to support his parents. That put Yuri, college, everything he wanted out of reach. He'd thought if he got away from Yuri he could forget her. But he knew he couldn't. She was everything he wanted in a girl. She was not only pretty and sweet, there were plenty of pretty girls, but she also had good common sense. She wasn't silly or giggly. She made a fellow feel comfortable when he was with her. She was someone you could share your hardships with as well as your good times. The reason he'd never talked to her about his rejection by the Army wasn't because she wouldn't understand how he felt but because he didn't want to talk about it at all. Yuri was someone you could see every day and never grow tired of. Living with some of those silly females would be like living on cotton candy. He wanted Yuri and no one else. But he could see no way that he could ever have her.

"I think I'll go up to the employment office tomorrow," he said casually to his father. "See what job openings they have now. If Tad should have to go, I ought to be earning more than what I get in here."

"You are a typical American, always in a hurry," Father Sato said, smiling. "Tadashi has not gone yet. Can you not wait until we hear from him?"

"Well, I could get something lined up just in case. I wouldn't have to take it."

Father Sato took out his knife and opened the blade slowly. Then he reached down in the pocket of the wicker chair and drew out an old magazine bulging with the carving he was working on. He spread the magazine across his knees and took up the piece of wood, which he was forming into the shape of a bird, and began carving. The whittlings fell on the paper. Tom glanced at his mother. Her eyes were closed and her mouth half open as she sat napping.

Tom waited patiently for his father to speak.

"I heard today that we may be allowed to return to California soon," Father Sato said slowly. "I would want you here to help with the moving and there to help get the ranch in shape again. It must be very bad, with no tenant for close to a year."

"That's only a rumor, Dad," Tom said. "We've been hearing them ever since we came. This one will never come to anything any more than the others have."

"One of the office girls overheard some of the head officials talking."

"Well, she shouldn't have blabbed it, getting everybody's hopes up," Tom blurted out in frustration. Seemed like there was something to stymie him in everything he tried to do. "Suppose it is true, it isn't going to happen all at once. Even if I could work only a few months at good pay, it would be that much more to help get the ranch planted again."

"Yes, money will be needed, but I have saved a nice sum from what Tadashi has sent. I can use that and pay him back when our crops are harvested. Once we are home again, it will be easy to get credit for seed, fertilizer, and the other things we need."

Poor Dad, Tom thought. He is living back in the days before the war, when all he had to do was make out his order and Mr. Wilson at the seed store would fill it and wait for the money. Tom had no heart to disillusion the tired old man.

"You wait, Son, until we hear from Tadashi," Father Sato said. "Less harm has been done by waiting than by being in too much haste."

"Yes, sir, if that is your wish," Tom said, giving in as he always had.

Ten days later, a telegram came from Tad. He was

reporting to Camp Shelby for duty, leaving Chicago the day he sent the wire. It seemed no time at all until a letter came, saying that since he had already had his basic training, it would not be long before he would be shipped overseas, for replacements were badly needed over there.

Then, one breathless, hot night during the first week in July, Tad arrived in Parker on the ten o'clock train, and an hour later walked in on his sleeping family. It was a great surprise.

Tad was wilted from the steaming trip in a crowded coach from Phoenix and smarting from the taunts of some men standing outside the station at Parker. Even his uniform had not been enough to protect him from their hatred.

All of the family got up and put on robes, and they sat in the living room talking into the early morning hours. Tad had not relished this trip back behind barbed wire to pay a farewell visit to his parents, but he carefully concealed all of his ill feelings.

After Yoshi and his father and mother had been driven back to bed from sheer weariness, Tom and Tad went outside and sat on the stoop. There was a soft, hot breeze rustling through the vines. Tad took off his coat and, folding it carefully, laid it behind him on the stoop. Then he stretched and relaxed, leaning back against the post which supported the trellis. But Tom's first question tensed him again.

"How long is your leave?"

"I'll have to start back tomorrow night." Then, seeing the look of surprise on Tom's face, he continued. "It takes so damned long to get here, three days on the main line, besides this side trip."

But even that didn't account for a ten-day leave which Tom had heard was what the fellows got before they went overseas.

"I didn't start right away," Tad confessed. "As a matter of fact, I didn't intend to come. I went to St. Louis with a couple of buddies and fooled around there for a couple of days."

Tad's still bitter, Tom thought. Too bad, when he's going off to fight for his country. Tom thought he knew why Tad had considered not coming back to camp, but he waited for Tad to tell him, if he wanted to.

Tom wasn't entirely right. Tad's hate was pretty well burned out. At least his reactions were no longer violent. He didn't hate anyone now, not even the Germans, in spite of all his officers had done to generate that emotion.

"Other fellows go home for their last visit before shipping out to their home communities, maybe where they have lived since they were kids. All their friends are there, and the community will give them a big send-off when they leave. They belong. But we Nisei come to concentration camps to say goodbye to our folks." There was no emotion in Tad's voice. He was merely stating facts in a hard, mechanical way, like a recording. "I only came because of Mom," he said after a moment. "Those days in St. Louis, I couldn't get her out of my mind. I almost went to Chicago to spend the rest of my time, but I'm glad now I didn't. Mom doesn't look so good as when I left. Has she been sick again?"

"She didn't have the flu last winter, if that's what you mean, but Dr. Nakata says her heart is weak. If you'd gone across without her seeing you again, it would have hurt her. Especially if she knew you could have come. And she would have known, too. Other fellows are coming to see their folks."

"Yes, she would have known. You can't keep much from her. Anyway, I'm here, so it's all right. If I hadn't been drafted, I would have got you all out of camp. I was working on it, but just try to find a house or apartment. And rent is terrific, in spite of controls. I hope you'll get out soon. You don't realize how bad it is to live this way now you're used to it, but once you're on the outside, you know how damned abnormal it is."

"Dad wouldn't have gone east, even if you had found a place to live. He thinks we're going back to California soon."

472

"Good Lord, doesn't he read the papers? There's as big a campaign on now to keep the Japanese out as there was to get them out in the first place. That includes the citizens, too. People don't make any distinction between the aliens and the native born." Again there was no emotion in Tad's voice. It was near to expressionless. He had complete control of himself.

"What makes Dad think you're going back?" he asked.

"Rumors. But he believes they come straight from the horse's mouth, the horse being a head administrator. Some secretary claims to have overheard, and spread the news."

"Well, don't be in a hurry. If you go back too soon, you might catch a bullet in the head. What else did the doctor say about Mom?"

"Nothing. Just said her heart is tired."

"I'm afraid I gave her a bad time when I was here. I wish I had a chance to make up for it."

"Write her often, funny things like you used to write from college. She loves to hear from you."

"There ought to be a lot of funny things to write from the battle front," Tad said, laughing harshly.

"Heck, you know what I mean."

They sat without talking for a short while. Heat lightning played across the sky. Beyond the ranges to the east, the first hint of dawn was creeping along the uneven horizon. Crickets chirped around the puddles of water under the coolers along the barracks. A coyote slunk off into the mesquite after a nightly forage around the camp.

"How's Yuri?" Tad asked suddenly. "Still in camp?"

Tom started, and the reaction wasn't missed by Tad.

"Yes, she's here. She works in the school office this year."

"Do you still like her?"

"What do you mean?"

"Well, I always thought you were kind of sweet on her."

"You had a lot of screwy ideas."

473

"Come on. You're holding out on me. Give, Boy, give," Tad teased. He gave Tom a slap on the shoulder. It seemed for a minute like old times back home when they had razzed each other about their dates. It made it easy for Tom to tell his brother how things stood between Yuri and him.

"It will be a long time, if ever, before I have anything to offer her. We'd both be old and gray. Say, have you noticed Dad's no spring colt anymore? He's not going to be able to do the heavy work on a ranch that he used to."

"He can hire it done. There will be a check from me every month as long as I'm in the Army, and ten thousand if I don't come back. That will help take care of him and Mom. Yuri's a swell little kid, Tom. Don't let her get away."

Tad sighed. No girl to wait for him while he was off fighting. None to come back to.

Tom noticed the deep sigh and wondered. Was Tad interested in Yuri? Tad always got what he wanted. Well, that would be a better match. Tad was a university man. He had a profession. He would be a success.

Tad, unconscious of the seed of suspicion he had planted in Tom's heart, began asking about his acquaintances in camp. He was loud in his denunciation when Tom told of the fellows who had refused the draft.

"The fools! But that's what being in camp so long has done to them. Maybe I would have done the same thing if I'd stayed here," he admitted. "Is Miss Brown still here?"

"No. She left at the end of the first semester. Gone into USO somewhere in California."

"She did a lot for the kids. And for all of us. But I don't blame her for getting away. What's news from back home?"

"The worst is that Allen Sullivan was in the naval battle around Guadalcanal, and his ship went down. Mari wrote she's heard from Peg, and the family haven't had any word about him."

"Maybe he wasn't on his ship. Could have been sick

or transferred or something."

"That's what they're hoping."

"Hey, look, the sun's coming up. Do you have to work today?"

"No. I can take time off whenever I want to." Tom didn't tell Tad he was just painting pictures, anyway. "But let's get to bed and get a few winks."

When they went inside, they found that Yoshi had been put on the davenport, and Mother Sato had made up his cot with clean sheets for Tad.

"Say, how do the four of you rate two apartments?" Tad asked, looking around the spacious bedroom.

"Dad just took possession when these folks moved out to go to Tule Lake. And no one has done anything about it."

Tad laughed.

"It didn't take Dad long to get on to the Poston ways," he said.

The two slept late, and when they came out into the living room, Mother Sato was preparing their breakfast. When she had told the cook Tad was home, he had gladly provided her with all the food she had wanted. She hovered over Tad as he ate. She noticed how thin he was.

"You get plenty of food in Army?"

Tad was about to give out with a soldier's gripes, changed his mind, and said, "Oh, sure. Meat, potatoes, vegetables, ice cream. And gallons of coffee."

"Why you so thin?"

"Well, I ought to be fat with all that good food, but I walk it all off between meals. You walk a lot in the Army, Mom."

"So?"

After breakfast, Tad went out to look up a few friends. But he found he didn't have much in common with them. They had stood still and were yet bellyaching over the little grievances of camp life. He was soon back at his own barracks, where he spent the rest of the day.

Father Sato had not gone to work and was waiting

475

for him. The time went all too fast for the parents, but to Tad, it dragged. He was anxious to get out of camp. He tried to hold fast to the atmosphere of the outside, to maintain the high morale of the training camp which had been built to a peak for the trip overseas. Many times during the day he visited with his folks, he had to get up and walk around to control his impatience to get away. Before office closing time, the three men went to a notary, and Tad signed power of attorney over to Tom. The ranch was in Tad's name. Now Tom could sign for him if they had to sell it for any reason.

At the mess hall that evening other folks respected their privacy, and the other seats at their table were left vacant. The cook brought them iced tea and a cake he had baked as a send-off for Tad.

"Wish Mari could have been here," Tad said, as he enjoyed the cake.

"It is vacation time. She would have come if she had known," Father Sato said.

But Tom knew she wouldn't have. What would she have come on?

"The doctor's family she works for took her to their summer house on Lake Erie," he told Tad. "She's having a good time. Willie's up there, too, working at a resort hotel. I think Mari's kind of falling for him."

"That punk?"

"Mari says he isn't a bit like he was in camp. Guess he was like someone else I know when he was shut up in here." Tom grinned at his brother. Tad poked him in the ribs with his elbow.

"Hey, Tad, listen, get me a German helmet, will you?" Yoshi shouted.

"I hear you, Boy. Sure, I'll get you a couple. What else do you want? Just give me your order."

"Oh, a sword, maybe. Just anything you find lying around."

When it came time for Tad to leave, Mother Sato did not feel like walking as far as the departure station, so he said goodbye to her at the barracks.

"I'll be seeing you, Mom, maybe back in California.

476

Take it easy, and be sure to write me some good, long letters. Write them in Japanese; there'll always be someone around who can read them if I can't."

Mother Sato sat smiling through her tears.

"Yes, I write. You be careful. Don't get hurt."

"I sure will. Goodbye, Mom." He patted her shoulder softly.

The four men walked across the firebreak. Yes, Yoshi was a man now, almost as tall as Tom. Two other soldiers besides Tad were leaving that night. There was a large crowd at the station, trying to make it a real send-off for the boys. Yuri was there. She had a small gift for Tad. She slipped it into his hand and have him a shy kiss on his bronzed cheek. Then she turned to Tom, impulsively grabbed his hand, and held it tight.

Now everyone was shaking hands with Tad, many he didn't know, all wishing him well. The pride in their faces showed they had all forgotten his tempestuous days in camp.

It came time to board the truck. Tad grasped his father's hand in both of his.

"Goodbye, Dad," he said in a broken voice.

"Goodbye, Son. I'm proud of you. You stand as tall as yonder mountain. May God keep you safe." Father Sato withdrew his hand and stepped back.

"So long, Tom," Tad said, not trying to hide his tears. He threw one arm around Tom and one around Yoshi. "You men take good care of the folks."

"Sure. We will," Yoshi said. He pulled a clean handkerchief out of his pocket and handed it to Tad. "Here, use this and take it with you."

"You're a good one," Tad said, taking the handkerchief and wiping his eyes. Then he climbed onto the truck and sat down beside the other two soldiers.

The driver gunned the motor, and they were off amidst waving and shouting. Out past the barracks now almost hidden in green foliage, up the open highway, now wide and gravelled, picking up passengers at each unit.

While waiting at the station in Parker, Tad strolled

across the street to the drugstore and bought cigarettes and a sackful of ice cream cones for his traveling companions.

"Dirty Jap. Dirty Jap," some onlookers called after him as he was returning to the station. One picked up a stone and threw it. It hit the ground at Tad's polished heel and sent a spatter of gravel over his boot.

Tad fought down the bitterness rising in his heart. Keep your mind closed. Don't feel anything.

The stuffy little train came puffing in, belching black smoke and sending cinders flying. Tad's leave was over. He was off to war. He climbed aboard with a grim face. Don't look back. Don't take the past overseas with you, he admonished himself. He'd be fighting for freedom for everyone. Yes, even for the bigots. Freedom for them to spew out their venom. Who cared?

Tad walked with head high into the hot, crowded coach and along the aisle. Not a vacant seat in sight. As he reached the end, a man in work clothes got up.

"Here's a seat, soldier," he said, and walked away before Tad could thank him.

Tad sat down beside an elderly woman, who turned and gave him a motherly smile.

Tad returned the smile, then settled into his seat, leaned his head against the back, and closed his eyes.

These acts of kindness had come at an opportune time for the Nisei soldier.

XXIX

A card came from Tad giving his APO address, and then nothing. The Satos assumed that he was on the high seas. They waited anxiously to hear that he had reached port safely. German submarines were making the transport of troops perilous.

As soon as Tad had left, Tom began to talk about getting out of camp, but his father was stubbornly determined. Rumors were flying faster that the evacuees were to be allowed to return to the West Coast, and even Tom began to believe there might be something to them this time. So he gave in to his father's desires without too much inner protest.

Tom had been thinking a lot about what Tad had said about Yuri, and he had come to the conclusion that his brother was serious when he advised him not to let her get away. Then Tad wasn't interested himself. Tom realized now Yuri wasn't the type Tad would want for a wife. He'd want a girl who would lean on him and not have a strong mind of her own. Yuri was independent; she'd never lean on anyone.

But where did all this brain work get him? Since he could never tell Yuri how he felt about her, what difference did it make if half a dozen fellows were after her?

There was no escaping seeing Yuri, for she and Tom went to the same places, movies, swimming pool, church, ball games; but Tom avoided being with her alone.

Now it was September, and Yuri was leaving to enter the fall semester at Berkeley. Against his better judgment, Tom had asked her for a date next to the last night before she left. He thought she would want to spend her last evening with her family. Yuri appeared pleased when he asked her and that made him think the pleasure wasn't all one-sided.

He dressed with unusual care. He had left work early and stopped at the barbershop for a haircut. He'd had a shower and shave before supper, and now he was all dressed except for his shirt. He'd put that on the last thing so it wouldn't be limp with perspiration before he even got started.

Tom looked back over the summer and thought it seemed short. It seemed no time at all since Tad was there, and now he was fighting in Italy. He had written a long letter to his mother and he had indeed found foolish little things to write about to make his mother laugh; but the letter he wrote to Tom was different. The enemy was throwing everything against them on the ground and from the air. A few inches either way and you would be just a white cross in a foreign country. It was hell, but don't tell Mom or anyone these things.

If Tad could have seen his mother now he wouldn't have cautioned. He would have known there was no need. Tom would keep mum. Mother Sato appeared to grow smaller and smaller as the hot days passed. She stayed indoors except to go to the mess hall, and even that short exposure to the heat seemed to drain her of what little strength she had. She would come back to the barracks gasping for breath.

While Tom and his father were at work, Yoshi stayed near the barracks and ran in often to see if his mother wanted anything. But now Yoshi was starting to school.

In the evenings Mother Sato talked to her family about going home to the ranch and kept asking how long it would be before they could start. Hearing her, Tom came as close as he ever had to cursing the government for evacuation. But for it and all the hardships and worries it had brought his mother, she might be well and strong.

Unknown to Tom, Mr. Takeda, suspicious that Tom and Yuri were in love, set about making the young man over into a suitable member for the Takeda family. He had spent a great deal of time with Tom, giving him instruction in art as fast as Tom could absorb it; and he had had a room cleared for a studio for Tom in the same barracks in which he worked. In that way Tom could work undisturbed by the constant chatter of the girls.

One of Tom's pictures was creating quite a sensation among the Caucasian personnel, although the evacuees themselves didn't care much for it. It was a young Nisei, slouching on a cot in a cluttered barracks room. His insolent face and sloppy dress depicted all the resentment and despair of many during the early years in the camp. The torn sweat shirt and the frayed pants cuffs blended with the vacant stare in the dark eyes and the spineless pose to make it a striking portrait of a soul adrift. Tom named it tersely, *Evacuee*. Mr. Takeda had insisted on hanging it in the Mojave Room, although Tom said it definitely was not for sale. He had been uncomfortable when it was finished to see how much the face resembled Tad's. Several people tried to buy it, and some of the offers were high, and Tom needed money, but he refused to sell. It wouldn't be fair to Tad fighting over there in Europe. When he once got it out of Industry and away from Mr. Takeda, he intended to destroy it.

Tonight Tom's mind was swept clear of everything except his date. What was he going to say to Yuri? Could a fellow tell a girl he loved her and not ask her to marry him? No, that was out. Well, maybe he could let her know how he felt without actually saying it. Yuri might have some ideas, if she really cared. Tom began to take hope. He had so much faith in Yuri that he persuaded himself that she might even have a solution to the whole problem. Poston would surely be a different place when Yuri was gone.

Yoshi came dashing into the bedroom just as Tom was giving his hair a last, futile brush. Tom noticed his younger brother was slicked up pretty keen, for him.

"Hey, Tom, can I use some of your shaving lotion, just for smell?"

Tom grinned. "Got a date?" he asked.

"Heck, no. I'm going to the show. It's Tyrone Power in *Suez*."

Tom had forgotten it was movie night, and he hoped Yuri wouldn't want to go.

"How come you're not taking that little number I've seen you running around with?"

"Susie?"

"I don't know her name."

"She lives clear over on the other side of camp. Think I'd walk all that way just to walk back with her?"

"No, I wouldn't, lazy. Help yourself to the lotion, but don't waste it."

Yoshi doused his face and head, and Tom grabbed the bottle.

"Say, that's enough. Don't you know this lotion costs money?"

Yoshi started to go.

"Oh, I may see Susie at the show if I feel like it," he said, feigning the grandest indifference.

"Yeah, and if you're real nice to her, maybe she'll bring you home, Romeo."

Lucky kid, Tom thought. No problems, no worries.

As Tom walked across the firebreak, people were converging on the movie from all directions. He noticed many uniforms among the crowd. Many fellows were coming back to camp now for their farewell visits. It was a good thing the USO had been set up and a room provided where they could hang out and where parties and dances could be given for them. It had been Yuri's idea, and she and Tom had both been active in getting the place furnished and providing refreshments for the affairs.

Tom hoped Mr. Takeda wouldn't be in a talkative mood and keep him in the apartment all evening, listening to a discourse on art. It was dusk now, and there were quiet places where Tom and Yuri could go to be alone while everyone was at the movies. He thought the seat beside the Japanese garden would be a good spot. When he reached the Takeda apartment, he found Yuri alone.

"The folks went to the show," Yuri said, when Tom asked about her parents as politeness demanded.

"I didn't know your father was a movie fan," Tom said, feeling lighthearted with relief. It was a good omen. He sank down on the soft divan.

"They don't go often, but Father thought there might be some scenery in this film which would interest him. It's *Suez* tonight."

"Yes, I know. Do you want to go?" He had to ask.

"No, not unless you do. I can see all the latest releases in San Francisco. I don't need to go to see an old one." The way she said "San Francisco" made it sound like heaven.

Tom took a good look at Yuri and noticed she looked different somehow. She had on a tiny checked silk that looked as if she had come straight from an exclusive shop in the city, and her hair was done up in a new style that made her look older and, well, sort of sophisticated. It scared Tom. Maybe he didn't know the real, outside-the-camp Yuri. Other people he knew had been different when they came to Poston from what they had been at home. Certainly right now he wasn't looking at the same girl he'd known these months on the desert. And when they began to talk, he soon found that her mind was already on the outside.

He watched her as she tripped around the room, too excited to walk, getting bottles of Coke from the refrigerator, extracting ice cubes at the sink, talking fast, not giving him a chance to say anything. Expensive new luggage was on the floor and chairs, half-packed, displaying new clothes, shoes with tiny high heels, filmy blouses, a pale green sweater.

"I'm so glad the folks wouldn't let me go east to school when Mari did. This is so much more exciting. And letting students go back to California schools means everyone can go back soon, don't you think?"

"Yes. It looks like it. But you seem mighty happy to be getting away from here," Tom said, resenting her gay mood.

"Wouldn't you be happy if you were leaving Poston, Tom?" Yuri asked pointblank.

"Yes, I would. But we've had a lot of good times

here, and I'd have a little regret over seeing things break up."

"But it's all over now. I'm going to forget it as soon as I get away." Yuri sipped her Coke.

"It isn't over yet for a lot of us," Tom said. His voice was heavy with reproof. He was stunned by Yuri's light way of dismissing these full years of friendship and hardship that they had all shared.

"But it soon will be," Yuri said. "Father believes that everyone can go by the end of the year, if they want to." There was a tinge of sarcasm in the last words. "Tom, do you mind if I finish this packing? I promised Mother I'd have it done and the luggage off the chairs by the time she got back."

"No, go ahead," Tom said, trying to sound as if it didn't make any difference to him what she did.

"Then I have to take sugar and cocoa over to the USO. For the big party after the show."

Tom had forgotten about the party. It looked as if his date with Yuri was fizzling out fast.

"If we take the stuff over before the crowd comes, we won't have to stay," Yuri said.

So they talked while Yuri packed. Or Yuri talked. When she finished, Tom helped her close the bags and set them back against the wall out of the way.

Then Yuri put the things for the USO in a paper sack, and they started out.

All the way over, Yuri talked of her plans. Some friends of the family were just returning from their round-the-world trip. They had bought a new car in New York and were driving across country. They were in Phoenix now and were going to come to Poston to get her and take her to San Francisco.

"That's just like the Formans. After all that long trip, they're coming this way to get me so I won't have to go on those crowded trains and maybe not be treated very nice, either. They're just lovely. I'm going to live with them for awhile until my folks come."

Tom was blind. He didn't know Yuri was talking so fast to hide her own feelings. Her pride had been

484

hurt. She and Tom had dated off and on over the years in Poston, and nothing had come of it. Other girls in her crowd had become engaged; some had married and relocated in the outside world. But Tom had never said the words she was always expecting. Now the parting of their ways had come, and she had to admit Tom didn't care. She'd never let him know how she felt. Only a little longer to pretend.

At the USO rooms Yuri got out the plates and cups and spoons and arranged them on the serving table. Then she put the sugar and cocoa in a place where they would be readily seen. By that time, people were passing, going home from the show. She and Tom hurried away.

Walking back, they took the long way around to avoid the crowd. Yuri was quiet now. A waning moon cast a soft glow over the camp. Yuri stopped and looked far out across the open desert.

"It's almost beautiful at night, isn't it?" she said.

"Yes." Tom's voice was husky.

They hurried on as if they were running for safety.

When they reached the Takedas' barracks, there was a light inside.

"The folks are home. Will you come in?"

"No, thanks," Tom said. "I'd better be getting home."

"Then I guess it's goodbye."

Suddenly Tom's armor collapsed like a paper shield. He threw his arms around Yuri and held her tight while he kissed her.

"I love you, Yuri." The agony of parting had drawn from him the words he had resolved he would never say.

The girl yielded to his kisses and was soft and relaxed in his arms.

"And I love you, Tom," she said with a caressing laugh.

Her words frightened Tom.

"Oh, no, you mustn't say you do. We can't . . ."

The door of the Takeda apartment opened. Mr. Takeda looked out.

"It's time to come in, Yuri. You will have a hard

day tomorrow with all you have left for the last minute."

"Have a heart, Father. This is my last night with Tom."

"Do you mean to say you've been here two years together and still have things to say to each other?"

"We're just beginning," Yuri answered.

"It's still time to come in."

Tom began talking fast, trying to explain and making things worse with every word.

"We can't be engaged. You will want to be free when you go to the university. You'll meet a lot of fellows there. And . . ."

"You don't want to be engaged?" Yuri asked coldly.

"Oh, no, it isn't that way. I-I have a lot of things to say. I . . ."

"I have to go in now. There's no time to talk. Goodbye, Tom."

When Tom tried to kiss her again, Yuri turned her head.

"I'll write. You'll understand," Tom said hurriedly.

If Tom could have told Yuri his reasons, she would have had an answer for everyone. But when she read his words back in California, they were hard and cold on the paper, and she was hurt, and decided the best thing to do was forget Tom.

Tom trudged back across the camp to his barracks like he was sloughing through a swamp. A swamp of despair. He had tasted one moment of happiness. Now everything was over between Yuri and him.

486

XXX

Tom's first thought was of Yuri when he awoke the next morning. He tried to put her out of his mind, but the few moments when they had confessed their love for each other was too sweet. They had to be relived. Maybe he would see her again before she left. He wondered if she had told her father anything about last night. He felt a little reluctant to face Mr. Takeda at Industry. However, he didn't have to, for the artist didn't come to his studio all day.

While Tom was at work, Yuri slipped over to say goodbye to Mother Sato, and when Tom came home at noon, his mother's face was bright with smiles. "She's had a letter from Tad," he thought. He waited to hear his brother's latest joke. But no. All Mother Sato could talk about was what a fine girl Yuri was, so kind and thoughtful to come on her last, busy day to see an ugly old woman.

"Very nice girl. She make good daughter."

Tom wondered what Yuri had said to her. Of course, he couldn't tell his mother how things were. He couldn't say that, because he'd have to stay on the ranch and help make a living for his father and mother, he couldn't make any plans to marry. So he just listened.

Mother Sato, sitting alone in the apartment, had been making plans.

"Papa-san will build a house for you. The north corner of ranch be a good place."

"Right next to Mr. Winters. We'll have fine neighbors."

They laughed together.

"Then build on other corner. No neighbors on that side."

Tom was amazed at his mother's assurance. Didn't she know they were practically penniless?

"Well, no hurry about a house. Yuri is just starting college. That will take her four years."

The little, faded woman considered a minute. She looked at Father Sato reading the paper as he waited for the mess hall gong. He came from work a little early each noon so he could read the latest war news from Europe.

"So? That not good."

"What isn't good? Yuri going to college?"

"Wife know more than husband not good. House can wait while Tom go to college. You go learn new way to farm, easy way. You teach Papa-san. He old-fashioned, only know hard work." She gave Father Sato a saucy glance and chuckled to herself.

Father Sato looked over the top of his paper and smiled. It was good to see his wife in such a fine humor.

The cool weather came, and Mother Sato sat outside in the shade and looked at the flowers and watched the people pass. Her mind was on going home to the ranch, and as soon as the men would come in the evening, she would begin to talk about it.

"You say high prices for everything now," she said to Father Sato and Tom one evening. "Higher than we ever got. We make more money. Maybe buy washing machine like over in laundry. No work. Just sit and wait."

"Yeah, if we could have stayed at home, we'd be sitting pretty now," Tom said. "Money for three years of good crops in the bank. We wouldn't have a thing to worry about, would we, Dad?"

"*Fukusui bon ni kaerazu,*" his father answered.

"What does that mean?"

"Spilled water never returns to the tray. One should not waste energy fretting over what might have been."

Tom had written his letter to Yuri not long after she left. She did not hurry to answer, and when she did, her reply was brief. If that was the way he wanted it, that was the way it would be, she wrote, and ended by saying she saw no reason for them to correspond.

She didn't understand, Tom groaned.

The break was complete.

Tom was embarrassed by Mr. Takeda's attitude toward him. The man talked to him like a father to a son. Apparently Yuri had told her father nothing, and he was guessing. Tom felt like a fraud. He thought he ought to explain to the artist, but how do you tell a man you're in love with his daughter but don't intend to marry her? Mr. Takeda was as proud as Yuri. He couldn't make him understand any more than he had her. As time went on, Tom felt more and more shabby in the artist's presence.

The Takedas had him over for supper one Sunday evening and showed him the snapshots Yuri had sent. Pictures of her on the campus, at the beach, in Golden Gate Park. Everywhere she was with other students, some of them Nisei, a couple of good-looking fellows among them. When Tom left, Mrs. Takeda asked him to come often, they were lonely now Yuri was gone.

By the middle of November, the camp was fairly buzzing with rumors. Something big was coming up. There was a feeling of excitement in the air, not only among the evacuees but in administrative circles as well. These rumors were different from the mill run from which the camp had never been free since the day of opening. These had the substance of authenticity about them. California was going to be opened for the return of the Japanese. Many people began to make plans for the trip back.

Mother Sato was the most eager of all to get started. Father Sato felt justified in telling her they would begin to make ready. Then, on Thanksgiving Day, she had an attack.

It was fortunate that it happened on a holiday when Father Sato was there to pick her up from the living room floor and lay her on her bed, while Yoshi ran for the doctor.

Dr. Nakata came rushing across the two blocks from his barracks and administered a stimulant. Yes, it was her heart, he said. He stayed for an hour or more, then, saying there was nothing more he could do, left some medicine and went back to his apartment.

489

Tom had gone up to Camp I that afternoon to a football game. When he came home, he saw deep lines of anxiety on his father's face. Yoshi was sitting quiet and solemn on the davenport.

"Where's Mom?" Tom asked, becoming frightened.

"She's in bed. She had a light heart attack."

Tom went to the bedroom door and looked in.

In the dusk he could see his mother turn her head toward him.

"Hello, Mom. Feeling all right now?" He went inside the room and stood by the bed. "Anything you want?"

"Tell Papa-san come."

Tom was shocked by her weak face. He could barely hear her words. He hurried out and sent his father in.

For days the woman lay hovering between life and death, and when, on the fifth day, she showed no signs of rallying, Father Sato sent for Mari. Dr. Nakata did not think Mother Sato had the strength to recover from the attack.

Tom would not trust the message to the office girls and rode into Parker on a provisions truck and took it to the Western Union office himself. It would take Mari at least three days by train. He was afraid that it would be too late. If he only had the money to send her a plane ticket!

The next morning it was cold and blustery. The wind whipped at unlatched doors along the barracks and sent them banging against the walls. It swooped down and whisked along the ground, picking up what dust had not been anchored by vegetation and dashing it against the buildings and into people's faces as they went to breakfast. Loose gravel from the road spattered against the cars. It howled down the deserted streets and shrieked like a demon as it bent double the bare branches of the mesquite trees. The sky was gray.

Outside the Sato apartment, the wind tugged furiously at the dead vines still clinging to the trellis, and inside, the rooms were cold, for the oil stove was inadequate in the drafty building when the chilly winds of winter blew.

Tom and his father stood facing each other across the bed. Mother Sato was only half-conscious of their presence. She looked so frail it seemed her spent body could not cling to life much longer.

Earlier, Tom had brought his father a tray from the mess hall, for Father Sato would not leave the bedside. Tom noticed that nothing had been eaten.

"Eat your breakfast, Dad," he said. "You'll be getting down yourself."

"My appetite is small."

"I'll make you some hot tea," Tom said. He couldn't stand the look on his father's face and wanted to get away. He wished Tad and Mari were there. He felt so alone in this crisis in the family.

While he was standing by the stove waiting for the water to boil, the door opened with a great gust of wind, and there stood Mari. His eyes opened wide in astonishment.

"How did you get here so quick?"

"I flew. The doctor bought my ticket. He's been wonderful to me. How's Mom?"

"Bad. Get hold of yourself before you go in."

Mari threw off her coat and hat and went into her mother's room.

At the sight of her, Mother Sato roused from her stupor.

"Mari! You come to go home with us. You help the men pack. I no good anymore." Her voice sounded strong. The presence of her daughter had acted as a stimulant.

Tom, who had followed Mari in, heard it and took hope.

"Yes, I will help them," Mari said. "Now you rest and take it easy."

"Yes. I rest. Tired . . . tired." Mother Sato closed her eyes.

"Your coming has done her good," Father Sato said to Mari. "She has worried because she was sick and there was no one to take care of her menfolk."

"Do you want to sleep awhile, Mari?" Tom asked.
"You can go in my room."

"No, I'll stay here. I'm not tired."

Later in the morning, Mother Sato roused and asked
if the mail had come.

"Yes. Tom brought it over a few minutes ago," Mari
told her.

"Letter from Tadashi?"

"None today. Maybe tomorrow."

"Tadashi ..." A gasp. Then silence.

Mari gave her father a startled look.

Mother Sato had gone home.

Mari clutched at her throat, turned away from the
bed slowly, and went out into the living room to tell
Tom.

As they talked, the outside door flew open and
Yoshi came bursting in on a gust of wind. His hair was
blown helter-skelter by the gale. He slammed the door
behind him.

"Hi, Mari. What are you doing here?" he greeted his
sister flippantly. Then he saw that she was crying. He
looked at Tom, then at his father, who had come to the
bedroom door.

Father Sato told him that his mother was dead.

Yoshi staggered back as if someone had hit him,
and he began to shake.

The utter look of horror which spread over his face
caused Mari to turn to Tom.

"Didn't you prepare Yoshi for what might happen?"
she asked in a low voice.

"I'm afraid we didn't," Tom confessed. "We were
both so worried over M-mom. I never thought of Yoshi,
and I guess Dad didn't, either."

"Well, you should have. Look at him."

"I want to see her!" Yoshi cried out in a shrill voice
and started weaving his way like a blind man toward
the bedroom door.

His father stopped him and looked at Mari. The
broken father was depending on her, and Mari knew she

must meet the situation.

She shook her head. The boy was in a state of shock and must not be allowed to see his dead mother until he had had time to recover. She went to him and took him firmly by the arm.

"Wait awhile," she said. "You cannot go in there now."

She heard the mess hall gong above the blowing of the wind.

"It is time for dinner," she said calmly. She took the scarf from around her neck and tied it over her hair. Then, with tender hands, she brushed Yoshi's hair back from his face. "We will go over and eat. No one knows yet what has happened, and we will say nothing to anyone."

Mari's strength had provided the anchor for Yoshi.

"You coming, Tom?" he asked.

"No," Mari said. "The men have things to do here. We will bring them some food."

They went out into the storm and fought their way across the block to the mess hall door.

That afternoon, Tom sent a message off to Tad which he never received, for the following day word came that he had been wounded and was on his way back to the states. His wounds were not critical, a leg injury, but he would not be able for further duty in the Army. They would have to wait to tell him of his mother's death until they learned to what hospital he had been sent.

After the funeral and cremation, Mother Sato's ashes were put in a box and placed on the shelf in the living room to await the return of the family to California.

XXXI

Two weeks after Mother Sato's death, Poston was electrified by the announcement of a mass meeting to take place in Camp I on the nineteenth of December. The purpose of the meeting was a poorly kept secret, and before the day arrived the evacuees were reasonably sure the ban on their return to the West Coast was to be lifted.

There was a strong undercurrent of excitement. However, it was only an undercurrent. On the surface, life in camp went on as usual. On the eve of the mass meeting, the Poston *Chronicle* published news common to a newspaper in a town that expected to go on forever. A list of new books at the library, election of officers for the Luana Club, Buddhist Church notes, movie program for the week, the beginning of the winter schedule of dances in the high school auditorium. Something new here, the Jukebox Saturday Night, an innovation in dances.

The day of the mass meeting came, and people from all three camps gathered in expectation. They were not disappointed.

Public Proclamation No. 21 of the Western Defense Command under the charge of Major General Pratt-- DeWitt had been transferred to other pastures-- rescinded the exclusion orders of 1942.

Rumor had become fact.

In the statement rescinding the orders, provision had been made for guarding against a mass exodus from Poston back to California. The order was not to take effect until January 2, 1945, and the evacuees would have to be cleared, just as they had been for relocation in the eastern states.

Immediately after the meeting, people began to make plans to return to the coast on exploratory trips to feel out the attitude toward them in their communities, as well as to make arrangements to take over their properties again. But there were many who had no place to return to and no money with which to look around and find one. To them, the prospect of the camp closing was a calamity. The order had said in "not less than six months or not more than a year." Plaintive, frightened voices were heard saying, "They can't put us out. They made us come here. They can't make us leave."

In grief and loneliness, the Sato family prepared to return to their ranch. There was little joy in it for Father Sato now that his wife was gone. He felt old and tired and unequal to the task of starting out again and building from nothing. True, they had the ranch, but with the real estate interests in California lobbying in Sacramento for a bill which would rob the Japanese of their land, they might soon lose that. Only his concern for his children and the desire to make their return as happy as possible gave him the strength to throw off the depression which weighted him down like a heavy stone.

A letter had come from Tad. He was in an Army hospital in San Francisco. The Red Cross had reached him with the message of his mother's death. He was so upset that he neglected to tell anything about himself.

Tom and Mari had both had letters from Yuri, expressing her sympathy in warm, easy-flowing language. And Mari had heard from Peg. Peg's letter was divided between grief over the passing of Mother Sato and pleasure at the thought of Mari's return. Peg wrote sadly of Allen. He was reported missing. They clung to hope that he was alive somewhere. Her mother wouldn't give up. Peg ended her letter by telling Mari to be sure to write and give the date of their return.

Mari had no thought of returning east to college. She would go back to La Vista with the others and make a home for her father and brothers. Perhaps there would be a way for her to attend classes at State College in the city, part time. If she couldn't, well, where her duty lay was clear.

Two men from La Vista went back to look around the community to see how things were there. They went

495

on the train, and Father Sato had them drive his car and truck back to Poston. They brought good reports. Their neighbors had been friendly. Farther north, there had been incidents. A Nisei had been shot in his home. In Orange County, a Nisei girl who was spending the night with her tenants had been waited on by a committee of prominent ranchers who had threatened her with death if she didn't get out before morning. She had stayed, and nothing had happened. There had been no incidents reported around La Vista.

Tad got in touch with Yuri when he learned from Mari that she was at the university, and Yuri went to see him. It was from her the Satos got more details about Tad's injury. The fellow next to him had stepped on a land mine. Tad had got only the side effects, which were enough to break his leg and give it several . . .

"It could have been worse," he told Yuri. "I could have been blown to smithereens. My buddy was." Then he had added, "It was Mom's prayers that saved me. She wrote she was always praying for me." Yuri didn't tell that when she wrote Mari.

Yoshi begged to stay out of school after his mother's death, but his father was firm in his refusal. And he was wise. The winter sports and Christmas activities at school helped him to forget. When he came home to the barracks, evening was the hard time of the day.

On Christmas Eve, Mr. Takeda invited Tom over for supper. After they had eaten, Yuri's mother withdrew to a corner of the room with her embroidery and left the men to talk together.

"Now that California is open to us again, I presume you are planning to return," Mr. Takeda probed.

"Yes, sir. We hope to go early next month."

"Back to the ranch?"

"Where else?" Tom thought. What was the man getting at?

"Yes, sir. That is our plan."

"What about your painting?"

Tom laughed.

"A rancher doesn't have the time for frills." He knew as soon as he had said it that it was the wrong thing. But Mr. Takeda let it pass.

"Tom, I saw your father the other day as he walked across the firebreak. He does not look well. Couldn't you persuade him to sell his land and have a home in town where he could take life easy?"

"Mr. Takeda, you don't know how an Issei feels about his land. Father will never part with the ranch."

"He may have to. From what I have been reading in the San Francisco papers, it may be taken away from him."

"I know. But if it is, that is the way it will be. He will never give it up voluntarily."

"You have talent, Tom. I have told you many times not to consider it lightly. Now I have done something which will give you a chance to see how far you can go. I have secured an art scholarship for you at the university at Berkeley. It will cover your university expenses, and a friend of mine would like you to live in his home and care for the grounds around his estate. That would take care of your living costs."

Bright stars sparkled before Tom's eyes. He was speechless. Four years on the campus with Yuri. A university education. A profession. Mr. Takeda had grown rich on his pictures. Why couldn't he? The barriers between him and Yuri were tumbling fast. He had her in his arms again, and this time it was for keeps.

Mr. Takeda was unhurried. He sat puffing leisurely at his pipe as he waited for Tom to answer.

After the brief flight into ecstasy, Tom came down to earth. Tad had said he would help pay for laborers on the ranch, but that was before he was disabled. The government would take care of him, but not in such a lavish way that he would have money to spare. And Tad himself would not likely ever be able to do the hard ranch work, even if he did come home to live. Tom pictured his father trying to run the ranch with only Yoshi, and maybe a crippled Tad, to help.

497

He felt anger toward Yuri's father for tempting him away from his duty. Why had he done it? Did he still think there was something between him and Yuri? Or was he so saturated with art that he felt compelled to find this opening for Tom to continue his work as a painter? Whatever the answers to these questions, Tom now had his answer ready for Mr. Takeda.

"Thanks a lot for doing so much for me," he said, "but I could not leave my father now. He needs me too much."

There was another silence.

Tom felt empty. He wanted to get away. He wondered if it would be all right for him to go now.

Mr. Takeda smoked his pipe. At the back of the room the oil stove burned with a steady, purring sound. Mrs. Takeda's embroidery needle flew back and forth through the cloth, pulling the colored floss through behind it. From the church in the next block came the sound of carolers' voices as they practiced before starting out to sing around the blocks.

With a quick, nervous gesture, Mr. Takeda tapped the ashes from his pipe and laid the pipe on the table beside him.

"Your deep feeling of obligation to your father is admirable," he said. "Of course, I am disappointed, but I have not given up. You do not know what lies ahead when you return to California. The way may open for you to accept the scholarship. It will be waiting. Do not hesitate to let me know if a time comes when you feel you can accept it." The man stood up.

Tom got to his feet.

"I don't know how to thank you, sir. You'll never know how hard it was to refuse. I'd like to say you will hear from me, but I can make no promises now. Good night. Good night, Mrs. Takeda." Tom moved toward the door. "Merry Christmas."

"Good night, Tom. Come to see us before you leave, or before we do. We have so much to pack, I don't know when we will get away. Merry Christmas."

Mr. Takeda opened the door and let Tom out, then

closed it after him.

Tom walked rapidly in the crisp winter night. How still the desert was! And how empty. Like his heart. He knew he had made the right decision, but it brought no elation.

As he passed a barracks, a radio was playing loud. A voice singing.

"Silent night, Holy night,

"All is calm, All is bright."

Beyond the Colorado River, the dark outline of the California mountains loomed close in the clear desert air. California ahead. Poston soon to be only a memory.

XXXII

Tom was awake at dawn in spite of having had only a few hours of sleep. His father and Yoshi were still sleeping heavily. Tom lay quietly for a few moments, looking about the bare room in the first light of day. This was the day. The day toward which they had looked from the moment they had been taken from the ranch so long ago. This was the day they were going home.

They had all worked late the night before, getting the truck loaded with all but the necessities for another night in the barracks. Tom yawned and stretched and looked for some sign of life from the other beds, and when he saw none, threw back the load of Army blankets and crawled out into the cold. He pulled his bathrobe on over his pajamas and tiptoed out of the bedroom. The bare, cheerless living room was like a refrigerator. Hardly worthwhile to light the stove, Tom thought. They would be out of there before the room warmed up. He took a squint at the oil gauge. Plenty of oil. Might as well have one more fling off the government. He turned the valve, waited for the oil to run, lifted the stove lid, and dropped a lit match in. A bright tongue of flame sent a warm current of air up over his hand.

As he went through these familiar motions, a pang of something like regret gripped him. Could he possibly feel regret at leaving? he asked himself sharply. Why not? he defended. Wasn't he bound to this place by the strong ties of deep experiences? His love for Yuri, and the wonderful months they had enjoyed together, then the heartbreak of giving her up. The Army doctor blocking his way to his cherished goal of serving his country in uniform. There had been a time when that was all he wanted. Afterward, Yuri's artist father discovering his talent and offering him an art scholarship at the university, implying that Yuri was included in the offer. How hard it had been to refuse, but he had a duty to his aging, grieving father. All these and many other crucial events bound him. The most tragic of all, his mother's death. Why shouldn't he feel for this place? He was leaving so much of himself behind.

He gave the purring stove a kick to get the memories out of his mind, then grinned at the similarity of his act to Tad's old gesture of frustration during those first cold winter days when they were freezing and waiting for the oil to come.

Leaving the stove and the memories it had started, he went out on the stoop to have a look at the morning. The overcast skies of the past week were gone. In the east there was the rosy glow of approaching sunrise. Everything stood out in startling clearness. The Needle Mountains far to the north looked only a short hike away. And across the Colorado, the vividness of the rocks and brush on the mountainsides brought them so near that already Tom felt he was in California. They seemed to beckon him home to start life anew. Well, he knew that returning to the ranch would not be merely taking up the old life where he had left off that cruel April day nearly three years before. There had been too many changes in him, in his family. He could not conceive of home on the ranch without his mother. She had been home to the children. How she had grieved to return and had never given up hope! How happy she would have been this morning!

Tom heard stirring of life in the apartment and, putting on a cheerful face, went inside.

"Gee, it's sure a swell day," he said. "Just made for our trip home."

"That is nice," his father said softly. Tom barely heard him above the rattle of the bedstead he was dismantling. Tom rushed to help him, and together they carried the mattress outside.

"We ought to make it home by early afternoon," Tom said.

"We will not drive fast," Father Sato replied. "The tires are old by now, and there is plenty of time. The

501

ranch has waited this long for us; a few more hours will not make any difference."

"No, I guess not," Tom answered, bridling his impatience, preparing for a long, slow trip.

Mari packed the last of the clothes and set the suitcases on the stoop for the boys to carry out. While Yoshi returned the Army cots to the block manager's office, Mari folded the blankets and had them ready for him when he came back.

"Heck, take them yourself. I've been working all morning."

"All morning? You haven't been up an hour yet," Mari retorted.

"Well, it seems like all morning, anyway. Look, I've even worked up a sweat on this cold morning." He brushed a grimy hand across his brow and extended it for proof.

"I don't see anything," Mari said without sympathy. "How do you expect to work on a ranch if you're all pooped out before breakfast?"

Yoshi's musings over his return home had never included anything about work, and the vision Mari's words called up was very unpleasant. He had no ready reply.

"Now go take the blankets over before the gong rings."

"Okay, slave driver, but no one's going to boss me around when we get home except Dad, and that's final."

"Gee, Dad, these mattresses take up an awful lot of room," Tom was saying as he tried to find a place for everything on the truck. "Why don't you sell them or give them to someone? There's still a year yet till the place closes down. Someone could use them."

"These are good innerspring mattresses, Son. Much better than the ones we have at home. These iron bedsteads we might leave. It would lighten the load on the tires a little. But it would be nice to have them. Then you and Yoshi could each have a bed, and we could put a good one in Norio's old room. You boys about wore that one out while you were growing up."

Already Father Sato was back home in his mind. Tom saw he wanted to take everything so withdrew his objections and helped him find room on the overloaded truck.

While the luggage was being put in the car, the breakfast gongs began to clang, and they went at once to their last communal meal in the mess hall. As they walked across the block to the side door, one after another around the camp the improvised gongs sent their discordant notes out upon the still morning air.

"Thank goodness we won't have to hear those again," Mari said. She had been more critical of things in camp since she had been out to college.

"You don't like them?" Tom exclaimed with feigned surprise. "Why, I was just thinking I would fix up something like that at home for you to call us in from the field. Maybe an old dishpan, and tire iron to pound it with. A person ought to be able to hear that quite a distance, even down to old man Winters's."

"You could starve to death before you'd ever get called that way," Mari declared.

The Sato family were among the first in the mess hall, and the pancakes and coffee were hot. They all ate heartily, for they did not know whether they could eat again before they reached home or not. Better not to give eating places along the way an opportunity to refuse to serve them, Father Sato had told his family the evening before, when he was advising them on their proper behavior on the trip.

After the meal, Father Sato stopped at the kitchen to thank the cooks for all their kindnesses to him and his family, especially during Mother Sato's illness. When he got back to his barracks, he saw Fumiki Saisho standing sleepy eyed and dishevelled beside the truck, talking to Tom and Yoshi. Under his arm he carried something in a blue cloth. As soon as Father Sato came up, the boy turned to him. It was apparent that his errand, whatever it was, had to do with the older man. Fumiki and Yoshi had never been very close since their sorry involvement in the incident of the stolen car.

503

"You're sure lucky to have a home to go back to, Mr. Sato," the boy drawled.

"Yes. It is very nice to have one's own home."

"Don't know what we're going to do. We ain't got a thing. We'll just have to stay here till they put us out, and then I don't know what'll become of us." There was a plaintive whine in Fumiki's voice. Such a helpless attitude went against the grain with Father Sato. "If the old man had lived . . . if he was here now . . ."

"Well, he isn't," Father Sato interrupted, speaking with unaccustomed sharpness. "Your father is dead, Fumiki, and you cannot depend on him anymore. You are almost a man. You must begin to make plans yourself."

The boy's mouth dropped open with surprise. No one had ever expected anything of him before. As he digested the thought, he watched Tom and Yoshi putting the last things in the car and Mari sweeping off the stoop. A few neighbors, up early, gathered around, waiting to say goodbye.

"You are a big, strong fellow," Father Sato went on, more gently. "You could work a ranch yourself."

Fumiki straightened his shoulders.

"Sure. I know how to do a lot of things on a ranch. I used to help my old man. Grew vegetables and sometimes strawberries. But it takes money to do anything."

"Yes. That is right. I see you have a head for business, too. But it doesn't take much all at once. You could rent a little land, and your brothers are big enough to help after school and on weekends. You have an older sister. She could get a job and provide the money you need. There will be a lot of California women waiting for some Japanese maids to do their housework for them. You talk to your mother about it. The first thing you'd know, you'd have some land of your own."

"Say, I bet we would," the boy exclaimed with more life in his face than Father Sato had ever seen. Then he lapsed into fear and hopelessness again. "Maybe no one would rent us their land. Anyway, you can't just start

504

out when you ain't got any place to go."

Tom and Yoshi were cooling their heels, anxious to get off. Why didn't their father get rid of that no account kid? Mari stood in the doorway, as if waiting for the proper time to perform some last-minute duty.

"We're all ready, Dad," Tom called.

"Yes, in just a minute." The kindly man turned back to the groping boy. "You talk things over with your family, then if you want me to, I will be looking around for a small piece of land you could rent." He took a pencil and an old envelope from his pocket and wrote his address. Handing it to the boy, he said, "Don't ever forget that a Japanese makes his own way."

Fumiki took the paper and stuffed it into his pants pocket.

"Thank you, Mr. Sato." There was light in his eyes. "I'll sure remember that."

Father Sato started toward the car. Mari disappeared into the barracks. Tom climbed into the cab of the truck, and Yoshi got up beside him. Everyone along the block was out by this time to wave goodbye.

Fumiki suddenly remembered the bundle under his arm. He came running to the car.

"Oh, say, Mr. Sato, I almost forgot about this." He unwound the blue cloth, bringing to light a grotesque piece of ironwood. "I don't s'pose you want anything to remember Poston by after all that's happened to you folks down here, but I thought this was kind of nice."

Father Sato took the piece of highly prized wood and turned it about in genuine admiration.

"I have seen many fine pieces of ironwood here, but this is the most unusual. Thank you many times for it. Did you find it yourself?" He felt quite sure the lazy fellow had not tramped the long journey to the hills and carried the heavy specimen back. But he was due for a surprise.

Fumiki hesitated, became shy.

"You was so good to me, Mr. Sato, not getting mad at me because of the trouble I got Yoshi into and all that, so I wanted to do something for you before I left.

My mom said she couldn't spare me no money to buy something, but I was telling her about all the pretty things you made out of wood, so why didn't I go find you a good piece of ironwood? So I did. I'm glad you like it."

"I like it very much, and I shall prize it, not as a souvenir of Poston, but as a gift from a boy who I am sure has iron in his soul. You will succeed, Fumiki. ¹ shall pray for you. Goodbye, my boy."

"Goodbye, Mr. Sato. Goodbye, Yoshi, Tom. See you in old Cal sometime." Fumiki left with a quick step, no longer interested in the Satos' departure, but in his own.

Father Sato got into the car, and Mari came out of the barracks carrying a small box in her trembling hands. She slipped in beside her father, holding the box of ashes on her lap.

Tom had the motors of both cars warmed up, and they started out, the father going ahead to set the pace. Everyone waved as they passed and called good wishes after them, then went about their daily tasks as usual. Another family had gone out to face an unfriendly world. Up past Units 2 and 1 they drove, and then the guard station.

Their baggage was soon inspected and passed. The MP waved them on. The last barrier was passed. They were on their own.

Yoshi was excited and full of talk. It was the first time he had been outside of camp since he had come in on the big bus that hot August morning many moons ago. Everything he saw he had to call to Tom's attention.

"Say, I'm driving a truck, Boy," Tom reminded. "You do the looking." But the boy soon forgot.

"Heh, Tom, look at that house over there behind the irrigation ditch. Look, there's a woman milking a cow. And they've got a horse, too. No, it's a mule. See it standing out there by that little shed?" It was his first glimpse of home life in so long.

"That is where some Indians live. This is on the reservation, you know."

Now it was the trees along the road.

"Look at those trees. Good to see something besides mesquite. Wonder what they are. Kind of feathery like."

"That's the kind Yuri's dad is always painting. Smoke trees."

"They do kind of look like smoke. Smoke trees."

Soon the first ugly buildings of Parker appeared on the horizon.

"Are we going to stop in Parker?" Yoshi asked.

"Are you kidding? Dad will probably bypass the town, and we'll follow him."

"Heck, I wanted to go through town."

"What on earth do you want to see that ratty place for?"

"I'd like to see that sign on the barbershop, 'Keep out Japs, you rats.' I'd like to get out and spit on it."

Tom took a quick look at his brother. The young people in the camp had been much aroused over the barber kicking a war-crippled Nisei out of his shop and throwing his crutches out after him. Yoshi's chin was thrust out belligerently, and he looked quite capable of doing just what he said he wanted to do. His attitude worried Tom a little. Maybe the kid was going to have some adjustments when he got back among the Caucasians again. Maybe he was too cocky for a member of a minority group. Indeed, right now he looked like anything but a member of a despised minority group. He didn't look as if he would take a thing from anyone.

The two cars arrived at Desert Center around the middle of the morning. Everything had gone well so far, and the men were beginning to have more confidence in their tires. They pulled up before the restaurant and all got out. Yoshi was keen to buy something at a real store and not just a camp canteen.

Inside the building, he swaggered up to the counter and bought a Coke and a package of gum. He smiled at the clerk as he threw his dime down on the counter. The man was caught off guard and found himself smiling back. The few "Japs" who had gone through before were very withdrawn and never looked a fellow in the eye. Now he asked the boy if he was having a good trip and how far he had to go.

"Yeah, swell, thanks. We'll be home before night."

When he and Tom were back in the truck, he told Tom about the man. "That guy was all right," he said.

"He's not all of California," Tom warned. "Watch your step, Boy, and take it slow at first." Then, afraid he might have intruded a sour note into the kid's first day out of camp, he added, "That clerk was probably friendly because you made such a big purchase." And the brothers laughed together.

That afternoon, when they began to climb the mountains beyond which lay their ranch, Yoshi became quiet. Carefully Tom guided the truck around the curves, watching for ice as they climbed higher. His father made better time on the climb and was now out of sight. When they were near the summit, Yoshi broke his silence with a wail of grief.

"It won't be like home without Mom." The words burst out like they had been dammed back for some time.

Surprise at Yoshi's outburst caused Tom to swerve the truck across the center line for an instant, but he quickly pulled it back into his own lane and steadied his voice to answer.

"No. It won't be the same. We'll have to learn to do without her."

"It won't ever be the same. I wish we hadn't come back." Now the boy burst into tears and hid his face in his hands. His body shook with sobs. All the braggadocio and cockiness were gone.

Tom felt a lump in his throat like a stone as he stared straight ahead and tried to think of something comforting to stay. What was there? Nothing. He must get the boy's attention off his grief.

"It's harder on Dad than on us," he said. "Be good to him and do all you can to make things easier for him. That is what Mom would want."

To this moment Yoshi had never once thought of his father's sorrow and loneliness. Gradually his sobs eased. Presently he wiped his eyes and began to look about him. They were on the downgrade now.

"Gosh, I bet Dad is lonesome. Who's he going to talk to evenings when we are all out running around somewhere? Remember how they used to talk so much and you couldn't understand a word they said, but they sure had a good time together? The way Mom looked when I told her the FBI had taken Dad was something awful. I tell you, Tom, it was awful, like . . . well, there isn't anything I ever saw that it was like. I was scared. And Dad was just away for awhile. He came back." His voice broke, and he was quiet for a minute, then went on. "It must be about all Dad can stand to think she won't ever . . ." He couldn't complete the sentence, but there was no need to.

"We ought to be able to see the ranch pretty quick now," Tom said. "When we come around that sharp curve with the old pine tree hanging out over the cliff, that's when we get the first sight of the house."

"I'll watch for it. I wonder if Malt will be glad to see me."

"Sure he will. Dogs never forget."

Yoshi was over a bad spot, and it was good that he had passed through his dark hour before they reached home, Tom thought.

Tom soon overtook his father and Mari on the downgrade and wanted to pass and hurry on to the ranch, but, no, his father should be the first to arrive. It was right that it should be that way. The winter sun was low when the two cars finally turned into the driveway. The family got out and stood looking about them. The place was a sorry sight. Only the first year had there been a tenant on the ranch, and he had given it little care. After that the weeds had grown rank after the winter rains of a year ago, died to unsightly stalks in the summer drought, and now formed a tangled mass from the very doorstep to the farthest corner of the land. Underneath, a fresh crop of new growth showed green in spots in the slanting rays of the setting sun.

Mari went toward the house, still holding the small box in her hands. Yoshi went racing about, looking for familiar things. The men stood looking.

Tom turned to his father. His spirits were as low as they could get. He was remembering the place as he had left it, the green fields free of weeds, the mown lawn, his mother's flowers.

Father Sato returned his son's dejected look with a smile.

"This is good land," he said. "It has grown a fine crop of weeds."

Tom laughed and marvelled that his father's inner resources were such that he could joke in the midst of such ruin. He felt his own courage returning.

"It is good land," he agreed. "And, come spring, we'll have it growing just as fine a crop of vegetables."

"We will get the machinery tomorrow and begin," the father said, and with a sigh he could not suppress, he turned toward the house.

"I found a note from Peg on the door." Mari greeted them with the news as the men entered the kitchen door and looked about in surprise. The furniture was there.

"And the lights and gas are on," Mari informed them. "And Peg said she was bringing our supper over."

"Someone has been very good to us," Father Sato said with trembling voice.

"You can bet it was the Sullivans," Mari declared.

"Well, now we've got something to sleep on, we won't have to unload the truck tonight," Tom said with relief. He was ready for bed right now. That is, after a good meal.

"Oh, yes, we must unload everything tonight," his father said quickly. "There will be many other things to do tomorrow."

"It's a good thing we've got lights, for we never could get it done before dark. How about waiting till after supper, Dad? Let's take a little breather first."

"I think that would be a good idea. But we will

need the suitcases, as we will want to get out of our best clothes. Where is Yoshi? Will you call him in to change before he tears his Sunday pants?"

When they had on their work clothes, there was still a bit of daylight left, and it found Tom and his father outside again, walking over the land, plodding through the dead weeds. In the greenhouse, Father Sato switched on the lights. Benches of flats full of dry dirt, and underneath the benches, piles of empty flats. No sign of life anywhere. He reached into a flat for a handful of dirt, eager to have the feel of his own land again, but it was caked hard as stone and defied his efforts to dig his fingers into it.

Tom saw, and spoke quickly.

"All it needs is water."

"Yes. Water is the great life giver. Without it, this area would be the same as the desert we have been crossing today."

As they walked toward the house they made plans. What would be the best crops to try? Had the markets changed? Would there be trouble selling their produce? Should they raise tomato plants for the growers, taking a chance that they would buy? The war was still on. They might grow a few thousand and see how they went. Many questions plagued them, and the small capital on which they must operate was a frustration. They must try to get a loan somewhere. Maybe the bank where Father Sato had always had his account would make him a loan. Tom recalled his experience at that same bank on the morning after Pearl Harbor.

"Why don't you see old Peter? He'd be more likely to accommodate you."

"I do not like to ask friends for favors."

"It wouldn't be a favor. He's got plenty of money, and a good, safe loan would be good business for him."

"We shall see. We shall see."

With so many things to do all at once, Father Sato felt suddenly old and tired and unequal to the task. He leaned heavily on Tom and would give him more of a share in making decisions in the future.

511

Peg was there when they got back to the house, but she left as soon as she had said a friendly hello to Tom and his father. Yoshi was eating a big hunk of cake Peg had brought, paying no attention to Mari's orders to wait until supper.

Mari had set the table so it would not seem to have a vacant place. But it did. As they ate the nourishing stew and the cake and fruit, Mari kept up a running monologue as if afraid of silence. She gave the others all the news she had gotten from Peg.

Allen was still missing somewhere in the South Pacific. They had all but given him up. Peg's mother had been the leader in getting the furniture moved in and the house cleaned. The Youth Fellowship from the church had helped with the work. If they had had more time, they would have cleaned up the yard, too, Peg had said. She also said not to feel indebted to her mother, for it was good for her to have something to do to take her mind off her troubles.

"When they went out for the furniture, they found old Peter Vandenheuvel laid up with rheumatism. His wife had died during the summer"--Mari hurried over this detail--"and he has a housekeeper. Old Peter told Mrs. Sullivan that she was a good worker but she talked too much. And the housekeeper told Mrs. Sullivan when she followed her out to the car that she liked the job and would stay on it, if the old man didn't talk her to death."

"Old Peter will never get too sick to talk," Tom laughed.

As soon as Yoshi had finished, he got up from the table and said he was going to bed. Tom looked at his father. What line was his father going to take with the kid now they were home again? Was he going to humor him as in the past, or was he going to make him work?

"Not until the truck is unloaded," Father Sato said. "We will need it the first thing in the morning."

"Oh, gee, Dad, have a heart," Yoshi began. Then he remembered Tom's words on the way home. "But I guess I'm good for another hour or two. Come on, Tom, let's

512

get started."

Tom gave him an approving nod, while Mari looked at her younger brother with open surprise.

Yoshi had been at loose ends ever since they had arrived at the ranch. While the men were looking over the place and talking plans for the spring work, and Mari had been busy putting things in order in the house, Yoshi had been going from place to place, seeking the thing he had expected to find by being home again. First he had gone to his room and begun digging into the cartons of his belongings he had had to leave behind with such reluctance when they were taken from their home. He had pulled out some books and games and tossed them aside, disgusted. Kid stuff. They meant nothing to him anymore. He found the old sweater his mother had made him leave behind and put it on. The sleeves came almost to his elbows. He couldn't even get into the shirts. He threw them on a heap on the floor and went outside in search of something to feed his hunger to feel at home. After he had tramped around in the tangle of dried weeds for a time, he went back to the house. He would go down to Jerry's in the morning and get Malt. With him back running around, it would be more like old times.

Now, while the men were taking the furniture from the truck in the light of the floodlight on the end of the greenhouse, Jerry came with the dog.

"Hello, Yoshi."

"Hi, Jerry," Yoshi said, looking at the little spotted mongrel at the boy's heels. Was this the dog he had shed so many tears over leaving? He couldn't even force any interest in the pet. He realized that along with the games and the books and the clothes, the dog belonged to another day. And another boy. A boy who liked to go chasing rabbits with his dog and who cried and ran to the house when he got hurt.

So when Malt hid behind Jerry and growled when a strange, deep voice spoke to him, Yoshi turned to his father.

"Would it be okay to give Jerry the dog for keeps if

513

he wants him?"

"Don't do anything in a hurry, Son," his father admonished, surprised at the request.

"He'll soon get acquainted," Tom said. "Hey, come here, fellow." He stooped and snapped his fingers at the dog, and Malt came dashing to him and leaped on his bent knees, trying to lick his face. "You old son of a gun, glad to get home, aren't you? Call him, Dad, and see what he'll do."

Father Sato set down the chair he was lifting from the truck and spoke the dog's name. Malt turned from Tom and looked at the man, wagging his tail in friendly greeting. He had never taken liberties with Father Sato.

"See, he remembers Dad and me. I bet it's because your voice is different. But he'll soon get acquainted."

"Sure he will," Jerry hurried to say. He was very much embarrassed. "Shut him up some place until I get away." He picked the dog up and waited for someone to indicate a place to confine him.

"No, I don't want him. I guess I've kind of forgotten him, too. I'm going to get a new pup sometime. One of those retrievers I can take duck hunting over on the Colorado. He's your dog, Jerry, if it's all right with Dad."

"Perhaps Jerry doesn't want him. He has been very good to keep him while you were away, and I can see he has taken fine care of him. You should thank him for his kindness."

"Oh, yeah, sure. Thanks a lot, Jerry. Do you want him?"

"Gosh, I sure do. I brought him over right away when I saw a light up here, because I kind of wanted to get it over with. But it don't seem hardly right."

"Go ahead and take him, Jerry," Tom said, wanting to get the ordeal over, too, but with a different ending than the one anticipated by Jerry.

"Well, thanks a million. I wouldn't hardly know how to get along without him now. Sure it's okay, Yoshi?"

"I said so, didn't I?" Yoshi said shortly. "Come on,

I'll walk a ways with you. I want to find out all about school."

The boys walked out the driveway, Malt sniffing at Yoshi's heels, unaware that he had just avoided another heartbreaking separation.

"We've got a winning basketball team this year," Tom heard Jerry saying as they passed out of range.

When everything was done that could be done that night, Father Sato went to his room. Mari had made up the bed, the one in which he and Mother Sato had slept for more than thirty years. And she had arranged the furniture as it had been before they had left the ranch.

Father Sato switched on the light and looked about him. His only company was his memories. He thought of Mama-san sitting there alone the night after the FBI had taken him away. How unnecessary it had been to persecute her so, dragging him off like a dangerous saboteur. Even if he had been, what harm to have allowed him to see her, to reassure her that everything would be all right? Never until now in his own anguish did he realize what hers must have been. That was the beginning of her decline. The anxieties and the exposure to the heat and cold, under conditions suitable only for an Army camp, had all taken their toll. Government officials had unjustly robbed him of two precious years of her companionship. Finally they had robbed him of his wife.

Searing hatred engulfed him. It frightened him more than the fires of hell. He had never hated anyone. He hurried to turn off the light to blot out the sight of the memory-laden room and fell to his knees beside the bed.

"Oh, God, give me the grace to forgive. They didn't know what they were doing."

He let his tired hand rest on the bed for a time, then he got up and undressed in the dark.

XXXIII

Nothing could be done on the ranch without the machinery, so that first morning Tom and his father drove into La Vista. While Tom went to get the tractor out of storage, Father Sato decided to pay a visit to the bank to see if he could get a loan if he needed one.

The manager, with whom Father Sato had done business for many years, was friendly enough, but his terms were harsh. The risks were very high, he explained. He is thinking we may lose our land, Father Sato decided. He said he would come in again when he was ready to consummate the loan and left the bank.

His shoulders sagged as he walked across the street and down the block to the seed store.

Mr. Wilson went so far as to say he was glad to see him back. Yes, he had fertilizer and could supply Father Sato with all the seeds and sprays he needed, but it would have to be on a cash basis.

"That is, for the present," he hastened to add. He did not want to lose a good customer, and if everything went well with the returning Japanese, Mr. Sato would give him much business.

"When you have crops ready for the market, we will talk about credit."

"When I have crops to sell, I will not need credit," Father Sato said, smiling.

With heavy feet, Father Sato went back to the car and drove around to where Tom had said the machinery was stored. He wanted to find out if Tom had been successful in repossessing their belongings before he went home and left Tom without a ride.

He found that Tom had already started home with the tractor and had hired a large truck and driver to haul the plow and cultivator. He did not think Tom should have gone to that expense, but he would not say anything about it.

Sunday morning Tom went to church with his

father and sat through the long Japanese service. He didn't want him to go alone. There were only a handful of people there. Tom didn't understand much of the sermon, but on the way home his father told him it was a good one and had given him strength.

Father Sato had told Tom of his visits to the bank and feed store, and Tom knew they were desperate for money. The small amount his father had saved from Tad's checks wouldn't even buy the fertilizer they would need. After dinner, he suggested that he and his father go to call on Mr. Vandenheuvel. He didn't mention money.

"He was so good to us after you left, and now he's shut in and alone, looks like we ought to go to see him the first thing."

"Yes, it would be a nice thing to do," his father agreed. He was not looking forward to the long afternoon.

Mari went with them as far as Peg's. She had prepared food for the men's supper, and she would stay at Peg's and go to the evening service of the Youth Fellowship with her.

Tom and his father drove on through town and out onto the west side to the roomy, tile-roofed stucco which Old Peter had built for himself and his wife after they sold the ranch.

The yard had an unkept look, but inside, the house was spick and span. And Old Peter was as fresh and clean as a newly washed baby. His bushy hair was as white as his shirt, and while living indoors had bleached his face of its coat of tan, his cheeks were rosy. His delight on seeing his guests made them glad they had come.

"You'll have to excuse me for not getting up," he boomed from his wheelchair, "but my legs have kind of gone back on me. Oh, I can stand all right, but it gives me pain." He extended a huge hand and shook Father Sato's hand, and then Tom's, most heartily. "Mighty glad to see you, Mr. Sato. You, too, Tom. Glad to know you're back on your ranch again, where you belong. It wasn't right to take you away. It hurt you and it hurt the country."

"Well, it's over now," Tom said.

"Yes, I hope it is. Take a seat. Take the chair here by me, Mr. Sato, so we can talk. Sit where you wish, Tom. Your hearing is better than mine."

Tom chose the davenport across the room from the men.

When they were seated, Old Peter spoke of the passing of Mother Sato. Tom had never heard the man speak in such gentle tones. He didn't know that he could. Then Father Sato offered his sympathy to the older man, who had lost his wife, too.

Their common loneliness appeared to draw them closer together, and they began going back over the years, reliving a happier past. Old Peter's voice was soon reverberating through the room and out into the yard, and Tom saw a spaniel, sleeping on the porch across the street, raise his head and give a reproachful look in their direction.

Tom became impatient, as the men talked on and on. He had hoped they would talk about the problems of the present, and Old Peter, always eager to help, would get around to inquiring about their needs. Tom had decided that if his father wouldn't ask the man for a loan, he would risk incurring his father's displeasure by asking himself.

Occasionally Old Peter turned to Tom and gave him a sly wink when he was recalling some amusing incident of Father Sato's early days in America. Then his hearty laugh would fill the room, threatening to burst the walls, and Tom would swear the davenport trembled beneath him.

The afternoon waned, and Tom was about to suggest it was time to go when Old Peter suddenly dropped the past.

"You didn't find the ranch in very good shape, I'm afraid. When land lies untended that way, it goes back. I tried to find a good tenant, but you can't do much when you can't get out and look around."

"You've done enough for us already," Father Sato said. "I want to thank you for your kindness to my family after I was taken away and for your letter to the hearing board."

"No more than anyone with a sense of justice would have done. Ridiculous, arresting you as an enemy. In my younger days, I might have gone into the city with my shotgun and sprung you out of jail. That's what someone should have done, a lot of someones. The whole community should have risen up in their wrath. Say, how are you off financially?" Old Peter said bluntly. "I don't suppose they paid you to be in prison, and I know you didn't have much income from the ranch, the land lying fallow that way."

"I think we will be able to get along," Father Sato said.

Tom fidgeted.

"You don't need to just get along. I've got plenty. I can let you have five thousand right now. Tom, look in the desk there and find my checkbook and a pen. And if you need more, I can get it. Money tied up in bonds isn't doing anybody any good."

Tom lost no time in finding the checkbook before his father could refuse.

"I will give you a mortgage on the ranch," Father Sato said, after Old Peter had brushed aside all of his objections.

"Nonsense. A man doesn't feel free when his land is mortgaged. He doesn't feel like it's his. You can sign a note, if you want to, but to me, your word is as good as your bond. Tom, there's some notes there in the desk, if your father wants one."

As Tom and his father were leaving, Old Peter said, "Now, Mr. Sato, it doesn't make any difference to me when you pay this loan off. It wouldn't really make any difference if you never paid it. I'm an old man, and I've got plenty. Partly thanks to you. And I've neither chick nor child to leave it to. If this housekeeper I've got stays with me to the end, I want her to have some. She'll have earned it." The old man laughed. "Now, goodbye and good luck to you. Come to see me when you can. And don't forget there's more where that came from," he said.

After more thanks, and some bowing from Father Sato, he and Tom left.

On the way home, Tom called to his father's attention the "For Sale" sign as they passed Harry Sakai's place.

"Wonder what ever became of Harry," Tom mused as he drove on.

"I never saw him after I was taken from Los Angeles. I think he was in deep trouble. The FBI were right in picking him up that day. He was an enemy of the country. This is a good ranch. I would like to buy it."

"What would we do with it?" Tom asked in surprise. "We've got all we can handle now." He was feeling good over having the money from Old Peter but not so good that he wanted to take on two ranches at once.

"More people will be returning from the camps. Some will have no place to go. We could rent the land. I could let Fumiki and his family have five acres. That would be enough for a start."

"Why don't you tell Mr. Vandenheuvel the ranch is for sale. He might buy it, and he would rent to the Japanese."

"He would not want the care that comes from owning land."

Yoshi started to high school on Monday morning. He was noncommital when questioned by Mari that evening on his return home.

"How was school?" she asked, as soon as he got inside the door.

"Okay."

"Are you behind the rest of the kids in your work?"

"Nope."

"Were they friendly?"

"Heck, what did you expect them to do? Have a celebration? I didn't know anyone in my classes except

Jerry in algebra."

Seeing it was hopeless, Mari gave up. She thought he must have got along all right, for he didn't act like anything had happened to upset him.

Mari soon discarded any school plans for herself. For the present, anyway. She wouldn't give up college altogether. And her music. It would have to wait, too. She hoped some day she could take up violin lessons again. She wondered if the maestro were still in the city.

When the Satos had been home a few weeks, Mari had a letter from Haruo, who was still in college. He had never explained why he had not been drafted. He and Willie had been called by their draft board at the same time. Mari opened the letter, eager for news from the college.

"I hate to be the one to tell you this," Haruo began, and Mari's heart skipped a beat. "But I don't know who else would. I had a letter from Willie's sister, Mame. Willie was killed in action in France about a month ago. I think you liked him a lot, and I know Willie was crazy about you. He wouldn't want you to be sad because of him, Mari, so try not to be."

The remainder of the letter was college news, but Mari scarcely read it.

Willie was dead. Willie, so active, so alive, so full of fun, so sweet to her when she left the camp and came to the new and strange environment of the east. She remembered his last letter before he had gone overseas.

"If you're still single when I come back, I'll have something to tell you." Now he wouldn't be coming back, but she knew what it was he would have said.

There was no time for grief. Soon the men would be coming in to dinner. Mari went to the bathroom and bathed her burning eyes, then came back to the kitchen and began to prepare the meal.

To see Father Sato at work on the ranch, one would think they had only one goal in life: to make all the money they could in the shortest time. Prices were high, and they worked with feverish haste to produce

521

all they could before the war ended and prices dropped. Father Sato had to rest sometimes when he felt a dizziness in his head. He chafed at the necessity for stopping work in the middle of the day. Some of his old customers had come to inquire if he were taking orders for tomato plants. Many growers wanted to double their acreage if they were sure they could get the plants. The mushrooming population in the city, and everywhere else in the area, had brought unlimited demand for produce. It seemed that the ranches could not grow enough to feed the hungry maw of Army, Navy, and industry.

Although Tom pushed his body to the breaking point with long hours of work, and although he had gained the separation from Yuri he thought would help him forget, neither had proved enough to quench the longing in his heart for the girl he loved.

To make money was a meaningless goal unless there was something at the end worth striving for. And for him, there wasn't. Just work, and more work.

However, by the first of April, when the Sato acres were green again, Tom could not but feel some satisfaction in his accomplishment. The thriving cucumber vines were yellow with blossoms. An acre of beans were climbing rapidly up their supports. The greenhouse was filled with flats of tomato plants, and outside, in the hot beds, thousands more for field planting. When he would come out early in the morning, he would stand a minute and look over the ranch, where the rising sun made diamonds of a million dewdrops on the growing plants. And he knew he loved it.

Why hadn't he found a nice farm girl while he was at Poston, instead of trying to travel in such high society? If he hadn't spent so much time mooning around about getting into a uniform to prove his loyalty, he might have given a little more thought to reality. Willie had proved his loyalty, and what did he get for it? A white cross in France. And Tad? A crippled leg. Who'd ever know ten years from now which Nisei was loyal and which wasn't? He knew in his heart; that was enough. He didn't feel any need to prove it to anyone anymore.

Sometimes Tom wondered about Tad. He'd been in that hospital four months now. He kept writing about coming home, but he never gave any date. Maybe he wasn't doing so well. Maybe one of them ought to go up to see him. He could get away from the ranch a few days before the cucumber picking began. A lot of the Nisei from around La Vista were back from camp now. Some didn't have work. He could get one of them to help his father while he was gone.

No, he didn't really want to go. It wouldn't be to see Tad. It was seeing Yuri again that he was thinking about. There was nothing but more misery to be gained from that. He dismissed the idea of a trip to San Francisco.

Mari knew Tom was unhappy, and she thought she knew why. That hungry look on his face when she'd tell him she had had a letter from Yuri. She knew he was dying to know what she'd said, but he wouldn't ask. So Mari would tell him the parts she thought would interest him.

Mari could read between the lines in Yuri's letters, and knew Yuri hadn't forgotten Tom. Yuri had always been so frank and straightforward, but her letters made use of all sorts of subterfuges to ferret out news about Tom without actually asking about him.

Blessed with common sense, Mari couldn't see why two people who loved each other shouldn't be engaged and eventually get married. She decided to take things in her own hands. Easter vacation time at the university was approaching. She wrote to Yuri and asked her down for vacation week. She would wait until she had Yuri's answer before she said anything to Tom. If Yuri refused, of course, she would never tell him.

XXXIV

The mail was late the day Yuri's answer came. Tom went out to the mailbox after he had finished his dinner to see if the carrier had come, so it was he who brought the letter in to Mari. He looked around for some excuse to wait until she had read it and discovered the knob on the kitchen door was loose. It had been loose for some time, but now, all of a sudden he felt it had to be fixed that very minute.

He was bending over the lower drawer of the cabinet, looking for a screwdriver, when Mari gave out a whoop of joy.

"Yuri's coming!" she cried.

Tom straightened up and stared at her.

"Coming where?"

"Here. She's coming down for spring vacation."

Tom kicked the drawer shut.

"What the heck is she coming here for?"

"Because I asked her, and because she wants to, I suppose. She wouldn't be coming if she didn't."

"Why did you ask her?" Tom demanded. He was angry. "You might have said something to the rest of us about it first. See if it was all right."

"Can't I ask my friends to come to visit me without having a family conference?" Mari was beginning to feel she had done the wrong thing, but she was going to stand her ground. "It is all right with you, isn't it?"

"Mari, you know I don't want to see Yuri."

"I don't believe you. I think you want to see her as much as I do, or more."

"A lot you know about it," Tom muttered. He forgot about fixing the doorknob and went out to the field.

"Was there a letter from Tadashi?" Father Sato asked as Tom passed the greenhouse.

"No. Just the papers and a letter for Mari from one of her friends."

Today Tom was doing some hand weeding along the

bean rows. Two seasons of weeds had scattered their seeds all over the place, and it seemed as if every seed had sprouted and grown. As he bent over the tedious task, careful not to disturb the vines, he nursed his wrath against Mari; but he couldn't generate enough indignation to overcome the joy that danced in his heart at the thought of seeing Yuri. The wonder of having her right there in his home, of finding her there when he went in from work, it was just too much. He forgave Mari. After all, it was a good idea to have Yuri come and see the ranch and how they lived, the little old house that would look like a shack to her, not much better than the barracks at Poston. Then she would understand why he had written as he had. She would see for herself, this was no place for her.

Inside the house, Mari worked like a slave to get everything looking its best for her guest. Mari had matured since those early days in Poston when she had been ashamed to have Yuri come to their apartment and see how shabby it was compared to the Takedas'. Her false pride was gone. She thought only of how nice it would be to see Yuri and of how she could make her friend's visit a pleasant one. Even if she had been wrong and Tom didn't want to see Yuri, she hoped he would be decent and not spoil her visit.

When the big day came, Mari put a fresh bouquet of pansies on the living room table. They were about the only flowers that were blooming so far of all the plants she had set out around the front porch and along the path to the gate. Then she went on a tour of inspection to see that everything in the house was the way she wanted it. Rugs still clean. The men hadn't tracked in any dirt from the fields. New curtains in bathroom and her bedroom, which Yuri would share with her, all hanging straight. Kitchen linoleum shining with a fresh coat of wax.

The impatient honk of the car in the driveway called to her. Tom had taken the morning off to drive her to the station. Since the traffic had become so heavy in the city, her father didn't want her to drive in herself.   She hurried to take the roast from the refrigerator, put it in a pan, and covered it with foil. If the train were late, they wouldn't have to wait so long for the meat to cook if it were at room temperature when she put it in.

Another long honk as she hurried out the door.

"Yes, I'm coming," Mari called, smiling to herself. Tom wasn't fooling her a bit with his gripe about having to lay off work a half day to go meet her guest. He'd preened himself like a peacock and now couldn't wait to get started.

It was a beautiful spring morning, and when they came to the top of the hill and looked down Broadway, the ocean was as blue as the sky, and the air so clear they could see men walking on the decks of the Navy ships anchored in the harbor.

How different from that April day three years before, when Peg had driven them to the station to depart for they knew not where.

Yuri had written she would like to take the night train from San Francisco, make good connections in Los Angeles, and arrive in the city at ten.

As they drove down Broadway, Tom began to feel uncomfortable. What would it be like to see Yuri outside of Poston? That was an interlude that belonged to nowhere.   Other people he had met and known well there had already moved out of his mind. He had no desire to see them again. He began to try to push Yuri away into that forgotten zone. Yuri Takeda, daughter of a noted artist, now a university student, someone he had met at a Poston which was now a thing of the past.

He had so convinced himself of his aloofness from this girl who was coming to visit Mari, and whose visit had nothing to do with him, that when the train pulled in and Yuri came tripping down the steps to the platform in a stylish blue suit and a chic little hat to match, he could take her outstretched hand and say, "Hello, Yuri. Glad to see you again," in the friendly way a fellow might greet his sister's guest. But when he felt the slight but unmistakable pressure of the small hand in his, a message from heart to heart, he was all agog.

Mari had greeted Yuri before Tom, and then she had turned away to leave them alone and was watching the other passengers coming down the steps. It was then that she recognized the tall, thin young man in uniform, slightly stooped and carrying a cane, who was being helped down the steps by the porter.

"Tad!" she cried, and rushed to him. Tom, hearing her, followed. Mari clung to Tad's arm with both hands, the tears of joy running down her cheeks. "Oh, Tad, it's wonderful to see you."

Tom pumped Tad's hand and slapped him on the back.

"Tad, you son of a gun. Where did you come from? Why didn't you let us know?"

"Hello, Tom. Hello, Mari," Tad said. "This was Yuri's little secret. Anyway, it isn't a good idea to announce your plans ahead of time unless you are your own boss. I was afraid the doc might change his mind. How are you all, anyway? Tom, boy, you're sure looking fine. Getting back to the ranch did you good, eh?" Tad's arm was now free from Mari's grasp and he threw it around his brother's shoulder. "Say, is it swell to be coming home. How's Dad . . ." He let the words hang. He had almost said, "and Mom?" from habit.

"Oh, Dad's as good as could be expected, the way he's working," Tom said quickly, hurrying past them a delicate moment.

Yuri had stepped back out of the line of traffic of passengers leaving the train, and she stood smiling as she watched the joyous reunion. Strangers looked, too, and some smiled compassionately as they noted the cane and saw the pinched face now bright with pleasure over coming home.

Yuri was thinking how near she had come to refusing Mari's invitation and how glad she was now she hadn't. For without someone with him, Tad would not have been allowed to come. She had intended to refuse, but she had made the mistake of telling Tad when she went to see him the afternoon after the letter had come.

527

That very night Tad had called her in great excitement. The doctor had said he could come with her. She was caught. She would have to watch her step not to do anything to give Tom the idea she was throwing herself at him. Let him make the decisions.

Mari took Yuri's arm, and they walked behind the boys down the platform, adjusting their steps to Tad's slow ones, all chattering and laughing, the happiest foursome at the station.

"Say, the old bus looks new," Tad commented when they reached the car. Tom didn't remind him it was old only in years, not in use. It had had three years of rest. Neither did he tell Tad he had stayed up late the night before washing and polishing the car to have it shining for Yuri's visit.

"That old fellow, what's his name, must have taken good care of the car," Tad said as he climbed in with some difficulty. No one dared to help him. "Looks as good inside as out."

"Peter Vandenheuvel. He took good care of all our stuff. And that's not all he's done for us. If you could see his heart, I guess you'd find out it was made of gold."

On the way out to the ranch, Tad asked Tom about his draft status.

"I see they haven't got you yet."

"And I don't think they will. I registered as soon as I got back, but I guess I'm being deferred because of the ranch work. At least that's what they told me."

"You're lucky. There's no glamor in it, Boy. How about your health? That okay now?"

"Oh, sure. It always was. That doctor in Phoenix must have had spots on his glasses."

"Or Jap hate in his belly," Tad said.

"I never thought of that."

Tad laughed without mirth. He looked at husky, sun-tanned Tom, and thought of his own crippled leg and his weary all-gone feeling.

"Well, either way it was your good luck. With all the fever you had to get into the fight, you'd have been

528

right up there at the front, an easy mark for some sharp-eyed Jerry."

"From what I hear, you didn't hang back much yourself," Tom answered, full of pride in his older brother.

"With shells bursting in front of you and behind you and on all sides, and mines exploding under your feet, it doesn't make much difference whether you're front or back. When you've got a job to do, you just go ahead and do it. Don't believe everything you hear about how heroic we were. I was just plain scared most of the time."

Tom was listening to Tad and trying to follow the conversation in the back seat at the same time. The girls were hashing over their experiences at college, and every time Yuri spoke the sound of her voice would send Tom dreaming.

When they passed Harry Sakai's place, Tom noticed the "For Sale" sign was gone. He remarked about it to Tad and said he'd like to know who bought it.

"Maybe that old man Winters, if he could get it cheap," Tad said scornfully. "I suppose he's still around."

"Yep, he's still here."

"Suppose he didn't roll out the red carpet for you when you came back."

"No, he didn't go quite that far," Tom said. He was glad Tad could joke now about the things he had been so bitter about before they left the ranch. "But he did bring us a basket of fresh vegetables the day after we got home and asked if there were anything he could do to help us clean up the place. I've heard the tenant on our place that first year gave Mr. Winters a bad time. And after the tenant was gone, the ranch grew up in weeds and the wind blew the seeds all over Winters's place. I think he's really glad to see us back."

"Well, don't expect too much. How have you been received by the other folks? Pretty good?"

"Everything seems okay around here. I hear the folks farther north have met some resistance, even violence. But if anything like that has happened down here, I don't know about it."

"We should never have gone," Tad said.

"We had no choice."

Fortunately the sight of the ranch as they turned the corner cut off any further pursuit of that subject.

Father Sato came out to the driveway to meet them. He had changed to the clean blue shirt and jeans Mari had laid out for him. She had told him she wanted him to look nice to meet Yuri. The father's surprise and delight at seeing Tad was overwhelming. For a moment he was unable to speak.

When he had regained his composure and had given Tad a warm welcome, Mari presented Yuri to her father. He had never met her, since Mari had left camp soon after he had come, and Yuri had no longer visited at the Sato apartment. But he had heard much about her from Mother Sato, and he was prepared to like her.

When Mari introduced Yuri, the girl stepped back and made a low, sweeping bow to the little man. As a rule the Nisei girls did not observe this gracious and respectful gesture so dear to the hearts of the Issei, and Father Sato was immensely pleased. Yuri had won his heart. Tom had never talked to him about her, but Father Sato knew that here was a girl he would like to have in the family.

After dinner, which was preceded by a longer grace than usual, for Father Sato must give thanks to God for Tad's return and the guest in his home must be called to the attention of the Heavenly Father, Tom changed into his work clothes and went out with his father to the field.

Tad wandered around the house awhile, restless, looking for someone he knew he would never find, then he went outside and limped around the yard. He was tired from the trip, and he soon sat down on the back porch steps. He listened to the talking and laughing going on in the kitchen as the girls did the dishes, and he wondered how such happy sounds could be coming from this bereft home. To him there was crepe on every door. He wondered how Mari could have forgotten so soon.

When the dishes were done, Mari and Yuri came out on the porch.

"What do you folks want to do this afternoon?" Mari asked.

"I want to see the ranch the first thing," Yuri replied.

"That's not very exciting," Mari laughed. "Do you want to show her around, Tad? And don't take long."

Tad didn't know how much longer he could keep going, but he agreed.

"But not in that outfit," he said, looking at Yuri's high heels and city clothes. "Didn't you bring country clothes with you?"

"Of course. I'll be ready in a jiffy." She ran into the house and changed from her suit to a pair of brown broadcloth slacks and a yellow sport shirt. In place of the pumps she put on a pair of low-heeled walking shoes.

Tad surveyed her as she came out and laughed.

"Do you call those farm clothes? Your idea of the country must be the country club." While he'd been waiting for Yuri he had slipped into his room and put on some old levis and a work shirt. He had the sleeves rolled up, and his arms were pale and thin. Getting out of his uniform had rested him.

"She isn't going to be digging irrigation ditches," Mari said. "Just walking around won't hurt her slacks any."

"You never know around a ranch what you're going to be doing," Tad warned. "Anyone who shows himself in a field is likely to have a job pushed on him."

"Oh, do you suppose I could really help? Our gardener let me help him once when I was a little girl, and I pulled up half a row of sweet peas before he caught me."

"You just try pulling up one of Tom's cucumber vines and you'll be in the doghouse the rest of your days," Tad threatened.

"Do cucumbers grow on vines?" Yuri asked in surprise.

"Where did you think they grew?" Mari inquired, suspicious that Yuri was joking. After all, they'd grown acres of cucumbers at Poston.

"She probably thinks they grow in the lugs at the market," Tad teased.

"Well, I guess I never thought much beyond that," Yuri said humbly. "Come on, Tad, let's get started."

"Got anything for snake bites around here, Mari?" Tad asked, winking at his sister. "We might meet up with a rattlesnake or two."

Yuri was undisturbed. "You should know better than to try to frighten with rattlesnakes someone who has lived with them for three years. Under the mess hall, under the barracks, along the river when we went fishing."

"Oh, yes. I forgot. My mistake."

"I never saw one around here, anyway," Mari said.

"Yeah, I was just teasing. But I'll bet there are some nice, fat tomato worms, big as my finger. Maybe Tom will set you to picking them off of the plants and squashing them under those fancy shoes."

"Oh, Tad, shame on you," Mari chided fondly. "If that's the way you are going to show Yuri the ranch, maybe I'd better do it."

"No, I'll be good. Come on, Yuri."

Yuri wanted to run everywhere at once, but she slowed her steps to keep with Tad.

"Are you sure you feel like walking so much?" she asked before they had even reached the greenhouse.

"Yes, I'm okay. I'll sit down somewhere when I get too tired. Do you want to see the greenhouse?"

"I want to see everything, and I want you to tell me all about the plants in the fields."

"Going to marry a rancher?"

"I might, if I get a chance," Yuri retorted smartly. Then the flippancy was gone, and she turned to Tad, the anguish of frustration in her eyes. "Oh, Tad," she cried.

"What is it, Hon, that's keeping you and Tom apart? Do you want to tell me?"

They sat down on a pile of flats on the shady side of the greenhouse, and Yuri told Tad about the letter Tom had written after she had left Poston and after they had spoken their love for each other.

"Just be patient," Tad said, taking her hand, after she had finished a recital of all the reasons Tom had why they could never marry. "Tom's a slow burner. He's like the peat up there in the northwest country. Once it's set afire, it never goes out. He'll get everything figured out some day, and he'll realize he can't live without you."

"It's hard to wait. We've lost so much time already, time we could have spent enjoying each other and making plans. Maybe I shouldn't have come down here. He made a clean break."

"Now don't say that. We're going to have a lot of fun this week. Say, I've got an idea that might help. How about us trying to make Tom jealous?" Tad thought it would be nice to have Yuri sweet on him for a few days.

"No, no. I wouldn't do that to Tom," Yuri said quickly. "It wouldn't be fair."

Tad got up.

"Well, if we're going to look at the crops, we'd better get at it."

After Yuri had seen the Sato acres, Mari took her for a ride. It was the first time Yuri had been in the southland, and she marvelled at the warmth of the afternoon. They were wearing fur coats in San Francisco.

Before they returned home, Mari drove around to see Peg, or maybe for Peg to see Yuri.

The Sullivans had good news. Allen was safe. He had been transferred before his ship went down. Everything was so hush-hush out there in the Pacific that he couldn't write much. Just said he was all right and not to worry. Peg invited the girls to dinner the following evening.

"Be sure to bring Tad and Tom," she said as they

left.

When Mari told Tom about Allen, he said, "Well, that's the best news yet. We ought to celebrate."

"We're going tomorrow night," Mari said, and she told him and Tad about the invitation to dinner.

"I think I'll stay home and visit with Dad while the rest of you are out of the way," Tad said. He looked very tired. Mari didn't insist on his going.

Yoshi came dragging home from the Sakemoto ranch, where Father Sato had sent him for what he was worth to help out in a crisis. One of the Sakemoto boys had sprained his ankle, and there were hundreds of pepper plants to be set out.

"Another man in the family," Tad commented, noting how Yoshi had grown while he had been away. Tall as Tom, almost. "How are you, Boy?" He gave Yoshi a friendly cuff on the ear.

"I'm doggone tired, that's how I am," Yoshi moaned. He had no sympathizers. "And I've got a blister. Look, Dad. Do I have to go back there again tomorrow?" Yoshi pulled off his shoe.

Father Sato, who had just come in from the greenhouse, looked at the inflamed heel.

"We'll see how it is in the morning," he said. "Wash it good and put some iodine on it."

The next evening, after Tom and the girls had left, Tad and Yoshi and their father ate the supper Mari had fixed for them. When they had finished, they put away the food that was left and piled the dishes in the sink and went into the living room. Father Sato took his place in the familiar old leather chair by the front door, while Yoshi, who had had to go to work that day, flung himself down on the davenport. Tad took his mother's rocker and pulled up a stool to rest his leg on.

"Dad will make a rancher out of you yet," he said to the weary boy.

"Not on your life. When I get through college, I'm going to join the Air Force and be a pilot. Just ride around in a plane all day," Yoshi bragged.

"Big ideas, Boy, big ideas. How do you know you're

going to college?"

"Dad put Norio through. And you. Why wouldn't he send me, too?"

Callous kid, Tad thought. Couldn't he see his father was an old man and four years before Yoshi would be ready for college?

"I'm here to tell you Dad didn't put me through," Tad said. "I made my own way."

"Working?"

"How else?"

"Did you have a car?"

"Are you kidding? No, I managed to walk to my classes."

"Heck, it'd be no fun going to college without a car."

"Maybe you've got the wrong idea, Buddy. College is where you study. If all you want to do is ride around, you can stay home and drive the tractor. Be a lot cheaper."

"Are you going to stay home now?" Yoshi asked, changing the subject.

"No. I've got to go back to the hospital awhile yet."

Before long, Yoshi was too sleepy to talk, and he got up and went out to bed. Mari had made up a bed in Norio's room back of the garage for him so Tad could have his bed.

Now Tad and his father were left alone, and Tad had the chance he had been waiting for to get some things off his chest. But first his father had to know all about his wound and what the doctor said about his leg.

"I will be good as new . . . in time," Tad lied. "It's a little stiff tonight and hurts, but that's because I've been doing too much walking since I came. I ought to be discharged in a month or two."

"Mr. Vandenheuvel, you remember him, sent word to me today that he has bought the Harry Sakai place. He wants me to find a tenant for him if I know of any Japanese who wants land. There was a family in Poston, you remember the boy, Fumiki, with whom Yoshi

535

was involved . . ."

"Yes, I remember him," Tad said.

"I think they are interested in leasing some land, but they would not need the whole ranch. We might take part of it, if you wanted to plant it. It is near enough for us to use the same machinery."

Tad sat silent. He knew he would never do ranch work, but he hated to disappoint his father.

"If you would like that, I will speak to Old Peter."

"Dad, you know I took business administration at the university with the idea of having a business of my own. When I volunteered for the service, I planned to start something of my own when my two-year hitch was up. Well, all those other things happened. Now after my discharge I can begin to carry out those plans. I'll tell you what I have in mind. I'd like to start some kind of business in the city. You know I was never much good on the ranch. When I had that florist shop at the university, I found out there was money in it. While I'm down here I thought I'd go into the city and look around. See what the prospects are."

Father Sato listened intently.

"I'm not surprised you don't want to do ranch work. I thought it might fill you in until you had other plans," he said when Tad was through. "I like the idea of selling flowers." The conversation had come to the subject Tad most wanted to talk about, his mother.

It took little prompting to get his father to tell him all about those last months before her death. She had been more like her old self, cheerful, and eager to return to the ranch. As he told of Tad's name being the last word she had spoken, Tad's cup of remorse was filled to overflowing. The anxiety he had caused his mother when he was in camp had weighed heavily on him even when she was still alive. But he thought then he could make it up to her when he got home from the war. How weak and foolish he had been. Willing to be shipped off to Tule Lake rather than answer a couple of questions the way he was supposed to. And his mother walking up there to the office in the heat to intercede for him. Oh, if he only had another chance to make it up to her.

When he began to put his dark thought into words, his father would have none of it.

"There is neither virtue nor comfort in placing blame on yourself," he admonished. "Bitterness and remorse are like moles that burrow along under the ground, destroying the roots and leaving the plants to wither. They can sap the very life from your soul. You would do well to expel all such thoughts from your mind, now and for all time."

"But how can I when I believe that worry over me had a part in breaking her health? I feel terrible."

"I'm not sure she worried so much about you," Father Sato said. He was probably as near to skirting around the edges of truth as he had ever been. "She had faith in you. She knew how you felt about your Army discharge and evacuation, but she knew that underneath the resentment which you expressed in your actions, was the good son. You are unjust to her memory to feel remorse."

His father spoke with such certainty that Tad was impressed and convinced. He began to feel free, like a heavy load had fallen from his back.

Father Sato began to talk of his family in Japan. He had tried to find a way to get word to them of Mama-san's death, but he had not been able to do so. And he was concerned for the welfare of his brothers. He had read the papers every day since the bombing of the homeland had begun. Other large cities had been destroyed by the American bombs. Tokyo, Osaka, Fukuoka, Kagoshima, and many others. All but Kyoto and Hiroshima. Perhaps Kyoto would be spared. It was an art center, with nothing of military significance there. But Hiroshima, he and Tad had seen for themselves the heavy concentration of training camps around there. Why hadn't it been bombed?

"It will be," Tad said. "But I imagine your folks have all left the city before this. They know the bombers will come."

537

"Yes, perhaps the women and children have gone to the country somewhere, but the men could not leave their work."

They were still talking about Japan and the war when they heard the car drive in.

As the girls came through the kitchen, followed by Tom, Tad heard Yuri saying how much she liked Peg and all the Sullivans.

"I feel just as happy as anyone that Allen is alive and safe," she said.

"I wouldn't say he's very safe out there in the middle of the Pacific with a war going on," Tad teased, trying to throw off the tension created by the emotion-filled talk he had had with his father.

"Oh, you know what I mean," Yuri replied, coming into the living room and dropping down into the rocking chair. "He was so fortunate to have been transferred to another ship just before his went down."

"Sure, I know what you mean. We are so close I can read you like a book." There was a touch of tenderness in his voice.

Yuri's face flushed, and she looked quickly at Tom, who was just coming through the door, to see if he showed any sign of having caught the note of tenderness in Tad's voice. If he had, he wasn't showing it. Apparently he didn't care what her relations to Tad were.

Father Sato went to bed soon after the young folks came home. Tad was ready to follow him. He had had a long, hard day.

"I think I'll turn in, too," he said, getting up slowly. On a sudden impulse, as he passed Yuri's chair he leaned over and gave her a kiss on the cheek. "Good night, Hon, see you in the morning."

Yuri drew back with a confused laugh. Tom, who had been about to sit down in his father's chair, suddenly remembered he had left something undone outside, and he bolted out through the kitchen as if he were being pursued.

"Need any help?" Tad called after him.

"No. It won't take a minute."

"Now see what you've done!" Mari cried.

And Yuri said in a chiding voice, "Tad, I told you I didn't want you to do anything to make Tom think there was something between us."

"You'll thank me for it," Tad said confidently. "I'll bet that old slow-smoldering peat is getting all aglow with fire this very minute."

"What have you been up to?" Mari asked. It looked as if Tad had hatched out some sort of plot.

"Nothing. I only wanted to make Tom jealous. He isn't being fair to Yuri. Anything wrong with that?"

"Yes, there is something wrong with it." Mari's sharp voice indicated that all Tad's battle scars or his weariness were not going to save him from what she had to say.

Tad sat down again and waited for the storm to break.

"You can't play games with Tom. I don't believe you really know your own brother. If you did, you could talk to him, let him know how you feel about the shabby way you think he's treating Yuri. And not make a fool of yourself, acting silly over her. Make him jealous. Rubbish! Don't you know that if Tom thought you were in love with Yuri he would never compete with you."

"Then he hasn't any guts."

"He's got something better than guts," Mari exclaimed in anger. "He's got courage and loyalty. You are his older brother. He has always given in to you and he always will, no matter what it costs him. I don't see why you had to give him a stab in the heart."

"I didn't mean to hurt him, Mari. Honest. Can't you believe me? I thought I could help." His last words were so low they could scarcely be heard. He had no strength even to talk.

"Well, you didn't."

"I'm sorry," Tad said, looking at Yuri. "I guess I did the wrong thing." He rose to his feet slowly and started for the kitchen.

"That's all right, Tad. Thank you for trying to help. Now go to bed and get some rest. The world hasn't come to an end."

"No. I can't go to bed yet. I have to go out to see what's keeping Tom so long."

In answer to Mari's warning look, he said, "No, I won't say a word about this 'much ado about nothing.'" Mari's sharp words had left bruises.

XXXV

When Tad got outside the house, the cool night air refreshed him, and he straightened his shoulders and called upon what reserve strength he had for the encounter with his brother.

Although he was tired in body, his mind was alert, and as he looked about in the bright moonlight trying to spot Tom, a thought came to him, something he could say which might help Tom out of his dilemma without arousing his suspicions.

He found Tom sitting on the stump of the big eucalyptus tree which had been cut down some years before because the branches had grown so large they had shaded the greenhouse.

"What are you doing out here?" he asked.

"I was just figuring out how I could get this stump out without disturbing the roots of these small fruit trees."

"Were you planning on doing it tonight?" Tad asked soberly.

Tom laughed.

"You've got a funny bone, just like Mom. That's the kind of thing she would say to take you by surprise and make you laugh. I suppose we'll never get over missing her around here." Tom sighed.

"Well, I guess people do forget eventually. But it takes time. She was a great mother. Say, it's getting close to midnight. You'd better be turning in. I suppose Dad still expects you up at five."

"Yeah, around five. But I'm not sleepy. Nice night. Think I'll stay out awhile. I didn't tell you, Mari moved your bed over by the window. She knows you like lots of fresh air. Mine's still by the door," Tom said, dismissing his brother.

Tad disregarded it.

"Mind if I stay out with you? There's something I want to tell you, and there's no chance to talk in the house with the girls chattering like magpies all the time."

"Suit yourself," Tom said indifferently. He moved over to make room on the stump.

Tad sat down and stretched his sore leg. He didn't say anything for a time, giving his idea a chance to develop into something tangible.

"I've met a girl up there at the hospital," he announced after a few minutes. "I knew the first time I saw her that she was the one for me. You know how you tell. Something clicks inside here." He made a vague gesture toward his heart.

Tom felt his own heart beating fast. So Tad wasn't in love with Yuri after all. Thank God.

"That's great, Tad. Just great," he burst out, slapping his brother on the back. "One of the nurses?"

The relief in his voice made Tad wince. Mari was right. He had hurt him.

"No. Not a nurse," he said. "A student at Berkeley. She had finished the first semester of her junior year when evacuation came. Now she's back, beginning where she left off.

"I'd have to wait a year until she graduates."

"Do I know her?"

"No. She wasn't at Poston. Folks from up her way were sent to Topaz Center, Utah."

"That's kind of a long time to wait, but if you're engaged, you've got something to look forward to." There was envy in Tom's voice.

"But we're not. That's what I wanted to talk to you about. I haven't even asked her yet."

"Afraid she'll turn you down? Have you got any idea how she feels about you?"

Tad shifted uncomfortably on the hard stump.

"I think I have. There are four or five other Nisei in the hospital, and she comes to see us twice a week. Brings us magazines, candy, games to help pass the time. The last few weeks she's been giving the other fellows their stuff and then finding a nice, cozy corner on the sundeck to spend the rest of the waiting hour with me.

542

I think she feels the same way I do."

"Well, for Pete's sake, what are you waiting for?"

"Oh, well, you know . . . this lame leg. I don't think a girl would want to marry a cripple, do you?"

"You won't always be lame," Tom said. And Tad didn't contradict him, although he knew better. "I don't think you're being fair to her, Tad. It's up to her to decide. That's her right." Tom's voice was serious.

Tad's plot was succeeding so far, but he must move with caution.

"Do you honestly think it would be right for me to ask her to marry me? You've always been more level-headed than me. You don't go off half-cocked. What you say would carry a lot of weight with me if I thought you really meant it and were not just saying what you thought would please me."

"Sure, I mean it. A girl's got a right to decide for herself. You ought to know that, Tad. You can't make decisions for other people."

"Tom, do you mind if I ask you a question about Yuri?"

"Go ahead. Shoot." Tom stiffened and took a defensive position.

"I was pretty doggone sure at Poston that you were in love with her. Did she turn you down?"

"She didn't get a chance. I never asked her. I wasn't in any position to ask a rich girl to marry me. Not a penny to my name but the fourteen a month I was making down there."

It was evident from Tom's words that he was making no connection between the rights of Tad's girl and those of Yuri. Tom wasn't stupid. How could he have missed the point?

Tad was dead tired. He was ready to give up, but it had never been easy for him to accept failure. He'd have to make one more effort or all his fish story about his girl up north would be for naught.

The night was quiet. The dew on the grass at Tad's feet sparkled in the moonlight.

Suddenly he broke the silence with feigned hot

anger.

"So you did say that just to make me feel good. All that baloney about a girl having a right to decide. Who do you think I am, a disabled soldier that you feel sorry for and have to humor? I call it a dirty, mean trick you've played on me."

"I wasn't tricking you!" Tom cried in dismay. "I meant what I said. I never meant anything more in my life. You know I don't pity you. I think you're great, fighting for your country after what it did to you. Believe me, Tad." Tom's voice was pleading.

"Well, if you meant what you said, you've got a chance to prove it. Yuri is right here in our home. I know you love her. She loves you. She told me so. But you are making all the decisions. Farm boy can't ask city girl. Poor boy can't ask rich girl. All that tripe. You didn't hesitate to spit out advice to me. If you meant it, why don't you take it yourself?"

Tom shot up from the stump like a released jack-in-the-box.

"Well, I'll be . . . I've been blind as a mole. When you were talking about your girl troubles, I could see as plain as day what you should do, but I never applied it to myself. Sure, Yuri's got a right to decide, and I'm going to give her a chance."

Tad smiled to himself. He felt he had lied in a good cause. He stood up, and the two brothers started for the house.

"Say, you never told me the name of your girl," Tom said as they approached the back porch. Tad was taken by surprise.

"Her name? It's . . . Kato. Wouldn't have to change it much if she married me, would she?" Tad laughed.

Tom went to work the next morning whistling cheerfully. He was freed from his self-imposed silence. Now he could tell Yuri how much he loved her, and then it was up to her. He decided he wouldn't be in a hurry. Give Yuri time to have a good look at ranch life. Lots of hard work and not much play.

Tom knew he wasn't going to spend his life on a

ranch, but he was tied to it as long as his father lived. When his father was gone, Tad would sell it, and Tom would be free to do something else. He didn't know just what he would do, but he knew he wasn't going to be an artist. If Yuri married him, he might paint a picture now and then to please her father, but that would be it. He might even go to college, learn a profession. He'd have his share of money from the sale of the ranch and he could work at college to help out like Tad did. He'd always thought he'd like to be an engineer. He wouldn't say anything to Yuri about all of this, though. It was an unpleasant thought to have Yuri waiting for his father to die.

Of course, she wouldn't do so intentionally. Such a thing would be as distasteful to her as it was to him. But if she hated the ranch, the thought would be bound to be in the back of her mind somewhere, and she would feel guilty. He wouldn't put that burden on her.

There were more than thoughts of Yuri to spur Tom on this morning. The cucumbers were ready for their first picking. Tomorrow when he took them to market he would receive the first income from the ranch since evacuation. With good weather, backbreaking labor, and plenty of fertilizer, there would be a bumper crop of everything this summer, and by autumn there would be money in the bank.

Tom had been in the city to see Mr. Imoto, who was back in business. Not in the same market, some Caucasians were running it now, but in a small space in a poor location. It was not because he was a Japanese, but simply because business was booming in the over-crowded city, and any space at all was at a premium.

"With the demand for fresh produce so great, the growers and retailers would find me if I was in a cave," Mr. Imoto had told Tom with a hearty laugh. "Everything goes out so fast, I don't need storage space. All I need is a loading zone, and I've got that."

He had told Tom to tell his father he could handle all he could grow. So it was good news that Tom had brought home to Father Sato.

Tom waited until Yuri and Tad's last day on the ranch before they would return to San Francisco. Then, as the family got up from the noon meal, he asked Yuri if she would like to go into the City for dinner that night. The invitation surprised everyone except Tad. He had been wondering all week what was taking Tom so long.

Pleased yet puzzled, Yuri said she would love it. Tom had been different since the second night she had been there, free and easy, enjoying the evenings together when he was away from work. She didn't know what it meant, or whether it meant anything. Now out of the blue this invitation to dinner. Tom was certainly unpredictable.

Mari thought it was a great idea, and Tom was afraid she might want to go along. He didn't see the wink Tad gave Mari over the back of Tom's head. When Mari began clearing the dishes from the table without further comment, he was relieved.

That evening he took Yuri to dine at the most exclusive restaurant in the city which had no color barrier. One time when Tad was home from college he had taken Tom there, saying he wanted his younger brother to know how to behave in society. Just to make sure the proprietor's attitude hadn't changed since the war, he had checked by telephone. Nothing must go wrong on this night of nights.

The dinner would take a big chunk out of what he had received for the cucumbers this morning, but Tom was reckless with money tonight.

They dined in style. Yuri was delighted to find abalone on the menu. Tom was not ready yet to indulge in that delicacy. Its connection with Pearl Harbor Day was still too close. He settled for a steak.

Occasionally he would see someone from another table give Yuri an admiring glance, and he was proud. She was so beautiful. His heart faltered. How could he ask such a wonderful person to marry him?

After dinner, Tom suggested they drive out to some high cliffs near Point Loma, overlooking the ocean.

There Tom parked the car, and they got out and walked, hand in hand, along the edge, enjoying the stiff, salty breeze in their faces.

They had gone only a short distance when Tom stopped and loosened his grip on Yuri's hand.

"This week down here, Yuri, you have had a chance to see for yourself what ranch life is like. You should know by now whether or not you would be happy living in the country. You know I love you, for I have told you so. I have loved you ever since I first set eyes on you that morning at church in Poston. The night before you left Poston, you told me you loved me. I'm sorry I wrote that letter to you after you were gone. I know now I was wrong, making the decisions for both of us. Do you still love me? Could you be happy with me on the ranch?"

It was a long speech for Tom, but he said the things he had to say and asked the questions he had to have answers to.

He walked away a few steps and stood looking down at the waves as they came in and dashed themselves futilely against the rock cliff. He braced himself for Yuri's answer.

Now that Yuri had the decision to make, she began to doubt. Was she the right girl for Tom? Or would she only be a burden to him?

Suddenly the truth dawned on her like a glaring light too blinding to be faced. Their love was a Poston affair. Isolated from the outside world, living in an unnatural environment at the age when they were ready for love, they had fallen for each other and thought it was the real thing. It had given them romance to brighten the ugliness of their internment.

But it couldn't last. There was no basis for permanence. They were entirely unsuited for each other. If they had met in the outside world, they probably would never have given each other a second look. If they married, they would never be happy.

She tried to stop the thoughts as they raced through her mind, but she knew they were true. At last she gave up.

She looked over to where Tom was standing on the edge of the cliff. How could she tell him? How could she make him see the truth as it had been revealed to her?

Slowly she walked over to him and took his hand in hers.

In the moonlight Tom saw tears glistening in Yuri's eyes; but they were not tears of joy, for he saw no smile on her face. He was puzzled. He waited nervously for her to speak.

Her voice was low but steady as she told Tom the thoughts that had passed through her mind.

He was stunned. If she had said, no, she wouldn't marry him, he would have been stricken but not surprised. But to tell him his love for her wasn't real and wouldn't last! That was too much. He began to protest vehemently.

But Yuri went right on talking, and now her voice was so earnest that he was compelled to listen. Gradually he became half convinced she might be right.

Maybe he couldn't live up to Yuri or make her happy. Maybe it was a mismatch. Although he couldn't conceive of such a thing now, maybe as the years passed he might grow tired of always trying to please Yuri and would wish that he had married someone with whom he could be more comfortable.

He felt the softness of Yuri's hand in his, and he couldn't see those hands washing the men's dirty work clothes or mopping the floor or washing and bunching vegetables out in the packing shed.

Finally, he agreed reluctantly that they should go their separate ways, unattached, and time would tell whether or not Yuri was right.

Tom now felt that Yuri would never marry him. She would find someone else up there at the university. Too bad Tad had fallen in love with that girl up north. The thought ran through Tom's mind and was gone.

He tried to take his disappointment in stride. "Just another Poston casualty," he quipped with a shrug of his shoulder as they walked toward the car.

But when he started the motor and headed the car toward home, Yuri weeping by his side, he felt a deep sense of loss. It was like someone had died.

AFTERWORD

During the spring of 1972 I taught a historical methodology course at California State University, Fullerton (CSUF), centered on the World War II Japanese American Evacuation, an event which occurred thirty years earlier. It was out of this educational experience that the Japanese American Project of the CSUF Oral History Program emerged. It was during this semester, also, that I became aware of a cache of documents in the university library's Special Collections bearing upon the Evacuation. Most of this material, explained Linda Herman, the head of Special Collections, had been donated about five years earlier by a former teacher at the Poston War Relocation Center in Arizona, Georgia Day Robertson. While all of the items--War Relocation Authority brochures, editions of the camp newspaper, and the like--possessed scholarly value, the prize donation was a large, boxed manuscript of an unpublished historical novel by the donor carrying the title "Harvest of Hate" (with the accompanying description on the title page declaring it "A novel based on the evacuation of those of Japanese ancestry from the West Coast during World War II").

Two immediate actions flowed from the discovery of this manuscript by those of us in the newly formed Japanese American Project. First, an archival finding aid was developed which consisted of a critical estimate of its literary and historical merits, a synopsis of its story line, and a running index as to its "historical" contents. Second, since it was agreed that the manuscript deserved wide dissemination, an attempt was made to locate the author.

Finding the manuscript, however, proved easier than finding its author. Herman, who herself had never met Robertson, gave us one lead, an Orange County address in Capistrano Beach accompanying the

Robertson donation. But this produced nothing useful about Robertson's current whereabouts. Therefore, we turned to the person through whom the donation had been made to CSUF--Dr. Giles Brown, formerly the Chairman of the Department of History and then the Dean of Graduate Studies. Brown remembered Robertson as a woman of advanced age whom he had met at a world affairs lecture series coordinated by him in south Orange County. I think perhaps it was from him that we were given a Palm Desert, California, address for her. In any event, a letter sent to this address, dated October 4, 1972 and containing a request to interview her, was returned "addressee unknown." One further step was taken at this point; since we knew Robertson to have been a teacher by occupation, we sought to locate her on the roll of California state pensioners. This strategy, too, went unrewarded.

During the next six years, while the Japanese American Project expanded its collection of oral histories and published several anthologies based on them, little concerted thought was given to "Harvest of Hate" or its author, whom we presumed to have passed away. But the manuscript and Robertson were never far from our minds. Indeed, when a colleague in the Department of History, Professor Warren Beck, was compiling a volume of readings for publication on the subject of American history through literature, we encouraged him to excerpt portions of "Harvest of Hate" for the section of the book on World War II. This he did. Moreover, a few years later, in a companion volume treating California history and literature, Beck excerpted still another section from the Robertson manuscript to illuminate California's home front experience during World War II.

Then in February 1978 Linda Herman notified us that she had just received a letter from an Oregon woman, Dorsey Morris, who was the niece of Georgia Day Robertson. She had written that only recently her aunt--who was living in a mobile home park in Costa Mesa, California--had told her that the manuscript

551

"Harvest of Hate" had been deposited at CSUF and wondered whether she could possibly read it.

Aware now that Robertson was not only alive but residing in Orange County, we immediately contacted her. By chance, I was then teaching a class focused on the Poston center and its impact upon the nearby community of Parker, Arizona. Accordingly, I assigned one of the students, Mary Skavdahl, to read "Harvest of Hate" and then conduct a taped inteview with Robertson for our project. I also informed Robertson that, while our project was very much interested in publishing her novel, she should first explore publication prospects with some large commercial and academic presses that had already published notable works on the topic of the wartime Evacuation. Acting on my advice, she wrote to these presses, though without eliciting serious interest from any of them. The opposite was true, however, when she sent the manuscript to several additional commerical houses. In fact, one major press, after mailing back her manuscript, requested permission to have it returned so that its editorial board could take publication of the novel by them under serious advisement. But when this publisher ultimately decided against publication, the door was open for our project, through the CSUF Oral History Program (of which I had become the director in 1975), to publish "Harvest of Hate."

Robertson's expressed desire to have us publish her novel in the spring of 1979 was coincident with my resignation from the directorship of the Oral History Program and my return as Director of the Japanese American Project. Before resigning, though, I secured the promise from the new program codirectors, Dr. Gary Shumway and Dr. Lawrence de Graaf, that they would back the publication of the Robertson manuscript provided I raised all the publication monies. I passed along this information to Robertson with the glib assurance that raising the necessary funds would occasion few problems and that she should prepare herself to see "The Harvest of Hate" (as Robertson had by then retitled her novel) published by no later than Christmas 1980.

How wrong I was! In spite of my steadfast efforts to locate the funding to underwrite a publication which I very much believed in, spiraling production costs combined with an acutely depressed economy undermined my intentions to put "The Harvest of Hate" into print. Although I never abandoned hope that the requisite financing would be someday forthcoming, I feared that this might not come about during the author's lifetime. After all, in 1980, Georgia Day Robertson celebrated her ninety-fourth birthday. She nonetheless kept writing me letters to the effect that probably the one thing keeping her alive was the prospect of seeing her book published, something which, as the years marched on--1981, 1982, 1983, 1984, 1985--induced in me acute anxiety and contrition.

But just when our correspondence had slowed to a trickle, largely because I could no longer bear to be reminded of my fractured promise to her, encouraging news came from two sources. First, the Director of the Oral History Program, Dr. Gary Shumway, who had always shared my high estimate of the book, urged me to proceed with publication and ensured me that the program would lend whatever fiscal and staff support it could muster. Second, the Japanese American Council of the Historical and Cultural Foundation of Orange County agreed that it would also provide some financial backing for the publication. Thus fortified, I enthusiastically relayed the news to Robertson in the spring of 1986 that the project was no longer dead in the water and that plans called for publishing "The Harvest of Hate" to commemorate her 100th birthday on October 9, 1986 (a date later pushed back by a month and a half so as to coincide with a fund-raising dinner sponsored by the Japanese American Council).

When the novel was first being readied for publication during the summer of 1979, I conducted two interview sessions with Robertson at her mobile home in

Costa Mesa. The first of these took the form of a life review; the second was focused on her novel. Since the transcripts are too lengthy to print here in full (they and the tapes from which they derived are on deposit in the Japanese American Project), what follows is a biographical summary of her life succeeded by some excerpts from her interview which bear upon the text and context of *The Harvest of Hate*.

Georgia Day Robertson was born on a farm in Van Buren County, Iowa, in 1886. There she attended a rural school though grade eight. In 1902, she moved with her family to the county seat of Keosauqua, where she graduated from high school two years later. She then taught for one year in rural schools before matriculating at Iowa State College at Ames, Iowa, in the fall of 1905. Supporting herself with a variety of jobs, she graduated in the class of 1900 with a major in mathematics and a minor in physics.

The next year she went to China as a Methodist educational missionary and spent a year studying Chinese. In 1911 she had her life threatened and eventually was driven out of her mission station at Chengtu by antiforeign revolutionaries, who were "determined to drive the Manchus off the throne after 300 years of rule," and fled to Shanghai. In early 1912 she was sent to Nanking to teach mathematics in the Men's Union University, which was established and supported by a number of missions of different denominations. In 1913 she returned to Chengtu and became the principal of a girls' boarding school, a post she held until her marriage the following year to a Canadian mining engineer, John Alexander Thompson Robertson, who was then teaching in a Chinese government school.

After giving birth to her first son, Angus, in 1915, Robertson, "fulfilling a promise I had made to my parents when I went to China that I would return at the end of five years," came home to Iowa the next year. Later that year she was joined by her husband. The family then went to Canada for a short while, and there John Robertson accepted employment at a Canadian-owned cobalt mine in Fredericktown, Missouri. At Fredricktown, in 1917, the Robertsons' second son, David, was born.

Three years later, with World War I over and a lessened demand for cobalt, the Fredericktown mine and John Robertson went back to China to work for a foreign mining company in Yunnan Province. Meanwhile, his wife and children waited in Ames, Iowa, for the mining company to construct them a bungalow in which to live. Owing to the Chinese government passing laws controlling foreign elements working in China, it was impossible for her husband's company to continue operating and so it closed its mine and he returned to the United States. In 1922 the Robertson family moved to Flat River, Missouri, where John Robertson worked for a lead mining company. Tragically, he developed cancer and died the following year at the age of thirty-six.

Georgia Robertson then returned to Ames in time to enroll in Iowa State College for the 1923 fall semester on a teaching fellowship and, the next year, she received a master's degree in economic history. Thereupon she taught high school in Ames for a year and a half and then, in the winter of 1927, moved to the West Coast to begin graduate study toward a second master's in education at the University of Southern California, which she completed that same summer at Iowa State.

Between 1927 and 1933 Robertson held teaching positions, respectively, at Iowa State--"the most beautiful year I ever had professionally"--Simpson College in Indianola, Iowa, and Morehead State Teacher's College in Morehead, Kentucky.

In 1933, with President Franklin Delano Roosevelt newly installed in the White House, Robertson and her two boys moved to the Orange County, California, community of Midway City. The next eight years, "by selling short stories and teaching at a Santa Ana evening high school and raising chickens and selling eggs," she was able "to make enough money to pay the rent and keep food on the table for all the family and buy a bit of meat for the cat."

And then it was back to college, this time to the University of Southern California's doctoral program. After "a couple of months of complete enjoyment," she reached the conclusion that a salary was temporarily more important than a degree and so accepted a position for a Salvation Army-managed USO club in San Diego. While working there as the entertainment supervisor, she heard the news of the bombing of Pearl Harbor.

H: Because it was a military town, was San Diego especially panic-struck by this thing? Was the whole town pretty much in a state of anxiety?

R: No, not the whole town, just individuals. Of course, we had a blackout that night. There was a line of streetcars just standing out there on the tracks not moving, no lights on them, no street lights or nothing. I couldn't get back to my room. I had to go across the street to a hotel. The lobby was loaded with people who couldn't get to their homes--some people who lived over on Coronado Island. There was no bridge over to Coronado at that time. Nothing was running. I stayed in that hotel overnight, and this woman where I was rooming out on Mission Hill--she was one of the hysterical ones--loaded up her car and she said, "Would you like to move out? I'm going down there, we're going to be bombed." Away she went to Arizona. I went back to the hotel and got a room and stayed in that hotel the rest of the time I was in San Diego.

H: How long did it take for people to regain some semblance of "business as usual" in San Diego?

R: I don't know, because I didn't know much about that side--I was too busy with USO.

H: So how long were you down in San Diego at the USO?

556

R: I wasn't down there too long, three or four months.

H: What did you do after that, since that only took you into about early 1942, didn't it?

R: Well, I came home for the summer and looked for a job for the fall. Along in August, I still hadn't found anything, so I went into the California Teachers Association's placement bureau in Los Angeles. They didn't have anything. Just as I was leaving--I had my hand on the doorknob, I was in a hurry to open the door, I guess--and the secretary called to me and said, "Would you be willing to teach Japanese?" I said, "Why not?" Then she told me about Poston. She gave me Dr. Miles Carey's address and said, "He's looking for teachers, write to him."

H: Had you heard anything at all about the Evacuation up to that point?

R: Oh, I knew the Japanese had been evacuated, but I am ashamed that I didn't protest against it. There were so many things happening then. So I wrote to Dr. Carey and asked for a job in math, and he wrote back and said that all the Nisei were going to teach the math in the high school but could I teach social science. I wrote back and said yes. I never had, but sure, I could teach it. Then I never heard a word from him. It came the last of September and I'd rented my house and I thought, "Gee, I wonder what's the matter; I think I'd better call him up." So one Saturday night I called him--the last of September--and as soon as I got him on the phone, he said, "Why aren't you down here, school begins on Monday!" I said, "I didn't know I had a job." You see, the Nisei girls were employed as the secretaries in the offices and they were so mad about being down there that they didn't give a darn whether they did things right or not. They had sent my letter telling me I had this job as head of the Department of Mathematics and had sent it to somebody else in northern California.

H: Oh, so they gave you a math job actually?

R: Yes. They wrote and told me I would be the head of the Mathematics Department and supervisor of teachers.

H: Who was the head of the school that you were talking about? What was his name?

R: You mean at Poston?

H: Yes.

R: Dr. Miles Carey--a wonderful fellow.

H: So you had to get down there over the weekend?

R: Yes, I had to pack up that night and went down that same night. A friend took me because I didn't have any tires for my car. You know how it was in those days, I didn't have a spare, so I was afraid to drive. My friend took me down and we drove all night. We got to Poston in the morning, dead tired and hot--it was hot! We had breakfast in one of the mess halls. My friend had gone down to visit one of her Nisei friends from Westminster [Orange County].

H: This was like in September of 1942?

R: Yes. So she went right to the block of her friend, and that was the only time while I was down there that I ate in one of the Japanese mess halls. You know what we had for breakfast? We had cold pancakes and syrup and hot coffee. And that was my breakfast. I don't know if it ever got better after that or not.

H: Where did you live after that?

R: They put us in the barracks, just like the Japanese had, only better furnished.

H: But you didn't live with the Japanese?

R: No. There was a school block, a block set aside for the school. The Caucasian teachers occupied two rows of barracks in that block.

H: Did all the teachers who were at Poston stay at Poston III?

R: Oh no, in Poston I, Poston II, and Poston III.

H: Didn't you only have one high school for all of Poston?

R: No.

H: Oh, you had Poston I High School, Poston II High School, and Poston III High School?

R: Right, the same with the junior high and the same with the grade schools. Each camp had its own schools and its own principals.

H: So you were the head of the Math Department for . . .

R: For all three.

H: Oh, for all three of them, I see. So you had to meet regularly with the heads of the other two schools. I mean, you met with the other math teachers at Poston I and Poston II.

R: Yes. All of the math teachers in the high school were men--Nisei men--and they all had at least one year of university. It was from them that I got a lot of material which is in the book [*The Harvest of Hate*]. The head of the social services for the administration, she appointed me to counsel with the Nisei men in our Poston III who had fathers in prison [alien enemy internment] camps. Some of them had real mental troubles and what they needed was a psychiatrist. At least I could listen to them.

They would tell their stories. They were having a hard time handling the situation, because they knew their fathers had never done anything wrong, and there was no reason why they had to put them in prison camps. They just couldn't take it, you know. Then there was the problem that they were putting up a camp someplace--it seems to me it was in Texas--you probably know, where the men in the camps could have their families with them?

H: Yes, Crystal City, Texas.

R: These fellows had to decide whether they'd stay at Poston or go with their families to these prison camps. They had a lot of problems. And I also learned just gobs of information from them about the years before Evacuation.

H: You weren't at Poston very long before they had a pretty considerable strike in the Poston I camp [November 1942]. That must be one of your first memories, isn't it?

R: Well, it amounted to so little that it didn't make much impression on me. I was up in Poston I that day of the strike and I was right in the midst of it. It wasn't very exciting. They just had built a platform and they had a fellow up there on the microphone and he was stirring up the crowd and they were listening and yelling and that was about all there was to it.

H: And you didn't feel any fear at all?

R: No, I went right in back of the crowd; I was close enough so that I could have touched them. I was right behind the crowd. See, I visited all these math teachers regularly and then we had all those teacher's meetings and we always wound up talking about the Evacuation.

H: Really? How did you evaluate the teaching staff over there?

R: Good.

H: Both from the point of view of the Caucasians who were in there teaching, like yourself, and the Nisei?

R: Oh, I thought you meant the Japanese American teachers.

H: I mean both really.

R: Oh, there were some of the Caucasian teachers that had no business to be there. One of them even called the kids "Japs" right in class. There were others that didn't use much judgment. Some of the missionaries were overly sentimental and sympathized with the evacuees too much. Although I was head of Mathematics, the Education Department still didn't have their full faculty at the beginning so I had to teach a class in social sciences. And I'll never forget that first morning when I went into the classroom--bare barracks and no seats even, and a little table for the teacher and a little chair and, back up on the wall, her own little blackboard. And that's all there was in the room. No textbooks, no seats. The kids came in carrying their little stools their fathers had made for them out of mesquite. Those high school boys were mad as hornets. I would say that the high school age Nisei were the mad ones and the college age Nisei were the hurt ones. Oh, were they mad! They were just there to break up the whole thing. They were used to the California school buildings and the big libraries and gymasium and all that sort of thing--and now this bare barrack. I said to them, "I won't say I know how you feel, because that would be impossible, it wouldn't be true. I can't know how you feel. But I have a good idea. You're here and there's nothing you can do about it, and nothing I can do about it, so there's no reason to punish yourselves by not getting an education while you're here. So let's get down to business." No textbooks! I did a great job of teaching then; really, it taxed all of my ability.

H: Did they get down to business?

R: Yes, I had a nice time with them.

H: Did you find it one of your better teaching experiences?

R: I just taught that class a month, and then they got another Caucasian teacher in--Louie Marquette, a Jew from Brooklyn--and he took it. We had a lot of fun with him and we loved him! But he said one day, "I'm sure getting tired of hearing the class talking about how Mrs. Robertson did it." (laughter) He'd hear that every day, "Mrs. Robertson did this; Mrs. Robertson did that."

H: Why'd they take you out of the classroom?

R: Well, I wasn't supposed to be teaching because I was the department head.

H: Oh, so the department head didn't teach there?

R: No, I wasn't supposed to be teaching, but I had to take this class because they didn't have a full faculty yet.

H: So your total teaching experience down there consisted of one month, really, of teaching?

R: No, after the government began to allow the Nisei to go out and relocate--you know, go east and finish their education or get jobs or something like that--some of our Nisei teachers left. I had to take classes then. Most of the time after the first year, I was teaching at least one class. That gave me contact with the high school as well as the college age.

H: How long did you stay at Poston, until it closed up?

R: No, I left in the spring at graduation.

H: Which year?

R: 1945. And they closed up sometime that summer, I guess.

H: And so you were there pretty close to the end then. You were there from 1942 to 1945, almost three years.

I'm curious about the contacts you had with people within Poston, the Japanese Americans. You've already mentioned some people who you talked with, but do you recall having long conversations with these Nisei about their experiences prior to the war and at the time of Evacuation and subsequent to that, regarding their families and the like?

R: Oh, I had numerous conversations. I couldn't pick out anyone special, because they were just continual--they wanted to talk about it.

H: Would you speak mostly to high school students or did you speak with their parents? Did you speak with first-generation Issei as well as Nisei?

R: I spoke both to individuals and to groups of people, outside of the classroom.

H: Do you remember having any friends among the Issei generation, the older people in the camp?

R: No. My contact with Issei was very little, I just saw them. The gardener who looked after the lawn and planted flowers and things around our barracks and the janitors at the school--of course, they didn't speak much English, the people in that group. So I had very little contact with the Issei. I don't know if the woman who organized the teacher's group was a Nisei or not--she came from Los Angeles--a very lovely woman.   She spoke very good English. But, of course, there are a lot of Issei who speak English well. My contact with Issei was just about nil, my personal contact with them.

H: What about with the Kibei, the Nisei who were educated and spent some time in Japan? Did you have any contact with them?

R: No, I don't remember knowing any Kibei.

H: So most of your intimate contacts were with the Nisei teachers who worked under you, right? Were they an interesting group of individuals?

R: Yes, marvelous, and all different. But they're just as American as the Caucasians, just as American. You can't classify them, you can't stereotype them, they're just as different individually as the Caucasian teachers are.

H: Where were most of the people from that were in Poston III?

R: San Diego County and San Joaquin Valley.

H: So most of your teachers were representative of that area.

R: My teachers were in all the camps. I visited all the camps.

H: So you had teachers from Orange County as well?

R: Oh, yes. I had teachers from Orange County. Then, of course, I've kept in touch with them ever since I came back here to live from Poston. Every once in awhile the Nisei in this county used to get together and talk over Poston days, and once in awhile they'd stop and take me with them. I was just sort of one of them, you know. I remember one night one of the fellows said--we had been talking about our experiences down there--and he said, "Well, I'm certainly glad I had that experience. I sure wouldn't want to go through that again, but I think I really got a lot out of it." I thought that was really interesting.

H: When you went to Poston you probably didn't have a very strong feeling about the Evacuation because, as you said earlier, you had only heard about it and knew in a general sense that it was going on. Once you got there and you were involved within the camp, did you start to develop the feeling that this was a terrible thing, or did that ever occur?

R: Definitely.

H: How fast did that feeling come about?

R: Well, it didn't take long, I can tell you. Just a barren desert and those ugly barracks. There wasn't even a green blade of grass or leaf or anything. Bulldozers had scraped off mesquite, everything off the desert, before the barracks were built. When I went

there, there was nothing but these black tar paper buildings and, of course, the administration buildings were
wood and painted grey and white and they had a little
group of them and most of them were in Camp I. We
had small groups of administration buildings in Camps
II and III. When I saw those Issei there sitting with idle
hands, just sitting, sitting, sitting and looking down at
the ground. Oh, the things I saw! It didn't take long
for me to decide that this was a shameful thing, a
tragedy, just a tragedy.

H: Do you think that the administration at Poston
was pretty much of a similar mind as you were, that
they realized that this was an American tragedy?

R: Oh, I think that that was recognized clear up to
the federal government. I think they had no longer accomplished the Evacuation than they realized they had
made a colossal blunder because it was so soon that they
began to make arrangements to let the people out to go
east. I kept wondering where Eleanor was when President Roosevelt was signing the proclamation [Executive
Order 9066]. She kept pretty good track of what he was
doing and if she had known about that, I think she
would have objected.

H: Do you remember her visiting the camps?

R: No, I don't remember a thing about it. I wonder
if it's true.

H: Well, she did visit Gila [River War Relocation
Center in Arizona], but I'm not sure that she visited
Poston.

R: She certainly didn't visit when I was there.
Some of the prominent visitors when I was there--and I
wish they would put it in a book--was the Congressional
committee that conducted that investigation in Los Angeles and took the word of that fellow that had been

dismissed by the Poston administration and who lied to them. When we read the morning *Los Angeles Times*, we just couldn't believe our ears or our eyes.

H: Which committee was this?

R: I don't know what the committee was, but they were the Congressional committee that investigated Poston because there had been so many things said--the evacuees were getting better food and they were storing food for the Japanese when they came over, and were poisoning the water in the dam way up there above Parker [Arizona]. There we were several miles below Parker, and how could poisoning the water down there get clear up to the dam? No one could figure that out. They never let up. The *Los Angeles Times* never let up on the Japanese, even after they came back home.

H: Is that the paper you were getting down there at Poston, the *Los Angeles Times*?

R: Well, the *Times* was what practically everyone was getting; that's what they sold at the canteen. All of them were lambasting them in the papers. Norman Chandler was the owner and editor of the *Times* at that time and I got so disgusted I finally wrote a letter and invited him down. I said, "I just wanted to give you an invitation to come down and meet some of these fine Japanese Americans and find out what good citizens they are and how patriotic they are." Then I thought, here I've invited the owner and editor of the *Times* down and never even said a word about it to the administration. I think I'd better tell them. I told the administration about it and they said, "That's o.k, I hope he comes." Well, I had a letter from him--a long one-- but it certainly wasn't an answer to mine. All he told me about was that several years before he had planned to get a large tract of land down in Mexico, and he was bringing over Japanese to farm it. And how glad he was now that he hadn't done it, because then he would have had a Japanese enemy and a Japanese army right here on our border.

H: When you came back from Poston, where did you settle in California. Or did you settle in California?

R: I still lived in Midway City; I had my home there.

H: Did you go back to teaching when you came back? Or did you go back to selling eggs and writing short stories?

R: No, I didn't get a teaching job because I came home in the spring of 1945.

H: Well, the War Relocation Authority supposedly had a responsibility to try and place the people that had worked for them during the war. You didn't get any assistance from them to place you in a job?

R: I didn't ask for it. Some of the folks did and some of the folks didn't.

H: So then what did you do for an income?

R: Oh my, I lived on what I made down at Poston. I probably sold my bonds--it was an order by the government to buy bonds every month, so I had several bonds. And, of course, I was alone then because David had gone to war and Angus was in the Merchant Marine. So I was alone and it didn't cost much to live.

H: So how long was it before you felt sufficient indignation to want to launch your novel [*The Harvest of Hate*]? Can you remember the conditions surrounding your decision to write that book? I'm sure you do.

R: Well, it wasn't until 1946 that I decided to write

it. I can't remember what I did in 1945. I don't know whether I ever told you or not, but I needed the setting for the novel to be San Diego County. I knew that I'd have to have the locale of the book down there because it was from the San Diego County people that I had gotten so much of my information. And although it probably would have been the same all over before the Evacuation, I still wanted to write from the place where I got the information. So I went down to Chula Vista, south of San Diego--they had a lot of Japanese ranchers down there. I had a friend in Chula Vista that I stayed with and we drove out to these Japanese ranches and looked them over and they were very accommodating and stopped their work and I told them what I was going to do. They showed me their land and their equipment and what they were growing and their buildings and showed me how they grew their different crops and told me what they grew in the summer and in the winter, and so I got a firsthand idea of ranching. That was very valuable.

H: What specifically prompted you to write the novel? After all, this involved quite an investment of time and energy and everything else?

R: It's pretty hard to say after so many years, but I think perhaps as I told you, the trip I made to Iowa right after the war might have had something to do with it, to find the utter ignorance of the people. And even after I talked to them about their indifference, they just looked upon it as a local problem. It didn't make any difference to them and they didn't do anything about it. Anyway, there came a time in early 1946 one night when I said to myself, "Someone has to write a book." Since I had done quite a bit of writing, it didn't seem like such a big task, so I decided that I would do it.

H: What had you written up to that point?

R: Oh, I had written two or three books on China and I had written a book about World War II concerning a woman that was very patriotic and thought her husband ought to go to war--and he didn't care to go to war, so she went to war herself, with the Red Cross.

H: Were these novels that you wrote?

R: I've never written anything but fiction.

H: Had any of these novels been published or not?

R: No.

H: Now, you were saying earlier that you were writing some short stories to subsidize your family and everything, so obviously some of your short stories were published.

R: Oh, I sold around twenty of them.

H: When did you start writing the stories?

R: After I quit teaching in 1932, after I got out of college teaching. I had probably written little things before that. Then it was the Depression and there wasn't anything to do and I liked to write. I think if my English teachers had given me a little encouragement in college, I would have started writing right away, and if I'd really put a lot into it, I'd be a successful writer.

H: Did you write anything during World War II during the time you were at Poston? Did you write any short stories or essays or sketches?

R: While I was at Poston, no. There wasn't much time for writing while I was down there.

H: Did you keep a diary?

R: No, they say only an introvert keeps a diary.

H: Aren't you an introvert?

R: I don't know. (laughter)

H: But you didn't keep a diary or a journal when you were down there?

R: No.

H: Did you do any other kind of writing other than that angry letter you sent to Chandler? Did you do any other writing, like for the newspaper?

R: No, I don't think so.

H: One of the things about *The Harvest of Hate* that impressed me the first time I read it and impressed me even more the second time I read it was something which went beyond its novelistic qualities. While you have developed some memorable characters and crafted a sturdy plot structure, as a sociocultural historian I'm really quite amazed at the sociological grasp you have of the events that transpired in the camp. I was wondering, in fact, if, at the time you were writing this novel, you had any assistance in the way of documents that were made available to you by the Bureau of Sociological Research at Poston? I know there were a couple of studies available at the time you wrote the novel--ones which were published in 1945 and 1946. One of them was by Alexander Leighton, who was the head of the Sociological Bureau at Poston, and it's called *The Governing of Men*. There was another book put out by the University of California by Dorothy Swain Thomas and Thomas Nishimoto called *The Spoilage*. Did you either have access to those two studies or did you have access to documents that were available at the camp or did you just read the Poston *Chronicle* and rely on your own memory, or just how did you construct this novel in a historical and a sociological sense?

R: No, I didn't have any of those books, although later I did read *The Governing of Men*. It was just mostly memory. It made a deep impression; you know, you don't forget things like that. When you go through something like that, you don't forget it.

H: So most of the situations you describe in the novel were things that you either picked up yourself or found out through conversing with some of these Nisei who were working under you in the Mathematics Department of the three high schools, right? So there's not too much in *The Harvest of Hate* that's "bookish," in the sense that it comes from a book, somebody else's observation? It mostly comes from your observations and your conversations.

R: Yes, I think so. I didn't limit my contact down there with the Mathematics Department, because I had very close contact with all the teachers; you see, we had teachers teaching all different subjects. We had teachers' meetings and we had contact with all of them. So my contacts were very large.

H: O.K., let me ask you a couple more questions about the novel. The Sato family--is that literally a family that you had as a specific living model at Poston or is it a composite invention?

R: No, it wasn't a specific family. I chose my characters so that I could represent the different things down there--Tad, the one who resented and fought the government every inch of the way; Tom, who tried to cooperate; Mari, to represent the young women; and Yoshi, the children. And, of course, Father and Mother Sato, the Issei.

572

H: How did you come to rivet upon an agricultural as against an urban family--what was the deciding factor there?

R: I suppose that's because all the Japanese I'd ever known here in Orange County were ranchers. I just never thought of them as city people. I've known Japanese in Orange County ever since I've been out here, but I've never known any of them that lived in town--they were all ranchers.

H: And why did you choose the San Diego area as opposed to Orange County? After all, you had been living in Orange County several years prior to the Evacuation?

R: Well, that's very simple. As I mentioned earlier, the people in Poston III were from San Diego, and that's who I got my information from.

H: Did you also feel rather comfortable depicting a farm family like the Satos because you were from a farm family yourself?

R: Oh, I don't know that that made a difference. It had been a long time since I'd been on a farm. Yes, I suppose, but I never thought of that.

H: It seems that there are a lot of things about the novel that correspond with your own background--there is, first of all, a farm family. Also, you had a choice of making the Satos either Buddhists or Christians, and you made them Christian. As for the San Diego setting, there was the fact of your USO employment in that city. So you did have some working knowledge of three central parts of the Satos' lives. Then, too, in a couple of key chapters you take up the experience of the Poston school system, which again you would have had personal contact with. So perhaps all of these things helped to impart authenticity to you novel. Maybe this helps to explain why the book speaks with such a commanding voice.

Did you feel that you not only had a good grasp of San Diego as a result of working there for several months at the USO, but also that you possessed a good knowledge of the Japanese American commnity in the San Diego area?

R: I knew nothing while I was down there. I was working for the USO and had no contact with the Japanese.

H: So most of your knowledge of the San Diego Japanese American community came once you arrived in the camp?

R: Yes, in Poston III.

H: What characters in the book correspond pretty closely to specific people that you knew in Poston, or before or after?

R: I don't think any of them do.

H: How about yourself? Do you figure in the novel, are you a character in the novel?

R: No. Miss Brown did the things I would have done, but no, I'm not in it.

H: What about Miss Carlson, which is a name like Robertson and is mentioned as having been a former missionary in Japan?

R: There were several missionaries from Japan at Poston.

H: Who were teaching in the school system?

R: Yes, and I think there were some in the administration.

H: What about individual members of the Sato family? I know the family is a fictive creation designed to illustrate certain points. But you mentioned before we started this interview that perhaps two of your favorite characters in the novel are Tad and Yoshi Sato. Does either or both correspond with someone you knew at camp?

R: No.

H: None of the math teachers who worked under you found their way into the Sato family in recognizable form?

R: No.

H: One of the things that you bring out a lot in the book is the resistance among certain elements within the Poston population. You have Tad participate with the camp dissidents for awhile, but dissenters are there as an undercurrent throughout the story. Where did you derive the feeling that there were people who really were against what the government was doing and that almost all authority at Poston was being undermined by this group. Where did you get that feeling?

R: Oh, we knew what was going on in the camp, we knew pretty well what was going on. There were these resisters and a lot of them were sympathetic to Japan. A lot of them were just disgruntled like Tad was. You don't live in a camp and not know about these things.

H: You felt it a lot, then?

R: It came through the grapevine.

575

H: But it comes across in something that should have been closer to home to you than just the grapevine. It comes across in the attitudes of some of the students and some of the teachers in the school system. You have Tad, in fact, depicted as a teacher and what you are basically saying in the novel is that as a teacher he, in effect, propagandized in the classroom. Did you have some models to base that portrayal upon from your direct experience, that Nisei teachers used theopportunity of being a teacher in order to make certain kinds of points that could be considered pro-Japan or anti-American, or however you want to put it?

R: Well, I can't say definitely because I wasn't in the classroom; I don't know what they were saying, but I am very suspicious that they were.

H: So it wasn't someone that you had in mind, or a group of somebodies?

R: It wasn't definite information, no.

H: But you had a sense that that was going on? I know you weren't in the classroom very long yourself, just at the outset, right, and then you became, more or less, an administrator.

R: Yes, then after the Nisei began going out--to jobs and out to finish their college, going back east-- then I did quite a bit of teaching the last couple of years. I had to take their place, because classes would be left without a teacher until they got another teacher in. So I did quite a bit of teaching.

H: What about your character named Hideo Yana? He was a Kibei and he was something of a firebrand. Did you have somebody in mind or was the character just created to conform to the Kibei element?

R: No. He was purely fictitious. However, I was familiar with Kibei and their problems even before I went to Poston.

H: Mr. Takeda, Yuri's father--the artist--we talked about him before we started taping this interview and you said you can't recall his name as such. But doesn't he closely follow along the lines of somebody you knew in camp--an artist that you knew in camp? A distinguished artist at Poston?

R: Well, he's real, I really used him. I said I didn't take anybody that was real down there, but I suppose, in a certain sense, he was.

H: And in what context did you know him?

R: Mostly through the Mojave Room. I'd go over there and he was always around and I knew him pretty well. He had a picture that I always wish I had bought.

H: Did he paint pictures of smoke trees like you described in the novel?

R: Oh yes, he had this beautiful picture of a smoke tree and I wanted to buy it. I asked him what he wanted for it and he wouldn't put a price on it. He said, "What do you want to give?" And I didn't know what to give to a well-known artist--whether to offer $30 or $50. Fifty dollars was about as much as I could have paid. And so I just never got it. He didn't put prices on his things and none of the artists did who had work in there. They had beautiful carvings. They'd go out in the mountains and get the ironwood--these Issei-- and bring that in and make beautiful carvings. Oh, that Mojave Room was a place of beauty! Wood carvings, paintings . . . what else did they have in there? I don't remember.

H: Did you have much contact with the agricultural unit at the camp? Since Tom works for the Ag unit at Poston, did you have very much contact with that group of people?

R: Oh, I didn't have any personal contact with them. I just saw what they were doing.

H: Did you used to read the Poston *Chronicle*?

R: Oh, everybody read the Poston *Chronicle*! That was our newspaper.

H: Did you read back issues again after the war before you wrote your novel? For background purposes?

R: I don't think I had very many back issues of the camp newspaper.

H: Is it fair, then, to describe you as writing this novel by sitting down at a table or sitting down on a sofa, without doing much historical research except recollecting things through memory?

R: I just sat at the table and wrote it.

H: So it wasn't something you ran to the library to get information for, or contacted other people about or anything else?

R: No, I started the novel up in Washington State at my son's. He had a little ranch up there.

H: What were some of the things about the novel that worried you? Like some problems in the novel that you had to wrestle with and that caused you a great deal of anxiety or just a lot of hard work to try to unravel or solve or whatever you were going to do?

R: Well, I can't think of any right now. You create

your characters and they just sort of take off. That's the reason I like writing fiction.

H: You write in the novel about the experience of Mrs. Sato going to the Poston I hospital. Tad goes over to visit her and he finds that in spite of all the rumors that he'd heard about the hospital that it was a pretty good hospital. Did you have any firsthand experience with that hospital so that you could validate the observations?

R: At first it was terrible and they said that babies died there because of the heat and the lack of moisture they had in the atmosphere. But it got better as time went on and they got competent doctors in there. It was difficult to get doctors from outside as it was during the war, because the Army was taking them. It improved, and by the time Tad was up there, it was a pretty good hospital. Nothing was right down there to Tad, you know.

H: You use a number of occasions in the book to make some fairly ugly commentary about the town of Parker, Arizona. Each time you mention Parker, it's in an unfavorable light--in fact there seems to be ...

R: Nothing good to say about it.

H: What was your experience with Parker? What was your contact with Parker?

R: Well, that was our nearest town. That's where we went to do our shopping. There in the hot summer days, the drugstore was always cool and we'd go in there and have ice cream. Then we sometimes went in for dinner--there were two nice eating places there.

H: Now you're talking about nice things, ice cream and good places to eat, but yet your book doesn't talk about those nice kinds of things. What did you sense in

Parker that caused you to characterize it in such negative terms?

R: Its relation to the Japanese.

H: What did you pick up, what kind of comments? Were people in the town calling you a "Jap lover"?

R: Well, signs on the doors "Keep out Japs, You Rats." You'd see that on many doors in town.

H: Did you have any unpleasant contacts in Parker with individuals who railed against the Japanese being out there or you spending your time with the Japanese?

R: No. I had no personal conversations with anyone in Parker. Just a buyer-seller relationship. I did have an argument with the owner of the drugstore because he wouldn't serve black people. During the second and third year we had several black nurses and teachers at Poston.

H: At Poston?

R: At Poston.

H: I didn't know that.

R: There was a woman that lived right next to me in the barracks--Mrs. Cook--a beautiful woman and a teacher. I wanted to take her into Parker and have something cool in the drugstore on a hot day. But I wasn't going to have her insulted, so I spoke to the owner of the drugstore and I said, "I have a very good friend down at Poston, but she's colored. I'd like to bring her in sometime for a treat." And he said, "Well, I'm awfully sorry, but we can't serve her." And I said, "Well, you're serving all these Indians, why can't you serve a colored person? You served these colored soldiers from the camp nearby. I guess you don't let them sit down and eat something--you sell them whiskey. Why can't you just serve this black teacher?" "Well, I'm awfully sorry, we can't do it." Well then, some of the teachers did take her in one time, and I don't think he ever saw her--she was a very nice looking person and very well-dressed and I don't think he ever realized that she was black.

H: What about the schoolteachers out there. Your comment in the book was that some were basically good and some were bad. That's a comment you put in a novel. When you step outside the novel, do you still maintain the same thing that . . .

R: Oh, as I mentioned earlier, some of the teachers called the kids "Japs" right in class and, of course, that was the worst insult you could call them. Some didn't like them.

H: Did things improve or get worse in this regard?

R: Well, I don't know, we had some pretty funny people down there. I remember one time, we had a woman there that Dr. Carey wanted to get rid of. She was a stout person and when the hot weather came, she was dismissed. I said to Dr. Carey, "What did Mrs. So-and-So do? Why was she dismissed?" And he said, "High blood pressure." And I said, "Whose?" That was the only time when I saw Dr. Carey a little bit angry. He just flared up and said, "Well, it wasn't mine."

H: You make quite a point in the novel about opposing the housing and the salary that the Nisei teachers were given as against what the appointed teaching staff received. You suggest in your novel, too, that the Nisei teachers displayed a remarkable degree of forebearance and didn't really comment upon this too much--at least not openly. Was it something that a lot of people felt guilty about--this arrangement for teachers?

581

R: Yes. I had a very fine Nisei teacher--I don't know what she was teaching, but she was a lovely girl--and she was trying to earn money to go to college. Well, you can't save much money on--I think the evacuee teachers got $18 a month for their top salary. And here I was--I wasn't getting a lot, maybe $300--and I offered to split my salary with her because we were doing the same work. She wouldn't consider it.

H: She said nothing doing, huh?

R: I would gladly have done it. Yes, I felt guilty. I don't know if anybody else did, but I did terribly. It wasn't fair. Eighteen dollars a month! And the farm workers got $14 and somebody got $16--I don't know who they were. Eighteen was the outside.

H: Would you say that the behavior of the character Yoshi Sato, for his age group, was something that you saw a lot of in kids his age at Poston?

R: Well, he's eleven. Oh, I don't know if I have it in the book or not, but when the parents tried to discipline their children, they said, "The government is supporting us, you don't have anything to say." You just can't imagine these Japanese youngsters saying that to their parents.

H: The same sort of breakdown, then, that you have depicted in your novel in the mess halls, where the families aren't eating as much together.

R: The young people ate together, the kids ate together and Father Sato was very shocked about that when he rejoined his family at Poston.

H: You mention a number of times in the story, too, that there was a lot of pressure brought to bear on people like Tad, or Tom at another point, to make certain decisions, that there was coercion that if they didn't say "No" in the loyalty questionnaire they were liable to be beaten up. And you talk about beatings that went on. This was not just at the outset of the camp, but it applies to the later years of the camp's existence as well. Signing up for the selective service was another case. Was that a pretty common thing that was communicated to you by the math teachers that worked for you--that they had to watch themselves, that they couldn't talk, or if they were overheard they'd be beaten up if they didn't say the right thing?

R: Well, the night Tom was lost in the woods and Tad was very much worried, because he thought that Tom had been beaten up because he wanted to volunteer and was going to sign "Yes" to the loyalty oath or something. Tad was very worried and was up and awake when Tom got home after daylight.

H: You have such a really good feeling for that, your empathy is so powerful here, that I'm wondering how it got communicated to you. That's not something you're writing about second-removed very much. Were you yourself ever intimidated?

R: No, no we just lived with it. You can't live in an atmosphere like that and not know about it. We lived in the camp right with the Japanese. We lived in barracks right with the Japanese around us.

H: But did anyone ever come to you with this very idea, "Look, I can't be seen talking to you, you are a Caucasian, you represent the administration here, and if I'm seen talking to you, that makes my reputation sort of suspect and I might be beaten up." Did people ever tell you that, or did you feel shunned by people because you were, so to speak, "the enemy"?

R: I can't remember such instances, but I suppose that a lot of the teachers that did come and talk to me told me about these things that were going on in camp. That's the way I knew about them.

H: Were you able to enter into many close relationships with Japanese Americans? I mean, would you feel free to go over to their barracks and eat a meal with them? Or would you invite them over to your place for a game of cards? Did you feel free to intermingle with the internees?

R: Well, sure. There was always somebody coming to my room.

H: And you didn't sense any reluctance on their part to do something like that?

R: No.

H: Now was that more true of the teachers than of other people? In your novel you characterize the schools as a great stabilizing force in the camps. Do you think that other administrators could have had that same access to the Japanese people as you did as a teacher, or not?

R: No, I don't think the Japanese ever really trusted the administration.

H: So teachers weren't really counted as being part of the administration?

R: No.

H: So there were the administrators and there were the schoolteachers and then the resident population. You were granted something of an exception, then, even though you were a Caucasian because you were a teacher.

R: Oh, they were so happy that the teachers were willing to come down. They thought at first that nobody would come to live under those kinds of circumstances. So they were very happy that we came.

H: Was that a real incident where in the novel you mention a Japanese American man who was found hanging from a mesquite tree? Was that a true incident?

R: Yes.

H: One final question: You originally titled your novel *A Harvest of Hate*. You retitled it *The Harvest of Hate*.

R: No, you're wrong. I originally titled it *Harvest of Hate*.

H: O.K., you didn't use an article at all. Now you've called it *The Harvest of Hate*. Why the change?

R: I thought that would put the emphasis on the harvest and I thought it sounded a little better, like *The Grapes of Wrath*. *The Grapes of Wrath* sounds better than *Grapes of Wrath*.

H: Was Steinbeck's novel something of a working model for you?

R: No, never thought of it.

H: Had you read it?

R: Oh, sure, who didn't?

After writing the first draft of her novel in 1946, Robertson taught at Costa Mesa Junior High School from 1947 to 1950. Then she went to Japan for a year during the American Occupation as a missionary and a language teacher. Upon her return to Orange County in 1951, she failed to find another teaching position. And so she wrote and sold a couple of serial stories with a Japanese background and worked on revising her novel, in addition to doing some substitute teaching and tutoring. By 1960 she was seventy-four years old, and feeling that she didn't have "a ghost of a chance of ever teaching again," retired for good. Now, over a quarter of a century later, she has become a published novelist and, in the process, laid her claim on posterity.

ARTHUR A. HANSEN
Fullerton, California
November 16, 1986